The Secret at Arnford Hall

To

Alison

Happy Reading

love

Mollie Blake

X

The Secret at Arnford Hall

by
Mollie Blake

The Secret at Arnford Hall by Mollie Blake
© Mollie Blake 2014
ISBN 978-0-9927200-4-9

Published by Live For Now Publishing 2014
c/o SRA Books
Minerva Mill Innovation Centre
Station Road
Alcester
Warwickshire
B49 5ET
United Kingdom

Printed and bound in Great Britain by
TJ International Ltd, Padstow, Cornwall

To Diane

Acknowledgements

I would like to thank Diane, Bob, Wendy, Ann and Elaine for their support and encouragement during the writing of this book.

Importantly, thanks to my family and friends who continue to put up with my obsession with writing stories and my desire to make people feel good whilst losing themselves in my books.

Thanks also to Sarah Williams, Sue Richardson, Katie Read and Lucy Lavers for their continued support and enthusiasm. I have to mention my editor, ˌne, who has helped to make this book even better.

And I thank Bentley, Porsche, Ralph Lauren, Armani, Jessica de Lotz, Richard Anderson, Angelo Galasso, Biba, Chanel and Einaudi, whose beautiful products and music inspired me.

Part One

Chapter 1

Gabriel Black sat on the black leather and chrome chair in front of the beech desk. It was Monday, the twenty-eighth of August, 2017, and the sunshine was streaming through the windows of the fourth-floor offices of Abacus and Cornworthy Solicitors in Manchester. The sunlight formed a vivid bright triangle on the corner of the desk next to Gabriel's coffee cup, and he was mindlessly creating the image of a sword in its sheath with the shadow of his pen; a slight distraction from the document in front of him. His dark expression matched his Hugo Boss black suit, dark blue shirt and deep grey silk tie. He had not taken his jacket off, despite the heat of the day. He took a sip of his coffee and frowned.

One of the family solicitors, Andrew Cornworthy, was sitting back in his chair observing his client through his rimless spectacles. Andrew was fifty-eight and had represented the Black family for the last thirty years. Over eight years ago, he had been instrumental in preparing the document now under review, and was mildly amused at his client's growing frustration with it. Of course, no one had actually expected something to happen to necessitate this document to come into effect … but it had.

Andrew leaned forward and spoke quietly to the man who was still staring at the shadow of his pen.

"It accurately reflects your and Eliza's wishes at the time of John's birth. Of course, its, let's say, unique character could make it unenforceable."

Gabriel looked up at Andrew and his frown deepened.

Andrew refused to be unnerved by his formidable glare. He knew his client well and continued, "But we both know that wouldn't be in the spirit in which it was written, and wouldn't follow Eliza's wishes. When you're ready, perhaps you could let me know how you wish to proceed."

He sat back again and, placing his elbows on his waist, formed an apex with his fingers and thumbs, and contemplated nothing in particular. If it were not for the tragic circumstances which were responsible for the necessary appointment, he would have almost enjoyed it.

"Don't patronise me, Andrew. I know what I agreed to. But I should consider what's in the best interests of the child."

"I think Eliza already did that, in getting you to agree to the conditions in the first place."

Gabriel stood up and walked to the window, his highly polished black shoes glistening in the sunlight. He had his back to his solicitor and couldn't see the faint smile on Andrew's lips.

Looking out across the skyline at the new skyscraper under construction, large billboards on the building site prominently promoting Black Construction, Gabriel wondered if it was still on schedule, and made a mental note to check with his managing director. He was very conscious that, since hearing about Eliza's death, certain changes needed to be made in the way he worked. This included lines of communication between the subsidiary companies and Black Holdings Ltd, of which Gabriel was Chief Executive Officer.

He turned to face his solicitor.

"Have you ever even heard of Arnford Primary School?"

"No, but I'm sure it's a perfectly acceptable institution for the education of small children. I'd imagine it won't differ significantly from John's current school: the curriculum, targets, parents' activities …" At this point, Andrew couldn't fail to notice the raised eyebrows of the man still standing at the window, and his smile became more evident as he continued, "…will be very similar."

"You're enjoying this, aren't you?" Gabriel returned to his seat and sat down, sliding the chair back slightly and resting his right ankle on his left knee.

Andrew thought he was finally beginning to relax, but was careful not to dismiss the huge change that recent events would bring to Gabriel Black's life. He remained silent while the other man continued.

"How well educated will the teachers be? How good is the curriculum? And I don't just mean reading, writing and maths. And what sort of children will he be mixing with?" His voice was filled with a superior scorn. "I should have made her see sense and got the boy a decent education, to prepare him for Eton! They were the best years of my life. What chance will he have in the ineffective state system?"

"I think you're exaggerating, Gabriel. Check the EdBest reports, go and see the head teacher, and form your own view on the competency of the school. There are other state schools and academies too, you know. What about the other conditions in the document?"

Gabriel Black sighed, resigning himself to acquiescing to the demands of his son's dead mother.

"Tell Carol I will adhere to the conditions. She has my word. When can I see John?"

Andrew pressed his intercom.

"Andrea, can you please get me Eliza Redfern's sister, Carol, on the phone."

A moment later his telephone rang.

"Hello, Mrs Beardly. I have just had a meeting with Mr Black and he has agreed to reconfirm the terms of the agreement he made with your late sister. May I take this opportunity to say how very sorry we are for your loss."

There was a pause, as Andrew listened to the woman's response.

"Yes, I understand, and I will, of course, be acting as intermediary, as had always been agreed with Eliza. I'll forward a copy of the signed agreement for your information. Mr Black will arrange to collect John in the morning." At this point Andrew glanced over to Gabriel for confirmation that this was in order, and his client nodded. "I presume that will be from your home in Mobberley, Mrs Beardly. Would 10 a.m. be convenient?"

There was a moment's pause.

"Good. I'll inform Mr Black and he can confirm this with you. Can you please ensure that all John's personal belongings are ready too? Thank you, Mrs Beardly, and please don't hesitate to contact me at any time in the future. I think you have my details." Pause. "Good. Goodbye." Andrew put the phone down.

Gabriel scribbled his signature on the document and slid it over the desk to his solicitor.

"This had better satisfy her, and she can damn well stay out of our lives."

"Don't alienate this woman, Gabriel." Andrew spoke disapprovingly now. "She is the closest relative John has now, after you. And, let's face it, he doesn't know you yet. You'll need to give him time and support to adjust to his new life, not to mention the fact that he has just lost his mother. Have you sourced a counsellor yet?"

"Roger is onto it. I thought I would try to spend a few days with my son; just the two of us." Gabriel was on the back foot now, sheepishly aware that Andrew was right about Carol. She and her three children were going to be part of his life from now on, starting tomorrow, when he would drive over to meet John for the first time.

"Ring and get my car out front, please." Not waiting for any response, Gabriel walked over to the door and headed for the lift.

Andrew let this abrupt ending to the meeting go. He realised Gabriel Black had a lot of thinking to do.

Chapter 2

Nine years earlier

Tall, dark and handsome, thirty-one-year-old Gabriel Black, probably the richest, most eligible bachelor in the north-west of England, was waiting in a boardroom for a meeting with his financial advisor. As he lounged in one of the high-backed leather swivel chairs at the oak boardroom table, Eliza Redfern walked in and poured him some coffee. Gabriel immediately took in her shapely five feet four inches, shoulder-length copper-coloured hair (no doubt out of a bottle), and air of apparent innocence. He liked the challenge that demeanour often gave!

As he was leaving, he stopped at the reception desk and leaned in towards Eliza, placing his hand palm up in front of her.

"Write your phone number on here."

Eliza stared at him, shock and embarrassment on her face. "I beg your pardon?"

"I want to take you to dinner. Give me your number." His voice was authoritative and his hand remained in front of her.

Hardly in control of her own actions, she picked up her pen and wrote her mobile number on his palm. He flashed a smile to die for and left the building.

Eliza Redfern was twenty-six. She had had three romantic relationships so far in her life, but was currently not seeing anyone, so what could be the harm in going out for dinner with one of the most handsome, richest men around? OK, he had a reputation for being a ladies' man, with a different woman for each day of the week. There'd also been press reports about prostitutes, and a fierce protection of the privacy of his family! And by all accounts it was a weird family. Didn't he have a twin brother that no one ever saw, a sister, and a mother who looked young enough to be his sister? Well, she was game for most things and so when he said he would pick her up at eight, she spent the preceding two hours getting ready.

He came for her in his jet-black Lotus Exige sports car, and wined and dined her with champagne and lobster. He then enticed her to invite him back to her place for coffee, which ended in her bedroom with one of the best nights of sex she had ever experienced.

To her amazement he called her again and she had three more dates with him over the next two weeks.

One month later she texted him.

I'm pregnant.

She was amazed to find him knocking at her door within an hour.

"You said you were on the pill."

"I am!"

"Are you going to get rid of it?"

"No."

"Do you want a relationship with me?"

"Not really. We don't know each other at all, and definitely have nothing in common."

"Do you want any money?"

"It would be appreciated, or I'll have to go back to work."

"Can I have a relationship with my child?"

"Well, you are the father!"

As the weeks turned into months, Eliza found herself spending a bit more time with the father of her unborn child. He took her out to dinner at least once a week, and they went to his family's villa in Monaco for a week, which was out of her world, almost to the extent of making her reconsider her answer to his question: did she want to have a relationship with him?

Then, quite by accident, she discovered his secret.

Her reaction was straightforward. "I don't want your money. You cannot have a relationship with my child. I *never* want to see you again."

Then letters from his solicitor started arriving through her letterbox.

My client will be seeking paternity rights …

He will approach the court for full access to his child, and will attempt to gain custody …

Eliza was worried sick she could lose her baby. Her sister couldn't understand why she had suddenly refused to see Black any more. She thought their relationship had been progressing.

"Eliza, you'll need the money. Think what a future your child will have with that inheritance to look forward to!"

"You don't understand, Carol. It's better that my baby has nothing to do with any of them."

Eliza Redfern never told anyone Black's secret.

However, she needed a compromise, and also needed to know what would happen if anything should prevent her from raising her child in the future, God forbid.

One night she sat at her computer screen and began to type.

This agreement will be in place until the child of Eliza Redfern and Gabriel Black reaches the age of eighteen. It will come into effect on the death or incapacity (total physical and mental) of the mother, Eliza Redfern. It will cease on the death of Gabriel Black.

Gabriel Black will have no contact whatsoever with the child unless and until this agreement comes into effect.

On the signing of this agreement by Gabriel Black, Eliza Redfern vows to acknowledge the father of said child to be Gabriel Black.

That father is to adhere fully to the following conditions:

The child is not to attend any private schools up to the age of eighteen. He/she is to be educated in the state system.

The child is never to sleep at Arnford Hall when Mrs Black is in residence.

He/she is to be allowed to choose his/her own religion, if any.

He/she is to be given the choice to join the family business, but under no compulsion.

He/she is to be free to leave Arnford Hall once he/she reaches age eighteen, with no restrictions to be put on where the child lives.

The child is not to be spoiled.

The child is to be allowed to play with children of his/her own age.

The child is to be allowed to join in his/her school's activities.

The child is to be allowed to go to football matches, tennis tournaments and other events of his/her choosing.

The child is to be shown love.

It was simple and heartfelt. In exchange for his agreement, Gabriel Black's name would appear on the birth certificate and the child would bear its father's surname.

Black realised this was as much as he was going to get without a threat of really bad publicity. All his lawyers put together would have great difficulty in keeping the press quiet, and he knew he could never take that risk.

He realised he would have no relationship with his own child until he or she reached the age of eighteen. Then they would probably want nothing to do with him anyway!

He visited Abacus and Cornworthy Solicitors and signed the agreement.

Eliza Redfern relaxed, tried to enjoy her pregnancy and looked forward to the birth of her first child.

Gabriel Black no longer gave a fuck about the world.

Chapter 3

On Monday, the twenty-first of August 2017, one week before Gabriel Black went to see his solicitor, seventy-year-old Mr Humphreys had a heart attack at the wheel of his car. He was on a busy dual carriageway. There was no central reservation and his vehicle careered out of control into the blue Ford Fiesta travelling in the opposite direction. Eliza Redfern died instantly. She had been on her way to work, having just dropped her son, John Black, at a summer holiday kids' club at High Legh Primary School.

Chapter 4

Black's Bentley Mulsanne drew up outside the Abacus and Cornworthy offices, and his chauffeur got out to open the door for his employer.

"Good morning, sir."

Black got in the back, giving a curt, "Thank you."

Michael Johnson wasn't surprised that his boss appeared to be in yet another dark mood, and he watched him open the refrigerator in the central console and take out a bottle of champagne, raising the privacy panel as he poured some into a crystal champagne flute.

Black was used to drinking on his own, but 11.30 in the morning was early, even for him. However, he needed a drink and the champagne was the best thing on offer for now.

His mind started to wander and he pictured Eliza and the shock on her face when he had asked her to write her number on his palm. He had never loved her, and had gone through the usual suspicions when a girl told him she was pregnant. This had only happened to him once before, and after his lawyers and doctors had threatened to carry out DNA testing, it quickly became apparent that that child was not his.

But Eliza had been different, and after a few dates with her, he knew she would never trick him like that. It wasn't the loss of Eliza that saddened him, as she had told him in no uncertain terms that she never wanted to see him again. And who could blame her? It was the realisation that somewhere in the world he would have a child, but may never have the chance to meet them, let alone get to know them.

His own lifestyle had got him into this situation, and even he had been unable to turn back time and undo his mistakes. Instead, he had to live with them, go on committing them even, and his world became blacker and blacker.

Two glasses of champagne later, he got out of the car at Arnford Hall and went straight into his office. He unlocked one of the filing cabinets, pulled a cardboard box from the bottom drawer and took it over to his desk. He sat down and removed the lid. He hadn't looked at the contents since last December, when John would have had his seventh birthday. The one thing Eliza had done, of her own volition, and with no note or any further communication whatsoever, was to forward a picture of John Black to his father on each of his birthdays.

Black laid them out on his desk. There were eight altogether, including one of the newborn John wrapped up in a blanket, with fists like boxing gloves just peeping out of the top.

Aged one, he was supported by someone's fingers (the adult had been obscured from the picture and he could only assume it was Eliza), evidently very close to taking his first solo steps.

At two, John stood alone in a fancy-dress costume, apparently some sort of swamp man.

At three, he was in trendy-looking jeans and blue T-shirt, on a bouncy castle.

At four, he was sitting at a table decorated with a tablecloth, cup and paper plate all depicting Lightning McQueen (whoever he was, Black thought). It was just possible to make out Eliza standing beside him, but she was looking away from the camera. Black thought she had changed her hair. Possibly the light brown was her natural colour.

At five, John wore a shirt emblazoned with a picture of a boy in a green jacket with the number ten on it, and what looked like aliens around him. Roger reliably informed him this was Ben 10, a young superhero often seen on kids' TV. Black didn't bother to ask his PA how he knew this piece of information!

At six, his son was wearing pyjamas and standing behind a robot made out of juice, egg and yogurt cartons; presumably his own creation.

At seven, John wore a plain grey T-shirt and blue jeans, and was standing beside a river, and in front of what looked like a man. Black used every device he could think of to try to analyse the picture, to confirm that it was indeed a man and even identify him; but he couldn't be certain. Did John call someone else Daddy?

Now there would be no more photos from Eliza.

12

There was a knock at the door and Black slipped the pictures back into the box before he responded.

"Come in."

A slim man wearing deck shoes, with light brown trousers and a dark green polo shirt, walked in.

"How did it go this morning?" Roger asked his employer and friend of the last fifteen years.

Black looked across at his PA and right-hand man, and took in his casual summer clothes. He had never been able to appreciate Roger's taste in dress, but he was one of the few men who could stand up to Gabriel Black, who could be confident in his presence, and who could put up with all his traits … and that took some doing!

"I've agreed to adhere to the agreement, and the boy ..." He hesitated for a second and then stood up and moved away from his desk as he corrected himself. "My *son* will be joining us from tomorrow."

"You're doing the right thing, Gabe." Roger was the only person to ever call Gabriel Black by this shortened name. "Things will work out and I'm sure he'll settle in well here. We'll just need to give him time to adapt, and comfort him through his grieving. It's tragic for a seven-year-old to lose his mother, but he has gained you."

Roger looked directly at the other man and, as their eyes met, an unspoken understanding passed between them.

"He is definitely being short-changed! If there is a God, why am I not dead and my son living happily with the woman who loved him?" Black's voice was filled with bitterness and Roger remained silent, no doubt asking himself the same thing.

Black continued. "Andrew asked me if we had sourced a counsellor yet. I told him you were dealing with it. Will you, please?" This was not a word Black used very often. He was used to simply telling people what to do.

Roger nodded. "I've arranged to meet a woman tomorrow in Wilmslow. I've also arranged for you to meet the headmistress at Arnford Primary School on Thursday at 10 a.m. I think you should go with John. The children aren't back until September, and he'll have the chance to have a look around. Miss Greaves is looking forward to seeing you both. The school can also offer support and counselling."

Black frowned. Or, rather, the frown that had taken up residence on his face since the police had called to tell him about Eliza Redfern's death deepened.

"I know you want to handle everything your way, and your way is usually best, but this is not business, nor is it about you." Roger had lowered his voice. He was not going to allow Gabriel to wallow in self-pity. They would all need to get used to the new "norm", which was going to become their way of life, with a young child living under their roof – or roofs, to be precise. And it was going to impact on all of them, one way or another, thanks to the agreement.

Black's phone rang out, indicating a message.

Roger started to head to the door. "If that's Elana, see her tonight. Have a good time and be ready to face tomorrow as a new day." He pulled the door shut as he left the room.

Black checked the message from Elana and composed his reply.

Be here at 8. Sorry, but the car will take you home tonight. Late. Black.

Yes, he needed a good screw. How easy was it going to be to carry on his bachelor lifestyle with a seven-year-old in situ? What time did he go to bed? Which one of the nine spare bedrooms should he be given? Hell, would he even sleep alone?

And what about when the child was not to sleep at Arnford Hall? Black thought again that there was no God.

Chapter 5

Black opened the door to Elana at precisely 8 p.m. that evening and stood for a moment as the former lingerie model slid her long slender legs out of the taxi. The short skirt that followed was just visible under the equally short jacket, which barely covered her thirty-five inch, C-cup breasts, as they pressed against her black lace top. Her stiletto heels crunched over the gravel towards him.

He smiled for the first time that day. He didn't give a damn about Elana; she could have been any one of the string of women he was seeing at the moment, most of whom knew about the existence of the others, though possibly not quite how many of them there were. He just needed sex, and here she was, on a plate, as it were.

He took her coat and she took the glass of Moët he offered and walked into the drawing room, sprawling onto the oatmeal chaise longue and smiling provocatively at her host.

"Your text sounded like you were in a hurry, darling."

Black smiled back selfishly. "I just have a lot to do tomorrow, so I'm sorry to have to push your sweet little ass out this evening. Come over here, and take my mind off all the work I have to do in the morning." He patted the cushion beside him on the four-seater sofa. Elana kept hold of her champagne.

After a few sips he took the glass from her hand and placed it on the ornate antique mahogany coffee table and slipped his hand down her bra, before nuzzling into her and finally kissing her.

He wasn't in the mood for much foreplay, and he forced her back to lie on the sofa as he pushed his hand up her skirt, lowering her knickers as far as he needed to gain access to the place he wanted to enter.

"In a hurry, are we, sir?" Elana pouted, feeling slightly short-changed not to at least have had the chance to empty her glass.

Black was already unfastening his trousers. He climbed on top of the former model and ungraciously inserted himself inside her. There was no passion, no embrace, no gentleness; just lust and selfish hunger on his part. His one redeeming act was to ensure she had a mind-blowing orgasm just as he emptied himself into her.

As the unloving couple adjusted their clothing, he handed her back her champagne glass. He had barely said more than a dozen words to her. Even for him, this was unusual.

"Are we going to go upstairs and get more comfy?" She glanced at him, hopeful, but his expression made it clear that comfort was not on his mind.

"No. Drink up and let's go downstairs," he said, his tone a mixture of lust and distaste.

"Oh," she said, with the feeling this was going to be the modus operandi for the evening.

He took her hand and led her out across the hallway to a small spiral stone staircase, which led down to the lower floor. He tapped on the remote control in his pocket and, as they progressed through the house, bursts of white light illuminated their way down and across a lobby leading to large dark oak double doors. This was the den. He entered a code on a number pad at the side of the doors and swung one open, moving aside for Elana to walk in first. Heavy brocade curtains were drawn across two tall windows opposite the doorway, blocking out any daylight that would have shone in through the south east-facing glass. With more tapping on the remote, a faint glow of yellow light fanned out into the spacious, sparsely furnished room.

Black walked over and raised the sash of one of the windows to let in a little fresh air as it had been a warm August day. He left a small chink in the curtains, as the air sifted into the room. There was a king-sized four-poster bed in the middle space, and ivory chiffon lace curtains had been tied back, revealing a black silk sheet spread over the mattress, and various loops of chain hanging from the posts. A large bedside table stood at each end of an ornately carved dark wooden headboard, and at the foot of the bed was a large sofa in a saddle-oak hide, with deep buttons extending over the back and the arms, with brass coasters cushioning polished wooden legs. Two additional identical sofas sat against the walls on either side of the bed. On the right-hand side of the room were two large wing-backed armchairs to match the sofas, with a mahogany coffee table between them. All of the seating faced the bed.

"I'm in the mood to play tonight," he said, his tone cold with a hint of menace.

Elana was taken aback by his lack of passion. She knew, after her five previous encounters with the man before her, that he was seldom gentle, never loving and occasionally cruel, but he was masterful, unpredictable, exciting, and even at the age of forty, incredibly sexy and erotic. No man – and there had been quite a few – had ever made her feel as good as he did, and she knew she would keep coming back for more for as long he would have her. No doubt that was how the others felt. Hell, she had even agreed to a threesome with one of them, but that really wasn't her bag.

"What did you have in mind?" she ventured to ask.

He glared at her and she bit her lip, regretting her question.

"Strip!" he ordered and he sat in one of the armchairs and slouched back to enjoy the performance.

This was different for Elana; putting on a stage show. Usually, they both undressed quickly and jumped into bed. Now she stared at him, still in his black trousers, dark blue shirt and deep grey silk tie. He had simply taken off his jacket.

Trying to appear confident, she threw her head back and strained to smile, unfastening her blouse and casting it off, followed by her bra. He did not take his eyes off her, nor did the stern expression on his face alter as she continued to remove her skirt and stockings. She moved towards him and thought about letting the stockings float over his shoulders, but somehow she thought he might not appreciate such a gesture. He was in a strange mood.

She finally removed her suspender belt and lowered her knickers, elegantly stepping out of them. She put her hands on her hips and pouted, making direct eye contact with him, and she was aware of him drinking in the vision of her slender, yet well endowed, naked body.

Suddenly he was holding her, his mouth hungry for hers, his hands roaming over her breasts, tugging on her hardened nipples, then lowering and moving towards her vagina. His fingers invaded her, first one, then two, then three, and he felt her wetness and licked his lips. He would keep her waiting a little longer.

"Now strip me," he said at last, and she sighed in relief that he was at least going to join in the play.

She hurriedly unfastened his tie and placed it around her own neck. She knew he liked that. She unbuttoned his shirt and pushed it down his arms and back. Then she fell to her knees and tugged at his trousers, her slender arms running down his legs as she removed the elegant, expensive garments. He tugged at the tie and raised her head to look up at him and, looking into his eyes, she slid his trunks down.

She kissed the end of his large, erect penis and then slowly began to take him in her mouth, her tongue circling him, pushing his foreskin back down his shaft, filling her throat, until he withdrew himself.

"Not yet," Black murmured.

He pulled her up using the tie and led her to the bed, indicating for her to lie back across it widthways. He tugged at two cuffs, which were permanently attached to the underside of the bed, and secured her widespread ankles in them. Then he pulled the chains on the cuffs further out, enabling Elana to slide across the bed and hang her head and shoulders off the other side, so her top half was upside down, her breasts full and yearning to be grasped. Black strode round to her and positioned one of the black silk pillows on the floor so she could rest her head on it. Two further cuffs were then pulled out from under the mattress and her wrists were bound in them. She was now draped, outstretched, over the bed.

He lowered his head to brush his lips over hers and she moaned in anticipation of his next move. Climbing onto the bed and straddling her body, he entered her. As he thrust she strained on the ankle cuffs, not wanting to evade him, but

18

struggling against his force and the nature of gravity to push her further off the bed. His fingers sought the spot that would give her the most pleasure and she pulled at her bonds, desperately wanting to touch him, kiss him and hold him to her. But she was immobilised. He was in control and he continued to push his penis into her and then withdraw, fingering her clitoris until she screamed out in orgasm. His cry combined with hers as his liquid flowed into her. He stayed inside her a while longer, finally caressing her breasts and sucking at her hardened nipples as she lay on the very edge of the mattress. Then he dropped the top half of his body off the edge and hovered over her as, inverted, his hands supported him on the floor. He kissed her and his tongue invaded her mouth, exploring, tasting and licking inside her.

"Gabriel," she exclaimed, as he withdrew, and she strained against the cuffs, uselessly trying to free herself.

He pushed himself up and then climbed off the bed. He released her arms and helped her up onto the mattress and released her ankles. She rubbed them to prevent cramp and then lay on her stomach on the silk sheet. Black lay next to her for a few minutes before standing and taking a black silk wrap from the back of the door and putting it on.

"Wait there and don't move," he ordered as he left the room, returning a minute later with the champagne and glasses. He topped the latter up and placed them on the coffee table, before proceeding to tip the bottle to drip the sparkling liquid on her back, creating a small pool in the curve of her spine. She flinched at the coldness and he slowly and sensuously began to suck it up from her body, trying to stem little streams which had started flowing over her waist onto the black sheet. It was one of his more erotic acts and she was intoxicated by it, raising her head slightly and exhaling, wanting the sensation to linger, as she felt a false hope that maybe she meant something to him.

But she didn't.

He raised himself up and went over to the sofa, making himself comfortable as he sat back, took his champagne and stared at her intently.

"Now turn over and pleasure yourself for me." He sipped as he watched. This was becoming easier for her, as she knew it was one of his games. She lay back and opened her legs as her hand moved down and she cupped her pubis, extending her fingers to stroke and cajole her clitoris, which still tingled from the memory of his tongue on her back, making it easy for her to reach orgasm for the third time tonight. Maybe he would change his mind and let her stay.

But he didn't.

As she slowly came down from her ecstasy, he patted the sofa for her to sit next to him, without offering her a robe, and passed her the glass of champagne.

He observed her revelling in the delicious bubbles, her long neck and lean naked body as she posed gracefully beside him. It was easy to see why she made a very good lingerie model.

They drank the last of the champagne and he leaned over and embraced her, running his fingers down her spine, cupping her hair in his hand as he tasted her lips and then explored inwards to her tongue. His hand moved to grasp her breasts and he pulled at her nipples, twisting them with his forefinger and thumb, and she moaned softly. Then his fingers slid inside her vagina one last time, and he brought them up to his mouth to suck her juice from them.

Her eyes were closed and he had to admit she was beautiful.

But it was time for her to go now. He wanted her to remember how good and bad he could be. He wouldn't be seeing her again.

At midnight he called for the car to take her home. Michael had known it wasn't worth going to bed until he had taken this woman back to wherever she had come from.

Chapter 6

At nine o'clock the next morning, Roger rang Mrs Beardly and advised her that Mr Black would be collecting John in one hour.

At precisely ten o'clock, the black Bentley pulled up outside 3 West Terrace in Mobberley. The property was a modern dormer bungalow, and Black saw, unnoticed through the dark-tinted glass of his car, four faces peering out from the large picture window overlooking the street.

Michael got out and walked round to open the rear passenger door to let his employer out. Black exited the car confidently, holding a *Phalaenopsis* "Lady Ruby" orchid. He strode up the path to the front door with the confidence of someone who owned the whole estate. Well, no doubt most of the residents subscribed to Black Power for its low cost energy.

Within five seconds of his knock a short woman with shoulder-length soft brown wavy hair opened the door. He immediately noticed her resemblance to Eliza, although he hadn't seen the mother of his child in the past eight years.

"Hello, er …"

"Black." His dark eyes under his furrowed brow gazed intently at Carol, and she immediately felt even more nervous than she had been feeling for the past hour, while waiting for him to come. Her eyes fell to the plant.

"This is for you. It should be fine in an east-facing window, preferably on a windowsill with a radiator below it."

Carol just stared at the plant, admiring its beauty, but not without thinking the petals appeared to have capillaries distributing – or could it be seeping? – blood along them. She looked up at him.

"Shall I come in, or are you just going to pass me my son out here in the street?" His face gave away no trace of what he was thinking, but his eyes showed that he had spotted a small suit-case and a large trunk just behind the woman in the hallway.

"I … I'm sorry, of course, Mr Black. Come in." She stepped aside, feeling clumsy and unsure of herself in her own home. He was so intimidating, and why did she feel he was enjoying it?

Carol led Black into the dining room.

"I thought I would bring John in here and you two could have a little privacy. I'm sorry, the other children are getting a bit giddy. None of them are used to strangers in the house."

He looked mildly amused at the term "stranger". He handed her the plant. She took it and hurriedly left the room, glad for the chance to gulp in some fresh air as she shut the door and left him alone in her dining room.

She had to admit he was very good-looking, and impeccably dressed, if somewhat formal for this warm late-August morning, especially considering he was here to meet a small seven-year-old boy. What would John make of the dark navy trousers, stark white shirt with blue stripes and dark blue silk tie, and sunlight bouncing off his highly polished black shoes?

Black looked around the room, waiting patiently. He was aware of protests and some shouting among the children. Then everything was hushed.

A moment later the door was opened and Carol walked in, not quite pulling John in behind her.

Black turned to see the small boy, looking down at his feet, short black hair crowning his head, wearing a familiar Ben 10 top with skinny blue jeans and trainers. John was kicking his foot into the carpet. Black wanted to tell him to stop and to look up, but remained silent. Then he noticed the bedraggled-looking dog in the boy's hand.

"Is that Gromit?" his father asked, his voice quiet and gentle. *Please, don't let him be afraid of me.*

Carol still had hold of his hand and John clung to hers as he slowly raised his eyes to see the large man standing across the room from him.

"Yes," he whispered and he hugged the toy to his chest.

Carol bent down towards him, saying, "Come and sit on the chair, John. Would you like to say hello to your father?" She thought of saying "dad", but Mr Black didn't look like anyone's dad. She led the reluctant boy to a chair opposite to where Mr Black was standing. Black sat down too.

In the same gentle voice, he spoke as he placed his hands before him on the table.

"Hi John. I am so pleased to meet you. I've seen some pictures of you. You're a big boy now!"

John shuffled back on the chair and Carol, who had crouched down beside him, released her hand from his grip and stood up.

"Let me go and get some water and tea." She looked questioningly at the man, who nodded silently, hardly taking his eyes from John. She left the room and closed the door.

"Who's the guy on your shirt?"

The boy didn't look up. Black pushed his chair back and walked round the table and sat on the one next to his son. He felt surprisingly relaxed and patient. The latter was not a trait he was known for.

"I used to love Batman when I was your age."

Now John looked up and Black could see he had been crying; his eyes were narrowed and he looked tired.

Suddenly he spoke up. "I like him too." Then he pulled his shirt out in front of him.

"This is Ben 10, but I think Batman is better … and Spider-man."

"Oh, yes." Black smiled warmly, fighting back an almost overwhelming urge to grab the boy and hug him to him. "I forgot about him. I think I have some movies at my house with these superheroes in them. Maybe we could watch them together sometime."

"I watched films with my mummy. I don't think I like movies much." Black was a little taken aback and slightly perplexed. Did John not know that films and movies were the same thing? How could he get on this boy's wavelength? He had never come within a hundred yards of a boy before, let alone tried to enter into a conversation with one. He really had his work cut out for him. Should he refer to Eliza now, yet, ever?

"I've got films too."

"Aunty Carol says I have to come and live with you." The boy shot him an accusing look.

Black hesitated a moment, choosing his words carefully. "I think we should give it a go. Your mother would be happy."

John looked at him, wonder in his eyes. "That's what Aunty Carol said."

Black sighed in relief. He had said something right.

Carol knocked and entered the room with their drinks. As she placed them on the table, she looked questioningly at Black, and turned to John. "Are we OK?" she asked, trying to sound cheerful.

He nodded.

"I … I wondered if your driver would like a drink. He's been waiting quite a while." She glanced at Black again.

He was about to say, "He's paid to wait," but thought better of it. "That would be nice. I'm sorry. You'll have to ask him what he drinks." His expression added, *I don't need to know such things!*

Left alone again for a few minutes, Black turned to study John. The boy was looking down at Gromit, his cuddly toy, which was grubby enough to show it was a well-loved possession. Black gazed at the young boy's black wavy hair and his sad brown eyes, reddened from shedding more tears than a seven-year-old should have to shed. Again, he was almost overwhelmed by a desire to scoop the boy up into his arms, to take away all his sadness and grief, to protect him and to love him.

"Do you like football, John?" His father's voice was quiet and unemotional.

"Yes."

Black responded to the monosyllabic reply, avoiding any awkward silence. "I used to love fencing at school."

He was pleasantly surprised when John turned to him and proudly announced that he knew what fencing was; one of his friends had done some in after-school club.

Feeling he was on safer ground, Black started to encourage John to tell him what he did at school, what he liked to do, and what his friends were called, and he smiled proudly as the boy's animated chatter began to get a little louder.

As Carol came back into the room, she couldn't fail to notice that the two appeared a little more relaxed and John was talking ten to the dozen. She gave his father a genuine smile.

Then she saw him glance at his watch. *He wants to go now, get started on his new relationship with his son.* She was surprised at the feeling of compassion that emerged within her at this.

Why had Eliza shut this man out so completely? It was obvious she had thought something of him; it had taken her eight years to seriously start seeing another man! Black seemed nice enough. OK, he was controlling, proud, arrogant and had a bit of a reputation as a playboy, not to mention as a ruthless businessman who didn't give a damn about anyone else, but he had an empire to run; you couldn't turn your head in the street without noticing something to do with at least one of his companies. And, by all accounts, the family empire had been left to him to run.

Carol was amazed that he was even here in person, having expected a call to say a taxi would come for John, or some other impersonal arrangement. Now he appeared genuinely desperate to get to know his son.

And what was with the agreement Eliza had entered into with him? How had she persuaded such a rich, powerful and influential man to commit to it?

She broke free from her reverie.

"John, why don't you go into the lounge for a moment and join your cousins? I just need to speak with your father."

John didn't need asking twice and he shot out of the room, not looking at Black again.

His father was surprised to feel a twinge of disappointment. He sat back in the chair and crossed his legs as he surveyed Carol Beardly. He regretted that she reminded him of Eliza: he didn't want to be reminded, didn't want to think what might have been if his life had been different. She wouldn't have been driving a small car, taking their son to a state school, if things had been different. She wouldn't be dead now!

Carol broke into his thoughts.

"Mr Cornworthy sent me a copy of the … er … agreement." She shot a glance at Black before looking away as she took a paper from her jeans pocket and continued to talk, examining the list a little too intensely. "I feel it my duty to make sure Eliza's wishes are followed."

She was clearly nervous and in awe of the man in front of her.

He knew she didn't know his secret.

He remained silent, letting her continue awkwardly.

"Well, er, is there a Mrs Black?" she was positively trembling.

"I'm not married, if that's what you mean." His tone was impassive and he didn't take his eyes from her face.

"Oh, OK then. I guess we don't need to worry about that point." Her voice betrayed the fact she couldn't comprehend why her sister had included a clause to say that the child could not sleep in the same house as a Mrs Black.

He smirked to himself, amused that she had raised point two before point one in the agreement.

"Which school will he be going to?" She spoke too quickly, and threw her head back almost petulantly. Why was this man so intimidating?

"I'm seeing the headmistress of Arnford Primary School on Thursday."

"Good." *I sound like an old school headmistress myself.* Carol cringed inwardly.

She opened her mouth, ready to continue her tirade of questions, when he spoke again.

"I said I would adhere to all the conditions I agreed with your sister. I think we ought to be leaving now." He stood up and walked out of the dining room, leaving Carol Beardly feeling exasperated, and a little silly.

She shot after him.

He entered the lounge and took in the bright, spacious family living area and the four children huddled over a Cluedo board.

He waited a moment, observing the innocent family life before him, which Eliza had thrown into utter confusion and despair, and which he was about to irretrievably break up.

"John?" He spoke quietly, with authority. "It's time to go. Say goodbye to your cousins."

Carol came in and the word "arsehole" echoed around her head, as John shot out of the room, crying as he ran upstairs.

"I don't want to go. Why can't I stay here?"

Black turned and looked imploringly at Mrs Beardly.

"What did you expect? His mother's just died, for pity's sake!" She almost spat the words at him. Somehow, she knew they would never be happy families, the Beardlys and the Blacks, but she was damned if she was going to give up her nephew totally.

"Look …" She could see that Black was completely confused, "what did I say wrong?" written all over his face.

"He needs to know when he will see us again. He's lost his mother; you're taking him out of the school he knows, and now you appear to be cutting us off too. None of us want that. The kids get along great." She hesitated as she added, "I was hoping he could come away with us sometimes, for holidays and the like." She looked at him, trying to appeal to the better nature that she was sure was in him somewhere.

"I think that may be sensible."

Sensible! Sensible? What is this guy, a bloody robot? "It would be compassionate and kind." She watched his eyes darken and his frown deepen.

"We are not all from the same compassionate and kind family background as you, Mrs Beardly. Let me know which holidays you were thinking of and I will consider it. Now, will you bring John down, or shall I go and get him?"

What's with this guy? She was taken aback by his formal, stand-offish and controlling manner. She had witnessed his gentleness and, she believed, genuine love for his son in the dining room. Was he now showing his true colours? Was he a monster? Would he harm John? No. From the warmth in his eyes when he gazed at his son, she somehow knew he wouldn't.

"I'll get him, but I think we need to be able to tell him when he will next see his cousins." She glared at Black. "Unless, of course, you want to make him even more unhappy than he already is?"

"I want nothing of the sort. Bring your children to Arnford Hall on Friday." He forced the words out, as an image of children at Arnford Hall evaded him.

"With respect, Mr Black, I think it would be better if John came here." She saw his accusing look. "I mean, we have toys and computer games and the like. It would just be easier. I'll come and get him if that helps."

"That won't be necessary." His eyes shot around the room and he took in the latest Wii console, which had only just been released. Presumably there were lots more gadgets in the house. He took his Black Communications Xphone out of his pocket and tapped the screen.

"I'll bring him. We will arrive at 2 p.m. for two hours." He raised his eyebrows to see if she concurred.

She was stunned by his formality, and the fact he was going to be accompanying John.

"Yes, that's fine," she said, thinking that if there was anything else in her diary it would have to be moved!

He strode confidently into the hallway and looked at the bags by the door, as Carol went upstairs to talk to John. He opened the front door and carried the bags to the car. Michael got out and opened the boot.

"Sir?" he said questioningly, aware there was a small boy missing, and wondering if they were about to leave.

Black placed the bags on the ground. "I'll be back in a minute," he said as he returned to the house.

Carol stood in the hall holding John's hand, Gromit clutched firmly in the boy's other hand.

"So, John, we're going to see you in three days, OK? You can choose what you want to play with, and see your cousins." She looked up at Black. He was observing the two of them, and Carol wondered for a moment if there was a trace of anxiety on his face. Just a trace …

"I've made your father a list." She continued to talk to John, and Black felt like an intrusive observer. "So he'll know what food you like, and which games you enjoy playing. Don't forget to brush your teeth every morning and every night. And be good going to bed when your father tells you. Promise me?"

John looked at his aunt through tearful eyes and nodded. "Did you tell him I like chocolate?" he whispered.

Carol smiled warmly and hugged her nephew. "Yes, darling."

Black crouched down in front of his son. "I love chocolate too, John." He looked at Carol, unsure how to suggest it was time to go.

"Come on, let's go and look at that big car," and she led John down the drive as Black followed.

Michael opened the car door, having inserted the newly acquired child car seat, and smiled at the little fellow, feeling a touch of sorrow that he was leaving an apparently happy home to take up residence at Arnford Hall.

Carol turned to Black. "Over to you, Mr Black." She stepped aside.

"Climb into your seat, John," his father instructed, his tone gentle and patient. He leaned in and secured the seat belt, then closed the door and turned to face Carol.

"Thank you." He held his hand out to shake hers.

Why do you have to be so formal? Aren't we like family now? She took his hand in both of hers and squeezed it, inwardly pleased to see the look of surprise on his face.

"Don't forget to come on Friday. Two o'clock, you said."

"Er, no." He quickly regained his composure. "We will see you then." He walked around the car and Michael held the rear passenger door open as he climbed in to sit next to his son. The chauffeur then shut the door and walked round to the driver's seat.

"Thanks for the drink," he called and then drove away.

Black just glimpsed the faces of the three children staring out of the window as the large black Bentley drove their cousin away.

John gazed out of the window and hugged Gromit. Black turned slightly to look at him. He knew the child would need time to adjust: Arnford Hall; the staff; the dog; a new school; new relatives; life without his mother; and of course, life with his father.

Black would treat it just like all his other projects. He was used to working hard to continue to expand the Black empire: he had taken the Black Group into energy, construction, communications, health, beauty and gambling; he had evolved from being a megalomaniac to attaining omnipotent status, a business force to be reckoned with and in some cases feared; he was known to be ruthless with competitors, adversaries and rebellious employees.

Surely there was a more humane side to this man; a hidden side to be discovered?

He glanced through the list Carol had handed him.

A few notes I hope you will find helpful in getting to know your son.

He likes chocolate bars for a treat.

His favourite food is pasta with a simple tomato sauce, and he likes breaded chicken, fish fingers, shepherd's pie, sausages, with just a few chips, boiled potatoes or a little mashed potato.

He prefers to drink water and may occasionally have apple juice.

He loves to play on the Wii or his DX and has some games in his trunk. He also likes to play board games and some simple card games like Go Fish and Uno.

He played football after school and had just started a judo class.

He is a keen reader and has plenty of books in his trunk.

He has some cuddly toys and his favourite is Gromit. He takes him to bed and he may choose some of his others too: they're all in his trunk.

He goes to bed at 7.30 p.m. and likes to hear a bedtime story.

He can dress himself and brush his own teeth but, like most boys aged seven, is happy to let someone help him. Good idea to brush his teeth with him occasionally for another year or so!

Please let us help you if you need anything – anything at all. And call me at any time night or day.

We will miss John and look forward to seeing him soon.

Carol and James, Abbie, Josh and Craig

He put the list back in his pocket. John had not looked away from the window and the silence in the car was palpable.

"What are your cousins called, John?" The question was unthreatening, intended to make his son feel at ease, in his comfort zone. *Isn't that what you're supposed to do with young children?*

John looked at his father. His cheeks betrayed streaks of dried tears.

Has the boy been crying since we left?

"It's OK. We can talk about things. Do you want to say anything?" The man sitting beside the sad boy looked desperate for a response from him.

"I play with Craig mostly. He's seven, like me. Can I see him soon?"

"Of course." Black smiled with relief. "And do you like to play with Josh and Abbie?"

"Do you know them?" the little boy looked amazed and Black's smile grew wider.

"Maybe you can help me to get to know them." The recognition of the importance of his cousins, the connection to normality for his son, made Black realise that, in the short term at least, the Beardly family was going to be important to him. He needed to know more about them.

"What can you tell me about them?"

"I don't know."

"Did they go to your school?"

"No. I live in High Legh with my mummy." His voice suddenly began to quiver and he let his head drop towards his knees as he whispered through uncontrolled tears. "I want my mummy."

Black put his hand across the central console dividing them, and took hold of his son's, squeezing it firmly, "It's OK, John. It's OK to cry."

31

The boy's sobbing became quieter as they approached the driveway to Arnford Hall.

While pausing for the electronic gates to open, Black thought of the small dormer bungalow on a road full of identical properties. He wasn't sure where John had lived with Eliza, but assumed it was somewhere similar. Of course, he could have found out, monitored all mother-and-son moves, but what would have been the point? He had never expected to even meet his son. As the car crawled along the tree-lined avenue, thick canopies of the woodland on either side blocked out the August sunshine. The unforeseen change in the lives of the two people in the back of the Bentley had begun.

As Arnford Hall came into view, John peered out of the window, taking in the sandstone towers and large turrets with giant crosses, some almost sword-like, adorning the facade, like some medieval knight's castle.

"Does King Arthur live here?" he asked, picturing the scene from the Disney film *The Sword in the Stone.*

For the millionth time in his life Black wished he lived somewhere else – a warm and welcoming home in another land.

His voice was solemn now. "No, John. This is our house … your house now. Come on. Let's go and explore." He suddenly felt the acceptance of this place by his tearful son was essential to his own life, his current existence, his modus operandi … all he knew.

Michael opened the car door and Black stepped out onto the gravel driveway. As the chauffeur walked around to John's door, Black called out, "I'll do it."

"Yes, sir."

Black leaned in to release the seat belt and took John's hand in his own and held it firmly as he climbed out of the car and stared up at the huge mansion, with its numerous windows glaring down at him, and the two gargoyles mounted at the bottom of the steps.

Chapter 7

Still holding hands, Black led his son up the stone steps to the huge front door. He turned the large iron ring and pushed the heavy door open. They walked into the vestibule together and continued along a corridor of highly polished parquet flooring, leading through double doors into an octagonal room at the other end of the house. Sunshine poured through the windows, providing a welcome as intimate as was possible for such a vast house. This was one of Black's favourite rooms and he seldom brought any of his lady guests here. He hoped this could be a room in which John would feel comfortable.

Keeping hold of the child's hand, he strode across the soft pale blue carpet to a window seat.

"Let's sit here," he said, tentatively, watching John as they sat down next to each other. "Do you think Gromit will like living here?"

Silence.

No problem. He's going to need time to adjust. I'm going to need time too!

Black was unsure whether to continue chatting or just give the boy a little time with his own thoughts … whatever they were.

The silence was broken by a loud knock on the door. Everything in this house needed to be loud to be noticed, and although the doors were open, it was customary for the staff to knock at all times to make the occupant – usually Black – aware of their presence.

"Yes?" Black responded, looking up at Roger.

Roger entered the room and approached the boy. "Hi, John. My name's Roger and I work for your father. I'm very pleased to meet you … and Gromit," he added as he saw the dog strangled by the boy's tight grip. Roger then turned his attention to Black. "We need to take the luggage up to his room. Have you decided yet?" Black knew he was referring to which bedroom would become John's.

Arnford Hall had eight bedrooms on the first floor and two additional ones on the second. Black had the master suite, situated in the west wing, which faced south-east and was connected to a morning room, which was directly above the octagonal room. To the north of Black's room was a short corridor leading to a smaller bedroom. This room faced east and was light and airy, with a large picture window looking out over the grounds. A doorway led to a shared bathroom. It had been decorated with a Chinese theme and was a welcoming guest room, but it was not a child's bedroom.

Black was very aware of how unprepared he was, the house was, the staff were, the whole bloody lot of them were, for his son's unexpected arrival. Things had happened so quickly since the news of Eliza's death, and he had reacted, without actually managing the situation. This was not his style. Business deals were planned; action taken quickly when necessary, but everything would have been calculated, investigated, amended and changed to suit his business needs; offers would be made and if the seller didn't like it, then he walked away: he was the one who always called the shots. Roger was the guy who knew how to work with him; the person with whom Black could work best. Now they were both out of their depth, baffled by a seven-year-old boy and his needs. Black had intended to take the boy up to the lake house for a couple of days and leave Roger to sort out the bedroom. After all, the PA did have a ten-year-old nephew and knew a little about these things. But now there was a school to visit on Thursday and an aunt and cousins on Friday.

So the bedroom needed sorting today!

"Get Amanda to prepare the Chinese room for now." He hesitated a moment. He tried to picture John alone in the double bed; it didn't seem right. Perhaps he should sleep with him in one of the twin rooms. Would that be setting a bad precedent? Yet the boy's mother had died, he had been to stay at his aunt's and now he had come to live with a father he didn't know, in a house which wasn't welcoming. A temporary measure seemed appropriate.

"Wait. We'll both sleep in the green twin room for the moment, until we get some proper furniture arranged."

Roger's face betrayed his surprise at this change of plan. He had not expected Gabriel to take such a drastic step, to vacate his own bedroom. But then there were, no doubt, going to be lots of changes from now on.

"Right. Do you want us to put John's things in there now?"

Black looked at John. "Shall we go and look at your things?"

The boy lifted his head and nodded. He still held his father's hand.

The suitcase and trunk were in the vestibule. Black opened the trunk.

"Why don't you tell me what everything is and then we can find a place to put it." Black's voice was quiet and a little apprehensive as he waited for a response.

John's face brightened a little as he saw the familiar toys and books in the trunk.

"This is my Star Wars lego, the Millennium Falcon which Mummy helped me to build." He finally let go of Gromit and began to pull the toys out, naming them and showing them to his father. Black's smile remained and he handled the toys, as though trying to reach out to his son via the physical contact with his belongings.

They spent the next half hour inspecting the contents of the trunk and placing some around the octagonal room, and taking others upstairs to reside temporarily in the green twin room.

The gadget in Black's pocket beeped. He took out the device and, using its voice activation, spoke to Steve.

"Yes, Steve?"

"Good day, sir. It's twelve thirty and I wondered if you were ready to have lunch yet?"

Black smiled at John as the young boy looked in awe, first at the gadget, from which he could hear Steve's voice, and then at his father, who towered over him.

"What would you like for lunch, John?"

"I don't know." His voice was nervous. "I'm not really hungry."

"Well, I'm sure you will be in a little bit. Steve's a really good cook." With a hint of laughter in his voice which Steve couldn't fail to notice on the intercom, he added, "I bet you'd love some pasta with a bit of sauce."

"OK," John replied quietly.

"Er, I'll see what I can do, sir."

"Just keep it simple, Steve, and I'll have the same, in about thirty minutes."

"Yes, sir."

Black winked at his son, and then shook his head, still smiling, as John asked, "Should I call you 'sir'?"

"No, you shouldn't! What would you like to call me?" replied his father, suddenly aware that John hadn't addressed him by any title yet.

John stared at his feet. "I always wanted a daddy."

Chapter 8

Gabriel Black remembered his own father. He had been twenty-five when George Black had died from motor neurone disease, having lived with the condition for ten years. Gabriel, his twin brother, Julian, and their younger sister, Ellouise, had all idolised their father, and had learned to shoot, fish and fence with him. The first symptoms of George's illness appeared as the twins turned fifteen: tiredness, cramps, lack of grip in his hands. Family life for them had changed drastically over the following few years.

The children had called George "Poppa". Gabriel Black never envisaged being called "Poppa", nor "Father", "Dad", "Daddy", "Pops", "Pa" or any other imaginable paternal label.

His face became grave as he looked down at John. Tentatively, he crouched down and gently hugged his son to him. He breathed in the smell of his hair, felt the warmth of his body and was sharply aware of the love in his own heart for this young person who had become the most important thing in his life.

"You can call me Daddy, John, if you like," he whispered.

"OK," was the reply.

Black closed his eyes and held onto his son for a few moments longer. As he released him, the boy's attention returned to the last remaining item in the trunk. It was a large paper bag containing several fancy-dress costumes. John pulled out a Batman outfit.

"Do you want to put it on?" Black asked.

"No, not yet, thank you."

"Let's put them in the drawer then." Black took the contents and placed them in the chest in the green room. "Now let's get some lunch."

It was evident and, of course, natural that John was nervous in this house. As he sat on a bar stool at the kitchen island, Gromit firmly in his grip once again, he was silent, fidgety and did not touch his food. Roger and Steve sat with them for lunch and Roger tried to make conversation, discussing Ben 10, with whom he had become acquainted thanks to his nephew.

Black's PA was well aware that he was regarded as the in-house expert on children now, and for once in his life he was a little nervous of the responsibility and his ability to live up to expectations. His saving grace was that he had to be better at it than Black, but he did have to admit his employer was a quick learner and adapter. Neither Roger nor Steve could believe their ears when John had responded to Black's question – "Would you like any garlic bread?" – with a "No, thank you, Daddy!"

The afternoon passed slowly. Black did not want to leave John alone, but he had some work to do and things to discuss with Roger. He also had an urge to speak to Carol Beardly … for advice. He considered letting his son watch television in the octagonal room, while he worked in his study, which was directly off that room, and then thought about the computer games in his trunk.

"John, do you want to play on your DX in my office while I do a bit of work in there?"

"I'm not sure."

The boy's voice was quivering. He had barely touched his food, except for a piece of chocolate cake, and had been staring blankly at a book about Spiderman for the past half hour. Black noticed he hadn't even turned a page.

I've got to do something.

"I know. I'll turn the TV on and you can watch something for a few minutes while I make some phone calls. I'll only be in the next room. Then we'll go for a walk. I've got something to show you."

As Black sat at his desk, he realised just how much he needed this bit of breathing space; a chance to take stock of how things were progressing and to come up with an action plan.

He called for Roger to join him.

"Did you get that book?"

"Yes," Roger replied, handing him a copy of *Coping with the Death of a Parent: A Guide for Children.* "I got a copy for Steve and me to read too."

"Good. I want you to get that interior designer in; the one who did the games room. Get her to give us some options for the Chinese room to be converted into John's bedroom. I'm going to arrange to go and see the room he had with Eliza." He paused a moment, as if confirming to himself that this was the right thing to do. "I want him to feel at home here, as soon as possible."

"Of course. Do you want me to come with you?"

"No. I want you to stay with John. I'll go alone. He needs to get to know you, and Steve. You're going to have to sort a room out at your place too." Black looked directly at Roger and a mutual understanding passed between them. Black added, with a touch of regret in his voice, "I'm sorry about this."

"Don't be. We'll get the spare room sorted, don't worry about it."

"Well, check that funds for any refurbishment will be readily available. I don't want any last-minute messing about with disinvestments, and I'll pay for it all directly. Don't let it affect the estate, unless you have a more efficient plan?"

"Let me have a think about estimated costs. We've had a good run with one of the global equity funds and it may be a good time to cash some of it in. I'll check for any tax hit and let you know."

"Thanks. And can you also speak to Paul at the Manchester development? I was looking at the site yesterday and just want to know how it's progressing. I might need you to keep a few balls in the air for me over the next few days."

Roger suddenly smiled, thinking about the green twin room, "And you're going to need to keep yours in your trousers for a while! Nothing like a challenge!" As Black picked up a notebook to hurl at his PA and best friend, Roger left the room, laughing.

Black sighed and picked up the phone.

"Hi, Mrs Beardly? It's Black." He arranged to meet her at Eliza's house at 6 p.m.

Afterwards, he took John for a stroll around the grounds of Arnford Hall, including the dog kennel where Satan lived. Satan was an aging Chesapeake Bay retriever gundog, who had been with the Black family for all of his thirteen years.

He was a working dog not accustomed to anyone except his master, Roger and Steve. As they approached the kennel, Black explained that Satan was not a family pet, but that he loved to work and help catch and retrieve things.

"I'm just going to introduce you," Black said reassuringly, squeezing John's hand.

Standing closely between Satan and John, Black instructed the dog to sit. Satan looked up at his master, his amber eyes bright, his posture one of pride and affection. Black stroked him, saying, "This is John, my son. He's come to live with us. Make sure you look after him, Satan." And, turning to John, while still patting the dog, he winked at his son and John smiled up at him.

"We'll take him for a walk later, if you like."

"Yes, please, Daddy."

Would he ever get used to hearing that name?

While Roger and Steve took John to the nearest McDonald's for tea, Black waited for Carol outside the house that had been home to Eliza and John.

"Thanks for agreeing to meet me here. I just need to get a feel for what John is used to. There's enough change going on in his life and I want to try to give him some normality, something he has been brought up with that he might regard as his own."

"I think that's a great idea." Carol led him into the lounge. "I guess we're going to have to sort everything out and arrange to sell this place. It all belongs to John now."

"I can get someone to do everything, if it will help. Have a think and we can discuss it on Friday. Right now, I want to see where John has been living. It's very different for him now." Black looked at Carol as he paused for a moment. *If you only knew how much!* "I need to make sure the change process is managed to cause the least upset to the child."

Carol didn't know whether to be in awe of this unemotional, controlling and reserved man standing in her dead sister's small living room, or infuriated with his manner towards "the child"! *He was his son, for goodness' sake!* She decided to bite her tongue, and at least be thankful that he was actually considering his needs, and how to help John's transition to his new life.

Black looked around the room. There was a small sofa and armchair, a coffee table, and a mantelpiece above a gas-flamed fire. He smiled faintly as he recognised the model from one of Black Power's most popular home-fire ranges. *She didn't hate me enough to never buy any of my products, then. I'd have given it to you as a gift, Eliza!* He turned his attention to two photographs on the mantel: one was of John in his school uniform, beaming at the camera; the other was of mother and son sitting on a bench in what looked like a park or wood. He wondered who had taken the photo.

"Did she have a boyfriend?" His voice was quiet and his eyes remained on the picture.

"She had started dating a guy a couple of months ago." Carol thought back to how she broke the news of Eliza's death to David. The relationship had really been too new to have any lasting impact on either him or John, who had met him twice. Carol and James had both felt it best to let David get on with his own life and not to seek any contact with John. From the look on Black's face she knew this had been the right decision; he didn't need to know any more about it.

However, he obviously thought he did!

"Who was he, and did he meet John?"

Carol tried to be patient and not appear exasperated. "His name was David. As far as I know, he met John twice. Look, my sister had a few relationships. They never lasted very long and she wasn't in the habit of introducing John to any of her boyfriends. But I think she did like this guy, and they had been on a couple of walks at the weekend, taking John with them. Other than him coming to the funeral," she realised she had his full attention now as he turned to look at her, noticing she was struggling not to let her voice show how upset she was beginning to feel, "we won't be seeing him any more. He'll move on."

Suddenly she fell onto the sofa and began to cry quietly. Black remained standing and waited a moment.

"I'm sorry," she sobbed, her head lowered as she fumbled in her pocket to find a tissue.

Black pulled a stark white handkerchief embroidered with "GB" in navy thread from his breast pocket and handed it to her.

"Don't be," he said authoritatively. "Your sister has just died. You're entitled to be upset. Wait here while I have a look around."

Carol felt obliged to do as she was told, and remained seated for what seemed like an age. This was only the third time she had been back to Eliza's house after she had died; the earlier times had been to collect things for John. She dreaded the thought of having to go through her sister's belongings, and every now and then her grief would come over her, and she would lament her loss, curse the waste of a vibrant life and the cruel theft of a young mother. It wasn't fair!

He came back into the room, carrying a Spiderman duvet and pillow.

"I'm sorry if this is painful for you, but can you tell me where to look for some photos of John's mother? There were none in his trunk or suitcase."

She looked at him apologetically, almost fearfully. "I'm sorry. I wasn't sure if you would appreciate them," she whispered.

"They're for John, not me." Although his voice was quiet, she felt as if he was admonishing her. He perceived her sadness and added, "But thank you for your concern. I'm afraid I have no feelings for your sister. I have few feelings for anyone." He looked out of the window onto the street momentarily. "So, please don't worry on my behalf. However, I am not totally heartless and do appreciate the chance I have been given to have a relationship with my son. I don't intend to waste that chance, but I am sorry it has come at such a cost to your family. If you could just show me where the photographs would be, or let me know if they are on a computer, you can leave then, if you prefer, and I'll lock up here and bring the key over to you on Friday." He waited for her response.

"I have her computer at home. I intended to go through the photos myself, and perhaps with John when he was ready, but there is an album in the dining room." She stood up and he followed her through some double doors into a sunny room with

French doors leading into the garden. He looked out at a swing and small climbing frame while Carol retrieved the album from a drawer.

He took it from her and put it on the table.

"Is it OK if I take a look here? I'd like to take a couple back to Arnford Hall, for John to have with him. I think it will help." He looked at her intently, awaiting her consent.

"Of course. Take whatever you like. I think you're right about it helping John. He may want to come back here one more time too – you know, before it's sold." She fought back the tears this time.

"We think alike, Mrs Beardly," and he began to turn the pages of the album.

After a couple of minutes he had withdrawn three photos: two of Eliza on her own and one of her laughing with John. He returned the book to the drawer.

They walked back into the lounge and he took the large framed picture of the two of them together in the park from the mantelpiece. *Who cares who took the damn photo?*

"Thank you. We can go now." He led the way out of the house.

As she watched his Bentley drive away, Carol wondered why she felt so compelled to do what he said.

Chapter 9

Black arrived back at Arnford Hall just as Roger and Steve returned with John.

Roger and Steve had been together for five years and had been married the previous year, since the law had been changed to allow same-sex marriages. They lived in the former coach house, within the grounds of Arnford Hall but not visible from the main building. It had three bedrooms, one of which was to be allocated to John, as the two men had discussed with their employer.

Roger had asked John if he would like to go to McDonald's with him and Steve, as it presented a great opportunity for the three of them to start to get to know each other. If life was ever to have any semblance of normality and peace at the Hall, this ease of being with each other would be vital to those living there.

Steve had driven the white Audi Q7 to the restaurant in Altrincham, while Roger explained, in the simplest possible way for a seven-year-old, his relationship with Steve, and how they both worked for his father: Roger as his assistant and right-hand man, and Steve as his chef.

John seemed to take things in his stride and, as soon as Roger started talking about the latest episode of *Ben 10* he had watched with his nephew, it seemed they would be friends for life, and that any friend of Roger's would be a friend of John's. The fact they all liked McDonald's was a bonus!

So far, so good.

"Come on, John," Black called as he climbed out of the Bentley, leaving Michael to park it in one of the garages. "Let's take that walk with Satan."

A moment of uncertainty passed among the four males standing on the driveway, as John looked up at Roger, almost for guidance as to whether to go to his father or not. As Roger smiled, John ran over to Black; the look of relief on his father's face not going unnoticed by Roger or Steve, and they watched as Gabriel lifted his son off his feet, hugging him tightly before setting him back down on the ground. It was an intimate moment and one his father cherished.

"Hey," yelled John in surprise. "That's my Spiderman duvet!"

"Let's put it on your bed when we get back. Come on." Handing the bedding and pictures to Roger, Black led his son down the steps to a store room to retrieve Satan's lead and a few treats for him.

As father and son walked the hound through the woods, Black needed all his wits about him to respond to the observations and questions of an inquisitive seven-year-old.

"Did you know Roger and Steve are married, even though they are both men?"

"Well, when two people love each other, it's good to get married."

"I don't think my mummy loved you. Is that why you didn't marry her?"

"Well, I think your mummy thought it best if we didn't get married." *Please don't ask me if I loved her.*

"Did you love her?"

"No, John. She didn't love me and I didn't love her. But I love you, John."

"That's probably good. I would feel a bit sad if you loved her and she didn't love you. If you love someone they should really love you back, or it would hurt your feelings. And my teacher says we shouldn't do that."

"I guess your teacher is right, then."

"Who do you love, Daddy?"

"I love you, John."

"Do you love a lady?"

"No, John, just you. Let's go back to the house now. I think Satan has had enough."

The man and boy climbed the stairs, carrying the pillow and duvet. Black placed them on one of the twin beds. He had also brought up the framed photograph of John and his mother in the wood.

"Where shall we put this?"

John took the picture and stood it on the bedside table next to his bed.

"Put her here so she can see Spiderman on my bed. She likes Spiderman. Do you, Daddy?"

"Yes, John."

They went into the bathroom and Black handed his son his toothbrush and the tube of toothpaste.

"My mummy always put this on."

Black squeezed the paste onto the brush. "Do you want to brush or shall I help you?"

"I can do it on my own." John began to brush, while walking around the bathroom, studying his reflection in the mirror, peering into the shower cubicle and stepping back as toothpaste dribbled onto the floor.

"Stand by the sink, John."

He did as he was told.

As he tucked his son into bed, Black sat beside him and read a few pages from one of his Mr Majeika storybooks.

Then he leaned down and kissed his son on the cheek. "Goodnight, John. Remember, I'll come back up in a little while and sleep in this other bed. I'll leave the lamp on. The intercom is on too, so if you need me just call out 'Daddy' and I'll come straight up. OK?"

The small child stared up at him, his eyes wide, one hand firmly clutching Gromit.

"Where are you going?"

"I'll just be in my office – you remember, the room downstairs – doing some work, and then I'll come to bed. I'll see you in the morning, John." He left the bedroom, leaving the door slightly ajar.

On the landing, he sighed and waited a moment. There was no sound.

In his office he checked through the notes left by Roger. The Manchester development was running two weeks late. Black called for his PA.

"What the fuck is going on? Why weren't we told about this?"

"There's been a delay on the delivery of a steel girder. They're hoping to make the time up during phase two, so haven't changed the final completion date."

"They'd better fucking not. What's the penalty on this?"

"Half a million."

"Bloody brilliant. Hell, I'm tired."

Suddenly the two men looked up at the ceiling. There was the sound of small feet pacing about.

Black got up and strode along the corridor to the main staircase. As he started to walk up, he saw John dragging Gromit behind him, coming down.

"I can't sleep. I don't like being here on my own. It's scary."

"Come on. I'll come up with you now." As he took the boy's hand and led him back up the staircase, he glanced at his watch and wondered when was the last time he had gone to bed – to go to sleep, that is – at nine o'clock in the evening!

Black tucked his son back into bed. Then he spread himself out on the top of the second single bed.

"You haven't put your pyjamas on," John observed.

"You know, you're right. Will you wait here a moment while I go and get them?"

"I want to come with you."

I thought you might! Black reflected a moment. He had deliberately not given his son a full tour of Arnford Hall yet. He needed to determine which rooms would be off-limits. A couple were obvious and he would have to get into the habit of keeping them locked: the den was a definite no-go area; the morning room off his own master bedroom was another. What about the master bedroom itself? Could he really expect to prohibit his young son from entering? Maybe he could simply be told to knock. After all, the house rule was to knock before entering. He decided if he didn't want John to have access to a room, that door was to be locked.

"Come on, then. You can help me get ready for bed."

The smile lighting John's face was enough to confirm that Black was getting some things right.

They walked along the corridor, following it as it turned to the left and then right along another corridor to access the west wing. This was where John's bedroom would be, opposite his father's. They crossed the galleried atrium in the centre of the wing, continued along a further corridor and turned left to face a large white-panelled door. Black turned the gilt handle and walked in. John followed him.

The door opened, revealing a huge, dark and foreboding space stretching out before it. A large four-poster bed, fully curtained in a deep red Toile de Jouy adorned with vines, thistles and thorns in gold thread, was positioned against the far wall, the canopy imprisoning the occupant of the bed, or prohibiting entry to anyone outside it.

Black looked down at his son and, seeing John's eyes widen in amazement and fear as the small boy stared across the room at the bed, he immediately went over and pulled the curtains back, tying them to the posts, and revealing a heavy bedspread of the same rich red and gold fabric.

"Do you sleep in a tent?" John asked, wonder in his voice.

"I guess it is a bit like a tent. I like it to be dark; it helps me sleep. But come on, help me find my pyjamas, because I'm going to sleep in the same room as you tonight."

Black turned to the large mahogany chest of drawers, trying to distract the boy from the formidable bed, and himself from the wish that he hadn't brought his son into his room yet.

He quickly grabbed a pair of navy checked pyjamas and hurried the boy out and back to the green twin room.

"Now, get back into bed and I'll get ready in the bathroom." A moment later he walked back into the bedroom and saw John sitting cross-legged on top of his Spiderman duvet, staring at the bathroom door, waiting for his father to return.

Gabriel kissed him tenderly on the cheek.

In the dead of the night, Black was awoken by a silent seven-year-old boy trying to climb into bed next to him. He slid over to make room, and his heart warmed, along with his body, as he enveloped his son in his arms. His life was changing; it had to be for the better.

Chapter 10

On Thursday morning Black informed Michael that he would drive himself to see the head of Arnford Primary School. After all, it was unlikely he would feel the urge for a drink after the meeting, wasn't it?

John sat on his booster seat in the front of the Bentley, feeling very small in the big car.

"Why do I have to go to a different school? I want to see my friends."

"This is nearer to the house, and you'll make lots of new friends." Black was beginning to tire of John's continuing protests to everything that had been mentioned that morning. The only thing the boy hadn't objected to was taking Satan for a walk. He seemed to have taken a shine to the dog, was relaxed, even happy, walking beside his father through the wood with the dog pulling his master along.

Father and son had made a deal: he would be allowed to sit in the front of the car in exchange for agreeing to visit his prospective new school. However, the embargo on complaints had not lasted long.

"My mummy wouldn't make me change schools."

"I think she would if she thought it was for the best, John, especially if she liked Arnford School."

Black was still surprised at how casually at times John could speak of his mother. But he didn't underestimate the boy's feelings, and the grief that gripped him at certain times too, as he had witnessed that morning when John had woken, sobbing for his mother, and holding her picture to him before finally agreeing to go downstairs with his father.

As the car pulled into the school car park, Black reached over and put his hand on John's.

"It's going to be fine," he said quietly, his voice not betraying his own fear that this was going to be a mistake, for both of them. "Let's go and meet Miss Greaves."

He pressed the intercom at the school entrance and, after a few seconds, a buzzer sounded the release of the door and they entered the reception area, to be greeted by an attractive woman in her late thirties.

"Hello. Mr Black, and John, I presume?" She looked down at the young boy and smiled. "Miss Greaves will be here in a moment. Can I get you both a drink?"

The man looked at his son, who looked at his shoes. "John, you are being spoken to. Please reply."

John reddened as he looked up, first at his father, then at the strange but friendly-looking lady.

"That's OK," the woman interrupted, and she also reddened as she saw the stern look cross Black's face.

"Tell the lady what you would like to drink." He waited.

"Water," John whispered.

"Water, what?" his father asked.

"Just water."

Black sighed. "Please!" he said abruptly, looking at the woman, and then adding, "and black coffee, no sugar, thank you."

"Just take a seat, please," she said nervously, and hurried out of the office.

A short, plump, smiley-faced woman approached them and welcomed them exuberantly, saying, "Hello! You must be John. I'm delighted to meet you," before turning to Mr Black and shaking his outstretched hand. "I'm Miss Greaves."

Her voice was warm and friendly.

Maybe today is going to get better, thought Black.

She led them into her office and motioned for the two guests to sit down.

"Thank you, Mrs Baker," she said to the receptionist as the drinks were brought in.

"Well, Mr Black. We are delighted you're considering sending John to our school. I'm sure you will both be impressed with it."

I doubt it, thought Black, remembering Eliza's terms and wondering how on earth he had ever agreed to them, any of them! He looked at Miss Greaves silently as he leaned forward in his chair and took his coffee.

But the head teacher was on her feet. There was no way she was going to let him intimidate her!

"Let me show you around." She stood up.

Black frowned and replaced his cup on the table. He and John followed their leader into the corridor.

For the next half hour they were shown the Year 3 classroom, along with examples of reading books, artwork, projects the children had been working on last year, maths worksheets, and "The very latest in interactive, voice-controlled coms boards for schools," as Miss Greaves was proud to point out.

The very latest from two years ago! thought Black, scornfully.

She then showed them the dining hall, the sports hall, the IT suite and a couple of the other classrooms, before taking them out into the sunshine to show off the school grounds: three fields, a large tarmacked playground and climbing frame area, behind which was a small wood, "for forest schools and other outdoor learning activities", Miss Greaves announced proudly.

Without waiting for any response from Mr Black, she then led them back towards her office, stopping off at reception and calling out to Mrs Baker.

"Mrs Baker, can you please take John back into the Year 3 classroom and let him do some crafts, while I speak with his father."

Black waited with bated breath, wondering if he would be expected to contribute to their conversation. Miss Greaves beckoned for Mr Black to take a seat at a small table in her office, while she walked over to a sideboard and flicked the switch on the coffee percolator sitting on its top. She then took out two white china cups and saucers, two silver teaspoons and a small milk jug from the cupboard, placing them on her desk.

"Now, Mr Black, let's have a good cup of coffee and you can tell me a little about John's background and the reason you are here." She sat back in her chair and surveyed him.

Black raised an eyebrow, but was beginning to like this woman's direct style.

"I believe my PA has already advised you that John's mother died, just over a week ago now." He looked intently at the formidable woman opposite him and she nodded in acknowledgement.

He continued. "I have had no previous relationship with my son, so we are only just getting to know each other. I'm respecting his mother's wishes that John be educated in the state school system, and as we live at Arnford Hall, your school seemed an obvious one to consider."

Miss Greaves continued to look at him, but did not interrupt.

"I'm not entirely in agreement with this arrangement, and I need to be certain that this school can provide my son with the best start one can hope for in the circumstances."

Miss Greaves wondered at this, but still did not interrupt.

"Of course, in addition to his education, I'm mindful of the need for him to settle in somewhere and be given any assistance that he may need in school to help him to come to terms with the loss of his mother."

There was a ping from the percolator and Miss Greaves smiled at her prospective new parent as she crossed the room to the door, saying, "Excuse me a moment while I get some milk."

A couple of minutes passed. Black had time to observe certificates the school had won: Status of Excellency awarded by EdBest to Arnford Primary School, North-West School of the Year for extra-curricular activities, a Green Flag award for Ecology school status, and a first-class honours degree from Oxford awarded to Miss Greaves.

The head teacher returned, and as she poured the coffee she announced brightly that John was playing happily with some lego in what would be his classroom.

Black accepted the coffee, admitting to himself it smelled much better than the first cup.

"I notice the school's certificates and your degree. I'm impressed." He had rarely said that to anyone in his whole life.

Miss Greaves beamed. "Thank you. We're very proud of our school. It's a shame you're here during the holiday and can't see the children and meet the staff – in particular Mrs McGuire, who would be John's teacher. But I can tell you we run a happy ship here, Mr Black. State education works well with the right leadership, and my senior management team and I are that right leadership. We have high standards, but also nurture our children and give them as varied experiences as possible to prepare them for the future. In John's particular circumstances, I think it will be important to try to get him into some routine as quickly as possible, while acknowledging there will be times, no doubt many at the beginning, when we will all need to take our lead from him, being empathetic to his wishes and needs.

"He's going through huge changes and upheaval. Stability will be important to him, more so as, from what you say, everything in his life is changing: home, school and family. We don't have a bereavement policy as such, but would work closely with you to pre-empt any harder times he may experience, and to understand how to best help John to cope.

"Mrs McGuire has excellent child psychology as well as teaching skills, and I know she will be someone who John will get to know and trust. I would have asked her to come here today to meet you both, but she is currently out of the country and not back until the weekend. I think it would be useful for you to talk with her and I can arrange that for lunchtime on the first day of school, next Tuesday, if that would suit you."

At last she paused for breath and awaited a response from Black.

Black consulted the diary on his Xphone and conceded that would be convenient. Having to rearrange a board meeting seemed a price worth paying to make sure he was comfortable with a prospective teacher who could be so influential in his son's first year at Arnford Hall.

Later that day, as the four males sat at the breakfast bar eating another meal of pasta with a simple sauce – this time John ate it all – Black relaxed as the boy told Roger, his voice filled with excitement, about the great lego his new school had.

Chapter 11

They had a more peaceful night's sleep that night, with Black senior able to continue working until midnight, after settling his son into bed at eight.

There would need to be quite a few changes within the Black business empire and this would affect many managing directors and senior directors. Black had asked Roger to issue a corporate memo stating that Group board meetings would begin at 10.30 a.m., instead of the usual 8.30 start. This would give Black the chance to take John to school every morning, which he felt was the right thing to do, during the first few weeks at least.

In addition, the Group Chief Executive Officer – Black himself – would be taking two weeks' leave – another rare occurrence – and Roger Courtney would be representing him. All matters were to be passed through Roger, who would decide what Black needed to know, such was the trust Gabriel had in his PA. The memo was to be copied to the Group chairperson.

Things continued to run smoothly for the Blacks as they were about to spend the next afternoon at the Beardlys' residence.

As father and son walked up to the door to 3 West Terrace, Carol opened it and John rushed to embrace his aunt.

"Hiya, darling," she exclaimed, giving him a big hug. "Your cousins are waiting for you in the garden." As he ran past her, she looked up at Black. "Hello, Mr Black."

He raised an eyebrow, a faint smile appearing on his lips. "Hello, Carol. Please, call me Gabriel." He entered her house as she moved aside for him.

Her mouth fell open from shock and fear as she wondered if she could ever call him Gabriel. She glanced at the Bentley and saw the driver taking a newspaper out of the boot.

"He'll be fine." Gabriel's tone cautioned her not to start fussing about drinks.

"OK," she said sheepishly. *How does this man manage to make me feel so uncomfortable?* She wondered what he was going to do as he walked straight into the dining room.

"It's doing well. Good." He turned away from the orchid, to face the lady of the house.

"It's beautiful," she whispered.

Yes, you are, almost; shame about your husband. His eyes did not give away the slight shock he felt at this thought. He hurried past her. "Where has John gone?"

"They'll be in the garden." Heaving a sigh of relief, she led the way to the kitchen and asked if he would like a drink. She didn't really know what you did with a billionaire in your house for a couple of hours while his son, her nephew, played with her children.

"I've brought this." He handed her a bottle of Chablis Premier Cru 2008, chilled.

"Oh." She was glad she hadn't already got out coffee mugs. "Just a moment." She went into the dining room, returning with two wine glasses and a corkscrew.

"Allow me." With ease, he opened the wine and filled the glasses, handing one to her. *So this was why he was chauffeured everywhere.* She didn't normally drink in the afternoons, but this tasted divine and hopefully it would help her relax and cope with being in this man's company for the next two hours.

"I would like to thank you for the notes you made about John. They were very helpful. We're still learning to get along, as I am sure you can imagine, and I'm appreciating the ups and downs of having a seven-year-old. Can't say I'm used to such steep learning curves, but I think we're making progress."

Carol tried not to appear surprised at his reserved manner and the restraint with which he spoke. He really was like a fish out of water, and she noticed he was wearing another suit, dark grey this time, with a pale pink shirt and light grey tie, in the middle of summer. Did he ever relax?

He continued. "Did you consider my offer to sort the house out?"

"I guess we would appreciate all the help we can get. James and I have never had to do anything like this before, and it's upsetting for both of us. We were all very close to Eliza and John." Her voice trailed off and Black waited for a moment before he spoke again.

"Right then. Don't worry about it. I'll arrange for the clearance and sale. Just let me know when you have taken what you want. We'll make sure we get a good price for what is left. I think I would like John to have the opportunity to go there one more time, while it still looks like his home; maybe even take some photos if he wants to. And with your permission I would like to move the swing and climbing frame I noticed in the garden to Arnford Hall."

Carol was stunned for a moment at how prepared he was, and thoughtful of John. "Of course. That all sounds good, and help yourself to the play equipment. James and I will get over there after the funeral if that's OK."

"When is the funeral?"

"It's on Monday the eleventh, at St Wilfrid's Church in Mobberley, at eleven o'clock."

"Do you think John should attend? Is it a burial or cremation?"

"It's a burial. I'm not sure about John."

"In that case, I think he will be best at school." The man paused a moment. "Do you think Eliza would agree?"

Carol hadn't expected this conversation and was suddenly beginning to feel sorry for John, his father, herself, and most of all her sister. She was dreading Monday but knew it was a day to be got through. She kept her voice steady as she admitted, "Yes, I think so."

"I won't come either, but will send a representative of John's family – the Black side, that is." His eyes softened as he looked into Carol's. She turned away and opened the dishwasher, looking around for something to put in it to legitimise her action.

"Join me in the garden when you are ready." And the senior member of the Black side of the family turned and left the kitchen.

Carol sat next to him at the garden table, watching him as he watched John and Craig playing with a football.

"Daddy, come and play with us!"

Carol nearly spat her wine out. *Daddy?*

Gabriel smiled at her and stood up, taking his jacket off and placing it over the back of the chair. "We all have to adapt, I guess." His eyes had a mischievous glint in them.

Carol looked away, hoping he didn't notice her blush. *It must be the wine.* But she knew it was this mysterious, handsome, charming man, who was the closest thing to a brother-in-law she would ever have. She watched thoughtfully as he kicked the ball around with the two young boys, clearly not used to such a sport. He was certainly trying hard with his son. *What on earth had Eliza had against him?*

Chapter 12

Black had instructed the staff at the lake house to have every-thing ready for him and John, as they would be arriving on Friday night and staying until Sunday.

At last they could be alone together, away from the bleak, sombre atmosphere of Arnford Hall. The house beside Lake Windermere was cheery and welcoming; it was Gabriel's own private property and one of his favourite places, holding no painful memories or current threats. He could be there alone, to enjoy the beauty of the surroundings and forget about things … for a while, at least.

Now he intended to use it as his sanctuary with John: a place where the two of them would be friends, share each other's joys and passions. He hoped his son would take to boating, shoot-ing, fishing, swimming and enjoying nature with him in this unsullied place.

Eventually, of course! Life with a seven-year-old would have to do for now. Black drove the two of them up to the house that night when they got back from their surprisingly pleas-ant afternoon with Carol and her family. He had yet to meet her husband, James, and in a way he regretted that he existed. He liked Carol, although she was far too ordinary for his usual tastes: she wasn't a model, she wasn't beautiful, she wasn't wealthy and she certainly didn't mix in any of his circles; but she was good-natured, discreetly attractive, and he loved the way she blushed. She had the same air of innocence that had attracted him to her sister in the first place. Maybe he was mel-lowing in his old age and he needed someone more like Carol than Elana in his life now.

He parked his grey Porsche 911 fiftieth-anniversary limited edition on the driveway and led John into the house. He had instructed his staff to set up bunk beds in the main guest room, and he placed their bags in there.

"You can sleep on top, John," he assured the boy as the latter stared hopefully at the ladder to the top bunk. John immediately shot up it, burying Gromit under the new Batman duvet cover. Black frowned as he saw the matching set on the bottom bunk, and imagined his staff's comments on the change in status of their employer. What the heck! He'd let that go for now. He was here to enjoy a short retreat with his son and nothing was going to stop that.

They spent the weekend swimming in the pool, rowing on the lake, exploring the hills of the Lake District, and visiting the Rheged Centre. Gabriel was impressed with John's confidence in the swimming pool, as he retrieved dive sticks off the bottom, swam underwater through his father's legs, and jumped in, splashing him with great delight. He was happy in the small boat when they took it on the lake and he enjoyed playing in the outdoor area at Rheged.

Black was delighted with the way their relationship was developing, and felt they were becoming friends. John didn't mention Eliza often, but Black was pleased that he seemed to be able to talk about her freely with his father, and he was getting upset about her death less often. Of course, John had many new things in his life to occupy his thoughts, not to mention that Black was cutting him a lot of slack, and it wouldn't always be like this.

In the evenings, John seemed happy to go to bed alone, knowing his father would join him shortly and be there when he woke up. He was so excited to be sleeping on the top bunk; the threat of going into the twin room with its boring beds, if he didn't go to sleep soon, was enough to make sure he did drift off, leaving Black to sit alone downstairs, weighing up the cost of having had no sex for nearly a week now. This couldn't go on much longer. He had a phone number for Juliette, who "operated" nearby, but he knew it would be inappropriate for her to come over.

He didn't want John to meet any of his female companions. He had read enough of the book Roger had given him to know now was not the time for his son to find out that he had many lady friends, none of whom he loved, and none of whom were suitable to replace a mother.

He needed a plan, but with all that had happened he hadn't had time to make one.

Chapter 13

It was Tuesday morning, the first day of the new school year for the children at Arnford Primary School, and Grace McGuire was happily driving along, thinking about the new child, John Black, son of the infamous playboy billionaire Gabriel Black. How strange that it had taken the death of the poor boy's mother for the father to bother to have any relationship with his only son! And why on earth would someone like that send his child to the local state primary school?

Miss Greaves had been right when she'd said it was all most unusual and that the child could be seriously mixed up, given everything that had happened in his life in such a short time. However, she knew her Year 3 were a good bunch of kids. There were only twenty-three of them and she should be able to ensure that young John Black was as happy at the school as possible in the circumstances.

She pulled up at the roundabout. There was a car coming from her right, and she braked, taking advantage of the time to reach over to her glovebox and get a CD out; she should just have time to listen to her favourite track before she arrived at school.

Suddenly there was a thud and the sound of metal on metal, and she was thrust forward in her seat. *What the hell?*

The next minute, her car door was yanked open and a tall, dark-haired man was looming over her.

"What the hell are you playing at? How much damn space do you want before you pull onto the roundabout?" She noticed the man's eyes take in the CD in her hand before returning to look at her face.

Grace extracted herself from behind the wheel and stepped onto the road. "Well, excuse me!" she yelled indignantly, "but you just ran into the back of me! Just look at what you've done to my car!"

She flung her arm out, before slamming her hand down onto one of the rear panels of her bronze-coloured Toyota Aygo. The back end was caved, in pushing a rear panel onto one of the wheels, and the rear windscreen wiper was on the ground, together with pieces of her lights. She turned and glared at the huge black Bentley, which was completely unscathed.

"You weren't paying attention! Too interested in putting a CD on, by the look of it."

The man's voice had a threatening, yet exasperated, tone, as though he was cross with her for allowing herself to be distracted, and ready to punish her in some way.

Who the hell do you think you are? Grace glared at him but struggled to get a word out. She breathed deeply, trying to stop herself shaking.

"Look. Are you OK?" His voice was a little quieter now, controlled and clearly expecting an answer as its owner stared at her.

"Yes, I'm fine." She exhaled and turned away from him to see the traffic backing up and passers-by staring at the cars. The giant of the still perfect Bentley contrasted with her broken, bent Aygo. "This is just great!" Grace had only just finished paying for the damn car and now she couldn't even drive it. Plus she had to get to work. *Bugger!*

She opened the passenger door and grabbed her handbag to get her phone.

Then she became aware that the man was already speaking to someone, asking them to come and move the vehicle and get it to a garage. He spoke with authority and a second later he walked over to her.

"The car will be taken to see if it's worth repairing," he said derisively, and glanced at his watch as he added, "Where are you going?"

Grace stared at him. His look commanded her to answer. "I'm going to work. And now I'll be late!"

"You should have thought about that when you were trying to put a CD on while driving."

How dare he? "You caused this bloody accident! I was stationary!"

"But you shouldn't have been. You should have driven off! Then I wouldn't have hit you!" His voice had risen again.

"Well, you did, didn't you? And they had better be able to fix my car. I don't have a spare one at home!"

"Wait a moment." The man went back to his vehicle and spoke to someone in the passenger seat; at least that was what Grace presumed, as the glass in the vehicle was totally blacked out. He could have been talking to a baboon for all she knew!

He approached her again.

"Get what you need from your vehicle and leave the keys in it. It's hardly likely anyone is going to take it." Again he appeared disdainful. "I'll take you where you need to go."

You must be joking. I'm not going anywhere with you, mate!

But she did need to get to work, and she would be late for registration if she had to walk. Besides, she needed this guy's insurance details. Would she be able to claim for a courtesy car? She knew she couldn't on her own policy. *Oh bugger, bugger!*

"OK. I would appreciate a lift to Arnford Primary School. And what's going to happen to my car? Can you give me your insurance details?"

"My PA will attend to everything, and we will sort you out with a car in the meantime. You may need to start looking for a new car, perhaps with a stacking CD system, or even an in-car music system."

You cheeky sod!

He held the rear passenger door open, "Get in, Miss ... er?" He looked at her enquiringly.

"Mrs!" She spoke more loudly than she had intended, and thought she may have sounded rude.

Well, too late now, she'd said it. "Mrs McGuire."

She looked shocked when he actually smiled at her. He looked like a cat that'd just been given a whole tankerful of cream.

"Well, Mrs McGuire. Get in the car and meet your new pupil, John Black. Looks like we're all going to the same place." And he closed the door on her and went round to the driver's side, still smiling.

Grace McGuire felt like a scolded pupil from her own class. She slid over the leather seat and leaned forward, saying, "Hello, John. I'm Mrs McGuire, your new teacher. I'm very pleased to meet you." She fastened her seat belt and sat back, wondering just how bad had her language been. Thank goodness John wouldn't have heard anything. But a parent? Oh, what must he think?

The child remained silent. Had his daddy just destroyed his new teacher's car? Would she be cross with them both? He shot a nervous glance at his father.

"Say hello to your new teacher, John."

"Have you broken her car, Daddy?"

"Well, sort of, but don't worry, we're going to fix it and make it better. Mrs McGuire understands and she isn't cross with you, John. Are you, Mrs McGuire?"

"Of course I'm not cross. It was my fault really." She gave a hard stare at the driving mirror – *like hell it was!* – as she made eye contact with Black. He studied her expression, but gave no indication as to his own thoughts.

She continued. "I'm really looking forward to getting to know you, John, and I think you'll like your new school. Year 3 is a great bunch of kids. What sort of things do you like doing?"

"I like my own school. I'm not sure I want to go to a new one."

"You know, John, you're going to make a lot of new friends and we have a lot of fun at Arnford Primary. Today, we're just going to get to know each other, and you and I are already starting to do that, aren't we?" Grace's tone was warm and comforting, encouraging the young boy to put his apprehension aside and begin to look forward to the day ahead.

John remembered the lego.

"I liked playing with the lego." He looked at his father, who turned and smiled at him.

"We have lots of lego, John, and you'll be able to play with some of it today, I promise. Look, we're here already. You have a lovely car, John. Thanks for letting me join you on the ride to school." She then realised Mr Black was driving straight into the car park, off-limits to parents before half past nine.

"I'm sorry, Mr Black, but you can't park here. It's staff only!"

"You're staff, Mrs McGuire," and he parked across two other cars, blocking them in.

He then got out of the car and, before she had the chance to do it herself, he had opened her door, and that of his son, and the two passengers climbed out.

Grace appeared infuriated and he smirked, taking John's hand. The latter looked sheepish, trying not to worry that his father had broken a school rule. *Mummy would never have done that …*

As Grace led the Blacks into the school building, she asked Mrs Baker to take John to his new classroom. It was almost nine o'clock, and no doubt the school bell had been rung.

"I'll be here after school, John, to take you home, OK?" His father reassured the nervous-looking boy.

"Yes, Daddy." John hugged him before following Mrs Baker down the corridor.

When they were alone, Grace turned to Mr Black.

"It's customary for parents to wait in the playground until the bell goes and the children go into school. I'm sure John will want his routine to be the same as all the other children's. Most children don't want to be different. There is parking in the streets around the school. You just need to respect the neighbours and park considerately." Her glare challenged him to disagree.

"I believe we have a meeting at noon, Mrs McGuire. You can make me aware of all your school rules then, if you like. And hopefully there will be time to discuss the appropriate care of my son, who has just lost his mother …" He seemed to tower over her as he continued, "… and is only just getting acquainted with his father! Now, if you'll excuse me, I believe I'm illegally parked in the school grounds. Until midday, Mrs McGuire." He turned and left, leaving Grace feeling furious at not being able to tell him exactly what she thought of him. *Arrogant, rude bastard!*

Black returned to his car and drove out of the school with a stern look on his face. He got Roger on his in-car phone.

"Cancel my morning appointments and rearrange them for Thursday. I need to attend to something in my office, and then I have to be back at this damn school. I presume Michael is dealing with the car?"

"He's loving it! He will, of course, be going over the Bentley with a magnifying glass. You know he doesn't like you driving his baby."

Black approached the infamous roundabout again and saw the Aygo being towed away. "He can do what he fucking likes with his magnifying glass, and if he says anything to me I'll tell him where to shove it!"

"That good a morning, then, is it?"

Black was aware of Roger's grin on the end of the phone. He sighed.

"Could have been better. Run me a check on Grace McGuire, John's teacher, and leave it on my desk. What mood is Steve in today?"

"He's going to work your butt off! Be ready."

Great, that was all he needed. Today could only get better. What were the odds of literally running into his son's new teacher! He couldn't wait to find out more about her.

On arriving back at Arnford Hall, Gabriel went straight to his office and locked the door. The report from Roger was already on his desk. He read every word.

Grace McGuire. Age 39 ▪ Address: 3 Willow Lane, Arnford, Cheshire. ▪ Resident for 15 years ▪ Marital Status: single ▪ Husband: unrecorded ▪ Mother: Jane Bright, deceased ▪ Brother: Michael Bright, address unknown ▪ Father: ACCESS DENIED ▪ Previous Address: ACCESS DENIED ▪ Education: ACCESS DENIED

Black paused for a moment. He tapped the intercom.

"I am not to be disturbed for the next hour."

The whole household would have heard. It was not an unusual order from their employer, but it was rarely heard so early in the day!

He unlocked the bottom drawer of his desk and reached underneath the drawer above it, retrieving an innocuous-looking key. He then went over to his bookcase and located a concealed button and pressed it. The bottom skirting board of the bookcase fell away, revealing a panel with a keyhole. He inserted the key and withdrew a palm-held electronic device. He took it to his desk.

Black Armour had recently developed some covert surveillance and monitoring software for the UK government. One of the databases contained information on all crimes – both culprits and victims – over the past fifty years. It was strictly confidential and the copy in Black's hand was highly illegal. There had been just a possibility, at the time the project was handed over to MI6, that the software could be useful; could act as collateral at some point in the future. That point was now. Black wanted to know who was going to be looking after his son in the classroom at Arnford Primary School.

He soon found out.

Grace McGuire's real name was Melanie Bright, and she was the daughter of the infamous child murderer, George Bright. He had been killed by some fellow prisoners, who had taken justice into their own hands. No prison officer had been convicted of gross misconduct; nobody had mourned the death of George Bright. His widow committed suicide shortly after his arrest, claiming not to have known about his crimes against pre-school children, and his son and daughter were given new identities.

Grace McGuire's life was closely monitored by the authorities and her record was exemplary. She had graduated with a first in English from Durham University before her father had been convicted, and had been on a fast track in law to the Bar. This career had come to a premature end as she was given a new identity and moved to Arnford. She had been provided with qualifications inferior to those she had actually achieved, but sufficient for her to be accepted at Manchester University on a three-year BSc degree course in psychology and, with another first under her belt, she had chosen to complete a teaching course, after which Miss Greaves was delighted to welcome her to Arnford Primary School, where she soon became a member of the senior management team.

Black sat back and paused to take in this information. He – of all people – knew that the faults of the parents did not necessarily transfer to their offspring. He thought of his siblings, Ellouise and Julian, leaving himself out of the equation for now.

He secured the palm book back in its safe hiding place and returned the key to its secret location in his desk, then unlocked his office door and walked down to the kitchen.

Steve looked up from the tray of chocolate brownies he had just taken out of the oven.

"Morning, sir. Thought I'd make a treat for John after his first day at school."

"Thank you. I won't be home for lunch today. What time do you want to start the training session tonight?"

"Half past eight, when John will be in bed?"

"Yes. I'll see you at the piste. Please excuse me if I'm a few minutes late." Black frowned.

Steve looked directly at his employer. "I understand."

Black took an apple from the fruit basket and went to find Roger.

Chapter 14

The Bentley pulled up in the school car park at three min-utes to twelve. Black let Mrs Baker know that it was his Bentley blocking in two cars and that he would be in a meeting with Mrs McGuire, should anyone require it to be moved.

As if anyone would dare! she thought.

He was asked to take a seat in the reception area and told Mrs McGuire would be with him shortly.

At five minutes past she greeted him with a very firm hand-shake and explained that they could use Miss Greaves' office. This time no coffee was offered.

She observed his confident manner as he sat next to her at the coffee table, leaning back and crossing his legs, smoothing the knife-edge crease of his black pinstripe trousers. His shirt was a brilliant white and the top two buttons were open; no tie. She allowed herself to appreciate the handsome features of his masculine, clean-shaven face, his dark, hypnotic eyes staring at her intently, waiting patiently for her to say something.

"Well, Mr Black, John has had a good morning. We have a buddy system here and I've put him with a young boy called Adam. They seem to be getting along well together. I believe your son likes Star Wars. We've done some reading and I'm delighted to say John is confident and accurate in his reading and comprehension. Of course, everything is new for him, not least of all navigating around the building, which is always a bit daunting when everyone else seems to know where they are going. There's a school information booklet written by the children themselves, especially for children who join the school in later years than reception, and it has details to help them to settle in quickly. I'll be going through this with John this after-noon and the booklet is for him to keep.

"Adam is a considerate boy, mature for his age and sym-pathetic to a new boy in school, even at this young age, and I hope they will become firm friends. John hasn't mentioned his mother yet, but I'll encourage him to speak about her if I feel he wants to." She paused, and glared at the man before her. "Unless you have any objections?"

"I think he will talk when he wants to. Our situation is somewhat unusual, as I'm sure your headmistress has informed you."

You condescending git! Grace tried not to let her agitation show.

He continued, "But it would appear you are the psychology expert, Mrs McGuire."

She stared at him questioningly. *Had he been checking up on her?*

He smirked.

She tried to maintain her composure. "May I suggest we proceed with a system of open communication between the school and yourself, Mr Black? By that, I mean if we are concerned about his emotional stability at any time – and I think we have to expect situations to arise during the course of the term – we can discuss this with you, either face to face or on the telephone if that's more convenient.

"Likewise, we hope that you would advise us of any issues arising at home that we could help with, or be on the lookout for when he is in school. We could bring in Family Services, if you wish, and someone would be assigned to you and John to offer support and counselling." Now she looked smug as her eyes met his. "To be on hand to guide and advise you about the emotions and stresses John could be experiencing."

He moved forward slightly, and his voice was low and intimidating. "I don't think that will be necessary, Mrs McGuire."

Did he say that mockingly?

"With your qualifications and background I'm sure we can manage the situation between us. As you say, we just need to ensure we communicate well. I think we should start with being honest with each other."

What the hell was he saying?

"After all, you appear to have excelled at Durham and Manchester. I'm sure you are more than capable of helping a child whose mother has just died." His eyes burned into her.

70

As the colour drained from her face, she stared at him. The silence hung in the air.

"Let me get you some water." He stood up and went to the door. "Take a minute to decide which name you wish me to call you by."

She watched his back disappear into the corridor and heard him asking Mrs Baker to fetch some water, as Mrs McGuire wasn't feeling too well.

Grace swallowed hard. *He can't know. How could he possibly know? I've done nothing to betray my past. Nobody knows. I've been Mrs Grace McGuire for the past fifteen years. He can't know.*

He walked back into the room with a glass of water, closing the door behind him.

He handed her the drink and she accepted it, grateful. Her mouth felt as dry as sandpaper, and she concentrated on drinking for a moment.

He sat down and stared at her, his face cold and impassive.

"I know who you are, Melanie."

She glared at him, her eyes wide with horror and her stomach churning. Her present, happy and fulfilling life flashed before her. Her voice was barely audible.

"How do you know?"

"That doesn't matter. Of more importance to me is how are you going to convince me you can look after my son while he is in your care?" His voice remained menacing.

She felt a cold chill run through her body. *Dear God, what do I do?*

She was shaking and her voice trembled. "I don't know what you are expecting from me, but I can assure you I am the best teacher for your son, Mr Black. I can empathise with his emotions and be attentive to his needs. I will be there when he needs me." She paused as she swallowed the bile surging up from within her. "I can even have dialogue with him at home if he needs it. My children are the most important things to me, Mr Black." She fought back a sob as she was enveloped by the fear of losing all that she had worked for since her father's arrest.

"Mrs McGuire ..."

The use of her replacement name gave her hope that he would change the direction of this conversation. But her hope was quashed as he continued, "We need to talk further. I'm sure you would agree." His tone was derogatory, daring her to challenge him, knowing she would not. "My car will take you home tonight and will pick you up in the morning. Tomorrow you will come back to Arnford Hall, and a car will be made available to you. We can discuss further how we can proceed with this situation then. I'll see you at quarter past three, Mrs McGuire."

Grace stared in disbelief as he stood up and left the room, closing the door behind him, leaving her alone with her thoughts and dread.

Chapter 15

John was happy to be going home after his first day at school, and was positively exuberant when he discovered that his teacher, Mrs McGuire, would be coming in the car with them again. Obviously, his daddy liked her, and maybe she had forgiven him for wrecking her little car. After all, she did like Daddy's big one!

The adults in the car were silent, but John chatted excitedly about the book he was reading. "It's about volcanoes, Daddy!"

"That sounds exciting. You can read some to me at home."

Grace was looking out of the window, balancing this paternal, caring side of the driver with the dark, threatening man she had met in Miss Greaves' office. Where was this going?

"Your address, Mrs McGuire?"

"Oh, I'm sorry." *Shit, how many times has he asked me?* "Er, Willow Lane, number three." Quickly she tried to make out where they were. "Turn left at the traffic lights."

Of course, he already knew where she lived. He just wanted to break her from her reverie. She needn't think the worst of him; not yet, anyway!

It was only a few minutes to Willow Lane, and the Bentley pulled up outside a small detached house with a single garage. It had two distinguishing features: there was a large monkey puzzle tree in the front garden, and her garage door was bright red, standing out from the mainly black or cream neighbouring ones. Black wondered what this said about the teacher he was going to get to know better.

Grace immediately opened the car door, on seeing that Black was already on his way round to open it for her, and started to walk up her path, aware he was following her.

The key was in her door when his low voice compelled her to look round at him. He remained about three feet away from her.

"What time do you need to be picked up?"

"I can make my own way, thanks." She regretted that she sounded petulant. She wanted him to know she was angry, but didn't want him to know she was frightened. She turned her back on him.

"That is not what I asked. Just answer the question, Mrs McGuire."

She stopped as she was about to cross her threshold. With her back to him she spoke clearly, her voice controlled and even. "Half past eight."

"Thank you."

She heard his footsteps as he returned to his car and heaved a sigh of relief, walking into her hallway and slamming her door shut. She needed a large gin and tonic.

How dare he? What could he possibly do to her? Would he threaten to reveal her hidden past? Was he going to take his son away from the school?

She pictured John Black, his hair as dark as his father's, and eyes too, now she came to think of it. He seemed to adore Black senior, as he had kept talking about his new daddy in school. She felt it was strange that he hadn't mentioned his mother, but that time would come. Mr Black was obviously making a very good impression on his son. Grace was struggling to determine what the former's real character was; did he have some sort of split personality?

She sipped her drink as she slumped down on the sofa. It was only quarter to four; a bit too early to speak to Jason, but she needed to hear his reassuring voice, to help her keep a grip on reality while she still could.

Jason Chesters was forty-five years old. He worked as a solicitor in London and spent Monday to Friday at his flat in Putney, and shared the weekends with Grace, either at her house in Cheshire or at his London flat. They had been seeing each other for just over a year now and both knew they would soon need to discuss their longer term living arrangements, but each was reluctant to commit to uprooting to move north or south.

"Hi Grace, is everything all right?" He sounded concerned, knowing it was unusual for her to call before seven in the evening, and especially at this time when she was normally still at school.

"I'm fine. I just wanted to say hello and hear your voice. Had a busy first day with the new children. Have you got a minute to chat?" *Should she mention the car accident?*

"Sure. I've just finished with a client: a messy divorce and too much money involved for it to be amicable. I was going for early drinks with a few others from the office. So how was your day? Whinging kids and stroppy head teacher?"

"Not at all!" she chastised him and knew he would be grinning on the other end of the phone. He was really supportive of her job and loved her passion and enthusiasm for it. She deserved to have children of her own, but it wasn't on his list, and this was the main reason why he hadn't yet been able to broach the subject of them living together permanently, in London, if he had his way. He needed to know it really was the right thing for Grace McGuire to do, and that she was the right woman for him.

She continued, "Actually, I had a car crash."

She heard him gasp. "It's OK, I'm fine. A new parent ran into the back of me, would you believe." She didn't want to say too much, as she knew Jason would be furious to think she could have been in any way responsible as she wasn't paying full attention. But what the hell; Black had run into her. She decided not to mention at this stage that the other driver was none other than billionaire Gabriel Black. She felt a chill again, remembering the implied threat about her identity. Jason must not find out.

"Are you sure you're OK? Do you want me to come up?"

"Honestly, I'm fine. They should be sorting me out with a courtesy car tomorrow." *At what cost, though?*

"Well, that sounds fair enough. I presume they're accepting responsibility and putting it through their insurance?"

Would he? Black didn't ask for any of my insurance details. He'd only said he would sort a car out for me tomorrow.

Jason continued, "I can draft a letter if you think they're going to be awkward about it."

"No, I'm sure that won't be necessary. I'll let you know if there are any problems, but hopefully I'll get a car from tomorrow, and mine won't take too long to fix. It did look a bit of a mess, though."

"Could you drive it?"

"No. The back's caved in." She decided not to mention that the other car was a huge Bentley and didn't even have a scratch that she could see. "Look, I just wanted to say hi, and hear a friendly voice. Go and join the others for that drink, and I'll see you on Friday night. Try and get here as soon as you can."

"OK, honey. Take care and let me know if you have any problems with this parent. Don't work too hard."

"Bye, darling."

Grace put the phone down and got her laptop out. She glanced at her lesson planner, but her mind was on the other side of the village at Arnford Hall, and she wondered what would happen tomorrow.

Chapter 16

By half past eight that evening, John was fast asleep in the green twin room, exhausted from his first day at school, which by all accounts had gone well. He spoke fondly of Mrs McGuire and was quick to tell Roger that he had made a new friend, Adam. He also asked his father if he could go upstairs and tell his mummy about it. Gabriel's heart went out to his son as he stood with him by the photo in the bedroom and listened as he explained that his new teacher seemed to like Daddy, which was good for him, because obviously Mummy hadn't, but that Mummy mustn't mind; John still loved her and he was sure she would like his new friend Adam. He then promptly ran back downstairs to watch a bit of TV before bed.

Gabriel was surprised at his relief that his son was sleeping peacefully. He felt a mix of emotions at bedtime, ranging from sheer frustration that John didn't seem to have any intention of going to sleep at the allotted time of half past seven, to pleasure at the opportunity for the two for them to be together, to share a bedtime story and sometimes, if John was forthcoming, to discuss what they had each done in the day. It curtailed Black's routine of working in the evenings, but he could make up for it with the time he gained from getting up earlier in the mornings.

Tonight, though, he had a training session with his fencing master, Steve – his chef. Their roles would be reversed for the session and Gabriel would be under the chef's command. He got changed in his own bedroom and made his way down to the piste. The master was waiting for him. The student expected to be in for a tough session, as no doubt the chef would want to get his own back for the recent addition of pasta and a simple sauce to the Black household menu, not to mention a trip to McDonald's.

He wasn't wrong, and later, as Black lay in bed, exhausted, listening to his son's faint snoring, he thought about Grace McGuire, and about his own lifestyle and character. John was the only good thing in his life. Was he really prepared to embark on a plan which could guarantee he would sink further and further into hell, just when his son needed him?

Fuck it! *He* needed this!

Chapter 17

Grace drifted off to sleep at midnight, dreaming of blue flashing lights, policemen taking her father away, standing at her mother's grave, and the handsome face of her younger brother, Michael, with blood streaked across it. She awoke, startled, as she heard his screams in her dream.

She was sweating and felt sick. She hadn't had any nightmares about her family for the last ten years – what was happening to her? *What if I have a bad dream when I'm with Jason?*

She went into the bathroom and splashed cold water over her face, eventually drifting back to another restless sleep, before waking at five o'clock.

She showered and dressed and went downstairs and did some work in the kitchen, then made herself a double espresso, but couldn't face anything to eat. She tried to concentrate on her second day with Year 3 and mentally visualised every face, putting a name to each of them and where they were sitting in the classroom.

The children were her solace, and she congratulated herself for the hundredth time that she had left the legal profession and gone into teaching. She smiled as she pictured Jason sitting across from some wronged wife or husband, having to listen to the sordid details of yet another case of infidelity. His steady flow of customers was never going to dry up!

But it wasn't long before her thoughts drifted to the driver of a large black Bentley, his words piercing her ears and stabbing at her memories. *The bastard!*

She wondered what would happen today. Maybe it wouldn't be as bad as she was making out. What had he to gain by revealing her former identity? Surely he wanted routine and stability for his son? That would be shattered before it had even begun if he took him away now. She was sure a bond had formed between John and Adam, and his father must see that.

She just needed to show him what a good teacher she was.

She glanced down at her black trousers, and then at her white short-sleeved shirt, suddenly very conscious of her appearance. She remembered the early days when she had first started seeing Jason. *For goodness' sake, I'm not going on a bloody date!*

Fuck it! *She* didn't need this!

Chapter 18

As he was finishing his second espresso of the morning, half-reading the *Financial Times,* and half-listening to John telling him what a great friend Adam was, Black asked his son to pause a moment as he called to Roger. "Get Michael to bring the Bentley round. I want him to drive us to the school this morning. We need to leave at quarter past eight."

Roger used the intercom to ask the chauffeur to confirm that the Volkswagen Golf would be there that afternoon, ready for Mrs McGuire. He then nodded confirmation of this to Black.

"Good," said the employer. "Do you want to go up front, John? We're going to pick Mrs McGuire up and take her to school too."

"Yes!" John exclaimed and punched his fist into the air, much to the amusement of Gabriel, Roger and Steve.

There was something very agreeable about having a happy seven-year-old in the Black household; it gave the adults a feeling of optimism for the future.

"The plans for the bedroom are being brought over this afternoon," Roger informed Black.

"Are you going to the construction meeting today?"

"Yes. I probably won't be back before five."

"I trust you made it clear to them that nothing is to be kept from us, whether they think it will all come good in the end or not, or I'll fire the lot of them!"

"Don't worry, they got the message."

"Good. John and I will go through the drawings this afternoon, and after school you can see how you want your new bedroom to look, John."

The young boy looked a little perplexed. His father had tried to explain that he would be having a different bedroom, all of his own, and that Daddy would go back to sleeping in his own bed. But John hadn't really thought about it very much. Now he suddenly thought about being alone.

"Will it be your new bedroom too, Daddy?"

"No, John. We already had this conversation. I will go back to my room, but it will be just across the corridor from yours." He paused and, on seeing the anxious expression on John's face, added, "Don't worry. We'll talk about it later and you'll be able to see what your new room will look like. It will be great, promise. Now come on, we need to get you to school."

John was still grumbling about not wanting to be on his own when the Bentley pulled up outside 3 Willow Lane.

Michael got out of the car and walked up the drive to knock on the door.

Grace felt relieved when she was greeted by a smiling, tall, blond-haired man in a light grey suit. *He's sent his driver!* She smiled back.

The chauffeur held the car door open and her face dropped as she saw Gabriel Black sitting in the back of the car. She climbed in slowly, grateful for the central console separating them. She felt as nervous as hell.

"Good morning, Mrs McGuire." His voice was clear, almost pleasant, and he turned to face her, his eyes penetrating, leaving her feeling the urge to envelop herself in some impenetrable shroud.

She spoke quietly, looking straight ahead. "Hi. Thank you for the lift." She was determined to make this look like no more than an offer of help with transport, caused by Mr Black's inept driving. She shot a glance at the driver's mirror and saw Michael staring back at her. *Did he know anything? Oh, for goodness' sake, stop being paranoid!*

"Hi, John." She tried to lean forward a little to put her hand around the seat in front of her, but the space was too great. She sat back. "Are you looking forward to school today?"

"Yes, Mrs McGuire," the boy said, proud that his teacher was travelling with them again.

"Mrs McGuire will be coming for tea tonight, John." Black was still watching the reluctant passenger. "You're not vegetarian, are you?"

"Er … no. But please ..." *Oh pleeease!* "… don't go to any trouble. I'll just collect the courtesy car, if that's OK."

"It's no trouble." He turned away and looked out of his window.

As they approached the school, Black addressed his driver. "Park on this lane somewhere. I'll be a few minutes while I take John into school." He then spied a small house for sale, about a hundred yards from the school gate, with a decent-sized driveway. It seemed to be unoccupied. "Find out who owns that house and get Roger to enquire about hiring a parking space."

"Yes, sir." Michael pulled the car up and got out to open the door for his employer.

As Grace started to move she recoiled from the touch of Black's hand on her knee.

"Wait until he opens your door," he commanded, and then added with a hint of bitterness, "You may not find it so distasteful when he does it."

Grace thought of the way she had quickly got out of the car yesterday, so he could not open her door for her. She blushed and looked away, remaining in her seat as Michael came round. In the meantime, Black went to the front passenger door and was gently helping John to unfasten his seat belt and climb off his booster seat.

Taking his son's hand and carrying his school bag, Black turned to the teacher. "We will see you at quarter past three." He led John towards the school.

Michael noticed a fearful look cross their travelling companion's face. She looked more than just pissed off at having her car smashed up, but his employer had a talent for pissing people off.

He smiled at her and then walked over to the house that was for sale, entering the number on the board into his phone before returning to the car.

Black stood at the side of the playground and observed some of the other parents. He didn't feel totally out of place, as there were several other fathers, a couple in suits, clearly doing the school run before heading to work. Children were running around and there was a feeling of happy anticipation in the air.

With John and his fellow classmates led safely into school by Mrs McGuire, Black walked back to the car. His phone buzzed and he read the message:

Sender: Ellouise

Message: Hi GeeBee. Heard about Eliza. Sorry. And John: fantastic. I'm so pleased for you. You deserve some happiness in your life. Can I come see you and meet him? I could be there Friday. Trying to get in touch with Julian, but no success. Have you heard from him? Please let me come Friday. Take care, big brother, El xxx.

Gabriel Black smiled. He had wondered how long it would be before Ellouise burst onto the scene. She was five years his junior and raving bonkers! But she had a great heart, and was a breath of fresh air whenever she came to Arnford Hall, which really wasn't often enough. However, he couldn't blame her. She only had to look at her big brother to remember why she'd left.

Still, she was coming to meet John and he was certain the two of them would hit it off. Ellouise would never be a traditional aunt – that would be Carol's role – but she would be a bright sparkle in John's life, and Gabriel would make provision for her to be there for his son if anything should happen to himself.

He replied confirming that Friday would be great, and no, he had not heard from Julian, nor did he know where he was, but he would find out.

Back at Arnford Hall, he spoke to Rick, one of the best IT geeks at Black Armour.

"Get hold of Julian and tell him to get his arse back to Arnford. He has a nephew to meet. And let me know where he is as soon as you locate him. Cheers."

After school, Gabriel waited in the playground for John to come out. He then waited a further ten minutes before Grace McGuire came scuttling across to him.

She didn't fail to notice that his face was like thunder. *Well, sod him!* She had work to do and she couldn't just drop everything! And no way was she going to apologise for keeping him waiting. She would have been more than happy to walk home, and even forsake a courtesy car if she could turn the clock back and never have met Gabriel bloody Black!

"You weren't going to forget us, by any chance?" He taunted her to say something upsetting in front of his son.

"I'm sorry I kept you waiting." *Damn! I didn't want to say that to him.* She quickly went on. "John," and bent down to the seven-year-old, adding, "I just needed to finish tidying the classroom ready for tomorrow. Shall we go?" She took John's hand confidently and walked towards the gate, leaving his father staring after them both. She would show him that his son liked her.

Her face dropped as they approached the car and Michael got out to open their doors. Black didn't fail to notice anything. He was enjoying his game and it made him hungry to carry on with it.

"John, choose some music with Michael. I just need to talk to Mrs McGuire a moment." He flicked a switch and she watched, almost unable to breathe, as the privacy panel rose, cutting her off from what felt like humanity.

"Breathe!" he commanded. "So, are you trying to tell me something, Grace? I'm concluding that is the name you wish to be known by."

She turned to look at him, spitting her words at him. "Just what do you want with me?"

"All in good time. For now, I want you to relax. We are going to the Hall and I will show you your car. We will then enjoy a meal together and hopefully you will get to know John, and he and I will get to know you. I hope you didn't have any other plans for this evening, as you and I will continue our conversation when my son has gone to bed."

He watched as the colour drained from her face, then lowered the panel and the bouncy sound of some boy band flowed into the back of the car. Black smiled as he heard John singing along with the music.

"Good choice, John," he said, though he had no idea who it was, and he picked up the *Financial Times*, which he was still trying to finish from that morning.

Grace felt glued to her seat, unable to move and not wanting to talk. The fifteen-minute journey seemed endless.

The car waited patiently for the huge iron gates to open, giving way to the long drive, with views of woodland to either side. As Grace stared out of her window with a child-like curiosity, she noticed a giant sculpture, a stem of gleaming steel, twisting and stretching into the sky, like some sort of psychedelic baton held by an invisible orchestral conductor, the sunlight casting rainbow colours from prisms along its length. It was exquisite, and she dared to glance at her companion, who was watching her intently. She looked away quickly and caught sight of another sculpture, this time of an enormous shining steel treble clef. They were both beautiful. *Was this another side to Gabriel Black? Did he like art? Music?*

And then she saw it as they rounded a sweeping bend, the trees now giving way to open meadow, wild and romantic with splashes of red from poppies and blue from meadow flowers: the dark stone of Arnford Hall, acting as a sensual and yet fearful magnet, luring you into its walls, but warning that it might not let you go again. It was like a majestic castle, threatening to captivate all who entered by its gothic beauty and its secrets; secrets it would not let you take back to the outside world!

"Breathe!" he commanded for the second time. "Welcome to Arnford Hall."

As Michael opened her door, she heard Black asking John to go into the house and let Steve know he was home and to ask him for a snack. She was vaguely aware that his father remained near her, observing her face as her eyes drank in the rise of the stone steps, flanked by stone-winged menacing gargoyles. She could hear them screeching, *Do not enter, do not enter ...*

The windows, with their leaded veils, were casting pitiful glances down on her, and she could imagine them chattering to each other, *Poor child, poor dear child ...*

She finally dragged her eyes away from the Hall and turned to its master. Her mouth fell open as he said softly, "It's OK. I used to hear them too." He walked up the steps to the huge doorway, knowing she would follow him.

Inside, the entrance was bright and sunny, the lemon of the walls providing a most welcome relief to the exterior. The corridors were lined with white busts of majestic-looking souls from days long gone, mounted on tall, dark plinths. Portraits and painted hunting scenes adorned the walls. As Grace gazed up, her eyes followed a line of them leading up a grand staircase. She quickened her pace to keep up with Black, following him down a small spiralling flight of stone steps and through a large doorway leading into a state-of-the-art kitchen. Here she was greeted by a smiley-faced John who was just being shown a tray of chocolate brownies by one of three men in the room.

Black was washing his hands at the sink. He turned to face her, the other two looking at him expectantly.

"Grace McGuire, this is Roger Courtney, my PA, and his husband, Steve Ford, who is my chef – and fencing master." At this latter title he turned to the second man and respectfully bowed his head, adding, "Who, it has to be said, gave me a right thrashing last night during training." The three men laughed.

"Pleased to meet you, Mrs McGuire," both men said, and shook Grace's hand.

"You must let us apologise on behalf of our employer," Roger's eyes twinkled kindly, and for the first time Grace began to feel at ease, "as we believe he ran into the back of your car. We give him the excuse of not driving very often." Roger smiled at his boss.

"Now, you have to admit, Mrs McGuire, you weren't exactly concentrating and you did have loads of room to pull out."

"I admit no such thing," she admonished playfully, unable to prevent herself from giving the shadow of a smile.

"Can we have one? Can we have one, Steve?"

The adults turned to John, who was eyeing the brownies hopefully.

"Sure, and ask your teacher if she would like one."

"Thank you, John." Grace took a brownie and felt herself relax for the first time today. *Oh, hadn't he told me to do just that?*

Suddenly his voice cut through like a downpour crashing onto a sunny day. "I need to go into the office. Roger, please can you show Mrs McGuire the car and discuss the arrangements with her." He turned to address Grace directly, "I will see you for an early dinner at half past five." Then he turned and walked out of the kitchen and back up the stairs.

Roger shot a quick glance at Steve and indicated towards John. Steve nodded and spoke to their young charge. "Come on, John. Let's go and feed Satan."

"Oh, great. Can I get his bowl?"

"Sure." They left through French doors leading into the garden.

Roger saw a look of disapproval on Grace's face and wondered if it was due to Black's abruptness, or Satan's name. He wondered about apologising for the former and providing some explanation for the latter, but he had a feeling this was not going to be the last the Arnford Hall household saw of Mrs McGuire, and decided it was probably better for the woman to make her own judgements and discoveries. He just hoped she didn't make too many.

"We've followed Gabriel's instructions, you understand. Life here runs smoother that way." He winked conspiratorially at her, a friendly schoolboy smile forming on his lips. "He believed you required a Volkswagen Golf, complete with in-car, voice-activated music system. He also believed you would like it in red." Roger raised his eyebrows as if to say, *I have no idea why!*

Grace couldn't help smiling back. She did like red and she thought about her garage door which she was particularly pleased with, but she felt indignant about the reference to the music system, and could just imagine the story Black had relayed to his staff. She wasn't going to let him get away with that.

"I'd just like to say that your employer drove into the back of me. I was stationary!"

"We know. And he has had no end of stick about it, especially from his chauffeur." The smile was still in situ.

Roger led Grace along a pathway down the side of the west wing of the house. They passed a long glass room, almost like a greenhouse, and Grace couldn't help peering in at rows and rows of orchids and seedling plants. Roger noticed her questioning expression.

"Gabriel's passion," he explained. "Only now surpassed by John. At times he will spend most of his time in there, and he has travelled all over the world for the love of his orchids. A few years ago he was obsessed with them, but it became clear the family empire needed him to take control, so he had to make a sacrifice – one of many, actually – and now he restricts himself to what he can grow here."

Grace tried to put together some of the pieces of the puzzle unfolding around this man.

As they continued walking, she realised they were heading to a row of garages. Grace held back a cry of protest as they entered one containing a bright red VW Golf. It looked brand new.

As Roger was patiently showing her the controls, she interrupted him. "I presume my car will be ready in a few days. I'm not sure why Mr Black has gone to all this trouble."

"No, Mrs McGuire, I don't think you understand. This is your new car. The garage was instructed to write off your car."

"You what?"

Roger waited a moment, for her to calm down.

"How dare he?"

"He dares—"

"Who the hell does he think he is?"

"The boss."

"Well, he's not *my* boss."

Don't bank on it! "Let's go back inside and have a drink."

It was quarter past five. On returning to the kitchen, Grace knew she needed to calm down, so she suggested to John that he read to her. He seemed quite happy to acquiesce, and as Steve busied himself around the kitchen, creating wonderful aromas, Grace and John sat at the breakfast bar discussing his book about volcanoes. She had no idea where Roger had disappeared to, but sincerely hoped he would be joining them for dinner; he made her feel comfortable. She was aware of every minute that passed, and couldn't help keeping watch for the master of the house to appear.

At half past five Steve announced that dinner was ready to be served and, as it was such a lovely afternoon, they would sit outside on the terrace. Plates of warm chicken and bacon with peas, carrots julienne and baby new potatoes were set out on the table, and Roger joined them. Grace sat next to John, and then felt a twinge of disappointment as the seat next to her was left vacant, with Roger and Steve sitting opposite. A moment later, the two men stood up. Annoyed with herself, Grace felt obliged to do the same as Black joined them at the table.

"Please sit down." He spoke formally, and Grace sensed the atmosphere begin to thicken. Only John seemed oblivious to the change.

Black kissed the top of his son's head and ran his hand over his dark hair. "How are you getting on with your book, then? Have you been reading with Mrs McGuire?" He settled down in the seat next to Grace.

"Yes, Daddy. We've finished it, haven't we?"

"You read really well, John. Maybe your father would like to listen to a bit after dinner." She hoped she sounded like a typical primary school teacher; the really annoying sort.

"Of course. I couldn't miss hearing the end about Mount Vesuvius, could I, John?" *Back at you, Mrs McGuire!*

"No, Daddy."

"And don't forget to eat your peas and carrots, after the trouble Steve has gone to for us. Thank you, chef."

"You're welcome." Steve continued to pour some sparkling water into lead crystal glasses for the adults, and still water into a Ben 10 cup for John.

Grace wanted to confront Black about the car, but appreciated it wasn't appropriate to do so in front of John. She would have to bide her time. She complimented Steve on the food, which was lovely, and under different circumstances she could have enjoyed the evening. But she was here under duress, and still couldn't make out why he was doing this to her.

Roger and Steve chatted about a film they had watched recently with Roger's nephew, something about a new version of the superheroes, the Avengers, and wondered if John might like to watch it sometime. John thought that would be a good idea, and he remembered that his father had told him they could watch films together.

John then seemed quiet for a moment and Black wondered if anything was troubling him. He knew that he was having an easy ride with his son so far; John had a lot to occupy his mind, but it was very early days, and Gabriel was concerned how they would both manage if and when unpleasant issues arose. John would long for his mother, and what if he stopped liking his father? For Black, his relationship with John was revealing a side to him he didn't know existed; a side which didn't want to live without his son. He fell silent, vaguely aware of the conversation going on around him. He needed to be patient until John was asleep, and he could then begin to put his much needed plan in motion.

On seeing that John had still not spoken to anyone, Gabriel stood up and walked round to his chair and crouched down beside him.

"What's the matter, darling? You're a bit quiet tonight. Tell me, is there anything wrong?"

"I was just thinking about Mummy and when I watched a film about Spiderman with her. I can't do that any more, can I, Daddy?"

The conversation at the table stopped.

"No, John, but I think Mummy would be happy to know you could enjoy watching films with new friends. We could all watch it together sometime."

"What about Mrs McGuire?" John buried his head in his father's shirt.

Gabriel shot a forlorn look at Grace and, for the first time, she pitied the single parent before her. Her heart warmed at the sight of him trying to comfort his child, knowing there was nothing he could do to take away the pain, and replace the loss of his son's mother.

Grace spoke quietly to the little boy sobbing next to her. "If you would like to invite me, John, I would love to come."

Black was taken aback at the sincerity in her voice, knowing that right now, Arnford Hall was the last place on earth she wanted to be.

John's plate was almost empty, with only the unwanted peas remaining stubbornly uneaten. Gabriel took his hand, saying, "Please excuse us now. We'll go and walk Satan and then you can have a bath before bed, John."

He looked directly at Grace. "Roger and Steve will keep you entertained until I return. Come on, son," and they went back into the house together. He had intended to show John the designs for his new bedroom, but decided to leave it for now, as John would worry again that he was eventually going to have to sleep in the room on his own.

Later, as they entered the green twin room, Black tried to quash any thought that he was being pulled from one gaoler to another.

Chapter 19

When John was asleep, Black walked into the hallway and spoke into the intercom to Roger. "Where are you?"

"We're back in the kitchen. I've just been showing Mrs McGuire the orchids in the plant room."

There was silence at the other end, and Roger sighed. He lowered his voice as he walked into the central hall, leaving Steve to continue the conversation about how he got into cooking.

"Gabe, you left over an hour ago. What did you expect us to do? You said you would show her the car yourself, and here's a heads-up, she's pissed off that she's not getting her own car back, and she seems genuinely interested in the orchids. I'm sorry if we've done the wrong thing, but we couldn't just leave her to sit on her own."

"You're right, of course. It doesn't matter. But leave her now. Tell her I'll be there in a minute. You two can go home." There was a pause. "Thanks, Roger. I'll see you in the morning. We need to catch up on how you got on seeing that counsellor." He switched the intercom off.

Grace was standing by one of the French doors looking out onto the patio area and the colourful flowerbeds beyond. It was a beautiful setting, and it seemed less threatening to be inside the house looking out at its wonderful landscape, rather than outside the house looking up at its intimidating features.

She turned as she heard his footsteps on the limestone tiles.

"Follow me," he ordered and walked out of the room.

Again she struggled to keep up with his long strides without actually running behind him, which she was determined not to do. She felt like an errant pupil being frog marched to the head teacher's office. And somehow she felt this was going to be a worse experience.

They were walking along the hallway towards the front door. She thought he was going to take her outside, to see the car maybe, but he turned to the door on the right and unlocked it. She followed him inside.

She imagined this to be one of Arnford Hall's smaller rooms. It seemed almost cluttered, with a two-seater sofa and two comfy-looking large armchairs, all in a pale blue velour fabric, inviting her to lounge on them, to read and sip wine, maybe. There was an ornate walnut coffee table and an oak dresser with china plates and cups and saucers displayed on its shelves. *Has anyone ever used them?* An antique-looking washbasin was set in a wooden casing, with brass taps. Elegant tea, coffee and sugar caddies, together with a sleek electric kettle, were positioned on a walnut sideboard to the side of the sink. As if this wasn't unusual enough, the back wall of the room was filled with shelves stacked high with books. The large sash window, facing the front driveway to the Hall, was beautifully framed with heavy, deep blue, exquisite curtains in Chinese silk. The eclectic mix of furniture and objects gave a strangely welcoming feel to this room and, to Grace, it looked heavenly.

Grace's emotions were swirling inside her; this room was beautiful, calming, welcoming, it even smelled lovely. She spied fresh lilies in a huge crystal vase and a beautiful orchid positioned in front of the window. *One of his?*

"It's a *Cattleya leopoldii.*" He walked over to the plant, which had a flower head of five green petals spotted with deep red, the white hood of the anther looming above the deep red base petal.

Grace stared at him.

He lingered next to the orchid a moment, as though inspecting it. Then he sat down in one of the armchairs, leaned back and rested his right ankle on his left knee. He beckoned for her to sit on the sofa before resting his arms comfortably on the sides of the chair.

"Well, Mrs McGuire. How was your meal?"

Grace glanced at him and then looked down at her feet. *What the hell was he doing? Chit-chat?*

With no intention of sitting down, she lifted her head. "Just cut the crap and tell me why the hell I'm here."

94

"As you wish." His tone was even and he spoke without emotion; his eyes were dark and seemed lifeless. "I want to offer you a deal, Mrs McGuire. It seems you are very good at keeping secrets, so we have something in common." His look intensified as he observed the discomfort on his companion's face. "I will share your secret and keep it for you, and you will give yourself to me for one year."

"Are you fucking insane?" Grace stared at him in disbelief, and her anger mounted as he smiled.

"Some would say my own secrets should have made me insane, but I don't think so. I'm a busy man: I have an empire to run, a son to care for, and I need a diversion in my life. You fit the bill perfectly."

He watched as Grace sank onto the sofa. The colour drained from her face.

He continued in the same even tone.

"Please consider my proposition with great care. You will put yourself at my disposal for one year from today. When I call, you will come; when I ask for anything, it will be given; I instruct and you follow. It will be our secret, and when the year is up I'll release you to live this happy life you have built for yourself. You will be the lucky one, Mrs McGuire. I will be the one left behind."

Grace sat on the edge of the sofa, rocking unsteadily back and forth, looking at her hands as she twisted them and inter-locked her fingers, then pulled them apart and repeated the ritual again and again. It was an impulsive nervous gesture she had not performed in many years. She summoned the strength to stop and put her hands down on her lap.

Gabriel continued to watch.

With a quiet, unsteady voice she looked at him, her eyes tearful, and asked, "Why are you doing this to me? I have a job which I love, and a boyfr—" She hesitated, as Jason's face flashed before her.

"A boyfriend? Whom you love?" He was curious, but unfeeling.

He waited a moment but she was silent.

He continued. "Don't misunderstand me, Mrs McGuire. I will keep your secret, and you can keep your job and your boyfriend. But you *will* be mine, and you must give your whole being to me. I'm sure you know what I mean. For one year." Black stood up and walked over to the sideboard. "Do you drink tea with sugar?" He started to fill the kettle with water and set out two of the fine bone-china teacups and saucers.

How could he act so bloody calmly? He's threatening me with slavery!

"Do you think I can just sit here and drink tea with you, you fucking monster?"

"If you do not accept my proposal, Mrs McGuire, the people that matter to you will get to know just what a *fucking monster* your father was. My crimes are against myself, not innocent, helpless children. Now, I think you need a cup of tea."

Grace sat in silence as tears trickled down her cheeks. She watched as he poured the boiling water into a china teapot, and after waiting a moment for it to brew, he poured the Indian tea into the cups and added a spoonful of sugar to one, and a dash of milk to both. He then sat down on the sofa next to his unwilling guest and handed her the saucer.

"I think it's time we began. Take it and drink the tea." His hand hovered in front of her until she took the cup from him.

They sat in silence, sipping the tea. Grace was aware of the proximity of his body to hers and she eased over to the arm of the sofa to distance herself from him as far as was possible. But she did feel thankful for the distraction the tea provided. Her mind was racing, considering her options: should she go to the police? Tell Jason? She knew she didn't want to do either of those things. She wanted her life just as it was: the job she loved, her relationship with Jason, even though she didn't know what that would lead to, and her home in Arnford.

What price was she prepared to pay to keep all of it? What would this man do to her? Could she have sex with someone she despised?

Black took the empty cup from her hand and placed it with his own on the sideboard.

"Let's discuss some of the rules, Mrs McGuire. I'm sure it will help you to accept the situation when you know what is expected of you."

Grace closed her eyes, expecting the nightmare to be over when she opened them again. Of course, it wasn't.

He continued to talk, but now his voice was gentler and she could almost imagine compassion in it, but could a man without a heart have compassion? She had seen him with his son: where was that man now?

"You will call me 'sir'. When I walk into a room in your presence, you will stand. When I tell you to come to me, you will come. When I require you to go somewhere, you will go. When I order you to do something, you will do it. When you are at Arnford Hall, this room will be your sanctuary. I will not come in here unless you invite me. Here is the key."

She watched in disbelief as he took the key from his pocket and held it out, waiting for her to take it from him.

If I take it, I'm accepting this hideous arrangement. Why would I need a sanctuary?

Grace McGuire raised her arm and opened her palm. She felt the cold metal of the key in her hand, and the cold chill of fear in her heart.

"Good. But be warned, Mrs McGuire; if you come to your sanctuary too often, or stay in here too long, there will be consequences. Now follow me; it's getting late and it will be dark soon." He waited, observing her while she got shakily to her feet. She was on autopilot, barely conscious of what she was doing.

This time he took her outside and led her to the garage, to the car. He flicked on a light switch and went over to a workbench to pick up a key fob and a mobile phone – the very latest Xphone, from Black Communications, complete with charger. Grace hovered at the threshold of the garage and he walked over to her, handing her the phone and its charger, saying, "Keep this with you at all times and leave it turned on. I will communicate with you using this, and I will know where you are."

He stared at her and, as she took the phone from him, she inadvertently spoke her thoughts out loud.

"Why me?"

"Because you will be looking after my son and I need to know you; to own you for a while."

"Is this about John, or you?"

"Actually, Grace, it's about you. Now let's look at your car."

He pressed the fob, held the driver's door open and waited until she climbed in. Then he leaned in to press the ignition button and she became aware of a spicy fragrance emanating from him. He spoke in a clear voice. *Even the car was programmed to follow his instructions!*

"Music. Adele, 'Skyfall'."

The music flowed round the interior of the car and escaped into the garage and out onto the drive. Grace recognised the tune and turned to look at him in incredulity. This was one of the tracks on the CD that she had been holding when he had crashed into her.

"Now turn the phone on and go home, Grace. I'll see you soon."

Chapter 20

At breakfast the next morning, Black advised Roger and Steve that Ellouise would be arriving at Arnford Hall tomorrow. A guest room was to be prepared for her; the one next to the green twin room would do. Steve would let the daily housemaid, Annabel, know.

Black turned to his son.

"You have a new aunt to meet, John, after school tomorrow. I think you'll get on fine with her. She's a lot of fun."

John hadn't paid very much attention to anyone that morning, and Black wondered if thoughts of his mother were still bothering him after the previous night. Satan was always a good distraction and, after breakfast, the two of them went to give the hound a short stroll through the wood.

As John was putting his school coat on, he asked "Is Mrs McGuire coming with us this morning?"

"No, John, but you'll see her in class."

On the other side of the village, Grace was climbing into the red Volkswagen, going through yesterday's events for the hundredth time.

What had she done? How was she going to get out of this? Why was she even using this car? Was the phone in her bag?

She had checked the screen fifty times so far. Nothing. She felt like she was in some sort of game but it was never going to be her turn to throw the dice.

At about half past five, after catching up on some work, Grace stood up in the staffroom, ready to leave. Her colleague and friend, Jane, asked if she was doing anything exciting this weekend, and Grace was just in the process of telling her that Jason was coming up, when the Xphone in her bag trilled. She grabbed it and stared at the screen.

Sender: Gabriel Black

Message: The car will pick you up at 8.15 p.m. Isn't it time you were going home, Grace?

Grace fell back onto the chair.

"Are you OK, Grace? You look like you've just had some really bad news!" Jane immediately went over to the sink and poured a glass of water for her friend.

"No, no, I'm fine. Something I wasn't expecting, that's all. I'm fine, really." But her hand was shaking as she accepted the glass.

Half an hour later she was sitting on her bed at home, staring at her dressing table. *What will I do now? Send the car keys and phone back in his car and tell him to fuck off?*

Would I? Dare I?

Melanie Bright is being pushed into the back of a police car. The policewoman who climbs in beside her glares at her unsympathetically, her face appearing ghoulish in the glow from the flashing blue lights of the four other police cars that have come charging to their house, to drag their father away. She can just make out her brother, Michael, being manhandled into the back of another police vehicle by an equally unsympathetic policeman.

Someone is telling her they will need to throw a blanket over her head to protect her when they reach their destination and she will have to get out of the car. The inevitable crowd will no doubt try to attack her – she will be judged guilty by association, no matter how loudly she protests. These people feel a need to represent the victims – innocent children, whom they don't know personally but for whom they want justice and, more frighteningly, revenge. Melanie and Michael must be questioned, dragged through the mud stirred up by their "loving" father. A father whose children are still alive!

It was six weeks of hell before Melanie and Michael were finally cleared of any knowledge of their father's atrocities. Six weeks she would never want to live through again. Melanie Bright disappeared after those six weeks, never to walk on earth again. Michael Bright simply disappeared.

Grace McGuire shuddered. She could not live as Melanie Bright. No one must ever know. The choice of what to do about Gabriel Black was not hers.

She realised she was wringing her hands again. She flung them out in front of her and sat still for a moment before going into the bathroom and getting under the shower. The water flowed over her and she felt calmed by its warmth. Jason had bought her some Crabtree and Evelyn spider lily shower gel, and she breathed in its tropical green citrus fragrance.

At half past six she pulled on a deep purple silk blouse, with an open V-neck, and soft, grey calf-length leggings. She felt cool and comfortable.

At half past seven she was reviewing her children's home-work books, and grouping them based on their end of Year 2 performance results. It occupied her mind, as well as her hands.

At eight, she was rereading everything, wishing they were further into the term and there was more to read.

At five past eight, the words no longer meant anything to her.

At ten past eight, she couldn't see the words any more.

At quarter past eight, he knocked at her door.

She opened the door and took in his dark eyes, his black Hugo Boss suit with a shadow of pinstripe, emphasising his tall, slim physique, and his stark white crisp cotton shirt slashed down the middle by his bright red tie. *Red.*

"Breathe, Grace!" he commanded.

She said nothing and did not move. She didn't know if she wanted to breathe. *Could you die of hatred?*

"Come, let's get in the car." He reached out and took hold of her hand.

She breathed at the shock of the warmth of his hand, the firmness of his grip, the fusion it made with hers.

He will never let me go.

She followed mindlessly as he took her to the Bentley, open-ing the passenger door for her, then went round to the driver's door, climbed in, turned the ignition on and drove them to Arnford Hall.

"Have you eaten?"

"Yes," she lied, looking straight ahead.

He noted her light brown, shiny, wavy, shoulder-length hair, remembered her hazel eyes, and acknowledged that purple suited her. She looked good for thirty-nine; she looked very good.

As they mounted the steps to Arnford Hall, the gargoyles and windows were silent, but she still felt afraid. They entered the vestibule, and he closed the large front door behind them. He waited a second and observed Grace as she took in the hallway and corridors, the paintings and busts, and then the door to her sanctuary. She didn't move.

Black had started to walk towards the grand staircase, when Roger appeared.

"John is sleeping soundly. Goodnight, Gabriel." He turned to Grace, who was still standing on the threshold of the hallway. "Hello again, Grace. Have a good evening," and he disappeared towards the stone steps down to the lower floor.

Black continued up the main staircase and Grace followed him. She quickened her pace and when she was just behind him she asked, her voice accusing and admonishing, "Does he know what you're doing to me?"

"No. No one does. It's our secret, and we're good at keeping secrets, remember?" He carried on up the steps.

They passed the paintings and came to the galleried landing around the atrium. They turned right and walked along the gallery and into an octagonal hall under a glazed roof. There was a large telescope positioned in one corner and Grace distracted herself for a second, wondering who was the astronomer.

He stopped at the first white-panelled door on the left and took a key from his pocket. He unlocked the door and moved aside to let her enter first. He followed her.

"This is your bedroom. The key to this room, Grace, is mine."

Grace turned her back to the room and looked at him so he could see the hate that filled her eyes.

She remembered the key to *her* sanctuary and put her hand to her shoulder bag.

"I want to go to *my* sanctuary," she said defiantly, determined not to let him intimidate her.

His expression was impassive.

"It's not that simple, Grace. You have to get there!" He blocked the doorway with his body.

Her face dropped as she realised what he meant, and stared in disbelief as he turned and locked the door, placing the key back in his jacket pocket.

"Don't look so worried, Grace. Treat it as an adventure."

"An adventure?" she yelled. "You're not exactly offering me a bloody holiday, are you? You're scaring me."

For the first time that evening, he smiled. *You're beautiful when you are angry.*

Before she had the chance to think about what he was doing, he grabbed the back of her neck, pulled her towards him and sealed his lips over hers. She struggled as his strong arm came around her back, pinning her arms to her sides. The kiss was hard and long, and she was aware of his power and his need as she felt him lean in towards her. He smelled of the spice she remembered when he had shown her the car, and she momentarily gave way to the sensual shock running through her, amazed that she could even think she liked this.

Suddenly he pulled back and released her.

"Take your clothes off, Grace."

She backed away from him, stumbling into an antique chaise longue.

"No. I won't do it." Her voice quivered as she regained her footing.

"If you won't, I will." He walked towards her, his smile now gone.

She moved around the chaise longue and made for the only other door off the room. It led into the en-suite; there was no other exit. He was already in the doorway and placed his elbow on the door frame, his hand resting on the back of his neck.

"So, who's it going to be, Grace? You or me?"

I will not cry. I will not cry. She stared at him and, silently, trying not to shake, she brought her hands up and began to unfasten her blouse, revealing a black bra. She tried to think of a poem to recite in her head. *The Lady of Shallot, imprisoned in her tower!*

As her blouse fell to the floor, he shifted his balance slightly, his eyes not leaving her; waiting patiently, confidently.

She slipped her feet out of the kitten-heel nude sandals, pushed her leggings to the floor and stepped aside. She stood before him in her black bra and thong.

Now her eyes did not leave his. She raised her arms behind her and unclasped the bra. She slipped her hands through the straps and then flung it angrily to the floor. She quickly lowered her knickers and hurled them over the room to land at his feet in the doorway. Then she stood tall and straight, determined not to let him see her embarrassment … her shame … her fear.

His stony face drank in her firm breasts with their taut nipples, her sides curving to form a small waist, flowing into her hips, her pubis crowned with wiry light brown pubic hair, neatly trimmed, giving way to her slender, long legs. He mentally savoured her taste like a fine red Bordeaux.

He wanted her. *But just how are you going to get her to agree to let you have her?*

To him, this was a minor detail for now, but he had never taken a woman against her will and had no intention of ever doing so.

He raised his eyes and looked at her face and her graceful neck. Then he saw her silver cross on its fine chain.

"Stand in the bedroom, beside the bed," he commanded.

She walked hesitantly to the foot of the bed, facing it, with her back to him, and was aware of him approaching her. Suddenly she felt his breath on the back of her neck. She flinched slightly at the thought of his touch on her skin, but he didn't touch her. Instead, he lifted her silver chain and unfastened the clasp.

"You don't need this here. He doesn't live in this house." He removed her cross and walked to the dressing table, placing it in a small dish.

"That's mine, and He lives with me!" she said quietly but firmly. She wasn't afraid of her nakedness; she had had more than her fair share of relationships and had lost her inhibitions long ago. But she felt humiliated in front of this man, this fully clothed man, and now he had taken something she treasured from her. Her eyes felt moist and her resolve to tough it out was beginning to weaken.

She focused on the bed, hoping he wouldn't see how much he was hurting her.

She turned her head to the two tall sash windows and momentarily admired the gold silk curtains. There were so many beautiful things in this house; why was there such an atmosphere of gloom and sadness?

Then he was behind her again. He placed something around her neck and she heard a click.

"Now you are mine, for the next three hundred and sixty-four days."

She put her hands to the band around her throat and turned to stare at him as she felt the small padlock at the back.

Her eyes moved to the mirror on the dressing table. She walked over to it, conscious he was still watching her.

In her reflection she saw an exquisite thin band of the palest yellow gold, with a twist of golden ribbon running through it. It was delicate and feminine, and she ran her thumb and forefinger along its curve, feeling the ripple from the ribbon within. It hung loosely around her throat, and felt light and surprisingly comfortable. Then she twisted it around and gazed at the padlock in the reflection. It would not come off without a key. She leaned in towards the mirror and could just make out the initials "GB" engraved on the lock.

She looked at him through the mirror. "Who has the key?" she asked quietly. She already knew the answer. A tear fell to her cheek.

He disappeared into the bathroom and returned with a large bath towel, which he placed over the bed.

"Lie down on the towel, Grace."

Her look said it all. *Fuck you!*

She no longer looked at him, but did as he ordered, and gazed up at the ceiling, desperately admiring the ornate coving around the rose of the crystal chandelier and along the edges of the walls. Then she closed her eyes. She knew what he was going to do. She hadn't shaved herself for a long time. She remembered having a boyfriend who had liked that, and she had done it for him. But Jason never seemed to mind her more natural, yet tidy, look.

Now she felt his hands on her, along with the coolness of a gel and the blade of a razor. He had raised her legs and opened her up as he knelt at the end of the bed, and she was lifeless in his hands.

There was a trickle of water and a gentle patting with a small hand towel, before she felt his fingers very gently dab some cream on her. He was taking great care over his task; he had done this before.

This ritual was carried out in silence and, now, as she lay motionless on the bed, she could hear water running in the bathroom and the sound of items being put down on hard glazed surfaces.

She raised herself up and looked down to observe his handiwork. She had to admit it was good. She got off the bed and walked over to look at herself in the mirror and for a moment, forgetting who was with her, she thought she looked young again!

Then she caught sight of his reflection. He was just behind her, watching her. She was aware that his features appeared softer and she almost believed he was admiring her.

He was still fully clothed and she knew he was deliberating over something.

"Are you on the pill?" he asked.

She wanted to tell him to mind his own business, but standing there naked before him, something within her made her nod.

He couldn't take his eyes off her. He wanted to touch her, taste her, smell her, enter her.

The minor detail had now turned into a major challenge for him.

"I want you to allow me to have sex with you." His eyes glistened and his voice was soft, gentle, hopeful.

Grace thought of his rule: *When I order you to do something, you will do it.*

"Are you ordering me to allow you?"

"Do I have to?"

"Will you take this collar off if I do?" She put her hand on the collar.

He looked at her for a moment and then stepped forward. She was directly in front of him. Slowly he put his hands out and touched her breasts, feeling her nipples brush his palms. She cursed herself as they hardened and she felt a tingling within her. He knew he was beginning to arouse her.

Grace realised now how much he wanted her. She was aware of his erection, trapped in his trousers, and she knew she would have power over him – for a short while at least. She lowered her hand and touched him.

A thrill ran through him and he closed his eyes tightly enough to let her know she had affected him.

Then he pulled away. A mask went up and his voice was firmer, though not harsh.

"I don't bargain, Grace. I control. Are you going to see Jason on Friday?" It had not taken Black long to find out the name of his captive's boyfriend.

"Yes."

"I will take the band off then; tomorrow."

"And how am I going to explain this?" she asked, sarcasm in her voice as she looked down at herself.

He smiled. "Tell him it's a gift. He'll like it. And so will you. Now may I show you?"

Grace nodded. *It was enough.*

"Aarrgh!" she moaned involuntarily as he lowered his hand and cupped her bare, soft pubis. As his hand lingered she felt the heat of his touch. He gently moved his finger to feel for her clitoris, his lips lightly brushing her cheek, and the warmth of his breath felt like velvet on her skin.

Thoughts of his undeniable love for John, his admiration of the orchids, his attention to her likes in music and colours – *even his tie is red* – his power, his threat, his control consumed her mind.

He took his hand away and stepped back as he started to unfasten his tie.

She watched as he hurriedly removed his clothes. For a moment she had a chance to gaze at his body and his large, erect penis. He was a very sexy man.

He gently took hold of her shoulders and guided her to the bed, casting the damp towel on the floor and stripping the top covers from the four-poster bed. She slowly lay back and felt the coolness of the silk sheets. She had consented to let him have her and now she waited to see what he would do.

He straddled her body and as his hand went lower, to help lubricate her and make sure she was ready for him, she was unable to prevent herself from reaching up to pull him to her, such was the excitement he created. He groaned in sheer pleasure, staring deep into her eyes as he slowly moved his penis into her vagina. The fit was perfect and he wallowed in the feel of his skin on hers. He positioned his hands on either side of her head and steadily raised and lowered himself along her body. His arousal was immense; was it the lack of sex over the past few days, or the fact that the woman beneath him hadn't wanted him, and yet now she was giving herself to him?

Grace felt lost in the physical sensations her captor was creating in her body. As he moved gently within her, she could feel his fullness and length. She was intoxicated by his sexual sensuality and she felt his hand move over her abdomen and continue downwards until his finger lightly touched her clitoris and began an erotic stroking of this most intimate part of her body. She reached a climax more quickly than she had ever done, unable to suppress her scream of sheer pleasure.

Her audible betrayal of her pleasure was enough to push him over the edge, and he gasped in unadulterated joy as his sperm flowed into her.

He lowered his lips to find her mouth and kissed her for the second time, watching as she closed her eyes, and he knew for those few minutes that she had given herself to him, helpless to resist the lust and desire he could arouse.

As he gently withdrew from her, Grace turned on to her side to observe him. She watched as he gracefully left the bed and walked over to his jacket, taking in his muscular legs, firm buttocks, and the dimples just marking his lower spine. She was surprised to see him take the key from his pocket and unlock the bedroom door before heading out to cross the hall and enter his own bedroom directly opposite.

Grace lay there a moment, waiting for her senses to come back to earth. Then she rushed into the bathroom, used the toilet, grabbed her clothes and bag, and fled downstairs, still naked, into her sanctuary, locking the door behind her. She leaned against it and breathed deeply. She could hear his voice whispering, "Breathe, Grace."

Feeling a little calmer, she looked around at the room. Her ordeal was over, for now at least. She dressed hurriedly, not without remembering her clean-shaven pubic area, and Jason.

She had betrayed her boyfriend – been unfaithful, however reluctantly. She even questioned just how reluctant she had been.

She had had sex with nine men in her life. As she got older, sex was less intense, less exciting and she wanted it less frequently. But this had been different: it was unwanted, fearful, without love and passion – it was just wrong, and yet it was exciting, erotic, intense.

She felt exhilarated. She acknowledged that he was good; very, very good.

And she loved this room. She gazed at the books and her heart leaped at some of the titles. She looked over to the sideboard and noticed that crystal wine glasses and champagne flutes had been added. She looked around for some sort of fridge. *Surely there must be some drink to go in these.* She pulled open a walnut door to reveal a cooling cabinet, with the bottom half holding bottles of white Burgundies, white and rosé sparkling wines and fine champagnes. Chocolate bars had been placed on the top shelf, along with strawberries and raspberries.

Suddenly the phone in her bag trilled. She looked at the screen.

Sender: Gabriel Black

Message: When you are ready, the car will take you home, Grace.

Was that disappointment she felt?

She felt her collar. *No! I am just his thing, to use and abuse and discard. He is still a bastard.*

She looked around the room again, took a chocolate bar from the cooler, and went into the hall and locked the door behind her. She went out into the fresh air and the Bentley was on the drive, Michael already coming round to open the rear door for her. She glanced up at the house, and thought she noticed a shadow at one of the first-floor windows. She climbed in the car and Michael drove off.

Alone at home, Grace went through the proceedings of her extraordinary evening. She suddenly realised. *Tomorrow is Friday. When is he going take the collar off? What can I wear to school tomorrow?*

Chapter 21

It was lunchtime and Grace was beginning to panic about the collar. She had decided how she was going to lie about the lack of pubic hair to Jason, but there were no words to excuse the collar. She put her hand up to her neck, over her sleeveless cream polo-necked top. The band protruded slightly under the thin fabric, but it wasn't obvious that it was a locked collar, and her hair shielded the back from sight. She finished her salad and was thinking about taking a walk down the lane for some fresh air before the afternoon's classes, when she heard the trill.

Sender: Gabriel Black

Message: Meet me in the playground when I collect John.

Grace went for her walk.

The afternoon lessons went well, and her mind was immersed in phonics and times tables. The children were still in the "just back at school and enthusiastic" phase, and it was her favourite time, giving her ample opportunity to get to know her new children. She couldn't help having a soft spot for John Black; he was friendly and good-natured, keen to learn and bright. She also couldn't help wondering which traits he had inherited from his father.

Just after quarter past three, she stealthily glanced out of her classroom window and saw the dark-haired man in a black suit, talking animatedly with John Black and occasionally glancing at the school doors.

He's waiting for me!

Fearful that he would leave and she would be "labelled" for the weekend, she hurried out to him.

"Grace." He was smiling and he glanced towards John.

Oh, this is a show for your son. Well, two can play at that game!

"I think you mean Mrs McGuire!" she said, a little louder than she had intended, but also glancing, exaggeratedly, at John Black. "Hello, John," she added, smiling at the young boy.

"Hi, Mrs McGuire. Are you coming for tea?"

"Not today, John. I just needed to check something with your father. Have a good weekend and I'll see you on Monday." She turned to Gabriel Black.

He looked at her, one eyebrow raised, clearly expecting some sort of acknowledgement, response – something – from her.

"Sir." She hissed the word at him, certain John couldn't hear.

"Come to the car." He turned to take John's hand and walked to the Bentley parked in the driveway of the house that was for sale.

He held the front passenger door open for John and helped him to fasten his seat belt. Then he held the rear door open for Grace. "Get in."

She stared at him. *What's he doing? I'm not ready to leave school yet. I want to go home. He had said nothing about going with him.*

He waited and she reluctantly climbed into the car.

He went round to the other side and climbed in the back. Grace relaxed a little, knowing the car wasn't going to go any-where. Apparently the man driving it today was sitting next to her!

He put his hand to her neck and asked her to turn around. He then put the small key in the lock and removed the collar.

Without looking at him, she whispered, "Thank you," and climbed out of the car. By the time she reached the school gate, the Bentley was heading back to Arnford Hall.

She felt she could relax now – until Monday at least. Perhaps this arrangement wasn't too bad; a price worth paying for her life, her happiness. Jason need never know – not while he remained in London, anyway. It seemed Black was going to be reasonable about weekends and, surely, holidays too.

By the time weekends and school holidays were deducted from three hundred and sixty-five days, it seemed a much more manageable proposition. Not to mention her comfortable, well-provisioned sanctuary! She was certain she could switch herself off from the sex rituals; after all, she had taught herself to switch

112

off from her past well enough! Besides, she had to admit the sex had been good; she had felt young and vibrant, and it reminded her of how exciting it used to be when she first explored the activity. And he was fucking good at it!

She cocooned herself in her little bubble. This was how she was going to cope for the next year.

Chapter 22

"We're going to meet your new aunty, John." Gabriel glanced at his son, sitting next to him, and smiled.

The young boy couldn't begin to know how important he was to the man at his side, and the power he now had over him, over the Black empire, and the thousands of people affected by it.

As they walked down the hallways of Arnford Hall, it became clear that Ellouise had arrived.

She launched herself at her big brother and hugged him lovingly. "GeeBee!" She always used the name she had given him as a small child when she had been unable to pronounce Gabriel. "I've missed you. You look great. How are you? Have you missed me?"

Finally she let him go and paused before crouching down to look John Black squarely in the eyes, beaming with delight and instant affection.

"And you must be John."

John stared in amazement at the lady facing him, who had long flowing dark brown hair, large, bright blue eyes, and was dressed in a multi-coloured flowing calf-length chiffon dress, with beads, bangles and rings hanging off virtually every part of her body (face excepted!). She resembled some 1960s flower-power girl.

Gabriel was laughing as he announced, "John, meet your aunt Ellouise."

"Call me Aunty Ell. Would you like that?"

John looked up at his father, shyly, and copied the nod Black senior made.

"Come and see what I've brought!" And Aunty Ell casually took John's hand and led him to the octagonal room. She had received inside information from Roger, whom she trusted implicitly, on what this particular seven-year-old boy liked, and had brought gifts of Star Wars lego, Ben 10 toys and T-shirts, superhero comics and, of course, several bars of chocolate. She was instantly John's new best friend, just behind Roger and Adam. Of course, she had to be aunty number two, just behind Aunty Carol.

Gabriel stared at their backs, and then went down to the kitchen to catch up with Roger.

Weekend plans had been made for the Arnford Hall household: the men were going to have a fencing bout this evening while Aunty Ell got to know, and no doubt spoil, her nephew (a sin the men were determined not to commit; well, not too frequently anyway!). The adults would share a celebratory evening meal, as it had been six weeks since Ellouise had joined them. They would spend Saturday going through plans for John's new bedroom and then all going for a walk with Satan, and possibly fishing at the mere in the grounds of the Hall; and in the early evening the Blacks would watch the new Avengers film Roger and Steve had already seen. On Sunday, provided Gabriel was satisfied that John and Ellouise were getting along well together, and he and his son could bear to be parted for a day, Aunty Ell was going to take John to the beach at Crosby and Roger and Steve would do their own thing. Black would entertain himself at Arnford Hall.

Jason arrived in Willow Lane to the open arms of his girlfriend at seven o'clock on Friday night. His face lit up when he felt and then saw the newly bared skin on his lover (Grace felt momentarily cross that bastard Black had been right), as they had sex under the duvet.

On Saturday they lazed around the house, and went for a drive in the new car.

"Just how long have you got this for?"

"A few more days, I think." *I still haven't had the conversation with bastard Black about my own car …*

In the evening they went to the local pub with some friends.

After more sex late on Saturday night, and a lie-in on Sunday morning, Grace glanced at the Xphone flashing in her handbag.

What now? And her face froze.

Sender: Gabriel Black

Message: The car will pick you up at noon. Time for him to go, Grace.

Fucking shit! You bastard!

"Are you OK, Grace?" Jason was just cooking eggs and bacon; it was half past ten.

Did I speak out loud? "Sure, I'm fine." *Think! Should I just not go? How do I explain to Jason that I need to go out?*

"I'm just going to the bathroom," and she ran upstairs.

Two minutes later she went back into the kitchen.

"Jason, I'm sorry, I've got a cracking headache coming on. I really can't face any food. I need to go back to bed with some Nurofen. I'm not going to be good company. Why don't you get an early train home? There's no point in hanging around here. I'm really sorry, sweet."

"You do look pale, Grace. Why don't you go and lie down? I'll bring you some water and tablets. I don't mind staying to see how you feel in a bit. My train's not till quarter past four. Maybe we could go for a walk later if you're feeling better?"

Grace was beginning to really feel sick – at her lies, at what she had already done to Jason, and at what she was about to do.

"I doubt I'll be up to doing anything, Jason. I'll just take the tablets and go back to bed. You go. You can catch up on stuff at your place, can't you? I need to go and lie down." She walked over to the cupboard to get the Nurofen, as Jason handed her a glass of water.

"OK. Are you sure you'll be all right on your own?"

"Yes. You just go."

Jason looked at the eggs and bacon. He decided to make them into a couple of sandwiches to take on the train. He checked his phone: it was a twenty-minute walk to the station and, if he hurried, he could catch the next train in thirty minutes.

"Call me when you're feeling better, OK?" He kissed her gently before she made her way upstairs, not turning to him to say goodbye, so he didn't see the tears streaking down her cheeks.

Now she really did have a headache.

Chapter 23

There was a knock on the door and Grace moved from the bottom of her staircase, where she had been sitting for the last five minutes. She had tried to analyse how she felt: self-loathing, anger at herself, her father, Black; bitterness at the cruelty of her fate; curiosity – *curiosity? Don't go there …*

She opened the door. He was there, wearing black Armani trousers, a pale grey shirt and plain purple silk tie. She remembered her purple silk shirt. He looked striking and confident.

Gabriel took in the woman standing before him. He had waited all morning to come and knock on her door. Her hair was pulled tightly back in a ponytail, the hazel of her eyes looked paler than he remembered and she wore very little make-up. She wore a short-sleeved blue and red checked shirt with navy slim-fitting jeans and Converse trainers. She looked tired and sad. He wouldn't permit himself to feel guilty for bringing this on her; he wanted this too much for that. Besides, feeling guilty had been the norm for him for many years.

"Hello, Grace."

She turned her back on him, saying nothing. Suddenly she felt his arm on hers as he pulled her back towards him, and she was aware of both his strength and control, as the grip was firm but not painful.

"You must remember your manners. Didn't they teach you that at school? I said hello, Grace." His tone was cold and unfeeling.

She stared at him, fearful for a moment, but he let go of her and looked down for a second.

She said "Hello, sir," with loathing in her voice. "Can I get my bag now?"

He looked at her intently, and she couldn't make out if he was angry with her or himself.

"Yes. I will wait by the car."

Grace grabbed her bag and locked her front door. She walked to the car, trembling slightly, fearful of what he had in store. Well, at least she would see John, and Roger and Steve.

He opened the front passenger door. *No Michael today?*

He walked round and climbed into the driver's side and the car filled with the sounds of Gustav Holst's "Jupiter".

"Bringer of Jollity." Grace stared into his eyes, which were fixed on her. "That's a laugh," she said quietly, mockingly. Then her eyes fell on the central console. The golden collar was twinkling in the sunlight. She raised her eyes to meet his.

"Turn around, Grace."

She did as he ordered and she heard the padlock click. Then she stared straight ahead.

The car started to move. He didn't speak, nor look at her. She broke the silence.

"You said I could keep my boyfriend. You knew he was here. Why have you come for me?"

"I'm taking back what is mine. You're on loan when you are with him, Grace, for this period, remember?" He kept his eyes on the road.

"You don't fucking own me!" she retorted.

He was silent. He admired her spirit. *Don't break it!*

It was only a short distance to Arnford Hall, but to Grace it seemed to take a long time. There was a definite chill in the car.

As it came to a stop by the steps he said firmly "Wait here." He went round to open her door.

She stood on the gravel and watched him run up the steps. This time he had to unlock the front door.

The gargoyles seemed to be mocking her today. *He's spoiling your weekend, isn't he?*

She wondered where everyone was. Was nobody at home? She suddenly felt nervous.

She followed him into the house. He was waiting in the main hallway. She hesitated by the door to her sanctuary, wondering whether to go straight into this room.

His voice broke her deliberation.

"I won't stop you going in there. But remember there will be consequences if you stay too long, or use this room too frequently." His eyes looked black as he stared at her. He had plans for today, while they were alone, and he didn't want her to lock herself away.

She walked past the door to her sanctuary, and she felt certain she noticed him sigh. *With relief?*

"Follow me," he ordered and walked up the grand staircase and around the galleried landing, to the room he referred to as her bedroom.

Will I ever be required to sleep in there during my year of slavery?

"Now take your clothes off. I want to see you – all of you."

She hesitated a moment, glancing around the room, wondering if she had any options. She thought of her sanctuary, but he was standing in the doorway, blocking her escape. She looked over at the dresser and saw her cross still lying in the dish; she had forgotten to take it with her when she left the other day. It was a welcome distraction, and she started to wonder why he was so vehement that God didn't live in this house, as she unceremoniously undressed. As her attire diminished, her resolve to find out more about this man staring at her now naked body strengthened. He knew her secret; she was determined to find out his.

Black's face didn't expose his mental comparison of this thirty-nine-year-old, respectable, proud woman, who didn't give a fuck about him, and didn't want to be with him, with the shallow exhibitionist, Elana. The latter would have done anything for him. Hell, she had joined him in a threesome with Cindy, just to please him, not out of love for him, but love for his money and power. Yet Grace was with him to save herself, her whole existence: she wanted nothing from him, except to be free. *You really are a bastard, Black!*

He broke the silence. "Good." He walked over to the large chest situated next to the dressing table and opened the top drawer.

As Grace watched him take out some sort of interlocking chain and cuffs restraint, she shuddered and sat on the side of the bed to prevent herself from keeling over.

"What are you going to do to me?" she asked with a fearful urgency.

His eyes made contact with her and she quickly added, "Sir?"

"We're going to play, Grace. Let's see if you like it."

She closed her eyes briefly, and then opened them to see him approaching her with the restraint. She made no attempt to move, neither to aid nor hinder him, as he placed a black leather collar around her neck. It rested over her collar of gold, and then he fastened her wrists in the cuffs, leaving her hands in front of her, linked to each other, creating a triangle of chain from her neck to her wrists.

He pulled gently on the chain and lifted her to her feet. She felt the leather collar against the back of her neck as the restraint became taut, forcing her to follow him closely as he led her out of the bedroom.

When she realised he was going to take her downstairs, she froze and pulled back against the chain in his hands, feeling the strain on her wrists.

"Wait," her voice was becoming hysterical. "What about the others? Please don't let anyone see me!"

He moved towards her, releasing the tension on the chain, and cupped her chin in his hands, raising her face to look at him. She was startled at his warm touch and his enticing smell as his face was so close to hers.

"We are alone, Grace. Don't worry," and he tugged gently as they continued to make their way downstairs.

After descending the grand staircase, they went down the spiral staircase to the lower ground floor. At one point Grace stumbled in her nervousness and he reached out to support her, his arm cradling her shoulders, and again she breathed him in. They walked through a small hallway and she watched, as though in a trance, as he entered a code on a number pad at the side of double oak doors and pulled one open.

"This is the den, Grace," he said, his voice laden with lustful expectation as he let go of the chain.

Grace looked around the darkened room, and as her eyes adjusted to the dim light, she saw the huge bed in the middle, the black satin sheets and ivory chiffon curtains tied back to the posts. She registered chains hanging around the bed, the seating and the fact that it all faced the bed. In readiness for some sort of exhibition, she thought, and shuddered in dread. This room frightened her. As she turned back to the door, wanting to get to the sanctuary, his voice boomed in her ears.

"It's too late, Grace. You won't make it. I won't let you this time." He took two steps to reach her, taking her hand instead of the chain, and he pulled her forward with him, to cross the room to a door in the far corner.

"I told you not to worry," he said calmly, a little taken aback by the fear in her eyes, and the realisation that he was genuinely scaring her.

Scaring women was not new to him, but he always did it intentionally; he liked the "game". But now, with Grace, he was hopeful she might enjoy his attentions, and he was disturbed by the fact that he was frightening her. *You should give her the chance to get to know your games! You have her naked and chained, what do you expect? She's not exactly your biggest fan!*

He squeezed her hand. Grace wasn't sure if this gesture was his attempt to comfort her or merely to let her know he was there and he was in charge.

"Stand there," he commanded as he positioned her in front of the closed door.

Grace watched in silence as he slowly undressed and revealed his strong naked body to her again, not realising he had done it to try to put her at her ease.

He finally opened the door, which led to a large wet room with grey tiles covering three walls. There were water jets protruding from each of these walls, at varying heights and distances apart, and several hoses were positioned on the tiles. The fourth wall was painted white with a large towel rail, washbasin and tall cupboard coming off it. There was a control panel in the wall alongside the doorjamb.

From the ceiling protruded one huge plate of steel, splattered with water jets of varying diameters, and all around the plate, embedded in the white ceiling, were spotlights.

Grace stared around her, trying to predict what was about to happen, and she noticed the warmth of the room and a fresh, clean smell.

Black released her hand.

"Kneel on the mat," he ordered.

Glad to take the tension out of her legs, she knelt down on one of the rubber mats that were placed around the room. Resting her hands on her knees, she looked up at him, not failing to notice his erection as his large penis betrayed the excitement he was feeling.

He looked proud and confident; a man who normally never disappoints, who is never rejected, who is admired, yearned for, even.

Well, not by me, thought the naked, kneeling victim, but she knew her resolve to be strong and defiant was weakening.

Black went to the tall cupboard and took out a spreader bar with two cuffs attached to it, and a teardrop-shaped bottle containing a purple liquid. He took these items over to where Grace was kneeling, and knelt beside her. She looked at the spreader and then at him, defiance in her eyes, as she was coming to terms with what she thought he was going to do to her.

"Despite what you may think of me, Grace, I want you to enjoy this. I want us both to enjoy it. You are my captive. Don't you play games and have fantasies?"

She scoffed at him, her bitterness ringing out. "You must be bloody joking! Do you think I can enjoy this?" She raised her bound hands to him.

He took them in his own, and to her amazement, he brought them up to his lips and peppered them with light kisses.

Then he stopped and let them drop, as if he realised he had gone too far, as if he had let his guard down and allowed her to see something of him she wasn't supposed to – tenderness, affection.

"Stand up," he ordered, his impassive tone back now, his eyes dark and guarded.

As Grace clumsily stood up, manoeuvring the chain so it didn't get in the way, he fastened her feet into the cuffs on the spreader bar, and she was immobilised before him, focusing on not falling over.

Then he stood in front of her. "I know you don't want to, but try to relax. It will be better that way." He unfastened the lid of the bottle and poured some oil into his hand. As he rubbed them together, spreading the liquid over his palms, Grace became aware of the sensual smell of lavender, rosemary and almond. He steadily started to rub the oil over her shoulders, along her arms, on her breasts, lingering there to pleasure himself with their softness, and then down to her abdomen, before kneeling in front of her and trailing his hands down her outer thighs. He continued to her feet, persuading her to lift them one at a time, and as he lightly oiled her toes and soles of her feet she placed her hands on his shoulder to steady herself and adjust to the unwieldy bar. He felt warm and firm. He paused a moment as he felt her touch, before returning to his task, stroking the inside of her legs, upwards this time, and reaching her inner thighs. She could not hold back a moan of pleasure and for a moment she was lost in the tingling sensation surrounding her vagina.

In silence and with gentle, methodical motions, he continued to smooth the oil over her skin, moving around her and covering her whole body. As he stroked her back, she couldn't refrain from lowering her head and leaning forward ever so slightly, wallowing in the pleasure this act was giving her, the chains and bar almost forgotten.

Once again he knelt before her. Her legs were secured, the distance between them revealing her cleanly shaven, most intimate part, and he looked up at her, his eyes drinking in the erotic vision above him and expressing his desire to touch her there. She lowered her lids and then felt his fingers lightly caress her vulva. He had raised himself high on his knees and he kissed and sucked her pubis, as his fingers continued their journey to her vagina, entering it and exploring around it, before searching for her clitoris, to feel it, play with it, excite her.

The smell, the restraints, this man were all alluring and her head was fighting a losing battle with the rest of her body – *this is wrong! You should tell him to fucking leave you alone!* But the sane side of her brain was isolated in this arena: the rest of her being wanted him to make her come, and she knew that would not be enough. She wanted him to fuck her.

As she wobbled slightly, he steadied her by taking hold of her thighs, before continuing to entice her into orgasm. He worked

123

gently and incessantly and her brain finally conceded defeat. This was wonderful. He was selfless in his desire to pleasure her, and Grace was aroused as she sensed this act pleasured him too. She couldn't think of any man who had even tried to make her believe that masturbating her gave him as much fun as it did her. Gabriel Black didn't need to try; his enjoyment was obvious and she revelled in it even more.

She began to tremble and wanted to protest as he ceased for a moment and reached up, pulling gently on her chain.

"Lie on the mat," he instructed, the urgency in his voice betraying his need for her to come.

With awkward movements, she lay back, open, shameless and desperate, and as soon as his fingers resumed their stroking, she cried out in an all-consuming orgasm.

His finger lingered for slightly longer than was bearable, and she moaned, "No, please," desperate to close her legs to him, but unable to.

He ceased touching her and brought his hands to the sides of her shoulders as he straddled her body. He pushed his hips down onto her. His penis was so erect, his control so assured and her opening so wide and wet that his penis easily found its way, entering her, filling her and shooting his sperm into her.

Grace became aware of a sexual awakening within her.

They lay side by side for a few minutes, Grace wondering if sex with him was always this good, Gabriel trying to work out what had just happened. *Was this the best sex he had ever had? Fuck! This was not part of his plan!*

Finally he stood up and went back into the den.

Grace closed her eyes. He had left her cuffed and chained. She tried to stand up but needed to manoeuvre her widespread legs and attempt to sit up first. She was struggling with her emotions and the paradox of feeling ashamed and degraded yet having just been made to feel wonderful, sensual and wanted. *Why, why?*

Suddenly he was standing in front of her, holding his hand out to help her to her feet before crouching down to unfasten the cuffs from her ankles, then standing and removing the restraints from her neck and wrists. Her collar remained in place.

They were both coated in the sweet-smelling oil. Grace watched Black move to the control panel and press the keypad. Suddenly water started to pour down on her from the steel plate above her head, and he pulled on one of the hoses. Staring at her apprehensive face intently, he said softly, through genuinely smiling lips, "Breathe, Grace," as he aimed the jet of water at her.

She inhaled as the warm water fell over her from above, luxuriant and indulgent, and then gasped as the jet of water from his hose sprayed her, with just the right amount of force and heat to feel she was having her own private shower by her own manservant.

He hesitated a moment, before turning and taking another hose from the wall.

"Will you do the honours, please?" and he held the hose out to her, hopeful she would spray his body.

She took it and aimed. They showered each other with the warm jets, drenching each other under the sensual sheets of water.

He turned the water off and, replacing the hoses, took two large, soft white towels from the rail, handing one to Grace.

They dried in silence. When they were dry, he enveloped her body in a soft, luxurious white bathrobe. He stood naked before her, then he took her hand and led her into the den. She watched his graceful steps, again appreciating the muscles in his legs and buttocks as they flexed with each movement.

She tried not to admire him, but she failed.

He went over to the bed, motioning for her to lie back on the black silk sheets. He pulled out a tube of gel from one of the bedside tables and gently rubbed her wrists and ankles.

"So, Grace, are you more comfortable with the prospects for the year now?" His voice was hushed and there was a confident smugness about him, as though he was so used to pleasing women that, surely, she could only admire his sexual expertise.

But Grace was wrapped in a robe, her nakedness no longer exposed. She had regained her composure, her "school teacher" persona. *No way are you getting inside my head!*

"I'm here because you are forcing me to be, sir." She glared at him, spitting that last word out.

His eyes flickered slightly, taken aback by her bitterness after the sexual pleasure she had just given him. Hadn't she been compliant in the end, desirous? Hadn't it been as good for her as it had been for him? He knew the answer to both those questions was yes.

His mask went up and his emotions returned to their hiding place. He moved off the bed and gathered his clothes together. He did not put them on.

"Let's go back upstairs." He walked ahead of her and her eyes soaked him up, admiring his body.

They returned to her bedroom.

"I presume you'll want to get dressed now." He folded his arms and watched her as she slowly put on her clothes. She hesitated, to see what he was going to do, but he continued to study her, confident with the role reversal as he remained naked before his fully clothed hostage. As if daring him to say anything, Grace walked over to the dressing table and took her cross from the dish and put it in her bag. Then, placing the bag over her shoulder, she headed out of the door and around the gallery towards the staircase.

He didn't attempt to stop her, nor did he follow her. He collected his clothes and walked over to his own bedroom. As she reached the stairs she heard his bedroom door close.

Grace unlocked the door to her sanctuary and walked in. She checked the phone, expecting a message to tell her the car was ready. There wasn't one.

The clock on the mantelpiece showed half past five. She suddenly felt very hungry and went to the fridge for the strawberries, raspberries and chocolate bars she had seen in there before. She ate some, and then studied the wine bottles.

Meursault Perrières 1er Cru sounded expensive, and Grace uncorked the bottle and poured some of the honey-coloured chilled liquid into the crystal wine glass. It tasted delicious.

She searched the book titles and selected Lord Tennyson's "The Lady of Shallot". She curled up in one of the armchairs with the wine and fruit on the coffee table beside her, deciding to make the most of her "imprisonment", and felt a pleasant tingling on remembering his actions in the wet room. She felt certain that if she had put her mind to it, she could have climaxed again at the mere thought of it!

Chapter 24

It was six o'clock. Black was unable to stop his mind oscillating between John and what he was doing with Ellouise, and Grace and what she was doing in her sanctuary. He couldn't bring himself to let her go yet, and he was concerned by his need to see her again. This had not been part of his plan.

The next minute, laughter and shouting came from the Hall's entrance.

"Daddy, Daddy, we're back!" and Gabriel ran down the stairs, the paternal side of his heart warming as his son came over to him and hugged him tightly. He had missed him.

"We've been to the seaside and Aunty Ell helped me win this on hook a duck." John proudly raised a bright red, cuddly lobster.

"Well, he's great!" Gabriel raised his eyebrow as he glanced at his sister. *Really?*

She started laughing and then went on to say what a fabulous day they had had: fun on the beach, racing down sand dunes, paddling in the sea (at which point Black glanced down at John's shoes, saying "Off!"), and a few rides and games at a travelling fairground.

As the two travellers sat on the floor removing their sandy footwear, both declared they were starving.

Then all three heads turned as the door to the former smoking room opened.

Grace stood nervously in the doorway, happy to have heard John's voice and suddenly wishing to see him, feeling safe that she wouldn't be left alone with his father.

John looked delighted to see his teacher.

Ellouise looked shocked and turned directly to face her brother, who was standing behind her, her questioning look at him unseen by Grace.

Gabriel looked relieved, and then his mask rose as he saw his sister's face.

An awkward silence hung in the air until John went over to his teacher, his face still beaming. "Mrs McGuire, hi. This is my new Aunty Ell."

Ellouise turned around to face Grace again and cautiously approached her. She held her hand out and gently shook the one extended to her by Grace.

"Hi, I'm Ellouise, Gabriel's sister." Although she smiled, Grace couldn't fail to detect a sadness behind her eyes and a feeling that she was sorry that Grace was there. Her eyes lingered on Grace's golden collar.

Am I intruding on a family reunion? But he hasn't sent me home.

Grace let her hand drop and suddenly regretted opening her door. *I shouldn't be here. I can't go on with this. What's he playing at?*

Then her eyes met his; dark, secretive, protective and determined.

Gabriel walked straight over to her and surprised her by taking her hand. In a voice too smooth and words emitted too quickly to be normal he said, "Ellouise, this is Grace McGuire, my guest and John's teacher."

The surprises weren't over yet, as Ellouise simply touched her brother's arm and said quietly, Grace just making out her words, "Oh GeeBee, what are you doing?" and she glanced behind Grace, into the sanctuary.

The teacher suddenly felt guilty about opening an expensive bottle of wine and tried to break the awkward atmosphere, saying, "Hey. Would you like a glass of wine?" as though it were the most natural thing to ask.

"Go to the kitchen." Gabriel had regained his composure and spoke authoritatively; no one was going to argue with him. "I'll bring the wine."

Nervously and wondering what the hell was going on in this little family gathering, Grace followed Ellouise and John down to the kitchen. Gabriel was only a few seconds behind them, wine in hand, and he asked his sister to fetch some glasses over to the island. He then went to the fridge and took out a platter of sandwiches, some salad and a chocolate cheesecake, courtesy of Steve.

He and Ellouise laid out four place settings on the island and the dysfunctional group sat down to share the supper. Grace felt like she was playing in some surreal drama, where, weirdly, the script was being written as the story unfolded.

She was seated next to John, and Gabriel sat opposite her, with Ellouise at his side. The young Black chatted happily to all three grown-ups, and Gabriel was particularly grateful for the distraction created by the child's amused recounting of the adventure to Crosby. Ellouise was quiet, and now seemed less hungry than she was when she first arrived back from their day trip. Black couldn't fail to notice that Grace was eating, and drinking, enough for all of them.

This was her way of making sure she wasn't expected to say too much. *Go on, girl, you can manage another mouthful!*

Eventually Black reluctantly took his son up to bed, clearly not comfortable leaving the two women to carry on drinking the second bottle of wine – and, of course, providing them with the perfect opportunity to talk.

As soon as he had left the kitchen, Ellouise got straight to the point. "So, Grace, how long have you been seeing my brother?"

Grace doubted she had concealed a look of shock at this direct question and hesitated, not knowing how to answer: the inference was so wrong; the truth was unspeakable. She remembered his words: *It will be our secret.*

"Well, er … I just met him through school, where John has started this term. I just want to help John to settle and let him know I'm here for him should he need to discuss anything at all. This is a really difficult time for him, with the loss of his mother, and all this change to his life …" She looked up at Ellouise and felt that she knew something wasn't right.

"I'm sure he didn't give you that necklace just because you're his son's teacher."

Grace put her hand up to the collar, regretting her blushes, and was about to say something, when the sister continued. "Is the old smoking room your sanctuary?"

Grace was dumbstruck. Then she heard her own voice, only just avoiding sounding hysterical, laugh out, "Ha! You know your brother! He thinks I need my own space ..." Grace wondered if his sister had been taken in by this explanation.

"Has he told you it used to be his?" Ellouise watched as Grace looked at her anxiously and then took a gulp of her wine.

Desperately trying not to splutter as she was getting over the shock of what Ellouise had just said, Grace put her glass down. She was taken aback as the other woman came around to her side of the island and took hold of her hand.

"I'm sorry, Grace. I didn't mean to shock you and I have probably said too much. But I love my brother very much and I don't want him to be hurt. Please don't hurt him."

Grace stared at the woman beside her: her long flyaway hair, hanging halfway down her back, the floating aquamarine, red, green and yellow floral dress, the beads and bangles adorning her neck, wrists and ankles, and the small tattoo of a bluebird on the top of her foot.

She had no idea what to say. *Wasn't their relationship a secret? Had he "enslaved" other women? What did she mean by* his *sanctuary? Why the hell would he need a sanctuary in his own home?*

As she took another sip of wine, she was beginning to regret her tactic of eating and drinking to keep silent, because she was now feeling quite tipsy and not only would she lose her excuse not to talk, she was also in danger of not being able to talk coherently! *Aha, new plan maybe? Let her think I'm completely inebriated!*

Ellouise let go of her hand. Her voice was suddenly quieter and she whispered,

"Are you staying here tonight? Let me come and see you later; there are some things you need to know ..."

Ellouise stopped talking, and Grace did not have to look round to know that Gabriel had returned to the kitchen, his shoeless feet striding silently across to the island.

"Am I interrupting anything?" His tone seemed to be daring his younger sister to say something.

Now it was her turn to take a drink.

Grace stood up, more out of trepidation about how the day was turning out, rather than remembering his rules. Gabriel looked at her, noticing an expression which told him that she was in possession of new information. About him.

Now it was his turn to take a drink.

"I was just asking Grace how long you have been seeing her."
Damn you, Ellouise! Give me a break!

"Right then, girls." He needed a diversion, a good one. "Grab your glasses and let's see what we can find out about each other."

To Grace's amazement, his eyes were shining, a slight smile touching his lips. Suddenly Ellouise became animated and grabbed her brother's arm.

"Are we going to play dare to bare?" and she turned to an astonished Grace. "Have you played this game before, Grace?"

As Black led the way out of the kitchen, Grace was vaguely aware of him saying, "I doubt it!"

He walked into the lower hallway. For one moment Grace was fearful he was going to lead them into the den, but instead he walked past it, turned right at the end of the hall and then left at the end of a long corridor. He entered a code into the pad on the wall and opened a panelled door. They walked into a small anteroom, which appeared to serve as some sort of cloakroom, as Grace saw two coat racks. Gabriel walked on, through another door, and as she followed him, her gaze fell on gambling tables: blackjack, roulette and poker.

This was the games room. It had seating for about fifty people, with what looked like a well-stocked bar area at one end. *Is this how the Black family entertain?*

He turned to see Grace's face; she was staring at the tables.

"So, take a seat and let's get started. We'll keep it simple as we don't have much time. I'll get some drinks while Ellouise explains the rules." He headed over to the bar and poured Jack Daniel's into three tumblers.

Ellouise took Grace's hand and led her to the roulette table, saying excitedly, "Don't worry, we're not going to play roulette, just use the wheel. You spin it and ask a question of the others, while the ball is still bouncing. If it lands in the black you have to answer truthfully; if it lands in the red you can tell a lie. Of course, no one will know for sure if you are lying. The aim is to try to find out more about the others than they do about you. But each question is at a cost – you have to take off a piece of clothing – dare to bare, you see; the winner nearly always ends up naked!" She started laughing at the look of horror on Grace's face.

"Don't worry. GeeBee always has a treat in store for us after a game."

"You don't mean sex?" Grace blurted out, not realising her mouth was spewing forth her thoughts.

Ellouise's laughter continued. "Of course not! And I don't know about you, but I don't do girls. I experimented a bit at Cambridge, but I prefer men. Of course, I can't say what you two will want to get up to later!" and her eyes twinkled as though Grace wouldn't be able to keep her hands off her brother!

"Er, I have work tomorrow, and what about John?" she asked, anxiously looking up at Gabriel.

"The intercom is on in his room and we can hear him any-where in the house if he wakes up. We'll make it a short game and just the one drink. No harm will be done, and we'll make sure you get to work on time." He handed her a glass and sat down opposite the two girls.

He took a long, slow sip of whisky.

"I trust my sister has filled you in on how we like to play? You realise we're not a prudish family, and were never brought up to be self-conscious of our own or each other's bodies." A look of amusement was in his eyes as Grace shuffled uneas-ily in her seat. "Surely you've been in communal showers at a gym, swimming pool or some such place? It's no different really. And you've already seen me."

Grace took a sip of the JD, too unnerved to wonder where the Coke was!

"Who's going to go first?" asked Ellouise, clearly wanting to break the tension mounting between her brother and his guest.

Well, you're welcome to! Grace really wanted to go home, get on with her school planning for tomorrow, tidy the kitchen, even scrub the floor – anything would be preferable to sitting here dreading what was going to happen.

"Guests should always be first. Go ahead, Grace."

Grace glared at Black. Well, she had already worked out that she had a shirt, jeans, two shoes, two socks, knickers and a bra – that made eight pieces of clothing, at least two of which she wanted to keep on. *So what was one shoe?*

"OK," she said, trying to appear nonchalant as she threw her head back. She was determined to rise to this challenge, and hopefully an opportunity would arise where she could call his bluff. She decided not to pussyfoot around!

"Have you ever used the sanctuary?"

"Spin the wheel and put the ball in, Grace." Gabriel's tone and face were veiled from her scrutiny.

She watched the ball jumping in and out of the red and black numbers. Black.

"Yes." Black looked at her expectantly.

She bent down and unfastened her shoelace and removed her trainer.

"Place it on the bench," he instructed. "We each keep our own pile."

"Oh." She stood up and walked over to the bench and returned with one shoe remaining in place.

"Yes," said Ellouise.

Gabriel looked expectantly at Grace again.

"But I only asked one question!"

Ellouise smiled. "Two answers equals two goes. You need to be more specific to whom you are asking the question. Didn't I mention that?" She was smiling at Grace as though she was actually doing her a favour.

This woman is raving mad! Grace angrily removed her other shoe and marched over to the bench and back. She glared at Ellouise. "Are you ganging up on me?"

"Yes." The sister laughed.

"No." The brother sipped his drink.

As Grace sat motionless, he added "Well?"

"You've got to be kidding me! I didn't spin the wheel."

He shook his head. "We'll make an exception with the wheel this time as it's your first game," and he waited.

Grace removed both her socks and placed them on the bench. "It's getting late. What time will we be finished?"

"Spin the wheel, Grace."

"For fuck's sake," she muttered under her breath, fearful the drink was erasing her wits. She spun the wheel. Red.

Brother and sister both replied, "When we're all naked."

Ellouise was smiling gently at Grace, as if to say, *Don't worry; enjoy.* Gabriel just watched her and Grace still had no idea what he was thinking.

She walked over to the bench and removed her shirt and jeans.

She returned to her seat in her bra and knickers. *How come I'm the only one who has removed any clothing? Do not ask that out loud, girl!*

Ellouise leaned over to her and whispered, "It's OK, Grace, I'm helping you, you'll see."

It was clear the Blacks were enjoying the game and it seemed to be at her expense. Well, no more questions from her mouth.

"Grace," Ellouise was still smiling, "Do you like my brother?" The ball was bouncing. Red.

"No." *Oh, this is going to be easy.*

Ellouise removed her dress, and sat looking very confident in a coral-coloured bra and matching knickers, her feet bare.

"Ellouise."

Grace turned to face Gabriel.

He continued. "What did you tell Grace in the kitchen?" The ball stopped in black.

"Not to hurt you." She wasn't smiling now.

Gabriel's expression hardened. He removed his tie.

"Grace." The ball started to bounce again in the spinning wheel. "Will you?" Black.

She looked at his sister.

Ellouise's expression had changed. Her smile had gone and she was staring at her brother intently. She had never known GeeBee to play this seriously before. He was clearly pissed off that Ellouise had been talking to his "guest". There was something not quite right between him and Grace.

"I don't think you are capable of being hurt."

The two girls breathed a sigh of relief.

Black removed his shirt.

Grace studied the bare-chested man sitting opposite her, a faint splash of hair defining his pectoral muscles, his nipples clearly visible, looking touchable, squeezable. *Oh, this has to be the drink talking …* She was finding it hard not to like what she saw.

Where is this game going? And what is the treat Ellouise seemed so excited about?

Ellouise broke her reverie.

"GeeBee, do you care for Grace?" Spin. Black.

"Yes." He stared straight at the school teacher, his expression firm, his eyes dark.

Ellouise removed a bangle, and smiled at the other woman as though she were her conspirator.

Grace was too consumed by digesting Black's response, not doubting the sincerity of it, nor understanding the meaning of it, to protest.

Gabriel leaned back in his chair and started to play with a spare coaster on the table. "Grace, do you love Jason?" Spin. Black.

Oh, this bloody game!! Can it get any worse?

"I can't say … I—"

"Too late. Forfeit." He stood up and walked round to Grace's chair. "I guess my sister forgot to inform you of this rule too. Stand up." He pulled her chair aside. "If you refuse to answer a question on black, you lose all your clothes."

"That's not fair!" Grace found herself yelling at him, as she stood in her underwear, her hand on the table to steady herself. "What about a bit of slack for my first time?"

He smiled and shook his head. "We don't want to spoil the fun." He waited.

Grace looked over to Ellouise. The sister smiled back and finished her JD.

"Well, fuck you!" said Grace as she ungraciously discarded her bra and knickers, walked over to put them on the bench and then sat down beside her clothes.

After a moment, aware of movement from the other two occupants, she looked over at them. They were both now naked, and looking at her with amused expressions.

Ellouise walked over and sat down next to her. "You may want to fuck him," her eyes were twinkling again, "but not me – thanks for the offer, though," and she laughed playfully as she saw the look of outrage on Grace's face. "I told you there would be a treat ..." She took her companion's hand and led her over to Gabriel, who was standing naked beside the door.

He led them back through the cloakroom and down a short corridor with double doors at the end. He pushed one of the doors open. The girls followed him in.

Grace gasped in awe at the large indoor pool, with the shimmering water reflecting off the white walls around it; her eyes feasted on sun loungers scattered along the sides, a Jacuzzi nestled at the end, a drinks area with bar and stools, and doors leading off, presumably to shower and changing areas.

"Now relax and swim." Gabriel's voice gave Grace the impression he was relieved the game was over, and she watched as he dived into the water and swam, using the butterfly stroke, up and down the pool.

It looked so inviting. Ellouise just touched her arm, saying softly, "Let's get in, Grace. He normally insists on swimwear, probably even more so now with John living with him. But sometimes we get the thrill of swimming naked. It really is lovely." With that, she dived in to join her brother.

Finally Grace smiled and joined them. For the third time she could remember, she felt relaxed in his presence. Ellouise was right – this was lovely.

Having struggled to complete two lengths and continuing to regret drinking so much, Grace rested her arms on the pool side as she watched the two Blacks effortlessly move through the water; he continued to do butterfly, looking powerful, graceful and focused; his sister did a neat breaststroke, creating slight ripples as she cruised through the water.

Grace closed her eyes for what she thought was a moment and then she felt him. He touched her feet and she felt his body glide up hers as he surfaced and tore into her soul with his eyes. Grace looked around hesitantly.

"She's gone, Grace," and he kissed her, wet, soft and warm.

What are you doing to me? They both thought.

137

Chapter 25

Gabriel lifted his school teacher out of the water and placed her on the side of the pool. She watched as he gracefully lifted himself out and strode through one of the doorways, returning with two robes, black for him and white for her.

As Grace wrapped herself in the fresh-smelling fabric, he lifted her up into his arms and carried her from the pool.

He entered the code on the panel on the wall and took her into the den, lying her down on the black silk sheet.

"You know what I want to do." He started to take his robe off and then walked over to a cupboard and withdrew what looked like a headband. "Let me make this easier for you," and he placed the band over her head to cover her eyes. He carefully secured it, making sure it was comfortable for her.

Then she heard the faint click of a switch.

Grace opened her eyes: she felt Black unfasten her robe and let it fall at her sides, but she saw Jason's face, gazing at her, with laughter in his eyes.

What the fuck has he done now?

She heard his voice, definitely *his* voice, saying, "Isn't this who you would rather see, Grace?"

She didn't know how or why he had done this. She wanted to ask him, why was he doing this to her, why was she even here with him, what did he want from her? Could she live like this for another three hundred and sixty days?

But she remained silent, staring at the image of Jason. His face was animated and he smiled, pouted and softly laughed at her. However, the hand she felt parting her legs, the lips she felt kissing her clitoris and the hands softly caressing the tops of her inner thighs, paying her more attention than Jason had ever done, belonged to Gabriel Black.

Jason never made her feel this sensual, nor this desperate to come.

Black was fucking with her mind as well as her body. But right now, she couldn't hold back: the truth was she didn't want to. Her climax was gradual, the tingling pleasure steadily building up to that most exquisite of sensations. She moaned softly, and then a little louder as she felt his tongue stroke and suck her, both of them sure in the knowledge that she was going to come tumbling off the edge.

And then she said it.

"Jason."

She shut her eyes tightly for a moment as she became aware of Gabriel stopping for the briefest of hesitations with his tongue and fingers, before he continued until he felt her hands gently pushing him away and she curled up, replete with physical pleasure.

Suddenly he was on top of her, his knees forcing her legs to straighten and part, his penis entering her vagina forcefully, roughly, desperately. He thrust and she felt him banging down on her hips, his balls pushing against her.

She shouldn't be enjoying this violation of her body, his selfish domination of her. But she was. She moved herself up towards him, intensifying the contact, the feeling of fullness inside her. He gasped, aware of what she was doing, and felt overwhelmed as he suddenly flowed inside her.

Now she closed her eyes again. Jason was gone, and she could only see blackness, with dark eyes piercing her.

Gradually, she felt him withdraw and get off her, and she became aware of feeling empty. She also became aware of feeling disappointed that she wasn't ready for him to leave her body and she suddenly felt sickened as, opening her eyes, Jason continued to smile at her. She pulled at the band and yelled "Get this fucking thing off me, you bastard!" as she yanked it over her head, pulling strands of her hair out, and threw it aside. She quickly grabbed the white robe and ran into the wet room, vaguely aware that Gabriel Black was standing naked at the bottom of the bed, his face darkened by a deep frown, staring after her.

She grabbed one of the hoses and searched for some sort of lever, knob, anything that might actually turn some water on, and as she remembered the events of earlier that afternoon, she began to walk towards the control panel in the room. He reached it before she did.

"Do you want to cleanse yourself of me?" His voice was controlled and calm and his frown was gone. He almost looked saddened. *This hasn't gone quite to plan, but what did you expect?* He wasn't waiting for a response, but pressed the buttons on the keypad and handed her the nearest hose, taking a second for himself. He turned his back on her as he hosed himself down, letting the water flow over his head and body, resting his forehead on the cool grey tiles.

Grace watched, unable to guess what he might be thinking. She poured the water over herself and then sat hunched up on the rubber mat and held the nozzle so that the hot water ran over her back. It felt relaxing and she had positioned herself so that she could continue to observe the man in the room with her. How long was he going to lean against the wall?

After a couple of minutes Black slowly stood up straight and turned to face her.

"Are you done?" he asked quietly.

Grace nodded and stood up.

He returned the hoses to their resting places and punched the pad. Then he grabbed two towels from the cupboard, passing one to Grace. He wrapped his own around his waist and, as he turned to go back into the den he said, "The car will be ready when you are."

Grace watched his back and then heard the door shut as he left the den. She didn't see him again that night.

Chapter 26

At 11.45 a.m. on Monday, the family, friends and colleagues of Eliza Redfern were beginning to depart from her graveside.

Carol Beardly spotted a tall man in a black suit standing beside his black Bentley. She said something to her husband, James, and then walked over to him.

"Hello, Mr Black."

"Gabriel," he said and smiled at her.

"Come and meet James and join us for a bite to eat," she said, her hopeful eyes searching his for agreement.

"No, thank you. I just wanted to pay my respects. I'll wait here awhile if you don't mind," he said solemnly, and she had a feeling that Gabriel Black wanted to be on his own with his own thoughts.

"Of course. How's John? We're all missing him."

"He's doing fine. My sister Ellouise is over and he calls her his number two aunty, right behind you." Carol felt her cheeks burning at his genuine smile.

"Come and see us again, please. Don't let's be strangers." Part of her felt that this strong, powerful, rich man standing before her actually needed her, the ordinary Cheshire wife, mother and homemaker. What had he said? *"We are not all of the same compassionate and kind family background as you, Mrs Beardly."*

As she was about to turn to leave, he took her hand, saying, "We won't. Will you introduce me to your husband?"

Now she really was shocked. His hand felt warm and strong, and there was something protective and safe about him. In another life she would have hoped to get to know him better, in every possible sense. However, she was happily married with three lovely children and would never jeopardise that happiness for any man or any thing, but she hoped they could be friends.

"Come on," she said nervously, glad of the opportunity to turn and walk away from him, giving her a chance to regain her composure as he dropped her hand and followed her to where James was talking with some other people.

Her husband tried not to appear intimidated, as he shook the hand of billionaire Gabriel Black. Black's formal, stand-offish, bordering on arrogant manner did not make it easy, and Carol was thankful that her husband hadn't noticed him touching her hand. Gabriel Black had a reputation with the ladies, and James Beardly might not be quite so understanding about such matters …

Carol sensed the tension between them and decided on a compromise to give them a chance to get to know each other a little better.

"Gabriel." As his wife spoke, James stared, in awe of her pluckiness. She continued, "Why don't you bring John over on Friday after school? He can stay the night with us and you could come over for breakfast on Saturday. We could discuss the house then too." She glanced at the two men for concurrence.

"That's a good idea, Carol. Thank you. I think John would like that. And it will give us a chance to get his bedroom ready." He continued to explain as he saw Carol's puzzled expression. "We're having the Chinese room redone for him. He's chosen Star Wars as the theme. I'll get the designers in for Friday and Saturday and it should be completed for when he comes back to the Hall. What time do you have breakfast?"

Carol smiled, noticing that Gabriel Black rarely referred to Arnford Hall as home, and wondering what he would think if she told him truthfully that breakfast was whenever she and James got out of bed, and not at a time when the staff were told to make it! "Let's say ten o'clock."

Chapter 27

It was Wednesday. Grace had not heard from Black since he left her in the wet room on Sunday night. She was having a busy week at work, including trying to fit in the children making Christmas cards so they would be ready for parents to purchase in time to post out for Christmas, three whole months away, so she hadn't had much time to wonder when she would receive a message from him.

She was sitting in front of the TV, alone in her lounge, when the phone rang. It was Jason.

"Hi honey, how's it going?" His voice sounded excited. He was up to something.

"Oh, OK. A busy week at school, and I could do with an early night tonight. How about you?"

"I'm going to the barber's tomorrow. Why don't you come down for the weekend and let's have some fun."

Grace hesitated. "I thought you said you had stopped." Her voice had become quiet and sober.

"Oh, come on. It's not like I do it every week," he lied.

There was a pause.

"Look, let me get you some of the New Blue. You know you like it, and it's been ages since we got a little high."

"I said I wouldn't do it again, Jason. I thought you had too. It's wrong in so many ways; you know it is." Her voice was rising but she couldn't help it.

"Hey, just come down Friday night and see how you feel when you get here. I miss you, Grace."

"I'm not doing it, Jason, and if you are, then I'd rather not come."

Grace put her hand up to her neck and her fingers stroked the collar. *And if I still have this on, I can't come.* She struggled to control her voice, suddenly feeling tired and tearful.

"No, still come Grace. I won't take anything. Unless you change your mind," he added and her heart sank. "I'll meet you at the station."

Too tired to protest, she relented, "OK. See you Friday night."

"Goodnight, honey, and don't work too hard."

She heard the phone go dead.

It was quarter past nine, and she decided to go straight to bed. She brushed her teeth, staring at the collar in the mirror. She had begun to feel comfortable with it as her hair hid the padlock and she got a lot of compliments on it, with everyone marvelling at how expensive the necklace must have been. *If you only knew what it was costing me!* She realised people called it a necklace: to her it was a collar, a symbol of captivity.

Well, surely he would summon her soon and take it off. He should know she would be seeing Jason at the weekend. He had said she could continue to see her boyfriend, and her existing life was to be protected; otherwise, why was she doing this if she was going to lose it all anyway? She went through everything that had happened on Sunday and could not push from her mind the knowledge that she had enjoyed some of it.

Mentally, she had found a way to accept what she was being forced to do and not let guilt over her betrayal of Jason consume her too much. But it wasn't easy; she had never cheated on any of her former lovers.

That night her sleep was restless and broken. She tossed and turned, captured in the vicious circle of being kept awake by the desperate desire to be asleep.

Meanwhile, across the village at Arnford Hall, Gabriel Black was studying the report he had ordered from Rick at Black Armour on Jason Chesters: a family lawyer working for a top firm in London; his list of ex-girlfriends, one of whom he seemed to have dropped just days before she was convicted for possession of heroin; frequent trips to the barbers, complete with list of illicit accessories purchased, including purchases to date, during his relationship with Grace McGuire. Which drugs did she take with him?

Black had already decided to put surveillance on Jason Chesters, even before hearing his name on Sunday night, and now the billionaire, who could afford to pay for any information he wanted, was made aware of the telephone conversation Chesters had just had with Mrs McGuire.

Black should arrange to see her on Friday to take her necklace off.

But he would have the Hall to himself that night: there was no John to worry about. It would be a shame to miss such an opportunity. He would be kind and give her warning. From the sounds of the taped telephone call, he would actually be doing her a favour …

On Thursday night, Grace was startled by the trill of the phone on the coffee table in front of her.

Sender: Gabriel Black

Message: The car will pick you up at 6 p.m. on Friday. Don't make plans for this weekend, Grace. You may want to bring a weekend bag.

Grace stared at the small screen and put her hand to her neck. What should she do now?

Well, fuck both of them. She was pretty certain Jason would take some ecstasy; he couldn't bloody resist it. And she would show bastard Black exactly what she thought of him.

Chapter 28

At half past three on Friday afternoon she rang Jason.

"I'm sorry, darling, I'm not going to make it this weekend. I've got a load of marking to do, and the house is a mess. And I know what you and the gang will be up to. I'm just too tired. I'll call you on Monday."

"OK, if you're sure …" he said, accepting it all too easily.

She arrived home at five and was opening her front door to Michael at six. The look of surprise, followed by his big grin, made her smile as she climbed into the back of the car, after waiting for him to open her door: she wouldn't put it past Black to have ordered the chauffeur, on pain of death, to let him know if she opened the damn door herself! She breathed a sigh of relief when she discovered the car was empty.

As she exited the vehicle and began to climb the steps she was aware of the gargoyles sneering, *Oh, you are really going to piss him off now!*

Gabriel opened the door and stared at the woman before him. Grace was wearing a sweater emblazoned with large hoops of brown and yellow, her knitted skirt was patterned with blue and green checks and her legs were wrapped in black knitted tights, with flat brown mules to complete the ghastly attire. She had a supermarket carrier bag with her, and Black didn't want to begin to imagine what underwear may be in there ready for the weekend, let alone what she was wearing under the dreadful clothes.

What in hell are you playing at, Grace McGuire? Revenge for Sunday, or for spoiling your weekend?

Of course, he was aware of the relief that had tinged her conversation with Jason when she told him she wouldn't be joining him and his friends in their illegal drug-taking this weekend.

Grace walked straight past him saying, in a voice laden with sarcasm, "Hello, sir. Don't let me spoil your weekend then," and he watched as she headed for the door to the sanctuary.

Suddenly she swung round as she heard him call out from the doorway.

"Don't even think about it, Grace. You're coming with me." Before she knew it, he was beside her, his arm under her elbow, leading her down to the kitchen.

Her sarcastic laughter gave way to sheer embarrassment when Roger and Steve looked up from the island as she entered the room. Shock was soon replaced by a warm smile from Roger as he quickly walked over to Grace and pecked her cheek lightly.

He said, "Nice to see you, Grace."

He whispered, "Tread carefully, girl."

Steve remained silent and stared at Gabriel, who now had a face like thunder.

"There's a change of plan, Steve. I'm sorry about all the hard work you've gone to, but get me a central table at Simon Radley's for seven thirty."

"Yes, sir." Steve gave Grace a pitying smile, as if to say "good luck, you're gonna need it" and she watched, beginning to feel regretful and very silly as Steve turned to look in a bucket and said, "Looks like you get to live another day."

Grace walked over and looked inside at the large lobster walking around the bottom.

"You guys have it if you want to," Black said in a voice louder than was necessary. "I don't want John thinking he has a new pet tomorrow." His smirk was too big for words. He turned to Grace.

"Come and see what Steve did for us, Grace," and unceremoniously he grabbed her hand and dragged her into the garden.

Her embarrassment grew as she looked out onto the patio and saw a dining table, complete with white tablecloth, a silver candelabra with three white dinner candles, two place settings with crystal champagne flutes, a bottle of champagne resting in an ice bucket, and the most beautiful orchid, a white *dendrobium nobile*, with its tall monopodial stem, lush green waxy leaves and sensual white flower heads. *Another one of his?*

"But never mind." His voice had become quiet and bitter.

The gargoyles were right; she had pissed him off.

Keeping hold of her hand, they went back through the kitchen and, as they continued up the two flights of stairs, he took his intercom out and ordered Michael to be ready with the car in ten minutes. When they reached Grace's bedroom, he held the door open for her to walk in.

"Wait here," he ordered and as he closed the door on her, she heard it lock behind him. There was no way he was giving her the chance to escape to her sanctuary this evening.

She stared at herself in the mirror and cringed at the appalling image standing in front of her. She didn't even have any make-up on.

Well, presumably he would be back in a minute and no doubt she would be divested of all her clothes anyway. She was now feeling very hot under her thick clothing and, yes, she actually felt like a good shag!

As she sat on the edge of the bed, she heard a key turn and the door opened.

He stood in the doorway, a determined expression on his face, and Grace was suddenly mesmerised by his appearance.

He was wearing a Richard Anderson black dinner suit with satin lapels and a white dress shirt with cuffs exhibiting Jessica De Lotz gold cufflinks, hand stamped with the Black family crest of a hawk, its talons at the ready, preparing to swoop down on its unsuspecting prey. His feet were encased in highly polished £4,000 Angelo Galasso black crocodile skin shoes. He looked like a million dollars.

Now she wanted him to fuck the arse off her. She stood up nervously.

"Let's go," he said, and he glanced at the plastic carrier bag she had placed on the dressing table, his eyes dark and threatening, and added, "Don't forget your bag, Grace."

Ignoring this remark, she followed him out of the bedroom.

As the Bentley pulled up outside the Grosvenor Hotel in Chester to end a silent journey, she turned to him. "You cannot be expecting me to come in there with you." Her voice quivered with trepidation.

"You will walk in, Grace, or I will carry you." His challenge made her want to sink into any hole available.

Michael had opened her door, not looking at her as she stepped out of the car.

She was vaguely aware of pedestrians walking by, unknown faces staring at her, and then changing direction to gaze at the handsome apparition who was accompanying her. She felt his hand under her elbow.

"Smile, Grace," he instructed through gritted teeth, as the doorman held the door open for them, unable to hide a look of amusement as he took in the spectacle this couple made.

They were greeted by the Simon Radley restaurant manager, who could not conceal his shock as he stared at Grace, before quickly regaining his professional, formal composure and firmly shaking Black's hand.

"Mr Black, it is a pleasure to see you again; I believe it's been a while since you last dined with us."

"Yes. Please meet my guest, Ms Grace McGuire."

The manager shook her hand, and again Grace would have loved a black hole to have swallowed her up.

She threw her head back and declared that she was pleased to meet him. *Ha bloody ha!*

The Simon Radley restaurant at the Grosvenor Hotel in Chester is the proud possessor of a Michelin star and four AA rosettes, and tonight, following a day of racing at the nearby Chester racecourse, it was particularly busy. However, a call for a reservation for Gabriel Black was immediately attended to.

"Sir, can I just double-check that you wanted to be seated in the main dining area near to the entrance, rather than your usual private dining room?" The manager appeared to be having difficulty accepting that this guest wanted to eat with members of the general public.

"Yes, that's right. I presume the table is ready."

"Yes, certainly, sir, I'll take you to it now. Please follow me."

A table for two was perfectly positioned in full view of all the guests entering the restaurant. Gabriel held the chair back for Grace to seat herself, and she now knew he meant to humiliate her in front of everyone.

Her spirit was temporarily broken and she sat down feeling totally miserable.

As he sat opposite her she heard him order a bottle of the Krug Grand Cuvée; a bargain at £270!

As the sommelier filled the champagne flutes, Black ordered starters of French rabbit with bacon macaroni, pumpkin and poached langoustine, followed by a main course of John Dory, sticky oxtail, star anise, candied and coppice-smoked shallots. For both of them.

Grace sat back and resigned herself to her fate as a constant stream of his acquaintances, both male and female, came over to say hello, to gloat at his companion and to go away whispering and sniggering.

"So, are we enjoying ourselves yet?" His fake smile penetrated his still dark expression.

"You are a cruel, mean bastard!" She spat the words at him.

"And you have acted like a petulant, irritable schoolgirl. Let me think. What would be an appropriate punishment for such a pupil?"

She stared at him, her eyes suddenly wide with fear. "You wouldn't dare!"

"Don't challenge me, Grace, I am definitely not in the mood. Eat your food and try to enjoy at least this part of our evening." He calmly sipped some more champagne.

Grace nervously gulped hers.

As she began to eat (after all, she thought, she may as well make the most of this; it smelled and tasted wonderful, and she had to compliment him on his choice, though not out loud of course), she forgot her predicament for a short while. She couldn't stop herself admiring this handsome man conversing with passing acquaintances confidently and authoritatively, and saw his expression gradually soften, an occasional smile on his lips as he looked at her.

For his part, his anger at first seeing her at the entrance to Arnford Hall, knowing she was ruining the evening he had planned for her, was finally subsiding and he was beginning to see a funny side: she was plucky and defiant, wanting to be her own boss and subservient to no man; nor did she show any need for a man, including Jason Chesters.

As he watched her eat, confident that at least she was enjoying the food, he wondered where his little game was going to take them both over the coming months. He was already beginning to feel the need for a change to his plan. Feelings were emerging within him which he had not anticipated.

Chapter 29

On returning after dinner, Black held her hand as he led his guest along the entrance hall of Arnford Hall, still allowing her no opportunity to escape into the sanctuary.

Instead of ascending the grand staircase, he carried on and turned to the right where they descended the stone spiral staircase to the lower level. She hoped he was taking her into the kitchen, from where she could hear laughter, presumably Roger and Steve, but her heart sank, as her real fear was confirmed and he entered the code to open the door to the den.

As she watched him close the door and turn the dim lighting on using the remote in his hand, she started to feel a tingling in her lower body, not sure if it was fear of her captor or an inappropriate erotic arousal at the thought of what he might do to her. She was hot and uncomfortable in her ridiculous clothes and she would have loved to have gone into the wet room and let the water cover her body from all angles, but she felt glued to the spot, unable to move.

He walked over to one of the bedside tables and took a pair of scissors out of the drawer.

Approaching her he said quietly, "Let's get you out of these garments, and just make sure you don't feel tempted to wear them ever again."

She stood motionless as he raised her right arm and cut through the wool of the jumper, straight across her chest and down the left arm, then completing a crucifix as he brought the scissors from the top of the neckline, revealing her collar as he did so, down to the hem of the waist, letting it fall from her. He cut the small bow on the front of her black bra, separating her breasts, and pushed it down her arms. Next the skirt fell victim to the scissors as he cut straight down her right side, and it joined the remains of the jumper and bra on the floor at her feet. He knelt effortlessly and grasped the top of her woolly tights and brought the blades of the scissors down the front of each leg, raising one foot at a time and pushing them off behind her. Finally she stood tall as he made two incisions in her turquoise knickers, either side of her freshly self-shaven pubis, and she felt the slight coolness as the cotton material fell to the floor.

He stood up and his eyes drilled into hers.

Without breaking the contact, he leaned in to whisper to her, "What were we saying about a suitable punishment for a petulant, irritable schoolgirl? I think a caning would be most appropriate."

Her eyes widened and her mouth opened. "That was banned twenty years ago."

She started to emit a quiet laugh, almost hysterical, trying to lighten the mood. "Why don't I write you some lines?" quickly adding "sir" as she watched him shake his head.

She was naked before him, but that was the least of her worries as she saw him go over to a large, tall cupboard on the wall on the left-hand side of the den. He withdrew a rattan cane, gently tapping his palm with the thinner end, his eyes still fixed on Grace.

"Bend over the bed, Grace," he commanded, his voice impassive as he stood and waited.

She didn't move. He saw her eyes dart to the door.

"It's locked," he said and added, "I have all night, Grace, but it's better to get your punishment over with, I think." He continued to look directly at her, his stony face unmoved by any compassion he should have had for the woman before him. He was denying himself that, though he could easily have gone to her, lifted her in his arms, and hugged her to him.

He waited.

After a moment Grace looked up at him imploringly.

"Please don't hurt me," she whispered tearfully and bent forward over the side of the bed, her cheek resting on the cool black silk sheet. It became damp as the tears began to run down her face, and she brought her hands up to hold on to the smooth, cool fabric to brace herself for the pain he was about to inflict on her. She was already hurt by the shame which had been steadily consuming her all evening.

She started to recite "The Lady of Shallot" silently in her head and held her breath.

She heard his footsteps move nearer and her fingers tightened on the sheet, her eyes shut fast and the tears falling, falling.

Then she felt the sharp sting and she cried out as the thin cane made contact with her buttocks, the just bearable pain smarting as he brought it down on her again and then one last time.

She waited a second to be certain her ordeal was over, and then she let her body slide down to the floor and she lay there, her hand rubbing her behind, the stinging refusing to go away just yet.

She heard a sound as he removed his clothes.

"Stand up." His voice was a little louder and made it clear to her that he would not be messed with.

She stood up, her back to him.

He glanced momentarily at the three faint marks on her bottom. He had not used much force; hell, he had caused *much* more pain to some of his female companions; but they knew him better, were stupidly willing to take any shit from him, just to be with him. He knew Grace McGuire was not like that.

"Look up," he said, and took a step to stand directly in front of her, as she raised her head to face him. He wrapped his arms around her, pulling her to him, his lips hungrily seeking hers, his chest stroking her breasts, his erect penis caressing her lower abdomen.

"Now a fresh start." His voice was a whisper but with a harshness to it, as if he were daring her to disagree.

She didn't care about a start; she just wanted it to be the end, the end of this damned year he seemed to have over her.

Just what is your fucking secret, you bastard? And yet, she surrendered herself to him, finally giving him what he had wanted from the moment he opened the door to her earlier this evening.

He eased her onto the bed, and she stared mindlessly at the ceiling as she waited for him to get on top of her. But he didn't.

Instead, she felt him gently pull her down the bed slightly, so that her legs hung over the bottom of it. She didn't bother to look up as she felt him open her legs and she wondered if he was going to fuck her as he stood over her at the end of the bed.

154

But then she gasped as he slid his shoulders under her legs, gently lifting them just enough to allow him access, and she felt his fingers very gently open her labia, making way for his tongue to touch her clitoris. He licked her, patiently caressing her most intimate part, arousing her with something: what was it? Passion. Her excitement grew, her pleasure became more intense and her climax started to grip her, all memories of humiliation at dinner and being caned, gone. There was a desperation inside her; she needed to climb to her pinacle of orgasmic sensuality and his patience, tenderness and persistent attention to her needs ensured she came, and came, and came.

Slowly and steadily he crept up her body, placing feathery kisses over her pubis, her abdomen, in between, around and on her breasts, a gentle sucking at her nipples and on the front of her shoulders before stopping as his face appeared in front of her. He pulled her further onto the bed and held his body above hers, with his hands on either side of her head, his eyes piercing her. Was he asking her for permission to enter her? Did she want him to?

Grace thought of the table in the garden, the lobster in the bucket. Had she ruined his evening?

The answer to all those questions was yes.

Hardly aware of what she was doing, she lifted her hands and placed them on his shoulders, feeling him, strong and muscular. She pulled him towards her and relief filled his face. His eyes closed for a moment as she felt his penis penetrate her, gently and then a little more forcefully, in and back and then in deeper, his steady motion exciting her more, making her want him. What was he doing to her?

He gasped as he came and he moved them both onto their sides, staying inside her and moving his hands over her breasts. For him, sex had never been this good, and feeling himself inside her still, he wanted to stay right there and forget all that had happened in his life before her. But he knew he would not be permitted to do that; he was too deep in his own shit.

Chapter 30

Finally he withdrew from her, and as he made to get off the bed, he held his hand out to her to help her up, saying "Let's go to your bed."

Still naked, he opened the door. Outside the den, all was dark and quiet, and from the confidence with which he strode out of the room, hesitating to check she would follow him, Grace guessed they were now totally alone.

She stood outside her bedroom door, waiting for him to unlock it, not sure what to expect to happen next; she had never spent a night at Arnford Hall. She was exhausted and confused by the fluctuating emotions he was forcing her to endure, and the thought of trying to get the key and evade him to her sanctuary seemed too great an effort right now.

As she studied the contents of the bedroom, she realised that he had remained in the room and locked the door. *Does he think I'll escape to the sanctuary?*

"Have you brought your toothbrush?" he asked, matter-of-factly.

She turned away from him and went to her carrier bag of shame, took out her brush and toothpaste and walked into the en-suite. She closed the door behind her.

He opened it, just as she was staring at what was presumably his toothbrush and paste on "his" side of the sink.

As they went through their dental routines, they watched each other through the mirrors above the two sinks, neither face giving anything away.

He finished first, and turned his back on her and peed in the toilet. She continued her marathon teeth-brushing session until he had left the room, leaving the door open behind him.

Well, bugger him. Grace sat down and peed too.

He was standing by the window as she entered the room, having pulled back the curtain slightly so he could survey the dimly lit garden below. He turned to look at her.

"Are you staying in here for the night?" she asked churlishly.

"Yes," he replied, somewhat uncomfortably, wondering if he was actually doing the right thing. But he was determined to make the most of what was left of a night without John.

"Are you going to tell me which side to sleep on? Or are you just going to fuck me again?"

"It's a big bed, Grace. I'm used to sleeping in the middle. You can sleep where you like."

"Right. That suits me just fine." She turned to get the key to the sanctuary out of her carrier bag. She searched. *Oh shit, she had forgotten to bring it. How could she?*

He was still standing by the window.

"Grace. Get in the damn bed." He sounded tired and not in the mood to be irritated by her.

She thought of his words "petulant" and "irritating" to describe her. Well, sod it, she was tired too. She pulled back the cool, fresh-smelling, luxurious sheets and accepted their invitation to get in and enjoy the comfort they offered. She was on the window side of the bed and Black walked around to the other side and got in beside her.

"Is it so bad to sleep with me, Grace?"

She was taken aback by his sincerity and apparent inability to believe there should exist a woman who didn't want to sleep with him.

"Do you forget why I'm here? I don't. Sometimes you act like I'm just your bloody girlfriend!" She lay on her side with her back to him, but her voice was raised and he heard her.

"No, I don't forget, Grace; you make it blatantly obvious you don't want to be here. And there's nothing 'just' about being my girlfriend," he added, quieter now. "However, it's a good similitude; it can be our cover, Grace."

Suddenly she felt his hand on her back, his fingers trailing down her spine. She tried not to move, but involuntarily her spine curved to accommodate his touch.

He continued confidently, his voice lower and more husky now. "You can't deny that your body tells me that's not such a bad thing. Just enjoy the sex, Grace. That is an order." He slid his body alongside hers, raising her top leg and using his hand to insert his penis inside her very wet vagina. Her wetness was the only invitation he needed.

As he began to pump and thrust, she felt the fullness of his balls pressing against her as his hand moved round to excite her clitoris. He raised his finger to her mouth. "Taste yourself, Grace," he whispered, and she closed her eyes and sucked, telling herself he could be anybody: but she knew this was not Jason, or any of the other eight men she had had sex with. This was Gabriel Black. There was something about him, and it wasn't just his secret.

They came quickly and simultaneously and, by mutual consent and desire, he lingered inside her.

Eventually she went into the bathroom and stared at the woman in the mirror. She felt invigorated, younger even, and frightened by the emotions he invoked in her.

When she climbed back into the large bed, she heard his steady breathing; he was asleep.

Chapter 31

Grace woke at half past seven, alone in the bedroom. She had no idea what time Black had left. As she went into the en-suite, she saw that his things were gone too.

She returned to the bedroom and went over to her carrier bag, casting a final glance at her cut clothes on the floor. She had brought a grey bra, which had been white in a former life, and two pairs of the most unsexy, large knickers she possessed. She wanted to wear none of them. *Why on earth had that seemed a good idea on Thursday when Black had summoned me?*

She went over to the chest of drawers and looked in the top drawer. She saw the triangular chain and cuffs and quickly closed it. In vain hope, she opened the second drawer. There was a white lace plunge bra and a black satin strapless one, both with matching thongs. The tags were still on.

In the wardrobe hung a purple silk shirt, a pair of black leggings, and a short-sleeved red dress with white polka dots with a floaty three-quarter length skirt. Again, they were brand new.

Taking the scissors to remove the labels, she dressed in the white underwear and red dress and, barefoot, made her way down to the kitchen.

Gabriel immediately stood up and walked over to her, saying a little too quietly for his normal confident self, "Good morning. You look lovely."

She was wearing no make-up and she felt anything but lovely, but there was something in his eyes, betraying his frustration that he couldn't hide a certain feeling from her. *Does he actually like me?*

Suddenly his mask went up.

"You have Roger to thank for the clothes. Come and have some breakfast," and he returned to the island, clearly expecting her to follow him.

She looked at Roger and said, "Thank you. They're a lovely fit."

"You're welcome." His warm, genuine smile put her a little more at ease. She really liked this guy. Steve was a lucky man.

She looked around the kitchen, seeing Steve come in from what looked like a large walk-in larder, his arms full of fresh vegetables.

Grace said, "Hi," feeling more than a little embarrassed at the memory of last night and how she had spoiled an evening that Steve had worked hard to prepare for his boss.

The chef approached her, asking if smoked salmon and scrambled eggs were OK for breakfast.

"That sounds lovely, thank you," and Grace hoped she was forgiven.

"Where is John?" she asked.

"John stayed at his aunt's house last night with his cousins." Gabriel didn't look up from the newspaper, which seemed to have his full attention.

"Is Ellouise still here?"

Now she had his attention.

He sounded disappointed as he said, "No. She doesn't live here and unfortunately she doesn't visit very often." He continued, almost as if he were talking to himself, "Maybe now John is here she'll come and stay more often."

Grace wondered if Black felt he needed his sister more now, to help look after his son. After all, it wasn't easy being a single parent, especially following the death of the other parent, and even more so when this parent had never had a relationship with the child. Now she realised why he had slept with her last night; he didn't feel he had to be with John. For a man who probably had sex with a woman most nights, this change to his life must be enormous.

His words interrupted her thoughts.

"Come and sit down, Grace." He beckoned to the stool next to him.

Steve started to set out the eggs and salmon, some brown toast and fresh orange juice for the three of them; Gabriel was breakfasting later with the Beardlys, and just having juice now.

"The bedroom fitters are due at half past eight," Roger started to inform Black. "They made good progress yesterday. Should be finished by two this afternoon."

"Good," said Black. "We'll stay out until tea time. I don't want John dwelling too much on the fact that he will now have his own bedroom, and I won't be sharing it with him."

"I think that's a very good idea. It's important for John to learn to feel safe in his own room, and before long he'll be glad of his own space; it will be important to him."

The three men turned to face the school teacher.

"I'm glad it seems I am doing something right then." Gabriel did not take his eyes off her.

Steve glanced at Roger, who glanced back at him with an "I'm not sure what game he is playing here" kind of expression on his face.

Black continued, "We have also decided not to pursue counselling for him. Do you think that is the right thing to do too?"

"Yes," was her reply, without hesitation. "I haven't witnessed any behaviour from your son to suggest any major emotional disturbance." Grace was speaking matter-of-factly but with a reassuring gentleness to her voice. "In fact, I think his new relationship with you is actually helping a great deal with his grieving process."

"But he hardly ever speaks of his mother. I'm worried he is bottling it up."

"He may not speak of her very often, but he talks to her; he involves her in his life. I remember when he read to me and he kept turning to his mother's photograph, involving her in the conversations. I think, at the moment, that is his way of coping." Now she looked directly at her keeper. "Something else you have got right, sir, as I am sure it was your idea to put the photos out."

Again all three men stared at her: Roger and Steve in surprise at hearing her call him "sir", though it wasn't unusual for his lady friends to use the title, and Black in awe of her wisdom, and hoping that perhaps she was beginning to despise him less.

Black drained the last of the juice from his glass and then got up.

"I'll have my coffee in my study, please, Steve. I've got some work to do." He turned to Roger. "I presume everyone knows it will be work as normal for me from Monday."

"Yes. And board meetings have all been rescheduled for later starts."

"Good. I'll see you later this afternoon, Grace," and he left the kitchen.

Grace glanced at Roger, who raised his eyebrows, and she went chasing after Gabriel.

"Hey!" She sounded indignant. "What am I supposed to do? I have a whole load of work to do too, you know."

He turned to face her. "Where is your work?"

"At home, of course."

"Give your keys to Michael and tell him where it is. He'll fetch it. You may also want to tell him where the key to your sanctuary is. But you are not leaving here until Sunday." He turned and left her standing, exasperated, as she watched him ascend the stone steps to the ground floor.

Grace spent the rest of the morning working in the sanctuary. Michael had brought everything she needed and, she had to admit, it was much more pleasant working in this lovely room than sitting at her small kitchen table. And the chocolate-dipped strawberries and pineapple in the cooler, together with the homemade lemonade, would never have made an appearance in her kitchen.

She was surprised at how absorbed she was in her work, when a knock at the door made her jump.

She remembered his words: *I will not come in here unless you invite me.*

Was he back? Had she spent too long in here? He had said there would be consequences. Would he punish her?

She was shaking as she unlocked the door and opened it.

"Grace." It was Roger, and he could see she was nervous, "It's OK. I just came to say that Gabriel has asked if you will consent to have dinner with him tonight; the one he planned for last night?"

She stared at him in disbelief. She remembered Black's suggestion they "pretend" she was his girlfriend. *Well, sod that!*

"Do you know what he is doing to me?" She tried to control the shaking of her voice.

"No, I don't: you can be assured no one will know except you and him. Surely you have found out by now, Gabriel Black is not your average sexual partner."

Grace's eyes widened, hardly able to believe that Roger could think they were simply having some sort of affair.

Roger continued, "I only know he is one of the most tormented men I know, and the greatest friend I have ever had. I love Steve as my husband; but I also love Gabriel Black." Now it was Roger's turn to stare at her, with a look of deep intensity. "You seem different from his other partners. I get the feeling it's not just about sex between you."

There was a pause as he watched the woman before him blush at his frankness and his innocence of the real relationship between Grace McGuire and Gabriel Black. Roger smiled reassuringly as he continued, "Sure, he can be a lot to handle, and I see he has given you your own space here to cope with some of his more obsessive traits, but if you don't see his friendship, trust and protection, then you're not looking. Give him a chance, Grace. I think you mean more to him than you know. Now I need your answer."

"I, I ..." she hesitated a moment, but as she looked at the man before her, his smile sincere, almost pleading with her to accept his employer's invitation, she responded, "OK, I will."

Roger's smile turned into a grin as he glanced over her shoulder into the sanctuary. "Come and have a drink with Steve and me."

Now she was able to smile. She felt an attraction to this man, as an ally, a friend – and she wanted to understand the relationships between the men of Arnford Hall: she wanted to find out as much as possible about her captor.

As she walked into the kitchen behind Roger, Steve greeted her with a huge grin.

"Tea? Peppermint?" he asked.

"Please, that sounds nice." She added sheepishly, "I'm sorry for ruining the meal plans last night."

He looked at Roger and they both laughed, remembering the spectacle of the couple getting into the Bentley last night.

"That's OK. I don't profess to being up to Simon Radley's standard, but I think we can all make you feel more comfortable tonight." He aimed a conspiratorial grin at Roger as he added, "Can we dress you?"

"What do you mean?"

Steve glanced at his watch. "It's one o'clock. Let's take you into Knutsford and find something ravishing!"

Roger looked at the startled expression on Grace's face, and made an attempt to reassure her. "What he means is let's go shopping. Come on, finish your tea."

Chapter 32

Meanwhile, Black had borrowed the boys' Q7 and driven over to the Beardly household. All apprehension about what had happened, and what was happening, at Arnford Hall was forgotten when John came running up to him shouting, "Daddy!"

"They've had a great time, Mr—" Carol stopped herself. "*Gabriel*, and John has spoken so much about you; you're making a great impression on your son." She hoped she didn't sound patronising as she looked up at the man in the pale grey suit, with a pastel pink shirt, no tie and shiny black shoes.

"Thank you," he said, his voice warm and friendly.

She felt brave enough to add, "In fact, he's been telling his cousins so much about you, they want to call you Uncle!"

"Oh, really!" Gabriel Black raised his eyebrows. This was unexpected. "Well, I suppose there is a first time for everything, and having made such a good impression, I would hate to disappoint anyone. What did you tell them?" He looked at her intently.

"Er … I said you were a very important man and they should call you Mr Black!"

Now she felt his look scolding her. His expression was serious, as though what title would be appropriate for his son's cousins to call him was of great importance.

"What does John call your husband?"

"Oh. Uncle James," Carol couldn't believe she was having this conversation with this man.

Suddenly James joined them in the kitchen. "Did someone mention my name?" He held his hand out to shake Black's. "Hi, Mr Black."

"Please, call me Gabriel. And I guess it's Uncle Gabriel then." He stared intently for a moment at Carol, leaving her feeling that if he regretted this decision it would be on her head! *Why was everything to do with him so intimidating and complicated?*

Carol proceeded to place breakfast on the table, cereal for the children and scrambled eggs and bacon for the grown-ups. The children started to giggle in the presence of their new uncle.

"John says you're rich."

"Josh, don't be so rude, and it's none of your business," Carol reprimanded her son and looked at James for support, avoiding Gabriel Black's eyes.

Uncle Gabriel spoke quietly. "He is mistaken. In some things I am very poor, Josh, isn't it?"

The ten-year-old stared in amazement and with head lowered and eyes raised, looked at his mother for some sort of permission before saying, "Yes. And I'm sorry."

"It's OK." The visitor continued to eat his breakfast, and then broke the awkward silence that had fallen on the gathering. "I was wondering, if you didn't have any plans for the rest of the morning, we could all go over to Eliza's house and decide what you'd like to keep. I can then sort things out, as we discussed." He was looking at Carol and James. "I've got the Q7; we could all go together, give the children a chance to play for a bit longer?"

James looked at Carol. Having breakfast with this man was one thing; spending the rest of the morning with him was another! Still, he was right; it needed to be done and maybe Carol would cope better if they all went together.

"I think that sounds a good idea," James said as he looked at his wife to see if she agreed.

"Sure. Let me clear these things and we can head over there. We can go in our car if you prefer."

"Not at all," said Black, who was obviously in charge now.

And so John and his cousins climbed into the one-year-old white Q7, arguing over who would go in the very back of the car, and the recently titled daddy, new uncle and effective brother-in-law drove them all to High Legh.

Black paid particular attention to John's behaviour while they were at his former home, and father and son were given some privacy while John proudly showed his father around. Gabriel acted as though it were his first visit. The young boy broke down in his mother's bedroom, saying he missed her, and as Gabriel hugged him, sitting on Eliza Redfern's bed, he wondered for a moment if he was doing the right thing now, and if he would be doing the right thing tonight, when John was expected to sleep in his own room at the Hall.

After a couple of minutes Carol opened the door.

"OK in here?" she asked quietly.

Gabriel looked up and the tenderness in his eyes, and the way John clung to his father, made her feel he actually had everything under control.

She walked over and sat beside them, gently stroking the small boy's hair. Slowly her tears fell as she shared her grief with her sister's son. Gabriel put his arm around her and the three of them sat for a few minutes, before he quietly lay John on the bed and left the room, saying, "John, comfort your Aunty Carol. Mummy would like that. I just need to see Uncle James."

He stood in the hallway and stared over the bannister. He felt guilty at not sharing their grief, fearful that his son would notice he did not shed tears for his dead mother: would John hold it against him as he got older and remembered this time? He had read enough of the book Roger had bought to know such a thing could happen. He would have a lot of explaining to do when John was ready to question him. He prayed to a god he didn't believe in that his son would not question everything in his father's life.

He went out into the small garden for some fresh air, and studied the climbing frame to distract himself. He had already planned where to erect it at the Hall.

Later, with items clearly marked for keeping, and Black assuring the Beardlys that they could all be stored in a lock-up at Arnford Hall until they wanted to retrieve them, they agreed that the house would be sold as soon as possible.

Dropping the Beardly family back at Mobberley, father and son decided to go to Tatton Park, Gabriel thinking a long stroll round the gardens would be good, John thinking a play in the adventure playground would be brilliant. Daddy had to agree, it was good fun.

Chapter 33

Back at Arnford Hall, Gabriel walked along the corridor past the sanctuary, immediately mindful of the fact the door was closed. *Has she been in there all day?*

John had raced him to the kitchen, and by the time Gabriel reached it, he could hear his son telling his school teacher about the sleepover with his cousins.

Carol had mentioned to him that her nephew had been reluctant to sleep in Craig's room initially, saying he needed his daddy to be with him. She was bold enough to reassure Gabriel that he was doing the right thing in providing John with his own bedroom, getting him to take ownership of it and, more importantly, to start to sleep in it, alone.

"It's never easy," she had said. "And sometimes we have to go through a bit of pain and heartache to give them their independence," adding that parents needed their independence and privacy too. He was glad it wasn't just him.

Now he felt relief that his reluctant guest had not shut herself away from his presence. Not yet, anyway. And Roger had confirmed that she had agreed to have dinner with him tonight.

As the master of the house entered the room, Grace turned to look at him. She was seated at the island. She remained seated.

Steve was busy preparing food, and Roger glanced over at his employer.

"Go well?" he asked.

Gabriel nodded, his eyes still on Grace. She had a little make-up on now, and looked almost relaxed, chatting to John.

"I'll go and walk Satan." With that Black left the room.

She had broken one of his rules. Why? He couldn't let her get away with it. *She will hate you for it.* He started to question whether he was punishing her, or himself. It was only Day 11 of their arrangement and already he was beginning to feel involved, too involved, with her, in a way he had not intended. He could always mentally remove himself from situations he got into; why was he beginning to feel he couldn't switch off in this one?

Suddenly he was aware of Satan stopping and looking up at his master, asking for a rest and to be taken back to his kennel.

"I'm sorry. Come on, boy."

It was half past five when he walked back into the kitchen. Roger and Steve were eating with John. Grace wasn't there.

"Have you seen your new bedroom yet?"

"Not yet, Daddy. I wanted to wait for you."

He sat next to his son. "Well, we'll go and check it out when you have finished here. What's for pudding?"

"Steve says I can have a cookie after some chopped apple."

"Sounds like a good deal." Then, unable to stop himself, he looked at Roger. "Where is she?" His voice was firm and conveyed his annoyance that she wasn't here, rather than letting slip his concern that she was avoiding him.

His PA glanced upwards.

"I'll be back in a moment, John." Black went straight to her sanctuary and knocked on the door.

Grace opened it with a smile, expecting to see Roger. Her face dropped as Gabriel glared at her.

"Are you deliberately trying to piss me off?" He loomed over her in the doorway.

She moved aside and waved her arm at the room, her papers laid out on the sofa and coffee table. "I've been working. And if that pisses you off," she said, seething at his rudeness and threatening attitude, "then tough. I have to earn a living, you know. A living so that I can hold my life together, a life which you said I could keep."

"You are breaking the rules!"

"What the hell have I done now?" She could only think she had agreed to have dinner with him; had almost been looking forward to it.

"Have you been in here all day?"

She hesitated a moment, thinking about the drink she had shared with Roger and Steve, the trip to Knutsford, the shopping, the lunch.

"Yes," she lied, feeling dejected, confused and helpless.

"No." The voice came from behind Gabriel. He turned and stared at Roger.

"She has been out with us. I need to speak to you, sir." He spoke quietly and impassively, and Grace wondered how he could show such control when surely he was annoyed with his boss and the way he was treating her.

"I'll be with you in a moment, Roger." Black turned to Grace. "I would like you to join John and me to look at his new bedroom. I would appreciate your assistance in helping him to settle in there." Before she could respond he turned his back on her and walked with Roger to his study.

"I don't know what you're up to, Gabe, and I know you're not going to tell me, but it's obvious this woman is not one of your 'little black book' girls, and she deserves a bit more respect from you."

Black walked over to his desk and made no comment.

Roger changed the subject. "Julian has been in touch."

Now he had his employer's attention.

"Where is he?"

"He's been in Patagonia. He's on his way here. He said to let you know he will arrive on Thursday."

Black consulted his diary on the Xphone. He had no meetings that day. "Order a Lamborghini to be at the airport for him and let him drive it himself; I want him in a good mood."

"What are you planning?"

"I want him back on the board."

Roger looked at him gravely. "Are you sure?"

"Yes." Gabriel sounded as though he had been thinking about this for some time. "Don't worry," he added, sadly, "it will only be to help manage the business. I know he can do that, and will do a good job. I will never ask more of him. You know I wouldn't."

A mutual understanding passed between the two men.

"I know," replied the PA. "Can I ask you something?"

"I don't need a hard time, Roger." He knew what was coming.

"Don't take it out on Grace. Ease up on her and I think she'll be good for you. If you don't, you could lose her."

He doesn't know she can't go anywhere, not for another three hundred and fifty-four days.

"She's just my distraction, Roger, like all the others. Don't make out it's anything special," he lied, looking down at the paperwork on his desk. This conversation was over.

"Are you ready?" He was standing on the threshold to the sanctuary; the door was open.

"Yes, sir," she said, making no attempt to hide the bitterness in her voice.

"Do this for John, please," he whispered and walked on ahead of her.

John was just finishing his cookie.

"Hello, Mrs McGuire. Are you coming to see my new bedroom?"

"Hi John, yes. Isn't it exciting?" She walked over to him, trying to avoid any contact with his father, without it being obvious to anyone else.

"Come on, then." Gabriel led the way up two flights of stairs, and across the galleried landing.

He opened the door into John's new bedroom and stood back as the young boy walked in, his eyes wide with amazement and pride. The room had a definite "wow" factor and Gabriel felt both pleased and relieved.

John stared at the wallpaper covered in Star Wars characters, the duvet cover with superheroes on it, the curtains with stars and planets covering them, and the main attraction, a large model of the Millennium Falcon spacecraft, looming out of a wall in a giant 3D sculpture. It was exactly the same as shown in the plans that Black had reviewed with his son, right down to the three-foot model of a mobile R2D2 standing at the bottom of the single bed.

"Do you like it?" his father asked.

"It's awesome!" John turned to him, beaming. All his toys, clothes and, of course, pictures of his mother, had been placed in here. "Do you like it, Mrs McGuire?"

Apart from it being totally over the top? "Of course I do. It's fabulous, John. I bet you'll love sleeping in here."

171

"Let's go and brush your teeth and then we can look at your school book before bed."

As the two Blacks walked into the interconnecting bathroom, Grace wasn't sure what her role should be.

Is he expecting me to just stay here?

She decided to sit on the edge of the bed and wait for them to return. She looked around at the "no expense spared" décor and contents of the room; the sign of a father desperate to please a son. She hoped he wasn't spoiling the child. But then, who was she to judge how he cared for a boy who had lost his mother and was only just getting to know his father?

When they walked back into the bedroom Grace stood up and glared at Gabriel, just managing to stop herself from sticking her tongue out at him. *Petulant and irritating? Don't go there again!*

"Why don't you read to me and Mrs McGuire and then I'll read you a story, John? I think Mrs McGuire has some work to do." This time he actually glanced over at her, looking for her consent.

Grace was feeling totally confused by his manner, what he was saying and the way he looked at her. Her emotions were causing turmoil and she was afraid she couldn't cope with much more.

As she closed the door on Black reading to his son, she walked around the gallery and into "her" bedroom. The door had been unlocked all day, and the bronze Biba cowl-backed maxi dress, from today's shopping expedition, hung in the wardrobe. Steve had insisted the gathering around the right hip was flattering to Grace's pear-shaped figure, the low cowl back, which would prevent her from wearing a bra, was just revealing enough to be provocative without being tarty, as he put it, and the colour absolutely complimented her own skin and light brown hair; it just had to be this one. She had to admit she felt gorgeous in it. *What was it about gay men and their ability to dress well and have a good eye for colour?*

She slipped into it and placed the new Dune champagne-coloured strappy sandals over her bare feet. She neither needed nor wore any underwear.

172

She re-did her make-up and ruffled her hair to give it a bit of life, asking herself why she felt it was so important that she looked good. She didn't want to think about the answer.

She heard footsteps across the landing and a door open and close. *His bedroom?*

Then she heard John cry out, "Daddy I need you. I'm scared …"

A door opened and closed, then footsteps, and his voice. "John, I told you it was all right. There's nothing to be scared of. Look, Gromit isn't scared. You need to get to sleep so you'll have lots of energy for tomorrow. We're going to have a great day, but if you don't go to sleep you'll be too tired to enjoy it."

It went quiet. Then Grace was aware of Black returning to his bedroom.

She waited until she heard his footsteps again and determined he was going downstairs. Quietly she followed at a safe distance and stood back watching as he glanced into the empty sanctuary, feeling a little empowered by his puzzlement as he wondered where she was.

He went down to the kitchen and was greeted by Steve.

"Ready when you are," said the chef cheerfully, trying to hide his concern that the guest of honour had not appeared. "Can I get you a drink, sir?" He looked over to the doorway and added, "and madam?"

Gabriel swung round and took in the vision. She was the ultimate contrast to the woman who had greeted him at the entrance to Arnford Hall only last night. His look of shock was soon veiled by the mask that slipped over his features.

"That would be lovely, thank you," Grace replied, and she simply couldn't help smiling at Black.

He approached and took her hand.

"Allow me," he said as he led her out onto the patio and over to the elaborately decorated table, with candles burning and the white orchid in pride of place. Gabriel pulled her chair back and waited as she took her seat.

He sat down opposite, while Steve brought the Dom Pérignon, followed by starters of goat's cheese soufflé with a honeyed pear and pecan nut salad.

Gabriel raised his champagne glass, his eyes holding hers, and waited for her to lift her glass to his.

"You look beautiful." His voice was low, mellow and sincere.

Grace flushed slightly and held her breath as his gaze burned into her, undressing her with the desire in his eyes.

"Breathe, Grace," he ordered.

He was wearing plain black Hugo Boss trousers with a white shirt, open at the neck, and his crocodile skin shoes. She could smell his spicy, seductive fragrance.

Would she do anything for him tonight?

"Has John gone to sleep OK?" she asked nervously, to break the tension that seemed to hang in the air.

"No." He began to eat his starter. "The intercom is on. Steve will let me know if he wakes. I guess it's a big change for him."

"Yes," she replied, luxuriating in the taste of the food, the surroundings, and the vision of masculine beauty before her.

"Did you get your work done?"

"Yes."

"I want you to join John and me tomorrow. I have plans."

"Is that an order?" She continued to eat, not quite ready to look at him.

"Yes."

As they finished their first course, Steve appeared and cleared the plates away, returning with a main course of duck breast, baby potatoes, green beans, carrots julienne, poached rhubarb and syrup. It looked and tasted divine.

"I thought you said you weren't as good as Simon Radley," she said accusingly to Steve as he poured more champagne. The chef smiled. Black looked surprised and considered how quickly, and with such ease, his reluctant guest was building a relationship with the staff; he thought of what Roger had said earlier. It would seem that Mrs McGuire was becoming a welcome visitor to the Hall.

Steve interrupted his thoughts.

"I'll leave now if everything is in order. The dessert is in the fridge, sir. John hasn't woken."

"Good. Thank you, chef, that's fine. Enjoy your evening and tomorrow. I'll see you on Monday."

174

Now the two of them were alone. Grace looked up at him as he was gazing at her, and their eyes met. Neither of them smiled; they each knew why she was there, though only she knew she actually wasn't too disgruntled by it at the moment.

"So why does a school teacher have to work at the weekends?"

"There are not enough hours in the day. It's par for the course."

"What are your contractual hours?"

"Eight forty-five until half past four. The children come in at ten to nine and leave at quarter past three. It's pretty much full on during the day, and then we have a bit of time to sort the classroom out for the next day, attend planning and staff meetings, and I'm also responsible for the needs of those children requiring a bit more help than the rest."

"Did Melanie Bright choose teaching, or Grace McGuire?" He was watching her now and noticed a slight hesitation as she started to shuffle the remains of her food around the white china plate.

She didn't respond.

His voice was matter-of-fact and she wondered if he was just thinking out loud, or if he really expected her to join in this conversation.

"It seems that you have chosen to protect those whom your father chose to harm. In my case, I just turned my back on everything. I can't escape my fate. I was living in my nightmare and now John has become my daylight. I wonder if you will be my breaking dawn, Grace." It wasn't a question. He had laid his cutlery to the side of his plate, having only eaten about three-quarters of the meal, and he started to sip his champagne, clearly savouring the taste, and looking out onto the flowerbeds.

"What is your nightmare?" Grace asked quietly, placing her knife and fork together on her plate.

Ignoring her question, he simply asked, "Are you ready for dessert?"

She nodded and smiled, trying to soften the sombre mood that threatened to envelop the evening.

"Excuse me." He bowed politely as he left the table.

Oh, Mr Darcy!

He returned with two plates, each containing a small, dark chocolate casing, with two spoons.

Grace watched as he placed one of the plates on the side of the table and then positioned the second in between them. He handed her a spoon.

"Crack it open," he instructed and, intrigued by his mysterious air, she carefully – and then more forcefully – brought her spoon down to crack through the case of chocolate. Slowly, liquid chocolate laced heavily with Grand Marnier flowed from the broken shell, and Gabriel collected some of the liquid and the chocolate shell onto his spoon and held it out to her, waiting for her to open her mouth.

She felt sensual and erotic as she drank the sensational liquid, and her eyes drank in his sexual magnetism. *Maybe he was right in thinking any woman would want to have sex with him …*

He studied her intently, feeling confident now that she was enjoying the meal and possibly his company, and he leaned forward as she boldly repeated his action and held her spoon out to him.

His lips lingered on the metal and its surface was clean as she extracted it.

After they had finished feeding each other, in his low, sexy voice he asked, "Will you enjoy some sex tonight, Grace?"

"Why not?" she whispered, and she felt a wetness at her vagina, too turned on to worry about it showing through the silk of her dress.

He picked up the plate with the second dessert and took her hand.

She wondered if he would lead her into the den, but he walked up the stone staircase, past her sanctuary without even glancing at it or his guest, and up the grand staircase to her bedroom. As he followed her inside, he locked the door.

"I like your dress," he murmured as he pulled her towards him and began to nuzzle at her neck. "Did Steve choose it?"

"Yes!" she gasped. *Just rip it off me …*

Without lifting his head from her neck he continued, "Do you masturbate, Grace?"

"What?" she whispered, too lost in her own lust to comprehend where he was going with this.

He repeated the question, still holding her to him.

"No." Her voice betrayed her apprehension. Well, not for years, she thought. With the men before Jason she had never really felt the need, although she and Richard had experimented with a vibrator a few times, and she had liked it … But since she had been seeing Jason, sex a couple of times at the weekend had been enough for her; she even had to admit to feeling tired sometimes and wasn't too bothered if the odd week or two went by with total abstinence: she had put it down to her age. But she certainly wasn't telling this man – whom she now really wanted to fuck her – any of this.

He held his arms out, firmly holding her shoulders. His eyes became darker, his lips set straight and the sexual magnetism that had been building between the couple was broken.

"Time for your punishment, then. Don't look so shocked, Grace."

He may as well have hit her in the face.

He ignored her questioning look as he pulled her dress up and lifted it over her head. She stood naked before him.

"Why are you doing this?" She spoke to his back now as he slowly hung the dress back up in the wardrobe.

"I'll see this gets cleaned for next time," he said matter-of-factly. He then lounged back on the chaise longue, not taking his eyes off her as he said, "I want to see you excite yourself, Grace, for my pleasure, not yours. Come if you want to; I doubt I'll be able to tell if you fake it or not. But I want to watch. I'll tell you when to stop."

She stared at him, her insides knotted with sexual frustration, her heart breaking at his cruelty.

"What did I do?" She didn't move and her voice was shaking.

"When I enter a room you stand, remember."

She recalled being in the kitchen earlier that afternoon, when father and son had returned from Tatton Park.

She looked at him, the hatred that should have been in her eyes not finding room as they were filled with a deep sadness.

Part of her had thought he liked her. Now he was reminding her she was there as his possession, to be controlled and humiliated if it suited him.

His voice brought her mind back into the room.

"I'm waiting. Do you want to stand, sit, lie down?"

She couldn't move.

"Let me help you, and do it my way then."

She had no idea what he meant and, like a puppet, she let him lie her down gently on the bed and then felt his hands take one of her feet. As he moved it over towards one of the posts at the bottom of the bed, he pulled the curtain aside and secured her ankle to the post with the rope from the tie-back. He repeated the process with the other leg, leaving her spread open, fastened to the posts. He returned to his front-row view of her vagina and waited.

Grace closed her eyes and slowly moved her hand down to the top of her inner thighs. She felt around the edge of her vagina, apprehensively curious at the feel of the soft folds of her vulva, before moving her finger to touch her clitoris. She lightly stroked it and, even now, hating him for putting her through this humiliating ordeal, she wanted to feel him on her, in her, holding her. What the hell was he doing to her?

He continued to watch and shifted in his seat as he grew harder and harder. Would she let him in? He wanted her. Fuck, he needed her more than he had ever needed anything in his life. But he couldn't let her know that.

Grace pulled her hand away and sat up.

"I can't do any more." She stared at him as if daring him to make her. She tried to lean forward and reach the ties to release her legs, but she couldn't. Frustrated and fighting back tears, she flung herself back down on the bed covers, putting her hands over her face.

"Don't move," he ordered quietly.

A moment later Grace felt the mattress lower and she opened her eyes to see that, now naked too, he was kneeling on the bed beside her.

"Punishment and reward. It seems to be your thing, Grace." He took the chocolate shell he was holding in his hand, and

178

broke it open above her stomach. She felt the cool liquid run over her, she could smell the alcohol and cocoa, and then she closed her eyes and luxuriated in the feel of his tongue lapping up the liqueur and chocolate from her body, before he carefully placed bite-sized pieces of the firm chocolate, its taste tinged with the alcohol, into her mouth.

"Enjoy the sex, remember, Grace."

And when he had ceased feasting on her chocolate-coated abdomen, he began to taste the saltiness of the skin on her breasts; he chewed at her nipples, nibbled at her neck and all the while his fingers stroked her clitoris and explored her vagina.

"Don't come yet," he whispered softly now, as she moaned with desire. "Wait for me."

He released her feet from their bindings. Then she felt his penis enter her, full and long. She raised herself up to feel more of him, moving her body in rhythm with his to maximise his pleasure, just as he was maximising hers.

They came together, crying out with passion, feeling hot and satiated. They lay together for a moment and gazed at each other. She could feel his fingers slowly trailing up and down her back.

"I should hate you," she murmured.

"But you can't," he breathed.

For the second time, he stayed in her bed.

Chapter 34

As Grace awoke the next morning and glanced at the light sneaking out from the heavy curtains, it took her a moment to remember where she was. She turned to see empty space beside her.

How did he manage to leave the bed and the room without disturbing her? She had always considered herself to be a light sleeper. Maybe she slept more deeply in this warm, luxurious bed?

She glanced at the clock. It was eight o'clock. She lay staring up at the ceiling for a moment, remembering the events of last night, what he had made her do, and what he had then done to her and with her. She struggled to reconcile the reason she was in his house with the emotions he made her feel.

I'm here against my will, doing things I don't want to do, and yet I feel energised and special!

She thought about the contrasting evenings: the pain and the shame of Friday, then the initial embarrassment followed by the sensual, passionate feelings of last night. She put her hand to the collar.

What am I to him? Someone to be controlled, dominated? What had Roger said? "If you don't see his friendship, trust and protection, then you are not looking. Give him a chance, Grace. I think you mean more to him than you know." But Roger doesn't know why I'm here; I'm his son's school teacher and he's blackmailing me. How bad does it have to be for me to hate him?

His words, *But you can't*, echoed around her head.

She went into the en-suite and surveyed the large claw-foot bath. There was a bottle of Chanel No. 5 bath gel on the shelf and she unscrewed the lid and smelled the heavenly fragrance. It was her favourite perfume, and she turned the gold tap and watched as hot water gushed from the swan's mouth and she added the fragrant liquid, breathing in the aroma.

Being in no rush to meet her keeper, she lay back, luxuriating in the bubbles for a few minutes, and wondered what his "plans" for today were. She was trying to deny that she felt a little apprehensive that he would walk in, or summon her in some way, and her feeling of calm would be broken.

But nothing happened.

She put the purple silk shirt and black leggings on, applied a little make-up which Michael had brought from her house, and turned the door handle to make her way down to the kitchen, hoping to find John. The bedroom door was locked. She turned it back and forth. *Why would he do this?*

She listened to the apparent silence on the other side of the door. She walked over to the window and pulled the curtains back, peering out over the gardens. She couldn't see or hear anyone.

She sat on the bed. And waited.

At ten o'clock she awoke from her snooze, brought on by the sheer boredom of having absolutely nothing to do – no work, no books to read, nothing to eat or drink – and she started to feel hungry and angry. *What is he playing at? How long is he going to leave me in here? Is he punishing me?*

She tried the door again. It was still locked and she kicked the bottom of it as hard as she could with her bare foot, making a tiny muffled sound and forcing a spider to come scurrying from beneath it.

Then she thought of the Xphone. She took it from the carrier bag:

Sender: Gabriel Black

Message: Wait for me.

Wait for me! What the hell is that supposed to mean?

Grace felt furious. *He's not showing friendship, trust or protection. He's a selfish, controlling bully. Don't dare tell me I can't bloody hate you!*

She tried to open the sash window, and was contemplating throwing the bottle of bubble bath at it to smash the glass when she heard the door handle turning and she stepped back, staring at the door.

He opened it and walked in, closing it again behind him. He didn't speak.

"Why the hell did you lock me in here? What are you fucking playing at?"

He stared at the bubble bath in her hand, and prepared himself to move, should she hurl it at him.

"I needed to attend to something, and I could do it better knowing exactly where you were." He walked past her into the bathroom, as if to confirm she had taken a bath. "Put your shoes on and come down." He turned and left her standing in the middle of the room, staring at his back, as he went out and made his way downstairs.

Deciding freedom from the room was better than being "petulant and irritating" and staying in it to annoy him, she followed and stopped in front of him at the bottom of the staircase.

"Let's get in the car; John's waiting."

Grace stood at the top of the steps of the Hall and stared at the grey Porsche 911 waiting for them at the bottom. It was a beautiful car, and for a moment she felt excited at the prospect of getting in it. But she was furious with him and what he was doing to her. How the hell was she going to get through today?

He held the door open for her, studying her expression, seeing her anger, but he knew she would say nothing; John was in the car. He felt confident that by the time they got to their destination, she would have calmed down.

He had spent two hours that morning trying to persuade Ellouise not to catch a plane to Florida. Roger had alerted him to the fact that his sister was determined to follow her latest boyfriend (and there had been many of them) to downtown Miami, where no doubt he would have spent her money on drugs, just like the others. Gabriel was on a mission to try to bring his family into some realm of decency and create the best possible family environment for John. It was never going to be an easy task, but did it have to be impossible? He wanted Ellouise to be around when Julian arrived. Roger had been instructed to arrange the purchase of the small bungalow near John's school, for Ellouise to live in. If she still wanted her generous allowance, she would have to put up with his rules; at least he wasn't insisting she lived at the Hall.

He had left her with Roger and Steve, together with the request, not to be denied, that she joined her big brother for dinner tomorrow evening.

Now, after some delay, and with a very pissed-off companion, he could get back to his plans for the day.

He hit the accelerator and zoomed over the gravel out of Arnford Hall, Arnford Village and Cheshire. Gabriel Black couldn't get to the house at the lakeside quick enough.

There was a dense silence in the car.

After only fifteen minutes John asked, "Are we there yet?", sounding bored and grumpy.

Gabriel wasn't sure why he shouldn't be happy at the prospect of going up to the Lakes; but then he hadn't shared his surprise with his son, and the seven-year-old was no doubt too young to appreciate the fact that he was in one of the top cars on the road. The Porsche 911 50 had been built to celebrate fifty years of this model, and only 1,963 had been made.

"So, what do you think of the car?" the driver asked the passengers.

"It's cool, Daddy," came a quiet, bored voice in the back. Was he saying that because he knew it was what Daddy wanted to hear?

Gabriel never ceased to be in awe of his son's wisdom, and was sometimes a little alarmed at how much he reminded him of himself. He remembered for a moment how he had spent his own early years trying to please his father, and how his final promise to his father before he died had led to Gabriel's life of hell. From the second he knew of the existence of his own child, he had vowed never to bring him into his nightmare.

He was grateful when the woman sitting next to him released him from his dark thoughts.

"It's very impressive. What's the significance of the 50 logo?" Grace could hear his passion and enthusiasm as he explained how and why he purchased this car three years ago, and that he rarely played any music in it so he could listen to the engine.

Really? she wondered.

The two adults then became aware of a light snoring sound from the rear of the vehicle, and Black watched his sleeping son through the rear-view mirror. Friday night had obviously been a late one, and no doubt last night, being his first night in his new bedroom and on his own, had taken its toll on the young boy too.

Grace immediately took advantage of this period of privacy.

"What the hell were you doing locking me in the bedroom?"

"You were asleep when I left and I didn't want you going anywhere."

"Escaping you by going to the sanctuary, you mean?" she asked, her voice harsh, as she looked straight ahead. "I could have got some more work done, or at least found something to do in the house. I wasn't exactly able to leave the Hall, was I?" She paused and, as he remained silent next to her, she continued to let him have it. "And what about my own car? What right had you to instruct the garage to write it off? It wasn't that badly damaged!"

"You weren't safe driving it."

"I've had it three years and never had an accident. How many bloody times do I have to remind you, you drove into the back of me!"

Then she fell silent. If she had been concentrating on the road that day, she would no doubt have proceeded onto the roundabout, he would not have hit her, and he would never have discovered Melanie Bright. She would not be here now. *Where would you be? Snorting coke with Jason?*

She looked out of the window.

"Where are we going?" she asked quietly. John had school the next day, so she was sure they would be back in time for her to get home at a decent hour and get a good night's sleep before work in the morning. In fact, hadn't he said he would be back at work on Monday?

184

"I have a house in the Lakes. We're going to spend the rest of the day there. Don't worry, you'll be home in plenty of time." He glanced over at her, his eyes dark, his expression veiled in a sorrow he couldn't quite mask.

Here was a woman who worked hard, had a boyfriend, a life she loved. Had he overstepped his own mark with his entrapment of her? Was she awakening a compassion within him, one he didn't know existed, outside of his new relationship with his son?

The rest of the journey passed in silence, and he finally pulled up outside the lakeside house. Having opened the gate, he got back into the car and drove through, parking in front of a block of three garages.

Grace stared out of the car window at the large three-storey house, clad in grey stone, set in private grounds with a short sloping driveway leading up to a large glazed door set in dark oak.

"Breathe, Grace," he said as he got out of the car. He walked round and opened her door.

As she climbed out, still staring at the house before her, he leaned into the back of the car, gently waking John and unfastening his seat belt.

"Come on, we've got things to do and not much time," he said, and Grace's eyes followed father and son as they went up to the front door.

As she joined them in the hallway, she was mesmerised by the modern, tasteful décor of the building. The walls were covered with light grey natural stone tiles, creating a peaceful, calm look, with a masculine design. *Is this his taste?* She couldn't fail to feel the contrast this house made with Arnford Hall. There were no gargoyles, no serious portraits or sombre busts here.

Gabriel led them into a stunning, modern kitchen with white gloss units contrasting with dark slate grey worktops. The walls and floor were covered in the same grey natural stone tiles which seemed to run throughout the ground floor. On the top of a central island stood a large picnic basket and three big cardboard boxes.

He went over to investigate the contents of the picnic basket and smiled. Then he walked out through a large open patio door.

There must be someone else in the house. Grace looked at John and they both followed him. She was curious to know who could be here. And why was she suddenly feeling excited about being in such contemporary, state-of-the-art surroundings? With him and his son?

As she peered out onto a huge decked patio area, she gasped again, her excitement growing as she looked out over Lake Windermere. The view was breath-taking. The decking area was elevated, as the house was on split levels, and it was artistically peppered with dark brown and beige garden furniture and enclosed by elaborate wrought-iron railings. Oh, she could live in a place like this and die a happy girl!

Then she saw him, talking to a grey-haired, portly woman of about sixty-five. As he heard John and Grace come out, Gabriel turned to face them and smiled. Grace believed this was the most relaxed she had ever seen the man who was commanding her to have sex with him.

"Nanny, I would like you to meet my son, John, and my friend, Grace McGuire."

The woman beamed and came over, leaning down to John and exclaiming how happy she was to meet him at last. She immediately mentioned she had heard he liked Spiderman and Batman, and that she had seen his wonderful bedding.

Unable to conceal her puzzled expression, Grace looked over to Gabriel, who remained a short distance away.

His smile was still evident. His eyes did not leave her.

By way of explanation, he told Grace, "I brought John here for a couple of days so we could get to know each other and have some quality time together. Nanny has seen the Batman characters on our bedding."

After John shyly allowed himself to be hugged by this warm, friendly old lady, Nanny turned to Grace and shook her hand with warmth and reassurance.

"How wonderful to meet a friend of Gabriel's. This is such a rare occurrence; you must be very good for him."

Now the smile was gone from his face, replaced by his lips set in a straight line, eyes deep in thought, still staring at Grace.

She couldn't quite get her words out properly. *This woman will think I'm a blithering idiot!* "Ha … I, er … do my best" – beaming smile – "I'm John's teacher." And as she saw a concerned questioning look pass from the woman to Gabriel, she felt obliged to add the word "too!" *Oh … have I just become complicit in his little game?*

"Well," Nanny was trying not to sound patronising, but all three grown-ups knew she wasn't doing a very good job, "I hope you're looking after him. I'm just sorry I can't still do it."

Gabriel walked up to his childhood nanny and put a loving arm around her. "I'm all grown-up now, Nanny, and don't need looking after."

Grace watched in stunned silence as he kissed the older woman respectfully on her cheek and said, "Come on let's grab the picnic and walk down to the lake. Will you help me, please, Grace?"

Too stupefied to do anything else, she followed her captor back into the kitchen, just like happy bloody families!

"What are you playing at?" she demanded when they were far enough into the kitchen not to be heard outside.

"What do you mean? You have a problem with spending a day at my house, with my son and my old childhood nanny?"

"I have a problem pretending I'm some sort of girlfriend. Are you going to tell her you locked me in a bedroom this morning?"

"I admit she has jumped to certain conclusions. I have never allowed any of my former acquaintances to meet her before. I'm sorry if this is offending you." Inwardly, he was asking himself why he had used the expression "former acquaintances" when in reality he had never consciously decided to stop seeing all of the women he had been seeing before Grace, just some of them! But outwardly his expression hardened, not appreciating his "guest" attempting to ruin another activity he had arranged. "Of course, if you don't want to come to play with John and me on the lake, I can lock you in a bedroom here until we get back." His tone was stern, in a "don't push me, Grace" kind of way.

He slung the strap of the picnic basket over his shoulder and picked up two of the cardboard boxes and headed back outside, saying, "If you are coming, please bring the other box. Otherwise wait right there and I'll be back in a second."

She didn't need any time to decide to pick the box up and follow him. *Petulant and irritating?* Hell, no. She was angry!

Nanny took one of the boxes from him and the group made their way through a gate in the railings and down some steps to a boathouse on the edge of the lake. Gabriel unlocked the door and John ran in after him, shouting, "Daddy, are we going out in the boat again? Are you coming, Mrs McGuire?" He sounded so excited, Grace actually felt wanted – suddenly appreciating for the first time today that Gabriel seemed to want her here; he just had a damned funny way of showing it!

"No, John. We're not going out in our boat, but we are going to play with boats. This one is yours." He started to open the first box.

He lifted out a remote control yellow speedboat, with a double cockpit, and the name *Sea Knight* written on the side. He placed it on the bench together with the control box. John was fascinated with it.

"Can I drive it, Daddy? Will it go fast? Can we take it out now?"

"In a minute, John. Show it to Nanny while I get Grace's and mine out."

Grace looked at him questioningly. "You got me a boat?"

"Well, you can't join in without one. This used to be a favourite pastime of mine with my father, when we used to have family holidays up in Scotland. I have always wanted to try it here and now John has given me the perfect excuse to do it." The smile and relaxed manner were back.

While Nanny and John were studying his yellow model, talking animatedly and already forming a friendship for life, Gabriel sat close to Grace and opened the second box.

He withdrew a beautiful sailing yacht with the words *My Grace* painted across the main white sail. He placed it on the floor and leaned into her, whispering, "Breathe, Grace."

She became aware of his breath on her neck as she closed her eyes momentarily, feeling herself falling under his spell; she felt his hand press against her back slightly and shuddered, trying to deny the thrill that ran through her, but failing, and they both knew it.

"Till later," he added and then pulled away.

In the last box was a black radio-controlled Viper high-speed boat. As Gabriel carefully placed it on the bench, John came to study it, declaring, "Wow, Daddy, it looks like a Batboat!"

The father just smiled, not quite making it a schoolboy grin.

"Come on then, let's get these toys on the water," said Nanny and Grace looked at her, amazed at the effect she had on Black senior; she said "jump" and he jumped!

Before she knew it, Gabriel, still wearing his Hugo Boss black trousers underneath, climbed into dark green waders, and they all carried their boats to the water's edge, Nanny helping John and asking Gabriel if he had arranged boat cover with Ian, should there be any unforeseen capsizing out on the lake.

"Yes. I'll just call him now and let him know we're ready." He turned to John, "Are you ready to try launching your boat, John?"

"Definitely!" came the confident reply as the young boy continued to admire his ocean-going vessel.

"Well, I don't think we'll get any racing done today, but let's just treat this as boat training and getting used to steering it."

Grace watched as Black patiently set up the controls and showed his son how to use them. He restricted the speed to reduce the risk of capsizing, and entered the water near his own jetty, with the aim of keeping the vessels relatively close to the shoreline. Ian would be on hand in a Zodiac RIB to retrieve any vessels in danger of being lost.

John was ecstatic when, with Gabriel's hand guiding his own, his yellow *Sea Knight* surfed out onto the lake.

"Don't let it go too far, Daddy, I don't want to lose it."

John very quickly mastered manoeuvring the small boat, which was particularly well balanced for young pilots, and Nanny replaced Gabriel as John's first mate.

Now he turned to Grace, who had been admiring both the view across the lake to the hills beyond, their peaks just capped by the mid-afternoon sunshine, and the man who now approached her, looking decidedly odd in his white shirt with the sleeves rolled up and his green waders.

He adjusted the tiny pieces of rope attached to the sails and rigging of *My Grace*. His actions were gentle, even tender, as if he were delicately tightening a woman's bodice. For a few minutes he was silent, absorbed in his task, hoping the school teacher beside him would smile and enjoy this time with him, his son and a woman who had been so important to him in his youth; a woman who had helped him live with his nightmare, survive the challenges life threw at him, until she could no longer bear it for him. It was then, when he was thirty, that he had given Nanny a home here in Windermere, just a few minutes' walk from his own home by the lake.

Whenever he came here, he nearly always tried to spend some time with her. He was also nearly always alone.

He couldn't quite figure out why he wanted a young woman, whom he would probably only know for a year, to be acquainted with the people who were important in his life.

He turned to Grace and held the boat out for her to admire.

"Shall we put her in the water?"

Grace nodded and her eyes told him she was happy here.

Good. It was important to him that she liked to be here. Here was not Arnford Hall.

With three people sailing three boats not too far off shore, laughter, exclamations and the odd competitive moment were shared, while Nanny admired all of the vessels and their pilots, and took picnic things out of the basket to feed the hungry group. The afternoon raced by and at half past three, Gabriel reluctantly announced it was time to get the boats out of the water, tidy things up and start to head back to Cheshire; two people had school tomorrow, and two had work!

"Is that a puzzle, Daddy, if there are only three of us? I know, I know …"

Nanny insisted that she would hose the boats down and put everything away and lock up when they had gone. She wanted to enjoy the last half hour with them. She made some tea and juice to go with the remaining sandwiches from the picnic.

While Gabriel and John visited the bathroom before their car journey, Nanny took hold of Grace's hand, squeezing it warmly between her own, and said, "I'm so glad he brought you and introduced us. I sense not everything runs smoothly for the two of you. Poor Gabriel, I'm afraid an easy life has never been his destiny. But keep working at it; all the best relationships are worth fighting for. I know he is definitely worth it, Grace. I think he needs you."

She stopped as she heard his footsteps approaching.

As Grace sat in the car, fighting off the desire to close her eyes and doze to the hum of the engine, she thought about Nanny's words: *He needs you.* Ha – what a joke.

Despite her best efforts not to fall asleep, she was awakened by his voice.

"Grace, we're here."

She climbed out of the car and waited while he helped John out of the back. It was seven o'clock and he told her to wait while he took John to bed, adding, "I haven't finished with you yet."

As she watched them ascend the grand staircase, she turned and unlocked the door to her sanctuary, not really caring if he had noticed.

The fruit had been removed but there were some biscuits in a container and she made herself a peppermint tea. Whoever was responsible for keeping the room stocked with things for her was doing a good job.

Half an hour later the phone trilled.

Sender: Gabriel Black

Message: The sooner you come to your bedroom, the sooner you can go home, Grace.

She thought about the tenderness, almost affection, he had shown her earlier today, the dinner last night, even the sex and the sensual ritual with the chocolate, the passion amid the need and the taking. Then she thought of the punishments – the humiliating outing to the restaurant, the caning, the forced masturbation.

Oh God, how much more can I take of this?

She remembered Nanny's words: *Poor Gabriel, I'm afraid an easy life has never been his destiny …*

Was it the same for her?

She collected all her papers and things together and was ready to go home. What was he going to expect of her now? She tried to blank her mind and thought, Let's just get it over with.

She walked up to her bedroom. The door was open. He was standing by the window.

"I just need you one more time. Is that too much to ask?"

Grace stared at him, silent.

"The answer is 'no', Grace."

"No, sir," she said quietly, not quite able to look at him now, as she felt his emotional torture begin to damage her soul. In another life she may have admired this man, perhaps even fallen in love with him. But now she was torn between hating him for what he was doing to her, and needing him – needing the sexual tension, the eroticism and the excitement he conjured up in her.

"Take your clothes off and lie face down on the bed." He spoke quietly, his voice soft as though he were about to reveal his undying love for her. Of course, he wasn't.

Grace faced him and began to take off her purple blouse. She was surprised to see that he undressed with her, and as he gazed at her revealing her curvaceous body, she allowed herself to admire his athletic one, his toned muscles, and the perfect amount of body hair showcasing his chest, penis and balls.

The silence bound them as they continued with their task, each aware of the other's scrutiny, and each going slowly, as if to allow the onlooker time to appreciate what they saw.

Both naked now, he waited a second for her to lie on the bed. She did what was expected and lay down, looking at the curtains pulled across the sash window, her hands resting at each side of her head and her legs together, stretched behind her. She counted the seconds before feeling the compression of the mattress as he climbed onto the bed, and then she became aware of his knees brushing the sides of her lower legs. Suddenly he started to stroke her buttocks, and she felt his hands part them and trail his finger from her lower spine, over her coccyx and continue down the crack between her cheeks, to her anus. He held his finger there for a moment, as if contemplating something.

"I … I don't like that, if that's what you're thinking about …" She couldn't hide the concern in her voice.

He continued to trail his finger down to her vulva, saying in the same quiet tone, "Beware of telling me all your fears, Grace. It's not safe for me to know all your weaknesses." The softness of his voice contrasted starkly with the menace of his words, and Grace clenched herself, dreading his hand moving back up to her anus.

But she did not move, and his hand did not return to that unauthorised entrance.

"Good," he said, and he steadily parted her legs, positioning himself in between them. She tensed as she felt his finger enter her vagina, circling inside her, coaxing her juices to lubricate his way as he inserted his penis into her. Slowly, maintaining their connection, he raised her buttocks up slightly. She complied, more eagerly than she intended, moving to her knees, pushing herself further onto him, wanting to feel full of him, have his balls pressing against her vulva. She lowered her head, resting it on her forearms, relishing the touch as his hand moved to her most excitable part and his fingers began to massage her clitoris sensitively, provocatively, as though her pleasure was more important to him than his own. She felt his breath on her neck and realised he was smelling her hair. As her desire grew, she raised herself further, almost upright now, pressing her back against his chest. His strong arms bound her to him, his movements in and, almost, out of her, mesmerising her for those few minutes.

Instinctively she bent forward again, lowering her head and raising her bottom, giving him direct access, feeling his testicles brushing against her sensitive skin, his penis deep inside her, desiring him to fill her even beyond her capacity … she felt feral and desperate and she loved it. She didn't want to deny herself this orgasm; it thrilled her, gave her a high like no drug she had ever tried, and it made her feel that he wanted her, needed her, even. *Is this why he is so schizophrenic with me: good guy/bad guy?*

As she cried out, his breathing quickened and he moaned, his grip tightening on her as he poured himself into her.

Her own pleasure was heightened by the feeling of power she got when she made him come.

Finally, they fell back and Grace rolled onto her side, feeling serene, which was so at odds to how she had felt when she had arrived at his door on Friday in her distasteful clothes. What was he doing to her?

After a few moments he ran his hand down her arm and leaned over to kiss her shoulder ever so lightly. "I'm glad that wasn't too much to ask, Grace. The car will be ready when you are. Don't forget your work things," and he got off the bed, gathered his clothes together and left the room, closing the door quietly behind him.

Chapter 35

That night, Black left his office at two in the morning, having reviewed his papers for the board meeting tomorrow. His holiday was over and he needed to adjust to a routine that would provide adequate quality time for John. Was he expecting too much of Julian to be able to come back to the fray, working for the Black empire? He hoped not, as he didn't have a plan B yet.

Besides needing time for John, he also realised he could no longer deny to himself that he wanted time for Grace: more time for Grace. He regretted the punishments; but that was his cover, wasn't it? She needed to be protected from him. He needed to be protected from the possibility – probability? – that she would hurt him. He remembered her answer in the game: "I don't think you are capable of being hurt." *If only she knew.*

He eventually got into his own bed and dreamed that he could reach out and touch her as she lay beside him. He woke at six and went down to the pool to swim for half an hour before John woke. He tried to get her out of his head, but he knew he probably never would.

As he walked into the boardroom at Black HQ in Manchester at half past ten that morning, he was faced with an empty chair where the chairperson normally sat.

"Where is she?" he asked Roger.

"She has sent her apologies. Her flight has been delayed." His look echoed Gabriel's thoughts: *She's not quite ready to come back yet, but she will.* "She has sent some comments and questions for you. They're in your file. I've read through them and nothing requires urgent attention. Everyone else is here and we're ready to start when you are, sir."

Black gazed out of the window across to the private residences above the skyscraper Hilton Hotel on Deansgate, wondering when she would contact him.

The meeting started with matters arising. Group figures were analysed, and company reports reviewed.

The Chief Executive Officer asked the MD of Black Construction where the provision for a potential half a million pound penalty was in his balance sheet. As the man shifted uncomfortably in his seat, it was agreed that the CEO and his PA (also known as the director without portfolio, or Roger Courtney) would be kept fully informed as and when matters arose which were outside the agreed project plan for this build – and any other build, for that matter.

There were ongoing concerns about the running of one of the subsidiaries at Black Communications, and Black decided he needed to sort the situation out and would fly to China to visit the management team in two weeks.

Fuck it! he thought in the back of the Bentley on his way to collect John from school. He now had to consider the most efficient way to get halfway round the world, sort out a bloody management team who couldn't be left to organise a piss-up in a brewery, and arrange for John to be well cared for. He realised it would be a while before he could spend some time with Grace.

Returning to Arnford Hall, he was surprised how calm he felt with John in the car beside him. Yes, his son was his daylight and he loved him more than anything in the world.

Chapter 36

It was Thursday morning and a bedroom was being prepared for Julian. Gabriel didn't want it to appear as though he had already decided that Julian should move back to Arnford Hall. It would be better all round if Julian believed he had made his own decision to do so. Therefore, the sleeping arrangements needed to appear temporary, and a couple of enticements put in place so that Julian Black was kept in a good mood and made to feel happy back at the Hall. The first thing was to suggest that if he came back onto the board, he could afford to have a nice car – a very nice car – and Gabriel was already dangling this particular carrot in the form of the Lamborghini. The second thing was to help him remember what a good time he could have at Arnford Hall, and so a gambling night (or two) would be arranged; this would take careful planning now that John lived there, and the involvement of a certain school teacher could be useful, not to mention it would definitely cheer Gabriel up. Finally, the third thing to do was to ensure that Julian Black did not, in any way, feel that he was at risk of being dragged into his twin brother's nightmare. Gabriel would need to set time aside to talk to his younger (by twenty minutes) brother, to reassure him, promise him that it would be OK. Gabriel himself would need to prepare for this little tête-a-tête.

Having taken John to school, Gabriel drove to Knutsford, to the Cottons Hotel where Ellouise was staying until the house purchase was complete. He had been surprised at how easily she accepted his proposal; maybe she recognised it was time for changes in her life too. Big brother had also made her realise what a huge mistake she would have made, had she gone to the States with the lowlife drug addict, as she had tried to do. She promised she wouldn't pull a stunt like that again, at least not without talking to Gabriel first.

"Are you ready?" he asked, watching his younger sister float around the room, grabbing a sandal, painting her lips, putting her second earring in … as chaotic as ever. *Can she really help look after John? She can barely look after herself!* But he remembered what a competent IT systems expert she was when she put her mind to it.

"I thought I was to come over in my car. Do you want to make some tea while you're waiting? How's John?"

"I want you to come with me and then I'll know where you are." He waited for her chastising look and smiled. "Just hurry up, Ellouise, there's no time for tea, and John's fine. He's getting excited about the party tonight. I think he'll have a shock when he sees Julian."

"Have you told him about you two?"

"Don't stop getting ready," he ordered, resigning himself to waiting for her as she continued to get ready. "I'm going to talk about it in the car later when I pick him up. And I need you to be supportive of Julian. I want him to stay."

Now she did stop. She looked at him and her eyes asked the question her lips wouldn't.

"It's OK, Ellouise. I want him to want to stay and I'll make sure that he will be willing to do so. I want him involved in the business." He paused and studied her expression. "But leave that to me. I want him to be happy to be back and for us all to have a good time tonight. Now finish getting ready. You have five minutes," and he pointed to his black and gold Graff watch.

Five minutes later they were leaving the hotel and heading to Arnford Hall.

As they were approaching a busy junction, Ellouise spoke. "Is Grace coming?" She felt brave enough to ask her brother this question, knowing he needed to concentrate on the road and wouldn't be able to scrutinise her too much.

Keeping his eyes on the traffic ahead, Gabriel frowned, knowing exactly what his sister was doing.

"No."

He had wanted to summon her (*ask her?*) but he knew he wouldn't want to let her go. He also knew she was a distraction from his work, and right now he needed to focus on his objectives, Julian and China included.

Ellouise broke into his thoughts. "What about her necklace?"

Now he did turn to her. His lips opened and then shut tightly.

Eyes back on the road, voice controlled and in a matter-of-fact tone, he asked, "What do you mean?"

"Have you left it on? What about her Jason?" The sister remembered his question to Grace in their game of dare to bare.

He had intended to take the necklace off her in the car on Friday, like last time. But perhaps he could make them both feel good, himself by having the pleasure of seeing her this evening, and Grace by being released from him early … He began to feel uncomfortable at the thought of Grace with Jason.

And was he ready for her to meet Julian yet?

"I'll think about it."

Ellouise knew the rest of the journey would be made in silence; even she didn't want to intrude into his thoughts. But at some point, she wanted to question her brother about his latest relationship: the necklace, the sanctuary, Jason …

Chapter 37

Just as her lunch break was coming to an end, the phone in Grace's bag trilled. She was sufficiently in control this time for no one to think anything of seeing her check it for a message, nor did she display any facial expression which could cause any concern as she read:

Sender: Gabriel Black

Message: The car will collect you at 5.45 p.m. Do not eat beforehand – unless you want to have two evening meals. Your dress will be waiting.

She went straight to her classroom and thought no more about his summons, but not before an image of being tied to a dining chair and force-fed flashed before her eyes.

Before she knew it, her school day was over and she was alone in the back of the Bentley, wondering what he had planned: tea with John and then sex? For some unknown reason, she suddenly began to contemplate the fact he could be seeing other women; how could she be sure the sex they were having was safe? He had only asked if she was on the pill. He had a reputation as a ladies' man, and she knew it wasn't a "one at a time" reputation. She needed to check this out; she was going to be at it with Jason this weekend. She hoped.

Do you really? Yes!

As Arnford Hall loomed in front of them, her eyes widened when she spotted a yellow Lamborghini on the driveway. *Wow, he's got a new car! Maybe we're going for a spin? Somewhere nice … he said my dress was waiting for me!*

Suddenly all feelings of deceiving Jason were forgotten in the thrill of being in yet another fast car.

You're in for a shock, sniggered the gargoyles.

Grace was surprised more than shocked as Roger opened the door.

"Hi, Grace. It's good to see you. Gabriel has asked if you could get dressed for dinner. We will be sitting down at seven." As he saw her puzzled expression, he added, "I'll be in the kitchen if you need me."

She followed him through the vestibule, and saw him hesitate when he reached the door to her sanctuary. Then he carried straight on and she knew he didn't expect her to follow him.

She unlocked the door and closed it behind her.

As she looked over at the bookshelves, she saw the Biba dress hanging from the rails, and her new shoes on the floor.

Well, it would seem she was not going to be driven in the Lamborghini. And dressing for dinner seemed a bit formal for tea with John. Now she really was curious.

It was six o'clock, and suddenly she didn't want to be in here alone; she wanted to know what was happening. She wanted to chat with Roger and Steve; that always seemed to make her feel more comfortable.

Leaving the door to her sanctuary open, she made her way down to the kitchen, feeling a little more relaxed as she heard the familiar voices coming from inside.

Walking in, she saw Steve deftly removing the skin from fillets of salmon. There were various cups and dishes holding a variety of ingredients and he was obviously preparing something special; from the quantity of fish in front of him, it was not just for four adults and a small child.

He looked up and smiled. "Hi, Grace."

Oh, how she wished this could just be a friendly gathering, in which she would be just another happy participant.

"Hi. Where's John?" she asked.

"Walking Satan, with Ellouise and Gabriel."

"Oh." She looked lost for a moment.

"Let me get you a drink." Roger approached her, carrying a large empty vase, which he rested on the island as he went to the fridge.

"Water is fine, thanks. Can I get it?" She felt like a spare part.

"No, it's OK," and he let iced water flow from the fridge door compartment into a crystal tumbler.

A young woman walked in, dressed in black and white and carrying a huge bunch of white oriental lilies, a peppering of gypsophila and several large Kentia palms. She took the vase from the island and walked into one of the rooms off the kitchen, presumably to create a floral display. Grace couldn't comprehend the different functions of so many rooms, but clearly the staff here did.

She felt very conspicuous sipping her water in the midst of the activity going on around her, and asked if she could help in any way.

"You're a guest, Grace. Relax." Roger took a handful of cotton napkins from a drawer and walked out of the kitchen, leaving her to ponder the irony of being called a guest.

Then she heard his footsteps, and got up from her stool, turning to stare at him. He was wearing white denim trousers, a long-sleeved white shirt, open at the neck, and a cream waistcoat with fully fastened mother of pearl buttons encased in circles of silver. White leather brogues completed the catwalk vision. His black hair made a magnificent contrast to all the white.

He looks incredible, but why is he making such a statement? This isn't like him!

"Hello, sir." She said it before she was even conscious of doing so. *Hell, he's got you well trained now!*

"Oh, I like the title. Hello, madam." He paused as he beamed at her.

Steve looked up and laughed, waving his large and very sharp-looking knife.

Grace looked puzzled for a moment and then she felt her jaw drop as Gabriel walked in, dressed in one of his black Hugo Boss dinner suits with a stark white shirt, dark grey bow tie and crocodile skin shoes.

"Hello, Grace. I see you have met my brother, Julian."

She stared from one to the other. Their height, build, hair, facial features … all were identical.

"Proper introductions, please," and the white Black looked pointedly at the black Black and walked over to take Grace's hand.

She pulled back slightly as he raised it to his lips and kissed it, bowing as he stepped back. Then she caught Gabriel's eye and he was startled to see a pleading look in them. He immediately walked over to her and took her hand, saying, "Introductions can wait. Come on, Grace. Time to get you dressed." He felt something surge up inside him as she actually squeezed his hand.

He led the way to her sanctuary in silence and stopped at the open door.

"I'll wait for you in the octagonal room." He pointed to the end of the hallway, and then left her.

Grace closed the door and sank onto the sofa. *Oh, my gosh, there are two of them!* She had never met identical twins before, and could not get the vision of the two brothers out of her head. Thank goodness they weren't dressed the same, and suddenly the fear of getting them mixed up filled her with dread. There was something about Julian … he looked like someone who wanted everyone to think he was untouchable, but who wasn't really. He was not the same as Gabriel; Gabriel Black was untouchable. Yet for some reason Julian scared her even more than Gabriel did.

She suddenly realised she had needed to hold his hand in the kitchen, to feel that he was protecting her. And she wanted to see him again, now.

Hurriedly she changed into the dress and discarded her underwear. She glanced at her face in her little compact mirror, and tried as best she could with the small image of herself to ensure that her hair was presentable and make-up unsmudged. Then she slipped on the Dune sandals and walked as quickly as she dared to the room at the end of the long hall.

She practically flung the large white oak door open and gazed at him as he turned away from the window to face her.

"Are you all right, Grace?" he asked, noticing how pale she looked.

"I ... I'm fine," she lied. She felt anything but fine. "Why have you brought me here?"

He didn't move away from the window, nor did he take his eyes off her.

"I'm asking myself the same question. It was Ellouise's suggestion, actually. She reminded me I needed to take your necklace off; to let you get ready to go to Jason."

Grace noticed a frown flash over his face at the mention of her boyfriend's name.

He immediately regained his composure. "And I want you to meet my brother. If all goes to plan, you would meet him anyway. I'm hoping he's going to come back to stay. With John in my life now" – he stopped short of adding "and you" – "I will need help with the business. And Julian is actually very good at it. When he puts his mind to it."

"Where has he been?"

"All over the world. Patagonia of late. Let's hope he's got it out of his system. Come on. They'll be waiting for us to join them. This will be the first time my brother and sister and I have been together in over five years."

He walked over to her and took her hand. He leaned into her and lightly swept his lips across her neck below her right ear and whispered, "It suits you, you know ... the necklace."

Then he led her through interconnecting doors into the dining room.

Julian, Ellouise, John, Roger and Steve were all assembled, the adults sipping champagne and John drinking water from his Star Wars cup. He was telling his new Uncle Julian about his yellow *Sea Knight*, which Daddy had taught him to sail. In his heart of hearts, John *knew* that his daddy was really taller than Uncle Julian, no matter what anyone said. He would always know the difference.

They all turned to see Gabriel and Grace enter the room, and Roger watched with interest as Grace, still holding the master of the house's hand, was formally introduced to Julian.

"I'm sorry for the unkind trick earlier." Julian took a glass of champagne from the tray proffered by one of the members of the Black staff assigned to look after them this evening, and handed it to Grace. From Steve's smart appearance, in a black suit with deep purple shirt and grey tie artistically splashed with purple, his work for the day was done.

"I'm afraid the Black twins were always playing tricks on unsuspecting business partners, not to mention girlfriends." Roger's eyes twinkled as he stood next to Grace. "But I'll let you into a little secret. If you look closely at Julian's jaw line, just on the left side, there is a small scar, more visible if you can get him to laugh."

Julian rubbed his hand over his jaw and grinned. "And I can remember how I got it." He shot an accusatory look at Gabriel. "Nicked me with the bloody sword, he did."

Gabriel frowned and looked at John.

"Sorry," mouthed Julian. "I can see I'm going to have to get used to quite a few changes around here," he added.

"Let's sit down to eat." Gabriel took his son's hand and led him to the table.

Gabriel sat at the head of the table, with John on his right and Julian on his left. To Grace's surprise she was asked to sit next to John, with Ellouise at her other side. Roger and Steve sat opposite them.

Grace was amazed at how easily the conversation flowed, with Julian talking about his travels, going into great detail describing his stay in Africa and encounters with lions for John's benefit. She encouraged John to talk about what they had been doing in school, including working on a project about volcanoes, and Ellouise was complimenting Steve on the salmon, including the fish finger version he had put together especially for John, despite Gabriel trying to insist the seven-year-old should eat the same as everyone else.

After a dessert of key lime pie with mango and yogurt sorbet for the adults, and chocolate brownie with chocolate ice cream for John, Gabriel excused himself from the table and took his son to bed.

The remaining diners continued to sip an Italian Brachetto D'Acqui, a sweet, fizzy red dessert wine, which Grace discovered tasted delicious, before walking across the hallway into the drawing room.

Despite having had two glasses of champagne and a glass of the dessert wine, Grace was feeling remarkably in control of herself and preferred to listen to the chatter going on around her rather than engage in it too deeply. She thought it was a rare opportunity to find out a little more about her captor, though she did admit to having labelled him her protector earlier in the evening.

Mindful of the duplicity of her role here, or perhaps because she didn't know any of them very well, Grace remained quiet as Ellouise commented on how well her older brother was coping with fatherhood, and how proud she was of him. She also declared her belief that he would need some help now: "… despite trying to hold this family together single-handedly for the last seven years, not to mention the business he has built up, with your help, of course, Roger." Her expression became serious as she glanced from Roger to Julian. "I think we owe him that, don't you?"

Julian looked at Roger.

"I'm sure he could do with some help at Black Holdings. Support on the board, maybe …" Roger was clearly sowing the seed Gabriel had wanted to be planted.

"Well, he has always been our sort of father figure," and Julian grinned as he looked at Ellouise, adding, "Let's hope John isn't quite so errant as we've been, hey sis?"

Ellouise smiled back, but couldn't hide the expression of guilt on her face.

Had these two given Gabriel Black a hard time? Well, he was certainly no angel; Grace could testify to that. What sort of a family was this? Were they just crazy? Or were they all disturbed in some way?

Then Ellouise stood up, a little unsteadily after the amount of alcohol she had consumed, and said bitterly, "Let's hope he doesn't have to live through what we bloody did." She walked over to the sideboard and started to pour some whisky into a tumbler.

Roger immediately went over to assist her – and perhaps to reduce the quantity destined for the glass.

Suddenly everyone turned to listen to the school teacher.

"I feel I know John as well, if not better ..." she glanced at Julian and Ellouise as she continued, "than most of you, and I have to say he is a lovely, intelligent young boy, with a confidence and ability beyond his years. Considering he has lost his mother at such a young age, and is only just getting to know his father, it's amazing how well he has coped. And I know a lot of that is down to the love and attention his father is giving him. I guess, in one way, his life has changed as much as his son's, and I think he's coping brilliantly."

She stopped. *Why the fuck am I praising him?* She thought of Gabriel's words earlier this evening: *... I'm hoping he is going to come back to stay. With John in my life now, I will need help with the business ...*

"You're right, of course." Roger sat back down again.

Julian looked directly at her. "And are you good for my brother, Grace?"

She shuddered as she heard the familiar voice, intonation, accent, just as if Gabriel had asked her himself. "I ... er ... I'm not sure."

"Oh, but you are, Grace." Ellouise appeared to have calmed down a bit now.

"You must be one very tough cookie." After saying this, Julian suddenly fell silent.

Grace knew Gabriel had returned to the room before she saw him.

"And why is that?" Gabriel walked in with what looked like a glass of water in his hand.

"To put up with you!" As Julian looked at his brother, Grace sensed a strong bond between these two brothers. She felt instantly that they shared everything – *including his secret?*

Suddenly she stood up, and everyone stared at her.

Roger looked at Gabriel and then got up and walked over to Grace.

"Do you fancy a walk?" Roger asked and, taking her hand, he led her over to one of the French doors leading out into the garden and pushed it open, leaving Grace no time to think about saying no.

Gabriel didn't move for a second as he watched them disappear. Then he sat down on the sofa next to Steve.

"We need to arrange a games night. What do you think, Julian?" As he spoke, Gabriel's eyes were still fixed on the door, betraying his concern.

"I'm definitely up for it. Looks like I may be around for a while." Julian looked from his brother to the French door, trying to gauge just how pissed off Gabriel was.

"Me too," added Ellouise and she walked over to the sideboard again, this time opening a drawer and taking out a pack of cards. "Fancy a quick game of blackjack?"

"I'll deal," Julian declared.

The four remaining occupants of the room sat around the coffee table and played, each glad for the break in the tension created by the exit of Roger and Grace.

Roger led Grace down some steps and round to the left of the Hall. It was nine thirty and quite dark, but provided they hugged the line of the building on their walk, there was enough light to enable them to continue easily without losing their footing on the pathway. It was cool and Grace shivered a little in her silk dress.

Roger still held her hand and he raised it up in front of him, saying, half-laughing, "It's a very long time since I held a female hand. I did try, you know, to be what is expected – straight. But I wasn't. And once I came to terms with that, my life got a whole lot happier. I guess most of us have skeletons in our closets, some easier to let out than others." He let go of her hand. "Do you want to talk about anything, Grace?"

She didn't speak for a second, trying to imagine what Gabriel was doing right now, knowing full well what his PA had just done.

"I don't come here voluntarily, you know."

"We figured that out – Steve and Ellouise and I, I mean. I hoped you might have got to like him by now … seen through the controlling front he puts up. I meant what I said the other day."

She remembered his words: *But if you don't see his friendship, trust and protection, then you're not looking. Give him a chance, Grace. I think you mean more to him than you know.*

She struggled to get her own words out. "I … I don't think I mean anything to him. He threatens me, punishes me, even …" and she swallowed hard to fight back tears she didn't want to shed. "I can't balance this with the tenderness, even passion," she blushed, glad of the darkness hiding this from her companion, "that he sometimes makes me feel."

Roger stopped. They had arrived at a bench and he sat down and waited for her to sit next to him.

"You must believe me when I tell you, you do mean something to him. Even Ellouise has noticed it. We live with torment in this place, Grace, and Gabe carries that for his family, for Steve and me, even. We would never find a happier place to live, and Julian and Ellouise would have no family, if it were not for the sacrifices Gabe makes, and has been making for more than half his life now. He never dared hope to be able to see his son, and now he has him, he will not let him go, at least not unless John wants to. And things will have to change. Hell, they've already started. Since he met you, he hasn't seen another woman. And, believe me, Grace, I know monogamy has never been his thing. He won't talk to me about you; and that has never been the case before. He has always kept me informed of his relationships, in case the blackmailing starts, as you can imagine. But not this time. I can't get through to him, at least not yet. But I hate to think what it will do to him if you stop coming here."

She stood up, feeling indignant towards this man, who was showing pity for his employer, friend – ex-lover, for all she knew!

"Hang on a minute. What about me, my life, which he …" She hesitated, on the verge of saying "has threatened to ruin", but felt it would be too difficult to explain. Gabriel Black was right; it needed to be their little secret!

"Well, talk to me, Grace. Let me try to help you …"

She stared out into the blackness across the fields before them. "I can't talk. I've been tormented and lost my family too. His family is inside now, reunited after five years, is it? I have a brother somewhere I haven't seen for over fifteen years. And society won't let me see him ever again. You are the protector, Roger, you are protecting him. I have no one."

She sat back down and started to wring her hands.

Roger placed his hand over hers. "I'm sorry, Grace, truly. I can only express my feelings for what I know. Let me help you. And I swear to God, Gabe would want to help you too. Maybe not when he first met you; he probably thought you would just be another challenge, someone to be conquered. He feels he has to control, dominate people even, and his relationships with women haven't exactly been your average boyfriend/girlfriend sort of thing. But I don't think he feels that with you. And he seems to be trying to come to terms with that realisation himself. I think he's scared and I think you're the one scaring him …"

She interrupted him with a laugh. "Ha, I think you're confusing him with a real human being!"

"Grace. Please give me a chance to talk to him. Hell, he's going to want my balls tomorrow for bringing you out here tonight." Now it was his turn to laugh, and Grace knew the man next to her was not afraid of Gabriel Black. "But he will listen to me. Please."

"I like you, Roger, and I really appreciate the friendship you and Steve have shown me. But your boss has serious issues. And I think he is killing me inside." After a moment's silence she added, "I need to go now. I need him to let me go."

"I don't think he will. And I don't think we want him to. You have become a part of us now, Grace McGuire. We just need to figure out a way for this to work for you, for him, for all of us. Come on, let's get back." He held his hand out, to see if she would take it. She did.

As they walked back in through the French door, it was Gabriel's turn to stand up. He looked questioningly at Roger, but Roger just turned to Steve. "Is now a good time to go home, honey?"

"Before he wins the shirt off my back," Steve smiled first at Roger and then at Gabriel. "Yes. Training tomorrow night, sir."

He took Roger's hand and everyone shouted "goodnight" as the only married couple in the room departed.

Gabriel looked down at the cards. "I think we're done, guys. I'm glad you're here, Julian," and Grace watched as Julian stood up and the two men hugged. She heard Julian say quietly, "I'm glad too, GeeBee."

"Come on, sis." Julian took Ellouise's hand and they left the room to go to their own bedrooms.

"Thanks for the car, by the way. Fucking gorgeous! I guess it's got to go back tomorrow?"

Gabriel nodded. "But I have a proposition for you. In the morning."

Ellouise kissed her older brother and then he and Grace were left alone.

He looked at her for a moment, wearing his impenetrable mask, before saying, "Turn around, Grace." As she did so, she felt him unlock the collar and he held it in his hand, gently rubbing his fingers along the prominent thread of golden ribbon. "I'll take you home now."

Grace didn't speak. She let him lead her out of the Hall, open the car door for her, wait until she was seated, and close it again. He got in the driver's seat.

"Are you OK to drive?" she asked quietly.

"Yes. I only had one glass of champagne. I wanted my wits about me to deal with my family tonight." He turned to face her, still not having put his key in the ignition, and was going to say, "and to be with you". But he knew he was screwing up. He knew he was losing her. He knew the only way he could keep her was to continue to act like the bastard he no longer wanted to be.

"My clothes!" she exclaimed suddenly, realising she still had the dress on and that her own clothes, including her underwear, were in her sanctuary.

"It's OK. I can arrange to have them delivered to you tomorrow."

"I want them now." *Why?*

She realised that she wasn't quite ready to leave him yet.

What is this torment he bears?

211

Why would he need a sanctuary?
Why does he live in a nightmare?
Am I his breaking dawn?

"Now?" he asked, startling her from her thoughts.

"Yes, now." She was determined not to let him intimidate her.

He got out of the car and scratched his head, as he realised she remained in the car, waiting for him to open her door.

They climbed the steps, and she smiled at the gargoyles as they giggled, *Oh, you little minx, go for it girl!* She felt like a twenty-year-old.

She unlocked the door to her sanctuary and walked in. He stood in the doorway and leaned against the doorjamb, his eyes closed. Then he opened them and looked at her, a stillness hanging in the air.

"You're welcome to come in." No "sir".

"Are you sure?" This was not expected.

"Yes." She turned her back on him and said, "Take a seat."

He watched her as he sat on the sofa, and a smile started to creep over his lips as she went to the door, closed it and locked it.

"Your rules don't apply in here. So no punishments." She raised her eyebrows at him.

"No punishments," he said quietly, the smile steadily replaced by a hungry look as she lifted the dress over her head.

"You know what I want you to do to me," she said in a sultry voice he hadn't heard her use before.

He stood up, beginning to realise she was playing his game. "Is that an order?" he asked.

Now she smiled. "Does it have to be?"

"No." He slowly took his jacket off and placed it on the armchair. His bow tie followed and he unbuttoned his shirt, removed his cufflinks and slid the shirt from his back.

Then she reached him and slowly began to unfasten his belt and trousers. She lowered herself onto her knees as she slid the trousers down his legs, her hands trailing over his thighs and down his shins and calves.

As he stepped out of the trousers, she stood up and stepped back to admire him in his black Hugo Boss trunks. She ran her fingers over the soft cotton, aware of him bulging to escape the fabric, and she heard his gasp as she slowly moved her hand inside and stroked his penis, lowering her head to gently kiss his tip.

"Grace ..." He pulled her up.

"Gabriel ..." It was the first time she had called him by his name, and she looked up to see an unexpected moistness in his eyes. She raised her hand and closed them, stroking their lids, and he leaned down and kissed her gently, as if she would break.

Then he lifted her in his arms, placed her on the sofa and removed his trunks. He lay down beside her and his fingers gently traced a line down her neck, over her shoulder and across to her breasts. He lightly circled her nipples and Grace sighed softly from the pleasure of his gentle touch. He moved his head lower and licked and sucked the brown buds as they lengthened and hardened. At the same time he slid his hand down to her waist, over her hip and cupped her pubis. His lips sought the soft nape of her neck and he nuzzled, luxuriating in the taste of her. Then he placed his fingers at the edge of her vagina, lingering for a moment to enjoy the feel of the folds of her skin, before moving them inside to prepare her. She was already wet. He pushed his penis into her, continuing to kiss her neck, his lips hungry, devouring her. His mouth returned to her breasts, sucking hard on her nipples, biting at their hardness, and she relished the delicious pain, feeling his desire for her. He began to thrust, easing out and then ramming back in, trying to get deeper and deeper, and his fingers desperately sought her trigger, rolling and strumming her clitoris with increasing intensity.

"Come for me, Grace, I need this so much. Come for me." He was desperate for her to orgasm, driven by his own desire, sucking her breasts harder as she moaned in exquisite abandon, getting closer and closer to where he ordered her to go.

She screamed and he gasped; she screamed and he gasped; she screamed and he was wasted.

An hour later she woke to feel him close by her side, pinning her to the sofa.

"Time to take me home," she muttered as she gently shook him.

He stirred and lay there a moment before he realised where he was; what he had done. And what she had done.

Quickly he dressed. Then, turning to leave the room, he said in a low voice filled with regret, "I'll wait at the door," and he left her to dress, staring after him and wondering what mood he was now in.

He was not in control, and he didn't like it. She had a hold on him, and he didn't like it. He had been in her sanctuary, and he didn't like it. Despite trying to forget, he remembered his own need of a sanctuary, and he slammed his fist down on the stone wall and waited for the blood to trickle down the side of his hand.

The journey to her small house on Willow Lane passed in silence. He got out of the car, opened her door, walked her up the path and waited until she went inside.

"Goodbye, Grace," he said as he turned and strode back to his Bentley.

She stared after the red lights as they disappeared into the distance.

Had she gone too far this evening? Roger had said he wouldn't let her go; for the first time since her entrapment, Grace wasn't so sure, and as she walked upstairs she asked herself how she would feel if it ended.

On returning to the Hall, Gabriel entered his son's bedroom and kissed the top of his head. He felt calmer. His duty to love and protect this young boy was his gift, his reason for living now. All his yearning for a woman he could never have, and didn't deserve to have, was pushed to the recesses of his mind.

In his en-suite he rinsed the blood from his hand and then climbed into bed through the heavy drapes, lying naked in the dark on the top of the bedclothes.

He had sinned too much to expect happiness, and he awaited his punishment.

Part Two

Chapter 38

The twins were due home from Eton for the summer. Nanny was making sure their bedrooms were ready, with sports kits in the drawers and their equipment in the garage. The tennis courts had been resurfaced and a brand new fencing piste had been installed in the games room as a surprise from their father.

They would be disappointed that their father had not gone to collect them; one of the rare occasions when he drove himself was to the school to bring his children home each holiday. But that was going to change, and Mr and Mrs Black were preparing to tell the boys about their father's illness – an illness which would affect all of them.

The two fifteen-year-olds ran up the steps and Gabriel hesitated as he heard the gargoyles whisper sadly, *It's such a shame, such a shame.* Then he ran after Julian.

"Hi Poppa, Mother, we're home …" They flung their coats over the nearest busts and raced downstairs to raid the kitchen for food, Gabriel just making it before his younger twin.

"Here you go, now get upstairs to your parents, they're waiting to see you in the drawing room." Cook presented them with a tray of chocolate brownies. They took two each and headed back upstairs.

"What happened to you then, Poppa? We missed you in the car." Gabriel hesitated as his father remained seated in his chair by the window. This was the first time ever he hadn't come over to hug, high-five, or even whack them over the head if the mood suited him. But to just sit there?

"Sit down, boys, and finish your brownies. And mind you don't get crumbs everywhere." George Black spoke quietly. He was tired, even though it was only half past three in the afternoon.

Julian looked at their mother, in her pale blue silk dress, with a red ribbon around her waist, and scarlet red lips and nails, as immaculate as ever. He went to sit next to her on the four-seater sofa.

"I'm afraid I have had a bit of bad news and we need to talk about it, as a family." Their father commanded the twins' full attention.

"What about Ellouise?" asked Gabriel.

"Your mother and I will talk to her later; she's not home for another couple of days. We need to speak to you first."

At that point Nanny walked into the room. The boys stood up and respectfully waited for a hug from their lifelong companion and confidante. Then she joined Julian and his mother on the sofa and Gabriel sat on the chair opposite his father. He started to pull at a piece of cotton on his navy trousers.

"Don't fidget, Gabriel!" his mother scolded and Gabriel put his hands behind his head, resting his ankle on his other knee.

George continued. "I have been diagnosed with motor neurone disease. I'm going to die. But not quite yet."

There was silence.

"When?" asked Gabriel.

"It could be in a year … or three, five, maybe even longer."

"We don't know," said Mother.

"And it's not worth worrying about. We have to be strong for each other," said Nanny.

"I'm going to my room." With that, Gabriel got up and left them, closing the door behind him. In the solitude of his bedroom, he pulled the medical dictionary from his shelf and began to read:

A rare neurological disorder … causing the degeneration of the motor system … cells of the brain and spinal cord … results in weakness and wasting of the muscles … is progressive and symptoms worsen over time … severely reduces life expectancy … most sufferers die within five years.

Main symptoms:

Muscle wasting, often first noticed in one hand or arm or leg

Muscle weakness, difficulty in opening jars, carrying heavy objects, climbing stairs

Involuntary contractions of part of a muscle, twitches

Speech problems

Swallowing problems, excessive saliva (drooling)

Cramps and muscle spasms

Muscles weakening in chest, back and neck

Most people experience difficulties with breathing

Does not affect intellect

There is no cure.

There is no cure. There is no cure. There is no cure. There is no cure. There is no cure. There is no …

For now, the fifteen-year-old with dreams of being a doctor could read no more.

Julian knocked on his door and walked in.

"Are you OK, GeeBee?"

"Not really. What about you?"

"What does your dictionary say?"

"Fuck it!" exclaimed Gabriel as he passed the book to Julian. *Our father is already dead.*

"He wants to talk to us after dinner. Alone."

Gabriel looked at his younger twin. "Why?"

"I don't know. Fancy a game of tennis?"

"Sure. Let me whip your butt ..."

"I don't think so …" and the brothers quickly changed into tennis whites and ran out of the house.

After dinner that evening, they went into their father's office. He told them to close the door. He poured a large whisky into one of the crystal tumblers at his bar. Then he turned to them and smiled, "Don't tell your mother, hey," and poured them each a small one.

They sat down as conspirators, the twins sipping their forbidden drink slowly, trying not to cough and splutter.

"I have something to ask of you. I get very tired and often my muscles ache and I get cramps. I can't do things I could do a month ago. This is not easy for your mother."

Cynthia Black was ten years younger than her husband, and had become a mother at the age of twenty. She was now a very energetic, horny and sensual thirty-five-year-old. She needed sex.

"I don't want her to go around having sex with other men. I need to know where she is and who she is with."

Gabriel gulped down the remains of his whisky and spluttered into his hand, wiping it on his black dinner trousers. He waited for Poppa to continue.

"I need you two to help, to keep our family together. I want you to … look after her."

"For fuck's sake!" Gabriel stood up and slammed his fist on his father's desk.

Julian remained seated, watching his brother.

"I want you to promise me that you will look after her and make sure she gets what she needs."

"And if we don't?" Gabriel raised his voice and there was a new horror at the back of his eyes.

"Then our family will break up. We will not be the strong, proud, united Black family of our ancestors." He took a small sip of his golden liquor and savoured its taste.

"We're fucking virgins, Poppa." Gabriel was close to tears as his father's death flashed before his eyes, and at that moment he knew he would do anything Poppa asked of him.

Then George Black did something he had never done in front of his children before. He cried.

The boys knelt at his feet and shared his grief.

Nobody in the Black household slept well that night.

Julian crept into his brother's bedroom at one o'clock, and slid into his bed beside him, seeking comfort and reassurance that something would save them and everything would be OK in the morning. Gabriel hugged him and ordered him to try to sleep, though he himself could not. When he finally did, he had a nightmare about raping his brother, and they both awoke in the early hours, wet from their mingled sweat.

Nanny lay awake, not certain, but suspecting why George Black had summoned his sons after dinner that evening. She knew Mrs Black too well. Nanny wasn't sure if she could cope with what was happening in the house. But she did know she couldn't abandon her children; not now, when they needed her the most.

George lay uncomfortably next to his wife, worried whether he was doing the right thing, desperate to ensure that she would stay faithful to him – in both life and death – and determined to be strong to support his children as they continued to grow and mature, while he still could.

Cynthia lay awake and thought about tomorrow.

The next day the gamekeeper took the twins shooting and for a few hours they forgot about everything else and focused on who could bag the most rabbits. They had a picnic in the field and didn't return to the house until late afternoon, leaving time for a quick shower before an early dinner at six.

Shortly after dinner, they were summoned to the room which was to become their mother's second bedroom.

They wore black pyjama bottoms with contrasting vests, Gabriel's grey and Julian's dark green. Their mother wore an ivory silk negligée.

"Take your pyjamas off boys. Come on, let's not be shy. It's just like getting ready to go swimming."

It seemed a simple request, really, as the Black family frequently swam naked together, and walked around the bedrooms and bathrooms, confident with their own and each other's nudity.

But this was nothing like getting ready to go swimming, or prancing around the house naked.

The twins had no idea what to do.

Cynthia Black had snorted some cocaine just before they arrived, and now she just wanted to get laid. She had told George that she couldn't live without sex and, if he didn't sort something out for her – well, she would go and find someone herself. After all, she had done it on more than one occasion in the past. Her husband had found out about three affairs over

220

the years and each time he forgave her and paid lawyers – and lovers – to keep it out of the press. His honour, and the family name, were more important to George Black than anything in the world. Including even the innocence of his sons and the loving relationship they had every right to expect from their mother.

George himself had suggested the twins – their strong handsome boys, who would have done anything for their mother or father, and it seemed like a solution. He could think of no other way to keep his wife satisfied and faithful, and the family name unsullied. Surely, with love and understanding, it could do the twins no harm?

"Let's just get undressed together, darlings." Cynthia let her negligée fall to the floor.

The Black twins' nightmare, the family secret, had begun.

Their father showed them their reward the next morning: their very own fencing piste, a specially marked strip, complete with electronic recording apparatus.

"Put on a show for your mother and me. We would like that."

Gabriel stared at his father. "How can we, Poppa? Nothing can be normal now."

"Yes, Gabriel, it can. And we will make it so. Far worse things happen in families, son. Let's just get on with it, shall we?"

It was hardly ever spoken about again, and during the day life continued as normal as possible, as they all tried to adjust to their father's increasing incapacity, and ensure that he was stimulated mentally, sharing the joys of his children, their achievements at Eton (and later at Oxford) for the boys and Wycombe Abbey then Cambridge for Ellouise, their sporting challenges and victories, and holidays. On very rare occasions the parents got to meet some of their offspring's friends too. But not many.

Gabriel and Julian's lives revolved around a system of "punishment and reward".

When they were at home, the boys knew what was expected of them. There was an unwritten timetable for their evening obligations. Father mostly went to his own bed. Ellouise would work in her bedroom, swim in their pool or chat with Nanny, who was always glad of the company of one of her charges.

During term time, their mother made allowances for the boys and tried not to visit her sons too often; just twice a month or so each.

George Black was approaching death as his sons celebrated their twenty-fifth birthday. It was a small family affair, with no friends, just Nanny.

As the men sipped port in the smoking room, Gabriel spoke to his father about the business. Gabriel was concerned that he needed help, at a senior level, to continue to grow the business. He had forsaken a medical career and had studied economics and management at Oxford. He had just been made Chief Executive Officer of the Black Group, the youngest man in the country running such a large business empire, but he needed support. Julian was excellent, with his background in law, but Gabriel had a feeling his twin brother wasn't going to be around for the long term; he expected to lose his brother just as surely as he was going to lose his father.

"Get recruiting, son. Make sure it is the right guy for you, your number two."

And so, six months later, Gabriel welcomed Roger Courtney onto the board of Black Holdings, as director without portfolio and his own personal assistant.

Roger's background was in international law; he was an expert in his field, had a photographic memory, was a keen fencer and was someone who showed compassion. He was two years older than his employer.

After the first week, working very closely together at Black HQ in Manchester, Gabriel invited his PA for a drink and a bite to eat at the Midland Hotel. At nine o'clock they booked a suite, cancelled all their appointments for the next two days and they started a passionate, experimental affair.

Roger was homosexual but hadn't yet met the right guy. Gabriel didn't want to be heterosexual – he didn't want to be with a woman, unable to stop thinking about his mother. With Roger, sex was new, exciting and safe; his head was clear, he revelled in his own sensations of pleasure and mind-blowing orgasmic delight, and he loved Roger for loving him.

The following week Roger moved into Arnford Hall, into a small suite on the second floor. The two men swam naked together, fenced seriously together, shared likes in classical music, and worked very, very, very hard. They shared everything, including their deepest secrets.

As Gabriel sat with Poppa on the night he died, George Black had two requests to make of his eldest son and principal heir. It was evident that Gabriel and Roger made a formidable team and were more than capable of running the family business with assistance from Julian, Ellouise and, of course, Cynthia. Now his father needed assurance that his son was also capable of looking after his mother, to ensure she would never need to be unfaithful to her husband, even after his death, to ensure her name would always be Mrs Black.

Gabriel Black, at the age of twenty-five and a half, uttered the words, "I promise, Poppa." His face was grim, his voice without emotion and his eyes dark and lifeless. He took a little comfort in the knowledge that Julian had not had to make such a vow. And at least he had Roger in his life.

But his father had one more request.

"I'm ready now, Gabriel." And the man who had given him life, love, intelligence, wealth, fun, and a condemnation to Hell looked towards the syringe full of morphine at the bedside.

Alone, Gabriel sat in his bedroom and turned the pages of the book he had studied at Eton, *Oedipus the King*, the ancient tragedy by Sophocles, about a man who murdered his father and slept with his mother. He took his pen and scored through every page.

Then he went up to the top floor and shared Roger's bed.

As the Black siblings' relationship with their mother evolved, Gabriel's heart turned to stone, his faith in God to dust, his protection of Julian and Ellouise reached new heights, and his affair with Roger became the precious elixir that kept him alive.

He loved both his mother and father. He hated his mother too.

And so Gabriel began the next phase of his life.

At Arnford Hall he took over his parents' master bedroom and denied everyone else access to it, especially the morning room, which was accessible only from his bedroom.

His mother took up residence in her second bedroom, just across the galleried landing from his.

When she called, he came.

She gave her sons the smoking room as a sanctuary, where either of them could go and she would not permit herself to seek their company. But there were rules. There could only be one occupant at a time, and they could stay for a maximum of four hours..

Julian always seemed to manage to beat his brother to the smoking room.

So Gabriel arranged to have running water, drinks facilities and a cooling cabinet installed in there. He refused to add a toilet.

It fell more and more to Gabriel to service his mother and fulfil the promise he had made to his father.

A year later, the cook died. Roger Courtney interviewed Steve Ford as a possible replacement. He was welcomed onto the staff by Gabriel, as chef to the Arnford household, and also held in high regard as a master fencer. The four males of the house formed a close friendship, to begin with on the piste, with Steve coaching Gabriel, Julian and Roger in the ancient art of fencing. It was in a free-play duel, unsupervised, and unmasked, between the Black twins that Gabriel gave Julian the mark on his jaw that helped distinguish him from Gabriel. When they confessed what they had done to Steve, he assumed total control of the piste, and from then on they were subject to Steve's training regime, discipline and rules.

Steve Ford had another influence on life at Arnford Hall. He and Roger fell in love. Gabriel and Roger's affair had lasted just under two years, but Gabriel was beginning to seek out women, not for love but for sex. He didn't hide this from Roger – they were too honest with each other – but Roger couldn't handle this infidelity; it wasn't what he wanted.

So a love triangle developed between these three men: Roger and Gabriel remained strong friends and work colleagues;

Steve and Gabriel had mutual respect for Steve's roles as chef, subject to the command of Gabriel, and as master fencer, subject to the obedience of Gabriel; and Roger and Steve began a relationship, to finally marry in 2014, when same-sex marriage became legal.

Julian was planning to leave Arnford Hall.

Gabriel didn't actually plan anything. He just slept with women, he fucked women, he abused those who would let him; he dabbled with cocaine, heroin, ecstasy, anything he could get his hands on, but never too much, and never cheap stuff. He gambled and played poker like a pro; few wanted to be at his table. And he sought Black domination of the corporate world.

Two years after Poppa's death, at the age of twenty-seven, Julian left the Black Corporation and Arnford Hall. He had had as much as he could take. He started to have relationships with both men and women, never sure what he really wanted. But there was one thing he was sure of – he could not face one more single time in his mother's bedroom. He cried with Gabriel, begged his forgiveness, but said he always knew his older brother was stronger than him; he could survive anything, he had Roger now, and Julian would always love him. He knew about the paternal vow that bound Gabriel to his mother and the Hall, and he could never thank his brother enough for the sacrifice he had made. But Julian had to leave: he just had to.

Nanny stayed with her charges for as long as she could. She watched Julian become obsessed by his bisexuality in the most unnatural way. She watched Gabriel Black grow blacker and blacker, thanks to the drugs, the gambling, his relationship with Roger and with various women – and, of course, his mother.

Three years later, when Gabriel Black turned thirty, and with her heart breaking, Nanny had to leave: she just had to.

Her favourite charge bought her a house in the Lakes, a beautiful three-bedroomed cottage with its own English country garden, close to the large lakeside house which he bought for himself – just himself.

Ellouise had always been there for her brothers. She had shared their tears and tried to make light of their situation, asking who else was getting that much sex. She always tried to

225

make sure they all had fun together – hunting, fishing, boating, gambling, partying – and supported her brothers in their favourite pursuit of fencing; she was always there for them. And her exceptional IT skills were a valuable asset to the family business.

But, three years after that, when Gabriel Black reached thirty-three, had a son somewhere whom he was probably never going to meet, and treated numerous women like possessions (and not very valuable ones), Ellouise had to leave: she just had to.

Thus it was that Gabriel Black began the next phase to his life, sharing his home during the day with Roger and Steve, and during the night with his mother.

Cynthia finally moved out to a multi-million-pound duplex apartment in Beetham Towers above the Hilton Hotel in Manchester, overlooking, and within easy reach of, Black HQ, where she was still chairwoman.

She tried to remain faithful to her husband, and his proxy, her son. But sometimes she bent the rules slightly. Her dead husband would never know, and what her son didn't know wouldn't hurt him, surely? She began to have the occasional sex session with other men. But she still required what Gabriel had been forced to promise her. She remained a regular visitor to Arnford Hall.

Part Three

Chapter 39

It was Friday the twenty-second of September, 2017.

By half past seven that morning, Gabriel Black was in his office, after having a solitary breakfast.

He was trying to break free from his thoughts of the previous night, the dinner with the reunited Black family and Roger and Steve. And with the woman he still owned for the next three hundred and forty-eight days.

On hearing a knock, he looked up from the report he was holding, but not particularly reading, as Roger walked in and closed the door.

Gabriel had been expecting this visit. Roger had clearly been pissed off with him last night. His PA was both angry and upset at the way he perceived his boss to be treating his latest female "friend". And it was clear the Arnford household liked Grace. She wasn't like any of the others.

"I'm not sure what's going on between you and Grace." Roger stood by one of the French doors leading onto an elevated patio area, looking out into the distance at the tall trees swaying in the strong breeze. "But you are going to hear what I think, Gabe."

"Take a seat." Gabriel put the report down. His friend had his full attention.

"You need to stop your controlling game …"

There was silence.

"She thinks you're killing her. She said she needs you to let her go. I don't know why the fuck you have to be such a controlling bastard with your women, but if you don't do something, you will lose Grace. And right now I think you need her. She's good for you – for all of us. Don't drive her away by trying to keep her. Don't you think it's time things changed around here, for you and John?" He waited for a response.

Gabriel looked at the man sitting opposite him, his eyes sad and dark.

"Right now I need to keep a grip on this." Gabriel held up his report on the China business. "I need to make sure John is taken care of, get Julian back onto the board of directors, and make sure Ellouise settles down. I need Grace to be there when I want her. I need her to do what I damn well tell her …" Gabriel's voice trailed off in his last sentence. He was beginning to loathe himself even more.

"Just listen to yourself!" Roger was on his feet now. "Who the hell do you think you are, *sir*?"

Gabriel suddenly glared at him, stunned at the use of his title in such a bitter way.

"Roger, I …"

"You'll lose her, then. You don't even deserve her. But you need to be careful. You forgot to mention your biggest problem when you just listed your heavy workload. And stop feeling fucking sorry for yourself. We're all here to help you, you know. Grace, too, if you stopped trying to control her and just let her help you. She spoke up for you last night when you were putting John to bed." Roger paused before shaking his head and adding sadly, bitterness in his voice, "With permission, I want to get over to Manchester now."

"Of course." Gabriel hesitated as his PA left the room. He slammed his fist down on the desk.

He had let Grace get under his skin, into his head and, he feared, into his heart, where only his son had been allowed. Now Gabriel Black needed to regain control. He emailed a florist he frequently used and gave very precise details of a particular bouquet he wanted to be delivered. Then, blocking Roger's words from his mind, he went to find John and Ellouise.

Later that morning, Gabriel stood in the playground with Ellouise at his side, as they waited for Mrs McGuire to come and lead Year 3 into their classroom. The teacher glanced at the brother and sister. Ellouise walked over to her, expressing her pleasure at seeing her the previous night, and saying she hoped she would see her again soon. Grace was very conscious of Gabriel staring at her from across the playground. Then she saw him turn and head for the exit.

After he dropped his sister off at the hotel, Gabriel made his way home, to spend the day with Julian.

"So, what's your proposition then, GeeBee, and will it help me buy a fast car?"

Gabriel raised his eyebrow. *Impatient, self-centred sod – just how I would like to have been …*

"I'll give it to you straight, Julian. I want you back on the board. Black Holdings. You can start on a hundred and fifty grand a year, and I'll double it after the first year." Black studied the expression of his younger twin to see if he was snared yet, before adding, "With a 'welcome on board' gift of another hundred thousand. You will work your arse off for me and the company, and you report to Roger, but you'll get play time, and leave of absence for good behaviour." Now Gabriel smiled as he saw his twin's eyes shine. "You'll live here at the Hall, at least for the time being; you can have the top-floor suite and come and go as you please."

A smile was still painted on Gabriel's lips, but inside he held his breath as Julian looked at him questioningly.

"Are there other duties I'll have to take up again?" Julian's voice was almost a whisper.

"No, Julian. I have it covered." Gabriel's eyes darkened and he quickly added, in a positive tone, "You just need to get up to speed with the corporate structure and the current growth strategy. Shut yourself in the office for a month and then be prepared to get stuck in and earn your keep."

"What's the alternative?"

"You get nothing."

Julian had spent all his savings, as well as a generous monthly allowance from his brother, over the last five years while he went backpacking around the world. He had met Simon Jones in Africa, and found himself in love with a man for the first time. They travelled to Central America together, but while passing through Honduras, they were mugged. Neither of them had any money or anything of value. Simon was killed. Julian was raped and left for dead.

He was found at the roadside by a local school teacher who took him to the nearest hospital.

Not quite ready to return home, he ended his travels alone, admiring the beauty of the glaciers and mountains of Patagonia in Chile. On hearing that Gabriel wanted him back to meet his son, Julian Black had been glad of the excuse to leave South America, and accepted that it was time for him to return to England.

He discussed none of his experiences in Honduras, nor his relationship with Simon, with anybody – ever. After all, the Blacks were very good at keeping secrets.

"Where do I sign?"

Gabriel hugged his brother.

He rang Roger and confirmed that Julian had accepted the proposal Black and his PA had drafted. Roger agreed to bring the paperwork home that evening for Julian to sign.

Roger's tone then changed. "You've had a phone call, Gabe. She wants you to call her back."

Gabriel simply said, "Right. Thank you," and put the phone down.

"Get Steve to start you on a training schedule and let's have a bout on the piste tonight, before John's bedtime. Check to see if Steve and Roger can join us. I need to make some calls." With that, Gabriel went up to his bedroom and closed the door.

He took out his phone.

"Hello, Mother."

"Hello, darling. I'm sorry I missed the board meeting; I just couldn't get away in time."

I bet you couldn't!

"Get Steve to cook something delicious for dinner tonight and I'll come over. You can update me on everything."

There was silence on the end of the phone as Gabriel thought through the implications of what his mother was saying.

She didn't know that Gabriel's son was now living with him and calling him Daddy, nor that Ellouise and Julian were both in Arnford, for the foreseeable future. He had hoped he would

231

have more time to prepare for a visit from his mother, but he had known he wouldn't be able to put her off for long.

"Mother, I'm sorry, can we make it tomorrow evening? I need to do some more work tonight and it will give the chef more time to prepare meals. Let me send Michael over to collect you tomorrow about five."

"OK, Gabriel, I'll look forward to it. Until tomorrow, darling." She hung up.

Gabriel walked slowly down to the kitchen. It was noon and Steve was just preparing omelettes and salad for lunch.

The chef looked up as his employer entered the room, and immediately knew something was bothering him.

"Mrs Black will be coming over for the evening tomorrow. We'll have pheasant. Where is my brother?" Gabriel's voice mirrored his expression – emotionless, lifeless and cold.

After a slight hesitation, the chef continued with his preparations, saying,

"I think he's on the piste, trying to get some practice in for tonight."

Gabriel's face relaxed as he smiled and left to go and search for Julian; they needed to talk.

The two men sat at the bar in the games room holding tumblers filled with neat Coke; after all, they were fencing this evening.

"She'll be here about half past five. I want her to meet John."

"Do you? Really?"

"She is his grandmother, Julian. He will be our heir; the only one, most likely." Gabriel stared into his drink for a moment. "I want her to be just our mother. She hasn't seen you for five years, and it's been quite a while since she saw Ellouise. If we can't make this work, why have I put myself through purgatory? For nothing? We all agreed to this – for Poppa, for the family, Julian. I can't let that break up now. That's why I have continued to look after her all this time. She is still his widow."

"He's been dead a long time, GeeBee. You need to let her go. She needs to let you go. You have John to think of now." Julian reached out over the table and touched his brother's hand.

Gabriel thought of Roger's words: *You forgot to mention your biggest problem when you just listed your heavy workload,* and of Eliza's conditions: *The child is never to sleep at Arnford Hall when Mrs Black is in residence.* He pictured Carol and the look of curiosity on her face and he thought of Grace and her secret, with which he was cruelly manipulating her. He knew he needed to do something, but how could he live knowing he had betrayed the father whom he loved and respected more than anything else in the world? Wasn't it better simply to carry on as his father had asked him to do, and to see his mother in that forbidden way, the way she claimed to need him? He was afraid of feeling that he had let his father down, but could he hate himself any more than he already did?

And what about John? Wasn't he the justification for the change to his life? In the grips of the cruellest of deaths, would he subject John to such a despicable fate?

No. Of course he wouldn't. Never.

Gabriel looked up at Julian.

"It will be a normal family dinner. She is our mother and we will respect her. Try to enjoy it like we used to."

"And after dinner?"

"I'll take care of that." He would not confide in Julian that he intended to begin to make changes in his life, including his relationship with his mother. He didn't want his brother to worry that any responsibility would fall on him. The brothers were just about to begin living and working together again, and Gabriel did not want to jeopardise that, nor give Julian any cause to fear his own mother; not any more.

Gabriel finished his drink. "Let's go get some lunch."

Later that afternoon, when John came out of school, his father held his hand and led him to the car, not waiting to spot Grace peering through her classroom window, wondering if she would see him.

Chapter 40

At a quarter to five, just before Grace was about to leave school to go to Jason's for the weekend, the receptionist came into the staffroom.

"This has just arrived for you, Grace."

Mrs Baker was holding a large bouquet in a glass vase and shrouded in black paper, as if ready to be laid on Dracula's tomb. There were only a handful of teachers in the staffroom, and they all turned to stare at the creation.

As Mrs Baker carefully placed the vase on the table, everyone moved closer to peer over the top of the black paper.

"Oh, my goodness, it's exquisite. Beautiful, but somehow dangerous. How unusual. Is it from Jason?" Jane was teasing the paper back to expose the arrangement.

Grace felt numb, glued to the spot. She didn't need to see a card to know who had sent it. Instead of looking at the foliage poking out of the top of the paper, her eyes were transfixed on the red liquid just visible in the bottom of the vase. Was that because red was her favourite colour? Or was it to depict the blood that would pour from your fingers should you touch the vase's contents?

Grace suddenly felt as though she was in an empty room, alone with the bouquet. She couldn't hear or see anyone or anything else. Her hands moved forward and she heard his voice commanding, "Breathe, Grace," as she ripped the shroud of blackness away to reveal sprays of thorns, thistles and headless rose stems, their rich green colour amplifying the woody, fresh smell that filled her nostrils. In the middle, like a sleeping beauty protected by the pain-inflicting barrier from anyone who wanted to violate her, was an orchid. Grace stared at the blackened green stem with its single, almost transparent, orange flower, its petals protecting a small curtained anther tipped with white. It was isolated from the water in its own tiny pot. To Grace it appeared imprisoned almost as if to keep it safe from the thorns, thistles and prickles of the rest of the bouquet. Orange petals; the colour of a breaking dawn.

I wonder if you will be my breaking dawn, Grace, he had once said.

"There's a card," Mrs Baker said quietly, passing her a small envelope.

Unable to regain her composure, Grace said, "Thank you," a little shakily.

Jane moved towards her and gave her a gentle hug. "It really is exquisite, Grace. Shall I bring it to your car for you?"

"It's OK, thanks. I'll manage." She was beginning to feel a little more in control of herself, and she put the card in her bag and slung the bag over her shoulder as she picked up the vase. "Have a good weekend," she called to her colleagues, who had returned to their own tasks.

At home she sat at her kitchen table and stared at the arrangement. She opened the small envelope.

Don't let me get too close, Grace. It isn't safe for you. GB

What did he mean by that? How could she stay away from him when he kept summoning her?

She focused on gathering her things ready to go to London, but she struggled to get rid of the image of the bouquet and the blood-red water in its vase.

That evening, as Grace stepped off the train at Euston, she saw Jason waiting for her at Starbucks. They kissed and his lips lingered on hers. He declared he had missed her; it was nearly two weeks since he had seen her.

Grace noted his light brown suit, white shirt and dark brown tie, with ordinary-looking brown shoes, and his grey hair, neatly cut, no doubt following yet another visit to the barber's. His bright eyes told her he was really pleased to see her.

He noted her flat black boots, black jeans and cream Fat Face sweatshirt. Her hazel eyes, appearing somewhat distant, told him she wasn't sure about being here.

He carried her bag as they made their way across London to Putney.

"I thought we'd stay in tonight and grab a takeaway. Is that OK with you? You look a bit tired, Grace." Jason was trying to hide a nervousness that she was going to tell him something he might not want to hear.

"I'm fine. It's just been a long week and I don't seem to be able to catch up with myself at the moment. I've brought some marking to do tomorrow, if you don't mind."

"No, no problem." He thought about their rule of not working at the weekends until one of them had returned home on the Sunday afternoon; that guaranteed that they would see the most of each other and maximise the time they could share together. He couldn't recall another time when she had actually brought work with her to his flat.

"Are these a particularly difficult bunch of kids this year, then?"

"No, not really. I've just been a bit busy, that's all."

With school? Jason studied her face as they travelled on the Tube, sensing she was a hundred miles away from him. He put his arm around her, to reassure himself as much as to try to comfort her.

But Grace was more than a hundred miles away: one hundred and ninety-five miles to be precise, wondering what a small boy with black hair was doing with his father, his identical twin brother uncle, his flower-power aunty, as well as the PA and chef.

Chapter 41

That evening all the members of the Arnford Hall household were in the games room. John was sitting on the bench, next to his father. The boy's favourite colour was red and so Gabriel Black had a red band around his left arm, otherwise he was dressed completely in white – leggings and long socks, an under-plastron covering the upper part of his sword arm and his chest, a gauntlet for his sabre hand, a fencing jacket and a mask, which he currently held on his lap.

They were watching Julian, who sported a green band, and Roger, who wore a blue one.

Steve was band-less, currently acting as referee; he would fight the winner in the grand finale, though it was usually a formality. The master was rarely conquered.

John was thrilled by the tension in the room, watching the coloured scoring lights as the men concentrated on their fighting, dared on the odd occasion to question the referee and, at the end of the bout, saluted each other and respectfully shook hands.

With Roger declared the victor, Julian swapped places with Gabriel and John excitedly cheered for Daddy to win.

But, before too long, the twins were sitting on the bench and the three Blacks watched Steve beat Roger.

Fencers needed to be athletic, quick-witted and agile in both body and mind, and fully focused on the matter in hand. Julian had the excuse of being out of practice; Gabriel couldn't think of one.

After settling his son into bed, he joined the men at the bar in the games room.

"So when do we get to play poker?" asked Julian, with a glint of hopeful anticipation in his eyes.

"Why don't you try and organise a game for next month? It's still the usual suspects."

"Is it the same wager?" Julian asked mischievously, excited at the thought of being with a woman again.

"It can be." Gabriel thought of Cindy for a moment, the girl who was game for anything.

Poker at Arnford Hall usually consisted of ten players, seated at two tables. The regular attendees were Steve and Roger, Kevin, an MP, Andrew and Daniel, who were accountants, solicitors Colin and Mike, Stefan, a consultant gynaecologist, and Leo, a corporate financier. Gabriel was the tenth player and this time Julian would join them. They would each bring a guest, usually a woman, and usually one willing to participate in various wagers that were played for during the course of the evening. More often than not, the women would be bought as well as brought along for the evening.

Occasionally morality and respect were thrown to the wind and proceedings would lead to the den. These had always been Julian's favourite games nights, and Gabriel didn't want to disappoint him this time.

The next day, as Gabriel and John walked in the grounds with Satan, Gabriel asked if John would like to have a sleepover at Roger and Steve's house.

John had visited them once before, and Roger had taken pleasure in showing his young charge a small bedroom with brightly coloured wallpaper and Spiderman curtains and bedding.

"This bedroom is here just in case you ever want to come for a sleepover. That would be fun, wouldn't it, John?" Roger had asked nervously, knowing how important it was to everyone at Arnford Hall that John would be happy to sleep in this house when necessary: when Mrs Black would be in residence. Gabriel and Roger had tried to ensure the décor and furnishings were similar to those in John's bedroom in the house he had shared with his mother. They had been delighted when the young boy had declared, "It will be great to come here, Roger, as long as Daddy won't be too lonely on his own without me."

"I'm sure he'll be fine, John. We'll arrange for you to come over soon, and get a good superhero film to watch, maybe with a McDonald's, hey?" and the deal was struck.

After the father and son had returned from walking the dog, Ellouise joined her brothers and nephew, all in swimwear for an afternoon by the pool. The family played with dive sticks, chased after inflatable balls, and lazed on loungers playing Go Fish and Uno, games easily played with a seven-year-old, and one who was quite capable of winning most of the time. The older Blacks were relaxing before the arrival of their mother.

At four o'clock, they left the pool area and went to shower in their rooms upstairs. Gabriel had got into the habit of showering with his son in the bathroom adjoining John's bedroom, and they chatted about the latest episode of Spiderman they had watched together, as Gabriel lovingly washed his son's hair, and towelled him dry, rubbing and tickling a very happy little boy.

The father then helped his son to get ready to have dinner with his new grandmother. He was to wear a navy two-piece Ralph Lauren boys' suit, complete with a white shirt and a red tie, which John had chosen himself. Gabriel stepped back and admired his handsome, proud-looking son.

"I want you to be on your best behaviour for Grandma, John, and eat all of your food, especially the vegetables; she'll like that."

"I never knew I had a grandma, Daddy. Mummy's mummy died before I was born."

"I know, John, but you've got a new one now. This is my mother, and I think she'll love you very much."

Standing behind John, Gabriel closed his eyes and hoped that this would be the case. He remembered his young mother, married to a healthy father. She had loved to join in all the family activities with her husband and children. Before it all went horribly wrong.

"I'm not eating peas, Daddy. Steve knows I don't like them, doesn't he?"

"Yes, John, don't worry. And don't forget, you have a treat tonight – you're having a sleepover with Roger and Steve after dinner. Come on; let's go and find Aunty Ell. You can stay with her while I go to fetch Grandma."

Gabriel had decided to go with Michael to collect his mother, so he could talk to her in the car and prepare her to meet her family and grandchild. This was going to be a very special evening.

Once in the car, he raised the privacy panel and took a pen from his breast pocket as he said, "Rachmaninoff Piano Concerto No. 2". The back of the Bentley became filled with the solemn, provocative playing of a grand piano. Its passenger mindlessly threaded his pen through his fingers, twisting it round again, and again and again.

He closed his eyes and prepared himself to see his mother for the first time in nearly five weeks. He tried to focus on the family dinner, but visions of what would follow, between him and his mother, kept creeping into his consciousness, until he gave in and conceded defeat, knowing that he would do this for her, for his father. Her regular visits to Arnford Hall every Monday and Wednesday evening would resume and his plan to end their abhorrent affair would have to wait until another day.

He walked into her two-storey apartment after entering the code to gain access. On hearing movement upstairs, he went over to a decanter and poured himself a glass of whisky, adding a shot of water. He took a large gulp as he sat down in a huge black leather armchair and casually sat back, crossing his legs. He rarely visited her home, and he glanced around to see if anything had changed. The portrait of his father still hung over the marble fireplace and the photograph of the three Black children took pride of place on the mantelpiece. In her home, to all intents and purposes, she had not moved on, even though her husband had been dead for over fifteen years; but outside these walls he knew she had. She drank, did drugs and had sex with other men.

It was becoming time for Gabriel Black to move on too. Completely.

"Hello, darling, I didn't hear you come in. What a lovely surprise to have you come and collect me." She stood before him, looking healthy, young, shapely and, he had to admit, very attractive for a sixty-year-old woman. Her platinum blonde hair was short, feathered around her neck and fashionably spiked on top. Her dark brown eyes shone as she smiled at her eldest (and, she had to admit, favourite) son. Her eyes were showcased in shades of sultry browns, a glow highlighting her brows, and her lashes perfectly coated with black mascara. Her cheeks were kissed with a bronze tan and her full lips were painted in a glistening fudge-brown. She wore a Versace trouser suit of black and white zebra stripes, with matching Jimmy Choos.

Gabriel stood up, putting his empty glass down on the coffee table, and walked over to kiss her respectfully on the cheek.

"Hello, Mother." He picked up the holdall that was in the hallway and they made their way to the waiting Bentley.

"Have I missed much?" Cynthia asked as they settled into the back of the car, the privacy glass still raised.

"Eliza Redfern has been killed in a car crash."

"Oh." Cynthia looked out of the window, remembering the scenes at Arnford Hall when the woman who was going to have Gabriel's child confronted him about his relationship with his mother; a relationship he said he could not end.

She turned to face him as she asked quietly, "And your son?"

"My son, John, lives with me now." His dark eyes met hers and she saw the emptiness that had been there in the early days of their illegitimate relationship, when his father was still alive, but which had gradually disappeared as he came to terms with his fate.

She began to feel apprehensive as they approached the Hall.

He was aware of her questioning look. "I want you to meet him; he will join us for dinner." He spoke matter-of-factly, in total control of himself and, Cynthia perceived, of everything around him. "Then he will stay the night with Roger and Steve."

She hoped her son didn't notice her relief. She desired Gabriel's company tonight.

He continued, "Julian and Ellouise are there too."

Now she couldn't hide her surprise – astonishment, even – that he had succeeded in getting the family back together again; it must be at least five years since she had seen Julian, she thought. She let out a gasp of shock, before quickly regaining her composure, thinking through the possible consequences of her other son being in her company tonight.

As if he read her mind, Gabriel again spoke. "I have reassured Julian that you will be only a mother to him now; you do know that, don't you, Mother?"

She looked directly at him, admiring him in a manner most inappropriate for a mother. Their incestuous affair had been going on too long for her not to feel a constant need for him: he was her rock, the shining light that had come from her beloved husband's illness and death; the one outlet for her sexual demands permitted by her late husband, George.

"Yes, of course, dear. So long as I have you." She smiled and patted the back of his hand as it rested on the console between them.

You bitch. He did not permit himself to flinch.

There was a feeling of nervousness in the drawing room as Julian and Ellouise tried to let themselves be distracted by John's soliloquy about his volcano project at school, and how Daddy had helped him to make a model of Mount Vesuvius with cardboard, papier-mâché and paints.

The adults heard the front door open and they stood up in anticipation.

Cynthia had just scolded Gabriel for not allowing her the opportunity to have brought a gift for John, her only grand-child.

"Can I see him now?" she asked tentatively, as she placed her black leather clutch bag on the side table in the vestibule.

Gabriel entered the drawing room first and John came run-ning up to him, grasping his father's hand as he sensed the tension now present among the grown-ups.

A few seconds later, Cynthia entered the room. For a moment no one moved. Then Julian and Ellouise watched as their mother walked up to John and crouched down to say hello.

"Hi, John. I'm so pleased to meet you." She went to take hold of his hand, glancing up at Gabriel, who slowly gave the small hand he was holding to his mother, placing his own hand on John's shoulder to reassure him his father was still there.

"John, say hello to your grandma." Feeling an intuitive compulsion to stay very close to his son, Gabriel also crouched down, his eyes meeting his mother's.

John looked down at his new black shiny shoes and whispered, "Hello." Then he carefully pulled his hand away from the strange woman, and returned it to his father.

Cynthia smiled. "Your father tells me you like superheroes and Star Wars. Did you know that is what he liked when he was your age? And Uncle Julian too." And now she stood and turned to face her second son.

"Hello, Julian. It's been far too long since I've seen you," and she waited expectantly, until Julian finally broke free from the spot he had felt glued to, and went up to her and kissed her cheek.

"Hello, Mother." He waited for a moment before adding, "Can I get you a drink?"

"A gin and tonic would be lovely, dear, thank you. You must tell me later what you have been up to, travelling around the world."

"Yes, Mother." He was glad of the excuse to turn his back on her as he went over to the sideboard. He then played waiter for everyone and as he moved around the room the atmosphere eased slightly and John became the centre of attention.

Ellouise was wearing wide-legged, slate-coloured silk trousers with a floaty silk shirt emblazoned with giant red poppies, complementing her multi-coloured bangles. She wore high-heeled black and grey gladiator sandals, her bluebird tattoo just showing through. She approached her mother and presented the obligatory kiss.

"You look lovely, Mother. How was Africa?" and the two women exchanged small talk, while the men listened, appreciating this slight distraction, though Gabriel was conscious of a small seven-year-old approaching his boredom threshold.

"Come on, John, let's go and feed Satan before dinner is served." And he breathed freely as they made their way downstairs.

Conversation in the drawing room moved on to the Black company business.

"Are you coming back to work, Julian?" Cynthia asked.

Julian hesitated a moment, not sure if his mother was aware of the generous package he had been offered by a brother determined to get him back on the board. He decided he would leave him to reveal the terms to her, merely saying, "Yes, Gabriel has asked me to return, and I'm looking forward to it."

"Good. And you, Ellouise, what are you doing with your time at the moment?"

There was an accusatory note in Cynthia's voice, and her daughter remembered the arguments they had had several years ago when she had declared her intention to leave Arnford and Black HQ. She had been integral in developing the Black Group's IT infrastructure, and they had all been concerned about the knowledge gap her departure would create, not to mention the fact that GeeBee didn't want to lose his sister. He had not yet asked her back, and she hadn't considered if that was what she wanted. However, she did know that Gabriel wanted her to stay around; he had made that perfectly clear when he stopped her getting on the plane to Miami. Maybe she should play a more maternal role and help care for John. Seeing Gabriel cope alone with the day-to-day needs and requirements of raising a young child, and observing his relationship with Grace (if that was what it was), she knew he needed some help.

As a compromise, she decided to pacify her mother, telling her only what she wanted her to know. "GeeBee's in the process of helping me to buy a house near John's school, and I'm doing some freelance work, so it should work out quite well. It will be good to see more of my brothers." She deliberately used this term rather than the word "family", and Cynthia knew it.

"You must let us have a note of your fee structure; we may consider giving you a project or two."

"Well, thanks, Mother, but I'm rather busy at the moment. I would have to look at my availability."

"Well, you know family should come first, Ellouise, but I'm sure Gabriel will talk to you about that."

Ellouise took a long sip of her more-gin-than-tonic to stop herself retaliating against her mother's unfair use of her brother as emotional blackmail. Cynthia was well aware that Ellouise would find it hard to refuse her brother anything, given the current situation with his son.

Cynthia had quickly taken in the family bonding that had taken place since the three siblings were reunited. She fully appreciated the impact of her grandson's arrival in their lives, but she felt there was something more to it. She had never doubted her own relationship with her eldest son: his promise to his father, his sense of honour and duty, his commitment to keeping the family together, whatever the cost. And she had seen his life become consumed by work, and by women – lots of them. She had never felt fear of a rival, of someone special, someone who could perhaps affect her own relationship with him. She believed there was nobody else good enough for him, and nobody would be able to live with his guilt and self-hatred. And she needed him too much to feel any guilt for her own part in the events that had led to her son's tormented existence. As the years rolled by, Cynthia had come to believe that Gabriel belonged to her – he was made by her, nurtured and raised by her. He should be hers. She had a supreme right to him.

But now she perceived that there was something else happening in his life, something in addition to the boy, which could force him to make changes to the way he lived his life. This, she did fear.

When Gabriel and John returned from their walk with Satan, the Blacks made their way to the dining room. Steve had prepared a starter of shrimp and melon salad, and a main course of roasted crown of pheasant with cavolo nero cabbage and chestnut stuffing. John's portion had been simplified to some meat with mashed potato and a very small spoonful of cabbage.

Cynthia sat at the head of the table with Gabriel on her right, wearing a dark navy suit, a Dolce and Gabbana light blue and white striped shirt, and a cerise tie. John sat next to him, and Julian, in a rich brown silk suit, stark white shirt and chocolate-coloured tie, was on her left, with Ellouise at his side.

Meals with the Black family were never permitted to be silent affairs. They were an opportunity to discuss business, update each other on their lives, even a chance to lodge a complaint if anyone at the table was not happy about something.

At the age of sixteen, Gabriel had found the courage to state, out loud, that he was getting too tired to keep "seeing" his mother, and it just wasn't fair. Poppa replied simply that his son therefore needed to do more exercise to get fit and, whether one was sixteen or sixty, one should never be too tired, but should be bloody grateful. He later spoke privately with Gabriel, in his son's bedroom, and made it quite clear that he was never to embarrass his mother like that again.

Conversation at the dining table this evening revolved around Cynthia's holiday adventures, Julian's travels, and Ellouise's current work assignments, the daughter squirming occasionally under interrogation by her mother as, truthfully, she wasn't actually working on anything – after all, she had hoped to be in Miami!

It didn't go unnoticed that Gabriel remained quiet, simply asking a few questions of the others, rather than volunteering any information about his own activities, and no one questioned him. It was understood by the adults at the table that he would be preparing himself for the rest of the evening.

John complained about the food, despite Steve's attempt to make it nice for him; he was still constrained by Gabriel's insistence that John eat the same as everyone else. He fidgeted in his seat, declaring he was bored, and knocked over his glass of apple juice onto the starched white tablecloth. At this final straw Gabriel took a firm hold of his hand, asked for the two of them to be excused from the table, and led John out of the room.

In the hall he reprimanded his son sharply. "I asked you to be well behaved and eat your food, John. You have done neither. What is the matter?"

"I'm not eating that meat, and I don't like cabbage."

"I thought it was peas you didn't like."

"I don't like cabbage either. It's rubbish!" John kicked the carpet.

"Stop that now, John. Do you want to go to your room?"

"You said I could have a sleepover with Roger. I want to see Roger." The boy was now talking to the carpet, and Gabriel slowly lowered himself down to hug his son.

"OK, John. I know this may be a little bit boring for you, but Grandma has been so pleased to meet you. Let's go back in and say goodnight to everyone and then I'll take you down to Roger. OK?"

"OK, Daddy."

Gabriel stopped himself from saying "thank you" as he felt relief – now he had another excuse to leave the dining room for a few minutes.

So John dutifully kissed everyone goodnight, with an extra hug for his new grandma, who told him, "I look forward to seeing you in the morning, John, and you can tell me what you like to play with. Then we can go shopping; what do you think?"

"For toys?" John asked, his voice suddenly heightened with excitement.

"Why not?" and Cynthia Black laughed a genuine, heartfelt laugh as she hugged her grandson again and seemed to be delighting in the anticipation of being able to spoil him.

Julian surreptitiously shot Gabriel a questioning look. *Are you comfortable with this, brother?*

For now, was the silent reply.

Roger was waiting in the hall.

"Are you OK?" he asked his employer and friend quietly.

"Yes." But Gabriel seemed anything but OK. The walls that he could usually command to rise around him, to cut him off from the rest of the world whenever he was required to be with his mother, were not rising now. He felt vulnerable, a state quite alien to him. His familiar sense of self-loathing was more intense, and now he had the additional torture of accepting the fact he would always fail his own son, as a father to be loved and respected. Eliza Redfern had inadvertently ensured he would always question that part of his life, which she loathed and which disgusted her beyond anything she could cope with.

He hugged his son and said softly, "Time to go to Roger's, John. Bed when he says, OK, and don't forget to brush your teeth. Have a great time; remember your manners and be good. I'll come over for you in the morning. Goodnight, son." He kissed him, trying not to let the seven-year-old know how upset he was.

"Come on, John." Roger took his hand and headed for the door, not allowing John time to become anxious about leaving his father. "We're going to have a great time and you'll be able to tell Daddy all about it in the morning." He closed the front door behind them, leaving the powerful Gabriel Black standing alone, full of despair.

Slowly, he walked back into the dining room and sat down as port was being served with a selection of cheeses. He ate and sipped a little, joining in the conversation about the forthcoming local by-election, about which none of them really gave a damn, but at least it occupied their minds for a few minutes. They discussed a proposal to develop an area of Knutsford for a new housing development. It could be a great opportunity for Black Construction, but the locals were deeply opposed to the project, claiming it would put too much strain on already stretched amenities for the current residents. There was almost an air of normality in the dining room; but not quite.

Cynthia asked about Julian's appointment onto the board of the Black Group.

Julian looked at Gabriel for a lead on this.

Gabriel seemed to tense slightly, his eyes dark and stern as he looked directly at his mother.

"In your absence, the appointment was made by me – and Roger. We'll ratify the decision at the next board meeting." His tone was firm, as if challenging her to declare anything to the contrary.

She didn't, and her son continued, "He has a month to get up to speed with our current strategy and to start to contribute to the strengthening of the Black brand across our markets, assisting in particular with the licensing of the new products targeted in Black Armour. You're going to be very busy, brother." He smiled at Julian, relieved and thankful that he had accepted the offer.

Cynthia remained silent, and tried to gauge her eldest son's mood. She wasn't going to risk annoying him further by questioning Julian's commitment to the family business; she just wanted him agitated enough to be fired up, aroused, impassioned; and if he was a little angry with her – well, she liked that too.

"I think I'll retire now." As Mrs Black stood up and stepped back from the table, her three children got to their feet and waited a moment. She walked to each one and proffered her cheek for their kiss before leaving the room.

Without speaking to or looking at his siblings, Gabriel followed her.

Hearing his footsteps, Cynthia smiled to herself before pausing to wait for him to reach her. As he reached her side, she took his hand, her thumb smoothing the skin over it. He didn't pull away but led his mother up the grand staircase. She paused ever so slightly at the door on the galleried landing, the door of the room he now kept locked for Grace. But he continued to lead her down the corridor to the left, to the east wing of the house, and they stopped before reaching the green room.

"Is this to be my room?" she asked, feeling unfamiliar here.

"Yes," he replied simply, sensing her nervousness at this change to what had become their routine over the past fifteen years. He took some pleasure in leaving her in the dark as to the reason for it, and had no intention of enlightening her.

He opened the door and stood back for her to enter. Her bag had already been placed on a Queen Anne leather chair.

"You are staying," she said, determined for it not to be a question, but unable to hide her nervousness. Again she sensed there was something her son wasn't telling her.

"Yes," he said, and he followed her inside and closed the door.

Gabriel Black rolled off his mother and lay by her side. He felt nothing; he deserved nothing; he was nothing.

He stayed in his mother's room until he was sure she was sleeping peacefully. He never spent the whole night with her. He never woke to find her there in the morning. He always needed to breathe in the air of another room, whether this was his bedroom or a separate hotel room. Now he gathered his clothes and walked to his own room, locking the door behind him. It was two o'clock in the morning, but he stood under his shower for a long time, longing to be cleansed of her. After drying himself, he went into his dressing room and pulled on a thick black robe before opening the door into his morning room.

This octagonal-shaped room sat above his favourite room below, replicating its shape, and blessed with the same flood of light pouring into it when the sun rose. Tonight, the moonlight shone in, casting shadows on the walls. He went over to a panel and gently tapped some keys. Music filled his ears and he opened a drawer, withdrew a box and pulled back the lid, removing a cannabis cigar. He reached for a lighter from the box and lounged back in a wing-backed armchair in soft green leather, closing his eyes, losing himself for a while with the drug and Tchaikovsky's Violin Concerto No. 1 in G Minor. He shared this room with no one; no one else enjoyed its perfect calm, with landscapes painted by Constable and Turner, and an early piece of work by the sculptor Benjamin Paul Akers. This was his room of beauty and perfection; he was the only blot on its landscape.

That night his sleep was restless and evasive. He had a recurring dream of reaching out to hold on to the woman he wanted, but never quite managing to catch her hand, and it tormented him more than any nightmare he had known.

He woke at six o'clock, drenched in sweat, and took another shower, this time hurriedly. He wanted to see John.

By six thirty he was knocking at the coach house door, and went inside to join his friends as they had breakfast with his son.

Chapter 42

It was Sunday afternoon and Grace was settling into her seat on the train to head home. The table tempted her to place her books on it to prepare for her week with the children, but she had done everything she needed to at Jason's. She had been glad of the distraction in his flat, the excuse not to have to go to the off-licence for wine, the park for a walk, the restaurant for an intimate dinner for two. Instead she worked, and so he worked; she made time to have sex with him, so he had sex with her; she was too busy to cook breakfast on Sunday, so he did.

He knew something was amiss; this wasn't his Grace. He tried to engage her in conversation on Saturday morning, but she wasn't really there with him; Grace McGuire was still a hundred and ninety-five miles away, wondering about her captor.

Jason took comfort from their sex on the Saturday night; it had been gentle and fulfilling. He was certain she enjoyed it as much as ever, her cry delighting his ears, her smiles reassuring his heart, and he tried to convince himself that the rest was just down to her work. But he left her at the station with an uneasy feeling, and he was apprehensive about the following weekend, when it wasn't absolutely clear that he would go up to see her. On returning to his flat, he delved into the bottom of his bedside drawer and took out a little packet. He needed something to give him a bit of a lift.

He didn't make work the next day.

Grace checked the phone from Gabriel Black on the train, in her kitchen, in her bedroom, in her classroom on Monday, Tuesday, Wednesday, Thursday and Friday. No messages.

Each day, she gazed at the disturbing arrangement of botanical species on her kitchen table, not quite able to call them flowers. They were dying, including the dawn-breaking orchid. You couldn't truly protect anything from death. She threw them away on Friday.

Jason came for the weekend. No messages.

She put on a good show of giving her boyfriend all her attention this time; she knew she owed him that. But she wasn't sure if that was what she wanted any more.

She started to study her boyfriend's behaviour, his agitation, his drinking, his yearning for something he didn't want her to know about. She was sure he loved her in his own way, and she had to ask herself if she would still be in love with him if a certain man were not fucking with her mind, as well as her body. And why was that man silent now? Shouldn't she be glad? Shouldn't she be relieved at the prospect that her nightmare could be over?

But she couldn't stop thinking about him. *For fuck's sake, you're obsessed with him!*

Chapter 43

Gabriel and Roger were on the plane on their way back from Beijing. Black had been away from his son for four days and he couldn't wait to see him. He remembered John's tears as he attempted to explain that he would be away for a few days on business.

"Why can't Roger do it, Daddy? Roger's good at everything and then you can stay here with me."

"I have to go, John. And I know you're a big boy and you'll have Aunty Ell to look after you. You'll have lots of fun and I'll be home very soon."

And "soon" couldn't come quick enough.

While in China, the two men had informed the management team of the action plan and timescale for implementation of changes and monitoring for improvement. If results didn't turn around within the next three months, they would install a new team. The CEO and his PA had not come to discuss things; that had been done during the recent teleconferences. It was now time to dictate and start to see good, sustainable results coming from this particular subsidiary.

During his absence, Ellouise had taken on the responsibility for taking John to and from school, and she was staying at the Hall with Julian.

Julian was working hard for his brother, shutting himself away in his second-floor suite during the day, and joining Ellouise and John for dinner in the evening. He enjoyed listening to his nephew's re-telling of events at school and even took the occasional turn to read a bedtime story.

Gabriel Black was also acutely aware that he had not seen Grace McGuire for fourteen days. He had resumed the old routine of having to have sex with his mother twice a week.

When he and Roger finally returned from their trip, John was already home from school. The young boy ran down the steps to greet Gabriel with a huge smile and a very emotional hug.

They had only spoken once on the phone during his absence as John had been a little upset that Daddy would not be coming home just yet. It was the first time since he had met his father that he had not seen him every day, and Gabriel didn't want to make a habit of being away from his son.

The two were left alone together so they could catch up with each other's news, having the rare treat of a light tea for the two of them in the octagonal room, and then bedtime with a story and lots more hugs.

Exhausted, Gabriel joined his siblings and Roger and Steve in the kitchen. Julian informed everyone that he had arranged a poker night for the following week, and had also lined up a guest of his own.

His brother eyed him cautiously, wondering whom his brother had been so quick to get back in touch with after his five-year absence. But Julian tapped his nose, determined to give nothing away.

As Gabriel lay in his bed that night he finally admitted to himself that he needed to see Grace. He could not let go.

Chapter 44

Another week passed, and Grace had stopped checking *his* phone every day. It was in her bag, it was charged. She tried to forget about it.

Her feelings towards Jason had settled down again and she wondered if her earlier doubts about her relationship with him had simply been due to the thrill and excitement that Gabriel had given her. Even the memory of her punishments made her tingle in a submissive way, which was so alien to her. She found herself wondering what games he liked to play with his female acquaintances. But she convinced herself that his silence, a silence lasting three weeks now, just proved that she had been a toy to him; he had used her, had his fun with her and was now bored with her. She remembered her conversation with Roger, and his words: *You do mean something to him … he probably thought you would just be another challenge, someone to be conquered. But I don't think that he feels that with you.* Well, Roger was wrong.

Grace was nearly forty and didn't have a large circle of friends beyond her work colleagues and Jason's acquaintances; maybe it was time for her to commit more to her boyfriend, consider moving down to London, think of finding a fresh position in a new school, even. But then she thought of his cocaine use, knowing she would be kidding herself if she believed that it would stop automatically the moment she was permanently on the scene.

She also thought of a seven-year-old boy, with hair as black as his father's. Her emotions were screwing with her head and she didn't know what she wanted.

Then, late on Thursday afternoon, as she was getting ready to go home, *his* phone trilled. Not quite sure how she felt, she took it out of her bag and read the screen:

Sender: Gabriel Black

Message: The car will collect you at 8.30 p.m.

Staring at it, she tried to fathom out what it meant. It was relatively late for the car to come; John would no doubt be in bed. He didn't mention food; would the car be bringing her home again too?

She thought of the collar. Tomorrow was Friday. Would she be free for the weekend? Did she want to be? She remembered the day when he had taken her and John to his lakeside house. She pictured the elegant yacht, *My Grace*, which he had bought for her, and she remembered the warmth shown by his former nanny. She had seen a relaxed side to him then, and she had liked it.

Driving home, her thoughts wandered, deliberating about what to wear. She felt as though she was getting ready to go on a date!

Having perused her wardrobe thoughtfully, seeking clothes in which she would feel comfortable, relaxed even, Grace chose knee-length black leather boots, a short black woollen skirt over thick black tights imprinted with diamond shapes, and a mohair mustard-coloured sweater that highlighted her curvaceous hips and accentuated her pert breasts. She paid more attention to her make-up than usual, and the reflection in the mirror filled her with confidence.

She opened her door at half past eight.

And there he was, in a Versace liquorice grey silk suit, the jacket accentuating his narrow waist, and a metallic light grey shirt buttoned to the neck but with no tie. Exuding beauty and elegance, Gabriel Black appeared much younger than his forty years, and there was an air of calm about him, his lips forming a smile as he looked at her appreciatively.

I've missed her …

After a moment, he regained his usual composure, breaking the silence as he said, "Hello, Grace."

Flushing slightly, she whispered, "Hello, sir," and turned to collect her bag, before joining him on her driveway.

256

Not sure why she was experiencing a feeling of nervousness instead of the usual anger, frustration and annoyance when he would come for her like this, she looked for the Bentley and wondered if Michael was driving. But it was not the black car parked in front of her house. Gabriel was driving his Porsche 911 50. He held the door open for her and waited until she was settled before quietly closing it and going round to the driver's side. In silence he turned on the ignition and gently pressed the accelerator. The car slipped out of the village, before heading for quiet country lanes, where he pressed his foot to the floor, the engine roared and the trees and hedges flashed by in a blur. They zoomed around bends, up and down hills, the car swallowing the road hungrily and demanding more.

He was driving for pleasure, with no obvious direction other than to seek out fast, winding roads.

Not knowing where they were going or what he was thinking, Grace simply smiled to herself and enjoyed the melange of noise, high-speed motion, and an unexpected feeling of calm and security from just being with him. Was she beginning to feel under his protection? *Didn't Roger tell me to find his protection … ?* She thought for a moment of the imprisoned orchid and the words on his card. Then his voice broke in.

"Are you enjoying the ride, Grace?" he asked, his eyes fixed on the road, his hands and feet controlling gear changes, speed variations and direction.

"Yes, sir." She found herself wanting to say what she thought he wanted to hear, and she moved slightly in her seat as she realised she was speaking the truth.

"Good."

He drove with more determination, and she wondered if he had made some decision – from her response maybe, or his own desire, she wasn't sure, but half an hour later they were pulling into a very secluded car park at the Wizard's Thatch in Alderley Edge.

At the reception he asked for the room key for the Black reservation, and the attendant led them to the Camelot suite.

Gabriel clutched Grace's hand as she saw the huge red and gold draped four-poster bed in the medieval room, the flames of a roaring fire flickering in the seventeenth-century fireplace.

"Breathe, Grace," he murmured and he leaned into her, his own breathing slightly laboured, as though he were fighting back a desire to kiss her.

Grace was mesmerised by the gothic beauty of the room, and her eyes fell on the orchid on the dressing table. *Had he arranged this?*

Noticing her eyes drawn to the plant, his words confirmed her thought.

"It's a *Phalaenopsis, Doritis pulcherrima*."

Seeing the delicate pink petals, edged with white shadows, which drew the eyes to a deep red orifice in the centre, Grace couldn't help seeing the flower's resemblance to a woman's vagina, with a lower tongue-like red petal streaked with fine white lines near opening; inviting penetration, offering delight.

She looked up at the man standing beside her. She felt like someone having a secret affair, stealing a romantic evening with a lover, cheating on her unsuspecting boyfriend. Grace shied away from asking herself if she really wanted to be here, or was it simply that she had to be? She felt his warm hand gripping hers.

She stood before him and looked searchingly at his face, trying to read his mood. There was something different about him: his calmness was still there but his usual dark stare had been replaced by a serene look, as though he was gazing at something that was good for him.

"No rules tonight, Grace." He removed his jacket and approached her. He took her hand and led her to sit on the bed with him.

As they turned to face each other, he gently stroked her cheek with his finger, caressing her soft skin, conscious of her nervousness as she closed her eyes. He raised his other hand and cupped her breast, feeling its roundness through her sweater. Aware of a slight swaying movement from the woman sitting next to him, he put his hand against her back and finally brought his lips to hers. The kiss was light and delicate but, as he felt her melt beside him, it became firmer, and he tentatively moved his tongue to taste her. She felt a thrill as he entered her mouth, entwining his tongue with her own, intimately exploring her, and they slowly began to lose themselves in each other. By mutual consent, they lay back on the duvet, not breaking their kiss, and time stood still for them as they each savoured the other.

Grace was exactly where she had wanted to be: in a room, alone, with Gabriel Black.

He was where he wanted to stay: away from Arnford Hall, with a woman who was beginning to consume his waking moments, a woman who could be his breaking dawn, his saving Grace.

Finally their lips parted and he began to unfasten his shirt, hardly daring to look at her, hoping she would see his desire and begin to undress herself. Something inside him leaped as she slowly raised her sweater over her head. Soon she stood naked in front of him.

Having removed all of his own clothes, he moved towards her and enveloped her in his arms, skin on skin, matching desire with desire. His erection pressed hard against her, and he gasped as she lowered her hand and held him, her fingers wrapping around his hard, thick member. She caressed it gently, appreciating the velvety texture and wallowing in the groans he was making.

Grace's body yearned for him, and for the second time, she said his name.

She relished his grip tightening around her waist and they gazed at each other as he sucked his fingers before placing them inside her vagina. Steadily he kissed her as he lubricated her and she became mesmerized by his focus on her body. After a few moments he raised her up and she wrapped her legs around him, aware of his strength and control. Then she felt his penis enter her and his balls touch her as he moved within her. Agilely he manoeuvred them both onto the bed and she gasped as he penetrated her even deeper, filling her vagina, sending quivers through her body. His hand moved down, his finger connecting with her clitoris, caressing, stroking, massaging it. He slowed his pace, wanting to prolong their pleasure, and they delighted in hovering on the edge of ecstasy. After a few minutes, desire took over control, and she screamed as he moaned and his seed flowed into her. It was all too much, and yet not enough …

Grace was losing herself in physical pleasure and emotional turmoil. *Don't need him, you can't have him, don't need him …*

As their lovemaking ended, Grace turned away so he couldn't see a tear fall onto her cheek.

He lay beside her, one arm hugging her to him while he gently ran his fingers along the curve of her waist, savouring the feel of her soft skin. At the age of forty, a new emotion came over Gabriel Black. He was in love; but he would add this to his secrets: no one must know.

The couple dozed for a while, and as he awoke he gently roused her.

"It's time to go, Grace. I don't want John to miss me in the morning."

She gazed at him through sleepy eyes, not wanting to leave now. The clock on the cabinet read 4.30 a.m. She watched him dress, and she slowly began to do the same. Neither of them had toothbrushes, clean underwear, anything which would make them look like a respectable couple leaving a hotel. But she didn't care. He had awakened something in her, and she couldn't believe that she hadn't done the same to him. Maybe Roger was right; maybe he would want her.

Then she thought of her own secret. The one Gabriel Black had somehow discovered. Who would want anything to do with Melanie Bright, daughter of a child killer? No one. Especially not the father of a beloved son.

Gabriel's voice broke through her thoughts. "Thank you, Grace. What a pity we don't live in another universe." He raised her hand to his lips, brushing them over the back, the palm and along her fingers.

In the car, they travelled in silence, each deep in thought, each afraid to disturb the other. They both knew something different had happened that evening; neither of them knew what to do about it.

As Grace climbed into her own bed for a final couple of hours of sleep before work, she wondered why he had not put the collar on her. Then she remembered his words: "*No rules tonight, Grace.*"

Suddenly she heard the trill of his phone.

Sender: Gabriel Black

Message: Rules back in play. Go to sleep, Grace. The car will collect you at 6.30 tonight. Don't see him this weekend.

Chapter 45

At the end of the school day, John ran to his daddy, excited that he was going for a sleepover with Aunty Carol and would be sleeping in Craig's bedroom tonight. Now that his father was home from China, he was happy, confident in the knowledge that Daddy would be coming to collect him in the morning. This point had been of the utmost importance to the seven-year-old when he had agreed to go to his cousins for the night, and Gabriel was becoming more aware of the father/son bond strengthening to a point where John could experience separation anxiety if he envisaged that he might not see his father for a while.

Gabriel made a mental note to check with Roger on the progress of the purchase of the house for Ellouise. It would be good for John to have more female company, and he took comfort from knowing that John was at ease with his aunty number two. All he needed now was to be able to take comfort from knowing that his little sister could responsibly look after her nephew.

The car took them straight to the Beardlys.

"Hi, Gabriel," Carol said as she stood at her door, having opened it as soon as she saw the black Bentley pull up. She was coming to terms with using her pseudo-brother-in-law's Christian name, and her children couldn't wait to see Uncle Gabriel! "Do you want to come in for a drink?" There was a hopefulness in her voice, but Gabriel's smile had to be enough reward for her as he replied, "I'm sorry, but I need to get back. I'll just make sure John is settled and say hello to everyone."

Oh, how things had changed over the weeks following his first visit to the Beardly home!

"Hi, Uncle Gabriel." Fifteen-year-old Abbie was standing beside her mother, her blush giving away her crush on the handsome older man.

"Hello, Abbie. How are you?"

"Good, thanks," and as the words came out, her confidence deserted her, and the young schoolgirl shot upstairs to her bedroom.

Gabriel raised his eyebrow at Carol and they both smiled. He then turned to his son, who was just entering a deep discussion with Craig about what they were going to play. He kissed his cheek, reminded him to be good, brush teeth and go to bed when told. Gabriel was suddenly speechless when his son asked, "Next time, Daddy, can Craig come and sleep in my bedroom?"

Gabriel Black had never contemplated having *any* children in his house, ever. That had changed when John came into his life; he had not expected any other children to appear. But, looking at his smiling son, at Craig standing next to him, and picturing John running around the playground with his friend Adam, and the other boys and girls at school, he had to admit he would need to think about the implications of having John's friends, and indeed family, at Arnford Hall occasionally. Was that so wrong?

"We'll see, John." Gabriel ended that particular line of questioning, but not without noticing the scrutiny of the woman standing beside him. "I'll see you in the morning, OK?"

"Yes, see you, Daddy," and with a final hug, the young boys shot into the lounge to check out the Wii games.

"He'll be fine," Carol said. "He can stay for lunch too if he wants to. You know he could stay for the weekend ..." She didn't want to appear to be interfering, and she couldn't hide her nervousness as she spoke, but she was sure Gabriel Black must be feeling restricted by his son's needs. Naturally a seven-year-old needed his parent, and in normal circumstances there would be a mother to help fill that need too, share the demands of parenthood, and take a turn to enjoy a break from it. This man had lost the absolute freedom he had before – or so Carol Beardly believed. She simply wondered if there was a woman Black wanted to be with sometimes, and she knew how much she and James appreciated their time alone together, without any children, whenever they got the chance. "It ... it's up to you ..."

"No, it's fine. I want to come for him tomorrow. But maybe after lunch as you suggest. I don't think he likes to be away from me for too long." His eyes were masked and Carol had no idea what he was thinking. However, she did wonder if the man didn't like to be away from the boy for long either.

Gabriel walked into the lounge to tell John that he would be over to collect him at two o'clock, after lunch. John was cool with that. Gabriel then opened the door to the dining room and examined the orchid he had brought, remembering the first time he had met Carol and his son. Carol held her breath, aware that there were no flower heads remaining on the plant. In fact, it resembled a twig, and a couple of the leaves had lost their rich green, waxy lustre, but she had been too afraid to throw it away.

"I'll bring some food for it tomorrow, and let's see if we can keep it alive a while longer."

"Of course. I'm sorry – I'm not very good with plants." *Why the hell am I apologising?*

He simply said, "I'll come over at two. See you then," and he leaned in and kissed Carol on the cheek, unaware that this act almost caused her to pass out in her own hallway.

The staff at Arnford Hall were getting agitated, and Julian was getting excited, as preparations for the poker night got under way. Gabriel decided to leave them to it and shut himself away in his office, going through some work papers, before allowing himself to ponder what could happen this evening. He knew he was taking a risk in having Grace with him. He doubted she would have experienced a night quite like it; he was certain she would not have approved of a night quite like it! But he was confident he would be in control tonight. They could share the experience, the fun, and he was actually looking forward to her induction into how a games night was hosted at Arnford Hall; to feel the excitement, the illicitness, the risks they took and in some cases the breaching of their own limits.

As he went upstairs to shower and dress for the evening, he ordered Michael to go and collect Mrs McGuire.

Chapter 46

Grace had rung Jason at half past seven that Friday morning to say she had too much work to do this weekend and it was better that he stayed in London. She reassured him that everything was fine, really, and she was certain that she would see him next week. She told him she would ring on Sunday.

She looked in her wardrobe and decided to wear a little black dress, which she only ever wore at Christmas, but she always felt good in it. She accessorised it with gold drop pearl earrings and a thin chain-link gold bracelet, total value approximately £20 from eBay. She didn't bother to look through her spaghetti of necklaces! She completed her attire with peep-toe black stilettos and her black clutch bag with its gold clasp. She checked that the key to her sanctuary was among its contents.

Not knowing what else to expect this weekend and trying to prepare for all eventualities, Grace had also thrown some clothes into a holdall, together with some school papers to work on, just in case.

Somehow, she had had a feeling Michael would be picking her up tonight, and as she sat alone in the back of the Bentley, she cleared her mind as best she could, unsurprised at Adele's dulcet tones floating around the interior. *Had Gabriel instructed Michael to play this music? Was he trying to please her?*

As she walked up the steps the gargoyles teased her, *"You'll have to show him what you're made of tonight. Good luck!"*

His grey Porsche was visible in the garage and she remembered the romance of last night. Could she hope for a repeat tonight?

Roger opened the door and greeted her with a gentle, reassuring kiss on the cheek.

"It's great to see you, Grace. You look lovely. Will you come and join us in the kitchen for a drink?" He looked hopeful and she smiled and took his hand. She hadn't seen him for three weeks and yet it was as if their evening walk in the garden was only yesterday.

Ellouise was in the kitchen talking to Steve. She went straight over to Grace and hugged her like a long-lost friend.

"How fab to see you, Grace. You look lovely."

Grace's eyes roamed over the blood-orange chiffon floating over a dark brown satin maxi dress and nude slave sandals. It was Friday, the thirteenth of October, and freezing outside. Grace shivered on behalf of the bangle-emblazoned woman standing before her.

"Hi Ellouise," she replied apprehensively, feeling at a disadvantage in not knowing what was going on, and very tense wondering where Gabriel, and, indeed, Julian were.

Ellouise handed her a Kir Royale.

"You must have some of these too, Grace," she said as she placed a white china plate piled with strawberries and garnished with lime-green leaves in front of them.

While the two girls sipped and ate, Steve put some finishing touches to a large silver platter of cold meats and red berries. As Grace looked at the spread of food over the worktops she imagined they must be having a buffet and, from the quantities, there were going to be some additional guests. She chatted with Ellouise, hearing that John was staying with his cousins tonight, that Julian was in the shower, and that Gabriel was attending to his orchids.

Oh, this is a side of him I really don't know. She felt curious as she remembered her first visit here the night Roger had shown her Gabriel's plant rooms, and heard him apologise to his employer for taking her in there.

"Hello, Grace."

She turned to face him, sure – by the formal black dinner suit, the scarlet bow tie and the shining crocodile shoes – that this was her Black.

"Good evening, sir." She spoke quietly, but with a certainty that portrayed her confidence for this evening. Her last meeting with him had been sensual, even romantic. OK, that had been without rules and his last text had clearly stated his rules were back in play. But she had no intention of being intimidated by him and if there were going to be plenty of people around, what could he possibly do?

"Good evening, sir," Steve and Roger said in unison, the former only momentarily looking up from his work.

"Oh, for goodness' sake, GeeBee. *Sir*? Really, when are you going to chill a bit with these house rules?" and Ellouise kissed her brother on the cheek. "I'll go and tell Julian to get a move on. He's taking ages to get ready for his date." She left the kitchen on her mission, armed with a strawberry and her Kir Royale.

Now Grace really was intrigued about this evening, her growing confidence feeding her mind with an assurance that she would be Gabriel Black's "date".

Black looked after his sister scornfully, and raised his eyebrow to Roger, referring to the "copycat" use of the title "sir" that Gabriel Black was so accustomed to. *Looks like this is probably another change to add to my to-do list, but let's not rush things.*

"Come with me, Grace." He waited for her to join him at the doorway, before taking her hand and leading her to her bedroom. He unlocked the door and stood aside to let her enter. He followed her inside and closed the door behind him. Without speaking he walked over to the dresser, took her necklace and then stood behind her as he placed it around her neck and clicked the padlock shut.

"You look lovely," he said, his voice low and serious.

Grace felt a shiver run down her spine, but within a second she gasped as he kissed the skin he had exposed in parting her hair to put the necklace on.

"Breathe, Grace," he commanded, and she almost wished he had locked the door so she would know they were in here to stay.

Instead, he moved away. "We need to go down before the guests start to arrive. You're going to experience a games night at Arnford Hall, Grace. Let's hope you enjoy it."

She felt there was something he wasn't telling her. She remembered playing dare to bare with him and Ellouise, and how she had been drip-fed the rules. She wasn't sure if she wanted to play anything like that again, let alone with other people.

267

He broke her reverie.

"Do you play poker?"

Oh, that sort of game! "No," she replied and quickly added, "Sir," as he looked at her enquiringly. She didn't want to incur any punishments. She felt this was not the night and her nervousness began to escalate.

He was wondering how she would respond to what was about to take place. Mrs McGuire the school teacher would definitely not approve, but what about the woman who joined her boyfriend in occasional drug use? What else did she get up to with him? Black doubted it would be in his own league. Well, he was about to find out.

At half past seven, a maid began to show guests down to the games room. Gabriel was there to greet them, with Grace by his side.

Grace noticed that each man arrived with a woman, most of them looking like models; their faces, figures and clothing all fitting the image. And some of them obviously knew each other, as they separated from the men and chatted at the bar. Roger and Steve helped to get drinks for everyone, and eventually there were twenty-two people in the room.

Ellouise wasn't joining the party tonight.

Grace studied the gathering, intrigued, as she realised the men were positioning themselves around two poker tables. The women sat at tables by the bar and chatted, drank and nibbled at the buffet laid out on a long table alongside the bar.

She watched as Julian walked in, wearing a cream suit, black shirt and cream tie. His clothing was a bigger giveaway to his identity, than his small white fencing scar, which was hardly visible in the dim light. On his arm was a woman Grace imagined to be in her early thirties, wearing a short cocktail dress of ruby-red silk, patterned with colourful Japanese cranes, her dainty feet encased in red silk stilettos. Her blonde hair was coiled on the back of her head. She was stunning. She appeared a little nervous, though it was obvious from the introductions that she had met at least some of the guests before.

Julian came over and introduced Lindsey to Grace.

"You two can look after one another," he said as he handed them both champagne.

The two women smiled at each other, and as they sat down with the other women, an unspoken bond of trust seemed to form between them.

Maybe this evening isn't going to be too daunting after all, thought Grace.

She started to chat to Lindsey and they laughed as they shared their surprise at first seeing their identical partners together, each disclosing their own technique for trying to identify which one was which. Lindsey had known Julian for many years, although she hadn't seen him in the past five. She just happened to be between boyfriends when he rang her and invited her on this date, and – well, she was game for most things and it had been a long time since she had attended a gambling night at Arnford Hall.

"It's not for the faint-hearted, but then, you're with Gabriel so you must know that already!" Lindsey's eyes sparkled with excitement as she gave Grace a friendly grin.

Small alarm bells began to ring in Grace's mind. *Not for the faint-hearted! What's that supposed to mean?* She remained silent about her "relationship" with Gabriel Black; she had a feeling that tonight was not the time to mention that she was his son's teacher!

She was surprised at the number of times within those first few minutes of the evening that Gabriel kept looking over to her. His face was serious, as though something troubled him. She smiled at him on one occasion, but he just looked at her intently. He did not look at any other woman in the room.

However, after a few minutes he turned his full attention to the men.

Gabriel was at a table with Roger, Andrew, Mike, Colin and Leo.

Julian sat with Steve, Stefan, Kevin, and Daniel.

Grace had half an ear listening to Lindsey telling her about her work as an audit manager for a firm of accountants in Liverpool. The rest of her attention was focused on Gabriel, who was reminding the men of the rules for tonight: no limit poker, ace is high, Roger and Kevin would be the bankers, the ante would be £100, players should select their choice of prize before the first hand is dealt, and the host retains his privilege, as usual.

Grace's eyes then shifted to Gabriel's table, as she watched cash being exchanged for chips by Roger, and pieces of paper being handed around, together with pens.

What are they writing down? Are they playing for money and a prize?

She wondered how long the game was going to go on for and if the two tables would come together. Then she became totally absorbed, her eyes fully engaged on Gabriel Black as he took a deck of cards and held them up in one hand as the cards fell with precision into his other hand. He split the deck and she watched as his fingers and thumbs deftly shuffled. He worked skilfully, expertly and confidently. He then offered the deck to Andrew to cut it, and brought the pack together before dealing five cards each to the players at his table.

Steve was going through the same process on the other table.

The women were chatting animatedly, two groups taking shape; those who had regularly attended games nights at Arnford Hall, and those who were less accustomed to them. There was a certain air of superiority, and even derision, emanating from the former group.

Grace realised she was probably the only first-timer, and she decided to ignore her fellow guests, and to concentrate, as much as she could from her vantage point, on the play. She was curious about the pieces of paper. Each man had written something down and positioned the paper at their side.

She also started to notice one of the players looking at her rather more often than was deemed acceptable.

Stefan, the gynaecologist, was fascinated by the attractive woman who had stood at his host's side at the beginning of this evening.

Gabriel wasn't at the table where Stefan was sitting and, concentrating on his own game, he was blissfully unaware of this guest's attention to Grace.

Gabriel's hand of four of a kind won the game at his table. No one was particularly shocked by this. Gabriel Black was a lucky and skilful player.

Stefan won the game at the other table.

Grabbing platefuls of food, the men then gathered around to watch Gabriel and Stefan go head-to-head in a final game.

Before the final game began, the chips were cashed in with the banker. No more chips were handed out. The men each kept their piece of paper at their side.

Now the women joined the men, each going to the man who had accompanied them. Except Cheryl, Stefan's partner. She remained seated near the bar, and Steve poured her another glass of champagne. He turned to Grace, who was watching the final game from her seat.

"Another?" he asked, his warm, friendly smile reassuring Grace that she was among friends.

"No, thanks, Steve. I'm OK for now."

Then Roger joined them and, together with Lindsey and Julian, the five of them sat at one of the tables at the side of the room.

"What are they playing for now?" Grace asked, looking at Roger.

Roger glanced at Steve before saying, "Their choice of prize for the evening. It's whatever they have written on their piece of paper."

Grace looked at him, conscious that he seemed reluctant to say any more.

"What did you write on yours?" she asked, wondering why she was suddenly beginning to feel cold, and as she glanced over at the two remaining players, she again became uncomfortably aware of Stefan staring at her. She also saw that Gabriel was now conscious that his opponent was staring at Grace.

Suddenly Gabriel made eye contact with her, and for the first time, Grace felt she saw a nervousness in the dark, normally masked, eyes of her captor.

He turned his attention back to the man sitting opposite him.

Grace turned her attention back to Roger. "What did you write?"

"Steve, in private."

Her inner voice asked what that meant. Her eyes begged, *You can't be serious!*

Grace stared at Cheryl as she sat alone at the bar. Then she looked again at Gabriel. He did not look comfortable. She looked at Roger and knew that he had also noticed that his employer was looking ill at ease.

She watched in slow motion as Gabriel Black showed his hand, looking defeated, and Stefan showed his, a huge smile revealing his ugly teeth, his gaze immediately landing on Grace.

The coldness in her bones increased as the nervousness intensified in Gabriel's eyes, and he took the paper from his conqueror.

Grace, in public.

His eyes darted to Grace, his face momentarily covered in confusion, and then he swiftly looked at Roger, before standing up and saying, "Host's privilege!"

Everyone stared at their host. Julian walked up to him and took the piece of paper out of his brother's hand. He immediately looked at Grace. So did Roger and Steve. They knew something had gone wrong.

Gabriel Black had brought the most important girl in the world to him to his games night, confident he would be with her in her bed, excited, aroused and passionate, after the fun and excitement of a game of poker, followed by a period of shared eroticism among the guests; no harm done.

Now he knew he had fucked up totally, had been a fool to think it would all go to plan, a bastard to subject Grace to such a risk.

But the show must go on. He took Stefan aside.

The rules of the house dictated that the winner for the evening chose his prize. It was usually a woman (apart from Roger and Steve, who preferred to keep it in the family, as it were), and was usually some sexual act, performed in front of everyone, involving everyone, or occasionally performed in private before the couple would re-join the other guests. The evening

272

would always end in naked romping, in couples or groups, sometimes with your own partner, sometimes with others: it was always an "anything goes" post-game affair, with guests leaving in the wee small hours of the morning.

Stefan Polski had chosen to have sex with Grace in front of everyone.

The host's privilege enabled Black to make the winner an offer to take his place.

Sex with Grace in front of everyone was a given; Gabriel could only hope to take the place of the victor, with some deal that the gynaecologist would find too attractive to refuse.

After a few minutes' discussion between the two men, Grace saw Stefan nod to Gabriel. She then waited as she watched her captor approach. He looked as if his world had ended. He took her hand and led her to a quiet, darkened corner of the games room and instructed her to sit down.

Her eyes widened as he began to explain the rules of the game to her, and the implications of the final outcome.

She couldn't believe this was happening to her. She felt cut off from her body. She was hovering above it, looking down on it, as she was forced to listen to what Gabriel was telling her.

"We are going to go into the den. We will get undressed. We will get on the bed and have sex. Then we can leave."

She heard herself ask, "Where will everyone else be?"

"In the den."

"I can't do it."

"Yes, Grace, you can."

"I won't do it."

"Yes, Grace, you will. This is an order. Let's go."

The hatred in her eyes cut through him. He squeezed her hand until it hurt.

"Just let me fuck you, Grace. Then let me make it up to you."

"Make it up to me?" She began to laugh hysterically and started to feel nausea rise inside her.

"I think I'm going to be sick," she whispered.

"Grace, stay with me. I will be with you, and we can get through this together." He breathed on her hair and stroked her cheek. Then he pulled her up from the seat. "Let's go." He led her out of the games room and across the hall into the den.

She stared around the room, realising that everyone else was already in there. *Everyone* – another rule of the game. The night was not yet over for anyone.

She looked at Roger as he stood with Steve and Julian and Lindsey. They talked quietly and none of them returned her look.

She became aware that Gabriel was leading her to the bed, and she heard his voice.

"Do everything I tell you Grace. Undress me."

She looked up and stared into his eyes. His mask was on and his face was expressionless, hiding his pain and self-loathing. The outsiders of Arnford Hall were standing around or sitting on the sofas and armchairs that faced the bed.

So this was the exhibition Grace had never imagined could take place in this room. She was aware of them all watching her as she undressed Gabriel Black.

None of them could remember the last time their host had done such an unwilling act. Normally he couldn't wait to get in the sack with any one of a number of the women who normally attended such an evening. The thrill for his guests tonight was knowing that he was not here willingly; he had lost the game, and the woman undressing him now was not like any of the others. She ought not to be here. Even the female partners knew that.

Grace's hands were shaking as she began to undress the man in front of her; her whole body was shaking. She tried to close her eyes, but was afraid that she would lose her balance and fall over. She could not believe this was happening to her. *How stupid to have thought I could have another enjoyable evening with him!*

Slowly she struggled to unfasten his bow tie while he lowered his shoulders to enable her to reach, eventually letting the tie fall to the floor. Clumsily, she unbuttoned the frilled dress shirt, vaguely aware of the exquisite softness of the cotton. Her hands brushed his bare arms as she pushed the shirt from him to join the tie on the floor. For a moment she raised her eyes to meet his before undoing the button and lowering the zip of his black Armani trousers. As she was about to push them down he placed his finger under her chin and gently raised her head.

"Take my shoes and socks off, Grace," he whispered quietly, and Grace detected a sense of regret in his voice. But she was feeling too frightened, embarrassed and angry with him to acknowledge him.

Slowly she knelt at his feet, raising one foot at a time, slipping off the glossy black shoes and shakily peeling the socks from his skin. His feet felt warm, with elegant toes and manicured nails. For a moment her hand lingered on the top of his right foot and she felt an overwhelming urge to stroke her fingers along its length, until she became aware of his hand coming to rest on her arm as he bent forward and beckoned for her to stand up. Then she remembered where she was, and why.

As her eyes filled with tears, she slowly lowered his trousers and eased them from him as he raised each foot. They lay crumpled at his side, to be crowned by his black Hugo Boss trunks.

Discreetly he leaned towards her so she could hear his barely audible praise, "Good girl," and feel his breath waft against her cheek.

As he stood naked in front of everyone, Gabriel slowly placed his hand round Grace's back, and steadily unzipped her dress, lifting it above her head and revealing her black lace thong and bra. He lowered himself gracefully and lifted each foot as he removed her shoes. Then he slid her hold-ups down her legs and raised her feet to discard the stockings. He deftly removed her knickers before standing up and releasing her breasts from her bra. Finally, he held her close to him, as though trying to protect her nakedness from the onlookers.

The thought of this invasion of her privacy cut through him and his demons were released to torture him, to force him to despise himself even more, when he had thought such a thing was impossible.

He pulled back the netting surrounding the four-poster bed, saying quietly, "Climb onto the bed, Grace, and lie face down." *At least this way you will be slightly less exposed, my darling Grace.*

As a robot follows commands, so Grace followed the command from the man she now hated with an intensity she didn't know she was capable of feeling; an intensity that could have been love.

Most of the guests were beginning to make their own entertainment, reaching various stages of undress, and too turned on by their own antics to pay too much attention to the star attraction. Steve and Roger and Julian and Lindsey had gone into the connecting wet room and were having their own fun, trusting Gabriel to look after Grace as best he could, and not thinking too much of what might face him in the morning.

Only Stefan sat a distance apart from his partner, Cheryl. She was seated in an armchair, her face like thunder as she knocked back more champagne. The gynaecologist sipped a brandy and watched the performance of his host and the woman he himself had hoped to be with tonight.

As if floating in space, Grace was only vaguely aware of Gabriel behind her. All she needed now to solidify her hatred of him in concrete was to have him fuck her up the arse. She closed her eyes and contemplated pressing her face into the mattress and suffocating herself.

Then she felt him raise her ever so gently, his hand coming around her waist, warm and strong. She felt his finger as he pushed it inside her, followed by a second, his circles enticing her juices to lubricate her, ensuring she would be wet enough for him, trying to minimise any discomfort. Then he withdrew and she was aware of him holding his penis, ready to enter her. His body covered hers, hiding her from the sole spectator, and she felt his breath on her neck.

"Stay close to me, Grace. I'm going to come on your back. I won't try to excite you. Unless you ask me to?" He hesitated a moment.

"Just get me fucking out of here!" Her words were barely audible but he heard them as they smashed into his soul.

It took a couple of minutes, pushing himself into her, feeling the warm, smooth, wet silkiness of her body, his lust dispelling his disgust, his libido blinding him from everything in the room. As he was on the edge of coming, he pulled his penis out and glazed her back with his juice, gently massaging the white liquid into her as he leaned over her.

For a moment Grace almost felt relaxed as he massaged her, the warmth of his hands calming her, the feel of his body protecting her and, as she closed her eyes, the vision of his beauty gratifying her.

Then he took her hand and began to ease her off the bed and through the wispy veil.

"We can leave now, Grace. Just walk with me."

And, as though he had saved her from a worse fate than he had subjected her to, he wrapped his arm around her naked body. She laid her head on his strong, muscular chest and let him lead her out of the room, up the spiral staircase, up the grand staircase and into her bedroom.

He closed the door behind them both.

She drew away from him and, without thinking to brush her teeth, remove her make-up or moisturise her skin, she pulled back the bedclothes and climbed in, wrapping them around her curled-up body. She gazed at the window and stared at the patterns in the curtains.

Gabriel went into the en-suite, had a pee, brushed his teeth and showered. Eventually he walked back in and silently climbed in beside her. He put his hand out to touch her back and she tensed and slid away from him. He lay on his back and stared up into the darkness.

Chapter 47

It was six o'clock and as morning took her hold on him, Gabriel lay still for a few minutes, going through the events of last night, his last hand with Stefan, the not-very-covert sex with Grace, her words, *Just get me fucking out of here!*, in his head.

Her steady breathing assured him she was sleeping peacefully and he turned on his side, watching the slight rise and fall of her chest.

His plan had failed and he would have to face the consequences. A further few minutes passed as he made the most of this intimacy and peacefulness with her by his side. He knew it wasn't going to last.

He rose and walked round to the window and peered out over the grounds stretching out below him. It was still dark and he sighed before turning away, about to go into the en-suite, when he became aware of Grace rousing.

He dared to approach the bed and sit beside her as she opened her eyes and stretched.

"Good morning, Grace," he said quietly, not sure what his reception was going to be.

She stared at him for a moment as her memories of last night returned to haunt her. She could see he looked solemn, even ashamed of what had happened in the den. *Well, fuck your feelings!*

"What the hell did you think you were doing to me last night?" She sat up, not caring about her nakedness, not remembering that she hadn't removed her make-up and so her eyes were streaked with remnants of eyeliner and mascara.

"It didn't go to plan. I thought I was going to win." He tried to keep his voice low, to stay in control, but it was taking a lot of effort.

"You thought you were going to win! A fucking poker game! What are you – a magician or a bloody cheat?" She scrambled out of bed and went over to the window, gazing into the semi-darkness.

"I'm a good player, and I can usually read my opponents well. Very well. But I wasn't prepared for Stefan to be drinking you in with his fucking eyes. I lost it. I'm sorry."

She swung round to face him. "You're sorry! *Sorry!* Well, I'm fucking sorry you ever ran into the back of my car!"

Suddenly he was off the bed. He grabbed her arms and pulled her to him.

"Let go of me."

"Calm down, Grace, and listen to me."

"What are you going to say? Tell the world what a child-murdering, total fucking bastard my father was? Or what a domineering, cruel bastard you are?"

He closed his eyes for a second, resisting the urge to let go of her. Instead his grip tightened and he raised his own voice.

"I told you I did what I could last night. I could only take his place. Or would you rather I had let him fuck you? He probably wouldn't even have bothered to use the bed!"

He felt her deflate, his hold on her being the only thing that kept her on her feet.

Tears started to stream down her face.

"I don't understand. I thought you would protect me; keep me for yourself. Not abuse me, destroy me … kill me."

He realised he really had gone too far last night, and he remembered Roger saying that Grace had said once before that he was killing her. Tenderly, he wrapped his arms around her and hugged her to him. She became aware of his heavy breathing, and his desperation as he spoke again, slightly quieter now.

"I let my guard down, I know. But I did protect you, Grace, though you may not see it like that. I bought his place. It was the most I could do under the rules."

"Don't you break rules?" Her spirit was broken and she felt degraded, cheap, worthless.

"I don't break gentlemen's codes, or my own promises …" His voice faltered and she pulled back slightly and looked up at him. "… I struggle to break promises."

And she knew then that this was something to do with his secret. *He's made a promise he can't break.*

He eased her down onto the bed and sat beside her.

"I want to make it up to you. I'm sorry for how things turned out. I tried to make it as bearable as possible." He paused, but Grace remained silent. "What can I do, Grace? Tell me how I can make it up to you."

"Let me go. Set me free."

"I won't do that … I cannot do that, Grace. I don't want to lose you yet."

Again she looked into his eyes. His mask was gone. There was a finality in what he said: *lose you yet.* She saw a need, a desperation, a plea for help.

Then he knew he had let her see too much. Just as he raised the privacy glass in his Bentley, he raised his mask and she could see no more. His moment of vulnerability was gone and he now needed to take back control.

He needed a plan.

He stood up and held his hand out to her. "Let's take a shower."

Not caring what he did now, she felt him take her hand and simply let him lead her into the en-suite.

She stared in the mirror at her tear-stained face, her eyes red and swollen and smudged with mascara. *Bugger, I look like shit!*

She cupped her hands and her face expressed disgust as she smelled her bad breath. She looked down for a toothbrush; there was one she had used before, together with toothpaste. He joined her as they each brushed their teeth, glancing across occasionally to catch the other's reflection in the mirrors.

Then he led her into the large shower and commanded water to pour from overhead; a hot, steamy, powerful down-pour rudely awakening the two of them. He took the bottle of Chanel No. 5 shower gel and poured some into his hands before smoothing it over her body, creating a white lather, which he began to trail over every inch of her, barely taking his eyes away from hers. She stood like putty in his hands, accepting his movements, but lifeless.

She could so easily have melted as his hands slid down over her breasts and abdomen to linger on her pubis, and she involuntarily widened her legs as he reached in with his lathered fingers to cleanse her fully. And this gave him hope that there was a chance he could gain her forgiveness. But then she pulled his hand away, staring into his eyes, trying to penetrate his mask again; he knew it was going to be hard work, very hard work. His erection protruded obtrusively between them, betraying his desire for her. But she ignored it. For now, he would have to wait.

His voice ordered the downpour to stop and he opened the shower door. Black and white bathrobes hung on the wall and he passed her the white one.

"Are you hungry?" he asked as he rubbed his hair dry.

Actually, now I come to think of it …"Yes," she replied.

He opened the bedroom door and stepped over their clothes from last night, which had been placed in a very neat pile.

By whom? Grace wondered as she followed him.

Descending the stairways to the kitchen she suddenly felt embarrassed about the possibility she would see Roger, Steve and Julian – even Lindsey if she was still here.

As if he read her mind he said, "No one will be here yet. The boys will have gone home last night and I doubt we'll see Julian and Lindsey before lunchtime. I expect things got a bit carried away after we left." He walked across the kitchen and began to fill the kettle with water, take a few things from the fridge and put some bread in the toaster. Without looking at her he continued, "It can actually be quite fun. If you're up for that sort of thing. It doesn't have to be an orgy, but it's a 'let your hair down and anything goes' sort of affair. I had hoped you would like to play. With me, that is."

She took the teacups from his hands.

Grace McGuire wasn't so naïve not to know that these sort of parties were held – but they were not held in her circles, and they were not anything that she wanted to be a part of. But now she came to think of it, it fitted perfectly with Arnford Hall, Gabriel and Julian Black, and no doubt, Roger and Steve, and

Ellouise of course. Hell, why was she suddenly beginning to feel prudish? She was the normal one around here!

She sighed and then asked quietly, her curiosity about how he had really expected the evening to go beginning to get the better of her. "What did you write on your piece of paper?"

"Grace, in private." He sat down at the island and waited for her to sit next to him.

She was intrigued now, and remembered his erection in the shower. She also remembered what he had told her last night – to lie face down – and how he had withdrawn his penis and come on her back, how he had tried to shield her body with his own, and how he asked her to undress him first, so his naked-ness would be exposed before her own was. *Was that his way of trying to protect me as best he could?*

As she spread some marmalade on her toast she questioned him further. "What would you have done to me?"

He raised an eyebrow, trying to determine if this was going to get him into even more trouble with her.

"I would have taken you into the wet room, closed the door while I soaked you, oiled you, made you come, several times." He dared to smile, both at her and to himself as he continued to describe his original plan, "then I would have come inside you, and again if I could make it."

Oh, his eyes are twinkling. And her own insides were begin-ning to tingle.

"And then I would have coaxed you, with more champagne, to join the others, to continue to take pleasure in your body, and to give you pleasure, in exciting and tantalisingly inappropriate surroundings, with everybody around us, and yet we'd be all too interested in what we'd be doing to even think about what anyone else was doing. Almost like a teenage romp." There was an unintentional pause before he added, "I imagine."

Now it was her turn to be deep in thought. *You never did that? You never went to "inappropriate" parties where you could have sex without the risk of a parent interrupting?*

Little did she know that since his youth, he had been having sex *with* a parent.

Their breakfast continued in silence for a few minutes.

He broke it as he asked, "Can I take you there now?"

She stared at him, not quite sure what he was referring to. Then she realised he meant the wet room.

Up in the bedroom she had had every intention of trying to spend as much time as possible in the sanctuary today. But she found herself watching him spread the butter on his toast, virtually scraping it all off again. She noticed the way he kept brushing the crumbs from his robe, clearly hating them. She smiled as he exclaimed 'Damn it!' when a blob of jam fell onto the worktop and he fumbled to wipe it up with a cloth. Oh how she yearned to discover so much more about Gabriel Black.

She knew so little of him, outside the controlling, domineering persona that he allowed her to see. And if she were ever to find out his secret she would need to spend much more time with him. *Isn't that what you really want? Why you were so willing to come to him this weekend?*

"OK." She carried on drinking her orange juice.

He immediately started to clear the dishes away, waiting not very patiently for her to eat the last piece of toast.

A minute later, unable to wait any longer, he took the remaining mouthful of toast out of her hand, swept her up into his arms and strode confidently out of the kitchen, across the inner hall, putting her down while he tapped the code into the door. Then he picked her up again and walked through the now cleared den and into the wet room.

He set her down before him and stared deeply into her eyes.

"Now let me pleasure you, Grace McGuire." As he spoke he loosened her belt, easing the robe from her shoulders and letting it fall to the floor. He unfastened his own and then slowly and provocatively rubbed his naked body against hers, his hard, large penis rubbing gently, warmly against her abdomen, his hands caressing her arms, from her shoulders down to her wrists, which he then held and raised outwards before slowly lifting them up to his lips as he breathed kisses onto the backs of her hands.

Grace was entranced by his seductive movements, which made her feel amorous, sexy and beautiful.

He led her over to the mats and ordered her to kneel. He then took the bottle of oil out of the drawer. He began to rub some onto his hands as he knelt before her, the familiar fragrances of lavender, rosemary and almond filling the room. He proceeded to cover her in the glistening liquid, sliding over her upper body, pausing to take longer at her breasts, sucking her nipples with a hunger that made her gasp, before he smoothed the oil over them, and then squeezed them between his fingers, the slight pain making Grace gasp and she arched backwards, her chin rising towards the ceiling as if the slightest thread of cotton were pulling it up. His hands continued to slide over her; he relished seeing her give in to him and to her own desire.

He steadily lifted his penis up towards her face and instinctively her tongue reached out to taste him. But he gently resisted and moved round her to continue to massage her back, with long, intense, sweeping movements, up and down, and down and up, covering her shoulders, her back, her waist, her arms, no centimetre of skin left untouched, unlubricated.

She leaned forward and wallowed in the sensual, romantic gesture; she was losing herself in his actions.

"Lie back, Grace."

She needed no persuasion and she stretched out on the soft mat, resting her legs before her, aware of the warm oil covering the upper half of her body.

He paused and looked up, saying, "Einaudi. *In a Time Lapse.* 'Burning'." Strings of violins and cellos accompanied stunning, mind-absorbing, erotic piano keys as the music filled the room.

Now his attention moved to the lower half of her body. With his eyes focused on the woman before him, he crawled down the mat to take hold of her left foot and slowly began to tease it with his fingers, pulling gently at each toe, coating them in the oil and continuing up her leg to her thigh, before repeating the process on her right leg.

"Now come up onto all fours." His command brought her back from the dreamy haven she had drifted to.

Apprehensively she got onto her hands and knees and waited. She moaned as she felt him caress her buttocks, his fingers probing into the soft flesh, massaging her in circular motions and, as she was losing herself in the sensuality of his touch and the hypnotic power of the music, she raised her head and whispered, "This is wonderful."

She heard his sigh.

His hands then moved to smooth along her waist and she felt him come up against her, positioning himself behind her thighs, his penis pressing hard to find an entry point.

"I want you to let me in." His voice was low and husky.

She bowed her body forward, her head and buttocks rising, to ensure he had access to where she wanted his penis to go. This gesture was enough and he gently entered her vagina, his movements falling into a rhythm with the music, his grip on her waist tightening tantalisingly. Gradually his movements escalated with an urgency that he could no longer contain. Grace pushed herself back onto him, wanting more of him, and wanting the exquisite orgasm his fingers could give her as they caressed her clitoris. His movements were slow and steady, and she could feel that most wonderful of sensations becoming more and more intense. She was overcome by sheer pleasure.

She cried out and lowered her head onto the mat, feeling him straighten, hearing him catch his breath, inhaling deeply as his sperm streamed into her. She peered round at him, seeing his eyes closed, and said softly, "Breathe, sir."

A few moments passed before he withdrew from her. As he lay on his back he pulled her onto him, absorbing the oil that coated her body. She slid along him as he pulled her up to his face. As her face came level with his, he continued to slide under her. As he turned onto his stomach, he coaxed her onto her back and rested his head between her legs, preparing to feast on her, his own semen serving as an hors d'oeuvre before he reached the gourmet of her main course.

He savoured her taste, slowly, deliberately, lightly brushing his tongue over her clitoris, sucking to increase the intensity of the wonderful feeling building up in her, until she screamed again. Gradually he moved back up her body and rolled onto his back, pulling her on top of him. She rested her head on his chest, her sighs telling him she was satiated.

His arms circled her and they lay together in a state of sensual contentment. He stroked her hair as he asked softly, "Am I forgiven?"

"I'm thinking about it, sir." Finally Grace admitted it to herself – she was beginning to enjoy his "game". She was also beginning to feel more powerful.

Chapter 48

It was eleven o'clock before they finally returned to the kitchen, Grace wearing her black jeans and grey sweater, Gabriel in black trousers and light grey Ralph Lauren shirt, the top button open and with no tie; this was about as casual as Gabriel Black got. He looked relaxed, even happy.

Lindsey was sitting at the island with Julian, both hugging cups of coffee and wearing that "just got up and not quite ready yet" look. Julian was dressed in dark navy jeans and a red and blue checked shirt, and Grace still couldn't get used to the identical physical appearance of the twins starkly juxtaposed with totally different tastes in clothing.

"Hi, Grace." His eyes shone in a friendly smile, and Grace's fears of embarrassment from last night were proving unfounded.

"Wow, you two look great," said Lindsey and she glanced over to Julian, smiling as she added, "I hope we don't look as shit as I feel!"

"Here, take this and go and drink it in the garden." Julian handed his girl a glass of what looked like swamp juice, claiming it would cure her hangover.

Gabriel looked intently at Grace, as if to seek assurance that things were OK between them, realising he was no longer able to tell himself that it didn't matter if they weren't. "You two go and sit outside and we'll bring some more coffee out."

Wondering if Black senior was up to something, Grace followed Lindsey into the garden and they sat together on a bench looking out onto a wooded area, lightly lit by the low October sun.

"Grace, do you know how lucky you were last night? You were the envy of nearly every girl in that room, with the exception of Cheryl, probably!"

Grace blushed, not sure if she wanted to have this conversation with someone she barely knew, even though she did quite like Lindsey.

"What do you mean? I certainly didn't feel lucky." She looked away.

"I know it's more than five years since I've been to Arnford Hall, but I have never known Gabriel Black to call host's privilege before. He wouldn't have given a shit about what happened to his girl, and neither would the girl, probably. Nearly every girl in that room would want to go with him. I was sure he would come back to join the … er …" Lindsey paused, smiling to herself as she tried to select her words carefully, "party and get stuck in, as it were. It's what he always would have done. But he didn't return. He stayed with you, didn't he?" She waited for a response but Grace continued to stare at the golden-leaved trees in the distance. "He loves you, Grace. I don't think he has ever loved anyone else before. Not a woman, that is."

Now Grace gave Lindsey her full attention.

"What do you mean?"

"I'm sorry, I shouldn't have said anything, but even Julian has noticed his brother is besotted with you."

Grace was trying to take in the matter-of-fact tone this woman was using; there was no malice, no taunting, just an expression of her view of the situation. She was determined to keep digging for more information. It appeared that Julian and Lindsey had been quite close a while back.

"What did you mean about him not loving a woman?"

Now Lindsey seemed embarrassed.

"You'd have to ask Roger about that."

Oh shit. Grace's mind went into overdrive. *They were lovers?*

Suddenly she saw her companion's eyes move towards the kitchen and she knew they were about to be joined by the twins.

"Here you go." Gabriel handed her a mug of steaming coffee, his face thoughtful, studying her expression, and Grace wondered if he could tell she had just heard something that shocked her. As if needing to take control of the conversation, he continued, "We'll go and grab a bite of lunch before we collect John.

Julian, I've asked Roger to walk Satan, but will you feed him, please?"

"Sure. We're going to hang around here today. Are you coming back with John?"

"Yes."

Suddenly, Gabriel's phone buzzed. He looked at the number and started to walk out to the wood, but not before Grace heard him say, "Hello Stefan. Yes, it's all arranged."

She remembered his words when he told her he had tried to protect her last night, from Stefan: *I bought his place.* She wondered what had been the gynaecologist's price.

Gabriel Black wore a stern expression when he returned to them.

"Finish your drink, Grace; we need to go."

She glanced up at him and knew something about the telephone conversation had angered him. Her first thought was, *Don't damn well take it out on me!* But she had a feeling he wasn't doing that. Something made her think he wanted to get away, away from Arnford Hall.

She put her half-drunk cup of coffee down on the table and said simply, "I'm ready when you are," and as they walked through the kitchen, she looked directly at him and said in her best petulant tone, "sir!"

She was stunned when he simply took her hand and said, "Not now, Grace."

They walked in silence out to the front of the Hall and she was surprised to see the Bentley parked outside, Michael-less.

The garage door was still ajar and Grace saw Gabriel stare at the Porsche. She wondered why they weren't going in that.

He held her door open and she climbed into the front passenger seat and waited for him to get in the driver's side. As they went down the driveway, Gabriel pulled in to the side to allow a car transporter to pass.

Grace suddenly turned to him.

"What was Stefan's price?"

There was silence.

"Sir." Her voice was raised now and she felt she had a right to know, "You said you bought his place. What with?"

"The Porsche is his now."

"Your Porsche! You said that car was irreplaceable!"

"It doesn't matter now."

Grace stared out of the window, seeing familiar roads and buildings pass by as she realised they were going into Knutsford. A feeling of guilt swept over her.

Why the hell should I feel guilty? He put me through that ordeal. He lost the fucking game!

But she couldn't shake the feeling that she had lost him his car.

His voice broke into her thoughts.

"I lost the game, and the car was the one thing I knew he would go for. It's done and that's that." He kept his eyes on the road as he added, "You're worth it, Grace McGuire. And you're mine for a while longer. Don't forget."

They spent the next few minutes in silence. Grace's feelings of guilt were steadily being replaced by trepidation. She was fearful of what he was planning, what he might be capable of, as she was becoming aware of a change in his mood.

He parked the Bentley in King Street and walked round to open her door, no longer needing to remind her to wait.

Then taking her hand, as if they were just like any other couple going for a bite to eat on a Saturday, he led her to the Loch Fyne restaurant. They were seated at a small table in an intimate corner and Gabriel ordered sparkling water for them both.

"Am I right to assume you intend to work later?"

"Yes. I wondered if you were going to take me home?"

He didn't raise his eyes from the menu he was studying. "Of course not. Not yet, Grace."

She watched his eyes quickly trace along the words on the card in front of him.

"Just a light main meal, I think – halibut?" and he looked at her, clearly expecting her to agree with his choice.

She was about to pick up the menu that the waiter had placed before her, to make her own choice, but decided not to. Gabriel Black was in a strange mood. She wasn't sure if it was because of the car, the fact he wasn't used to losing at poker, or if he was thinking about his time with Grace; this was the third time this morning he had referred to his hold on her, and not letting her go yet. Today was the fourteenth of October: Day 39 of her enslavement. Was it really going to last for a year? Could she stand the mental turmoil he was putting her through for much longer?

How will I feel when he does let me go, when he won't want me any more?

She played with the cutlery, balancing the knife on its edge, switching the fork over and over. Suddenly she felt his hand on hers. It remained there a moment and she didn't dare look up at him.

Then she remembered Lindsey's words and she raised her head, letting her eyes make contact with his, to watch for his reaction, sure that there would be a chink in his mask, as she asked quietly, "Do you love Roger?"

A fleeting look of shock crossed his face, and he glared at her, before slowly and deliberately leaning back in his chair and bringing his fingers together, resting his elbows on the arms of the dining chair. There was a hint of menace in his eyes, as though someone were threatening him but he was letting them know he would not be messed with.

That's it! That is his secret! And now Roger loves Steve!

Grace squirmed uncomfortably under his scrutiny, fearful that she had overstepped his mark for her.

He waited, as if he knew she was growing fearful of him, and that she thought he was going to deride her. But he merely said, "I did love him. But, as you can see, we have both moved on." He waited for her to say something.

"Oh." She looked at him.

"I'm forty years old, Grace, and there's not much in this life that I haven't done – sexually, that is." He raised himself up in his chair, an air of authority and superiority emanating from him, and his eyes glistened as he added in a hushed tone, "Though even I draw the line at having sex with an animal!" He revelled in her shocked expression. "But, as it appears you are so interested in my love life, it's easy for me to say, I have had one real lover, and yes, that was Roger – a long time ago. He was there when I needed him. The women in my life have been more like fuck buddies."

Grace was stunned into silence for a moment. He had said far more than she had expected.

Then, before she knew it, the words came out, "So, I've discovered your secret. You have to let me go now!" She glanced quickly around the room, worried that someone might have heard her, but the tables nearby were unoccupied and she sighed with relief before letting her eyes return to the man in front of her.

Now he was smiling, and his eyes appeared to be mocking her, laughing at her, as he sat there smugly.

"Oh no, Grace, you are very much mistaken. My love of Roger was a wonderful, life-saving elixir. I'm not ashamed of it, and never have been. He remains and always will be my best friend. However, my secret is both shameful and evil."

He became silent and sat back in his chair as the waiter began to serve them a dish of steamed halibut with minted peas and green beans.

Alone again, he continued: he hadn't finished with this conversation yet.

"So you are trying to find out my secret. I'm not sure that is permissible."

Grace stared at him as he picked up his knife and fork and deftly began to remove the skin from his fish, evidently delighting in the suspense he was creating.

"It was not one of your rules!" Grace exclaimed indignantly. She could almost hear his mind whirring over the possibilities open to him.

"Oh, I'm not averse to implementing new ones, retrospectively."

She pushed her chair back; she wasn't taking any more from this schizophrenic power-crazy man.

"Don't even think about it, Grace! Eat your lunch."

Wondering just how much of a scene he would permit the two of them to make, believing him capable of anything, she remained seated.

She tried to eat. But couldn't. As she nearly gagged on a mouthful of green beans, she pushed her plate away, and spat her words through gritted teeth, "Guess what? I'm suddenly not hungry."

As he continued to place carefully filled forkfuls of food into his mouth, he motioned for the waiter to come to the table.

"My friend is no longer hungry. Please take her plate away, and bring a glass of chilled Meursault Perrières 1er Cru. Throw the rest of the bottle away. Thank you."

Both the waiter and Grace stared at him, as he continued to eat.

Grace remembered the delicious, expensive-looking wine she had opened and drunk in her sanctuary, when she had first met Ellouise at the Hall. She had shared that bottle with Gabriel and his sister.

How could she possibly judge this man, who could be so thoughtful, so intimate, even considerate (and, yes, she had to admit, protective at times), with the cruel, controlling, proud, yet haunted and self-loathing man she was slowly getting to know?

God give me strength. Grace gulped down half the glass of wine, luxuriating in the taste, needing the distraction it created.

The voices of the BeeGees suddenly echoed around the restaurant: "You don't know what it's like to love somebody ..." and Gabriel's fork hovered between the table and his mouth. His eyes darkened as he stared at Grace.

He became conscious that his perverse mood was deserting him. He had let her get too close to him today and was now determined not to allow that to happen again. But his usual MOs were failing him – his walls to protect him from his mother, his mask to hide him from Grace, and his perverseness to protect him from Grace. He was running out of options. *Can you make her hate you any more, you bastard? Go on – tell her your secret and have done with it!*

"Fucking hell!" he exclaimed and Grace stared in disbelief as he pushed his chair away from the table, having just spilled his forkful of fish and mint peas onto his pristinely pressed black Armani trousers.

As he frantically used his napkin to wipe the white fish and green peas deeper in to the fabric of his trousers, Grace started to laugh. The waiter hovered a few paces away, holding a cloth, but was fearful of offering to help a man as imposing as this particular guest. He visibly relaxed as he saw the tall, black-haired man begin to smile at his companion.

"Can I help you, sir?" The waiter handed the cloth to Gabriel.

Gabriel Black continued to smile at Grace and half-laugh to himself before taking the cloth. "Just the bill, please."

"Let me take you shopping, sir." Grace stood up and took the cloth and the napkin from him.

The dark tension between them was broken.

Gabriel had to concede he needed to change his trousers, and there was no time to return to Arnford Hall and still be in time to collect John from the Beardlys by two o'clock. Not knowing Carol's plans, he didn't want to be late: plus he was eager to see John. So he found himself being led to the Rohan shop on Princess Street and handed a pair of charcoal chinos by a still-amused Grace.

Reluctantly, he tried them on, and the female sales assistant asked if he would like to come out and show his girlfriend. Gabriel Black stared at himself in the mirror and saw Julian. *Oh well.* As he stepped out, he had a huge grin on his face.

"Welcome to the casual me!"

Grace smiled appreciatively. She too thought of Julian, but Gabriel without his mask had very, very kind and protective eyes. She knew now she would know him, no matter what he was wearing, when he was with Julian.

"Leave your shirt out," she dared to instruct, and watched with amusement as he pulled his pale grey shirt-tails over the much darker grey trousers, and stared at himself in the mirror.

You could have knocked her over with a feather, when he turned back to her and asked, "Will I do?" Regaining her composure, she nodded and waited patiently while he donned his overcoat and paid for the new trousers, requesting the soiled ones to be put in a bag.

At 3 West Terrace, Mobberley, Carol Beardly saw a very different Gabriel Black at her door, wearing chinos, even though they were dark grey. And he was with a woman.

"Hi, Gabriel."

He didn't fail to notice that Carol smiled approvingly and looked at Grace, happily awaiting an introduction.

As was now customary, he kissed Carol's cheek before taking hold of Grace's hand, saying, "Carol, this is my friend, Grace McGuire, who is also John's teacher." His smile widened as he added, almost conspiratorially, "So he'll no doubt call her Mrs McGuire!"

The two women smiled and shook hands, genuinely declaring how pleased they were to meet each other. Carol was glad to see the man she now regarded as her brother-in-law with an attractive woman; Grace was pleased to see a woman who wasn't a whore of some sort and who seemed to be able to touch this man in some way.

Grace McGuire was seeing yet another Gabriel Black.

"They're in the dining room, just finishing lunch. Excuse the mess." Carol followed Gabriel, who needed no further information to go in search of his son.

"Daddy, look, we made these crispy cakes." John pushed forward a plate with three remaining chocolate-coated cornflake cakes, empty wrappers betraying the fact that many more had been consumed.

"Oh, well done, you guys." Gabriel went over to John and hugged him.

Grace watched quietly from the doorway, soaking up this vision of relaxed father and son, in an ordinary family house. She immediately thought of the intimidating structure of Arnford Hall and wondered for a moment how that building had helped to shape this man.

"Shall Mrs McGuire and Aunty Carol and I have these last three cakes, then?" A resounding "yes" came from all four children and Gabriel offered the plate to the two women.

As John was politely saying hello to Mrs McGuire, following a sharp look from his father to remind him of his manners, Grace's face became a vision of astonishment as Craig said, not too quietly, "Uncle Gabriel, can we show you the pictures we've all done for you?"

As Black took in what the young boy meant, he only just remembered to give the packet he was holding to Carol. "Food for the orchid. I've written easy-to-follow instructions, and I'll check it next time."

"Great, thanks," said Carol, trying to stop herself biting her lip as she wondered just how much trouble she would be in if the plant were to die! She glanced at Grace, who was still adjusting to the use of the term "Uncle".

"OK," Black said, "show me these works of art, then." He tried not to make it appear obvious that no child had ever given him a picture, or indeed anything, before John came into his life. He followed the gang into the lounge, and was proudly presented with pictures of things that possibly resembled flowers, and, with a very vivid imagination, might even be orchids. He smiled to himself as he spied a brand new copy of *The Orchid Expert* on the floor.

Carol entered the room and immediately began to tidy the papers and pens that were lying on the carpet, along with an attempt to discreetly remove the orchid book, but a look from Gabriel told her she was too late, and she smiled and shrugged her shoulders.

"I must tell you, the children had an ulterior motive in drawing the pictures for you." She paused, thinking of her own complicity in the proceedings. "They really want to come and see John and his new house." Now she smiled shyly, lowering her head. "I thought pictures of orchids would make you happy. There, I've said it." All she needed to add was "I rest my case" as Gabriel stood in judgement over the four children looking up at him, and the woman now standing beside him, all awaiting his verdict.

"I see," he said solemnly, and he put his hands on John's shoulders. "Well, we'll see what we can arrange." Suddenly the room came alive, with the children asking excitedly, "When can we come?" and John proudly saying, "You'll see my bedroom, and Daddy might let us go for a swim."

Gabriel watched as his son then turned to Grace and said in his most polite voice, "Will you come too, Mrs McGuire?"

He waited for her reply, bestowing more importance on it than he could have imagined.

"I would love to, John."

As he watched her give her pupil a heartfelt hug, he felt a strange tightness in his own heart.

Carol offered to get some drinks, but Gabriel wasn't ready yet for Grace to start talking to more of his acquaintances. He was still mulling over how Grace had found out about him and Roger: *Lindsey?*

He also needed time to think where his little game with her was going, and what she was doing to his life.

Declining the drink, Gabriel helped John to gather his things and the Bentley was soon pulling away, leaving the arm-waving Beardlys behind.

As they came to a halt outside Arnford Hall, both Grace and Gabriel looked over to the open-doored and now Porsche-less garage.

There was a man clearing leaves from the west side of the drive and Gabriel called over, "Get that damn garage door locked," before taking hold of John's hand and climbing the steps, clearly expecting Grace to follow them.

She hesitated as the gargoyles warned, *Watch out for your behind!* She shuddered.

What mood will he be in now?

Gabriel waited for her in the inner hall. As she entered, his eyes followed hers to the door of her sanctuary.

Grace needed to get away from him for a while, and he couldn't blame her.

John looked up at her. His father had suggested in the car that they go shooting rabbits this afternoon. John wasn't too sure about this and Gabriel had said not to worry, they would talk about it when they got to the Hall.

Now the young boy asked, "Are you going to come shooting with us, Mrs McGuire?"

"I need to do some work, John. I'll probably see you later, but you have fun with your father."

Her eyes made contact with Gabriel, who looked at her intently for a second before taking John's hand in his, saying, "We'll see you for dinner, Mrs McGuire, half past five in the kitchen. Come on, John." His voice and manner made it clear this was an order; she had two and a half hours before he would expect to see her again.

Grace unlocked the door and breathed in the freshness of the room she was becoming quite attached to.

Chapter 49

Gabriel spent the next couple of hours showing John the gun-room, which was a small space, accessed from an external stairway leading down below the front of the house, with security gates at the top and bottom of the steps. There was an arrangement of guns in a secure cabinet, belonging to Gabriel, Roger, Steve, Cynthia and Ellouise. Cynthia Black had requested that she be permitted to buy John his first gun; it was a given that the young heir would shoot.

Gabriel had agreed, but he made it clear that no gun could be presented to John until he had been introduced to the family tradition of hunting. Even Gabriel Black had to admit, his mother was one of the best shots in the county.

Julian was the only member of the family who no longer took part in the sport. He just wasn't interested any more, and had hardly ever gone shooting with his family after the summer he was fifteen and first had sex with his mother.

A lot of things had changed that summer.

Now John stared in awe at his daddy, as Gabriel carefully showed him each gun and explained that Grandma would like to buy one for John so he could join Daddy and Roger and Steve and go shooting with Satan. The young boy remained quiet, pictures of the rabbits he had held at Stockley Farm when he had visited there with his mother last summer fresh in his memory.

"Do we kill the rabbits?" His voice was nervous, and he was only just holding back the tears.

"Yes, John, and we can eat them." Gabriel spoke authoritatively, trying to keep the boy's emotions at bay, as if it were the best way of educating the boy to treat animals as food or beings to be mastered, and admired even, but not to be fussed over. He thought of his own relationship with Satan, and the other dogs the family had had for as long as he could remember. None were ever brought into the house; they were there to do a job.

Gabriel Black suddenly heard his sister's words: *Oh for goodness' sake, GeeBee … when are you going to chill a bit with these house rules?*

Things were changing, and he wondered what Grace was doing in her sanctuary.

"Come on, John, we'll leave the guns for now. Let's just go out into the woods and I'll show you where some of the best shooting is. Uncle Julian and I used to go there a lot when we were young." Taking no nonsense from the reluctant heir, he locked up the gunroom and gates and headed out across the meadow at the back of the house, enjoying the mild autumn air, and not failing to notice how comfortable his new trousers were.

Meanwhile, Grace completed the work she needed to do over the weekend. There was a small platter of oat biscuits on the coffee table and a selection of pâtés and French cheeses in the fridge. Remembering she hadn't eaten any lunch, she helped herself to a selection and nibbled as she worked. By five o'clock she was contemplating going for a walk around the Hall. After all, what harm could it do? There were some lovely paintings and sculptures she would like to see in more detail.

Feeling a little nervous and wondering who else was in the house, she ventured into the main hallway and studied a large portrait of a handsome man in his forties. He was quite a bit stockier than the twins, but his hair and jawline were similar. Grace felt his eyes possessed the same warmth and kindness as Gabriel's, and there was something about his stance, as he leaned against a mantelpiece over a roaring fire, that portrayed an air of pride but also a strong, fatherly protection. She guessed this was Gabriel's father.

Grace stepped back and continued to absorb George Black's features.

Then she heard John's excited chattering. "OK, so Grandma is going to buy me a gun, but I can shoot pigeons with clay and they won't be killed?"

Grace hurriedly moved back to stand, unseen, just inside the sanctuary.

His frustrated father was heard to reply, no doubt for the umpteenth time, "No, John, you shoot at clays! They're discs made of clay and will just break if you hit them. Look, let's go and get ready for dinner and we'll go through everything when you get your new gun."

"When will that be? Can we ask Craig to come and he can shoot too? Can we, Daddy?"

The Blacks were approaching the sanctuary now.

"I think it would be better if Craig comes for a swim, John."

Grace held her breath, as she spied them walking past, aware of Gabriel gazing at her open door. Becoming conscious of one pair of footsteps stopping and heading back towards her, she heard him say, "You go on upstairs, John, and get ready to take a shower. I'll be right up in a minute."

There was silence for a few seconds and Grace wondered if Gabriel was waiting for John to disappear up the grand staircase. Then she heard a knock on the door.

"Grace?"

She slowly emerged from the shadow and stood before him, taking in the unaccustomed appearance of Gabriel Black in chinos. He seemed a little surprised and she realised he hadn't expected her to be in there.

"I … I thought you might have gone into the gardens." He paused, looking over to the window in the sanctuary, before adding, "I think it's going to be a lovely evening." He was still hovering in the doorway, looking uncomfortable.

For a moment their eyes locked onto each other before Grace turned away from him, saying, "You know what? I think I will take a stroll. I need to clear my head!" She tidied her papers into a neat pile and walked past him, leaving him still on the threshold of her sanctuary as she proceeded down the stone steps towards the kitchen, hoping the French door to the patio would be open.

Finding herself alone, she breathed in the cool, dry air as she stepped out and headed towards the woodland. She imagined Black senior had gone to have a shower with his son, and smiled, wondering if their discussion about shooting and cousins coming to stay would continue. She was well aware how frustrating some conversations with children could be, with constant tirades of questions, requests, miscomprehensions and sometimes temper tantrums when things didn't always go the way the small person wanted them to.

Then she let her mind drift to the thought of having her own child to care for, to love and nurture. A few years ago, it had been high on her priority list. For a while, at least. Then she realised she hadn't met the right man, probably never would, and the occasional subconscious memory of her father seemed to deny her the right to expect to have a child. In the cold light of day she knew there was no sense to this feeling, but it lingered. And now, approaching her fortieth birthday, she had resigned herself to the fact she would not become a mother – and probably wouldn't get married either.

As she continued her walk, she let her mind drift, and she had a vision of the Blacks' nanny living all alone, grateful when her former charge visited on the odd occasion when he was staying at his lakeside house. *Who would visit me? A year with your primary school teacher hardly develops into a lifelong relationship.*

She tried to picture Jason happily living in Cheshire, the two of them growing old together, snorting the odd line of cocaine. Or the two of them living in Putney and snorting lots of lines! She shuddered. Was that the relationship she wanted? Was that the best she could hope for?

Then she looked up and found herself standing in front of the tall sculpture of the conductor's baton, the one she had seen glinting in the sun on her first visit to Arnford Hall. What did this say about the master of the house? It was obvious he had a passion for instrumental music, and it would seem he also loved art. She glanced around to see if she could spot the treble clef sculpture, and as she turned she saw him walking towards her, his strides long and determined, and she could even feel his eyes trying to read her mind from the distance. She quickly glanced at her watch: was she going to be in trouble for being late for tea? But it was only 5.25 p.m., and she felt herself relax. *Oh girl, he's got such a hold on you now!*

As he came closer, Grace took in his deep navy shirt, black jeans and Caterpillar walking boots; his eyes, which looked as though they were asking for forgiveness – or was it acceptance? – and the smile, which seemed to say, "I'm sorry for being me, but hope that's OK with you," and she realised it was Julian.

For the second time since meeting him, she asked herself, *What torments him? What secret does he share with his brother?* And Roger's words echoed in her head: *We live with torment … and Gabe carries that for his family … Julian and Ellouise would have no family, if it were not for the sacrifice Gabe makes, and has been making for more than half his life now.*

"I hope I didn't startle you, Grace." Julian held his hand out to take hers in a sincere, caring gesture, as if to put her at ease.

She felt his grip and smiled warmly at him, and he returned a schoolboy grin.

"He's sent me to make sure you haven't run off and left him."

It was clear to Grace, now, that Roger had spoken the truth when he said no one would know what Gabriel Black was doing to Grace McGuire, or why she was really here at Arnford Hall.

She smiled at Julian. "I doubt those were his words."

"Well, no. I was instructed to find you." He brought his two hands before him, proudly, "Job done! And to remind you, and I hope I don't do it in quite the intimidating way my brother can," the schoolboy grin grew wider, "that it is tea time. Shall we go before we really piss him off?"

As they made their way back to the Hall, Grace felt quite at ease chatting with her captor's brother. *What else can I find out this weekend?*

"Who had the sculptures erected?"

"Gabriel had four installed about ten years ago. There are two musical ones, and two nudes. He likes to have beautiful things around him to admire." Julian hesitated as he stared at his companion. "And I can see why," he said quietly.

This was the side of Julian she was afraid of, and she remembered being glad to see Gabriel on the first night she had met his twin. *Are you jealous of your brother?* Grace carried on walking and felt his grip on her hand tighten.

There was silence for a moment and Grace looked at the Hall as it got closer and closer.

"I would like to say my brother is a very lucky man, Grace. But I'm afraid he's not." Julian stopped walking, causing Grace to stop too, as he maintained his grip on her. Slowly he raised her hand to his lips and kissed it chivalrously. "Don't look so worried, Grace…"

Oh, you sound just like him!

Julian continued. "Much as I'm tempted, I never take what is his. And I never hurt him; I owe him too much for that. Let's join everyone."

She caught a glimpse of a brotherly smile.

As the couple entered the kitchen, Grace couldn't fail to feel Gabriel's eyes on her and his brother, his questioning look lingering on Julian, and relief flashing across his face as Julian announced, "Delivered safe and sound." He made a majestic show of leading Grace to a stool at the island.

All eyes were on her: John, his father and Ellouise.

A very informal supper of roast chicken, baked potatoes and carrots and broccoli was enjoyed by all, including John. He delighted in telling everyone about his walk with Daddy to see where the best shooting was, and how great it was going to be when Grandma bought him a gun, and when Craig would come for a sleepover.

The forks of the Black adults then froze in mid-air as John asked his father, "Why do I always have to go for a sleepover with Roger when Grandma comes?"

Chapter 50

Grace studied the faces before her as time stood still.

Julian was the first to break the tension. His voice filled with nervous laughter as he leaned over to his nephew and said playfully, "Believe me, John, you'll have much more fun with Roger and Steve. Grandma doesn't like too much noise."

Uncle Julian was right, everyone was a lot quieter round here when she came, especially Daddy. Maybe her ears hurt!

Ellouise was the next to return to present time, as she confirmed Roger and Steve really enjoyed having John sleep over, and hoped he loved his room there; it was pretty special, wasn't it?

Yes, Aunty Ell was right too; he always had fun with them, and sometimes he got to have a McDonald's, even though Daddy didn't always approve!

Gabriel was the last to react. He moved back from the island, placed his cutlery together on his plate to indicate he had finished his half-eaten meal and, without looking at anyone, asked to be excused.

Grace stared after him as he left the room.

Ellouise touched her gently on the arm.

"Why don't you go to him, Grace? Tell him I'll see to John's bedtime tonight and I'll stay over. He doesn't need to worry about getting me back to the hotel."

Grace stared at Ellouise and Julian. She was shocked to see compassion in their eyes, and a plea for her to go after their brother.

Grace couldn't comprehend what had just happened, but somehow she knew that a nerve had been touched, a deep wound opened, a secret almost betrayed.

Feeling confused and a little apprehensive of how she would be received, Grace went in pursuit of her captor.

She reached her bedroom. The door was locked.

She swallowed deeply. Not sure why she was doing it, but feeling it was the right thing, she walked across the galleried landing and knocked on his bedroom door.

A moment passed before the handle turned.

Grace couldn't conceal her shock as he stood before her, his eyes glistening with a moisture she had seen only once before. That time, it had been extracted from him by passion, a passion that had been tangible between them when she had invited him into her sanctuary.

Now he looked desolate, and Grace was so moved by his sadness that her own vision became blurred. *What is this man going through? What – or who – is doing this to him?*

Suddenly she wanted her controlling, domineering, arrogant, even cruel and heartless at times, captor back. She wanted his protection, but she felt that, at this moment, he needed hers.

Very quietly, she heard herself say, "Ellouise thought you might like some company."

Gabriel stared at the woman before him, his bitter self-hatred consuming him, his shame enveloping him, his fear of failing John as a father, to be respected and loved, sickening him to his core.

"She said to say she'll put John to bed and stay here tonight." Grace was shaking, afraid that, since she was getting no reaction from him, her presence wasn't welcome. Shaking his head, he looked down for a moment before stepping out of his bedroom and pulling the door closed behind him. His body heaved as he sighed heavily, trying to regain control.

Slowly he took her hand and stroked it, feeling its softness, trailing his fingers across her knuckles and then caressing her thumb thoughtfully. His thoughts turned to John. He wanted to see his son, but was fearful of continuing questions. Maybe it would be better to let Ellouise put him to bed tonight. His confidence in her abilities to look after her nephew were growing and he was sure she could handle the young boy's innocent questions and verbal meanderings.

However, he was furious with himself for allowing Cynthia to dictate the return to her routine of coming over to Arnford Hall to see her son on Mondays and Wednesdays. Why the hell was he putting up with this now? It was ridiculous to think John could go on sleeping at Roger's for two days a week. It wasn't fair on his best friend and his husband!

Wouldn't his father release him from the promise that should never have been demanded, never have been made?

Grace waited for what seemed like an eternity for him to respond to her in some way. He just kept caressing her hand, deep in thought. Going over the strange events of a few minutes ago in the kitchen, she was trying to work out what it could all mean. Finally he broke the silence.

"Come with me."

Still holding her hand, he led her down the two flights of stairs and into his plant room.

"Wait here a moment," he instructed as he let go of her hand and went over to check some readings on a panel at the entrance.

During her first visit here with Roger, the PA had shown her the first "inner room", which he described as the warm house. Grace had been too nervous to pay much attention to anything back then, but now she looked around at the rows of orchids at various stages of flowering, the network of hoses running along tables, various gardening tools on a two-tier table. The inner wall was covered with photographs, charts and hand-written notes depicting prize specimens, seasonal tasks, temperatures and watering times.

As her eyes took in the display, he returned to her side and reached to take her hand again.

"Welcome to my retreat, my labour of love – although I don't attend to it as well as I used to. I have help in here now, and we have tried to automate as much as possible, but let me show you some of my favourites."

He was relaxed now, confident and master of his house once more, all awkward and dangerous questions forgotten for the time being.

"I guess I fell in love with the sensuality of the orchid. Did you know the name comes from the Greek word *orkhis*," and he smiled with a touch of mischief as he added, "or testicle.

Although I think some plants look like a beautiful, inviting vagina."

Grace tried to prevent herself from blushing, but doubted she was very successful, as she felt his hand squeeze hers. She remembered the orchid he had arranged to be in their room at the Wizard's Thatch, and how it had reminded her of a vagina.

He continued, talking to himself as much as to Grace. "I used to be besotted with these rooms, visiting every day, afraid to miss a flower which may only open for two or three days. Some species take on the pseudo-female appearance of an insect, to lure the male into pollinating the flower. Come and look at this *Stanhopea* and smell its fragrance." Gabriel led her over to a hanging basket full of flowers with cream and crimson petals, and lips of bolder yellow, falling downwards, and he held one for Grace to breathe in – it smelled of chocolate. Grace stared at him, respecting his knowledge, his skill in growing these beautiful plants, and his sensual enjoyment of them.

She closed her eyes a moment before declaring, "They're beautiful, sir."

He stared at her, her use of his title unexpected, and all the more appreciated, as emotionally he was still battling with his own self-hate, his desperation to be the best father he could for John, and his fear of losing the woman standing beside him.

He checked his watch. It was half past six; too soon for John to be in bed. Gabriel couldn't be certain where he and Ellouise would be, and he wasn't quite ready to see them again just yet. Besides, he needed some fresh air. He took Grace's hand and marched out of the plant room, grabbing two Barbour full-length wax coats from the cloakroom, and headed out to the garden.

"Put this on," he ordered and Grace could tell his mood was changing yet again.

She was swamped by the coat, which she imagined to be Julian's, and Gabriel raised his eyebrow as he watched her struggling to fasten it.

"Allow me." He took her hands away and deftly zipped it, pulling it up to her neck.

It felt warm and she could smell the wax and feel the weight of the fabric. Gone was the chill of the wind. And, apparently, gone was the vulnerability of the man now leading the way towards the wood.

They walked in silence and Grace listened to the crunching of the golden and yellow leaves beneath their feet, being replaced by silence as they walked across a mossy patch of open grass, a full, bright moon lighting their way. Gabriel walked with determination and she sensed this was not simply a pleasant stroll to lighten a strange mood.

At a fork in the path, clearly lit by the moon, he turned down a narrow footpath. Grace looked ahead of them and saw a faint glow of light in the distance.

As they got nearer she found herself looking at the two nude statues Julian had referred to. She stared in awe at the life-sized male and female, positioned to spend eternity back to back. They were placed approximately two feet apart. The female's hands were reaching out behind her, not quite touching the male's buttocks. The male's large, erect penis betrayed his "never to be satisfied" arousal and his face was immortalised in a look of pity and sadness. Grace walked around to the female's face, to see her tears of stone.

Gabriel stayed on the path and watched her.

She shivered and turned to stare at him. Her curiosity got the better of her as she heard herself ask, "Who chose such a strange pose? Was it the sculptor?" She hoped he would say "yes". She didn't want it to be Gabriel who had felt the deep sadness and loneliness that would have led someone to create such a desperate pose.

"No. I commissioned and designed them. You must know by now, Grace, I can never be satisfied. Nor loved."

"John loves you," she whispered, trying to block this artistic creation of torment from her mind.

"I hope so. And I hope I will never lose that love."

"Weren't you in love with his mother?"

His response echoed through the silence of the night. "No. And she never loved me. Let's head back. It's getting cold." The conversation was over.

Grace pulled the collar tighter to her neck and headed towards him. "I'm quite warm in this coat," she said, trying to lighten their mood.

"We'll take the longer way then." He reached for her hand and wrapped his fingers around hers. Feeling his warmth, she clung to the hope that he was beginning to relax again.

As they eventually approached the Hall, Grace noticed a swing and climbing frame placed on a well-manicured lawn. They looked a little out of place in the grounds of this stately hall.

Gabriel picked up on her gaze and explained, "They were from John's home. I thought it would be good to have them here for him. Hopefully they'll get a lot of use in the summer." He turned to see if there was a reaction from his companion.

"I think that's a good idea," she smiled, as she added, "they just look a little odd in a place like Arnford Hall."

"Mmm, yes, I guess they do," he sighed and squeezed the small, warm hand he was still holding.

After a few more minutes they entered the Hall through the French doors leading into the kitchen. Only the floor lighting was on, suggesting the household had retired upstairs for the night. It was half past seven. Gabriel was still not in the mood to bump into Ellouise or Julian just yet, so he decided to play it safe.

"So, my sister thought I needed cheering up, Grace," he smiled, in a threatening sort of way. "Well, let's see what you can do. Come on."

Still holding her hand, he led her across the hall towards the den, entering the code and pushing the door open.

Grace hesitated at the threshold, resisting the pull of his hand as he entered the room.

She stared at the bed. Memories of last night overshadowed the more pleasant ones of this morning. She tried to pierce the mask he had now raised, to judge what mood he was in. Were they going to share another passionate interlude, like the one they had enjoyed earlier in the wet room?

She entered the room. He released her hand and closed the door before flicking a switch on the wall and, as he came to stand behind her, dreamy sounds from an oboe began to fill the room.

"There will be no one else here tonight, Grace," he whispered, hoping to ease her tension, and she could feel his breath on the back of her neck.

"What is this music?" Grace tried to steady her voice as she struggled to hide her nervousness from him.

"'Gabriel's Oboe', from the film *The Mission*. Do you like it?"

She hadn't expected a question. "Oh … I usually need to hear something a couple of times before I can make up my mind but, yes, I think I do."

"Well, it's on repeat, so you'll have the chance to make up your mind. We'll change it if you decide it's not to your liking."

He came to face her and appeared thoughtful as he stared at her and licked his lips. He wanted her to be relaxed. Totally relaxed. And ready to do anything.

It was no longer the sad and vulnerable Gabriel Black before her. Now she knew he was ready to take control, to dominate, to threaten.

He's up to something! A mixture of erotic expectation and fear flowed through Grace's body, an exciting tingling welling up from deep within her. She clenched and felt a need to touch him, to feel him inside her, to be fucked by him.

Not knowing what he had in mind, Grace nervously shifted her weight from one leg to the other, as he continued to stare at her. A smile flickered across his lips and as they curved upwards, his eyes joined in and suddenly Gabriel Black was in game mode.

Grace's eyes fell to the bulge in his trousers, before darting back to his face as she gulped back her growing anticipation.

She lingered by the bottom of the bed, watching as he opened a drawer in one of the bedside tables and pondered over its contents.

After a moment he took out a teardrop-shaped black glass bottle; he studied it for a moment, before turning to his companion. Slowly he placed the black bottle beside the bed and approached her.

311

"Undress me, Grace; I want to be excited." His eyes were gleaming, challenging her to do as he commanded.

Her face expressed shock at his words. She had partly undressed him once before, in her sanctuary, where she had felt in control. She had completely undressed him in the den last night, where she had felt mortified. Now he was the master again, and this time she felt vulnerable. What was he expecting her to do?

"Grace. Do this for me." He waited.

With a determined look she approached him and began to undo the buttons on his shirt, letting it fall to the floor as his skin and dark chest hair were revealed. She found it easy to caress him, to trail her fingers over his chest, to squeeze and pull at his nipples. She felt his breath on her hair and heard his breathing begin to deepen, aware that he was luxuriating in the smell of her. She glanced up at him and felt empowered to see inside him as his mask began to fall, and she began to feel him need her. She nuzzled against him and slowly ran her tongue around his nipple, biting it with a libidinous intensity. As he moaned pleasurably, her desire to have him began to consume her. She wanted him. She wanted to excite him. She was hungry for him and her head swirled with earlier memories of the passion they had shared. This was easy. As she continued nibbling, she trailed a hand down and felt his hard penis trying to escape from his navy pinstriped trousers. He placed his own hand on top of hers and pressed hers deeper into him, whispering, "Feel me, Grace. I want you to feel me."

"You must wait." She breathed the words into his chest as her tongue and teeth turned their attention to his other nipple, the first one reddened and swollen from her attentions. His arousal was beginning to test his own self-control.

As he moved his hand away from his groin, she steadily eased hers down inside his trousers and trunks. She took hold of his long, thick penis, feeling the warm, velvety skin as she began to rub him, clasping her fingers around him before withdrawing completely to unfasten his trousers and push them to the floor.

312

"Sit on the bed." Her voice was controlled, and her confidence grew as he did her bidding, his eyes not leaving her as she knelt before him and slowly removed his socks, leaning down to kiss his foot, remembering how she had admired his feet last night. Barely realising what she was doing, she found herself sucking on his big toe, peppering her teeth along it, hearing him groan erotically as she aroused him further.

Then she raised herself up on her knees, her eyes level with his chest and, again, she rubbed his erect penis, which was still waiting to be freed. He placed his hands on her shoulders and she could feel their strength and their desire.

"This is good, Grace. Release me." He was almost pleading and she put her finger on his lips to silence him.

"Not yet. You asked to be excited." It was her turn to feel powerful as she pushed him back to lie on the bed.

Oh, how easily she was playing his game. She came up on the bed and straddled his chest. She leaned forward and placed her mouth over his, her tongue seeking and finding entry into his mouth, her hand seeking and finding re-entry into his trunks.

Again he groaned as he thrust his hips upwards and broke their kiss, repeating, "Release me, Grace."

"Please, sir." She smiled down at him.

"Please, Grace." His whole being was desperate to have her feel him, hold him, explore him.

Now as he raised his buttocks off the bed, Grace eased the elastic of his trunks under them and turned to face his feet as she rolled the CKs down his legs and cast them onto the floor.

His naked body lay beneath her fully clothed one; his erection begged her to take him. She took hold of his penis and delighted in hearing him moan more deeply. He was rock hard and she did what she realised she was most desperate to do. She tasted it.

"Oh, Grace." His words declared his pleasure at the erotic sensation she was creating within him. "I knew you could do this to me," and it was as though only she could do this for him.

"You need me." The words spilled from her mouth.

"I need you." His words were clear and certain; no masking, no disguising. He reached out and took hold of her waist. "Let me see you."

She paused a moment, sliding further down to settle between his legs to continue her task.

"All of you," he said. "I want to see all of you." He leaned up on his elbows to watch as she slid off the bed and slowly began to undress.

Now they were both naked and they lay on their sides in a circle, each pleasuring and exciting the other. His warm, soft fingers parted the lips of her vulva. His tongue lapped at her clitoris, and sighs escaped him as he drank her juices. All the while her hand gently pulled and pushed his penis into her mouth, her tongue licking the end, pushing into his slit, and then she pressed her mouth down, taking as much of his length into her throat as she could.

Slowly, they each became more intense in their actions. Grace paused to cry out in her own orgasm before greedily resuming her task, her movements becoming quicker and more forceful as she felt him tense and then release himself into her, his liquid coating her tongue, intoxicating her, empowering her.

She had just given her best blowjob ever, and was shocked by her own pleasure in it. He had just experienced exactly what he expected – the best blowjob he had ever received. He was shocked by his fear of what this woman was doing to him. However, that was going to change. He hadn't finished yet.

Confident that she was as relaxed as he was, he reached across to the black bottle on the bedside table. He placed it on the bed between them and sat back on his knees, as Grace sat up in front of him. She looked down at the bottle.

"I want you to feel *all* of me, Grace."

His emphasis of the word "all", and the dark look in his eyes, put her on edge. She wasn't quite sure what he meant until he asked, "Do you like postillionage, Grace?"

Chapter 51

Grace was hesitant. "I take it you're not referring to horse-riding." Her eyes widened in apprehension as she stared at the confident naked man before her. She moved back a little and swung her legs over the side of the bed.

He reached for her hand and she was surprised at the gentleness with which he took hold of her.

"No, I'm not. It's something rather more intimate." His eyes drilled into her, trying to gauge her reaction. *Was this asking too much of her? No matter.* He was desperate to feel her touch inside him and he needed to know how far she would go for him. Never before had he desired a woman to touch him as Roger had all those years ago. Yet he was now responding to urges which had begun to infiltrate his dreams, and he experienced a sensual desire to discover if this woman really was above all others. Would she do anything for him? Was her need to protect her current life enough to make her obey even this command? More importantly, he needed to know – could she take pleasure in pleasuring him in such a way?

He opened the bottle, took her hand and pumped some clear gel into her palm. Then he rubbed it over her fingers. Continuing to stroke her hand, his dark eyes, filled with lust, held hers. "I want you to enter my body and touch me where I haven't been touched for a very long time." He studied her face for a reaction, hopeful of detecting a willingness, however small.

Grace lowered her eyes and watched his fingers stroking her hand. It was an intimate gesture of need and confident expectancy.

He waited to see if she would pull back from him. She didn't.

She simply watched as he began to pump some more gel into his own hand. He shimmied closer, pulling her towards him, causing her to put her legs back on the bed and lie beside him. Lowering himself onto his back, he raised his knees and brought her left hand to his face, encouraging her to stroke his cheek.

He moved his other hand down to his buttocks and began to lubricate himself with the gel, watching her face the whole time. Then he took her gelled right hand and firmly moved it over his body, downwards, running it along his now semi-hard penis, touching his balls and then lower to his perineum. Here, he pressed her hand to him and moaned as his passion and desire for this most intimate time with her intensified. His head fell back onto the soft pillow and his body arched upwards in sheer pleasure.

Suddenly his eyes flashed open as Grace raised her hand, pulling it from underneath his. "Grace." His murmur was barely audible as he struggled to control himself, fearful of coming right then, but praying that this overwhelming sensation wouldn't end just yet.

"Sshh," she whispered. He felt her hand caress his cheek and move further to explore his face. He sighed before pressing his back into the bed, bowing his body, raising his buttocks as he felt her right hand gently, yet firmly, stroke his perineum. Then her fingers moved lower. He was breathless as he craved her touch, his desire hanging by a thread as he waited.

"I have never done this before," she breathed into his ear. "Am I doing it right?" Her hand moved lower and her slippery finger pressed slightly at the opening he wanted her to enter. Steadily she pressed and he moaned in bliss as she gradually buried her finger within his anus. He curved his spine into the bed, his eyes shut tight, turning his face into the hand that was caressing his cheek, his mouth eager to nibble and lick her fingers and palm.

"It feels so good, Grace. Please. Don't. Stop."

She placed another finger inside him. His skin felt tight around hers, but the lubrication ensured she could move and rotate smoothly. Carefully she crooked her finger at a slight angle and his moans confirmed that she was fulfilling her task. Her fingers explored him, the warmth of his body surrounding them, and finally she touched his prostate. His gasps and moans revealed a pleasure she didn't believe a man could express; an intense pleasure she didn't believe she was capable of giving.

Then she felt him take her hand from his face and move it down to his now very hard, throbbing penis. He couldn't hold back any longer and, as she took hold of him and moved that velvety skin up and down, up and down, his sperm gushed out and coated her hand. His eyes were shut tight and his body shuddered. Eventually he stilled and Grace withdrew her fingers as he pulled her close, hugging her to him.

She just lay with him, feeling intensely aroused by what she had just done. For him.

An eternity seemed to pass in the depth of their embrace until Gabriel leaned over to the bedside table and withdrew some wipes from the drawer. With the tenderness one would show to a lover, he gently wiped Grace's hands clean, kissing them passionately, staring deeply into her eyes, his own filled with an ardent gratitude. Then he gently pressed her back onto the bed, raising her knees and pushing them apart, fully exposing her most private part. "You are beautiful, Grace, all over," he whispered. He held her legs open to give his tongue full access to her clitoris and the entrance to her G-spot. He savoured her taste and craved her release.

Grace felt her orgasm build quickly, pleasurably, excitingly – and she knew it would not be long before she would climax. The pressure and rhythm of his tongue was exquisite, perfect, and she came.

He moved up her body and, as his lips reached hers, she could taste herself in his kiss, before feeling his tongue deep in her mouth. It was paradise.

"What are you doing to me?" she whispered.

"Punishment and reward, Grace. You ask too many questions, remember."

"You are wrong, sir."

He stared at her, his face covered with a puzzled expression.

"There was no punishment tonight."

Grace moved her hands down and stroked his buttocks. She traced her fingers along the crack between them and over his anus. She smiled. She liked it.

He closed his eyes, then lifted her hand up and rolled her onto her back.

317

"My breaking dawn," he muttered quietly, adding, as if to himself, "What am I going to do with you, Grace?"

They lay side by side, softly stroking each other for a while, each deep in their own thoughts.

Eventually, he got off the bed and held his hand out to pull her up.

"It's late now. Everyone will be in bed. Let's go upstairs."

As they reached the galleried landing which separated his bedroom from hers, he paused, appearing to contemplate which door to open.

"Wait here. I just need to get something."

He entered his bedroom, closing the door behind him. A moment later Grace heard the click of a lock, coming from a short, darkened corridor she hadn't noticed before.

Then the bedroom door opened again and he returned to her side.

Taking her hand, he led her down the short corridor and opened the door at the end of it. This was a second doorway to his private bathroom, only ever used by the cleaning staff when he didn't want them to enter via his own bedroom.

Feeling excited and nervous, Grace glanced around the room. It was a large space with soft lighting absorbed by matt grey stone tiles on the walls and floors, and modern white porcelain fixtures. Thick black towels monogrammed with a silver "GB" hung on a chrome towel rail. In the middle of the room, taking centre stage, was a large double bath sunk into the floor, surrounded by oak-coloured stone, and inlaid with lights to shimmer beneath the water.

It was beautiful, and Grace couldn't move, overcome by the enigma of this man and his world.

Gabriel bent down to the bath surround and raised the lever of a tap to let water gush in, adding splashes of Chanel bubble bath to create a frothy, fragrant pool. He held her hand as she lowered herself into the water. He followed and they lay back, resting their heads on white bath pillows, facing each other.

Grace had closed her eyes and a satiated tiredness was consuming her when she suddenly heard his voice, aware that his dark eyes were staring at her.

"Am I forgiven for last night, Grace?"

She hesitated a moment and remained still before replying, "Will you make me go to another games night?"

"Yes."

She ducked under the water a moment, escaping the air and his eyes, denying him the ability to read her thoughts.

"No, then," she said as she pushed the water from her face, again shielding her expression from him.

He suddenly leaned forward and took hold of her hands.

"Best try to avoid punishments then, Grace." He hesitated, remembering her willingness to perform the task he had requested tonight. "Or perhaps we can teach you to like it."

His look became even more intent and Grace shivered.

He started to climb out of the bath. "Stay in for a little longer and relax."

She didn't need telling twice. The water was wonderful and she felt concealed by the bubbles. She lazily watched her captor dry himself and then walk out of the room. Her eyes closed and time simply disappeared.

She wasn't sure if it was a few seconds or a few minutes later before she heard him come back into the bathroom. By the time she forced her eyes to open he was standing at the side of the bath, holding a towel up, expecting her to leave the water. She complied and he wrapped the luxurious, warm fabric around her body and gently patted her dry. He then let the towel fall to the floor. He grabbed a small towel as he took her hand and led her to her bedroom. He sat on the end of the bed.

"Sit here, Grace."

He held the towel aloft and motioned to the carpet between his legs. She realised he intended to dry her hair.

She settled down with her legs stretched out before her and leaned her head back. She felt his fingers massaging her scalp as he gently rubbed. He then reached for a brush and carefully ran it through her damp hair, heeding the inevitable small knots, trying not to hurt her. The actions were gentle and they shared a sensual enjoyment. As he completed this task she could feel his hands rub the top of her shoulders. He moved further back onto the bed, creating a space between his legs, and eased her

319

up to sit in front of him. He took hold of her wrists and held them behind her back, tilting her face towards him. He placed a light, tender kiss on her lips.

"Thank you for tonight, Grace." He smiled at the look of surprise on her face. Then he let go.

"But it's time to go. I'll get your clothes," and he left the room.

Grace glanced at her watch. It was half past ten. She sat back down on the bed and tried to assess how she felt. There was a part of her that was beginning to feel like she belonged in this house, as though she could be another one of its occupants. She wondered about Roger and Steve and the triangle of the happy couple virtually living with an ex-lover. It seemed to work. The three of them managed it. She tried to imagine what changes John had brought to their lives, and she remembered his question at dinner, "Why do I always have to go for a sleepover with Roger when Grandma comes?"

What would make a young boy go and stay with his father's PA when his grandmother came to visit?

The racing of her imagination slowed as Gabriel returned with their clothes.

"Did you like the bouquet, Grace?" He broke the silence as they continued to get dressed.

"It was unusual," she replied. "What did you mean by not getting too close to you?" She laughed nervously, glancing over to him as she continued, "Ha! Why on earth should I want to get close to you?" She immediately looked away, regretting the distance her words had put between them, and was shocked at her own feeling of regret that she wasn't close to him; couldn't be close to him.

Was she just going to be a fuck buddy like the other females in his life?

He stared at her intently, a brief look of hurt in his eyes. "It was a warning. Unnecessary, it seems."

Then he too looked away, remembering how she had touched him in the den, how he wanted to feel her touch him again.

But it was not to be.

"Come, Grace. I'll take you home."

She stared at him. After all they had been through. The poker night. The plant room. The den. Touching inside him. His bathroom. The intimacy. The pleasure. This man.

Oh, help me! I don't want to go …

She couldn't look at him. All her physical effort was concentrated on putting one foot in front of the other. He stopped outside her sanctuary. Her work papers had been placed in a supple, red leather document carrier.

Where did this come from? She ran her fingers over it, admiring its softness. Before her admiration became too evident, she quickly pushed it into her overnight bag, which had been placed next to it.

She walked to the front door and stopped to wait while he opened it, not looking at him.

The Bentley was at the bottom of the steps.

Goodbye, Grace. The gargoyles were solemn and sober and Grace felt a finality in their words. She hurried past them and climbed into the car as he held the door open.

Their silent journey was over within minutes.

Then he asked her to turn around and she heard the faint click as he took the collar off.

At the threshold of her door, he simply said, "Goodnight, Grace. Thank you."

She stared into his eyes. They were impenetrable. He turned and walked to the car without looking back at her.

Chapter 52

Grace lay in her bed staring at the ceiling. It was Saturday night, nearly Sunday morning, and she tried to analyse how she felt; decipher her feelings to determine what he was doing to her. She believed his need for her was growing, becoming a passion; she was sure she had interpreted his emotions correctly tonight. He said he wanted her to touch him as no woman had done. Only Roger had touched him like that. He had embraced her, caressed her. She believed he had made love to her. But he didn't love her. He made her think he wanted her. But he didn't need her. He had enslaved her. Now she had a feeling he had just let her go. She knew he wouldn't send for her tomorrow.

She struggled to get to sleep but eventually tiredness consumed her and she opened her eyes to Sunday morning.

It was ten o'clock and Grace was on her second cup of coffee, as she stared at the red leather document carrier on the table in front of her. Was this supposed to be a gift? Or was it just another sort of tag to show he owned her? It was inscribed with the letter "G" – for Grace or Gabriel?

She withdrew her work papers and placed the empty case in one of the cupboards in the kitchen, to sit alongside all the other odds and ends which had no proper place in her home, but from which she didn't want to be parted. She closed the cupboard door, feeling oddly satisfied with her decision to ignore the gift, the tag or whatever the hell it was supposed to be.

It had been a while since she had a Sunday to herself and she was still pondering what to do when her phone rang.

"Hi, Grace. It's Ellouise Black. I wondered if you would like to meet for lunch today?"

Grace hesitated. Why had his sister rung? Did Gabriel know she was ringing?

Oh sod it! Maybe she could find some more out about Black; she had nothing to lose.

"OK. That would be nice. Did you have anywhere in mind?"

"Join me at the hotel, here at the Cottons. The restaurant isn't too bad and they have a lovely Prosecco. I'll pick you up at twelve and we can get Michael to take you home."

"Oh no, it's OK, I can drive."

"No, no. It'll be nice to have a drink and chat. And don't worry. I know you won't want to be too late, since you have school tomorrow. See you at twelve," and Ellouise put the phone down.

Grace was wearing cream skinny jeans and a black polo-neck sweater, courtesy of Marks and Spencer. She pulled on knee-length black leather boots and felt confident in her appearance, although she suspected there would be quite a contrast with Ellouise's attire.

Of course, she was right. At five past twelve – she wasn't as punctual as her brother – Ellouise was knocking on Grace's door, dressed in a Roberto Cavalli silk trouser suit in midnight purple, emblazoned with rows of fuchsias and white beading leading down to multi-coloured, oversized flowers of crimson, lemon, jade and tangerine. Her stature was enhanced by high-heeled Jimmy Choo black lattice boots. She could have stepped straight off the cover of *Grazia*!

"Wow!" Grace exclaimed. "You look amazing, Ellouise."

"Thanks, Grace. It's lovely to see you. You have a delightful house," she exclaimed as she peered inside, over Grace's shoulder, and then stepped back to look up at the house.

As the two women headed to Ellouise's car, she continued talking. "Gabriel is buying me a bungalow similar to this."

By the word "similar", Grace knew she meant "small too"!

"It's the one near school. So I can help look after John."

"Sounds a good idea. And very generous! When do you get the keys?" Grace asked, genuinely interested. After all, if Ellouise was going to be dropping John off and picking him up from school, Grace was going to be seeing less of Gabriel, surely?

"Oh, I've no idea. Roger, bless him, is sorting everything out. He's such a treasure. Intelligent and lovely. I guess you've noticed that."

Grace smiled as she pictured gentle, caring Roger. "Yes. I like him a lot."

As the journey continued it wasn't difficult for Grace to remain quiet, listening to the other woman's ideas on decorating her bungalow, including another bedroom for John. What with the Hall, the lakeside house, Roger and Steve's and now Ellouise – how many bedrooms did a seven-year-old need?

It was about a ten-minute drive to the Cottons Hotel, and Grace wasn't surprised at how easily she was able to chat with Ellouise, who didn't seem to have any of the dark hang-ups which appeared to be embedded in the characters of her two brothers. She was like a free spirit, capable of adapting to the environment around her and changing if and when the need arose. Or the desire took her. Added to this, she seemed happy, genuinely happy.

To be close to her brothers again? Grace wondered.

As the two women waited for their starters, they sipped their Prosecco. Grace agreed it was delicious. One or two glasses wouldn't hurt her.

"I was surprised you weren't at breakfast with us this morning, Grace." Ellouise had become more serious now. She had pulled her long hair away from her shoulders to hang down her back and her features became leaner as though she had shed several pounds by this simple act. Not that she needed to lose any weight from her already willowy figure.

She continued. "Gabriel said you wanted to get home last night."

There was a pause, but it was clear Ellouise hadn't finished this line of conversation. "I'm surprised he let you. I thought you wouldn't want to miss the opportunity to have the whole day with him and John." She paused, her eyes resting on Grace's, expecting her to say something.

Grace remained silent, pondering over whether she should just play along with the fantasy girlfriend/boyfriend façade that Gabriel Black had so easily let those around him believe. If she did go along with it for now, would she be able to find out more about him? Perhaps why he used to have a sanctuary?

Grace decided to pick her words carefully. She needed to think of an excuse for going home, although Black had all but thrown her out of Arnford Hall last night. Even she wasn't sure why. But her explanation to the woman before her needed to be carefully thought through.

"I was expecting a visitor this morning and I needed to be home for them." Really? On a Sunday morning? She hoped her awkwardness wasn't too obvious.

"Was it Jason?"

Grace had just swallowed some Prosecco to hide her nerves and, as it sprayed across the table, she wished she hadn't. She started to cough .

"I'm so sorry." Grace tried to regain her composure and to stop herself looking like a dribbling idiot. "Yes, it was Jason." Well. So much for trying to carry on the girlfriend/boyfriend deception. Now she was portraying herself as a two-timing bitch. Grace leaned back in her chair and waited for Ellouise's reaction. She was surprised to see her smile.

"It's rather ironic, isn't it? My brother appears to be going monogamous" – Grace couldn't help noticing that Ellouise held her breath a moment at the word "monogamous" – "for the first time in his life, and the woman he does it for is having sex with someone else!" The younger woman stared intently at Grace.

But Grace was determined to maintain her dignity here, or to try to at least!

"We never agreed to exclusivity in our relationship." Was she really saying this?

"No. He wouldn't. He probably never expected to want that. Where did you pick Jason up?"

I beg your pardon?

"Er ... I've known him a long time. Way before your brother." Grace somehow found it hard to say "Gabriel". Had he trained her so well with that bloody title "sir"?

"Oh." Ellouise started to eat her melon. "Do you mind me asking if he pays you – you know, for the sex and stuff?"

For fuck's sake! What is this woman saying?

Grace was beginning to feel angry. Just exactly why had Ellouise invited her out for lunch?

"No, Ellouise. Of course he doesn't." Suddenly Grace stopped. *Was she prostituting herself for this man? Was his silence, his promise not to reveal her true identity, payment for the sex they were having? Hell, yes it was. Who are you kidding, Grace?*

"I didn't mean to embarrass you, Grace. But you do know he does do that. Or, rather, he did."

Grace gulped her wine. Then she suddenly thought of what Gabriel had said at the restaurant yesterday. "Of course I know, Ellouise. Your brother and I are just fuck buddies. Jason is my actual boyfriend." She sipped some more, her eyes watching for the other woman's reaction.

Ellouise picked her napkin up and gently dabbed at her lips before saying, "Oh. I see. I presume Gabriel knows this. Funny how you seem to be the woman for whom he has given up all the others, and yet you still have a boyfriend."

At that moment the waiter came to clear their dishes and she paused.

Grace leaned back in her chair, not quite sure where this conversation, or indeed the afternoon, was heading.

Their main course, of tiger prawn linguine, arrived.

"Well, I didn't ask him to give them up."

Ellouise smiled. "I'm sure you didn't. That would probably have guaranteed that he would see them more often! For an older brother, he can be a right jerk at times. But don't tell him I said that. Come on, let's eat and talk about something else."

Her mood suddenly seemed lighter and her eyes twinkled.

"I think we can be friends, Grace. You never know, Gabriel may even sweep you off your feet, and I'm pretty damn sure he could make you forget all your other boyfriends."

Grace was about to point out that she only had one man, but somehow felt that minor detail would not alter Ellouise's plan. This woman was up to something.

"Will you help me decorate my new home, Grace?"

Grace didn't see that coming. "Oh. I'm not sure I would have time, Ellouise. I'm really busy with work and don't have any free time really."

"I'm sure you could fit in a few evenings with a bottle of wine and we could go over colour schemes and fabrics and the like. It would be such fun. And, don't worry, I'm not expecting you to actually *do* any of the decorating. I'll be able to manage that and get help with anything I can't do."

The arrangement seemed to be set. Grace had a feeling she was going to be seeing quite a bit more of this woman. It might just be fun – and she was sure she would find out a lot more about her captor over the next few weeks.

Chapter 53

That night Grace stared at *his* phone, surprised and, she had to admit, a little disappointed that he hadn't summoned her. Did he know Ellouise had seen her? Had she told him that Grace had said he was just her fuck buddy?

She wondered how much of their conversation Ellouise would share with her brother. A smile came to her lips as she felt proud of herself for turning the table on him and his own fuck buddies. Two could play games. Maybe Grace could start throwing some dice, after all.

She finally went to bed, feeling she couldn't wait to see him again and see his reaction to the recent events. Would he want to punish her for asking questions, for calling him her fuck buddy? She closed her eyes, remembering the power she had felt over him when she had touched him so intimately last night, in a way she had never touched anyone before. It wasn't just power. It was pleasure. She had enjoyed it. All of it. She wanted to see him and have a chance, again, to hear him under the spell of the pleasure she knew she could give him. But she tried to quell her desire. It wouldn't work. Their relationship wasn't real. He was enslaving her for one year. That was all. She needed to remind herself of that fact.

Chapter 54

The next morning, as Grace McGuire led her class from the playground she glanced briefly at John Black's father, as he walked steadily away from the school.

The children were particularly lively today and, before she knew it, Grace was reminding them to collect their book bags to take home. As she tidied her papers together, she glanced through the window and caught sight of Black talking to the mother of Adam, John's school friend. She was alarmed at the intensity of her curiosity, startled to realise she was trying to think of a reason to go into the playground, to interrupt them, simply to find out what they were saying.

Adam's mother was married. Adam would like John to come and play at his house. Adam's mother would ask John's father if his son could come for tea. John's father would go to Adam's house. Adam's father would probably be at work. Black would have a drink with Adam's mother. Adam's mother was tall, slim, dark-haired and attractive – very attractive.

Grace slammed the book she was holding down onto the desk in front of her. *What's the matter with you?* She felt furious with herself for her stupid thoughts as she grabbed her bag and headed to the staffroom. What did she care about who Gabriel Black saw? It was good that John should go to play with his friends and do the normal things that boys his age did. But as she sat at one of the tables and began to prepare her planning notes for tomorrow, her mind kept wandering back to what was being said in the playground.

"I said, do you want some tea, Grace?" Jane was looking directly at her.

"Oh. I'm sorry. I didn't hear you."

"No. You looked miles away," Jane said as she turned to take cups from the cupboard. "I think you could do with a cup of tea. Peppermint?"

"Yes. Thanks. I just want to get these spelling tests marked and then I'm going to call it a day."

"Is Jason coming up at the weekend? Maybe we could all go for a drink on Saturday?"

Grace glanced at the bag that contained *his* phone. She really had no control over her life at the moment. He could summon her at any time. How many more times would she have to change her plans at the last minute in order to make herself available for Black? She felt deflated and wondered if it was really worth the effort to arrange anything, knowing he could ruin it.

"I'm not sure," she muttered.

Jane sensed something wasn't quite right with her friend. "Are you two OK?" she asked, surmising the couple had had some sort of tiff over the weekend.

"Oh, yeah. We're fine. I didn't see Jason this weekend, but let me check with him and see if he can come up. You're right. We could make an evening of it on Saturday." Then wishing to divert the conversation away from her own relationship, Grace added, "Have you guys seen that new film with Matt Bomer in it?"

Having successfully distracted Jane from her own problems, Grace enjoyed her cup of tea and got the marking out of the way before leaving school.

Once home she made herself some cheese on toast and picked up the phone to speak to her boyfriend.

"Hi. How was your weekend? Sorry I didn't get to ring you on Sunday."

Jason sounded tired. "That's OK, Grace. I went to watch the Saracens rugby with Nick on Saturday, and spent most of Sunday recovering from the celebratory drinks in the pub after the game."

"I trust it was just alcohol you were recovering from." She tried not to sound too accusatory, as her boyfriend hadn't mentioned buying any stuff recently.

"Yes, Grace," he replied quietly. "I haven't used anything for over a week now, honey. I missed you this weekend. Can I come up on Friday?" There was no attempt to hide his concern that all may not be well between them, or the pleading in his voice.

With her fingers crossed, and a forced eagerness in her voice, Grace replied, "Of course you can come. And I'll try to make sure I won't need to work too much. I can arrange for us to go out Saturday, with Jane and Carl and maybe some others. What do you think?"

"Good idea. We haven't done that for ages."

Grace sensed a smile on his lips as he added, "I can't wait till Friday, Grace. So tell me, how was your day?"

By the time Grace put the phone down, she felt a bit more relaxed, a little less guilty and a lot more tired. As she brushed her teeth, she tried to convince herself that she was only doing what Black was forcing her to do. She wasn't being unfaithful to her boyfriend through choice. In fact, ironically, she was going to her captor to save her relationship with Jason. She was certain they would have no relationship if he ever found out about what her father had done. She was convinced that no man who knew the truth about her past would want a relationship with her.

Yet, Gabriel Black did know. And he had shown her tenderness and affection. He also asked her to keep her distance, not to let him get too close to her – didn't that imply that he actually wanted to be with her? He asked if she were his breaking dawn, his saving Grace.

Am I nobody to him?

Chapter 55

The next four days came and went uneventfully, unmemorably.

Friday soon came, and the children were just putting their coats on to head home for the weekend. They had slips of paper in their bags with details of the forthcoming parents' evening, to be held after the half-term holidays. Grace went among the boys and girls, helping to ensure nobody left anything behind. She stood by John Black and Adam.

"What are you boys up to this weekend?" *So? It's just an innocent question!*

John beamed at his teacher.

"I'm going to play at Adam's house. My daddy said I can, as long as I'm good, and I can stay until six o'clock."

"Yeah, and we're going to play superheroes," added Adam, proudly.

"Oh, that sounds great fun. Have a lovely time, boys, and enjoy the weekend."

"Will you come over for tea again sometime soon, Mrs McGuire?" John was smiling and the question was spontaneous and innocent.

Grace realised she missed seeing this lovely boy out of school, who had been dealt such a cruel blow in his young life, but whose father was protecting him and apparently helping him to cope with his new life. She admitted it said a lot about the character of the man, whose own life had been changed so completely and irrevocably.

Was John the reason for the change in his father's sexual habits? The new monogamy, his relationship with a woman which was guaranteed to end within the year, and from which he would walk away with a blank page upon which to continue to write his life's story?

She looked down at John. "Maybe, John. That would be nice. Now go and find your parents and have a lovely weekend."

By half past four she was getting into her car to go home and wait for Jason, Gabriel Black pushed to the back of her mind, her fingers still crossed that he didn't call upon her and spoil this weekend with Jason. She felt she had some work to do on the relationship she intended to keep once Black had cast her aside and moved on.

On Monday Gabriel Black had listened condescendingly to Adam's mother, uncertain whether he wanted his son to go to a stranger's house and play with a boy whom Gabriel didn't know. But John's pleading, together with Adam's undeniable eagerness, made Black realise it wouldn't be wise to simply say no. He had immediately arranged for Adam Bretton's family and all known associates to be checked out. After all, whether Eliza Redfern would have accepted it or not, John Black was not an ordinary boy in the playground. He stood to inherit millions of pounds. For his own safety, his identity – and family background – needed to be kept hidden as much as possible, and his safety was of the utmost importance to his father, the Black family and their friends. The money was not the reason for the protection Gabriel insisted on for his son; it was his love for John, the most important person in the world to him. The money merely added a layer of complication, which couldn't be ignored.

So when someone wanted his son to go to their house for tea, Gabriel Black needed to know exactly who that someone was, and all possible connections to them. By Tuesday evening, he was able to confirm to Mrs Bretton that John could go. The chauffeur would take them all home from school that afternoon and would wait outside the Bretton residence until six o'clock to bring John back to Arnford Hall.

Having discussed the protocol of school friendships with Carol Beardly, Black also accepted there would be occasions when John would want to bring friends home. To Arnford Hall.

He remembered the excitement in the Beardly household at the prospect of going to John's new house.

Back at Arnford Hall Gabriel got his phone and dialled Carol's number. After exchanging the usual pleasantries, he said, "Come over for the afternoon on Saturday with the children and bring your swimwear."

Carol's face lit up. "That will be lovely. We're looking forward to it already! What plans have you guys got for next week?"

"What do you mean?" Gabriel sounded perplexed.

"It's the school holidays, Gabriel. The children won't be in school."

There was no response for a moment. Gabriel mentally went through his appointments for next week: he had planned to spend Monday and Tuesday with Roger and Julian going over group structure and strategies as part of Julian's induction back into the family empire; on Wednesday he was going to review correspondence and weekly business reports from the operating units; on Thursday he had been invited to a charity luncheon; on Thursday and Friday, he was going to prepare for the Black Communications board meeting on Monday.

Carol's voice broke into his thoughts. "John can join us. I was planning a couple of days out to break the week up: Chester Zoo and the Crocky Trail if the weather holds up. We'd love to have him with us."

"Thanks, Carol. It seems I have overlooked this. Let me talk to John – I'm sure he would love to come over to you. I'll also see what I can rearrange to free up some of my own time to spend with him. I'll get back to you when I can confirm everything."

Carol smiled to herself. *He needs to feel in control, leaving no loose ends, nothing to happen spontaneously. Well, if you don't count the fact he totally forgot about the week's holiday, that is!*

And so Gabriel's busy schedule led to an undisturbed weekend for Grace; a weekend to spend with Jason, but one that left her slightly on edge, not knowing if her captor was going to summon her.

Chapter 56

Gabriel Black sat by his intercom on Friday evening, waiting for notification that his son was on his way back to him.

Saturday afternoon was spent with John's Aunty Number One, Carol, and his three cousins. They all swam, played with balls, dive sticks and inflatables, and enjoyed a picnic tea of pizza and chocolate brownies, with some healthy fruit forced on everyone by the host.

The Sunday passed slowly, with the two Blacks staying around the Hall, walking Satan, and the son watching his father try out the new clay pigeon machine before John got his own gun from his grandma. The day ended with a kick-about with a football and Black junior hanging off the climbing frame.

By Sunday night, an exhausted Gabriel had finally put his "not really tired yet" son to bed. He made his way down to the octagonal room and poured himself a large whisky. Roger and Steve were not around this evening and Julian was out with Lindsey. He hadn't seen or heard from Ellouise since last Sunday morning. Although he was curious about her movements, he also respected her need for privacy and independence. They had always been important to his little sister. Now that he had her agreement to stay in Arnford for the foreseeable future, he was also careful not to frighten her away with his tendency to monitor and control those around him. He was confident it wouldn't be too long before he heard from her. She loved her nephew and hated to be away from him for too long.

At that moment, his mobile phone rang and he found himself sounding tired as he answered. "Hi, Ellouise. I was wondering when you were going to call and come and see us."

"GeeBee, hi. You sound exhausted."

You don't say. He took a sip of whisky, knowing he wouldn't be called upon to partake in the conversation just yet.

"I've had quite a busy week, thinking about my new home. Grace is going to help me decide on the décor. I've been to

Manchester, Liverpool, Chester and Birmingham looking for ideas and meeting with several interior design consultants. But I'm going to go down to London and see Andreas. You know I love what he can do with colours and textures. I know I don't have much space, but I can make it really cosy and welcoming, and I think I can extend off the dining room without losing too much of the useable garden space. I'm so lucky the bungalow is on a great plot. Of course, I want to keep some garden for John and his friends. It will be great for them to play after school before you or Michael come to collect him. Of course, I could bring him back to the Hall. But not on a Monday or Wednesday." She suddenly went silent.

Gabriel was still at the "Grace is going to help me …" part of the soliloquy. It took him a moment to realise she had stopped talking.

"I'm sorry, Ellouise?"

"No. I'm sorry, GeeBee. I didn't mean it to sound like that. But I really have to be in the mood to see her. You don't mind, do you?"

"See who?"

"Mother! Are you listening to me?"

"Yes, of course." He sat up straight. "When did you see Grace?"

"What?"

"You said Grace is going to help you …"

"Oh, dear Lord. You do love her!"

"Fuck, Ellouise!" He stood up and walked over to a side table by the window seat, mindlessly caressing a piece of Lladro – two beautifully detailed nude lovers, entitled "Passionate Kiss". "I merely asked when you saw her. Don't make assumptions, damn it!"

There was a moment's silence and Gabriel suddenly felt a little nervous. When his sister paused, she often followed it by saying something quite profound. He wasn't sure he was in the mood for the way this conversation was going.

"GeeBee. I just spoke about our mother."

Silence.

Then he managed to say, "Oh."

"Look. Can I come for tea on Tuesday? I can pick John up from school and I could stay over."

"Yes. He'd like that." Gabriel ran his hand over the back of his head and sighed. "So would I. Goodnight, Ellouise. We'll see you on Tuesday. By the way, there's no school next week. Apparently they get a week's holiday."

"Oh, great. Let me take my nephew out for the day. I'll think of something. Goodnight, darling. I love you, GeeBee."

"I know. You too."

Chapter 57

On Sunday night, Grace lay alone in her bed, mentally going through the events of the weekend.

She had been genuinely pleased to see Jason. He had picked up flowers on his way to her house, a bouquet of luxurious lilies in autumnal colours. He was wearing a cream-coloured V-neck sweater, paired with black jeans and brown leather boots. He looked handsome.

Grace had made an effort with her own appearance, having showered and put on pale grey lounge pants with a pale blue cashmere loose-fitting sweater. Her feet were bare and displayed her pedicured nails, which were coloured pearly grey.

"You look lovely." Jason hugged her and nuzzled at her neck, smelling her familiar Chanel No. 5 perfume.

Grace raised her chin to allow him easier access to her neck and felt herself relax into his embrace, warmed in the knowledge that he was glad to see her, and confident that she felt glad he was there.

She had already decided she wanted this weekend to go well. They needed to reconnect as a couple. Gone was her guilty conscience, banished was her self-blame, evicted were her emotions connected with a certain other gentleman. She had spent the last twenty minutes clearing her mind, resolving to forget all about Gabriel Black, his hold over her and her submission to his bidding. This weekend it was just her and Jason – she mentally crossed her fingers – and she was going to do all she could to make sure they both enjoyed it.

Sex in the bedroom was tender and more passionate than it had been over the recent weeks, and she slept more soundly, wrapped in Jason's arms, than she had done all week.

All in all, it had been a lovely weekend. But Grace shamefully acknowledged that, on more than one occasion, she had wondered why *his* phone had not rung.

Jason caught the late train home. If it hadn't been for a meeting he had to get back for on Monday morning, he would have stayed another night, seeing as Grace didn't have to go into work. But he knew his teacher well enough now to realise that school holidays for the children didn't always equate to holidays for the teachers – especially if those teachers were part of the senior management team, and had additional duties too.

Grace had plans to work on the files for her pupils with additional needs and to review some notes from a training session she had attended last week. Still, if all went to plan, and she was still in control of her own time, she had agreed that she would go down to Jason's on Thursday and stay until Sunday morning.

Suddenly life took on an air of normality.

On Monday morning her telephone rang and Grace recognised Ellouise's number.

"Hi, Ellouise."

"Hi, Grace. Hope you enjoyed your weekend. Are you doing anything tonight? I thought we could make a start looking at some schemes I'm contemplating for the bungalow. I could come over to you, if you like?"

Grace was planning to work at home all day. She had bought some ingredients to whip up a chicken casserole without too much effort, and spending some time with the vibrant, unpredictable Ellouise Black seemed a pleasant proposition for the evening.

"That would be lovely. I'm not sure what I can add to the proceedings, but it will be nice to see you and I'd love to go through your ideas with you. I can remember how excited I was when I first bought this place." Grace didn't mention that her excitement had been coupled with the immense relief of having confidence in her new identity and the opportunity to start her new life afresh without the scars from the shame of her father's vicious crimes. "I'll cook dinner for us. How does seven o'clock sound?"

"Perfect. Look forward to seeing you then."

Chapter 58

Gabriel, Roger and Julian were sitting around the table in Gabriel's office at the Hall, going through the group structures. The younger twin's initiation into the complexities of the Black Corporation had begun in earnest. Julian had worked hard over the past month and he had a good grasp of the company structure, the various objectives at operational levels within the individual organisations, and the overall strategy of continued growth and improving returns for the Group as a whole. Over the next few weeks, Roger would introduce him to all the directors and members of the senior management teams across the globe. For some of the older members of the Black empire it would be a re-introduction, and the sceptics among them would no doubt wonder how long the prodigal brother would hang around this time. But for most, it would be a shock, as they would be unable to distinguish Black junior from Black senior. Nobody wanted to upset Mr Gabriel Black. So nobody wanted to upset his copy, Mr Julian Black.

However, Julian Black was a lawyer. He was bright, quick and always cut to the chase. He took no prisoners. But, most importantly, he was loyal to a brother who had saved him from a life of hell.

His main involvement would be with Black Armour, and Gabriel excused himself for the remainder of the afternoon, while Roger began to go through the main contracts in place with various governments around the world, re-examining some of the files Julian had recently been studying.

Gabriel went up to his bedroom and rang Carol.

"Are you all having a good time?"

"Yes. It's been great. Even got to see the jaguars. We're just deciding where to go for tea. What time will your sister come for John tomorrow?"

"I think she said eleven, if that's OK. I really appreciate your help, Carol." Gabriel was still feeling guilty for not realising

John would be off school for a week, and for not making more time available to spend with his son. It was unfortunate he had such a busy schedule.

"It's no problem, honestly. And you know we love spending time with John. He really is a lovely boy. I know Eliza would be so proud of him." She took a breath before adding, "You must be proud of him, too. You're doing a very good job as his father, you know. He never stops talking about you and what you do together."

"I'm not sure I'm worthy of such praise. Especially this week. But thank you. And you're right. Eliza should be proud of him and of herself. She raised a wonderful child and gave him an excellent start. I don't intend to let her down."

He was silent a moment. Today was Monday. His own mother would be arriving shortly.

"Can I just say hello to him, please?"

"I'll just put him on."

Gabriel became aware of the chattering of excited voices as Carol passed her phone to John. He longed to hear his son's voice, and felt calmed by John's happy banter as he recounted the highlights of the trip to the zoo. The boy's earlier anxieties were gradually easing as he was becoming more relaxed with the short breaks from his father and more confident that he would return to him before too long.

After the conversation, Gabriel pulled on a thick black V-necked sweater and went down to grab his coat and scarf, pull his boots on and brave the weather to take Satan for a short stroll through the woods. The hound wouldn't be too enthusiastic about battling against the cold breeze that had arisen after the relative calm of the day. But his master needed the brisk walk and the blast of fresh air to invigorate him in readiness for seeing Cynthia Black. He had learned over the years that his ability to cope with his lot was strengthened if he remained as positive and as strong as possible throughout the ritual. He had long ago denied himself any expression of shame or self-pity – they were futile. But now John was in his life, he couldn't deny the shame, and he was finding it much harder to cope.

By eight o'clock that evening he was sitting opposite his mother at the dining table, waiting for Steve to serve the main course of pheasant, Cynthia's favourite game. Steve joined the diners, sitting down opposite Roger. Julian had gone out for the evening, as had become customary for him on Mondays and Wednesdays. However, they all knew this habit would have to be broken more frequently as Julian's input to the obligatory business discussions at the dinner table would be required.

For now the chairwoman was pleased with the company results; in particular, the new strategy put in place in China. Of course, she had every faith in the abilities of Gabriel and Roger. Their track record was second to none. The unanimity of the board of directors and the shareholders was essential to the continuing success of the business. Gabriel knew that his mother knew this. But she could still wield her power, with her own personal holding of fifteen per cent of the voting shares and her considerable influence over the trustees of the two trusts, totalling another forty per cent. And she knew that her son was well aware of this.

So business would continue to be discussed at the table and, if necessary, decisions would even be made and ratified at the next board meeting.

Cynthia turned to Roger. "And how is Julian's return to the fray coming along?"

Roger placed his cutlery down and turned to the woman sitting beside him. His loathing for her and her treatment of her eldest son had long been pushed to the recesses of his mind, imprisoned there by his love for Gabriel and his loyalty to the employer he respected more than anyone. As was the case for all the residents of Arnford Hall, certain relationships had to be managed, and Roger Courtney had learned very well over the years exactly how to "manage" Mrs Black.

"He's quickly grasped a good understanding of our objectives and the structure we've put in place to enable us to achieve them. Not only from a legal point of view, and you could be forgiven for forgetting he has been out of practice for five years! But also from an operational level. He hasn't lost his ability to cut to the quick where key decision-making is concerned. We had a good session today and have a bit more ground to cover tomorrow. Then he's in at the deep end."

"Well, let's hope your confidence is well placed, Roger. I know you are more than capable of watching his backside." Cynthia continued to rip her pheasant apart.

"I don't think that will be necessary, but naturally I'll be there if he needs me."

Gabriel cut in quietly, but firmly. "He's going to do fine, Mother. And it's going to mean Roger can concentrate on the new acquisition we're looking at. Weren't the disclosures due today, Roger? I didn't see anything come in."

"The guy rang to say they'll be with us first thing tomorrow. I'll start to go through them when Julian and I are done, just to check there's nothing we weren't expecting."

Gabriel nodded. Then he turned to Steve. "Ellouise is taking John out for the day tomorrow, so they'll not be eating here. But could you make some sandwiches for the early evening? Last time she took him to the beach they were ravenous when they got home. I'm not sure where she's taking him tomorrow."

"No problem," said Steve. "I'll do breakfast for eight o'clock if that's OK for everyone."

"Yes."

"How is the shooting going with John?"

He turned to his mother as he replied, "I think he's finally getting the concept of clay pigeon shooting. The kit seems to work quite well. I haven't mastered the top speed myself yet." A brief smile appeared on his lips.

"Why don't we all have a quick shoot before breakfast? It would be lovely if Julian could join us too." Cynthia almost sounded imploring.

The men turned to stare at her.

She forced out a laugh. "You wouldn't mind doing breakfast a little later while I remind my boys what I can do, would you, Steve?"

Gabriel gazed at his chef's face as Steve confirmed it would be fine and he'd aim breakfast for quarter to nine. It was decided.

"I'll stay over on Wednesday and then I can take John gun shopping on Thursday," suggested Cynthia.

"No," Gabriel said a little too vehemently. "We've made plans for Thursday." He had, of course, done no such thing, but … "I'll be in Manchester anyway on Wednesday. I'll call you."

An unspoken message passed between the son and his mother.

With the plans to buy her grandson a gun left hanging in the air, conversation became stilted, until Cynthia got up from her chair, thanking Steve for a lovely meal and excusing herself as she retired to her room.

She soaked in the bath as she waited impatiently for her son to join her.

It was a full half hour before he knocked at her door and walked in.

Gabriel Black had not had sex since he had last seen his mother five days ago. Yet he was struggling to get hard, to feel anything but distaste and disgust. And his unequivocal sense of duty.

He felt her touch him and, without thinking, he immediately pushed her hand away. With a few brutal strokes he made himself stiff and, silently, expressionlessly, fulfilled the task he had been set.

He closed his eyes as his unwanted release came. Cynthia immediately climaxed, feeling dizzy with the mixture of sin and sex and, above all, with the pleasuring she could command from him.

But she knew something was wrong and she waited until he was ready to speak to her.

She watched him get off the bed and wrap himself in his black robe. He walked into the bathroom to discard the condom he had used. Ever since her return from Africa he had insisted on using one until she had had tests to confirm she was "clean". He then returned to the room and sank down into the armchair.

Cynthia sat up in bed and pulled the silk sheet up to cover her breasts. She waited.

"I can't do this here any more." He looked over to her.

Her eyes were wide and her lip quivered slightly.

He summoned his strength and continued. "I know what he wanted." He looked over towards the window, the image of his

344

father appearing before his eyes, Poppa's voice saying "you can do this, son".

"But I can't, Poppa," he whispered.

"Gabriel. I …"

"No," he said. "Don't say anything. I will come to you on Wednesday. You're not to come to the Hall any more."

He simply stood up and walked out of the door, closing it behind him.

He strode through his own bedroom and into his morning room. He eventually fell asleep in his armchair, finally wakening at three in the morning and climbing into his bed to try to steal another couple of hours of much-needed sleep. His plans to change had begun.

Chapter 59

By the time Gabriel had showered and dressed to go shooting the next morning, it was seven o'clock. He ran up the flight of stairs to the second floor, now occupied by Julian, to give his brother a heads-up on shooting with their mother. He wanted to tell his twin himself, to gauge his reaction and to make sure that he could handle the situation. It was clear Julian was struggling with his emotions whenever he had to be in Cynthia's presence. Added to this was the fact that, as far as Gabriel was aware, Julian hadn't held a rifle in over fifteen years.

Julian ran his fingers through his hair.

"She knows I haven't been shooting for years. She just wants to humiliate me."

"It's just to shoot a few clays, Julian. You might even enjoy it. And you won't be able to keep avoiding her, you know. You're going to have to work with her in the boardroom."

"Yeah. I know." Julian looked at his brother with resignation. "I'll see you in the kitchen in fifteen," he muttered before disappearing back into his quarters.

Gabriel returned to his own bedroom and took out his Xphone. He had his own tension he wanted to relieve!

Sender: Gabriel Black

Message: The car will collect you at 8.30 p.m. Your so-called "FUCK BUDDY" (!) will be waiting.

He pressed send.

With a stern expression on his face, Gabriel walked into the kitchen and made a double espresso in the machine. He grabbed a banana and sat at the island as he began to read the *Financial Times*. He read with interest about the money problems of one of Black Construction's main competitors and smiled to himself. He would give Mark, their managing director, a ring and see if they needed any contracts taking off their hands, knowing Black Construction had a little spare capacity to fill. It always helped to have an upper hand with someone on the brink of struggling to survive; that way, deals were cheaper and quicker to close.

Cynthia walked in, elegant in her L. K. Bennett grey twill flannel trousers, black low-heeled soft leather boots and chunky knitted black V-neck sweater, exposing the winged collar of a white silk blouse. His mother loved the feel of silk on her skin.

Gabriel looked up as he said, "Good morning, Mother." He put his paper down and made her some coffee.

Julian joined them a minute later. "Good morning, Mother, Gabriel."

"Hi Julian, how was your evening?" Cynthia smiled broadly as she spoke.

Gabriel resumed his reading but paid some attention to the conversation between Cynthia and Julian, ready to support his brother if necessary.

"I'm seeing Lindsey," Julian said by way of reply to their mother. "We dined in Knutsford. Is Ellouise joining us for the shoot?"

"I'm surprised Lindsey is interested in you again, after the number of relationships you had when she was around last time," Cynthia's lips hardened into a straight line of bitchiness. She remembered her feelings of jealousy when her youngest son refused to visit her any more. Lindsey had appeared on the scene, together with several other women – and men.

Julian's eyes widened and he remained silent. He didn't need to be reminded of his behaviour before he left to go travelling. He wanted to say that it was thanks to his mother that he wasn't able to remain faithful to any one woman – or any one gender. But he didn't.

Gabriel sensed his twin was trying to prevent an atmosphere descending on the three of them. He folded his paper, resigned to the fact it would have to wait until later.

"Well, it looks to me like you and Lindsey are getting on great, Julian. I'm glad at least one of us in this family is finding happiness in a relationship." He walked over and put his arm around his shoulder. "Ellouise isn't coming. She's picking John up from Carol's later and taking him out for the day. Come on – let's go shoot some clays." Gabriel glanced at their mother. "We may well be about to get our butts kicked!"

The two men walked out, not waiting for their mother to catch up with them.

A short while later the three Blacks stood in the meadow and took it in turns to aim at the clays, each keeping their own score. Julian got into the swing of it remarkably quickly, but it wasn't long before the two men conceded that Mrs Black had by far the best shot. She had always won family tournaments and was a tough competitor in competitions around the country. She was a member of the National Rifle Association and her passion for the sport had grown following the death of her husband. She had told her children, at the time of his death, that this was one pursuit her deceased husband had not denied her the freedom to follow. Her children knew she was trying to justify her treatment of her sons – to herself and to them. Her pursuit of sex had indeed been restricted – in the most distasteful, illegal way imaginable. Nevertheless, it continued, her enjoyment and need outweighing any feeling of guilt or shame.

United in defeat, the Black twins headed back to the kitchen.

Cynthia informed them she would join them shortly; she just wanted to visit the nude statues she admired so much. Seeing the lovers back to back, she paused and for the first time in over eight years she allowed tears to fall down her cheeks. She thought of her grandson. She knew why Gabriel wouldn't allow her to stay over at Arnford Hall any more.

The image of her husband's writing on a sheet of paper in a small envelope passed before her eyes. She looked up to heaven.

"God, forgive me. But I'm weak, and will go on sinning to satisfy my own need. You must accept me for the weak woman I am. I know my son will not. I don't want to lose him. God, forgive me."

She took one last look at the stone statues of the tortured lovers and strode back to the kitchen to join her boys for breakfast. Michael had been asked to take her home. She wondered if she would ever return to Arnford Hall.

Chapter 60

The colour drained from Grace's face when she saw his message that morning. The fact that he was pissed off with her was written all over it. *What was she in for?* Well. Hadn't he said that punishment and reward were her thing? She hadn't seen him for over a week, and she realised she missed him.

How could she miss someone she hated? How could she hate a man who made her feel young, invigorated and important to him in a way no other man had done?

Seeking distraction, Grace set up her ironing board and began to iron with obsessive care. It gave her a chance to go over in her mind the conversations she had had with Ellouise the previous night. She found herself genuinely liking her captor's sister. She was vibrant and fun-loving, yet driven to get what she wanted. She had told Grace about her work for the Black family business, her skill in putting robust IT systems in place to add to its value and growth, and how she had finally admitted it was time for her to move on. She had been brought up with wealth at her fingertips, but had turned her back on that and sought to make her own way. Ellouise had laughed as she admitted her own way hadn't actually worked out too well, and she was grateful for her allowance from her brother! Grace enjoyed her company, her honesty and her kind nature. And she loved her enthusiasm for her new decorating project. She also admired Ellouise's love for her brothers and nephew, which shone from her.

Try as she might to busy herself in order to keep from thinking about her captor's message, about what could happen that evening, Grace's mind kept picturing the tall, dark, proud man.

She forced herself to recall Jason and his attentiveness towards her that weekend. It had reminded her of their first few dates, and she had tried to focus on her relationship with him, allaying her concerns about his drug-taking and what their future might hold.

She didn't need reminding that today was Day 49 of her enslavement by Black; it was embedded in her mind. But she did need to remind herself that she could get through this ordeal, that she could keep her boyfriend, that the life she had built for herself would be safe.

The day dragged. She ate lunch flicking through the TV channels, desperately seeking a distraction to block out her thoughts.

She showered. She dressed. She did her make-up. She got changed. She made a cup of tea, then poured the cold tea down the sink and sipped a gin and tonic. She had another gin and tonic.

At half past eight, she opened her door to Michael. She climbed into the back of the car. At Arnford Hall, she got out of the car and ascended the steps. She listened out for the gargoyles. *He's not upset; he's angry!*

He opened the large oak door and stood to one side to let her in.

"Good evening, Grace."

Grace looked at him and quietly said, "Hello, sir."

It had been seven days since she had been at Arnford Hall. She felt nervous and waited to see if he would chastise her.

He said nothing. He took her hand and led her down the hallway. It was clear he was not going to slow down at the door to her sanctuary.

She felt relieved that he did not take her downstairs, towards the den. But her relief didn't last for long, as he unlocked the door to her bedroom and locked it again, when they were both inside. He walked to the dressing table and took the collar in his hands. He placed it around Grace's neck and fastened it shut. Then he stepped away. No kiss. No nuzzling at her neck.

"Strip, Grace."

His words cut through her: cold and heartless, bitter and unmoved. She had not seen this side of him before.

He turned his back to her and gazed out of one of the large sash windows. The curtains hadn't been drawn and, against the blackness outside, the window acted as a mirror, providing him with a perfect reflection of her motionless image.

Without turning to face her he asked, in the same impassive tone, "Well?"

Grace moved towards the en-suite, certain that he would no longer be able to see her reflection.

"What are you going to do?" she asked, determined to keep the anxiety from her voice. She succeeded and sounded confident. But it wouldn't last long.

Now he turned and looked directly at her, his mask in place, his dark eyes piercing her, as he answered, "I'm going to fuck you, Grace, just like a fuck buddy should." His words were without feeling. He stood and waited.

For a moment Grace thought about locking herself in the en-suite. But, as with most bathroom doors, it was not impossible to turn the lock from the outside and she accepted the futility of trying to avoid her fate for this evening. The gargoyles were right; he was angry.

She glared at him defiantly and then turned her back as she lifted her black polo-necked sweater over her head. Pushing her jeans down, she couldn't resist peering around her legs to see him. Her defiance slowly began to ebb away as she saw that he had turned back to stare at the window. There was no way he could see her reflection. He showed no interest in her whatsoever.

Not until she had unclasped her bra and taken her knickers off did she hear his voice.

"Lie on top of the bed. Face down."

Grace felt sick. He hadn't treated her so callously before. Was this because she had called him a fuck buddy? Wasn't that the sort of relationship he was used to? He'd told her that himself.

She felt uncomfortable and clumsy as she climbed onto the bed and rested her cheek on the covers as she lay, waiting for him. She closed her eyes.

A minute passed before she heard movement. She moved her head and watched as he removed his trousers and trunks. She strained to keep him in sight as he climbed onto the bed. He was still wearing his shirt, the top two buttons unfastened.

351

Then she felt his hands on her buttocks. She clenched her muscles, afraid he was going to hurt her. But he didn't. Not physically, anyway.

His warm palms moved over the softness of her buttocks, and she relaxed. She thought she heard him sigh. He smoothed his hands over her skin, as if carefully easing out any small wrinkles from a delicate piece of silk. She felt him kiss her bottom lightly. Now she sighed, a yearning beginning to build up inside her.

But he stopped. He grasped her hips firmly and pulled her onto her knees, and she manoeuvred herself onto her forearms for comfort. Then she felt the tip of his penis at the entrance to her vagina. One of his hands moved away momentarily, until she felt a moistened finger being inserted inside her to lubricate her. She felt slightly self-conscious, as she didn't think she needed lubricating; even in her fearful state she was libidinous.

Then he thrust his penis into her, deep and hard; it felt tight and uncomfortable. He withdrew to her edge before pushing inside again. Other than holding her hips up, and the pressure from his penis and balls behind her, he did not touch her. His rhythm and speed intensified and soon he spilled himself into her. His breathing quickened but there was no other sound.

As he withdrew from her, he moved off the bed. "Now lie on your back and masturbate. I want to see you and hear you come." And he calmly began to get dressed as he watched and waited.

Grace curled her legs beneath her and placed her forearms on the bed, her back arched. She held her head in her hands and sighed softly.

"Are you going to disobey me, Grace?"

He had raised his voice. In it there was a trace of emotion – was it sorrow, regret?

She sat back on her heels, glaring at him. "You seriously think you can just fuck me like that and then expect me to pleasure myself?" Her voice contained a mix of anger and incredulity. And she hadn't finished. "Well, you can do what you like with my body. But you can't make me come! I have to want to do

352

that. So yes. I'm bloody disobeying you. Are you going to beat me?"

He stared at the naked woman on the bed. He wanted her. He knew that now. But she wanted her boyfriend. Gabriel Black wasn't used to competition of this sort. And he didn't like his odds. He didn't like himself. How could she ever like him? *Fuck it.*

He walked over to the chest and opened the top drawer. He withdrew two pairs of handcuffs.

"Yes, Grace. I'm going to beat you. This is how fuck buddies like to play."

He walked over to her and eased her onto her side. She neither resisted not aided him. She felt stunned. Her mind was no longer connected to her body.

He took hold of her ankles and cuffed them together tightly.

Grace watched as he untied the curtains around the bed and removed two of the tie-backs. He flipped her onto her stomach and secured her feet between the two posts, leaving no room for Grace to move her legs. They were fastened firmly.

He moved to the top of the bed and Grace lifted her head to see him. He cuffed her wrists together and secured her arms between the other two posts. She was unable to move except to raise her head. She sank into the mattress as her body and spirit deflated. She waited.

He must still be in the room. She could hear nothing. Then the moonlight was extinguished. He had closed the curtains. She pushed her head further into the bed, wishing she could escape from this room.

Then she heard a cupboard door close. He must have the senses of a bat because the room was now pitch black and he was still moving around.

Suddenly she let out a shriek. He had brought some sort of paddle down harshly on her buttocks, making them sting intensely.

"You fucking bastard!" she cried as she pulled on the cuffs.

Within a couple of seconds he had beaten her five more times. Each time he smacked a slightly different spot, until Grace's whole lower body was stinging.

Then he returned to the first spot and repeated the process.

She begged him to stop. Tears poured from her eyes and she hurt horribly – with pain and anger.

He had stopped. She was aware of him moving; there was the sound of the cupboard door again, followed by the turn of the key in the door and then the door opened and closed.

Grace was left alone in the room, immobile. She sobbed quietly, her mind spinning with confused emotions.

After some time, she heard the door open as he came back into the room. She felt something cold on her bottom and thighs. Then the warmth of his hands permeated the coolness, his fingers massaging a gel into her sore skin. She didn't move: she couldn't move. As his hands roamed lightly over her legs she muttered into the sheet, "Are you going to release me?"

"No. Not release, Grace. I will untie you, but you are mine for a while longer." His voice was quiet but firm. His anger had subsided.

She felt herself being freed from the cuffs and slowly she curled up like a foetus. Without further words, Gabriel switched on the bedside lamp and left the room, closing the door behind him.

Grace glanced at her watch. It was 11.15. She wasn't sure whether he was going to let her go home now, or if he was going to return to the bed and expect more from her. She wanted to escape to her sanctuary, but she felt sore and exhausted and just wanted to sleep. She dragged herself into the bathroom, hurriedly brushed her teeth and then climbed under the sheets, sleep consuming her almost as soon as her head hit the pillow.

Chapter 61

Gabriel lay in bed, staring into the darkness around him, sleep evading him. He had been more than cruel tonight. He had been brutal and pitiless.

When Ellouise had revealed to him parts of her conversation with Grace, she thought she was helping him to keep her. She encouraged him to be gentle with her, to sweep her off her feet and make her fall in love with him. Instead of Jason.

However, her brother didn't feel encouraged to be gentle. He was furious. With himself for letting Grace get to him, for letting her mean something to him, for giving him a hope he had never dared have before – a hope for a happy future, with a family of his own. And he was furious with Grace for being Grace. She would never be subservient to him. She was strong, confident, intelligent and loving.

Ellouise had advised him to make her fall in love with him.

But Gabriel Black had never played that game before. He hadn't wanted anyone to love him. He hadn't intended to love anyone. But now he knew he was in love. With someone who hated him. With someone who would hate him even more if she ever found out his secret. With someone who loved someone else.

He needed reassurance that he had something good in his life. He got out of bed and wrapped his robe around him before quietly walking along the landing and creeping into John's bedroom. He sat on the edge of his son's bed and gently stroked his hair. He began to feel the calmness he needed.

He couldn't undo what he had done tonight, and he would have to face the consequences. He still had a hold over Grace, but he felt anxious that his ability to keep it was weakening. His desire to keep it was also weakening. He was beginning to realise that she had a hold over him.

He wanted her to want him. *Fat chance of that. Especially after tonight.*

But they had a connection. Grace was his son's teacher and he thanked a God he wasn't sure existed. Maybe he did have a chance.

Chapter 62

Grace stirred in the large, comfortable bed. She had slept like a log. She rolled onto her back and felt some pain from her spanking. She didn't know what to expect from today, but she just wanted to go home. The next best thing was to go to her sanctuary.

She went into the en-suite and showered quickly, brushed her teeth and got dressed. Tentatively she tried the door handle, remembering the time he had locked her in this room. The handle turned, and she stepped onto the galleried landing. She could hear nothing, so she stealthily made her way downstairs, hoping she would meet no one.

She took the key from her bag and entered her sanctuary. There was a hint of jasmine and grapefruit in the air, essential oils aimed at bringing optimism and faith into your life. Grace breathed in the smell as she spied a vaporiser on the mantelpiece. Her eyes turned to the walnut coffee table, which bore a starched cream cloth, a tray containing croissants, melon, grapefruit, kiwi and strawberries in serving platters resting on it. Over by the sink, a china cup had been placed on a saucer with peppermint teabags at the side.

Grace filled the kettle with water and then waited for it to boil as she wondered who had put these things in here for her.

Suddenly the trill of his phone stole her from her thoughts.

Sender: Gabriel Black

Message: You are welcome to join us in the kitchen for breakfast. John and Ellouise are here.

Grace stared at the screen. No command. No dominance. Just formal politeness.

What is he playing at now?

Did he want her to put on a show in front of his sister and his son? Grace knew he wouldn't expect her to be anything other than herself for John. She wondered how he felt about her newly-formed friendship with his sister. For some reason, Grace wasn't sure if she could trust Ellouise. It was obvious she had told him about Grace's use of the term "fuck buddy". Yet Ellouise possessed a warmth and generosity of heart which was to be treasured in a person, and Grace couldn't help but like her. And she remained convinced that she could learn more about Gabriel from her too. Maybe she and John could lift her spirits right now.

She popped a strawberry into her mouth and, leaving her bag on the sofa, together with his phone, she made her way down to the kitchen.

She felt nervous as she entered the room. Ellouise immediately went over to her and hugged her warmly. "How lovely to see you here, Grace. GeeBee said you had stayed last night. I didn't realise he had kept you all to himself. I hope you had a lovely evening."

Grace turned to the man in the olive-green pinstriped suit, his buttoned waistcoat concealing the end of a green tie patterned with hunting scenes, standing out against his white shirt. It created an austere vision but did not detract from his strong, handsome features. He moved towards her.

"Good morning, Grace. I trust you slept well."

She froze as he leaned in to kiss her on the cheek.

"Breathe," he whispered.

Ellouise didn't notice the tension between the couple as she helped John to crack his hard-boiled egg.

"Hi, Mrs McGuire!" the young boy called before asking Steve, who was busy adding ingredients to a food processor, if he was sure he would like this egg.

"Trust me, John. It will be nice and soft on the inside for you to dip your toast soldiers into."

The chef turned to Grace.

"Hi, Grace. Lovely to see you. Can I get you some eggs and bacon?"

"Come and sit down," Ellouise called to her and motioned to the bar stool next to her.

Grace's head started to swim. What was happening here? Her behind was hurting from a thrashing Gabriel had given her, and they all seemed to think she had been here on a romantic date with him. And what was with the food in the sanctuary? She had assumed that was her breakfast.

"I …" She looked at Steve and then at Ellouise. "I think I just …"

There was a sudden crash as John's glass fell onto the tiled floor and shattered.

"I'm sorry, Daddy, I'm sorry." The small boy ran immediately to his father and hid his face in his jacket.

"It's OK, John. It was an accident and it's only a glass. Stand still and be careful of the broken pieces." Gabriel crouched down and hugged him close. "Let's have a treat and take our food into the octagonal room. You take Mrs McGuire up and I'll help Steve clear up here and then we'll join you with the breakfast things. Ellouise, will you go with them?" With that, John led Grace from the kitchen, followed by Ellouise, as Gabriel picked up the pieces of broken glass.

As the three entered the octagonal room, the master of the house bounded up the stairs and strode down the corridor to join them.

"Take a seat here," he called to Grace, pointing to the cushions on the window seat.

She realised he had brought her here to sit on soft padding, so she wouldn't have to sit on a hard leather bar stool. Was he feeling guilty, by any chance? She doubted that word was in his repertoire.

She sat down gingerly and glared at him.

"Steve has sent this for you." He handed her a small plate with a bagel and some bacon and scrambled egg at the side, a drizzle of maple syrup across the bacon.

She wasn't feeling hungry but she appreciated what Steve had done and she took the plate. Her emotions were swirling too much to trust herself to speak without crying, so she remained silent.

359

Gabriel opened his mouth to say something but was interrupted by Steve entering the room carrying a large tray with more breakfast things on it.

"Here you go," he announced to the ensemble and set the tray down on the sideboard before disappearing back to the kitchen.

Grace tried to relax, and quietly asked John how he was enjoying the holiday so far. She was conscious of dark eyes observing her as Black sat across the room, sipping his coffee. Ellouise joined John in telling his teacher about their day at Little Moreton Hall near Congleton and a quiz they had done wandering around the charming Tudor building.

"Why don't you three go swimming when your breakfasts are settled?" He broke into their conversation. "Then Ellouise can take you home, Grace. Can you just walk to the door with me please?"

He stood and waited for her to join him before leaving the room.

They walked along the corridor until they couldn't be heard by the others. He turned to face her.

"When are you going to see him?" His mask was up and his voice was direct and impassive.

"What the hell has it got to do with you? Sir!" she hissed through her teeth, her eyes staring beyond him to the hard oak of the door.

"I presume you will not want to wear your necklace."

"Then take it off me." Her eyes met his.

"Don't tell me what to do, Grace. It's not the role of a fuck buddy. I'll be in touch," and he turned his back on her and went out the front door, leaving Grace to stare at the oak once more.

"Damn him!" She stormed back to the octagonal room.

She didn't feel fully relaxed until an hour later, when, squeezed into a pale lemon swimsuit belonging to Ellouise, she was floating around the beautiful pool with John and his Aunty Ell, diving to the bottom to see who could do the best handstand and having a lovely time, the master of the house forgotten.

In the car on the way home she and Ellouise discussed the bungalow and their ideas for the lounge, which was the first room they thought should be tackled. Grace had almost forgotten about last night, provided she didn't make any sudden movements. But she still needed to consider when he was going to take her collar off.

Chapter 63

Gabriel Black drove the Bentley into Manchester himself today. He parked in his reserved spot and made his way to his office. The receptionist brought him some coffee and asked if he would need lunch.

"No, thank you. And see that I'm not disturbed." He immediately set about looking at his speech for the charity dinner tomorrow and the reports for the board meeting on Monday. He was sure that Roger and Julian would wrap things up on his brother's induction today. They would introduce him, over the next couple of days, to members of staff, and then Julian would be ready for his first board meeting in more than thirteen years. Gabriel needed to make sure he would not be intimidated by the chairwoman.

It was Wednesday, and he planned to see her later at her own apartment. This was not something he normally did. The surroundings made it even harder for him to find a place in his mind to escape to while she took her pleasure from his body. And he always wanted to retire to his morning room afterwards. But that couldn't be the case any more. Mrs Black would not be residing at Arnford Hall again, and John's home would be the secure, stable place a child's home was meant to be. Perhaps he could make further changes so that it became more welcoming, more friendly. Another project for Ellouise, maybe?

Black turned his attention back to his papers.

Over the next four hours, he called for two more drinks, made seven phone calls and sent fifteen emails. He checked back with Roger and Julian on a video conference call.

Then he toured some of the offices of his senior management team, keeping them on their toes as he enquired about the various businesses, their results, progress for the current financial year and their future budgets. They were used to the CEO popping his head in on the odd occasion, knowing they needed to be on good form to deal with his questions, but also knowing that he would be patient and wait for them to get back to him when necessary – he didn't always expect them to have all the answers at their fingertips. Most men and women occupying these offices had ascended the ranks of the Black business empire and knew what to expect. For the few who had been brought into senior positions from other organisations, Gabriel's visits tended to be much more daunting experiences.

Black returned to his own office for a final video conference with Rick from Black Armour. Rick Casey was expected to travel all over the world. He was single, thirty, very well paid and loved his job. He was one of Gabriel's favourite employees and his salary package, which included his choice of luxury car wherever he was (and currently that was Canada, with a Maserati Granturismo), ensured he stayed Black's employee. Whenever Rick was in the UK, Gabriel made a point of meeting up with him.

"How's it going, Rick? Not too cold for you out there?"

"No, sir. The skiing's fab!"

"You've got time to ski?" Black was smiling.

"I make time, sir."

"I'm sure you do. How's the car?"

"Drives like a dream, goes like the clappers." Rick reached out for a photo frame from his desk and placed it in front of the camera.

"Very nice. Just stay safe in it." Gabriel's smile grew as he heard Rick's pleasure and enjoyment in life from over four thousand miles away. "How is the project progressing?"

"It's all going to schedule, sir. Nothing to report other than it's on target."

Still smiling, Gabriel compared this man with the managing director of Black Construction, who had not kept Black informed of progress on a major build for that subsidiary.

"So you'll be back here in January?"

"Yes, sir."

"Great. Good work, Rick. I'll see you when you get back and I might have another assignment for you. Enjoy your skiing."

With his work list ticked off, Gabriel sat back in his leather and chrome chair and considered what needed to be done over the next couple of months outside of work. John's birthday was on the first of December, and he planned to speak to Carol to see how he had celebrated them in the past. Would it be best to try to do something similar or different? He felt sure it would be an upsetting time as John would be reminded of his mother. His conversation with Rick had also made him think that he would like to take John skiing for Christmas. He would need to make sure that the chalet was available and also arrange skiing lessons between now and their holiday. He would also include a certain woman whose company they would both want. Could she ski? He chose to ignore the other question that arose in his mind – *would she want to spend Christmas with you?*

At seven o'clock he closed his office door and made his way to the lift, saying goodnight to one of the night watchmen. He then walked the short distance to Beetham Tower and took the lift to his mother's apartment.

As soon as the sex was over he soaked himself under a cool shower. Normally he would leave straight away, but Cynthia, feeling slightly nervous at the change she could perceive in her son, asked him to take her to dinner. She suggested they share a meal in the Podium restaurant on the ground floor of the Hilton Hotel. Gabriel really wanted to go back to Arnford, but he wouldn't be in a very talkative mood no matter where he went now, and he knew Cynthia was anxious. Hell, he almost felt sorry for her. Almost.

Over their meal, he warned her not to give Julian a hard time at the meeting on Monday. He was doing well and would be a great aid to Roger, who was working too hard. He also decided to let his mother know that he and John wouldn't be around for Christmas. They were going to take the chalet in Meribel. She would not be invited.

"Will the two of you manage alone? You'll need to care for him all day and all night, Gabriel."

"I'm sure I can manage. But, actually, I'm thinking of inviting his cousins. It may be more fun for John to have other kids to ski with."

And as Gabriel drove home that night, he started to formulate a plan.

Chapter 64

The following afternoon, Carol put the phone down and turned to her husband, James, wondering how to explain she had just committed them to spending Christmas away, doing something none of them had ever done before, with someone they were all a bit in awe of. She could hardly say it was going to be relaxing!

"That was Gabriel on the phone."

"Oh. What did he want? Is he bringing John over?"

"Er, no. He's taking him up to the Lake District for a few days. I think they have another house up there."

"I bet they've got houses all over the place."

"Well, I think they have a chalet in France."

"What? You mean like a ski chalet?"

"I guess so. He wants us all to join him and John on a ski holiday over Christmas."

"You must be joking! We've never been, and it will cost a fortune."

"He wants to pay for all of it, including lessons between now and Christmas. He says it can be our Christmas present."

From the look on her husband's face, Carol knew she had a lot more explaining and persuading to do. For now, she let James get away with pulling his paper up and muttering something which sounded like, "Don't be bloody ridiculous!" while she began to prepare their meal. She needed to pick her moment to tell him that she had already agreed to Gabriel's offer, that the children would love it, and after six weeks of lessons, they should all be quite proficient!

The trill of *his* phone startled Grace as she flicked through a Farrow & Ball colours brochure that Ellouise had asked her to look at before they met up next week. She looked at the screen and at the same time put her hand to her collar. He had not removed it yesterday, and she was due to go to Jason's tomorrow. She was desperate to be rid of the collar, but she was also

365

afraid to see Gabriel Black again. Something had changed in him. He had been cruel and heartless. She still wasn't sure if it was his reaction to her calling him her "fuck buddy", or if he was simply getting bored with her. She had spent most of the past twenty-four hours trying to decide how she felt about it. Would she be relieved if he said he would release her from the "deal" he had struck? At least she would be free of the fear he would betray her identity. But she would also probably only ever see him again as a parent dropping his son off at school. She would never hear him, feel him, touch him, be a part of that crazy, dysfunctional – but also friendly and interesting – group of residents of Arnford Hall. And she knew she would miss it. She would miss *him*.

Her thoughts were quickly brought back to reality as she read his text.

Sender: Gabriel Black

Message: The car will be with you in ten minutes

That was it? Was the car going to "collect" as usual? Would it bring her back tonight?

Ten minutes later there was a knock at her door.

She was shaking as she went to open it, not knowing what to expect.

Gabriel stood there, wearing a black woollen overcoat, the collar pulled up. His dark, piercing eyes were expressionless and his tone was devoid of any emotion.

"Hello, Grace."

Grace looked at him questioningly, and she gazed at the Bentley beyond. She knew he would expect her to say hello, but the memories of their last night together and the pain from the spanking came flooding back and a fearful expression crossed her face.

For a moment she thought she detected a flash of remorse in his eyes.

"Turn around. We don't want to ruin things for your week-end with your boyfriend, do we?" he said sarcastically.

In different circumstances, Grace McGuire would think this man was jealous. But there were no different circumstances.

She heard the click and Gabriel took hold of the collar. He hesitated a moment and glanced into her hallway. He appeared to be contemplating something, but then his mask was back up.

"Goodbye, Grace." He put the collar in his pocket and walked back to the car, climbing in the driver's seat.

Grace slammed the door shut and went back into her living room.

"That damn man!" she said out loud, sitting on the edge of her armchair and putting her head in her hands. She felt the tear fall down her cheek before she realised she was crying. She wanted to cry; she needed to cry. This man was fucking with her life and she was struggling to keep a grip on it.

Well, she would go down to London tomorrow to spend the weekend with Jason and she was determined to keep her black-haired captor out of her head.

Chapter 65

The first two weeks of November passed uneventfully. School life resumed as normal. Gabriel saw his mother at her apartment. John slept at home every night and Grandma didn't come to visit. Grace received no texts from him.

Until Monday, the thirteenth of November.

Gabriel was in the Manchester office and picked up the phone to speak to Gilles Ypres.

"Hi, Gilles. Thanks for your offer to help us out over here for the next few weeks. I know it's a lot to ask, and I'll make it up to you when we come over to Meribel at Christmas."

"No, don't worry, Gabriel. I am glad to 'elp an old friend, and I look forward to meeting your son, you sly thing!"

His French accent did not detract from the ski expert's excellent English. Gilles had long given up expecting the formidable Gabriel Black to ever master enough French for the friends to hold a conversation in his own tongue. But, not having seen the English playboy in over eight years, he was really looking forward to helping to teach a small group of people, who were obviously important to Black, to ski. And the prospect of doing some ski guiding with them in France was too good to miss. Even if it meant travelling across the Channel every week to carry out the teaching. At least the Brits had attempted to take skiing seriously and the lessons would take place on real snow at the Chill Factore in Manchester.

"You said you wanted to start on Thursday?"

"Yes. Your e-tickets will arrive by email – I've booked for every Thursday until the fourteenth of December, and then we'll join you on the twenty-third. My car will pick you up at the airport and bring you over to the Hall for a bite to eat before the lessons start. How is Sandrine?"

"Formidable, as usual."

The two men laughed at his double meaning. Sandrine was Gilles' wife, ten years older than him but still more than capable of keeping the roving Frenchman in check.

"You do know she's already mailed me to make sure your trips over here are purely business?"

"I live a – what do you say? – feltered life, old friend."

Gabriel laughed again. "I think you mean fettered, old man. I know it hasn't been bloody sheltered! And it's about time she kept you under control. Anyway, it's your skiing expertise I want now. I don't need leading astray any more."

"Ah. Those were the days, non?"

"They certainly were, Gilles. I still can't order a Sex on the Beach cocktail with a straight face."

"I still haven't got over your last stay in Monaco either. It's been too long, my friend. *À bientôt!*"

"Yes," sighed Gabriel. "I'll see you on Thursday. Say hi to Sandrine for me. Oh, and can you arrange for me to have the old hut for a night? And I might need a skidoo."

"You old dog! How many beautiful women do you want to take?"

Gabriel could virtually see the grin on the Frenchman's face, although he felt too pensive to share it with him. "Just the one."

Sitting in the back of the Bentley as Michael drove him to pick John up from school, Gabriel tapped into his Xphone.

Sender: Gabriel Black

Message: The car will collect you for the next six Thursdays at 5.30 p.m., starting this week.

He wondered what his school teacher would make of the message. He wondered how she would react when he told her where she would be spending Christmas this year. He hoped he was doing the right thing. Doing the right thing wasn't something he normally thought about. He would make anything he did be the right one. But now he was apprehensive about her reaction. It mattered to him. What would he do if she didn't want to go?

369

Next, he dialled Carol Beardly, blissfully unaware of the sacrifices she had had to make to her husband so he would accept the fact they were going to go skiing. Not that she was complaining, as sex with him was always good! But first they were going to have skiing lessons.

By the time Gabriel walked into the playground to wait for John, everything was in place for cars to collect nine people to take them to the Chill Factore in Manchester on Thursday evening.

Chapter 66

Grace had chucked the phone into her bag after she had read his message in disbelief. What the hell did he mean by the next six Thursdays? What was he expecting her to do? Did Ellouise know about this? She resolved to ring her as soon as she got home.

But now she was home her courage had deserted her. What if it was something she would prefer Ellouise not to know about? She had already kept so many secrets: the real reason behind her relationship with her new friend's brother, his recent treatment of her, the spanking, his rudeness to her, followed by him ignoring her over the past two weeks. And now he was telling her he wanted to see her every Thursday for the next six weeks. What could she possibly expect Ellouise to say?

The more she thought about it, the more convinced Grace became that Gabriel Black would have shared his plan with no one. Ellouise would not be able to help her.

But damn it, she had her own life to live – work, Jason. She needed to know where she would be and when. Surely he would appreciate that? She resolved to try to talk to him, and find out what they would be doing and where she would be sleeping on those evenings.

Over the next couple of days she waited for an opportunity to talk to her captor in the school playground. That opportunity arose on Wednesday. It was a cold morning but the sun was out, hanging low in the sky and making her drive to school quite treacherous as she squinted in its blinding light. As she drove past Ellouise's bungalow, she saw the Bentley on the drive.

Having parked her car in the school grounds, she rummaged through her bag and retrieved a spare copy of a pamphlet she had been given at a recent seminar on children and bereavement. She wasn't sure how he would react to her passing it to him; whether he would see it as an intrusion into how he chose to raise his son, or if he would be grateful for the help.

But Grace felt that the one lasting thing about her "association" with Gabriel was his son. John would be at her school for the next four years and she was confident that Black respected her relationship with him, valued her opinion and appreciated the fact that John obviously felt close to his teacher. Although she had no major concerns at how John was coping with his mother's death, there would still be times when memories would be stirred, pains resurface and the feeling of loss would consume him. Dates such as his birthday, which she knew was the first of December, Christmas, Mother's Day, his mum's birthday and the anniversary of her death. She wondered if John would be aware of the latter two dates. At the age of seven it probably wasn't of great importance and could cause more upset than would be necessary. But as he grew older he would need to know and make his own decisions about how to grieve for her and commemorate her death. And advice on how to deal with these delicate matters was exactly what the pamphlet aimed to provide.

So with a determination which masked her apprehension, and the overriding feeling that this was the right thing to do, Grace walked into the playground and headed over to the tall, dark-haired man watching his son play tag with a few of his friends as they waited for the school bell to start the day.

She quickly became aware that he had seen her, and he waited with his eyes fixed on her as she approached him.

"Good morning, Mrs McGuire." His tone mocked her slightly and she wondered if it was his use of her "school teacher" title or the evident change in their relationship since she had called him her fuck buddy.

"Hello, Mr Black."

Now he held her gaze. Clearly he believed she had not finished her sentence. She glanced around to check they would not be overheard by anyone as she glared at him and said, with more than a hint of sarcasm, "sir!"

She tried to quell the anger that was beginning to build up inside her. The school playground was not the place to let her emotions come to the fore. She took a deep breath and handed him the pamphlet. "I thought there might come a time when

372

this may be helpful to you and John. It's quite self-explanatory, simply offering advice on coping ..." She hesitated as he quickly took in the title and flicked through the pages. "I hope you don't mind ..."

Then he took hold of her hand, saying, "Thank you. I'm grateful for your concern."

His words took her completely by surprise, forcing her to look up at him, and for a moment she saw his solicitude for his son. As his eyes moved to focus on the young boy, Grace felt the warmth of his fingers as they clasped her hand. She gently withdrew it and hoped that, to anyone in the playground who had noticed the contact, it would look like nothing more than a handshake.

Her withdrawal brought his eyes back to her, and she was aware of an apology in them now. She paused, realising that she could read quite a lot from this man's eyes when his mask was lowered. Why was it raised most of the time? Then she came to her senses and remembered the real reason she had sought the opportunity to talk to him.

"What did your message mean by every Thursday for six weeks? Will your car take me home each night? Can I assume that for the rest of the week I will be allowed to live my own life? I need to know what is going on ..." Her voice was low, for fear of being overheard, and she spoke quickly, betraying her anxiety. And she hadn't finished speaking.

But he had finished listening. In a flash his mask was up, the leaflet was in his pocket, and there was a determination in his voice. "Do not assume anything, Mrs McGuire." Then he discreetly leaned in and whispered in her ear, "Don't worry. You will be taken back to your own bed each Thursday. Now, if you'll excuse me." He turned and left her staring after him.

Grace quickly looked around her, seeing a flurry of activity as schoolbags were handed out by parents, cheeks kissed, hugs given and the children lined up in response to the school bell. Time for her to start work.

Chapter 67

Gabriel awoke after a night of broken sleep at half past five on Thursday morning. His visit with his mother the previous night had been particularly burdensome for him. He felt vulnerable and wronged. Gabriel Black rarely allowed himself any self-pity. He had accepted his fate over a decade ago, in honour of his father. He had blocked out all thoughts that his respect for his father could be misplaced. The threads of life which kept him together were his father's love, his sadness at the "duty" his father had bestowed on him and an intelligent, relentless determination to make the Black name synonymous with power and success in the business world.

But now he was questioning his past lifestyle and the sin he was continuing to commit. This internal interrogation acted like an infected wound, spreading through his soul, silently and unknowingly at first, but slowly beginning to fester, causing pain and decay.

He had felt relief when he told Cynthia he would no longer have sex with her at Arnford Hall. At last he could feel released of his burden as far as John was concerned. The other conditions Eliza had laid down paled into insignificance compared with the one implicating Mrs Black. He could work on ensuring John had a "normal", happy childhood: Carol was proving to be a great help to him for that. And he wanted to thank a God he still wasn't sure of, for Eliza's demand that John go to a state school and the opportunity that had given him to meet Grace. Grace, who was revealing so much of him to himself. Grace, whom he was beginning to believe could save him.

As he showered before going downstairs to grab a solitary breakfast, he questioned whether that was why his sexual relationship with his mother was becoming even harder for him to bear now. Because he was missing the lovemaking he had started to cherish with Grace. Lovemaking that was erotic and exciting, and yet romantic, and needed. He missed her. He ached for her. He didn't want to be with any other woman. And at the age of forty, after having sex with his mother almost every week of his life from the age of fifteen, he conceded to himself that he hated Cynthia Black.

But it wasn't just his own feelings that were … unusual. His mother appeared nervous, quiet, even evasive, during the little conversation they shared. It was as though she was hiding something. In the past she had been anxious after she had slept with another man. And she knew that Gabriel knew. He had always been furious with her on the odd occasions when it had happened. In his twenties he had informed her that he had a private detective monitoring her and, if she didn't stick to his father's dictate, then neither would he. The thought of not having her Gabriel for her pleasure was unbearable enough for her to comply. Well, ninety-five per cent of the time, anyway. It was different when she was on holiday and her son was not available to her. Mostly, Gabriel turned a blind eye in these circumstances, simply insisting that he use a condom on her return until the test results showed her to be clean.

But as he focused on her behaviour last night he was certain there was something troubling her, a fear he had not perceived before. This thought occupied his mind several times during that day, as he travelled to and from school, and again when going into Manchester to pick Gilles up from the airport, when he had time to ponder the matter over a glass of whisky in the back of the Bentley.

On returning to the car with his friend and ski instructor, he had no opportunity to muse. The trips down memory lane shared by the two men brought some light relief to his day and he banished all thoughts of Cynthia Black for a while, along with his haunting thoughts about his captive; he was beginning to find these too painful.

Meanwhile, Steve was in the process of rounding up the Beardlys and John in the Q7 to take them to the Chill Factore for their first skiing lesson. The children were wild with excitement, confident that skiing would be easy, and impatient to get started. Carol and James were quietly nervous, fearful of getting injured (James was a busy man and a broken leg would

375

not go down well at work) and secretly praying they would not make complete asses of themselves on the snow slope, piste or whatever it was called! Gabriel had left instructions for them to arrive at quarter past six to kit up – whatever that entailed – before an intense hour-long lesson with a ski instructor called Monsieur Gilles Ypres. James had Googled him and found that he lived and worked in France. They had no idea what to expect, except that it seemed unlikely that Gabriel would join them.

Roger had volunteered to escort Grace to her first lesson. As he met her at her doorway at half past five that evening, he was surprised by her surprise at seeing him. Did Gabriel ever tell her anything? How did he ever expect to have a normal relationship with her? Roger resolved to have a chat with him about common pleasantries between couples. Well, as far as his experience went anyway. But he felt pretty confident that what worked for a boyfriend under "how to behave on a romantic date" applied pretty much to a girlfriend too – chocolates and compliments would always be appreciated, as would feeling involved and being an equal partner in the relationship.

"Hi, Grace. I can see you weren't expecting me." He smiled and leaned in to kiss her cheek.

"Er, no. I thought it would be Michael."

"He's with Gabriel."

"Oh, right." She pulled her door to and checked it was locked before following Roger down the path towards the waiting black Jaguar XKR.

She climbed in as he held the door open for her and asked, "Do you know where we're going?"

"He hasn't told you?" The surprise in Roger's voice was tinged with anger. *What the fuck!*

"No. He just said I needed to be available for the next six Thursdays." She added reluctantly, to maintain the boyfriend/girlfriend façade, "I guess he wanted it to be a surprise."

Roger climbed into the driver's side and pulled away. Within minutes they were speeding down the motorway.

"So, how are things between you guys? We haven't seen you at the Hall for a while." He smiled warmly as he glanced over to her.

Roger always had a way of comforting Grace. She appreciated his concern and she felt sure his interest in her relationship with his boss was genuine. She imagined his fury if he ever found out what Black was doing to her. For the second time she thought of confiding in him, but something held her back. She felt alarmed at the possibility that it was concern for Black and his friendship with the man sitting next to her. Why the hell should she give a damn about that bastard, Gabriel bastard Black?

"Oh. I've just been busy with one thing and another." She turned away and looked out of the window, curious about this little trip and just what her captor was up to.

Her inquisitiveness getting the better of her, she asked, "So. Where are we going exactly?"

"Well. I'm not sure Gabe will appreciate me spoiling his surprise. But we'll be there soon and you're going to find out anyway. That is, if you haven't already put two and two together with the Christmas he's planning." Roger beamed a huge schoolboy grin, not doubting for a second that Grace was excited and looking forward to this evening. "He's arranged for you all to have skiing lessons so you'll be able to make the most of Meribel. Gilles is a great instructor, and he'll look after you for the next six weeks and meet us in France for some skiing too."

Her look of shock, open mouth and wide eyes indicated to Roger that his companion knew nothing about any of these arrangements. He concentrated on his driving a moment and waited for a verbal reaction to go with the visual one.

"I ..." Pause. "You mean he's ..." Pause. "He thinks we're going to go skiing." Pause. "At Christmas." Pause. "Him and me?"

Now she stared at Roger. "He can't be serious!" Grace's voice was raised, but as she saw an apologetic "I'm sorry you didn't know" expression on Roger's face she leaned back in her seat and sighed.

That bloody, arrogant, cruel, controlling bastard.

"Well. It's a fucking good job he isn't here. And who the hell are 'we'?" She hesitated a moment before adding, "I'm sorry to take this out on you, Roger, but you're the only one telling me anything!"

She stared straight ahead as Roger parked the car.

"Hey, take out whatever you like on me, Grace. As I said before, you're good for him. Maybe he's met his match and you're just what he needs to make him start acting like the thoughtful and caring guy he really is, instead of the controlling bastard he wants everyone to see. Except for John, of course." Roger hesitated a moment, wondering whether he had said too much. But, from Grace's outburst, he felt that perhaps his employer and friend could do with a bit of help in this relationship and he would actually be doing Gabe a favour.

He turned off the engine but made no attempt to leave the car. Instead he turned towards the angry woman sitting next to him and took her hand.

"Look. I'm not sure if you know …" He looked down at the hand he was holding before continuing, "Gabriel and I used to be in a relationship. We loved each other. It was a long time ago."

With each sentence he studied his companion's expression. He felt he knew Grace and could count on her compassion and understanding. His encounters with her had showed her to be loving, caring and forgiving, especially after the games night and the fact that her relationship with Gabriel had continued.

"I know him. I know he has a heart full of love just waiting to be given to a woman. And I truly believe that woman is you, Grace. Of course, he has John and he loves him more than anything in the world – anyone can see that. But he needs passion. He needs a companion. He needs someone to share the rest of his life with. I think he wants that person to be you."

Grace started to feel tears well up in her eyes.

"I'm sorry, Roger, but I think you're wrong."

He put a finger on her lips. "Don't worry, Grace. Everything will be fine. Let's go enjoy the snow." And his enigmatic smile left her wondering how he could seem so confident. She just wanted to get through tonight and go back to her own bed, as the bastard Black had assured her she could, where she could take in the implications of what Roger had said about Christmas. Implications which were far bigger for her than anyone else would realise.

As she stepped into the entrance of the shopping arcade leading to the ski slope, Roger continued into the ski shop, Snow and Rock. There they met Steve with John and the Beardlys. Grace immediately recognised Carol and her children. She assumed the man standing with her was her husband.

Her face lit up momentarily when John came running over, saying, "Hi, Mrs McGuire. Daddy said you were coming to learn to ski too. Look, we've got ski suits."

She looked around, bewildered by the glowing faces of the four children, contrasting with the overwhelmed looks on those of the two adults.

Roger and Steve kissed each other and were now observing the gathering with some amusement. Only Black could ensure that a sport to be enjoyed and a Christmas to be remembered could cause such trepidation in the three adults before them.

Carol walked over to Grace.

"So, dare I presume this is a first for you, too, not just us?" She smiled warmly at the woman whom she supposed to be her "almost" brother-in-law's girlfriend.

"Er, yes. I had no idea he was doing this. For Christmas." Grace was trying to get her brain to catch up with her eyes. Was Black taking them all to France for Christmas? She glanced around at the skiwear and saw assistants arranging for the children to try ski boots on out of the corner of her eye. This must be costing an absolute fortune.

"Oh, we're so glad you can't ski either." Carol turned to James, hoping that he would take comfort in the fact they would all be novices together – all for one and fall for all! "Oh, Grace, this is James, my husband. James, Gabriel's girlfriend. She's John's teacher. But I guess now we can call you Grace?" Carol's eyes seemed to be pleading with Grace for some sort of moral support.

"Of course, Grace is fine. I have no idea what we're expected to do. I've never contemplated going skiing before. It's just too expensive in the school holidays." She tried to focus on talking sense, appearing to be in control of her own actions, though the truth was far from this. She glanced out to the entrance of the complex. "Have you seen him?"

They knew she was referring to Gabriel. Grace still struggled to say his name.

"No. I don't even know if we will see him. Some guy called Gilles is going to give us lessons over the next few weeks. There are some suits over here they want us to look at. I guess we'd better get started."

Just then a young, trendy-looking assistant approached the two women, dressed like a snowboarder, with the crotch of her trousers hanging down around her knees and wearing a thin long-sleeved tangerine-coloured top with "A Bad Day on the Slopes Beats a Good Day at Work" emblazoned on the back.

"OK, guys, follow me and we'll check that this gear fits you."

Numbly, the two women followed her, leaving James in the capable hands of an equally young and trendy-looking boy with orange hair, the same baggy trousers and a black top with an identical logo.

Shortly after, Grace emerged from the changing room wearing a sleek, white, slim-fitting jacket with a black panelled body and black tabs detailed on the sleeves. It hugged her waist and accentuated her curves. Figure-hugging black ski pants completed the picture. What a pity she couldn't actually ski! On her feet were white ski boots. She neither knew nor cared about the make and she was desperately trying to convince herself they were comfortable and that she didn't look as stupid as she felt walking in them.

Carol was similarly attired, in a royal blue and white ensemble, and equally concentrating on trying not to look stupid in the boots.

James emerged, cutting a dashing figure in a lime-green jacket and black salopettes. He glared at his wife, the words, "This had better be worth it" written all over him!

Steve and Roger joined them. "Let's get you in the cold where you'll be more comfortable," the boys laughed and they walked to the snow dome. As the group entered, it was apparent they had the whole place to themselves. They stared up at what looked like a not-too-big mountain of snow and saw the children lined up at the side of the slope just a few metres up. The man standing in front of them gave them an instruction and one by one they turned to face across the slope before turning to face down it, their skis pointed inwards and their knees bending as they made a zigzag procession, led by Gilles, down to their proud-looking, if somewhat surprised, parents a short distance away from them.

Gilles turned to his young pupils, exclaiming, "Excellent, *mes chers*. You see what can be done in such a short time, *non*?" and then he turned to the adults, who looked more confident than they felt.

"So now the children have shown us 'ow it can be done, it's your turn. Let's get the skis on."

An hour later, students, instructor, PA and chef were sipping hot chocolates, sharing bowls of chips and chatting excitedly about the amazing progress they had made. James was grinning from ear to ear and couldn't wait to tell his colleagues about his new favourite hobby in the morning.

"I have to say, I was not looking forward to this one bit, and thought I would never get the hang of it, but your instruction was perfect. Thank you, Gilles." James glanced around and then turned to the children. "And we must all thank Uncle Gabriel." He winked at Carol, who had been encouraging him to use that title in front of the children; they all loved it and she felt it made John feel that his father was a part of their family too. "Where is Mr Black?" he asked Roger.

"I'm not sure. I thought he would have joined us by now. Something may have come up." He glanced at his phone, but there was no message from Gabriel.

He decided to wait five minutes and was just about to hit the speed dial when Gabriel appeared at the doorway to the bar. "I'm sorry I'm late, everyone."

John immediately ran over to his father, wrapping his arms around his hips, and began chattering about the ups and downs of their lesson. Uncle James had been the fastest. Everyone had fallen over at least once. Mrs McGuire had fallen three times, but then she skied really well. And Monsieur Gilles was brilliant. He could even ski backwards!

Gabriel squeezed his son and glanced at Grace. She looked radiant. Her cheeks glowed and she had been smiling and talking to Roger and Carol as he arrived, unnoticed. Now she had seen him, she appeared apprehensive and her brow furrowed.

He took John's hand and led him back to the table. Then he leaned in to Grace and kissed her cheek. She turned to look at him and he moved his hands to her face, his fingers delicately raising her chin. He kissed her lips, lightly and fleetingly, but he had the taste of her that he needed. The act was quick and no one seemed to think anything of a boyfriend going to kiss his girlfriend. Even John had simply carried on chatting with Craig, not even noticing his father kissing his teacher.

Grace blushed slightly, confused at the gesture, which felt as if it were more than just putting on a show for those present. She leaned down to take a tissue from her bag, giving herself time to regain her composure, to adjust to being in his presence.

As her captor went to sit next to Gilles, Grace resumed her conversation with Carol. She couldn't resist the occasional glance in his direction, wondering what he was doing or saying or thinking. Each time, he was looking directly at her. She shifted slightly uncomfortably and then watched as John took his father's hand and led him to the show window looking out onto the now empty ski slope. She heard the boy say, "Come and see, Daddy. It was brilliant. Will you come on the snow with us next time?" and then they drifted out of earshot.

"So we get to do this for the next few weeks and then go skiing in France. It's so generous of him. I wonder if we'll be ready to tackle the slopes by then?" Carol had clearly enjoyed her experience so far and was happily sipping the remains of her hot chocolate. "And, I have to confess, it will be lovely not having to cook Christmas lunch. I'm looking forward to the luxury of having someone do it all for us. Gabriel says he has hired a French chef for the week. I hope it won't be anything too fancy for the children, though."

"I think I'm still getting over the shock. Of both the fact that I have just been on skis for the first time in my life as well as the Christmas arrangements. He didn't really have time to go through the details with me. What has he told you?" Grace felt a little embarrassed at her economic use of the truth with Carol. She was certain Gabriel had deliberately kept her in the dark about all of these arrangements because she was really just his "fuck buddy". But she was going to make the most of this opportunity to find out as much as she could. Especially while Black was otherwise engaged with all the children and Gilles, as they excitedly brought him up to date with the events of the evening. She continued her fact-finding mission with Carol. "Who's going, do you know?"

"Well, I'm not certain, but I think it's us, and Roger and Steve. I have to say I've only met them a couple of times, but they seem really lovely. And we had a super lunch at Arnford Hall, made by Steve. I have never tasted better pizza."

"Yes. He is a wonderful chef. They're a great couple. I'm glad they'll be joining us." Grace was secretly thanking God that Roger would be with them. She was beginning to regard him as her guardian angel, although what he could do to save her she didn't know.

Grace had her own special reason for dreading the Christmas holiday period. It was a time when she wanted to be alone at home with the door shut and the TV turned off. It was a time when the families of the children her father had murdered sought to commemorate their lives, and more often than not it was reported in the news. Alone, she could confess her sorrow, her shame, her regret. But she did not need to be reminded of it. She had paid her respects as one of her final acts as Melanie Bright, informing the world of her sorrow and her innocence. Since then she had wanted to be a million miles away from any memories of it. Last year she had spent the day with Jason walking in the hills of Snowdonia. She had expected to do something similar with him this year. Now she dreaded watching TV in a

French chalet with the adults watching the English news and Gabriel Black watching her.

"Right. Well, it sounds as though everyone has had a good time and a great start to ski school, Gilles style."

Grace looked up, suddenly realising the wanderers had returned to the table. Gabriel put his hand on Carol's shoulder. He appeared to be seeking assurance that she, too, had enjoyed it. Her beam confirmed this and he visibly relaxed.

"I think we can look forward to the holiday and the skiing a little more eagerly now. Thanks for all the trouble and cost you're going to." James had joined them and even he was becoming a little more comfortable in this man's presence. Maybe Christmas wasn't going to be so bad, after all. And to be doing something so different would help John and the Beardlys cope with their first Christmas without Eliza.

It was getting late, and the children gave in to pressure from the grown-ups to get ready to go home. There was school tomorrow. They changed, gathered their clothes and boot bags, and the group made their way to the car park.

Gabriel caught Grace's hand, holding it for a moment as he stroked it gently with his thumb. "Michael will take you home." Then he let her hand drop.

"What is happening at Christmas?" she asked, involuntarily touching her hand where he had touched it. As soon as she realised what she was doing, she shook it, as if to get rid of a bug that had landed there.

"I will tell you when you need to know." He raised her chin with his hand and kissed her lips, lingering a little longer this time to savour their taste and feel their warmth. She was a beautiful woman to kiss. Then he pulled away. "Now go home, Grace."

She watched him walk over to John and Roger, the PA squeezing John's newly acquired ski gear into the tiny boot of the Jaguar.

She couldn't help smiling as she watched Gabriel manoeuvre his tall body into the back of the coupé to sit beside John, leaving Gilles to sit up front with Roger.

Then she became aware that the rear door to the huge Bentley was being held open for her.

"Thank you, Michael, but let me sit in the front. I'll feel much more comfortable." She smiled at the chauffeur as she noticed him glance towards his boss, apparently nervous of upsetting him by allowing his "girlfriend" to sit next to his driver.

"Er, I'm not sure that's such a good idea."

Grace simply closed the door he had opened, opened the front passenger one and climbed in, declaring, "Oh, it's absolutely fine. Mr Black won't mind." Her eyes made contact with Mr Black's as the Jaguar pulled away and into the darkness. She was sure she heard Michael gulp. She hoped he wouldn't get into trouble for her action; she was past caring whether she would!

"So, tell me, Michael, how long have you been driving for your employer?"

Michael turned to look at her a moment before replying. "It's been seven years now." He faced the road again.

"I guess you must really like the car. It must help to make up for having to put up with a man as arrogant and controlling as Mr Black." A part of her felt a little disloyal to be discussing her captor like this in front of his staff. But why should she be loyal to that bastard?

Michael half-laughed as he responded. "Well, the car is beautiful. But the main reason I stay and put up with him, as you say, is because he is generous with the package he gives me."

"Oh." She tried not to sound surprised. 'So he pays well, then?"

"As I said. It's the package." He sounded mysterious, and she felt she was being teased.

Her curiosity was not going to let this drop. "What 'package' is that then?" Surely Black couldn't have had an affair with his driver too?

"He pays for the best schooling available for our daughter." The driver hesitated a moment, clearly deciding whether to say any more by way of explanation. He decided he would. "Marie has cerebral palsy. She has the best medical attention and schooling we could wish for. Sharon and I couldn't afford that. Mr Black pays for everything, and makes sure my salary is enough to ensure Sharon doesn't have to go to work either. I'll take any shit he wants me to. I just don't like it when he damages the car!" He grinned at her, aware that he had silenced her.

Another side to Gabriel bastard Black. Obviously not a complete bastard to everyone. Just me.

She looked out of the window to avoid Michael's gaze, not really wanting him to know that this revelation of another caring side of her captor was messing with her emotions more than she could bear. She remembered his kisses. Were they just for show? They felt like more than that to her. She almost thought he was glad to be with her for the first time in nearly three weeks. She couldn't believe he hadn't wanted to have sex with her! She refused to acknowledge that she wished he did, that she was missing him, his body, his smell, his dark eyes. *Damn it!*

"I'm sorry?" Michael looked at her.

Shit! Had she said that out loud? Had she said anything else?

"Mmm. I was just asking, how old is your daughter?" She hoped she would get away with this one …

Michael was watching the road. "She's ten. She's a great kid but her legs are severely affected and movement is difficult for her. She needs a lot of physiotherapy and has had surgery a couple of times. But she's a confident and bright young girl. She's doing really well at school and we're very proud of her." The father was gushing with pride for his daughter.

Putting her own selfish concerns to the back of her mind, Grace started to ask about her treatments and about how she coped at school. She was alarmed to discover that Marie attended St Barts, a private school about ten miles outside Arnford. She couldn't think why Black would pay for a private education for his chauffeur's daughter, when his own son went to the local state school. Cost was obviously no issue to him at all. And somehow she knew he was definitely not the sort to snub the private system out of some perverse ideological commitment to protecting education for the "poor" people!

By the time the Bentley pulled up in front of her house it was ten o'clock and she felt exhausted both emotionally and physically. She said goodnight to Michael and went straight upstairs to get ready for bed. She left the bags of ski gear in her spare room, where they would stay until the following Thursday. She just wanted to sleep and escape her mind's constant analysis of the man who could fuck her body whenever he wanted to and fuck her mind whenever she couldn't get him out of it.

Chapter 68

The next few days seemed to be gone before Grace knew it.

There had been no messages to summon her to her captor. Somehow, she hadn't expected any. If she could say there had been any "routine" to Black's requirement to see her before, that elusive routine had changed. In fact, it had stopped.

Black hadn't had sex with her for a month. Even when they saw each other, barely a dozen words passed between them. If it weren't for the skiing lessons and the fact everyone was talking about Christmas at Meribel, Grace would have been beginning to believe her enslavement was over; he had let her go, but was just too cruel to tell her. And as her own relationship with John grew, she wondered if now Gabriel really just wanted her to help him care for his son. Maybe she was expected to play a "Nanny" role in France? Maybe he had another woman to take as his girlfriend. After all, surely he wasn't suddenly abstaining from sex, for a whole month and beyond? Of course he would be fucking some other hapless woman; a prostitute or maybe a stupid bitch who would be taken in by his wealth and power.

Her blood boiled when she imagined him fucking another woman. Did he use a condom? How did she know if he was clean? He had never used one with her.

And what did Roger think of the school teacher and his employer now?

Would things be any different if she hadn't called him her fuck buddy?

Well. She would never know. Her relationship with Jason, at least, had gone back to what it used to be. They were seeing each other every weekend, the sex was OK, and she even continued to shave regularly, for herself as much as for the two men she slept with. She was enjoying her work too. The run-up to Christmas in a primary school was always a very special and rewarding time. Children were keen to be good for Father Christmas. There were school plays, parties, Christmas craft activities and children's carols. There was a lot to look forward to in December and a lot to prepare.

However, first there was parents' evening. Grace had already starting preparing her reports for the following week, and she was confident of her assessment of each of her pupils' progress.

Yet, this afternoon, as she was handing out letters stating the date of the forthcoming parents' evening for the children to take home in their school bags, she felt hesitant as she handed one to John Black. Was his father really going to tick a box to indicate his preferred time to come into school to discuss his son's progress with Mrs McGuire? She smiled as she tried to picture him in his navy pinstripe Armani suit crouching on a small chair at a desk suitable for seven- and eight-year-olds. She shrugged at the waste of paper she had just given to John. No doubt Gabriel would request to see Miss Greaves; she didn't think, somehow, that he would want to see his captive in this particular role.

"Will I see you when we have our skiing lesson tonight, Mrs McGuire?"

Oh. Grace looked down at the black-haired boy smiling up at her. He seemed a little embarrassed to be asking his teacher a question that wasn't about school.

She smiled to put him at ease. "Yes, John," she said quietly. "I'll see you in a bit," and she couldn't help feeling sadness, tinged with concern, as she wondered how her relationship with his father could be affecting him. And how it would affect him when it was all over.

She hadn't actually thought of that. Had Black?

Chapter 69

By the time the novice group of skiers on the slope had finished their second lesson, they had an overwhelming need to take their ski boots off, sit down and have a hot drink.

Once again their benefactor joined them at this point. But tonight he was not whisked away by his son to hear a piecemeal account of the proceedings. The children were too tired and the grown-ups were too engrossed in chatting about their progress this evening. Clearly, they were not going to be competent skiers after only two lessons. Now they were all apprehensive that they may never be competent. Were they really expected to face down that hill – the hill Gilles had made them climb higher on the drag lift this time – which suddenly appeared to have grown taller and steeper? James had excelled tonight and made the most progress, so Carol was relieved that he wouldn't be complaining about the forthcoming holiday. In fact, his excitement was growing as his skiing proficiency increased. It was the girls who were beginning to worry, including Abbie. It had not been their night, despite Gilles patiently demonstrating time and again the position to take on the slope, how to point their skis, how to use their legs, knees and boots to flex and instigate turns, how to position their shoulders, arms, even face, and where to look. The girls had fallen, their skis had crossed, caught edges and slid underneath them; skis had even come off altogether, and this lesson had been very hard work. Roll on next week.

This time Gabriel had arranged that Roger would take Gilles back to the airport, Steve and his Q7 would take care of the Beardlys, and Grace and John would travel home in the Bentley.

As Black helped settle his son into his car seat in the back of the car and fastened his seat belt, Grace wondered about the significance of Gabriel sitting in the front next to Michael. There was going to be no discussion between captor and captive this evening.

The two occupants of the back of the car were tired and before too long, they were both asleep. Gabriel's voice woke Grace as the car pulled up in front of her house.

"We're here, Grace."

He walked round and opened her door. As she climbed out, he gathered her bags from the boot and then followed her up the path.

There were no kisses this evening. No one to put on a show for. As she walked into her hallway, he followed. It was the first time he had ever entered her house. She turned to face him. He was staring at her.

He could smell her in the house. It was womanly – musk and vanilla. He wanted to reach out and touch her skin and inhale. He missed her.

Then he saw the picture in the frame on the hall table. Grace and Jason.

He tensed as he placed the bags on the floor.

Grace followed his glance and saw the picture too. It had been taken several months ago, when they had been having drinks with friends. Jason's arm was around her shoulder and they were both laughing at the camera. For a moment she remembered the band Black had made her wear, and the image of Jason swam before her eyes. Black obviously knew what her boyfriend looked like. She didn't need to tell him who was in the picture with her.

Well, what did he expect?

She looked down at the bags. "Thank you," she said.

He simply turned and headed out of the house, quietly saying, "Goodnight, Grace."

She closed the door before he reached the end of her path.

She leaned her back against the door and closed her eyes. She was trying to come to terms with this change in his treatment of her. It was as if he had put up a wall between them and she couldn't understand why this was causing her more pain than even the spanking had done. Yes, the beating had physically hurt her, and she hated him for it. But this ongoing frosty, indifferent treatment of her was harder to bear. Now she really felt used, and she simply couldn't imagine what he expected of her on a skiing holiday. Why was she even included?

Memories of their sexual encounters started spinning around her head. Lustful, erotic, sensual acts she had only experienced with him. She wasn't sure she could cope with this mental torture – *he controls me but he doesn't want me.*

If he's had enough of me, why doesn't he just let me go?

She dragged herself to bed, hoping things would seem better in the morning.

Chapter 70

At the morning break, Miss Greaves popped her head around the staffroom door and asked to have a word with Mrs McGuire.

Gabriel Black got out of his chair in Miss Greaves' office to welcome Grace, and smirked when he saw the look of shock on her face.

"Good morning, Mrs McGuire."

"Oh. Hello, Mr Black." She had not been expecting to see him and she felt nervous in front of Miss Greaves. What was he doing at school? He was wearing a three-piece chocolate-brown suit in Italian silk, the jacket hanging loosely to reveal a waist-coat covering a cream shirt, his neck hugged by a brown silk tie. Grace fought off an urge to take a bite out of him!

As she remained at the doorway, watching him, she returned to reality when she heard Miss Greaves say, "Take a seat, Mrs McGuire. Mr Black has called in to make a very generous offer to us."

The head teacher was beaming and Grace relaxed a little. At least he wasn't here to take his son away from the school, or to tell Miss Greaves just who Grace McGuire really was.

She took the seat next to Black.

"He has offered to make a gift to the school of new electronic communications boards for all our classrooms."

"Er. That's very kind of you, Mr Black." She looked at him and felt his dark eyes gazing at her. Had John told him they had been experiencing problems with their own facilities recently during lessons? She knew that the current year's budget didn't extend to replacing any, let alone upgrading them all to the best ones available.

"Yes. He has suggested you accompany him to the Black Communications offices for a demonstration. I know you are more than capable of carrying out an assessment and making a recommendation." Miss Greaves looked at Mr Black, clearly expecting him to contribute to the conversation.

"I had noticed your current equipment was a couple of years out of date, and we have just launched a new model with additional functionalities. There is nothing to compare with it on the market. We've been working very closely with BestEd and the National Foundation for Educational Research. I've suggested to Miss Greaves that you could come along for a demonstration before I arrange to have the product installed here."

Grace glanced at her head teacher. Was he suggesting taking her out of school for a day?

"Yes. I think we can agree that we could accommodate your absence from school on Wednesday next week, if that works for you, Mrs McGuire?"

"Oh. Well, yes, of course. I would normally be planning that afternoon so I would just need to request cover for the class in the morning."

"Yes, yes. I will enjoy doing a bit of teaching again myself."

Black smiled, a look of victory on his face. He stood up and extended his hand to Miss Greaves. "Good. I'll arrange for my car to pick you up next Wednesday, Mrs McGuire." He then took Grace's hand and held her gaze as he shook it firmly. "By the way, may I suggest we discuss my son's progress in school then, too? It would help me immensely if I didn't have to attend your parents' evening."

"Of course." Grace felt tense as she sensed Black revelling in his control of her and glanced at Miss Greaves, wondering if she could pick up on this tension.

"Well, it is normally advantageous to come into school and see the children's work, but I'll leave it with Mrs McGuire to advise what is best. I can understand what a busy man you are, Mr Black, and we're grateful for your time to come in and discuss this proposal. Will you show Mr Black out, please, Mrs McGuire?"

Grace needed some fresh air and she led Black out into the school car park.

"Breathe, Grace," he commanded as he leaned into her ear.

"I'm not sure why you have asked me to accompany you. We have another member of staff who is more involved with our IT needs at school. I don't know why Miss Greaves didn't recommend that Miss Hall come to make the assessment."

"Oh, she did. I just persuaded her otherwise. I have needs of my own, Grace, and Miss Hall would be most unsuitable to fulfil those." He started to turn away, as though he didn't want to see her reaction to his words. "I look forward to seeing you soon."

Grace stood and watched him get into the car as Michael held the door for him. He didn't look back at her. She was reeling from his words and the change in him. He had virtually ignored her over recent weeks and now he had contrived for her to spend a whole day with him.

Chapter 71

On Tuesday evening his phone trilled from the depths of her bag where she had thrust it.

Sender: Gabriel Black

Message: The car will collect you at 8.30 a.m.

Grace had been expecting this text. She just didn't know what to expect during the day. She had determined she would ask him about his other sexual relations. He can't possibly have gone this long without sex. She needed to be sure she was not putting herself, and Jason, at any risk. For all his faults, Grace was certain her boyfriend wouldn't cheat on her. There was no way she wanted to risk her own or his health because of bastard Black's immoral lifestyle. The thought turned her stomach.

She was also determined to find out his exact plans for Christmas. She was going to make the most of this time with him, and that involved doing more than just assessing some potential new equipment for their school and discussing John's progress.

In the morning she put on her favourite black trousers and purple silk shirt. She remembered it was the shirt she had worn when he had first summoned her to Arnford Hall, almost three months ago. She pulled on her black Dune stiletto-heeled boots. They fit snugly around her ankle and were perfect with her slightly long tailored trousers. The heel was quite a bit higher than she normally wore, but she guessed they wouldn't be walking around too much, and presumably they would be seated for most of the demonstration. Any discomfort would be worth the elegance her boots gave her when she stood to interact with the coms board. The image of a sexy teacher standing before Gabriel Black, demonstrating the use of phonics for Year 3 reading skills, flashed before her eyes. She undid one more button on her shirt, checked her lipstick, which she had applied a little more liberally than usual, then went down to her kitchen to listen to the news for a few minutes before the car was due to arrive. She was sure they would be taking John to school before going to see the demonstration.

As she opened her door in response to the knock at half past eight, she was greeted by Gabriel Black wearing a black woollen overcoat. A scarf she recognised as that of Balliol College, Oxford, hung loosely round his neck.

"Put your coat on, Grace, it's cold." He commanded her to perform this basic task, no doubt setting the tone for the day.

Grace recalled one of his rules: *When I order you to do something, you will do it*.

She also remembered his appreciation of civilities.

"Are we simply going to see your prototype coms boards, or are your rules in play?"

"*Our* rules, Grace. And, yes, they're in play." He watched as her cleavage, visible through the opening of her blouse, was covered by her long black coat. He knew it wouldn't be for long.

She turned her back on him as she locked her door and said, "Good morning, sir" with just a touch of sarcasm.

As she got into the Bentley she said hello to John, pleased he was sitting in the back with her. She leaned forward to greet Michael too.

The short journey to school was a pleasant one. As Grace chatted happily with John about their skiing experience, she was able to forget who was sitting next to the driver.

However, she knew her ability to ignore him couldn't last for long.

He asked her to wait in the car while he took John into the playground. For the next ten minutes she made polite conversation with Michael, asking how his family was and whether they had any plans for Christmas. She assumed the chauffeur would have time off over the holiday period as his employer was going to be in France.

Then their time was up as Gabriel climbed in beside her and raised the privacy glass.

"Turn around, Grace."

As she did so, he placed the collar around her neck. She simply stared straight ahead.

He took two champagne flutes from a compartment and proceeded to effortlessly open a bottle of chilled Dom Perignon from the in-car refrigerator. He handed her a glass.

"To teachers and fuck buddies, Grace." He tapped her glass and took a long sip, his eyes resting on hers.

"I'm not toasting to that!" Grace sounded indignant and determined as her glare held his gaze.

Her captor smiled wickedly. "I assume it's the term 'fuck buddy' you object to, given your apparent love of the profession you'll do anything to keep."

He was taunting her and Grace had no intention of rising to his bait. But she needed to make her point. She wanted to end this cold, cruel game he had played since she had turned that phrase on him. She thought for a moment about her response.

Then it was her turn to smile, this time with genuine smugness.

"You seem to have an odd interpretation of the words 'fuck' and 'buddy'."

For a moment he looked perplexed until she continued, aiming to enlighten him. "I wouldn't relate either of them with the cruel, callous treatment you seem to show yours!"

Finally she raised her glass in triumph and took a much-needed gulp of the delicious liquid. Who gave a sod that it was only just after nine in the morning!

"Oh," he said, with a hint of menace in his voice. "I see. So it's not the fucking per se that you object to?"

She remained silent as she wondered where this conversation was going.

"Good. At least we're clear on that." He sipped some more champagne. "Well, stick to the rules, Grace, and I'm sure we can stick to the fucking. And the teaching, of course."

She took a sip of her drink and turned to look out of the window. He gained her attention by reaching towards her and taking the glass from her hand. Her questioning look was soon replaced by one of resignation as he leaned across, having unfastened his seat belt, and started to undo the buttons on her coat, one by one, peeling the garment back to reveal her purple silk shirt. He ran his long fingers over the lapels and, as one lapel reached the middle of the V to join with the other, he continued to move his fingers lower, this time feeling the skin encased by the silk. Slowly he slipped them inside her lace bra and traced the mound of her left breast. He eased himself forward slightly to move his thumb over her nipple and then to roll it between his thumb and forefinger, feeling it harden. Grace fought the urge to sigh, but as her body felt a spark of arousal, she couldn't prevent that sign of passionate response escaping her body. And as a predator is trained to react to the body language of its victim, Gabriel cupped her breast with his right hand as he turned her chin towards him with his left and leaned in to cover her lips with his own.

Grace didn't make any attempt to pull away and, as she inhaled his scent, she succumbed to the warm, sensual feel of his hold on her breast. She opened her mouth to him and savoured the taste and feel of his tongue as he explored. Now she felt his fingers make haste in opening her shirt and easing her breasts over the top of her bra and she let out a moan as his lips left hers and moved down to suckle, gently nibbling on her nipples, lapping over the softness of her chest.

She didn't feel like a fuck buddy now. She felt like a woman who was desired. His touch was sensuous and gratifying and she couldn't be sure who was getting the most pleasure. Grace undid her seat belt and moved her hand over to his lap, through the opening of his coat, and stroked the front of his trousers. His erection was long, thick and very hard. She pushed her palm onto him as he groaned into her bosom. Instinctively she fumbled for his zip, her need to feel him blinding her to their surroundings, but Gabriel looked up and took her hand.

"No, Grace. Not here."

Grace swooned as she saw his eyes: bright, shining, unmasked. She was breathless as he slowly covered her breasts with her bra, fastened her shirt and wrapped her coat around her.

Buckled up once more, he handed her glass back to her as he whispered, "Finish your drink. We're nearly there." Then he wriggled in his seat, trying to reposition his erect penis, which was pushing painfully against his trousers.

Grace leaned back in the comfort of the Bentley, her eyes closed as she wallowed in the lasting sensation his touch had given her. She knew this was the sort of fucking she could put up with. The sort that she didn't really want to miss. The sort that she knew would end when he had had enough of her, when his game would be over, after another two hundred and eighty days. That's if their attachment was really going to last that long.

As the car drew to a stop, she was still smiling. It must be the champagne, she told herself. She had the urge to cuddle the bottle to her. It seemed a shame to waste it.

Chapter 72

Black was greeted at the reception desk by an officious-looking blonde woman in her mid-forties.

"Good morning, sir. Everything is ready for you."

Gabriel gave a curt "hello" and walked through the gateway that had just been opened, with Grace following, concentrating on walking elegantly in her very high heels.

The offices of Black Communications were ultra-modern with walls of glass separating smaller offices and meeting rooms. Some were frosted in a pale green colour, with "BC" etched into the glass in Lucida Blackletter font, giving it an almost gothic air. The furniture was in maple and steel. Running along a cream-coloured wall was a display of awards – silver cups and platters, crystal glass decanters, figurines and paperweights, plaques adorning globes, giant golf balls and shields. Best Invention. Best Design. Best Engineering. Even Best Employer! Gabriel smiled as he saw Grace admiring them.

"I'm impressed, sir," she said, his title falling from her lips spontaneously, appropriately even, as everyone they passed addressed him in this manner. The Group CEO commanded respect from his staff. Grace was beginning to concede it probably had been earned.

"We like to be the best," he said in response. "We all work damn hard to achieve it. Come on."

He led her into a room which, although encased in glass on two sides, was made private by closing integral blinds which somehow still managed to let a lot of light into the huge floor space. It was more like an auditorium than an office. There was a raised floor, like a stage, across one end of the room. A large maple table, with twenty black leather and chrome chairs positioned around it, ran down the middle of the room, and one wall was lined with low-level cabinets.

The aroma of coffee emanated from a percolator, with white china cups and saucers laid out on top of one of the cabinets. An elderly lady entered the room and smiled warmly at Grace.

"Ah, Joan. This is Grace McGuire, representing Arnford Primary School. We're going to try to impress her with our latest coms board."

"Mr Black …"

No "sir", Grace noticed.

"It's lovely to see you. You won't have to try too hard!" and Joan grinned at a man she was obviously fond of. "It's lovely to meet you, Mrs McGuire. How do you take your coffee? Or would you prefer tea?" She was already pouring a cup for Mr Black.

"Coffee, white, with no sugar, will be lovely, thank you."

The sound of china cups wobbling on saucers, teaspoons hanging perilously close to the edge and the shuffling of feet across the grey office carpet alerted anyone present to the fact that Joan was past retirement age, and none too steady on her feet. But the smile on her face and the way that smile broadened when she looked at her employer made it obvious that she enjoyed her job and wanted nothing more than to make Mr Black a good cup of coffee.

"Thank you, Joan, you know exactly how I like it. I presume you put the canteen staff in their place after the last purchase of coffee beans?" Gabriel Black was actually smiling and making polite chit-chat with a member of his staff, who wasn't Roger or Steve!

"Oh yes, Mr Black. I told them it had to be Peruvian for you. Now just you buzz if you want any refills. I'll be right outside," and with that Joan left the office, closing the door behind her.

"Let me take your coat." Gabriel smiled at the look of confusion on Grace's face.

"Take a seat," he instructed. "I guess you're wondering why she is still working here, and what sort of slave labour camp we're running?"

"Well, not exactly." Grace was hurt by his supposition of her interpretation of what she had just seen. "I'm just surprised at her age" – she paused before adding, "and familiarity. With you." She sat down, glad to get the weight off her stiletto heels.

"She's one of the longest-serving employees in the Black Group. She used to serve refreshments at all board meetings many years ago and always managed to make the best coffee ever. Now she won't stop, bless her. We based her here to service small meetings. Transport is arranged for her to and from the office. She collects her pension and insists on her normal pay rate only for the time she works. She doesn't know it, but we increased her pension anyway, so she feels she's only getting what she earns. I guess she's one of those people who'll drop dead the minute her routine and purpose in life is taken from her. So, long may we enjoy her coffee." He savoured the flavour as he drank, his eyes on Grace.

She inhaled the aroma and smiled. She took her first sip, letting the liquid swirl around her mouth, tantalising her taste buds before swallowing. "It's very good," she concurred.

Gabriel checked his watch. "The team should be here now to demonstrate the product."

As he started to frown at the threat of said team being late, there was a knock at the door.

"Enter," he called out.

Three men walked in. "Good morning, sir, madam." They spoke in unison and then began to set up cables and press buttons which lowered the coms board into view, just above the stage area. Two of the men finalised setting up the equipment. The third man approached his employer.

"Sir, we have selected the software we normally use for primary school demos." He struggled to hide his nervousness, and Grace guessed the CEO of the Black Group was not normally present at such demonstrations. "Of course, we can use a different one if …" He stopped mid-sentence.

"Mrs McGuire," Black said curtly, apparently disappointed that this member of staff hadn't remembered the name of their prospective client.

"Yes, sorry." Black's glare had made the man blush, and he shot an apologetic look at Grace.

"That's OK, Mr …?"

"Robinson, madam."

"Mr Robinson. Thank you. I'm sure the usual software will be fine. As long as I can see that the product is user-friendly, interactive without any delays that allow time for children to fidget or, even worse, become distracted, and offers something more than other products on the market, I'm sure you can impress me," and she smiled warmly at Mr Robinson.

She hadn't intended to sound as if she was teasing the man standing in front of her, let alone appear to flirt with him. She simply wanted to put him at his ease.

But Black's harsh tone conveyed that he thought otherwise. "Please start, Robinson."

"Yes, sir," and the man turned away, preventing his audience of two from seeing further blushes rising from his neck.

However, at the end of the demonstration, Black shook hands with the three men. The demo had been impressive, with no hitches, and the new prototype was proving that the development costs had been worthwhile. The CEO knew they had an excellent product which would outclass its competitors. Grace knew this too.

Now they were alone, Gabriel reached over to the telephone on the table and pressed the intercom button.

A female voice responded. "Hello, sir. How can I help you?"

"Is the dining room ready?"

"Yes sir. Lunch is laid out now, sir."

"Good. We are not to be disturbed."

"Of course, sir."

"So, Mrs McGuire? Do you think the product will meet your needs?" Gabriel collected their coats as he spoke.

"Well, it's certainly impressive. I particularly like the apparent ease with which we can interface some of our own tasks without the need to rely on third-party software. That often only covers eighty per cent of what we would actually like, and is full of gimmicky features we'd never use."

"Yes. Product Development have put a lot of hard work into this."

He held the door open for her as they walked out of the large office. Their guise of seller and prospective purchaser seemed to be easily accepted by all the staff they passed. Grace wondered what they would think if they knew the real relationship between their employer and the woman at his side.

She was also beginning to wonder what would happen in the car going home after lunch.

She followed Black along the corridor and was relieved to enter a lift. Worrying about being alone with him here was nothing compared with the suffering her feet would have gone through if she had had to climb too many stairs in her stiletto boots. As it happened, the lift only had to go up one floor and Black made no move towards her during the short ascent.

As the lift doors opened, Grace felt the tension between the two of them heighten as they exited and she followed him down a short corridor. This floor differed from the first one as it had individual offices leading off the walkway, concealed behind brick walls. She noted the "ladies" sign above one of the doorways.

"I could do with paying a visit." She stopped outside the door.

"There's a private one off the dining room." He simply continued to walk, clearly expecting her to follow him.

As they entered the room at the end of the corridor and Grace surveyed her surroundings, the sound of a key turning in the door caught her attention and she spun round to see Black returning the key to his jacket pocket.

"The bathroom is through there." He pointed to one of two doors leading off to the right.

Grace looked around the room once more and then went into the bathroom. She shut it behind her and leaned against it, her eyes closing as she pictured in her head the layout of the dining room.

She had seen a small table laid out for two, with a white orchid in the middle. White china crockery, silvery cutlery and crystal glasses were impeccably positioned on the starched white cloth. There was a wine cooler with a champagne bottle cradled on the ice inside. She assumed this was the Dom Perignon from the Bentley. So it wouldn't go to waste after all.

The setting reminded her of their night in his garden when they enjoyed a wonderful meal, culminating in the chocolate-encased Grand Marnier pudding they had shared.

Grace swooned at the memory of the erotic scenes that ensued – her punishment as he had forced her to masturbate, followed by her reward as he had broken the second pudding over her body, licking her clean of the liqueur and chocolate. She could almost taste again the broken chocolate pieces he had sensuously fed to her. This had all been followed by passionate, intoxicating sex he had told her to enjoy.

Now their relationship had returned to captor and captive. Sex without passion. Cold and even cruel.

She pushed herself away from the door and hurriedly used the toilet. Then she studied herself in the mirror, trying to regain her composure, before walking back into the dining room.

Black had his back to her as he stood at a sideboard which was laden with cold meats, breads, salad, rice and pasta dishes. It seemed a lot of trouble to go to for a quick lunch for two people. But of course one of those people was Gabriel Black, the Group CEO, who would expect no less.

"I've taken the liberty of selecting some food for you." He turned to face her now and carried a plate to the table. He glanced at her boots. "I expect you would like to sit down." He raised an eyebrow and his lips formed the trace of a smile, as if he were teasing her.

"Oh, I'm fine," Grace exclaimed as she walked over to the table, head held high, concentration focused on placing one stilettoed foot in front of the other. The chair looked tempting but she didn't want to give him the satisfaction of sitting down immediately. She carried on walking to the far wall and studied a painting of a grand-looking woman from the 1920s. She was wearing a fur stole around her shoulders and pearls at her neck and ears. Her face immediately reminded Grace of Ellouise.

Suddenly she felt his hand on her shoulder.

"My grandmother, Cordelia Black. Her husband founded our business." He spoke in a hushed tone and Grace felt his breath at the nape of her neck.

She moved to the side, her eyes still on the picture as she said, "She's beautiful. I can see the resemblance to your sister."

Black had stepped back, trying not to show his annoyance that she had pulled away from him. His need for her was growing, and he felt the strain on his trousers.

He had gone over so many scenarios for today, mostly consisting of him fucking her over the table and then simply taking her home. But the memory of her touch in the back of the Bentley and the feel of her hand at his groin had left him wanting more. He wanted to see her smile, hear her cry out and feel her need for him. It was the last part that scared him. Grace McGuire didn't need Gabriel Black, and he still didn't know what to do about it. But he did know his stupid attempt to treat her like a fuck buddy was not going to help him achieve anything, and he already hated himself for the cruel spanking he had inflicted on her the last time they had had sex.

He now found himself in unknown territory. How could he make her want him, need him?

He walked over to the dining table. "Come and eat."

Grace finally conceded and sat down opposite him, studying the plate he had filled with food for her. As she began to eat she appreciated the lightness of the food; even the bread was light and the flavours of the pasta and rice complemented each other.

"This tastes good." She kept her head down, not sure how composed she would feel if her eyes were to meet his. "Who's the chef here?"

"Joan will have put this together for us. It's not often I attend these offices and she doesn't like to miss an opportunity to prepare a meal for me." He seemed to be picking at the food, which was not something Grace had ever noticed him do before.

Something was distracting him.

That something was causing more than a distraction. His whole body was tense and his mind was conscious of time ticking away. They would need to leave soon and he had unfinished business with her.

He poured champagne into the crystal flutes. Both glasses were only half filled. He sat back in his chair as he took a sip.

Now Grace did look up at him.

"Are you not eating?" She sounded as hesitant as she felt. He was up to something but she didn't feel afraid. His eyes were warm and unmasked. As she suspected, they were burning into her, but they looked to be questioning her. She waited a moment, certain he was going to ask her something.

When he didn't, she placed her cutlery at the side of her plate to indicate she had finished eating. His body language had seemed to ask her to do this and now she waited again. She remembered that he had locked the door, and this room had brick walls and windows that only overlooked manicured lawns. They were on the first floor and had complete privacy.

Gabriel pushed his chair away from the table and stood up. He reached for Grace's hand.

"Come with me."

He led her to the large table which occupied the remaining space in the room. Silently he lifted her on to it and then bent down to remove her boots. He took her socks off and then pulled her to her feet.

As his hand moved to the zip of her trousers, she placed hers on top of it.

"I need to ask you something." Grace spoke quietly but with determination. Part of her didn't want to piss him off. She didn't want to spoil this feeling of anticipation building up inside her. He seemed so gentle, she felt sure that she could enjoy this with him. But she needed to know the answer to her question.

"Have you been having sex with other women?"

His eyes connected with hers.

She maintained her courage and continued.

"I need to know. You … you never use a condom with me and I …" Her voice implored him to understand her need to be safe. "Well, I need to know that you're clean. I need to protect myself." There she had said it. She waited for his reaction.

"I'm clean, Grace." His voice was controlled and calm. "All the senior executives of the Black Group undergo regular health checks. I need to avoid embarrassing situations, just like everyone else." He resumed unzipping her trousers. "Besides, I don't want to catch anything either, and I certainly don't want my son's teacher to." Then he locked his gaze on her once more.

"But, yes, I do have sex with another woman and, yes, I do use a condom with her." *At the moment, anyway ...*

Grace held her breath. She hadn't been expecting such an honest answer.

"Breathe, Grace." He moved his hand to her cheek and gently stroked it. "After all, you have sex with another man. I won't ask if he uses a condom." He didn't need to, as he already knew condoms never appeared on any shopping bill of Jason Chesters. And he knew the guy's health records were good. Lucky for Black that Jason's firm of solicitors also carried out regular health checks on their senior staff. Part of him almost wished the fucking solicitor was riddled with some STD or other and then he would have a chance to break Grace away from him. Hell, even his illicit drug purchases had reduced recently. But, thankfully, they hadn't stopped entirely. The last thing Black needed to know was that his competition was now starting to be fucking perfect!

Shit, what was he thinking? Jason Chesters was his competition?

"You're hurting me," Grace murmured, still struggling to breathe but for a different reason now. Black had pulled her into him and his grip around her waist was so tight she couldn't get air into her lungs.

He immediately let go. "I'm sorry." *Fuck!* Today was not going to plan and they would need to leave shortly if he was going to be in time to pick John up from school.

No. He wasn't ready to let her go just yet. He was desperate to enter her and to smell and taste her. It had been too long.

"Excuse me a moment." And without any further explanation he left her standing at the foot of the long table as she watched him disappear through the doorway which didn't lead to the bathroom.

"Carol, hi, it's Gabriel." He paused a moment as she greeted him affectionately. "I have a favour to ask. Something has come up at work." He stared down at his hard penis pushing to escape the confines of his trunks and trousers. "Is there any chance you could collect John from school? I'm really sorry to have to do this."

Carol confirmed she would be happy to help, saying how pleased she was that he would think of her at a time like this.

He frowned, feeling guilty.

Of course she would be happy to pick John up and take him back to theirs for tea.

Good. It was arranged. Gabriel would collect him at six thirty.

He walked back in to the dining room.

"So. Where were we?"

Grace turned to face him. She was standing, barefoot, at the sideboard and had just bitten into a piece of pineapple.

He approached her and took hold of her hand. He brought it up to his own lips and took a bite of the pineapple. Then he placed the last piece in Grace's mouth.

"Do you want some more?"

Grace shook her head, lost for words and trying to clench her legs as she felt a tingling at the entrance to her vagina. He still had a sexual power over her and when he was being gentle with her, she struggled to deny it.

"Good." He placed his hand on her head, his fingers stroking her hair, while still holding onto her other hand. Then he lowered his lips to meet hers and Grace felt herself melting.

She breathed in his spicy fragrance and tasted the juice from the pineapple on his tongue as he gently pushed it inside her mouth. She entwined her tongue with his and felt sensations coursing through her body as the kiss intensified and she became aware of his hard penis pushing against her lower abdomen.

"I want to have sex with you, Grace."

"I know."

He lowered them both to the floor, placing more soft kisses on her lips and finally undoing her trousers. She was lying on the floor as he peeled them off and then slowly placed his fingers either side of her black-laced thong, gradually sliding it down her legs and casting it to the side.

He knelt over her. Having kicked his shoes off, he hurriedly pushed his trousers and pants off, setting his hard penis free. Seeing her lying before him, nearly naked, he was afraid he would ejaculate before he could even feel her warmth from the

410

inside. He took a deep breath to try and slow things down. He wanted to savour this feeling of sexual desire that was threatening to break him. He moved his hands to rest at the sides of her head, holding his body above hers, ignoring the pull on his muscles to hold himself in place. His desire was far greater than any strain he was feeling.

As he became aware of Grace's body rising slightly to meet him, the arching of her back to make a connection between her pubis and his penis, he lowered his knees and quickly moved his hand down, taking hold of himself, positioning his erection at the wet entrance to her vagina. He knew she didn't need lubricating. He could smell her, and he slid inside, easily, indulgently, hungrily. Her warm, moist skin engulfed him and he felt drunk on the pleasure that came over him.

He wasn't thinking straight. He didn't want to think of anything, other than the pleasure consuming him from being inside her, feeling safe, fulfilled and ecstatic. Steadily he located her clitoris with his fingers and gently stroked it, sensing his success from the moans emanating from the beautiful woman beneath him. His eyes held hers and he fought the need to close them as his orgasm threatened to end his pleasure all too soon. He stilled, desperately trying to prolong the experience. He had missed it so much, this sheer sexual euphoria he never got from the other woman he was fucking, the other woman who was fucking with him.

As he felt Grace, beneath him, begin to reach her pinnacle, his tireless stroking of her clitoris bringing her close to her climax, he finally let himself go and felt the ecstasy of his semen flowing into her. He revelled in her cries as she came with him.

He lowered himself on top of her and rolled them onto their sides. Remaining inside her for as long as he could, he stroked her hair and peppered her face with kisses.

Grace tried to comprehend the meaning of his tenderness and passion, afraid it would end and he would distance himself from her once more, punish her for some misdemeanour, block her out of his life …

She wanted to be a part of his life.

She closed her eyes and fought back tears.

411

As he softened, he withdrew and stood up, pulling on his trunks and trousers. Grace rolled away, grabbed her own garments and went into the bathroom. She took her time to dress, analysing how she felt now that their latest sexual encounter was over. Considering they had been only half undressed, on a carpet in an office, she knew it had been wonderful. They had taken pleasure in each other and she hoped they could move on. Although he still had the power to scare her, she now felt deep down that he would never reveal her true identity – not to Jason, not to Miss Greaves, not to anyone. She had continued to see a side to him that showed his humanity, his compassion, his heart. The man who loved his son, cared for his chauffeur's daughter, looked out for the well-being of an elderly employee and was loved by Roger Courtney could not be all bad.

She checked her appearance and went back into the dining room. He was staring out of the window. He held her coat as she approached. "Time to go, Grace."

As they walked through reception, he spoke to the officious blonde woman. "Please ensure that Joan takes the orchid from the dining room home with her."

Grace checked her watch as they sat in the back of the car. It was three o'clock. There was no way they were going to be back in time to collect John from school.

"Did you make arrangements for John?"

"Yes. He's gone for tea with his cousins. I wasn't going to miss the chance of some fun with my fuck buddy." There was no smile and Grace sensed his mask was about to go up.

"Look." She glanced down at her hands as she spoke. "I'm sorry I told Ellouise that we were just fuck buddies. You had used the expression yourself, and I was angry. She was asking about Jason and I needed to explain that he was my real boyfriend without giving too much of our, er, secret away." She turned to face the window, not sure how he would react.

"Truce, Grace. Our relationship …" – his tone as he said this was one of conspiratorial sarcasm, and Grace's heart sank – "… isn't about fuck buddies. I'm hardly your buddy. But we seem to fuck well together, don't you think?"

Yes, his mask was up. It was back to captive and captor. But Grace needed to check her theory.

"I don't think you will tell anyone about me. You can be cruel, but you're not that cruel." She stared at him, daring him to contradict her, to say that he would ruin her life.

Gabriel Black was silent. She had only said what he already knew, what he had known when he first started seeing the qualities of the woman sitting next to him – her pride and accomplishments in her work, her friendship with John, her steadying influence on Ellouise – and he knew that was no mean feat. But most of all it had been the way she brightened things up at Arnford Hall, the breaking dawn she represented for him. And he knew his efforts to fight his feelings for her were futile. But she was with another man.

He remained silent.

As they approached Arnford he finally spoke.

"Don't test how cruel I can be, Grace. Remember, I like to get my own way and I hate to break a deal. We have a deal." Then he lowered the privacy glass. "Mrs McGuire's home first, Michael."

The car finally pulled up outside 3 Willow Lane. Gabriel got out and walked round to open the door for Grace.

She hesitated for a second, frustrated at his words, nervous of their meaning, and angry at the torment he caused her to feel. She climbed out and walked to her door in silence. It had been a lovely day for the most part. Now, again, he reminded her of their real relationship. She was his to control for a year and he obviously intended to see it through.

Then she would be free of him. Then she would know how much she was going to miss him, for good or bad.

His words broke into her thoughts.

"Turn around, Grace." He removed the necklace and then stepped back as she turned to face him. "Goodbye, Grace. Enjoy your lesson tomorrow."

His eyes pierced his mask and looked into her soul. He had a look of sadness that almost took Grace's breath away.

Her words came out before she even knew what she was saying. "Goodbye, sir."

He walked back to the car, glancing at her briefly as he climbed in before she closed her door.

With a conviction so strong he could feel it bind him, there in the back of his Bentley, Gabriel Black resolved to entice the only woman he had ever loved to love him back, and to spend her life with him and John. He would put his plan into action at Christmas.

Of course, there was the minor problem of her boyfriend. But he was sure he could sort that.

But there was the major problem of his mother. Gabriel Black was a man of his word and he had no idea what to do about that.

Part Four

Chapter 73

The following day, Grace joined everyone at the Chill Factore. Much to the girls' relief, the skiing lessons went well and everyone made good progress.

This time Gabriel Black made no appearance. His pseudo-girlfriend made light of the fact she wouldn't be seeing him tonight when Carol asked how things were. It was no big deal. Yet, despite having enjoyed the evening with everyone, including Steve and Roger (who joined the students on the slopes this time, showing off their prowess on the snow), Grace was glad to get back home.

She hadn't heard from her captor; she hadn't discussed John's progress at school with him yet; and she still didn't know what the arrangements were for Christmas. She just knew that she needed to make up some excuse for Jason. He would be expecting them to spend the holidays together and Black wasn't going to let that happen.

As for the outstanding matter of the missed parents' evening, Grace decided to jot down some notes on John's performance at school in a letter to his father. This was preferable to trying to see him. John was a bright boy and she had no concerns over his academic abilities. And the way he was coping with the death of his mother and adapting to life with his father was exemplary. Grace was thankful that she had an insight into his life at Arnford Hall, and she knew there were no concerns that needed her attention.

But she remained in the dark about Christmas. She felt as though he was making some sort of statement that she still belonged to him and he still controlled her life.

Her friendship with Ellouise continued to blossom and they saw each other at least one evening every week. Ellouise had confessed that she had chastised Gabriel about his relationship with Grace.

"I told him he needed to win you over from Jason and confess his undying love for you. I hope you don't mind, Grace, but I think my brother needs a bit of help with his love life!" Ellouise had exclaimed during one of their telephone conversations.

Grace had been mortified. She tried to explain that they didn't need any help and perhaps in future it would be better if she and Ellouise didn't discuss each other's sex lives. Grace couldn't quite bring herself to say "love life". Ellouise had said that was fine, because at the moment she had neither a sex nor a love life, and if they talked about it too often she'd be ready to blackmail any number of past acquaintances into having sex with her!

Grace shuddered at the thought.

So their relationship developed around their interest in decorating, and a shared passion for old films and classic literature.

On more than one occasion, Grace asked Ellouise about the arrangements for Christmas. She simply said that she had been sworn to secrecy by her brother and she was to tell Grace nothing: it would be a lovely surprise!

Then, on Friday morning as Grace was finishing breakfast before going to work, the phone trilled.

Sender: Gabriel Black

Message: The car will collect you at 5.30 p.m.

Well, fuck you, bastard Black! Today was John's birthday. Her captor had given her no prior indication whether she was to be included in any celebration or not. And now, on the very morning, he sent for her. *Why couldn't you have let me know with enough advance notice to buy John a gift?*

She had hoped to be part of John's special day, especially as it would be his first since his mother's death, and no doubt not an easy time for any of them. She could have helped in some way, she felt sure.

But, no. She was just someone for his father to manipulate. Someone he could use when it suited him. A girl to have on show because the other woman he was fucking was probably some slut, unfit to expose his son to. Oh yes, Grace could be the prim school teacher who would be presentable at a party teatime. Then Gabriel would send her home and go and fuck his other woman.

How dare he do that to his own son?

How dare he do that to her!

Grace stared at her coffee cup, fighting back – yet again – the irrational feelings of jealousy and resentment that had refused to stop engulfing her since Gabriel Black had told her that he was having sex with another woman. Again she reminded herself that Black was not her boyfriend; what he did with his life was his business. She was suffering the punishment he had imposed on her, thanks to her own father, and she got the occasional reward of great sex with a handsome, powerful, controlling bastard.

Was she jealous? How pathetic! *How the fuck can you be jealous, Grace McGuire?*

And before she knew it, her cup had flown across the room, coffee streaked her walls, worktop and floor, and the sound of her sobs filled her kitchen.

When she got into school, she was surprised that John Black was absent. There was a message from home. John had had a very disturbed night and would not be in school today.

Grace immediately thought of the young boy mourning his mother. She also couldn't stop herself wondering how his father was coping.

At lunchtime she went into the village and purchased a birthday card and a book about volcanoes. It had been one of John's favourite school topics and she hoped he would enjoy looking at the beautiful pictures and finding out more about them.

Back in school, she rang Jason to apologise for cancelling their weekend at such short notice. She told him she needed to do a lot of work as she was really busy in the run-up to the Christmas break and it was the price she had to pay for having spent the last few weekends with him. He understood, and said he would ring her next week, reminding her not to work too hard.

Now she resigned herself to play her part at what she presumed would be a birthday tea for John. She was determined to do her best to make it a happy one for him. After all, she knew him nearly as well as his father did – he had only known his son a couple of weeks longer than she had. For goodness' sake, John needed her; she was a damn good influence on him and he had fast become one of her favourite pupils. Not that teachers had favourites! But she would do this for John.

And Black could go to hell.

When Grace heard the Bentley pull up in front of her house, she grabbed her bag and went out, not waiting for the usual knock on the door. She was feeling angry with Black for summoning her at the last minute, for not summoning her for nearly two weeks, for sleeping with another woman. She was angry with herself for caring about it.

She was within a few paces of the car when Michael climbed out and hurried round to open the rear door for her.

"Er … Mr Black asked me to remind you to bring your swimming costume."

"Oh." Grace frowned. *Tell me, more like!* "I'll just go and get it. Sorry." She hurried back into the house and returned a minute later.

She climbed into the car, fastened her seat belt and tried to remain calm during the short drive to Arnford Hall. As she got out at their destination, Gabriel opened the large oak front door. Going up the steps towards him, the gargoyles whispered solemnly, *We've missed you.*

"Hello, Grace." He moved aside to let her in.

"Sir." She spoke quietly and didn't look at him as she walked through to the inner hall. She paused at the door to her sanctuary. It had been so long, she wondered if it was still available to her. Or had he changed this rule?

He walked towards her. "I would appreciate it if you would join us for a swim. It's John's birthday."

She finally looked at him. "Yes. I know. You could have told me. I've brought him a gift. Of course I'd like to see him."

Gabriel drank her in with his eyes. This was all so new to him. His seven-year-old son's first birthday with him. Without his mother. His crying in the night and his struggles to comfort his son.

And then there was his desire to have Grace here – not to have sex, although he desired that too, but to share family time with her. For some reason that he wasn't quite sure of, this was important to him.

"Everyone is in the pool hall. Will you come down and get changed?"

Grace watched as his eyes darted to the door of the sanctuary and she sensed a nervousness about him. She pulled tighter on her shoulder bag and carried on walking, wondering who "everyone" was.

He quickened his pace and caught hold of her hand, causing her to turn to face him.

"It's kind of you to bring a gift. Thank you."

She looked at his face and saw that the confidence nearly always present in his eyes had deserted him. Grace wondered how today had gone. Why had John had such a disturbed night? Was he grieving for his mother?

As they walked down to the pool room, Grace asked, "How is John? We missed him at school today."

Black let go of her hand. "He's fine at the moment. Unfortunately Ellouise can't make it today, but his cousins and Carol are here. Of course, you know them from the skiing lessons. John was upset going to bed last night. We had been talking about the party arrangements, Carol has been helping me, and it made him think of his mother." He hesitated before continuing. "He hasn't really spoken about her for a while. I guess I hoped he had come to accept that she was gone and he was enjoying his new life …"

They had reached the turn in the corridor which led to the pool entrance. He stopped. "Look. I think I need a bit of help. I haven't really prepared myself for this and I don't want to let him down. I need you to stay tonight."

Suddenly he seemed to stand taller. He was visibly regaining his composure, as sure as he was reminding Grace that she was at his command. "We'll talk more later," he said, and suddenly the two of them were walking into the party atmosphere of the swimming pool room.

There was laughter and shouting. The four children were in the pool, together with Steve and Roger, playing volleyball, with various cries of "Goal!" and "Cheat!" and splashes galore.

Carol immediately came over and embraced Grace, kissing her cheek like a close friend. Her wet bathing costume was testament to the fact she had been a participant in the games, but the plastic glass of champagne in her hand showed she was taking a well-earned rest.

"Hi, Grace. It's lovely to see you again. Are you going to change into your swimsuit? Maybe then Gabriel …" – his name just slipped off her tongue these days – "will join in too. The children have been outnumbering us!" and her eyes shone with fun and affection.

Grace turned to her captor.

"Come on, let's get changed and then we can go in." Gabriel's warm grip tightened around his school teacher's hand; he was not letting go.

"Oh. See you in a minute," Grace called to Carol as she was being led away.

"Hi, Mrs McGuire!" she just heard John call out amid more laughter, and she gave a wave before disappearing into the changing room.

Gabriel started to unfasten his shirt. His eyes watched her to check she was following suit. As she began to remove her trousers, he turned and placed his shirt on a hanger. They could have been in the changing room of an exclusive boutique rather than of his private swimming pool.

Grace smiled to herself as she watched him meticulously fold his Ralph Lauren grey trousers. There was something very sexy about the vision before her now, as he stood in black trunks, embossed in white Armani signatures, a light covering of dark hair on his firm chest, his nipples erect from the slight chill, and his short black hair crowning his stern face, a face concerned at the coolness he felt from his reluctant companion.

Grace changed quickly, pulling her costume on to cover her bottom half before removing her sweater and bra and pulling

421

the costume up. There was a look of disappointment on his face as he realised he would have no opportunity to see her naked. And she knew he would do nothing about that. For now. In fact, she was beginning to doubt they would even have sex tonight. She appeared to be needed as the girlfriend on show and to assist with his son. Well, she didn't mind the second role. She would be glad to help John.

Meanwhile Grace waited, as he revealed his body to her, sensing her admiration of him, his penis half-hard, before he slowly encased that particular member in perfectly fitting black swim shorts.

"I hope you liked what you saw, Grace." His eyes penetrated her but, like his voice, his expression was impassive. "You'll be seeing it again later."

Oh, so they would be having sex.

He inclined his head towards the entrance to the pool. Time for them to join the others.

Within a couple of minutes everyone was in the pool. Gabriel, John, Craig and Steve formed one team and Grace, Roger, Carol, Abbie and Josh were the opposition. The males took it very seriously, which inspired the females to try to win. Unfortunately, to no avail. It was clear that Gabriel and Steve had their own formula for guaranteed goal-scoring, and it seemed John Black's genes were definitely his father's, as his swimming and throwing skills combined to make him a very worthy member of their "elite" team. It was slaughter with a huge dose of laughter for good measure.

Then Gabriel scooted out of the water.

"OK. Come on, everyone – let's have some races before the birthday tea."

"I thought Julian was joining us," Roger exclaimed as he joined Gabriel on the poolside.

"He should be here any minute. He was going to collect Lindsey."

"Those two serious, do you think?"

Gabriel raised his eyebrow. "As serious as Julian ever gets with a woman."

"Ah, here's Julian now." Gabriel walked over to his brother and his girlfriend. "Hi, Lindsey. Are you guys going to get changed? We're getting ready to have a swimming competition."

Then everyone saw double! Julian stood next to Gabriel. The brothers started talking about some work documents. The children and Carol just stared at the men. Grace, of course, knew what to look for to distinguish who was who: Julian's scar, if you looked closely, and the fact that, today, he was wearing light blue swimming trunks, but that only helped if you remembered Gabriel's were black. But for the Beardlys this was new.

"Er, boys." Roger interrupted the Blacks' discussion and his eyes indicated Carol, whose mouth was still open.

Gabriel's smile revealed himself. "I'm sorry, Carol. Allow me to introduce you to Julian, my twin brother."

"Hi. Pleased to meet you," and Julian, with his usual charm, leaned forward and kissed his brother's almost sister-in-law.

"Welcome to the family." He then beamed at the kids. "So who have we got here? I guess you're Craig and Josh." Right first time, and the Beardly boys smiled back, still in awe of seeing two men who looked exactly the same. "And you must be Abbie. Pleased to meet you." Julian smiled at the blushing teenager. "This is my girlfriend, Lindsey. So who's first to be thrashed in the swimming race?" With that, Julian grabbed his nephew's hand and walked to the edge of the pool. "Come on, John, we'll show them." The races began. They were fast, competitive and very, very splashy. Waterproof watches were awarded as prizes to each of the children and Gabriel thanked Carol for her suggestion of the gifts.

As they all finally exited the water, Grace's heart was warmed at the sight of Gabriel hugging his son, congratulating him on his superb skills, and then holding his small hand as he led him to a long table positioned at the back of the room, outside the splash zone and laden with sandwiches, salad and fruit. Taking centre stage was a birthday cake decorated with Star Wars' Luke Skywalker and Darth Vader, with "Happy Birthday, John" in blue icing and topped with eight candles.

It was a strange choice of son-and-father image, but Grace wasn't going to say anything. She knew John loved Star Wars.

As the children loaded plates with sandwiches, Carol and Grace added fruit and salad.

"I'm glad you're having a lovely time, John." Grace smiled warmly at the black-haired boy, who smiled back.

"Daddy told me you would come. I'm sorry I missed school today. I …" He looked down at the floor.

Grace immediately lifted his chin and looked into his watery eyes. "Hey, it's fine. We can all sing happy birthday to you on Monday. Now, I would love a hug from the birthday boy." As she pulled him to her, he wrapped his arms around her waist and pressed his head into her stomach. It took all of Grace's strength to hold back tears as she felt the small boy's need for her touch, her embrace.

Gabriel was standing with Roger discussing the handover of the latest building by Black Construction. He fought back his own tears as he watched this woman hugging his son.

"I'm losing her, you know," he muttered under his breath.

"Gabe?" Roger's question was barely audible but it brought Black into the present.

"Oh, sorry. It's nothing. So we can confirm handover the week before Christmas?"

"Yes. And Mark's been in touch about the Salford development …"

Roger noticed a faraway expression in his friend's eyes. This was not normal and, for the first time in a long while, he wondered if he should be worried about Gabriel.

Steve joined them, with a plate laden with food. The three men moved to the loungers and ate as they chatted about participating in a forthcoming fencing tournament. Gabriel had already conceded he wasn't up to entering any competitions at the moment. Night times with John were challenging, as Gabriel was having problems in getting John a) to go to bed and b) to settle once he was there. Reading self-help books and the leaflet Grace had given him didn't appear to be making any difference. John's behaviour didn't seem to be following any of the patterns listed, and this made all the "foolproof" methods to solve the problem futile.

He glanced over again, to see Grace and John admiring his birthday cake, the animated expression on John's face signalling his affection for his teacher. He was at ease with her.

Now everyone congregated around the food table for the cutting of the birthday cake.

As John was distracted by his cousins' chatter, Carol turned to Gabriel and said quietly, "John seems to have been much better this afternoon. This pool party was a lovely idea."

"Yes. It seems to have cheered him up." He looked at Grace. So did Carol.

"Grace, will you be staying tonight? Otherwise I can stay a bit longer and help to put him to bed." Carol was obviously concerned about her nephew's welfare, and it was clear that she had been helping Gabriel today. It was also clear that she noticed the bond between John and his teacher. She seemed to be expecting Grace to put the young boy to bed.

Grace glanced at Gabriel. He nodded.

"I think you need to tell me about John's behaviour. Was there a problem last night, and was it the first time?" Grace looked directly at Gabriel. It was very much the school teacher talking, but it was the woman's heart which was stirring.

"It's not the first time, but it's been the worst so far. We can talk about it later, Grace." His eyes seemed to be asking for understanding. And help.

"Shall we do the cake now, John?" asked Gabriel, placing his arm around his son's shoulders. He was worried that John would find it too much to hear singing and to blow out candles.

But earlier today the little boy had confided to him that he wanted a cake and candles. He would say a prayer to his mummy to tell her he was having a lovely birthday with his daddy, and that she would know he was happy with him, "because I do love you, Daddy."

Now, choked with more emotion than he could manage, Gabriel received a big hug from John. He lit the candles on the cake and everyone sang "Happy Birthday" to John Black, now aged eight. No one cried, but everyone hurt just a little in some way or other.

After eating some cake, the children huddled together to compare their watches and try out the different functions of lights, stop-watches and alarms, before dressing, and, amid lots of shouting "goodbye" and waving, Michael drove the Beardlys home.

Julian, Lindsey, Roger and Steve went up to the drawing room for more champagne and to wait while Gabriel and Grace took John to bed.

Gabriel carried his son up to his bedroom and Grace dutifully followed them. She looked around the large room, with the model of the Millennium Falcon "flying" out of the wall and the life-sized R2D2 model at the bottom of the bed. It was only the second time she had been in the room. She had brought her present for John, and Gabriel stood back as she sat on the bed next to the birthday boy and handed him the gift.

His eyes shone as he exclaimed, "Awesome! Look, Daddy, a book about volcanoes. It's even better than the one I had at school."

His father stepped forward and looked over his shoulder. "That's great. What do you say, John?"

"Thank you, Mrs McGuire."

"I'm glad you like it, John."

"Daddy got me a bike. Can we show it to Mrs McGuire, Daddy? Please."

"In the morning, John. It's too late and dark now. Come on. Let's brush your teeth and then it will be time to get into bed."

"Will you read me a story?"

"Yes." Gabriel led him into the bathroom. Grace followed them. She watched as he put toothpaste on John's brush and filled a beaker of water. The boy was jumping around like he had ants in his pants.

"John, do you want to go to the toilet?" Gabriel asked, his voice tinged with frustration.

"No!"

"Here, John," Grace stepped forward and raised the seat. "It looks to me like you need a wee." Her tone was gentle but

426

authoritative, and John did exactly what his teacher wanted. He peed in the toilet.

Gabriel smiled at Grace through the mirror.

Back in the bedroom, Gabriel picked up the book they were in the middle of reading. *Stig of the Dump*, by Clive King. The book was worn and well read. John looked at his teacher. "This was my daddy's book. He's reading it to me."

"OK, John. Get into bed and we can read a few pages." Gabriel pulled back the duvet and John dutifully climbed in and snuggled down as his father tucked the cover round him. Sitting on the bed, Gabriel began to read.

Grace sat at the bottom of the bed and took in the scene of domestic bliss. But it was one she couldn't really be a part of. As the reading continued, her mind wandered. What did his other woman look like? Some beautiful, sexy model, no doubt in her twenties, probably never coming within a hundred yards of any children. It just didn't seem right. She felt sad that she, Grace McGuire, would probably never have children of her own.

"Right. Goodnight, darling. Go to sleep and we'll see you in the morning."

"Will you be here, Mrs McGuire?"

"Yes," she said as she glanced at Gabriel.

"Sleep well, John, and we can all have breakfast together." He turned to switch the main light off, leaving a bedside lamp on. He bent down and kissed his son.

Then, as if it was the most natural thing in the world, Grace knelt next to John, held his hand and kissed his forehead. "Goodnight and God bless you, John. See you in the morning." She slowly got up and walked out onto the landing.

Gabriel joined her, leaving the door slightly ajar. He walked over to the rail surrounding the gallery and leaned over, looking down thoughtfully. He was waiting a moment to see if John would call him. Recent experience had proved that the minute he got downstairs, he would hear John's cries on the intercom and he would have to go back up to him. Over the past week or so, this had been happening several times a night. So he waited. Silence. Gabriel sighed and looked at Grace, who was also patiently waiting.

He watched her walk slowly over to the telescope that pointed up through the glass atrium and into the starry sky.

"Is this another of your hobbies?"

"No."

Their voices were hushed and Grace felt that he didn't really want to talk. But then he came to stand next to her and adjusted the height of the telescope to enable her to see through it.

"It was a gift for Julian from our father." He paused, as if he was very tired. "We used to get a lot of gifts from him. Bribes, you could say."

She pulled away from the lens and looked up at him. His voice sounded bitter, but his eyes were dead.

"Why would your father bribe you?"

He walked to the top of the stairs. "It doesn't matter. Let's join the others. It's getting late."

Chapter 74

As they entered the drawing room, Julian got up and poured them some champagne. Grace sat down on a sofa and slowly savoured the taste of the bubbly liquid. It seemed like it had been a long day. She was probably tired from her exercise in the pool, not something she was used to.

Gabriel sat next to her and they listened to the on going conversation about past ski holidays, going back to the time when the twins had been in their late twenties and Roger had just come into Gabriel's life.

Suddenly they heard John's cries over the intercom, and all eyes turned to Gabriel, who sighed and stood up.

"I'll go and try to comfort him, if you like," Julian offered.

"It's OK. I'll go."

Grace stood up too. "I'll come with you." Without waiting for a response from her captor, she followed him out to the hallway. As they mounted the stairs, John's cries became louder. Gabriel raced ahead. His son was screaming and by the time he reached his room, John was thrashing around in bed, the duvet was hanging off the end and the lamp was just about to topple off the bedside table.

Gabriel surged forward, just managing to catch the lamp and prevent it from falling.

Although John's eyes were open, it was clear he was still asleep. He was shouting out, "Daddy, where's Mummy? I need her, Daddy," and his body was wet with sweat.

Gabriel crouched beside him, attempting to put his arms around the child, but John was still thrashing about in the bed. He was inconsolable and Gabriel turned to Grace.

"I don't know what to do."

"I don't think there is anything you can do. Just be here and make sure he is safe." Grace had never experienced anyone suffering like this, but she suspected John was having a night terror.

Gabriel lowered his forehead to the bed.

"Where are his pyjamas?" Grace asked, looking around the room.

Gabriel got up and walked over to a white chest of drawers and withdrew a set emblazoned with stars and spaceships.

"When he calms down, we'll wake him and change him into these. Then hopefully he will settle back down to sleep peacefully. Is this what has been happening?"

"Yes. For over a week now. Nearly every night. I've thought about consulting a therapist. But having checked it out on Google, it could be night terrors and apparently they won't cause him any harm. He doesn't remember them in the morning. But it's very upsetting and I just want to help him." He looked forlorn and Grace felt saddened at the feeling of loneliness emanating from him.

"Of course you want to help him. No parent wants to see their child distressed in this way. But at least he's all right; he's not coming to any harm, sir." Grace's voice lingered over the word "sir". She felt like Jane Eyre for a moment, beholden to Mr Rochester for her job, frightened of him as her employer, her master. And she recalled Rochester's "other woman".

Black interrupted her thoughts. "Let's drop the title, shall we?" His eyes were black and intense and he stared at her hands. "Call me Gabriel. No punishments."

"Is that what your other woman calls you?" The words poured from Grace's mouth and she was suddenly edging away, placing her hand at the base of her neck.

"What? What are you talking about?" He remained motionless, staring at her before turning his attention back to John, who was beginning to calm down, coming out of the terror that had seized him.

"I'm sorry. I shouldn't have asked that. Not now. I … I need to go." Shit! She was supposed to be helping with John. Stupid idiot. She didn't move.

"No. Wait. Help me. Help me to help my son. Please." Gabriel reached out and placed his hand on her leg as if to prevent her from getting off the bed. "You said we should change his pyjamas."

Grace tried to regain her composure. She closed her eyes and took a deep breath. *Focus on John. Focus ...*

She leaned over the child and gently lifted him up. "John. John. Let's wake up and we can change your pyjamas. Daddy and I are here. You're safe now."

"Mummy?" John looked at his teacher through sleepy, watery eyes.

Grace's heart lurched. Was this night going to get any worse?

Now it was Gabriel's turn to want to get away. "For fuck's sake." Although he spoke under his breath, his words bellowed in Grace's ears. Now he was angry with her. And she couldn't blame him.

She did what came naturally to her. She wrapped her arms around John, who was now coming round and sitting up. "No, honey. It's Mrs McGuire. I love you very much, John. Don't cry, darling." And she rocked him as tears poured down her cheeks.

Gabriel left the room and wiped away his own tears.

A short while later, Grace walked out of John's bedroom, leaving him sleeping peacefully in fresh pyjamas. She closed his door, knowing the intercom would pick up any sounds of further disturbances.

Gabriel was nowhere to be seen.

Grace felt exhausted and in no mood for company. She made her way downstairs and went straight into her sanctuary. There was a white orchid on the sideboard. It was her favourite. Instinctively she took her own phone from her bag and took a photograph of the exquisite flower.

There was a knock at her door. She startled and then dreaded opening it. She thought it would be Roger and she didn't want to face him just now.

The knock sounded again and then she heard his voice.

"Please come to your bedroom, Grace, or – so help me – I'll smash this fucking door down."

Grace trembled. She pulled the door open; it wasn't even locked.

She saw the change in him. He was slumped against the wall. His eyes looked swollen. He had been crying, and his hair was ruffled from where he had run his fingers through it.

"Let's go. The sooner this bloody evening is over, the better." He marched up the grand staircase, taking it as given that she would follow him.

The door to her bedroom was open. There were no sounds from John's room. They entered Grace's room and closed the door to the outside world.

Gabriel went straight into the bathroom and started to brush his teeth. Not knowing what else to do, and a little fearful of his mood, which was even stranger than usual, she followed him. The brush she usually used here was placed on the "hers" washbasin and, as if on autopilot, she stood beside her captor and brushed her teeth too. Their eyes made occasional contact through the mirrors, but neither held the other's gaze.

It was clear he intended staying with her tonight. She felt so tired she was sure she would be asleep as soon as her head touched the pillow. She remembered his words in the pool changing room, implying they would be having sex tonight. Yet her outbursts and his dejected state convinced her there would be no activity this evening.

He turned to pee and she walked back into the bedroom, removed her clothes and climbed into bed. She wrapped the covers around her and turned on her side, staring at the curtains.

A couple of minutes later she felt him wrap himself around her. His warm, strong arms enveloped her own as they crossed her chest. His abdomen pressed against her back and, as he brought his legs up to follow the contour of her own, she felt his soft penis against her lower back. His breath floated across her neck and shoulders and then she felt a gentle kiss where her neck merged with her back. He steadily peppered the top of her back, from one side across to the other, with sensual, feathery, intimate kisses. When she sighed, he slipped his hands away from her arms to smooth them over each breast, steadily caressing and making them tingle. She was enthralled by his gentleness and pressed her buttocks back, ever so slightly, intensifying the connection of her skin with his, with his penis. She held her breath and he whispered in her ear, "Breathe, Grace."

432

She felt him harden, and raised her leg to let his penis rest between her inner thighs. She moved her hand down and her fingers felt it, stroked it, cradled it.

After a few minutes of this loving intimacy, he turned her to face him. He stroked her cheeks with the back of his fingers and then played with strands of her hair. His erection was becoming painful, he wanted her so much, but he hadn't planned this. Grace had been angry with him and he was fearful of driving her away. His earlier intention to have sex with her had been replaced with his wish that she might stay of her own free will. He would have been happy to simply hold her tonight, to sleep peacefully with her.

But now she seemed to be coming on to him. He felt her need and couldn't resist the urge to enter her.

As Grace's hold on his penis tightened, he rolled her onto her back. He tried desperately to slow down but was overwhelmed as he felt her hips rise up towards him and he finally drove himself into her. His hand sought her clitoris, wet and warm. His fingers stroked it and she lost herself to the sexual urges, the exquisite sensations that his touch could create. They moved in a rhythm that satisfied their mutual hunger. As she arched her back and cried out in ecstasy, his eyes burned into her, his lips tightened, and he gasped as he filled her with his sperm. As their climaxes gradually subsided he hugged her and kissed her, revelling in the moisture of her lips, their taste and texture. She opened to let his tongue in to explore and enjoy her.

"Thank you," he said as he withdrew from her. "I didn't know how much I needed that." His last word stung. "I needed *you*," he said silently.

Would things have been different if he had not made this mistake?

Chapter 75

"Daddy, Daddy …"

Gabriel shot out of bed, grabbed his robe and strode across the landing to John's room.

"I'm here, John. Daddy's here." He sat on the bed and hugged his son, wiping the tears from his eyes. "There, there. It's OK, everything is all right, darling."

"I want my mummy. I want her…" In his half-awake state, John sobbed and moaned, rocking gently in Gabriel's strong arms.

"I know. I know you miss her." He picked up the photograph from the bedside table. He had no idea whether it would help or not, but he held it in front of them both and said quietly, "Tell Mummy what a nice day you had yesterday, with Craig and Josh and Abbie. She would be so pleased to know that you were happy, John."

He continued to cradle him, pulling him onto his lap.

John took hold of the photograph and kissed the glass cover. "Daddy let me have a pool party. I won the swimming race, Mummy." Then his sobs continued.

Grace appeared at the doorway, wrapped in a bathrobe.

'Can I help?" she asked, refraining from entering as she absorbed the intimate scene before her.

Gabriel glanced at her. "Go back to bed. I'm sure it's really early."

"It's five o'clock. Please let me know if I can do anything." She approached the couple and sat down next to them on the bed.

John's sobs had eased a little and he peered at his school teacher from behind his father's back. He smiled weakly. "I know my mummy can't come back. But I miss her."

"I know. She would be very proud of you, John. You're being very brave."

"Can you stay in my bed, Daddy?"

Since John had first moved in with him and they had shared a room, Gabriel had always tried to resist these requests. He valued his own need to sleep alone too highly to give in easily, and he was determined not to let John form bad habits.

Recently, however, John had been getting more upset at bedtime, and Gabriel knew he needed to spend more time with him. He was just still managing to do the school runs, but the pressures of work were increasing and, until Julian was fully on board, Gabriel was juggling more than he was comfortable with. He knew he had one other person he could go to for assistance at work, but he was loath to see any more of his mother than he had to. He would just have to manage.

"OK." He conceded defeat. "Go back to bed, Grace. I'll stay here with John," and he climbed into bed and stroked his son's hair.

Grace turned and left the door ajar as she returned to the bedroom he referred to as hers. She lay in the huge bed, feeling unable to go back to sleep. However, she must have dozed because five o'clock had suddenly become seven o'clock. She dragged herself out of bed and stepped into the large shower. The warm water and the aroma of the Blenheim Bouquet shower gel, which seemed to have been set out especially for her, awoke her senses and confidence. She wallowed for a few minutes in the fragrance of citrus oils and spices, reliving the sexual tenderness she had shared with Gabriel last night. Then she remembered his words: *I needed that.*

They lurked in her head and steadily infected her mind, hurting her.

He didn't need her. He just needed sex.

She stepped out of the shower and wrapped herself in the soft white bath towel. She wrapped a smaller one around her damp hair and walked back into the bedroom. Her clothes were neatly folded on the chaise longue. She tried to put them on quickly, but her hands were clumsy and she couldn't balance. She had to sit down to put her socks on. She fumbled with the legs of her trousers and the zip just wouldn't come up. She rubbed her hair as dry as she could and then proceeded to put her sweater on back to front.

435

"For fuck's sake, what's the matter with me?"

Finally dressed, she picked up her bag and walked down to her sanctuary. She didn't encounter anyone else on her way to the small, welcoming room and she simply closed the door behind her and sank into the armchair.

She suddenly felt lonelier than she ever had in her entire life. She was surrounded by a family that had been reunited and which extended to include those close to them: Roger, Steve and even Lindsey. Naturally, her heart ached for John, but he was surrounded by people who loved him and she knew eventually time would ease his pain of missing his mother. His father would no doubt get married, and whether that woman would be suitable or not, John would be part of a family unit. From what she knew of the love Gabriel had for his son, she believed it would ultimately be a happy one.

But she was an outsider and had nobody. Where was her brother? Why couldn't she have stayed in touch with him? Why hadn't he tried to find her? They had loved each other, been there for each other through the hardest times as the public judged them guilty of their father's crimes. Their mother had committed suicide; their father had been murdered in jail. People wanted someone to blame. The public didn't want to know that the murderer's daughter and son were innocent.

And now she was alone. She needed Jason. He was all she had. She no longer loved him. Gabriel Black had spoiled any love she used to have for Jason Chesters. But she didn't want to be alone.

Grace cried, feeling numb. She curled her legs under her and rested her head on the arm of the chair, closing her eyes in an attempt to alleviate their soreness. She had no idea how many minutes, even hours, had passed, but she was roused by a faint knock at the door. She remained still, hoping whoever it was would go away. But it was in vain. The second knock was louder.

"Can I come in, Grace?" Gabriel waited, resisting the urge to try the handle. Whether the door was locked or not, this was his captive's sanctuary and he had no right to enter if she didn't want him to. He knew only too well the importance of that rule.

He and John had been searching for her. Gabriel had hoped she was just taking a late shower, or had gone down to the kitchen for breakfast with the others. He thought that, after what they had shared last night – caring for John, and intimate, passionate sex – Grace would not have felt the need to seek her sanctuary. But as their search for her proved fruitless, he realised he was wrong.

"Please, Grace. I will arrange for you to go home if you wish. But please don't stay in here."

The door opened. She looked down, but not before he had caught a glimpse of her red eyes. He wanted to tell her that John was waiting to see her, to show her his new bike. But his own guilt and sadness silenced him.

"Yes," Grace said and she picked up her bag and put it over her shoulder. "I would like to go home. Please tell John I'm sorry. I don't feel well."

"If you're not well, stay here. You can go back to your bedroom and get some rest. Or Steve could make you some soup or something to make you feel better. Tell me, Grace. Is there anything you need? We can help you." His voice was low and hesitant.

"I need my brother. So, no, you can't help me."

Twenty minutes later, Michael opened the car door for her and she walked down her path and into her house.

As she removed her coat, she instinctively put her hand to her neck. He had simply unlocked her collar and placed it in his pocket with the key. That wasn't his usual MO. He had always wanted her to wear his "mark", to be locked into him. She was used to worrying about when he would take it off. She flung her hand down. *Damn! You're acting like you're missing it!*

She rang Jason. By three o'clock that afternoon, she was drinking coffee with him at his local Starbucks. She didn't really feel better, but she hadn't cried for the last three hours, so that was something.

Chapter 76

Gabriel stared at his computer screen. It was six o'clock on Monday morning. He had just risen from John's bed, where he had spent the last two hours, having been woken by John's screams yet again and decided the only way either of them would get any more sleep that night was if he stayed with his son.

Now he was caffeined up – and furious. The weekly report he received on Jason Chesters informed him that on Saturday morning Chesters had visited a jewellery shop – Madison Diamond and Wedding Ring Specialist. The bill was £3,500.

Fuck, fuck, fuck!

He emailed Rick at Black Armour. It would be the middle of the night in Canada but he knew Rick would respond to him as soon as he got the message, and Gabriel Black was suddenly on a mission.

When he had first discovered Grace McGuire's true identity, Black had dug further into the whereabouts of her brother. If he was ever going to expose her identity, he would also need to know more about her brother. At that time, it had been sufficient for him to discover that the latest known location for Michael Bright was Nairobi, Kenya. And that for some reason he appeared not to have taken up any new identity. Now this elusive brother had become of vital importance to Gabriel Black.

Rick.

Need info on Michael Bright now; cannot delay until January, as first discussed.

Let me know what you have got so far and also your schedule.

Reply to this private email address only.

Black.

He continued to read the reports for the board meeting to be held later this morning and tried to remain focused.

It was clear to all at the meeting, including Cynthia Black, that their CEO was in a foul mood. It was a short meeting and everyone was glad to get out of the room. Except Cynthia Black. Her concerns about the secrets her son may have been keeping from her had eased over the last few weeks. Although he had made it clear he would not be having sex with her at Arnford Hall again, he had continued to honour his promise to his father. Their encounters were usually short, but she mostly got what she wanted. On those days when there was a board meeting, she got to enjoy more of his time. Ellouise often collected John from school and Gabriel would have tea with his mother. They discussed the business and, as they were both driven by increasing its net worth, they usually agreed over what needed to be done. His mother even conceded to herself that Julian was beginning to make a valuable contribution and she was gradually becoming more comfortable with the idea of Gabriel stepping back a little to spend more time with John. She had no reason to suspect that her elder son had any other intentions. She was also convinced now that there was no other woman in his life, and probably never would be.

But today he was worse than a bear with a sore head. His curt remarks made it clear to everyone present that he wanted this meeting over as soon as possible. At one point the chairwoman had to force proceedings to slow down a little as she reminded the CEO that the board had not been notified that completion of the Black Armour project in Canada was to be certified three weeks ahead of schedule. Nor had they been told that their top man on the project was coming back to the UK early. Gabriel would confirm no more than to say everything was in order and he was taking personal responsibility for the early completion of the project.

Now she waited in the boardroom until they were alone.

"What is the matter, Gabriel?"

"Nothing."

"You seemed to be in a rush. Not to mention a foul mood."

"I have a lot on at the moment, and there seemed to be no reason to deliberate over issues when things are generally running very smoothly."

"I thought you were starting to offload more work onto Julian."

"Yes. He can ease some of my workload. But ..." Gabriel hesitated a moment and tried to choose his words carefully. His mother was a shrewd woman and if he let slip any part of his plan to go on a manhunt to Africa, she would be onto him in a flash and do everything in her power to stop it from happening. Not to mention she may find out about Grace. His mother's hold on him had become too great and he needed to weaken it. "But I just found out about some potential opportunities for Black Communications in Kenya. Armen is setting up some meetings with potential contacts and I need to arrange to go out there. It's just a busy time." He continued to pack his things into his briefcase. As far as he was concerned, this conversation was over. He was about to leave the room.

"What about this evening?"

"I'll see you at five. I won't be eating with you." Now he left. He closed the door to his office and sank into his chair.

"Where are you?" Gabriel was calm, and Roger detected a need he hadn't heard in his friend's voice for a very long time. It wasn't for sex or drink or drugs. It was for companionship, for love.

"I'll be there in a minute."

Roger knocked on his door then went into the office and closed the door behind him.

The men looked at each other. Over the years they had formed a strong platonic friendship. Roger was very happily married to Steve and their relationship was monogamous. But Steve accepted the fact that there was a special bond between Roger and Gabriel. He knew his partner would do anything for Black and would never desert him. The three men had lived together for the past fourteen years. They knew each other well and a web of love, friendship and secrets bound them together.

Roger walked over to Gabriel's desk and perched on the end of it.

"Are you going to tell me what's happened?"

His friend was twirling his pen between his fingers. It was a habit he practised when he was deep in thought, usually in troubled thought.

"I think Grace is getting engaged."

Roger didn't know about Jason, nor the fact that Black had him under surveillance. He looked perplexed. "What do you mean? To another man?"

"Yes."

"You're telling me Grace has been seeing someone else all along?"

"Yes." Gabriel looked down at the pen in his hand. He suddenly felt guilty for not having confided in Roger. Not that he wanted to reveal any of Grace's secrets to his PA, but he now felt he should have let him know that their relationship was never a traditional boyfriend/girlfriend one.

"Did you know this? Was this other guy there before you?"

"Yes, and quit the interrogation, please." Gabriel got up from his chair and walked round to Roger.

The two men stared at each other and, seeing the regret in Gabriel's eyes, Roger reached out and hugged him.

Gabriel had needed him all those years ago, for friendship and passion. Now he needed him for comfort. And help.

As they pulled back from their embrace, Roger took his hand and led him to the sofa under the window looking out over the Manchester skyline. They sat down and remained silent for a couple of minutes. Then Roger turned to him. "Do you love her?"

"Yes." Black stared at the carpet. "But it seems she loves someone else." He gave a faint laugh.

"Have you told her you love her?" Roger already knew the answer. Gabriel Black wouldn't have thought about being honest with the woman Roger had watched him fall in love with over the last three months. Gabriel Black didn't love himself, so how could he possibly believe a woman could love him? His employer was too proud to admit that he could love someone who couldn't love him.

441

"No. I've only recently admitted it to myself. But to be in love has never been my destiny, has it?" Gabriel got up and gazed out of the window. "She's waiting for me, you know. My *mother*." He spat the last word out. "I feel so helpless. I'm suffocating in my own sin. Even if Grace wasn't going to marry Jason, there's no way she would accept me, want to be with me, let alone love me, if she knew … My life is a fucking mess. Thank God I have John."

Gabriel glanced at Roger. He hadn't thanked God for anything over the past twenty-five years, and yet now he suddenly wanted to pray for his son and a woman called Grace.

"What are you going to do?" Roger's question demanded an answer which did not start with the word "nothing".

"Try to make her happy. She has a brother she's not seen for many years. We've located him in Kenya. I'm going to go and get him. Then I'll stay out of her life."

"Gabe, I can't believe she hasn't got feelings for you. I saw the way she looked at you on Friday, the way she talked with John and helped to comfort him. Hell, before you just mentioned an engagement, I would have said I've watched her falling in love with you just as I'm sure I've watched you fall in love with her. You should have seen how she's been acting at the last couple of skiing lessons, looking over her shoulder waiting for you to arrive. But you never did and you could see her disappointment."

Gabriel remained silent, remembering Friday night: the compassion she had shown both him and John, and the sensual lovemaking they had shared. What happened after that night? Then he recalled his words, *I needed that,* and his regret at not saying what he really wanted to. Would it have made any difference if he had said, "I needed *you*"?

"Are you really going to go to Kenya to bring her brother back?" Roger grew thoughtful as he recalled Grace telling him she had a brother she wasn't permitted to see.

"Yes. I know how having my family around me again has helped, and given me renewed hope in life. At least I will feel as though I've done something for her and our time together won't have been totally unwanted for her."

442

Roger didn't understand why Gabriel should refer to their time as being unwanted. He was still convinced Grace loved his friend. Now he was even more certain that it was his friend's ability to conceal his feelings from her so effectively that would cost him this woman's love. There had to be something they could do.

"OK. So what have you got on this Jason guy? I presume you've had him under surveillance." He raised his eyebrow and let his employer know they needed to take action; the Blacks and their staff did not take things lying down. There was something here worth fighting for.

Gabriel smiled at Roger's determination. "He's a solicitor in London. Does recreational drugs. Not seeing any other women. Been dating Grace for the last year and a half or so."

Roger looked puzzled. "Grace doesn't strike me as the type of girl who would two-time a steady boyfriend. What did you have on her to make her start seeing you?"

"I can't tell you. But I haven't exactly been fair with her, nor honest with you."

"OK," Roger said firmly. "It looks like you are punishing yourself enough as it is over this, so I won't remind you that you've probably brought this on yourself with your controlling, egotistical ways. But it seems as though you've a lot of making up to do."

"Roger," Gabriel spoke quietly and he placed his hand on his friend's shoulder. "I know you're thinking I've got what I deserve. And you're right. Now it's too late. But cover me here while I go to Kenya. Then I can start to get on with … my existence. It will be as though I never met her. At least I have John and Julian and Ellouise. You'll stay too, won't you, Roger?"

Roger embraced him again. "Steve and I aren't going anywhere."

But we are going to help you through this. You deserve more than an existence. And you deserve to be free of your mother. We'll do our utmost to make you happy, Gabriel Black.

Chapter 77

In the staffroom on Monday lunchtime, Grace stared at the ring on her finger – a solitaire diamond shining prominently on a simple band of yellow gold, rainbow colours bouncing off it.

"It's beautiful," said Jane. "You must be so happy. Have you set a date yet?"

"Y-yes, it is." Grace continued to rock her hand to reflect the light. "We haven't got a date. Jason wants to go off and 'do it', as it were, as soon as possible. But …" Grace could think of a hundred and one excuses to delay things, but she only allowed herself to acknowledge one of them. Gabriel Black. "I need to finish this school year here and start applying for a new job. Hopefully I'll at least get some temporary work in London to begin with. Miss Greaves has been really understanding and will help with references and the like." She paused again. "But it's going to be really hard for me to leave here." She pictured a small boy with dark eyes and black hair.

"Were the children excited for you?"

"They all wanted to see the ring, and the girls were asking about a dress and bridesmaids. I won't upset them by telling them it will be a registry office do – no fuss, and we'll be glad to get away for a couple of weeks." Grace finished nibbling at her lunch and got ready to start the afternoon's lessons.

Everything over that weekend had passed in a blur. Grace had been desperate to leave Arnford Hall and she had been desperate to feel loved. The fact that it was the wrong man who had proposed to her seemed to have passed her by. Jason had been frantically happy when he met her off the train. Her visit was unexpected, and he had been waiting for the following weekend to propose to the woman he felt he needed to hold on to. But what luck! As soon as Grace had rung to tell him she would come down to see him, he managed to get a late booking at the Winter Garden, the magnificent eight-storey building with a glass atrium revealing the stars at night and its Victorian elegance and glamour. It was busy and noisy but they shared a wonderful meal of scallops with artichokes, macadamia nuts and lemon thyme followed by chicken with truffle boulangère potatoes, mushrooms and glazed shallots. A pleasant quantity of Sancerre was consumed and, as the waiter brought them a vanilla cheesecake with apricot and white chocolate, Jason reached in his pocket and placed a small dark blue ring box in front of Grace's plate. She stared at him, her mouth open but unable to speak.

He reached for her hand and uttered the words, "Grace, will you marry me?"

He then removed the ring from its bed of velvet and placed it on the third finger of her left hand. Summoning the waiter to order a bottle of Bollinger in celebration, Jason beamed at his fiancée.

Grace had never said yes.

On the Tube going back to Jason's flat that night, Grace felt numb. On the train going home on Sunday afternoon, she felt numb. She played with the ring, pulling it off her finger and pushing it back on. It should have been a token of Jason's love. It should have been a symbol of their future life together. So why did she feel that she had lost a collar and gained a band? It didn't make sense. She had gone to London because she wanted to feel loved. Wasn't that what Jason had declared when he placed the ring on her finger? Why, then, did he mention, having just finished his last glass of champagne, that being married would ensure he was offered a partnership at his law firm?

Now, as Grace talked about her future to Jane, she didn't feel numb any more. She felt that she was losing. She was losing the job she loved. Not just any job in any school, but the one here in Arnford Primary School with a head she respected immensely, a constant flow of lovely children she could educate, with knowledge and life-enhancing skills. She was losing her independence. She was losing her belief that she might have children. She was losing Grace McGuire.

She left the staffroom. The afternoon passed quickly and soon the children were filtering out of the classroom to go home. Grace kept back from the windows, refusing to give in

445

to her desire to see if Black was waiting in the playground to greet his son. She wondered what his reaction would be when he found out about her engagement to Jason Chesters.

So she never saw Ellouise holding John's hand as they walked back to her car parked on her drive.

"How was your day, John?"

"Not so good." He was kicking the pavement as they walked the short distance. "Mrs McGuire is going to marry somebody else. Somebody called Mr Chesters. And she's going to be called Mrs Chesters. And she's going to leave."

Ellouise stopped. She let go of her nephew's hand and crouched down to look into his eyes. The small boy looked up at her, his eyes clouded and sad.

"I thought she liked my daddy. I thought she liked me. I guess she won't come to tea any more." He carried on walking and kicking.

Ellouise straightened. She looked back at the school, desperate to go and find Grace and find out what the hell was going on. But instead she hurried to catch up with John.

"Come here, honey." She pulled him to her, embracing him tightly. *How could she take away his hurt? What was she going to tell GeeBee?*

"Mrs McGuire does like you, John. A lot. And I'm sure she will still come for tea with you and Daddy. Come on. Let's get you home. Steve has made some chocolate brownies for you." She crossed her fingers behind her back and decided to call at the deli on their way to make a secret purchase just in case Steve hadn't.

With the emergency purchase left in her bag – Steve hadn't let her down – Ellouise left John enjoying his cake in the kitchen and went up to the octagonal room to ring her eldest brother.

"GeeBee, it's Ell."

"Hi. Is everything OK? Is John all right?"

"Yes. He's fine. He's with Steve. But he's been told something at school." Ellouise paused as she heard Gabriel sigh on the other end of the phone. "You already know, don't you?"

"Yes." There was silence before he leaned forward and continued. "I hadn't allowed for this in my plan."

"Your plan! GeeBee, what the fuck have you two been playing at? How come she has still been seeing this Jason? I thought she had spent the weekend with you and John, for his birthday. You said you were going to take them both to the lake house. What are you not telling me?"

"Nothing, Ellouise. It's over, and that's all there is to say." He had no intention of saying anything to his sister in her current state of anguish mixed with anger. Hell, he didn't know what to tell himself. He held the phone away from his ear as her next tirade began.

"Oh no. Don't go being 'I don't give a shit about anything,' GeeBee. You have a future to think about. A future with John. A future with a woman you love. And I think she loves you."

"Don't, Ellouise. Please."

"What time will you be home? Are you seeing our bitch of a mother?" Ellouise's voice was raised and she was pacing around the room. Her anger held back her tears. "If you had heard John asking if Mrs McGuire would ever come for tea again, you would not be fucking saying *it's over*. We need to talk. And I'll come over there if you're not coming home tonight!"

"For fuck's sake!" Gabriel slammed his fist on the table. "I don't need this. I'll be home at half past seven to put John to bed." For the first time in his life he put the phone down on her.

His day was just getting better and fucking better!

Chapter 78

He walked into his mother's apartment at precisely five o'clock. Cynthia heard the chink of crystal as she walked into the living area and saw him pour a small whisky and down it in one quick gulp. He wiped his mouth with the back of his hand. Clearly his mood had not improved since this afternoon.

He heard her footsteps and swung round, his mask up, his eyes black and his posture exuding defiance.

Over the years, the mother and son had shared each other's moods, successes, the occasional failure and even – on the very rare occasion – joy. Now Cynthia braced herself for his anger. She wasn't aware that she had caused it. She was like a virus that was with him every day and, although he wasn't immune to her, he had found his own way of living with her, coping with her in his life.

So this was a first for Cynthia. Something – or, she guessed, some*one* – else had caused it; someone she didn't know about. Thoughts of another woman returned for a moment.

"Do you want to take a shower?" She tried to sound matter-of-fact, hopeful that her desire to share a shower with him didn't show.

"No."

He took three strides to reach her, grabbed her hand and led her to the master bedroom.

"Let's just do it, shall we, Mother? I need to get back home to my son."

Gabriel withdrew from his mother and went into the bathroom. He flushed the condom and fastened his trousers. He stared at himself in the mirror. Perspiration glistened in his reflection and he felt sick. He splashed some cold water on his face and breathed deeply for a minute. Then he walked back into the living area and grabbed his phone from his jacket.

"Michael. Bring the car round now. I'll meet you at the front."

As Cynthia walked from the bedroom, fastening the tie on her ice-blue silk wrap, his hand was on the handle of the door to the apartment.

"I'm going to Kenya. I'm not sure when I'll be back. I'll be keeping in contact with Roger if you need to tell me anything." And he left.

Chapter 79

When Gabriel returned to Arnford Hall he went in search of John. He found him with Ellouise in the octagonal room and it was clear that the young boy had been waiting for his father to come home. John ran to him, wrapping his hands around him for a hug.

"Hey, big boy. How are you? Have you been looking after Aunty Ell?"

He felt John squeeze him tight. He peeled him from his body and crouched down to look at him, taking hold of his small hands.

"I'm sorry, Daddy." Big dark eyes stared into Gabriel's and pulled at his heart. John had been crying.

Gabriel glanced over to Ellouise, who stood back from the father and son and smiled at her brother in an "I'm sorry too" sort of way.

"My mummy's gone and now Mrs McGuire is going to leave us too. She doesn't like me."

"Oh, John. That's not true, darling. I know Mrs McGuire likes you. She is so pleased you're in her class." Gabriel choked back his guilt and felt Ellouise's regretful look burn into him.

"But she's going to marry someone else and she's moving away." The tears were flowing down his small, flushed cheeks. "I thought she loved you, Daddy. Why aren't you marrying her?"

Gabriel closed his eyes. "We're just good friends, John. And we still can be. Maybe she will come and visit us sometimes." If Black had worried that he had made a mess of things before, he now had concrete – or, rather, tear-filled – proof that he had well and truly fucked up, not only his own life but John's too. For the shortest of moments he wondered if John Black would have been happier living with Carol Beardly and his cousins. The love he felt for John, the need he had for him, and the relationship which was developing between them told him otherwise.

There was something else touching the soul of Gabriel Black. The guilt he felt over the grief he was causing his son equalled the guilt he felt over his treatment of Grace. He resolved to ensure Grace got something of value from her time with the Blacks, and just maybe she would be willing to keep in touch. He wasn't sure how, but he could wait until Jason Chesters made a mistake, proved himself unworthy of her and then perhaps, if there was a miracle, Black could have a second chance and this time actually tell Grace he loved her.

Feeling stronger and calmer than he had since reading the report this morning, Black took his son's hand and led him out of the room, saying, "Come on. Let's go get a shower. Daddy feels dirty."

"I'll be waiting for you, GeeBee," Ellouise called after him.

It took longer than usual for Gabriel to settle John into bed that night. His words of comfort to reassure the boy stung his own lips as he uttered them.

"You will have the rest of the school year to see her … you'll be able to stay in touch and send her emails … she can come and visit whenever she wants to … and she's still coming skiing for Christmas …"

Who was he trying to kid?

Grace would want nothing to do with him, and it was his fault that his son would feel heartbroken for the second time in his short life.

Eventually, John drifted off to sleep and Gabriel left his bedroom to go down to the kitchen.

"Would you like to eat your supper in here, sir?" Steve asked as he opened the oven door to remove a beef casserole.

"Yes, that's fine, thank you," he said wearily. "Have you all eaten?"

Steve nodded and Ellouise confirmed she had eaten early with John. Roger was out walking Satan but he was expected back within the next ten minutes.

Gabriel parked himself on the bar stool at the island next to Ellouise, seeing little point in trying to avoid the inevitable. *Best to get it over with.*

"Can you bring the Pavillon Rouge de Margaux? I need something to leave me with a better taste today."

Steve glanced at Ellouise as he placed the single plate of food on the island and went into the wine room to retrieve the bottle.

Gabriel collected four crystal glasses. "Let's all enjoy this, at least."

Ellouise got the corkscrew. "So. You've made a right fucking mess of a relationship with the one woman I know could have made you happy!" She couldn't hide the bitterness that had been eating away at her all afternoon. Then she gave a weak laugh, waving the corkscrew like a truncheon. "And I thought you had finally got it together, GeeBee. You would finally stop seeing whores and money-digging sluts and settle down with someone who would be good for you. And John."

"This is not the time or place, Ell." Gabriel glared at his sister as he added, "I'm sorry about this, Steve."

"That's OK, sir." The chef poured the rich red liquid into the four glasses. "I'll just go and check where Roger is." Not waiting for a response, he headed outside into the cold night, certain that there would be less of a chill in the garden than there was in the kitchen. He hoped that the wine wouldn't be allowed to cool; that would be bad!

When the two of them were alone, Ellouise sighed and turned to face her brother.

"I can't say I'm sorry for what I said, you know. I simply don't understand what you've been playing at. Why have you carried on seeing her, even arranged the skiing holiday for Christmas, if you knew she was never going to leave Jason? This just isn't like you." She tried to hold back her tears, but her voice wasn't co-operating. "You know how fond John is of her. She announces to the class that she is marrying someone he's never even heard of, and he's heartbroken and thinks it's all his fault. I can't begin to count the number of times he has said that."

Gabriel pushed his half-eaten meal away from him and reached for one of the wine glasses. He savoured the aroma of plums and cherries and basked in the flavours as he swished it around his mouth before swallowing. Then he took Ellouise's hand.

"I'm sorry. To you, to John, to everyone. I seem incapable of holding on to anything I can't pay for." He stared at his glass. He thought about mentioning Grace's brother but he didn't want her to know the real reason he was going to Kenya. "I … I need to ask a favour."

"You know I'll try to help with anything. For you, for John. Let me talk to Grace …" She already knew he wouldn't want her to do that. She also knew she wouldn't go behind his back; not this time.

"No. At least, not for me." He shot her a warning look, confirming her own thoughts. "But I would be grateful if you would ask her to speak to John. See if she could possibly reassure him that she might stay in touch, even visit him. You could tell her she wouldn't have to see me. It could be with you. Or Carol." His throat hurt and his heart ached as he realised he was admitting that he would not be part of Grace's future.

"Are you and she finished? It's not like you've ever worried about your women being single before. And she isn't even married yet. What about the skiing holiday?"

He sipped his wine and his eyes darkened. "Oh. She will go skiing." There was no way he was going to let John down, or deny himself her company one last time.

Ellouise was about to ask him how he could be so certain, but the look on his face was the only deterrent she needed. She knew there was something strange about her brother's relationship with Grace. The necklace, the sanctuary, Jason fucking Chesters. But, then, there had always been something strange about the Blacks. Since the twins were fifteen, that is.

Black finished his wine and pushed his stool back from the island as he stood up. It was half past nine.

"I presume you are staying tonight."

"Yes. I'm sleeping in the grey room. I'll leave the bathroom doors open so I can hear John if he's disturbed."

Ellouise knew about John's night terrors, and she had been at her brother's side a couple of times to help to calm her nephew and comfort Gabriel. The grey room shared a bathroom with

453

John's bedroom, so she would hear John and be able to walk through the bathroom to comfort him if he disturbed. She knew Gabriel would be glad of a good night's sleep. Then again, she also knew that he had plenty going on in his mind which would probably keep him awake anyway.

"OK. Thank you." Gabriel kissed his sister's cheek. "I'll see you in the morning."

He went straight to his office and messaged Roger to meet him there as soon as he could. Ten minutes later, Roger walked in carrying two glasses of wine.

"There was a bit left in the bottle. I knew you would appreciate another glass." Roger slouched in the chair at the side of his employer's desk. He leaned over and put the second glass on the table before taking a sip from his own.

"Thanks." Gabriel shut his computer down. "Has Rick landed yet?"

"No. He's not due in until nine in the morning. Are you going to tell me exactly what you're up to?"

Roger drank his wine, trying, and mostly succeeding, to appear relaxed and normal. However, he was well aware that Gabriel Black travelling to Kenya for something not work-related was anything but normal. Add to that the fact he intended Rick Casey to go with him, and it was downright suspicious – with an element of danger!

"You know I'm going to Kenya to find Grace's brother."

"Why don't you just mail the guy and ask him to come over?"

Gabriel looked at his friend. He took a moment to decide how much he could tell the man he trusted more than anyone else; the man who knew Gabriel Black better than anyone else. He felt guilty that he couldn't tell him everything and he knew Roger would be hurt to know that.

"It's not quite that simple. The guy doesn't want to be found."

There was a pause and they both sipped some more.

"Is that why you want Rick to accompany you? Is that why you took him off one of the most lucrative projects we've had, before it was fully handed over to the client?"

"I already said the project was completed early and I would take full responsibility for the successful handover."

"And you're sure it will be successful?"

"Yes …"

From the way Gabriel frowned, Roger knew there was a "but" coming.

"But should there be any last-minute handshaking to do" – now Black actually smiled – "Julian will need to get over there and see to it. He may want to brush up on my signature, too." He pushed his chair back, willing the conversation to be over; keeping things from Roger didn't sit comfortably with him.

"Wait a minute. I hope you're joking. You guys might have got away with your pranks when you were younger, but you can't seriously expect Julian to carry it off now!"

But Gabriel was leaving the room. "Well, let's hope it won't be necessary then. I'll get Ellouise to take John to school in the morning. Tell Michael to pick Rick up from the airport and bring him straight here. We are going to Kenya on Wednesday."

Roger watched him disappear up the staircase.

Chapter 80

As John was getting ready to leave for school the next morning, Gabriel hugged his son tightly and tried for the umpteenth time to reassure him that Mrs McGuire still liked him and his daddy and that they would still be able to see her, even if she wasn't teaching at his school any more. He then turned to his sister.

"You can talk to her about this. Ask her to let John know she won't abandon him, even if she doesn't want to see me again …" He tried to control his voice. "I know she wouldn't want John to be so upset."

"Yes. I will. Are you going to collect John tonight?" Ellouise couldn't look at her brother as she fought back the lump in her throat. She busied herself with fastening John's coat and checking his shoes. Again.

"Yes. Then I need you to stay here and take him each day until I get back."

"How long will that be?" Her voice was quiet.

"Why? Have you got somewhere else you would rather be?"

Ellouise felt cut by his accusing question. "Of course not." The sudden rise in her voice alerted him to the fact that his sister was upset too. "I'll stay with John for as long as he needs me. But it would be good if I could tell him when *you*'ll be back. He needs you more than ever at the moment, GeeBee."

"I know. I'll be back as soon as I can and I'll keep in touch. Now go on or you'll be late. Have tea with us tonight, OK?"

"Yes. I'll see you then."

When the house had gone quiet, Gabriel went into his office and rang Andrew Cornworthy, his solicitor.

"Andrew, hi, it's Gabriel. I need to talk to you about my will."

The moment Gabriel heard Julian shout "Fuck, it's been a long time", he knew Rick had arrived. He left his office and walked down the hall to see his brother hugging the man who had just flown in from Canada. Gabriel joined the two men and couldn't

456

help feeling relief that he could now fully share his plans with someone.

Having shown Rick where he could shower and change, Gabriel went back into his office to wait for him.

He brought up the information they had gathered so far on his screen. Michael Bright was living in Nairobi. He was known locally as Kit, a nickname from the fact that he was good with tools! When he needed money, he repaired Toyotas. Nearly everyone drove one, and most of them were falling to bits. Kit could have made a lot of money. But often he was too drunk, hungover, or going cold turkey to even move, let alone get to work and fix cars. He had been a pilot on flights from the Masai Mara to Mombasa, but lost his licence thanks to drug and alcohol abuse.

And just to make it a full set of addictions, Kit had gambling debts big enough to make his eyes water. It looked as though the guy was a piece of shit, in shit.

Gabriel sighed and wondered why nothing in his life seemed simple. He hated the thought of going anywhere near this man, who appeared to be trouble with a capital T, let alone on a mission to bring him back. He felt sick when he thought about the risk he was about to take and its impact on John should anything go wrong.

He had already made provision in his will for Ellouise to have custody of his son in the event of his death. He had hoped to include Grace too, but that wasn't going to happen now. However, it did strengthen his resolve to make one more request to Grace McGuire – and he needed to do that today. He just needed to work out how he was going to see her.

Suddenly Rick knocked at his door and entered his office. The men went through the file Rick had compiled and scrutinised the town map of Nairobi.

"Sir, I think we've got all we're gonna get in this continent."

Gabriel raised his eyebrow as he glanced at the younger man and appreciated his laid-back, confident manner.

"Let's just get after the dick and reunite the happy couple." Rick beamed, with the words "thanks for letting me help" written all over his face.

457

"Look. I know you're keen, Rick, but we need to make sure this is done properly. I don't want some fucking loan shark or gangster trailing him back to the UK and I won't risk Grace being put in any danger because of him. We need to make sure we know the full extent of the shit he's in and get him out of it and cleaned up to bring home. Armen will meet us at the airport and give us an update on the money this guy owes, together with his physical state. We need to keep our heads low, do what has to be done and then quietly get him out of there. It may take a few days."

"I know. Trust me, sir. We'll get this sorted."

"OK. I've set the funds up so they can be wired to whichever fuckwit he owes the money to. Have you got the codes sorted in case we need to increase the funds?"

"Yes, sir."

"Good. Let's go get a drink."

The two men made their way to the kitchen. Gabriel was surprised to see Roger sitting at the island with his laptop.

"I thought you were going into Manchester today."

"Oh. Change of plan. Steve wants me to help shift some furniture this afternoon so I decided to work from here."

Gabriel thought it strange; the men's home was minimalistic, to say the least, and he couldn't imagine for the life of him what furniture could possibly need moving. And why didn't Steve just ask Michael? But he had too many other things to think about and so he just got drinks for the three of them, still planning how he was going to see Grace.

"So, Rick," Roger piped up, "I presume you're as confident as the boss about the completion of the Canadian project."

Fuck it, Roger, are you going to let that drop? Gabriel busied himself with the *Financial Times*, trying to ignore Roger's dig.

"Wouldn't be here if I wasn't, would I?"

Gabriel silently thanked Rick and glanced over the top of his paper at his PA. *Satisfied now?*

"Look, it's the lawyer in me." Roger had every intention of sticking his neck out, not caring whether he pissed his employer off or not. There was something he needed to do, and he needed a little time alone with Rick. "Humour me and run through the

458

completion document with me. If you two are buggering off, I want to make sure we can cover you, just in case."

On a good day, Gabriel would have wondered what the hell Roger was up to. But it wasn't a good day. He didn't know if he would ever have a good day again! He needed to see Grace.

"Right, I'll leave you two to it. I'll be in my office."

Roger breathed a sigh of relief as Black finally left the room.

"OK, Rick. I don't know what you two are up to but I need you to go through something with me."

Rick looked at the other man. He was well aware that Mr Black and Mr Courtney shared everything. But he wasn't sure just how much this man knew of Black's objective, and the possible danger involved, in going to Kenya.

Roger glanced over to the kitchen door to make sure they wouldn't be disturbed and then got straight to the point. "I need you to show me how to activate the tracker."

Rick stared at him for a moment. He visibly paled. Roger's demand made him appreciate the gravity of the situation. Black must really want this Kit guy.

Gabriel Black had a tracking device implanted in his left arm. His mother and the trustees responsible for forty per cent of the Black Group shareholdings had insisted that it was put in place to be used in the event of the disappearance of the head of the Group. Gabriel Black was worth too much money to be allowed to disappear. Or more to the point, to be kidnapped. He had agreed to this invasion of his body on the condition that only Rick Casey had the ability to activate the tracker and also to monitor it.

Now Roger was going to demand that that responsibility be given to him.

Rick glanced at the door. "Does he know what you're asking?"

"No. And he's not going to find out. Hopefully it won't be necessary. But we can't take that risk. *You* can't take that risk, Rick. I'm not asking you to do this. I'm telling you."

Seeing the anxious expression on Rick's face, the older man added, "I'll take full responsibility for it. You don't need to worry about upsetting him. But I know he is putting himself at risk with this task he's set himself. And I know it's no use trying to talk him out of it. But if it goes tits up I want to be able to do everything I can to help him. And you."

Without hesitation, Rick looked Roger in the eye and nodded. "My kit's in my bag upstairs. It will take me about half an hour to go through it with you and another hour or so to download the files you'll need."

"Let's get started, then. It's about time you had a nap to get over your jet lag. I'll let Black know you'll be sleeping for a while. Just let me know what you need now and what I need to do."

The two conspirators left the kitchen.

Chapter 81

On hearing from Roger that Rick had gone to get some sleep, Black went to find Julian.

"Look, there's almost zero chance you'll need to go over to Canada. Rick and his team have done a great job, and we should give them credit for completing everything early. But just in case you do," the older twin raised his eyebrow in a knowing look, "you know you can pull it off. Just have a bit more taste in the clothing department – and wear a dark suit!" Gabriel dodged as Julian hurled the pair of socks he was about to pull on at his brother.

"There's nothing wrong with my dress sense. You need to get with it, you old bugger! And you'll owe me if I have to drag myself over there and be you all week. It's going to cramp my style. I suppose I won't be able to take Lindsey with me?"

"Afraid not. No women for Gabriel Black." Gabriel started to reposition the toiletries on Julian's dresser. "Have you heard about Grace?"

Julian finished fastening his tie and turned to look at Gabriel, who had suddenly become quiet. "What's happened?"

"She's got engaged."

"Not to you, then? Are you going to tell me about it?"

Gabriel walked over to the armchair beside the window. He sank into it and gazed out at the vivid blue skyline streaked with thin, wispy cirrus clouds.

"I …" He swallowed. "I used her to entertain me."

Julian sat on the end of the bed. "I thought she was different. It looked as though she really meant something to you. Especially after the poker game …"

"I thought she would be just like the others. But I let her get to me. I'm not sure how it happened, but I had begun to hope there was something real between us. But it's just been a game. A stupid game – and I'm the loser."

461

"Then who the fuck is she engaged to?" Julian stared as Gabriel headed to the door.

"Her real boyfriend."

Julian watched the door close after him.

A minute later, dressed to go to his meeting at Black Construction, Julian caught up with his brother on the galleried landing.

"We need to talk, GeeBee. When did we stop being honest with each other?" He looked down for a moment before turning to look his brother in the eyes.

Gabriel hesitated a moment before glancing at his watch. It was midday.

"Have you got time for a drink?"

The twins headed down to the games room and Gabriel poured two Jack Daniel's and Coke.

"What happened in South America?"

It was Julian's turn to be quiet and thoughtful as he stared at his glass.

"How do you know anything happened?"

"You stopped contacting any of us – me, Ellouise, Roger. Everyone. Then you agreed to come back way too quickly, agreed to come back on the board and live here. And hooked up with Lindsey. So what happened?"

Julian scrutinised his brother's face. Gabriel was excellent at distraction; he had managed to turn a conversation which was supposed to be about him and Grace into confession time for Julian. How did he do it?

"I met someone on my travels. He made me forget everything when we were together; you know. Our relationship didn't need to be brutal or dominating or perverse to help me not think of *her*, not see her damn face or hear her vile words …" He swallowed and wiped his eyes. "It was just passionate, gentle and loving. I loved him, GeeBee. For the first time since that summer with Poppa, I was happy and in love."

Gabriel waited a moment, not wanting to interrupt. He hadn't realised how badly Julian had coped with the memories of Cynthia. He hadn't had sex with her for over thirteen years, yet it now seemed that it had taken him over ten years to find any sort of relationship to help him forget his nightmare experience.

Gabriel had just continued to live in his nightmare; week in, week out. He hadn't sought love, not after Roger anyway. He just wanted sex with anyone who wasn't his mother. But it had always been a purely physical act, with no friendship, no passion, no feelings other than lust. He pushed his own as well as his partners' limits. It excited him, gave him what he needed for a short while, and then he could walk away, never leaving anything behind. He had nothing to give and therefore he had nothing to lose.

Until he entrapped Grace McGuire in his life. Someone who wanted nothing to do with him.

Julian remained silent, the memory of Simon's face before his eyes, the feel of his touch on his body, the sound of his laughter in his ears … and the tears streaked down his cheeks and his body quivered gently as he cried his heartbreak out at last. Gabriel wrapped his strong arms around him, pulling his head into his chest.

"Let it out, Julian," he whispered, waiting patiently until his brother was calmer.

After a few minutes his crying subsided and Gabriel eased his arms away. Julian stared at his now empty glass and let the words pour out.

"We met in Namibia. His name was Simon. Would you believe, he was exactly our age? Same date of birth." He smiled momentarily. "I guess you could say it was love at first sight. He made me laugh. And, for the first time, he made me truly forget. It was so different and so good with him. He made me feel normal, unashamed of who I was. Blameless." Julian fell silent before raising his eyes to his brother. "I told him, GeeBee. I'm sorry," he whispered.

Gabriel reached his hand out and placed it on top of his brother's. "It's OK, Julian. I realise it's what you had to do. I always had Roger, remember. So what happened to Simon? Have you kept in touch with him?" He was already fearful of Julian's reply because he knew that his relationship with

Lindsey had been rekindled and Gabriel couldn't see how another man could figure in the equation.

"He was killed in Honduras." Julian closed his eyes tightly, trying to block out the memory that had haunted him for the past few months; his own physical pain from the brutal attack on them both, and the mental heartache from witnessing the callous, violent murder of his lover.

Gabriel tried to remain calm as he saw the fear on his twin's face. He knew this was causing him great pain and, when Julian finally looked at him again, he saw the deep sorrow in his eyes. He felt his heart ache for his twin as he waited patiently for him to continue, certain he would now tell him the truth.

"There were five robbers. One with a machete. Two of them held me while one attacked Simon. I … I couldn't help him. Oh God, I couldn't save him!" Julian held his head in his hands, his body shaking as sobs consumed him once more. "They … two of them raped me …" He struggled to speak through his tears, appearing to need to offload his nightmare, to share it with his brother and to feel his burden lessen.

Gabriel went to him, gently lifting him and pulling him into his chest, embracing him, calming him, loving him. "You're safe now, Jules. No one can harm you now; it's over." But Gabriel knew it wasn't over yet. After such an ordeal, his brother would probably need professional help to move on and put this horrific experience behind him.

He had so many questions for him. Did Julian have any contact with Simon's family? Did they know what had happened to their son? Did Lindsey know, and was she helping him in any way? He was almost certain Ellouise wouldn't know, but could Julian talk to her now about it?

Fuck, his timing was crap. Here he was, about to hunt for a man who clearly didn't want to be found, to bring him back to a country he, no doubt, didn't want to return to, to reunite him with a woman he no longer knew as his sister. A woman whom Gabriel Black had fallen in love with; a woman who was going to marry someone else.

And then there was their sister, Ellouise, with her long list of worthless, drug-addicted hangers-on, and not a cat in hell's chance of finding love with any of them. Why were their lives so fucked up? Was happiness to be denied to all of them? Would John inherit the Black family curse?

Gabriel suddenly felt lonely, isolated and outcast. His behaviour prevented him from letting anyone get close. It had driven Roger away, the one person who had accepted his incestuous relationship with his mother, but who could not accept the way Gabriel chose to treat other women. Until Grace.

Grace had been the only other good thing in his life, along with John. She would have been a good mother for John. She would have made Gabriel a very happy man if she had been his wife. But who was he kidding? Grace McGuire would have abhorred him just as Eliza Redfern had done. No woman was ever going to accept him as a man worthy to be loved, knowing the burden he carried. But he had one last request of the school teacher. Something he needed to do for his son.

He gradually released his grip on Julian, making sure he was calmer now and capable of holding himself up. "We need to talk some more, Julian, and we need to get you some professional help. Are you going to be all right for the next few days while I'm away with Rick?"

Julian put his hand on his brother's arm. It was a firm, reassuring gesture.

"I'll be fine. I feel better for having told you. I wish I'd done it sooner." There was a faint smile on Julian's lips. "And work is really good for me. It's what I need right now. That, and Lindsey. She makes me forget things too."

"I'm glad you guys have got back together. Make sure you take care of one another. Don't lose her, Jules, like I lost Grace. Love escapes me. Don't let it escape you. Keep hold of her."

As Gabriel made to leave the games room, Julian called after him. "Hey. What has gone wrong for you two?" Then his eyes widened and his voice lowered as he added, "She hasn't found out, has she?"

Gabriel shook his head. "No. She hates me for what I have been doing to her. You see, I can fuck things up all on my own. I don't need Mother's help." And he turned his back on his twin and left the room.

465

Chapter 82

Having made arrangements for Ellouise to collect John from school, and for Roger to let him know when Rick woke up, Gabriel sent a message to Grace.

Sender: Gabriel Black

Message: I need to discuss the delivery of the coms boards. I will come to school at 4 p.m.

He knew the situation was not ideal, but he needed to spend his last evening with John before he left for Kenya tomorrow, so he could see no other appropriate opportunity to talk to Grace before he left.

When Grace saw his message, her face dropped. She had been expecting some discussion to take place about the coms boards, so part of her hoped the message and its reason for his visit were true. But mostly she was afraid; she was afraid of Black's reaction to her engagement to Jason. He could be about to end their "relationship" or he could enslave her in his collar. She wasn't sure which she was more afraid of.

At two minutes past four, Mrs Baker came into her classroom and advised Grace that Mr Black was waiting for her in Miss Greaves' office. The head teacher had a meeting to go to and had said they could use her room to discuss the coms boards; all the staff were excited about the latest addition to the school equipment and couldn't wait for the installations.

As Grace walked into the room, Gabriel stood up.

He waited until she had closed the door before saying, "Hello, Grace," his voice solemn.

Grace's eyes connected with his for a moment before she felt her knees weaken and she hurriedly sat on one of the chairs at the coffee table. Her mouth felt dry and she struggled to control her voice as she responded quietly, "Hello, sir."

She felt annoyed with herself. Why was she so nervous? Things had changed now, he must see that. His message had said he was coming to discuss the equipment. *Fine! Let's do that and get it over with. Maybe now he'll let me get on with my life!*

But John's face flashed before her eyes. She remembered he had hardly spoken in class today and his eyes were less bright than usual. She suspected he had been crying. She also recalled the night terrors she had witnessed and she wondered if they were still occurring.

Well, she needed to know if her favourite pupil was all right, and there was only one way to find out.

"Before we talk about the coms boards, can I ask if John is OK? He was very quiet in school today …" She hesitated and realised that Gabriel Black was staring at the engagement ring on her finger. "I … I wondered if he was still struggling with night terrors or if anything else was upsetting him?" She looked at the man, questioningly, unable to hide her concern.

Gabriel had resumed his seat and was sitting back, one ankle resting on his other knee, patiently seeking the right words before responding to the nervous woman beside him. The desire to touch her, kiss her lips and hold her distracted him for a moment but he remained detached.

"I believe my son is upset that you are going to be leaving …"

Grace opened her mouth to protest, though she realised she had little to protest about, at this factual statement of her forthcoming resignation from Arnford Primary School. However, Gabriel Black was not going to allow her to interrupt. "Now that you are engaged to be married. It seems he had the impression you would continue to come and see us, have tea, watch a film with him, as you had promised." He looked at her accusingly.

Wait a bloody minute! Is he trying to make out I'm the baddie here?

"And just how in hell were you planning to tell him why I would suddenly stop being a part of his life next September, when you had had enough of me?" Grace gasped in horror as the words poured out of her mouth.

I will never have enough of you. Gabriel's thought cut through him, making him only vaguely aware of her next words as she whispered quietly, "I never wanted to hurt John. I want to let him know that."

Gabriel's dark eyes drilled into hers, though he remained impenetrable.

"Then I would appreciate it if you would let him know that you would agree to have tea with him sometimes at Arnford Hall and watch a film or share a book with him. Everyone will make you very welcome there. And now I guess we will never know what would have happened next September, will we?"

Grace squirmed under his scrutiny.

"Don't worry, Grace. I'm only going to order you to come skiing with us all for Christmas and then you will be free of me. And should you agree to visit Arnford Hall in the future, I will absent myself, if that will make it easier for you."

Grace could hardly believe her ears. Was he going to end it at last, make it easy for her to get on with her life again? Isn't that what she wanted? *Then why do I feel so—?*

"But I have one final request."

Oh. She searched his face for a hint of any emotion he could be feeling. Her own were in turmoil and she felt physically sick as images of his beautiful naked body, John's smiling face and Ellouise's fun-loving smile flashed before her eyes, reeled around her head and pounded at her heart.

"I want John to have a sibling and I would like you to be the mother. I would like to have a child using your eggs, Grace." He uncrossed his legs and leaned forward as he added quietly, "I'm only asking you to donate your eggs. I will donate my sperm and the foetus will be carried by a surrogate mother. I will arrange everything and I believe the procedure shouldn't take too long. I will, of course, recompense you for your trouble and any discomfort." He leaned back and observed the woman before him through his dark, masked eyes.

Grace stared at him. Had she heard him right? He wanted her baby? But he didn't want her! *Oh, my life!*

"Is that how you had John?" Her voice was quivering and she hoped he would think it was because of anger and not an

468

attempt to hold back the flood of tears which threatened to breach the dam of her eyelids.

Well, her question certainly made an impact.

He stood up, looking aghast, his hands coming up to flap in the air, before he dragged them through the blackness of his thick hair.

"Is that what you think of me? You think I would have left my son with some woman for seven years, never seeing him, playing with him, holding him?" Emotion flowed through his face and body as he paced around the room, almost talking to himself. "I got John's mother pregnant. She found out my secret!" He laughed the words out before his tone changed to become heartfelt and sad. "She wouldn't let me have anything to do with her or the baby. I didn't love her, but that didn't ease the pain and self-loathing which I continued to live with. I actually feel guilty for being glad that she is dead. Yes, fucking glad, because now I have my son and I love him." He fell into the chair.

Grace continued to stare at him, her eyes glued on the man before her. What could he have done that was so terrible? Sleeping with other women, even men, surely wasn't such a big deal to deny a father access to his child? And why hadn't he fought her? He could afford the top lawyers in the country.

She wanted to go to him and take his hand. She wanted to kiss his lips and soothe him. She wanted to wrap her arms around him and hold him tight, take away the pain that seemed too much for him to bear.

Suddenly he straightened, composing himself a little, but still looking hurt and regretful.

"I just want you to understand that John has grown fond of you and I would appreciate it if you could find it in yourself to maintain some informal contact with him, beyond that of pupil and school teacher. And I don't want him to be alone. Not now and not when I'm gone. I want you to be the mother of his sibling. I need to go away for a few days and won't be troubling you to see me again. I will make the necessary arrangements with Stefan." He looked at her for her reaction to the name of the gynaecologist who had wanted to fuck her after the poker

469

game at Arnford Hall as he added, "Don't worry. I'll arrange for Roger or Ellouise to be with you the whole time, but he is one of the top consultants in his field. Roger can let you know the arrangements. Enjoy your skiing lessons, Grace."

He started to walk towards the door but looked back when Grace said quietly, "I will be very happy to stay in touch with John. For as long as he needs me …" She wanted to say so much more but she heard him say gently, "Thank you," as he disappeared out of the door.

Chapter 83

Gabriel arrived back at Arnford Hall in time to join everyone in the kitchen for a light supper. John had been playing on his Wii with Uncle Julian and Ellouise had been encouraging her nephew to go faster round the track to beat him. The three of them were happily discussing the racing, and Gabriel was finally able to smile and feel calmer, knowing that John would be safe and cared for during his absence.

Having talked further with Rick, who – surprisingly – still looked a little tired, although he had presumably slept for the last few hours, the two men didn't know how long they were going to be away. Black hoped it would be about four days and didn't want to think about what could happen to prolong their stay.

After tea, Rick joined the Blacks for a swim and a game of water polo, John style, before Gabriel took his son upstairs for a shower and bedtime story and kissed him goodnight. He had explained that he needed to go away for a few days and Aunty Ell would look after him. If Daddy wasn't home by the weekend, John could go and see his cousins too.

Everything had been arranged with Ellouise. As well as knowing that his will was in order, his sperm had been deposited at Stefan's clinic, with clear instructions for a future baby to be accepted into the Black family. He had asked his sister to try to persuade a certain school teacher to make her contribution to said baby, if necessary. Gabriel tried to convince himself that everything was in order, should anything go wrong during his venture to Kenya.

He now had to focus on ensuring that nothing actually did go wrong.

The two travellers left Arnford Hall at ten in the evening on Tuesday, the fifth of December, exactly ninety-eight days into his year with Grace. Their flight would get them to Kenya the next morning.

His love for Grace, and his desperation to try to ensure she would remember something good about Gabriel Black and the ordeal he had put her through, drove him to find her brother and bring him back to her.

He was too consumed with this determination to consider that he was expecting her to give up a child to him, a child she wouldn't see or have the chance to love …

Chapter 84

Armen made his way through the chaos of Nairobi airport to Gabriel Black and Rick Casey. Gabriel introduced him to Rick and they shook hands before Armen hugged Black then led them out to the waiting car.

"It's good to see you, Black. It's been a long time. How's Cynthia? I hope she enjoyed our hospitality when she was here."

Gabriel studied Armen for a moment and decided that this was the guy his mother had been having sex with. And, from the look in Armen's eyes, he would like to have something a bit longer-lasting with his mother. Another solution to something on his to-do list?

"She's good. She talked a lot about you and the time you spent together," he lied.

"Yes," Armen looked sheepish. "I'm sorry – it was my fault she was a little delayed in returning home," and his beaming smile confirmed his affection for the woman who was not permitted to commit to another man.

"Well, I think she'll be planning another trip shortly. Maybe you can keep her away for a bit longer."

As his smile turned into a full-blown, delighted grin, Gabriel had all the evidence he needed that Armen wanted to take care of his mother. And probably not for just a short holiday.

"So. What have you got on this Kit, Armen?"

As they entered the national Kenya police headquarters, Armen took them into his office and ordered coffee, the finest Kenya had to offer. Gabriel had never forgotten how good that always tasted, almost as good as Joan's Peruvian beans.

The Black family had known Armen, the Deputy Commissioner of Police, for the last fifteen years. Although they no longer took family holidays together, whenever any family member visited the country, they always met up with Armen and exchanged news with him like an old friend. Of course, internal relations within the Black family were never discussed, and Gabriel had always wondered if there was some sort of attraction between the policeman and his mother. But right now he had more pressing matters to engage him.

"Your guy is quite a character, and unfortunately too well known by us." Armen looked at Rick, who, at six foot four with broad shoulders and muscles to complement his big frame, looked very capable of taking care of himself. However, the policeman in Armen also saw twinkling eyes and a youthfulness that said, "Hey, I can catch the moon if you need me to", and the wise policeman perceived a lack of fear for his own safety and an eagerness that could lead to carelessness in a nasty situation. As someone Gabriel Black might need to rely on over the next few days, Armen felt a rare nervousness about the task these two Brits had set themselves.

"Sure, he's drunk and disorderly regularly enough, and does the drug shit enough to get himself locked up on the odd occasion. But he's in with some pretty dirty loan sharks. He's way too good at using their money in the casino, and way too bad at playing poker to keep them off his back for much longer. As far as my guys can tell, he owes about five million Kenyan shillings."

Gabriel interrupted as he turned to Rick. "That's about thirty-five thousand pounds. Sorry, Armen."

"No problem. So we figure you two fairy godmothers have arrived at just the right time to magic him away from here." Armen winked at Gabriel.

"Look," Gabriel's expression was as serious as his tone of voice. "I don't want to leave any loose ends here, Armen. There must be no chance of these sharks trying to find the guy once we get him back to the UK. I want to reunite him with his sister, and there is no way that she is to be put in any danger. Just let us know where we can find him and the best way to clear his debts, and get him the hell out of here."

"OK, my friend," Armen smiled. "Right now he's sleeping off the drunken stupor he ended up in last night in the garage where he works. It's a fucking shame really, 'cos when he's sober he's one of the best mechanics in the city. And by all accounts he was a damn good pilot. But he seems to have a chip on his shoulder. He's an angry young man and quick to pick a fight. It seems drugs and booze give him some comfort and respite from his anger, but the guy doesn't know when to stop. Let's get you two to your hotel, where you can rest and freshen up. The hire car is here and the map with details of his hang-outs are all ready for you. I've called my man off the case now 'cos I can't really spare him any longer. But listen' – and Armen looked intently at Gabriel – 'any signs of trouble, you call me. You don't want to mess with any of these guys, Black. I'll get right over to you and we'll move in if anything kicks off." Armen opened the middle drawer of his desk and took out two pieces of paper, placing one each in front of Gabriel and Rick. "I have processed these licences for you." As he spoke, he withdrew two small hand guns and passed them over the table. "I take it you know how to use one of these?" The question was directed to Rick; Armen knew the Black family could shoot.

Rick shot a quick look at his employer. "Yes, sir."

You didn't work at Black Armour and not have a little play testing some of the equipment out!

"I take it these are as a precaution?" Gabriel studied the weapons as he directed the question at Armen.

"Sure. Just want to know you can defend yourselves if you get into any difficulties."

Black glanced up and then folded the licence and put it in his wallet, placing the small handgun in his jacket pocket. Rick copied him before gulping down the last of his coffee.

"Let's get to the hotel." Gabriel waited for Armen to show them to the car.

Rick drove the Toyota RAV4 painted red, covered in rust and minus its front bumper: if nothing else, this car would definitely blend in with the traffic. They followed the directions to the Serena Hotel on Kenyatta Avenue. Just in view further down the road was the DiamonDeck Casino. It looked dingy and cheap. Well, hopefully they would be able to avoid going in there at all, if Kit would play ball and accept the clearing of his debts and a one-way, first-class plane ticket back to the UK to be reunited with his sister. Gabriel sighed and walked into the brightly lit, well-appointed hotel.

The men checked into their rooms and showered before meeting in the restaurant for a bite to eat. Despite the long journey and little sleep, even in the comfort of the first-class beds on their flight, both men were alert, restless and ravenous.

As he watched Rick attack his steak, Gabriel wondered if he had been wrong to bring the young man along with him. He knew he would have been stupid to come alone, and Rick was one of the few men he could trust and who would work with him on the level that Gabriel Black needed – respectfully, but independently enough to question his employer if he felt the need to, and with a level of intelligence that Black respected. Apart from Roger, there were few men who could live up to his expectations; Rick Casey was one of them.

"Right," said Gabriel, "we're going to stick to plan A. When we get sight of Kit, I'll make contact. We get him to think I'm here alone. Then if anyone else gets involved they'll think the same. If things get a bit heavy, that leaves you to call Armen, OK?"

"Yes, sir."

"No heroics, Rick. Just get straight on the phone to the cops."

"No problem."

"So if everything goes to plan, I'll persuade him to come back with us, give him a couple of days to sort his affairs out. If Armen is right, he hasn't got much to keep him here – no assets, no ties with anyone. Just debts to clear and then walk away. Hopefully the colour of our money will help to persuade him."

"Sounds like the guy would be a real jerk not to accept the offer. If he's racked up over thirty grand of debt, it doesn't look like he would have much chance of paying any of it back, and where would that leave him with the loan sharks?"

"Well, let's hope he sees it like that."

A couple of hours later, the two men were walking down Navasha Lane. Rick hung back as Gabriel headed for a dilapidated building with a broken sign over the front garage door, declaring "Kit's Repair Den".

"Hey," Gabriel called as he walked into the darkened workshop. A moment later a man with an unshaven face and dishevelled appearance walked from the shadows at the back of the space. Gabriel caught his breath at the smell of oil, cleaning solvents, grease and dirt. The unabated heat from outside accentuated the odours and Black wondered how the guy didn't choke from being cooped up in here all day.

"Can I help you?" the man asked, eyeing the unlikely-looking customer, who was dressed in black trousers with a white short-sleeved cotton shirt and highly polished black shoes. You could hear the slick of the oil as it clung, unwanted, to the soles of the smart man's shoes.

"I'm looking for Kit."

A worried expression shot across the younger man's face.

Gabriel smiled as he realised the man probably thought Black was there to collect money for the loan shark. "I just want to talk to him," he said, hoping he sounded more confident than he felt.

"Look, mate, we just fix Toyotas here. You don't look like the sort to drive one of them, so why don't you just clear off my property?" Black glanced around the workshop. The floor space was a reasonable size and there were a couple of pieces of decent-looking machinery, together with numerous tools hanging on walls and lying on benches. But there was nowhere near ten thousand, let alone thirty-five thousand, pounds worth of assets in the garage. And he seriously doubted that the scrawny, unshaven beanpole of a man standing before him owned the building. Surely this guy would jump at the chance to walk away from all his problems and start afresh? For a moment, he wondered how he would react to being reunited with a sister he hadn't seen for years.

"Look. I take it you're Kit. Can we just talk somewhere?" Black looked around. He quickly took in the mattress on the floor and an array of clothing heaped in one corner. It seemed this was not only Kit's workplace; it was his home too. There was no sign of any vehicles currently being worked on, and the guy looked as though a good meal wouldn't go amiss, not to mention a good shower. "Let me buy you a bite to eat and tell you why I'm here."

"If you want to buy the fucking garage, the answer is no. I already told you fuckers that." So Black was wrong about the

477

ownership of the building. Suddenly the scrawny guy didn't look so scrawny. As he tensed, there was confidence and defiance in his hazel eyes. Black had seen the same look before. In Grace's eyes.

"I don't know who you think I am, but my name is Gabriel Black and I'm a friend," he paused ever so slightly, "of Melanie's."

Now Kit glared at him, with a look of disbelief before he spoke again. "Is she all right?" He started to walk to the back of the workshop.

Gabriel stepped towards him, concerned the guy might try to do a runner, but relaxed as he saw him collect a bunch of keys from a bench and come back to the front of the building.

"She's fine, but we need to talk." He hoped he had put Kit's mind at ease – but also that he had made it clear he wasn't leaving until he had spoken with him.

"Take me somewhere decent then, 'cos I'm fucking starving!" and Kit led the way out of the garage, pulling the large, rust-covered metal door down and locking it.

As they stood on the street, Gabriel glanced up at the structure and realised that the one-storey, dilapidated building was surrounded by modern, four- or five-storey upmarket offices. Kit's garage was an eyesore on a landscape of luxury real estate which could no doubt demand much higher rentals if his building was bought, demolished and turned into another modern office block.

Rick, who had been scrutinising fruit and veg at the street market on the opposite side of the road, discreetly acknowledged Black and followed the two men towards a restaurant a short distance away. Kit sat down and took the menu from the waiter. He ordered a T-bone steak, fries, onion rings and coleslaw on the side with a Guinness and whisky chaser. Black ordered a Jack Daniel's and Coke.

On hearing Rick order an iced tea from a couple of tables away, his boss smiled to himself.

"So how do you know Melanie?" There was a pause. "And how the hell do you know she *is* Melanie?" Kit leaned back in the metal chair and gave his lunch provider all of his attention.

"She teaches my son. And she now goes by the name of Grace. Grace McGuire." Black waited a moment to determine how co-operative, or otherwise, he could expect Kit to be with his plan to take him back to the UK.

"Has she sent you to find me?" The man's voice was quieter now, and it was clear he was pensive and preoccupied.

"She doesn't know I'm here. But she does want to see you. It's been a long time and she misses you."

There were a few minutes of silence and Black wondered what Kit was thinking – was he contemplating Grace and the life she now led, or remembering the horrors that had led to their separation? The man looked more regretful than angry, so Gabriel guessed it was memories of his sister that were occupying his mind.

When Kit's food arrived he tucked in, ignoring the fact Black wasn't eating at all. But soon his hunger deserted him and Gabriel watched as his body sagged with tiredness. Kit pushed his plate away. He hadn't touched his drink, but instead poured some water from the carafe the waiter had placed on their table.

"She won't want to see me. Not now. Not like this."

"She won't care what you look like. But she would care if you looked ill. Finish your meal and get some flesh on your bones. Get cleaned up and come back to the UK with me." Black wasn't just referring to a shower. The guy stank of alcohol, and Armen had already told them that wasn't the only stimulant he was used to taking. Was Kit going to have to go cold turkey, and could he cope with that? Back in the UK Black could get him the help he would need. But he didn't want to have to hang around in Nairobi waiting for the guy to get clean.

"Who says I want to go back? My life is here now, and it suits me just fine." He reached for his Guinness, and Black's hope for a quick flight back to Manchester steadily disappeared as the black liquid and the whisky chaser disappeared down Kit's throat.

He sat and drank his JD as he watched Kit. A new Kit might need to be dragged out of the old one. Well, Black had known this wouldn't be an easy task.

"It doesn't look like you've got a lot to lose by leaving here." Gabriel would not leave Kenya without Grace's brother.

"I fuckin' own that garage and I ain't signing it away to anyone."

"Who's asking you to?" Why did Gabriel get the feeling that Kit was being forced to hand his property over to someone?

There was a moment's silence.

"It doesn't matter," mumbled Kit, finally realising that Black had nothing to do with the men who were threatening him.

Gabriel took a breath before saying, "I hear you've got money problems."

"None of your damn business," Kit hissed, anger welling up. He pushed the chair back from the table. "My glass is empty; it's time for me to go. Enjoy your holiday."

"I can help you with your problem. All of them, if I have to. I want your arse on a plane out of here."

"You don't know what you're talking about. And it's better for you if it stays that way."

Again, Black got the feeling there was more than just poker debts involved here.

"Try enlightening me and let me decide what's better for me."

"Just fuck off!"

"Are you being threatened?" Gabriel decided to lay his cards, or rather his thoughts, on the table: he never declared his cards until the very end of a game.

For a second Kit looked like a rabbit caught in the headlights. His eyes darted around the restaurant before coming back to stare at Black. "Who the fuck are you, and what the hell are you doing here?"

"I told you. I want to take you back to your sister, who needs to see you. It's as simple as that. After your reunion, you're free to come right back here and pick up where you left off. And, quite frankly, I don't give a shit what you do then."

"Weren't you listening when I said she won't want to see me?"

"You're wrong. She does. I said we can clear your debts and get you back to the UK. Have you got a passport?"

480

Kit cast another furtive glance around and slumped in his seat. The guy was living on a pendulum: one minute he looked half-dead, then he was pumped up with anger, then he was agitated, as though concerned someone was following him.

Gabriel was beginning to wonder whether someone was threatening him or whether the guy was simply hallucinating through some drug dependency. He wasn't sure which was the most concerning, but he wasn't going to let it stop him taking Kit back to the UK.

He remembered his last conversation with Julian; the pain and heartache his twin brother must have gone through caused a deep sense of guilt in Black that he hadn't been there to help him and that their relationship had deteriorated so much that Julian hadn't felt able to talk to Gabriel about it sooner. He realised his brother and sister were a major part of his life, no matter how often he saw them. They would always be there for each other. He began to understand the loss Grace must be feeling for her brother and not having anyone on earth to talk to about it. Would a sober, stable Kit feel the same and want to see his sister?

He hoped so.

"Where are you staying?"

Gabriel quickly returned his focus back to the man now looking at him.

"The Serena Hotel. Will you join me for dinner? I can meet you somewhere else if you prefer. I've hired a Toyota." Black raised his eyebrow at the mention of the make of the vehicle, and he hoped it would break some of the ice between him and Kit.

Kit's lips formed a faint smile. "I'll see you at the bar in your hotel at eight," and he turned and left.

Once it was clear he had gone, Rick joined his employer.

"I think you had better wire me up when I next meet him. I'm not sure if he is afraid of someone following him or suffering from some form of paranoia. I'm glad he's agreed to come to the hotel. I just hope they'll let him in! Let's go to your room and see what else we can find out about him."

"I've already been through the files Armen gave us. Couldn't see any more than he's already told us. Except Kit Bright owns the garage."

Gabriel frowned. *He hasn't changed his surname.* "We may need to sort a passport out for him."

Rick gave Black a questioning look, but wasn't surprised when he received no explanation. Black had no intention of Grace McGuire's cover being blown.

Thanks to a licence to get surveillance and security equipment through customs on the pretext that they were travelling on business, Rick had brought some of the latest electronic devices and software from Black Armour, just in case.

Chapter 85

As Gabriel entered the bar at eight o'clock, he scanned the room and took a seat on a bar stool, ordering a JD and Coke. Ten minutes later he was beginning to feel pissed off, and worried that Kit wasn't going to show, until he felt a tap on his shoulder. He turned to see the thin man, not quite so scruffy-looking now, dressed in mushroom-coloured chinos with a black polo shirt and tanned loafers. His fair hair was slicked back, revealing short sideburns and a clean-shaven, smooth jaw line. Grace's hazel eyes stared at Gabriel, and he wore the trace of a smile. So this was cleaned-up Kit.

"Hey. Black, isn't it?" Kit asked as he sat on the stool next to him. He turned to the bartender, saying "The same," as he eyed Black's drink and added, "and a bottle of water."

When he had got his drink he asked, "Can we go sit somewhere more private?" and looked over towards a darkened corner in the bar area.

"So you really know Melanie?" Kit's question sounded ruminative, as though he had spent the afternoon reminiscing, as well as scrubbing up. Black barely had the chance to nod before Kit continued, almost as though he was simply thinking out loud. "I guess she's nearly forty now. She was always so smart, the way she could hold her own in any discussion or argument. She'd have made a great lawyer. You said she's a school teacher? What does she teach? Law? I bet she's still as pretty. Always had plenty of boys following her around. All my mates wanted me to introduce them to her. Even though I told them they were too young and too fucking thick for her!" Kit laughed. "Is she married? Got any kids?"

There was a pause. Kit swirled his drink around in the glass but then picked up the water bottle and took a swig.

"Your sister is called Grace McGuire now, and that's very important to her." Black didn't know Melanie Bright and he felt he was betraying Grace to use a name she had done her damnedest to forget. "She teaches at a primary school. She doesn't have any children of her own but she loves her job working with them."

"She's moved on, then. Got over it." Kit took a long sip of the JD. "I take it you know all about our *family*." The last word was filled with sarcasm and hatred.

"That wasn't Grace, or you, Kit." Black remained solemn.

"You wouldn't think so to hear the police drilling us, and the reactions we got from the public in the street, the courtroom, in the press, on the TV, every-fucking-where. And every year the families mourning their losses everywhere you looked." His head was lowered and he was slowly shredding a beer mat. "Don't get me wrong. I felt for them, really I did. I was only nineteen when the fucker got caught. I should have been having the time of my life at college. All I wanted was to be a pilot. But we were assumed to be murderers, paedophiles, psychopaths. Innocent until proven guilty? Ha, what a bloody joke! And there was nowhere to hide. I was Michael Bright. I had done nothing wrong. And, believe me, if I'd known what that sick bastard was doing I would have fucking killed him myself. Why couldn't I just live my life? My sister," he glanced up at Black, respecting his wish not to use the name, Melanie, "moved on. She accepted their rules. She wanted to have another life, start afresh.

"Me? I wanted to tell them to fuck off and leave me alone. Why the hell should I change for them? But no one wanted to know me. It's funny how you think you have friends until you actually need them and realise they're not friends at all. Not bloody one of them. And the person I needed the most wasn't allowed to have anything to do with me. Not even acknowledge I still existed. I knew if I hung around for too long, she would try to see me. But our wounds were still too fresh, even two years after the trial.

"So I left. I joined the Kenya School of Flying and trained at Wilson in Nairobi. I got on the Masai Mara to Mombasa run, earned good money and loved it. But the nightmares never stopped. I kept on thinking I had driven him to it in some way. Maybe I had been a really bad kid and I had made him want to kill children. I couldn't stop thinking about it. And then I started cutting myself."

Kit's voice had become hushed, almost a whisper. His features contorted as though he was re-experiencing an old agony.

Gabriel glanced at his arms and noticed, for the first time, scars, lots of small scars running along both forearms. He looked back at Kit, who smiled briefly.

"Yeah. I cut my arms, my legs, my chest, even the fucking soles of my feet, hoping the pain would take away my guilt. I was punishing myself for something he did! And, when that didn't stop the nightmares, I started drinking. Then I lost my job and my friends – my real friends. They tried to help me. But when I couldn't tell them why I had to hurt myself, or drink myself stupid, I realised I had to protect them from me and leave. So I ended up in this shithole. I was good with my hands and there are plenty of clapped-out Toyotas that need fixing, and I can breathe extra life into the fuckers." He hung his head. "When I can be bothered."

Finally he finished his drink.

Gabriel sat back and ran his hand through his hair. He wasn't sure when he had last felt so out of his depth. He had not expected to hear such a confession from the dishevelled angry man he met earlier. He felt sorry for the guy, but Gabriel Black lived by the rules of "help yourself" and "cope any way you can". He had done exactly that. And so had Grace, in her own way. It looked as though Kit had simply given up.

"Come back with me. We can get you a new identity. I know it wasn't what you wanted back then, but you'll have the chance to get your life back on track. A fresh start if you want, or at least a decent lifestyle. You'll get to meet Grace. Do something good for someone, something good for your sister." Gabriel hoped he was getting through to him.

"I've been thinking about what you said. I do owe some money. But I own the garage and I know some guys will pay a small fortune for it. They want the land …" Kit looked hesitant and Gabriel knew there was something he wasn't telling him.

"Who wants the land, Kit?"

"Moody Jirongo."

Chapter 86

As soon as Gabriel knocked on his bedroom door, Rick was pulling up a report on the MooRon gang, one of the criminal gangs operating in Nairobi. Their aim was to create wealth and power by "owning" as much land as possible; their tactics were extortion, blackmail and protection racketeering; their methods included arson, torture and murder.

"Shit." Gabriel breathed out. "We need to act fast and get us all out of here. Can you work on a new passport for Kit, in the name of Kit Stockton?" He wasn't sure where that name had come from, but it would do! "We'll work out full identity requirements for him back in the UK. Get a value on his garage and we can arrange to buy that from him. Or it may be safer to just give Kit its value and leave it for this MooRon lot." Black knew that he was thinking out loud. He realised that things could get very nasty if they hung around for Kit for too long. "We need to find out exactly how much he owes, get the cash ready and arrange delivery of the money. I want us out of here by Saturday."

"Right on it, sir."

Gabriel then called home. He desperately wanted to hear John's voice, but he knew it was too late in the evening and past experience had told him it was better not to talk to his son when he was away; John seemed to get so upset to hear his daddy, knowing he wouldn't be able to see him for a few more days. This time, Gabriel couldn't even confirm exactly when he would see him again. But he needed to know that John was OK and sleeping peacefully.

So he apologised for the late call when Ellouise answered the phone.

"John's fine, GeeBee, no nightmares. And apparently Grace has told him she is looking forward to their skiing lesson tomorrow night and wondered if they could have tea together too.

She's going to drive straight here and travel to the snow dome with Roger and John. I presume you spoke to her."

"Yes. I'm glad she's talked to John." He paused before asking, "Have you had a chance to talk to her yet?" He wanted to know if Grace had agreed to his request for her eggs, and he wondered if she would discuss the matter with his sister.

"I have asked her if we could meet up sometime over the weekend but …" Ellouise wasn't sure how to say that Grace had confirmed she was going to Putney. She knew her brother would know exactly what that meant.

"She'll be with him, won't she?" He didn't wait for a reply, but continued, "Just tell me how it is, Ellouise, and don't pussyfoot around. I want her to maintain some sort of relationship with John. It doesn't matter about me."

He couldn't hide the sadness in his voice from her, or the bitter feeling in his heart from himself. But he felt comforted that Grace had taken on board his concerns for John and she was being true to her word. He hoped she would stay in touch with him for as long as he needed her.

After a restless and predominantly sleepless night, Gabriel put on the jacket Rick had attached the wire to and went to meet him for breakfast. After Rick had checked that the communications devices were working and well concealed, Gabriel made his way to Kit's garage as arranged. Kit appeared from the back of the workshop, still looking presentable and in a much better state than he had the previous morning. He seemed relaxed, and headed to a pot of coffee as Black entered. "Want some?"

Gabriel nodded. "Thanks. Have you thought about our proposition?" He had offered to buy the garage from Kit, and they had also discussed a new identity for him.

"I've thought about it. I'm not sure I'm ready to settle back in the UK yet, if ever." He handed a mug of delicious-smelling coffee to Black, who was glad, as the aroma overpowered the lingering smell of oils and solvents. "I'll accept your offer to clear my debts; I'd be stupid not to" – he looked at Black to see a nod of agreement – "but I want to keep the garage. I need something to come back to."

Gabriel had thought that the younger man could view his workshop as his identity, the one thing that got him sober for some of the time. But he had also conceived a counter-offer which he now hoped Kit would find more attractive; the sober Kit, that was.

"Well, I've been thinking too. You said you had got your pilot's licence. How about you consider getting it back and go back to the job you loved? I would finance the business; I could be the silent partner in a safari operation with you."

Kit looked astonished. Would this stranger really give him the chance to start afresh in a job and way of life he had often yearned to regain?

"Do you love my sister?"

The question was unexpected. For both men.

Kit didn't know Black, didn't know that he was the head of one of the largest private businesses in the UK, if not the world, didn't know that he had a playboy reputation and was definitely not the loving kind.

Black never discussed his personal feelings with strangers. He had questioned his own decision again and again; his desire to make this business proposition to a man he knew very little about and to whom in normal circumstances he wouldn't have given the time of day, let alone consider entering into a business arrangement with. But he knew he would do anything to help Grace. And helping her brother was helping Grace.

"I think a lot of your sister. I'm doing this for her. Because she has helped me with my son." Then he remained silent. He was not about to divulge the importance of his relationship with John to this man, or the newness of it. He just wanted Kit to feel confident that Black would be true to his word and that he really could help him.

Suddenly a tall, thin black guy entered the garage. "Hey, Kit, man. I need you to take a look at my truck. Help me get it in here, will ya?"

"I'll be right with you, Dino." Kit turned back to Black. "I'm interested. Let me get Dino and his truck sorted. Come back at four."

At four o'clock on Thursday the seventh of December, Black walked into Kit's workshop. It seemed unnaturally still, making him wonder where Kit was.

Then he felt a sharp pain across the back of his head, and Gabriel Black fell to the floor.

Chapter 87

Roger was standing by one of the coffee machines at Black HQ. He was no longer cross about the way Gabriel had taken off to Kenya. He hoped that Grace would see his attempt to reunite her with her brother as a demonstration of Gabriel's true feelings for her. Maybe she would even have second thoughts about her engagement to this other guy, Jason. But then he frowned as he thought about Mrs Black. Would Gabriel ever break his promise to his father? He walked back to his office feeling saddened by the fact that if he didn't do it for this woman he had obviously fallen in love with, then he would never do it. It upset Roger to think that his best friend would never find true happiness.

He picked up the papers he had been working on and was trying to focus on them when his mobile rang.

"Roger, it's Rick Casey. I need you to activate the tracker on Mr Black." Rick's voice was tense.

"What's happened?"

"They've got Gabriel. I need you to operate the tracker."

Roger froze. "You'd better tell me what the fuck is going on, Rick." He immediately shut his computer down, grabbed his jacket and headed for the door.

"We think they're members of the MooRon gang. They've been after Kit, the guy we came here for, and now we think they've kidnapped both of them. Shit, Roger, can you get the tracker on?"

"I'm in fucking Manchester. The equipment's at Arnford Hall. Have you told the police?"

"Yes. Armen is involved. But there's a damn terrorist attack at Nairobi airport and so he can only spare one man to help at the moment. And we've just found the tracking device I had on Mr Black – but not Mr Black."

Roger could hear the panic in the younger man's voice. "Rick, keep talking to me and I'll get you on speaker when I get to my car. Let's hope there are no speed traps on the way home. Right, start at the beginning and tell me everything."

"We came to ask Grace's brother, Kit, to come back to the UK with us. Mr Black wants them to be reunited. I don't even know why they were separated. Anyway, this Kit owes some gambling debts, about thirty-five grand's worth. But he also owns a garage and I think the gang members have been after his land. At least, that's what I've been able to gather from the conversations Mr Black has had with him. I had a wire on him so I could hear them."

"Does this Kit know you're with Black?"

"No, I don't think so. Mr Black wanted it to look as though he was alone. And it's a fucking good job he did. He was supposed to meet Kit at his garage at four o'clock this afternoon. I hovered in the street waiting until he came out. About five minutes after he went in, a black Toyota Proace pulled out of the garage on to the street. At first, I thought it was just a customer. I didn't even make a note of the bloody number plate." Rick paused, feelings of guilt adding to his fear. "After a few minutes I realised I couldn't hear anything from Mr Black. I wondered if the transistor was working properly, but we had tested it. I walked past the front of the garage and peered in. There was no sign of life. I called, pretending I was looking for a part for my car, and there was nothing. The fucking place was empty. I'd put a wire on Mr Black's jacket and I checked it." He paused again. "I could see he wasn't in the vicinity. I rang Armen straightaway. Like I said, he could only spare one guy, so we started following the tracker. We traced Mr Black to the outskirts of town heading towards Nakuru. The signal was coming from some petrol station just off the main road. We ended up finding Mr Black's jacket, and his other clothes, on an attendant at a petrol station. Some guy had sold him the gear!"

"Fuck." Roger hit the accelerator and prayed the traffic out of Manchester would not be too bad at three-thirty on a Thursday afternoon. Kenya was three hours ahead of the UK, so that meant it was six thirty their time. Gabriel Black and Kit had been missing for two and half hours.

By four o'clock, Roger had reached his office at Arnford Hall and started to assemble the equipment to track the electronic device which was embedded in Gabriel's left arm. He prayed that his location would show up, quickly.

An orange light started to glow on the screen, and he watched as co-ordinates and grid references appeared. Suddenly some sort of coding sequence began to scroll across the bottom of the screen. *What the fuck is that supposed to mean?*

He rang Rick.

"OK, it's on, and there appears to be some sort of activity, but I don't know what the hell it means."

"That's OK. Now you've got it on I can take control of it from here." Rick sounded calmer.

As Roger saw instructions appearing on the screen, he felt confident that Rick knew what he was doing. Feeling confident of finding his employer and friend, and getting him home, was another matter.

"Have you worked out where he is?" Roger hoped his voice didn't sound quite so high-pitched and desperate to Rick's ears as it did to his own.

"It'll come up any second now. That's it, baby, tell me what you know …" Rick was in the zone. He could have done without the danger, but right now he just needed to focus.

"Gotcha!"

"Thank God." Roger sank into the chair. "So where is he?"

"Baringa Street, Nakuru. Do you know where that is?"

"Of course I don't know where the hell that is!"

"Not you, Roger, I'm asking Kanja here … OK. Roger, it looks like it's near the racecourse. Kanja thinks the kidnappers are arranging to meet someone. Possibly more gang members."

Roger couldn't believe he was hearing this. He felt as though he was on some sort of film set, and expected a Jack Reacher figure to be shipped in to take over the situation.

Shit, shit, shit.

"Rick, I'm going to ring Armen. Call me back in fifteen minutes. Don't forget." He put the phone down.

"Armen, it's Roger Courtney."

By five o'clock, Roger had been brought up to date on the situation: Gabriel Black and Kit were being held in an old warehouse just off Baringa Street. Armen confirmed that the MooRon gang were holding them. The motives weren't clear at this stage, and he believed it highly unlikely that any member of the gang would know who Gabriel Black was. The man had at least been wise enough not to wear his expensive watch, and his wallet carried no identifying cards or passport. Rick confirmed that passports, the gun licence, credit cards and anything else that could have identified him were all locked in the safe at their hotel. Unfortunately, so was the gun Gabriel had been given!

Armen had believed that the gang members were only after Kit for the gambling debts he owed them. However, he realised that this was small fry, as further investigation revealed that the plot of land on which his small garage and workshop were situated was worth a small fortune – and that was what the gang were really after. They wanted Kit to sign it over to them.

Armen wanted to handle the situation in a low-key way. If there was too much police involvement, the gang might wonder who the hell their other captive was. Hopefully, they thought of him as simply a tourist caught up in the wrong place at the wrong time. It wasn't unusual for tourists' rental cars to break down and require some help from a local mechanic. The fact that Kit's shop was situated on a busy road made him the number-one guy to turn to.

Everyone was also silently anxious that Gabriel's clothes had been found on a guy at a petrol station.

Chapter 88

Earlier that day Gabriel had woken to a banging headache, with his hands bound behind his back, propped up against the inside of a windowless van with Kit, also tied, opposite him. He was aware of two men in the front of the vehicle.

"What the fuck is going on?" he hissed at Kit.

"I think they've come for their money." Kit's expression was deadpan. He knew this might happen. Hell, he'd seen it happen to other gamblers. And on some occasions the gambler had never been seen again.

He had never really given a fuck about his own life before but he sure as hell didn't want to lose his garage, and now he realised how desperately he wanted to see his sister.

"I'm sorry you've got caught up in this."

Their voices were low and drowned out by the rattling engine on the bumpy roads. The other two occupants seemed unaware of the conversation taking place in the back.

"Well, tell them they can have their bloody money as soon as they let us go and get it." Black pulled on the rope at his wrists. It held fast.

"But what about my land?"

"For fuck's sake, Kit. Forget about your bloody land. We talked about you getting your pilot's licence back, remember?"

"Hey, what's going on back there? Shut the fuck up," came a heavily accented voice from the front.

Black was dripping with sweat.

"Get us some damn air in here, it's like a bloody oven."

"Oh, we'll soon cool you down."

The next minute, the vehicle pulled over to the side of the road. The two Kenyans climbed out and one opened the back doors. Black noted his brown skin, shaved head, the piercing through one eyebrow and a small scar sliding down his left cheek. He spoke English with a thick Kenyan accent.

"Get out of the car." He waved a small handgun at them. The two white men struggled out, their hands behind their backs. They were on a dirt road and there was no sign of life anywhere. The second Kenyan came forward and untied Black's hands, the gun still pointed at him. "OK. Strip."

Black shot a glance at the guy with the gun and then at Kit. His eyes seemed to ask, *Are they fucking serious?* and Kit gave a slight nod. As he started to remove his jacket, Gabriel tried to assess the situation: the jacket was wired and a tracking device was sewn into it. What deeper shit would they be in if he lost the jacket? What would the Kenyans' reaction be if they discovered the wire in the jacket?

He didn't like his answer to either of these questions. He was scared and angry that he had allowed things to get so out of hand without having put more safeguards in place. He simply hadn't seen this situation arising.

He threw the jacket back into the van, hoping that he would soon be climbing back in as well, so the fact he was no longer wearing it wouldn't make any difference to it still being a lifeline to Rick.

The Kenyans didn't say anything. As Black unfastened his shirt, Kit's hands were untied and he too began to undress. Naked from the waist up, Black hesitated. The guy waggled the gun pointing at his trousers and Black got the message.

"All of them," the driver hissed.

Standing naked on a dirt track away from any sign of human habitation with a gun pointing at him, Black feared for his life. John's smiling face flashed before him, memories of playing with boats with John and Grace at his lakeside house whirled in his head and regret, shame and sorrow gnawed at his heart. He expected to be told to turn around and be shot. Oh God, he wasn't ready to die yet, not yet.

Then the first guy walked behind him, grabbed his hands and bound them together again. He did the same to Kit. "Now get back in the van and shut the fuck up!"

The back door of the vehicle was slammed shut and the journey continued. Despite his fear and humiliation, Black felt relief that his jacket was still with them. But about ten minutes later, that relief turned to dread. The vehicle stopped at a petrol station. The guy sitting in the front passenger seat came round to the back of the truck and grabbed all their clothes, including the jacket.

"Hey, what are you doing with those?" Black yelled.

The guy ignored him and slammed the door shut.

He then entered the garage store and sold all the clothes for five thousand Kenyan shillings to the guy behind the counter and bought a crate of beer, pocketing the change. He chatted to the driver, laughing, as the journey continued.

Shit! thought Black as he realised what must have happened.

Chapter 89

At half past five, UK time, on Thursday afternoon, Grace parked her red Volkswagen Golf on the drive in front of Arnford Hall. It felt strange to be walking up the steps knowing he wouldn't be there. He wouldn't be there to put her collar on or visit her in "her" bedroom.

He's sorry. He needs you. Really he does …

Grace hurried up the steps, away from the weeping gargoyles. For the first time she rattled the huge brass ring on the ancient front door.

"Grace, it's lovely to see you!" Ellouise's smile immediately made Grace forget the gargoyles and her trepidation about coming here. "Come on in. There is a very excited young man here who can't wait to see you."

Grace followed her down to the kitchen and heard John shouting, "She's here," before he ran up to her, just stopping short of hugging her as he nervously looked up at his teacher.

"Hi John." She crouched down and her heart melted as her favourite boy let her wrap her arms around him and breathe in his smell.

"Hello, Grace," Steve called as he loaded the dishwasher. "Have you eaten?"

"Yes, thanks." She took John's hand and stood up. "So, John, are you ready for our next skiing lesson?"

"Yes, Mrs McGuire."

"I think you two are going with Roger and I'll go over and collect the Beardlys. We've got half an hour. John, do you want to come and feed Satan with me? You're welcome to join us, Grace."

John had already released his grip on Grace's hand, getting ready to go with Steve.

"No, thanks. Do you think it would be OK if I borrowed one of the books from my sanc—" She stopped mid-sentence,

497

feeling awkward referring to her sanctuary without the master of the house being there.

Ellouise soon put her at her ease. "Of course, Grace, go ahead and help yourself. It's good that the books are being read again. I think it's been a while since any of us have read them."

As she walked along the corridor, Grace couldn't help thinking how strange it seemed to still have the key to this room, and that its door was locked. It would appear that it really was a sanctuary just for her.

She glanced at the sideboard and couldn't help peeking in the fridge. It was bare.

Was it Gabriel who kept it stocked with the things she liked?

She wondered if someone else would come along and take possession of it now that she would be leaving. Hadn't he confessed that he was having sex with another woman? Who could she be?

Once in the room, Grace concentrated on looking at some of the books. She glanced at some of the titles before pulling out a beautiful first edition of *Lady Chatterley's Lover*, designed and signed by Sir Paul Smith. It felt exquisite as she traced her fingers over the delicately embroidered silk cover. She carefully replaced it, not wanting to take that particular book away.

She knelt and gazed at the titles on the bottom rows. These books looked as if they had been unread for many years. The pale blue, worn cover of *Oedipus The King* caught her eye. She had studied this at Durham, in another life, and she immediately wondered if it belonged to Gabriel. She wanted to read something he had read. She wasn't sure why. She pulled the book out and opened the front cover

Gabriel Black. College, Eton. 22nd June 1993

She placed the book in her bag and went back down to the kitchen.

Julian looked up from the *Financial Times*.

"Hi, Grace. Ready for your lesson?" He was wearing a dark navy suit. It could have been one of Gabriel's, and she shuddered inwardly at the image Julian portrayed of Gabriel. She made herself smile as she imagined the tricks the younger Blacks could have, and no doubt had, played on unsuspecting girlfriends. Of course, Grace wasn't aware that the young Black twins didn't really have any girlfriends. Not for a very long time.

"As ready as I'll ever be," she laughed.

Then John came running into the room. "Oh please, Steve, just one more snack before we go. Please."

Steve came in and went over to a cupboard, removing a container of homemade oat biscuits. "OK. Ask your teacher if she would like one too, and Uncle Julian."

John did the rounds just before Roger came in. He looked ashen. Steve immediately walked over to him and ran his hands down his husband's arms. "Honey, what's the matter? You don't look good," he said, his voice filled with concern.

Not wanting to startle those present, Roger replied, "I'm OK. But Julian," he turned to the younger twin, "can you take Grace and John to the snow dome? Something's come up and I need to deal with it straight away."

Steve felt the tension in Roger's body and decided to wait until they were alone before questioning him further.

"Sure. No problem. I'll take the Bentley," said Julian and he grinned at John as he added, "Come on then, you ski experts, let's go break a leg!"

Ellouise went up to her bedroom after seeing them off to their lesson. Before Steve left to pick up the Beardlys, he took Roger's hand. "Tell me what's wrong."

Roger's voice trembled slightly. "Gabriel has gone missing. Rick thinks he may have been kidnapped."

"Oh, fuck!" Steve exclaimed.

"Look, I don't want to cause alarm. I'm working with Rick. You just get on with the skiing lesson and get back here as soon as you can. Then we'll discuss it, with Julian too. Let's not say anything to Ellouise until we have more information. Now just go, please."

He could tell Steve didn't want to leave him, but he wasn't giving him an option. He hoped that by the time they returned from Manchester he would know more about what was happening in Kenya.

By nine o'clock Julian and Steve had joined Roger in the office. He set up a video call with Rick and the four men discussed the current situation.

"For some reason, Mr Black's jacket and his other clothes have ended up on a petrol-station attendant in Nakuru." Rick explained, not giving the others time to ask themselves, was Gabriel Black still alive? "The good news is the tracker in Mr Black is working and we're able to trace his movements. As far as we can tell, he is still alive."

"Thank God." Roger closed his eyes a moment in silent prayer.

Steve was standing behind Roger and he rubbed his shoulders, feeling his husband's tension and fear. Julian perched on the end of the desk. He ran his fingers through his hair and tried to calm his breathing to help him concentrate on what was being said around him. The news from Roger, that Gabriel may have been kidnapped in Kenya, had hit him like a kick to the chest. He had felt winded and unable to breathe. How could GeeBee have let this happen: the man who controlled everything that went on around him, who planned everything in his life so he could keep his secrets, and who built walls around himself so no one could harm him? Yet, since Julian had returned to Arnford Hall, Gabriel Black had been in turmoil over his relationship with his mother, which he had grown to live with and accept, and had let his heart be broken by a woman whose brother had led to him being kidnapped. A week ago Julian had felt that things were starting to go right for his family. Now he felt like he was in a living hell. He was grateful that Ellouise was there to care for John. The men were still not intending to say anything to her just yet.

Rick continued. "Armen is organising a police helicopter. It's just taking a while to sort, thanks to this attack on the airport. I'm going to get ready to go with them. I'll create a streamed link to your Xphone, Roger, which will stay open and you can keep up with what we're doing." He broke off and stared at them from the computer screen. "And don't worry. We'll get him."

Then the screen went blank.

Roger grabbed his Xphone from his briefcase and placed it on the desk. A few minutes later, they heard voices, as Rick had linked Roger's phone to his, and the events happening around him were being transmitted to the UK.

"I'll make some coffee," said Steve as they headed to the kitchen, aware of Rick asking Armen what time the chopper would be there.

Chapter 90

The black Toyota van finally pulled up, and the two Kenyans got out.

"Have you any idea where the fuck we are and what these guys are planning to do?" Black hissed. His behind was hurting from sitting for so long on the hardwood boards and being bumped all over the place, and his arms ached from the pressure of awkwardly trying to steady himself with them tied behind his back. He was frightened and exhausted and he imagined Kit felt the same. He certainly looked like shit.

"I don't think they're going to kill us, if that's what you're worried about." Kit's voice was quiet and unconvincing. "They need my signature to get their hands on my land and the documentation needs to be witnessed and signed by a conveyancing guy. The site's too valuable to risk not having the documentation right. They won't be able to develop it or sell it on if anyone thinks their ownership is dodgy. That's how I've been able to run up so much debt with the bastards."

"So they need you for a signature. What the fuck are they going to do with me?"

"I … I don't know. Did you come to Kenya on your own, just to get me?" There was a hint of disbelief in his voice, and Black felt a slight embarrassment at how it must have seemed.

"No, I'm not on my own. And there was a fucking tracking device in my jacket. I should have kept my damn mouth shut about this bloody heat." He was furious at his own stupidity.

"A tracking device? What the hell were you expecting, and who the hell are you?" Kit spoke more loudly, his disbelief more evident.

"It's better that you don't know, and hope they don't find out either." Black couldn't bear the thought of being held to ransom, and he suddenly felt sick at the thought of the pain and hurt he would cause John if anything went wrong. He grimaced, trying not to throw up. He suddenly thought about the tracker in his arm, but decided not to mention that to Kit, at least not yet.

A silence fell between them for several minutes before the back doors to the van were yanked open. "Get out," yelled one of the men, waving his gun at the two captives. They clumsily got to their feet and climbed out onto a dirt yard, scattered with rubble, leading to a corrugated-iron building with a large window that was covered in dirt. They were directed inside and Gabriel glanced around at the small, dingy space, a single ceiling bulb casting dim light. There was a desk in the far corner and a third Kenyan was making some notes on a document. The driver of the van was lurking at the side of the window, drinking from a mug of coffee, and there were three wooden chairs positioned a short distance from the desk.

The man at the desk looked up and stared for a moment at the two nude men.

"Well, it's good of you to come and see me at last, Kit. And for fuck's sake get them some bloody clothes." His English was perfect, with very little trace of an accent. Black assumed him to be at least slightly higher up the food chain than the two thugs who had brought them here.

A moment later, the guy with the gun flung two pairs of dirty pale blue overalls at his captives. He untied their hands and they quickly climbed into the overalls. Gabriel grimaced in disgust at the smell and wondered who had worn them before. He really did need to throw up.

"I need the bathroom," he said, his voice controlled enough not to let the Kenyans hear the fear that was pumping through him.

The man at the desk immediately looked up at him. "And you are?"

"John Vickers. And like I said, I need the bathroom." Again Black sounded strong and sure of himself.

Kit shot a glance at him at his use of a different name.

"It's out the back. Go with him." The man at the desk directed this instruction to the driver, who was still standing by the window. He turned and spat on the floor as he pushed Black towards the door and around the back of the building. Black

503

glanced around, expecting to see some ramshackle shed that served as a toilet. There was nothing, just more dirt yard, and through the dim, evening light he could make out several other dilapidated structures in the distance. They appeared to be on some sort of neglected development site that consisted of several workshops and warehouses, all looking about to crumble. There was no sign of activity, but it had to be about nine o'clock at night, so presumably that was to be expected.

The driver stared at Black as he put a hand against the wall of the "office" and threw up his guts. Then he lowered the zip of the overalls and peed, directing his stream onto the dirt track. He couldn't bear the thought of having to enter a shack of a building he had just urinated on. He gave a silent prayer to a God he now fervently hoped existed, and forgave, that he would live to see John and Grace again.

Back in the "office", Kit was sitting on one of the chairs in front of the desk. Black went and sat on another. The driver resumed his position by the window. His companion sat on the floor by the door, carelessly passing his gun from one hand to the other, smirking – until the man behind the desk said menacingly, "Put the gun down." He quickly placed it on the floor beside him and started to pick at some ugly sores on his arms.

"So. What brings you to Kenya, Mr Vickers?" The man picked up his mug of coffee and sat back in his chair.

"Do you care to tell me why we've been brought here at gun point?"

"Why don't you enlighten your friend, Kit?"

"I told you, Moody, my land is not for sale."

Ah, the very top of the food chain, thought Black.

Moody Jirongo stirred in his chair and his lips curled to form a smile. "And now I'm telling you. You have no choice. Your time is up. We want the money you owe us and the only thing you have is that land." He leaned forward and took hold of the document on the desk. "You've been brought here to give you time to consider your options. The first one is to agree to sign the papers to hand your land over to me. We'll go to the lawyer's in the morning." He stared at Kit. "Your second, and only other, option is to refuse to do that, and we'll shoot you. As you can

504

see, Jonah can't wait to use his gun. We can start with practising on your friend here." Now the gang leader turned his attention to Black. Black stood up and leaned over the desk. "You don't want to be doing that, Mr Jirongo. That's your name, isn't it? Not if you want to carry on running your little operation here."

Kit glared at Black, horror pasted on his face. *What the fuck are you playing at?*

Moody Jirongo shuffled back in his seat, looking slightly uncomfortable. He was silent a moment as he puzzled over John Vickers. *Where have I heard that name before?* Then a look of recognition appeared on his rounded face. "Are you the guy who works for Africa Land Partners?"

"Yes. And you're interfering with the piece of land my client wants." Black was impenetrable. His eyes were black and lifeless as they held Jirongo's stare. An air of dangerous confidence emanated from him.

"You fucking, lying bastard!" Kit leaped out of his chair at him. "You just wanted my land too."

Black sneered at him, regretting that he had to deceive his companion in this way, but he hoped his last-minute plan would get them both out of the mess they were in. "Yes, and if I'm not at my office by 9 a.m. tomorrow morning, my employers will be sending forces out to find both me and Kit." Black turned to face the man, who was now looking uncomfortable. "And you'll be the first person they'll come looking for, or at least their *security* people will." Black left the statement hanging in the air.

A couple of years ago, Black Construction had had the opportunity to get involved with Africa Land Partners, headed in the UK by John Vickers. Armen had warned Gabriel that the Kenyan arm of this organisation had strong links with one of the most formidable criminal gangs in the country. If Africa Land Partners couldn't get what they wanted, they sent in the heavy mob. Gabriel had wanted nothing to do with such operations and he turned down the offer John Vickers had made him.

Now, by pretending to *be* John Vickers, Gabriel was hoping to make Jirongo nervous; nervous enough of this other gang not to threaten one of their paymasters. Pretending to be after

505

Kit for the same land that Jirongo wanted seemed to be the best, if not the only, plan to try to get the two of them out of here.

Black's eyes were still drilling into the Kenyan's and for a moment he thought he detected surrender in the man's face, but suddenly everyone looked up as they heard the distinctive noise of a helicopter. It was so loud you could've been forgiven for thinking someone was trying to land it on the corrugated roof of the building they were in.

The guy on the floor grabbed the gun and shot to his feet. He headed outside and stared up. The driver was peering out of the dirt-covered window and the glow of blue flashing lights infiltrated the room.

They could hear commands being shouted over a megaphone, and Jirongo glanced at the driver. The next minute there was the sound of a blow, followed by a cry of pain, as the Kenyan who had ventured outside was disarmed. Suddenly Armen, dressed in black combat gear and a bulletproof vest, stormed in, aiming his CZ 75 pistol at Moody Jirongo.

Black grinned at his friend and put his arm around Kit's shoulder, who was still looking as angry as hell and completely gob-smacked.

. "I have some explaining to do," he said. As he saw Rick, also sporting combat gear and a bulletproof vest, appear behind Armen, he walked over to him and hugged him. "Am I glad to see you."

As Black, Kit and Rick exited the building, a second policeman, who had just cuffed the Kenyan – who was now staggering around, holding what looked like a dislocated shoulder – came in to arrest the other two gang members inside.

"Kidnapping British billionaires is not a good idea, Moody," Armen said as the gang leader stared after Black.

"That's not John Vickers, is it?"

Armen laughed at the man being cuffed by his officer. "No, it's not." He left him to wonder just who was the tall English gentleman who had successfully stalled the three gang members for long enough to be rescued.

"Wait here for the police van and I'll see you in the morning to write this one up," Armen called to his officer as he left to join the others in the helicopter.

The men shared anecdotes of the kidnapping, joking about nudity and tracking, first jackets and then body parts, during the journey back to Nairobi. Gabriel chatted with Roger on Rick's Xphone and arranged for first-class plane tickets back to the UK for the morning, for three adults. He also told him to ask Ellouise to invite Grace to lunch at Arnford Hall on Saturday.

Kit sat quietly and wondered what the fuck had just happened, too relieved and too tired to protest about going back to his own country. But there was one thing for him to protest about – vehemently.

Gabriel had arranged for Kit to have a room at his hotel. After showering and changing into clean clothes, Rick loaning some of his to Kit, the three men shared a meal before finally retiring and sleeping soundly. During the meal, Kit learned Black's true identity, and Black told him why he'd used John Vickers's name. Black was not giving Kit any opportunity not to go back to England with them now.

"After all I've been through for you, you're coming back to meet your sister. Like I said, if you don't want to settle in the UK you can come back and we'll see about setting you up with the safari flights to Mombasa."

Kit enjoyed his food and non-alcoholic drink. He also enjoyed listening to Rick and Gabriel sharing stories about past weapons and securities projects. The younger man clearly led an exciting life and when he mentioned that he was looking forward to getting home for a few days to drive his Aston Martin Vanquish, Kit's occasional desire for oblivion from a shot of heroin was far from his mind.

However, at nine the next morning, it came right to the forefront of it. Not the desire for drugs so much as the fact that Gabriel Black knew about his habit and was about to start getting him clean.

They were giving statements to Armen's officers when Armen came to join them.

"What time is your flight?" he asked.

"Noon," said Gabriel. "So there's just time for one last check," and he turned to Kit, who was just getting up from his seat.

"How much?" Armen asked as he headed for the door to the corridor. He stopped outside a white metal door, opening it and standing aside to let the other two men enter. Then he joined them in the sterile-looking environment and said hello to the dark male nurse who was placing some steel implements on a trolley.

"One hundred per cent," Black said, and folded his arms and leaned back against one of the pristine walls. He looked intently at Kit. Armen nodded to the nurse, who turned to Kit.

"Please take your clothes off, sir," he said quietly as he pulled on a pair of surgical gloves.

"What the fuck for?" Kit asked, glaring at Black. Without moving from his position, Black answered, "You're going to be sitting on an aeroplane next to me for the next ten hours. We'll be going through customs and I need to know that you're clean."

"Of course I'm clean."

"You have a record of concealing drugs about your person – for personal use, I've been told. I'm just making sure you're not doing that now. So do as the guy asks and then we can go."

As the penny dropped, Kit realised he didn't have a choice. There was no way his life here in Kenya was going to remain as it had been before he met Gabriel Black. For a start, he was tired of wondering when someone would come knocking on his door for their money, or his land. And he had started to think through what he needed to do to get his pilot's licence back. He was ready for a change, whether that was back in England or between the Masai Mara and Mombasa. He pulled the T-shirt above his head. As he stood in his underwear, he looked at the nurse.

"OK, sit up on the bed, please."

Kit then followed the nurse's instructions to open his mouth, and the nurse moved a swab around inside it, dipping it into a solution before inserting his fingers into Kit's mouth and feeling all around. He then picked up a torch-like instrument and began to examine Kit's ears, inside and out. Kit glanced at

Black, who was watching. Armen had his back to them, as he was perusing some papers on a small desk.

"Good. Now please stand up and hold your arms out."

Again, Kit did as instructed and the man frisked the top part of Kit's body, pausing at the couple of puncture marks visible on Kit's forearms.

"Can you take your underwear off, please?"

"For fuck's sake," Kit murmured before reluctantly pushing his trunks to his feet and stepping out of them, placing them on the bed in front of him.

He turned his back on Black as the nurse placed his hands at the top of his groin, prodding his skin before holding his testicles and then travelling lower over his perineum. The nurse then smoothed his hands down each of Kit's legs and raised one foot at a time, checking each toe and the skin between them.

"Now bend over the bed, please."

Kit closed his eyes and took a deep breath. He heard the rustle of a sheet of paper as Armen turned a page, and he felt Black's glare as he remained silent and observant.

"Get a kick out of watching, do you?" Kit sneered.

"Just protecting myself and my reputation," Black replied, thinking about his own stash of cannabis back home.

Kit placed his chest on the bed and rested his head as he turned to look at the steel trolley. He saw the nurse pick up a clamp and then it disappeared from his sight.

He heard a squirting sound and then suddenly felt the man's hand clasp his buttock. One gloved hand entered his crease and traced the channel from his lower back, leaving a trail of cool gel. Then his buttocks were prised apart and he felt cold, wet steel at his anus. A moment later he tensed as the head of the clamp was attempting to make its way inside.

"You need to relax, sir."

Again Kit breathed deeply and tried to relax the tight muscle, wanting to get the ordeal over with as quickly as possible. He groaned as the clamp was inserted and tried to hold in the sounds he wanted to spew forth as he became aware of his anus being stretched open by the expanding clamp. Then he felt gloved fingers exploring his body from the inside. He shut out the light and tried to blank his mind. Only the quiet sound of latex on skin could be heard.

Then he felt the clamp being retracted and withdrawn.

"All clean, Mr Black," the nurse announced, before turning to dispose of the gloves in the rubbish bin and completing his paperwork.

"Good," replied Black as he stood up straight. "Thanks," he said as he shook Armen's hand, "for everything."

"I hope to see you in better circumstances next time, Black. Maybe with your mother. Give her my regards," and the two men embraced for the last time.

Kit concentrated on putting his clothes back on. "You didn't need to do that."

"I did. I need to know that I can trust you. I put my life at risk to get you. I don't want any more surprises."

A few minutes later they were in a taxi, picking Rick up on the way to the airport. They got through customs and security with no problems, Kit Stockton's new passport not questioned. Finally Kit made himself comfortable in his first-class seat to head back to his home country after an absence of fifteen years.

Chapter 91

Back in Arnford, as Grace lay in bed after the skiing lesson, she opened Gabriel's book at the first page. She turned the page, and the next, and the next. She suddenly sat bolt upright. Every page had been scored through with a pen. Then an unsealed envelope fell out to land on her duvet.

In the soft glow of her bedroom lighting, Grace turned a deathly shade of white. She read the letter again.

Dear Gabriel

I will no longer be with you by the time you read this letter. But I know how happy I would have been that you have at last found peace with yourself and happiness in your life.

I have instructed your mother to give you this letter when you finally meet a woman you can truly love and whom you wish to marry. I pray you will be blessed with children, good health and much happiness.

It is all I ever wanted for my family. I pray you will cherish that union, that togetherness, which loves and forgives and lasts above all else.

Always be there for one another; share your joys and strengths. Heal each other's heartaches and help each other to conquer your weaknesses; embrace your family for what they are.

There can be no greater bond than that of a family.

And in the creation of your very own family, with your wife by your side, you are free to relinquish the promise you made me. I renounce the vow you made and release your own will back to you.

You will be faithful to your own Mrs Black.

You no longer have to fulfil your mother's sexual needs. My Mrs Black will be free to move on, as she will have served our family purpose. You are free of her, my son.

Your oath enabled me to die a happy, comforted man, knowing that our family would survive. I love you, my son, and am only sorry I can't be there to share the happiness you will have in the future with your wife.

Poppa

Grace's mind went into overdrive.

The envelope and letter were yellowed with age, but unmarked. Had anyone ever read this letter? And what did it mean? What was the significance of the book in which it had been kept? And why were the pages of the book defaced?

Oh. My. Life.

His secret. His shame. His darkness. His condemnation.

His mother.

The other woman.

Gabriel Black was having sex with his mother!

Grace gasped and put her hand to her mouth. Could it be true? What on earth would make him commit such an act? How could he? And if it was true, why hadn't it stopped when he met John's mother? Why had they never married?

She stumbled into the bathroom and splashed her face with water, before gulping some down. She thought she felt sick. But, no. She felt desolate, unbearably sad and overcome by the need to see Gabriel. To talk to him, to show him this letter.

But she didn't know when – or even if – she would see him again. To all intents and purposes, it looked as though she would be joining everybody for skiing at Christmas. But that was over three weeks away. She felt she couldn't even get through the night without him, let alone the next few weeks.

Chapter 92

By three on Saturday morning, Gabriel, Rick and Kit were walking up the steps to Arnford Hall. By now, Kit had begun to get to know the man who had inadvertently risked his life to reunite him with his sister. As the three men entered, Roger came up from the kitchen to greet them.

"Am I glad to see you!" he said as he hugged Gabriel, not bothering to conceal his relief and delight to have him home. "Don't ever scare me like that again," he whispered, for his ears only.

"I'm sorry, Roger. Thanks for activating the tracker. I'm not going to think about what could have happened." He pulled away from the embrace and turned to Kit.

"Kit, Roger, my friend. Roger, meet Grace's brother, Kit Stockton."

"You must all be exhausted. Let me show you to your rooms and we can hear all about your adventures in the morning."

As Roger led Kit and Rick to their rooms, Julian appeared at the bottom of the grand staircase. Kit stared at Black's double walking towards them.

"We'll do introductions in the morning, and I'll let Steve know we'll have a late breakfast."

Alone in the hallway, Julian stood in front of his brother. "Hey," he said. "Welcome home." He looked haunted, and Gabriel smiled warmly and wrapped his arms around him.

"I'm sorry for worrying you, Julian. If nothing else, it looks like we're born to survive."

In the silence between them, they both knew they were lucky to be alive, and there was a sense of optimism in the household.

"Come on. I need to see John and then we both need to get some sleep. Does Ellouise know anything?"

"No. We needed to know you were safe before telling her anything, and then we realised there was no need to worry her."

"Good."

513

Gabriel stood in the doorway to his son's bedroom. The faint sound of John's breathing filled his ears in the stillness and he walked over to the bed and leaned in to kiss his son. He almost wanted to wake him up, to kiss him and hug him tightly. But he just stayed for a few minutes, watching him sleeping peacefully, before finally retiring to his own room.

In the morning, everyone gathered in the kitchen. Kit stood on the periphery, witnessing the reuniting of a father with his son, a brother with his twin and sister, an employer with his staff and friends. He was introduced as Grace's brother.

The small boy came over. "Hello, Mr McGuire."

"Er ..." Kit looked confused. "My name's Kit. You must be John," and he tried to conceal his awkwardness.

Ellouise floated over in a rich brown velvet dressing gown. She smiled at the man with curly, sandy-coloured hair, who was wearing a navy blue sweatshirt and shabby jeans and looking uncomfortable.

"Kit Stockton, isn't it?" she asked and extended her hand.

Kit took hold of it nervously. "You're not Grace."

"I'm sorry, no. I guess we're a lot to take in. I'm Ellouise Black, Gabriel's sister!" Her eyes shone kindly. "I'm not sure what Gabriel has planned." She saw Kit's puzzled expression and laughed. "He's the one in the white shirt and black trousers. Their choice of clothes is the easiest way to identify them."

"Thanks for the tip," he said.

"I've laid food in the breakfast room, when you're ready, sir," Steve announced and everyone made their way through the kitchen.

Gabriel indicated to Kit to sit next to him, with John on his other side. The rest of the gathering sat around the table and tucked into eggs, bacon, sausages, tomatoes and mushrooms. Kit finally began to relax as he joined in the recounting of their experience, leaving out all reference to their kidnapping, which could upset John, not to mention Ellouise.

At the end of the meal, Gabriel asked Kit to join him in his office.

"I need your help in arranging for you to meet your sister," he said.

"Where is she? Does she know I'm here?"

"No, she doesn't know. I didn't want to worry her. She takes her new identity very seriously. That's why I insisted you have a new name on your passport. I thought you would be glad of the chance to start over again, as it were." Black paused for a moment. "I take it you didn't have anyone special back in Kenya?"

Kit shook his head. There had never been anyone. He had been burdened with guilt over what his father had done, and his youthful fear that he could have been in any way responsible for those hideous actions. He'd been driven by self-hatred, self-destruction and rage; a rage he mostly took out on himself, unless driven by alcohol or drugs to attack anyone who got in his way.

He hadn't exactly been a popular guy. And now, as he thought of Grace, he questioned, yet again, why on earth she would want to see him.

Gabriel broke into his thoughts.

"So, do you think it would be better if you guys met in private and had a chance to get to know each other a little?" Although his dark eyes gave nothing away, inside, Gabriel was trying to balance his own desperate need to see Grace with his sense of propriety that brother and sister be reunited privately and left alone to form a new relationship; he was certain that was what the siblings would desire.

Kit thought for a moment. He felt overawed by his surroundings. He had never been anywhere like Arnford Hall before. It reminded him of a stately home he had visited on a school trip. Black made him nervous and he still didn't know if he could trust the guy. And, no matter how helpful and philanthropic his gesture of reuniting brother and sister was, Kit couldn't understand why he would have gone to all that trouble for his son's teacher. There was something he hadn't been told; something weird about the Black family and their staff.

"I think I would like to meet her alone."

Gabriel nodded. "Yes. I suppose that would be best. Let's join the others and I'll see that it's arranged."

Black was suddenly formal and remote, and Kit couldn't help noticing the change in him. The two men had shared a life-threatening experience and there had been some unspoken bond between them. Now they were worlds apart. He followed the older man out of the office, relieved when Gabriel left him with the other adults, as father and son went out to take a dog for a walk.

Chapter 93

A short while later, Black climbed out of the Bentley and walked up the drive to 3 Willow Lane. Grace's surprised expression told him she wasn't expecting him. *Maybe she thought Ellouise was going to call for her?*

"Oh … I didn't realise you would be …" Grace's voice trailed off. She had assumed she was joining Ellouise and John and they would be going out for lunch before going back to Ellouise's bungalow.

"Hello, Grace," he said quietly, and she thought how tired he looked. There was something else in his eyes, and she wondered if she was letting her imagination run wild, now knowing the secret that tormented him.

"Hello, s—"

He cut her off. "Gabriel. Just say my name." His eyes captivated her as she stared, unable to move. Then she glanced over her shoulder. "I'll just get my bag," and she picked it up and held it close as she placed the strap over her shoulder. It held the key to her sanctuary. And the book containing the hidden letter. Her mind started swirling with questions and fears, but she took a deep breath. She needed to pick the right time to talk to him.

At his car, she waited as he held her door open. She glanced at the console as he started to drive. There was no collar. She was startled as he asked, "Are you well, Grace?"

"Yes. I'm fine." She gazed out of the window.

Piano music was drifting from the sound system and she enjoyed its tranquillity.

"How is John?" she ventured to ask.

"I have been away for a few days, so I've only caught up with him this morning. But he seems well and I think he is sleeping a little more peacefully at the moment."

After a minute he added, "Have you been enjoying your skiing lessons?"

She took a moment to respond to the unexpected question. Gabriel Black didn't normally do chit-chat, or even light conversation – with her at least. There was something different about his manner, and she thought again of the collar.

"They've certainly been different! A ski holiday has not been on my list of things to do. But I have to confess they've been more fun than I'd expected. And it's been nice sharing them with John and Carol and her family."

She was smiling and he detected a note of happiness. He wondered if he had ever managed to make her happy in the few months he had known her.

The car came to a halt in front of the Hall.

"Please, let me get your door," he said as he turned away from her to get out of the car.

She realised her jaw had fallen open. Was he actually being civil, even nice, to her?

He didn't take her hand as he climbed the steps beside her.

Breathe, Grace, teased the gargoyles.

"I'll let Ellouise know you're here." He hesitated as he looked towards the door to her sanctuary. "Do you want to come down to the kitchen?"

Oh! He's giving me a choice.

"Er, yes, OK." She followed him down the spiral staircase and into the kitchen. Everyone greeted her and she was introduced to Rick Casey.

"Pleased to meet you, Mrs McGuire." Rick held her hand tightly and had a strange look in his eye, as though he were examining her. *So you're the reason we went to Kenya, the woman he risked his life for.*

She felt herself blush and her confusion continued to grow.

"Peppermint tea, Grace, or would you like a glass of wine? Some of us have already started on the alcohol." Steve's voice was reassuring, just as it had been on Thursday night, when he had seemed even more attentive than usual, albeit a little preoccupied.

"Tea would be nice, thanks." Grace approached the island where Roger, Julian and Rick were sipping wine. She wondered where Ellouise and John were, and where Gabriel had disappeared to. She thought about her need to talk to him about the book and the letter, but she found herself in the midst of cheerful conversation about skiing, cars and fencing. She would have to wait, and she tried hard to concentrate on what was being said.

"Hey, why don't we have a bout tonight?" suggested Julian. "Are you going to stay over, Grace?"

All eyes turned to her.

She had no idea what was expected of her. She hadn't brought an overnight bag. The lunch invitation had meant she had let Jason know she wouldn't be seeing him this weekend; she was busy with Christmas preparations at school anyway, so it wasn't an unusual excuse for her to make.

"I wasn't really expecting to," she said, hoping she didn't sound as nervous as she felt.

"Well, why don't you? If you have nothing else planned, that is?" Julian persisted, "And I can get Lindsey to join us. We can have a bit of a party." *And, I hope, celebrate your reunion with your brother, and winning you back for my brother.*

"Good idea," agreed Roger.

Grace looked at the cheerful faces around her.

"I guess so, then." She drank her tea and remained quiet for the next few minutes as the men spoke about the order of play for tonight, with Rick declaring he would be a spectator, but wouldn't say no to a taster session with Steve. He was going to head back to London tomorrow before his next project for Black Armour began, and he wanted to make an evening of it. Julian slipped away to find Gabriel, hoping he hadn't overstepped the mark by inviting Grace to stay. He found his brother in his office, with Kit.

"Am I interrupting anything?" he asked as he entered the room. "The door was open."

The two men turned to face him.

"No," said Gabriel. "We're done. I've just told Kit that I thought it would be best if I brought Grace up to the octagonal room and the two of them could spend some time together. Michael could then take them both back to Grace's.'

"Oh. Well, I thought we could have a fencing bout after dinner. Grace has said she'll stay. We could make a bit of a party of it, you know. Celebrate family reunions. After all, GeeBee, you managed to get Ellouise and me back here and Grace's brother over from Kenya. They're both achievements worth celebrating, aren't they?" He paused and waited for a response.

"She said she would stay?" Gabriel didn't move from where he was standing by the desk.

"Yes."

Kit felt a slight tension in the room, and tried to decipher if this was a good thing or not. Gabriel's reaction hadn't looked particularly positive. And, from the conversation they had just had, Kit had got the distinct impression that Black thought it best that he and Grace return to her house. Which had been fine by him, because he was feeling uneasy in this great house and hemmed in by the Black family and the other guys here. It seemed a very strange set-up.

"Ahem!"

The men turned to the door again to see Ellouise. "Isn't it time we put Kit out of his suspense and let him see Grace?"

"Yes. I'll go and bring her up." Gabriel left the room, still wondering why Grace had agreed to stay the night.

"I'll show you the octagonal room, Kit," and Ellouise led him into the welcoming room just off Gabriel's office. It was bathed in yellow winter sunshine and Kit felt a little more at ease. He stood by the window and stared out across the terraced garden and down to the meadow and woodland.

"You have a lot of land here," he commented to Ellouise as she lingered at the doorway.

"Yes. I'll show you around sometime if you like." She smiled, then turned and walked down the corridor to find John to see if he wanted to go swimming.

Kit stared after her.

He started to feel nervous. He hadn't seen Melanie – *No, Grace, remember* – in nearly fifteen years. He rubbed his hands on his jeans, hoping they wouldn't feel sweaty when he touched her. Should he shake her hand, hug her, kiss her? Would she remember how they used to play and fight together when they were young? Would she remember that awful night, and the following horrendous weeks before they were separated?

Of course she would, just as he did.

He ran his hand over his hair, grateful he had been able to take a shower this morning.

Grace didn't notice Gabriel enter the kitchen. He tapped her shoulder gently and asked, "May I have a word with you, Grace?"

She had been listening intently to Steve and Roger as they explained some of the etiquette behind the ancient art of fencing to her and Rick. The atmosphere was relaxed and friendly and everyone seemed to be feeling festive, like an early start to Christmas. She noticed that the master of the house didn't touch her and she began to feel uneasy again in his presence. She nodded and followed him as he walked towards the breakfast area at the back of the kitchen as the others decided to join Ellouise and John in the pool.

Grace found herself alone with the man who had been her captor. But he wasn't acting like that now. Under different circumstances, she might have felt like a true guest.

"Let's sit down," he said quietly, his dark eyes clear and unmasked as he looked at her solemnly. She wondered if he was going to make some speech about their relationship being over. Or perhaps it already was over and she was simply here to be with John, although she still hadn't actually seen him yet. She thought about the book in her bag, which she had left by the island. Should she talk to him about it now?

"I need to tell you something, Grace," he said quietly, his hands clasped on the table in front of him.

He looked so nervous, Grace didn't know what to say or what to expect to hear.

He continued. "I know that you had a brother, Grace, and you've not been able to keep in contact with him."

"Michael!" she gasped, as the colour drained from her cheeks. "Is something wrong? Is … is he all right?" She recalled one of her recurring dreams where she could hear her brother cry out in pain, his face covered with blood.

521

Then she felt the warmth of Gabriel's hands as they gently clasped her hand, which she had unconsciously raised to her mouth.

"He's fine, Grace. And he's here. He's come to see you."

"What? He's here? He's here at Arnford Hall?" Her eyes were wide in disbelief, clinging to the hope that what she thought she had heard was true.

"Yes. He's here and you can see him. If you want to, that is." Gabriel stood and, keeping a tight hold on her hand, helped her to her feet. As Grace moved from the table, he pulled her to him. "I hope this is what you wanted, Grace. I hope I can give you what you want." The words were out before he realised what he had said. But his thought, "Let me be what you want" remained in his head.

Shaking with emotion, Grace allowed herself to be led up the spiral staircase and towards the octagonal room, his favourite room. As they approached the doorway, Gabriel turned to her.

"He's in there. I'll be in the plant room if you want me." He planted a light kiss on her cheek, the words "I love you" swirling around his mind, but remaining stubbornly unspoken. He turned and left her alone.

Grace entered the room and saw a thin, sandy-haired man standing near the window. She watched him for a moment, as the thick carpet cushioned any sound her feet made. She was shaking. She had thought so often of trying to find him, wanting to disregard the warnings from the police. But the nightmares of her father's arrest, the pain of her mother's suicide and the weeks of hell spent proving her own and Michael's innocence convinced her she couldn't do it. As the years had rolled by, her yearning to see him had grown, not diminished, and seeing Gabriel Black reunited with his family had only fuelled her own futile desire.

And now he was here.

"Hello, Michael."

He turned and looked at the woman before him. She had the same colour hair, but not quite long enough now to tie in the ponytail he remembered from their childhood. He hesitated before slowly walking towards her. "Grace. That's your name now?"

"Yes," she smiled, thankful not to be called Melanie. That part of her had died, but Grace was still Michael's sister.

He was close to her now and he could see her familiar hazel eyes look up at him. He had probably grown another couple of inches since he had last hugged her before saying goodbye forever.

Slowly, he reached out and his apprehension dissipated as she closed the gap between them and hugged him as he wrapped his arms around her, squeezing her in a tight embrace.

"Oh, Grace, forgive me, forgive me ..." Kit cried as he lowered his head to her shoulder. He couldn't release his grip on her. He needed their connection to fight the sickness and hatred consuming him as the memories of their father's crimes flooded back. His sister had been the strong one, the sensible one who kept her grip on reality and demanded compassionate treatment for herself and her brother. She had been an intelligent twenty-four-year-old, studying law, and she was innocent. He had been nineteen, headstrong and angry. But most of all he had been frightened; frightened that he could have somehow influenced his father to kill small children. He had been convinced that he had behaved badly as a small boy, but his father drew some insane line at killing his own child, so he killed other people's instead.

He had refused the counselling victim support had wanted him to have, and had vanished. After living rough in rural Wales for a few months, he finally left the country and sought a better life in Kenya. At first he thought he had found it. But his constant nightmares and his misplaced guilt began to eat away at him, leading to his desire for oblivion, and his ensuing alcohol and chemical abuse.

Grace eventually stepped back, taking his hands and bringing them to her lips. "Hey, there is nothing to forgive. It was never your fault. Never. I ... I can't believe you're here. I've missed you every single day." She reached up to his cheeks and wiped the tears from them. "Don't cry, Mikey," she whispered and he melted at the use of his pet name when they were children.

She laughed gently and then led him to the sofa. Still holding hands, they turned towards each other.

"You haven't changed, you know," he murmured through his sobs, thankful his shoulders had stopped shaking.

"You're just being kind, like always. I have more wrinkles," she said, her eyes never leaving his face, "and you have whiskers," and she touched the stubbly sideburns and ran her hand over his afternoon shadow. "And you're way too thin." She wanted to add, "and too grey, too sad, too lonely," but she bit her lip and fell silent, determined not to cry.

It was one of the happiest moments of her life.

Slowly, they began to relax with each other and shared stories of their "new" lives, very carefully referring to happy times in their childhood. They had a silent, mutual pact not to let the horrors that marked the end of their time together intrude in this joyous reunion. Kit confessed that he had stubbornly been using the Bright surname until Gabriel Black had insisted it had to be changed to protect his sister.

"What has he got to do with you being here?" she asked, suddenly serious and anxious.

"He came to drag me back from Kenya. He said you wanted to see me. He wasn't going to come back without me." As Grace listened incredulously, Kit told her about meeting Black, his offer to clear his debts, to set him up as a pilot if he wanted to return to Kenya. If the guy hadn't been so damned determined and controlling, Kit confessed, he might never have come back. "I thought you wouldn't want to see me. Not now that I've made such a mess of my life." Kit told his sister everything: about the flying, the alcohol, the drugs, the gambling and the resulting kidnapping and Black's quick thinking, which had led to their rescue, and which ultimately set Kit free and brought him to Grace. He explained how Black had suggested he donate his land to the SOS Children in Kenya charity, in order that they could benefit from it.

There were more tears and hugs and then Kit began to ask her about her life.

"So you're engaged to him, then?" he asked fingering the engagement ring. "I knew you were more than just his son's teacher. It was so obvious he's in love with you."

Grace pulled her hand away.

"Why do you say that?" She looked down at her ring so that her brother couldn't see the concern on her face.

"A guy doesn't go halfway round the world and risk so much for someone unless he cares for them – really cares for them. He got me out of a lot of trouble. Probably saved my life as well as cleared my debts. And I believed him when he said he would help to set me up in business with the safari flights. Why would a guy like him do that for a shit like me?" He smiled to take the bitterness out of his words. He had been in Black's company for a considerable amount of time during the last couple of days and his respect for him, the examination at the police HQ excepted, only continued to grow. "He told me he was doing it because you needed to see me, and I'm so glad he did what he did. I don't think I can ever repay him, but I'm going to make the most of the opportunity he's giving me. I'm going to make a fresh start with my life, Grace. And with our new names, I don't see why we can't keep in touch, see each other, be like a proper family. I'm not sure that I'll ever be bosom pals with my brother-in-law. He doesn't look the sort to invite down to the local pub, but you never know," and again he smiled playfully.

"You've got it wrong, Kit." Her brother's new name rolled easily off her tongue. "It's not his ring."

Kit could see that she was upset and distressed. "Oh. I'm sorry if I've upset you. I just assumed you would be marrying the man who loves you. So there's another lucky man, is there?"

"Mmm. You're not the only one who can make a bit of a mess of their life." She smiled sadly, thinking that's exactly what she would be doing with her own life if she married Jason. "But at least we have each other now, hey? And no matter what happens in the future, we must stay in touch. We'll never be strangers again."

She stood up. "Do you mind if I go and find someone? I need to do something. Have you met Roger?"

Kit nodded, feeling more than a little concerned at the change in his sister's behaviour. But he decided to let her out of his sight for a moment, fearing that the mood could be spoiled if they continued this line of conversation.

"Let's go and find him then and see what everyone is up to," Grace said, hoping it wouldn't take more than a minute to find Roger.

She's as strong as ever, Kit thought.

The pair made their way down to the kitchen, where they found Steve alone preparing lunch. "Everyone's gone for a swim. Go and join them, they'll have spare swimsuits. Oh, but Mr Black is in the plant room if you're after him."

Grace took Kit down to the pool and left him with Roger. She crossed the corridor to the plant room. As she entered, she saw his black hair among the flower heads as he stooped, attending to some part of a plant. She cleared her throat to make him aware of her presence. He looked up and put the small knife he had been using down on the bench.

"I hope I'm not disturbing you," she said quietly.

"No. Not at all." He walked towards her, wiping his hands on a gardening apron he was wearing. "I think I've done enough in here for now anyway."

As he came within arm's length, he frowned slightly, concerned that she looked agitated. For a brief moment he wondered if the reunion hadn't gone well.

"Is there something wrong, Grace? Is everything all right for you and Kit? You are pleased to see him, right?"

"Yes, of course I am. And I believe I have you to thank for him being here. I had no idea. And he got you into a lot of danger. How can I thank you for doing that for him, for all the help you have promised him?" She was doing her utmost to keep her tears at bay and she bit down on her lip to stop it from quivering.

Gabriel's eyes bore into her. He watched her for every movement, every emotion that would tell him what she was feeling. He could sense joy, tinged with sadness, and a fear he couldn't fathom. He deliberated about the importance of protecting her identity. He had reminded Kit to call her Grace; surely he had done so.

"Has he upset you?" he asked hesitantly.

"No, not at all. It's so wonderful to see him. I can't thank you enough. I …" Her voice trailed off. She fought back the lump in her throat.

"Breathe, Grace," he whispered and he came close to her, not touching, but she could feel his breath on her face and smell his fragrance.

"I … I need to talk to you, sir, I mean Gabriel." She gave a very weak smile.

"Shall we go to the sanctuary?" He moved slightly and Grace waited for him to take her hand, but he seemed to change his mind and just left the plant room.

As they reached the door to the room Grace had grown to like, he opened it. It was unlocked. She followed him in and he closed the door behind her.

"Sit down, Grace, and tell me what's the matter."

He waited for her to sit on the sofa before he sat in the armchair. He leaned back and crossed his legs. Grace observed his movements and he appeared relaxed. She suddenly felt afraid to speak, to confront him, knowing that his relaxed state was about to change.

"I borrowed a book on Thursday,"

He looked at her. His mask rose. He remained silent.

"It was *Oedipus The King*."

With no outward show of emotion, he brushed his hand over the leg of his trousers.

"I see. And what have you concluded, Grace?" Although his face remained impassive, his voice was quiet and gentle, with a hint of sorrow.

"I think I know who your other woman is."

He stood up and moved towards the window, turning his back to Grace. "And what makes you think you know?" His words were barely audible as he stared out of the window across the driveway, wishing he were somewhere else.

"I … I studied the book at school … I know the story … and I found a le—"

He interrupted. "So. Now you know my secret." He clenched his hands and squeezed his eyes shut.

There was silence.

"And now you can truly hate me."

She remembered, weeks ago, when she had said she should hate him and he had replied, "But you can't."

"I don't hate you." She got up and went to stand next to him. "I want to understand. Understand why. Why you did what you did."

"Ha! Am doing, remember, Grace, the other woman?" His voice was dripping with bitterness. He gripped the windowsill.

Grace felt afraid for a moment, but tried to quell her fear, knowing that she needed to make him talk, for her own sanity and maybe his too.

"I need to know why. Tell me about it. Please."

She placed her hand on his and softly stroked her thumb across the back. She caught her breath as he placed his other hand on top of hers. His head was lowered, looking down at their hands, and he started to talk quietly but steadily, his body sagging as though he was wearing a heavy garment that was weighing him down.

"I did it for him. I loved my father and I thought he loved us. She was our mother. He said it was our duty. We owed it to him and our ancestors and ourselves. It was to save our family. I know now he was wrong. Oh, I think he loved me. It was just misguided; warped, even. And we weren't a proper family. Julian couldn't wait to get away from here. And Ellouise soon followed. It's ironic that the two black sheep, the two depraved, perverted, incestuous damned reprobates, were the only two left. When I realised I would never be allowed to see John, my own son, I lost any hope of salvation. I had made a promise to my father. And I hate her." He slowly sank to the floor, bowed his head and cried. The tears flowed uninhibited down his cheeks and his shoulders shook. Grace slid down the wall to sit next to him. Her heart bled its sorrow out, to be replaced by a feeling of compassion and tenderness but, most of all, love.

"There was a letter in the book," she said hesitantly. He wiped his eyes and cheeks before turning to face her. "What letter?"

She could tell it was taking him a lot of effort to control his voice and focus on what she was saying. She wondered for a moment whether it would have been better to leave him alone for a while before mentioning the letter, but she felt sure he didn't know about it. If he did, then it changed everything. There was no reason on earth to justify why he would have carried on a sexual relationship with his mother if he knew he didn't have to. Grace couldn't believe he would do that, seeing him crying beside her confirmed that belief. She slowly got up and headed for the doorway. "I'll be back in a minute," and she closed the door behind her.

A few minutes later, she was sitting beside him on the sofa, waiting. His reaction seemed to be delayed. How long was it taking him to read the letter from his father? Eventually he leaned forward, holding the open letter between his knees, staring at it.

"She kept this from me, she fucking kept it." His hushed tone added to the anger and hatred in his voice. "Even when we found out Eliza was pregnant. She never said a damn word. Just made me keep going to her. Oh, God, I ..." He hurried over to the washbasin and was sick, retching until the vomiting ceased. He turned the tap and let the water flow around the basin before splashing his face with the cold liquid.

As he grabbed the towel, Grace got to her feet. "I should go now and leave you alone." She didn't move. He faced her, his features pale and overcome by a haunted expression.

"No. It's OK. You can stay in here, if you like. I need to go." He turned away again as he added, "Julian said you were going to stay. Are you?"

Grace looked to his back. "Do you think it would help?"

"Do you mean me? Or John?"

"Can I help you?"

He turned to face her. He seemed serene now, focused on some new thought.

"Will you wait here a moment, Grace? I just need to freshen up."

As she nodded, he picked up the letter from the sofa and went out. As he raced up to his room he reread the letter, his anger turning into a determination to finally take control of his life. He freshened his mouth with mouthwash and toothpaste, combed his fingers through his hair and stared at his reflection in the mirror. There was no point in dwelling on what had just happened and Grace's revelation. He would deal with his mother once and for all on Monday. He just needed to make a phone call to his solicitor, Andrew Cornworthy, first.

But he needed to go somewhere.

Before going back to the sanctuary, Gabriel went down to the pool. There was a game of water polo in full swing, and he was pleased to see Kit getting stuck in, noticing how he carefully aimed his shots so John could reach the ball and aim to score. He smiled appreciatively and wondered momentarily if Grace had considered co-operating with him to provide a sibling for John.

But things had changed now. She knew his secret.

Chapter 94

Gabriel beckoned to Roger, who was getting his breath back after chasing down the pool in an attempt to fend off Julian's attack. He looked glad of an excuse to get out of the water.

"You OK?" he asked as he approached his friend and noticed his concerned look.

"I need to talk to you for a moment. Can you dry off and come into the games room?"

Gabriel prised off the tops of two bottles of San Miguel. It wasn't their usual drink but neither man wanted a whisky, and Roger wanted something to quench his thirst. They sat at one of the tables.

"Grace has seen my old copy of *Oedipus*," Gabriel informed him as he balanced the edge of his beer bottle on the wooden surface of the table.

"Oh," responded Roger, as if to say, *That explains it, then.* "Is she still here?"

"Yes. I left her in the smoking room. She found a letter in it. From my father. I swear, Roger, I had no idea he had written it. She fucking kept it from me." Gabriel lifted the bottle to his lips and drank half of it in one go. Then he hung his head and continued to roll the bottom of the bottle on the table in front of him.

Roger waited a moment before asking, "What does the letter say?"

"That if I ever fall in love and decide to get married, start a family of my own, I will have served my duty to him and it would all be over. He would give me his blessing to start a family of my own. I could have done that nine bloody years ago, when Eliza got pregnant." Another slug. "I know I never loved Eliza, but we had enough between us to have made a go of it. And I would have been rid of *her*. It would have been over."

Roger sipped his own beer. Then he reached out and took Gabriel's hand.

"You can make it over now, Gabe."

He let out a sarcastic laugh. "Yes. Except the woman I love is going to marry someone else."

"It doesn't matter. You have started your family with John. Who knows what might happen in the future? But for fuck's sake, end it now, Gabe. Take control of your own life for once. You're pretty good at trying to control everyone else's." He squeezed the other man's hands before letting go and adding, "We've been through a lot together, and I want nothing more than to see you settled down and happy. I always knew it would be with a woman," he smiled and raised his eyebrows, "not that it wasn't good between us. But you need to talk to Grace and tell her how you feel."

Gabriel remained silent. He knew he needed to see her. *If she can bear to look at me.*

Knowing what his friend would be thinking, Roger declared, "She's a strong woman who knows what she wants out of life. I think a family is at the top of that list. You've brought her a brother. You can give her a son. And other children too."

He got to his feet. As Gabriel stood up, Roger placed his arm around his shoulders.

"I'm glad this has come out. And I'm glad Grace found the letter. Start living your life how you want to. Maybe now you won't be so angry with the world."

The two men walked out together.

Gabriel hovered at the doorway, wondering if Grace was still in the room. She was curled up on the sofa, her head resting on her arms. She looked up as she became aware of him and she smiled.

"I need to go somewhere. I wondered if you wanted to come with me." He looked at her expectantly and, as she came towards him, he held his hand out. He felt the warmth of her skin as she placed her hand in his. He wrapped his fingers around it and then slowly leaned in and brushed her lips with a light kiss. As he felt her tense, his lips sought hers again but with a deeper need now, an honest passion and a sense of long-awaited freedom. Freedom to hope that she could now accept him for who he really wanted to be.

Then he pulled back, taking hold of her left hand. "I need to know if you are going to marry Jason Chesters." His voice was solemn and firm and his eyes waited for her answer. Grace knew she owed it to Jason to talk to him first. Ever since that weekend in London, she had felt uneasy about the engagement. His enthusiasm had stopped her from questioning their future together. He took it for granted that she would quit her job and move down to London. And he took it for granted that she had agreed to marry him, even though she hadn't actually said yes. And yet she had worn his ring, and handed in her resignation at school. She simply hadn't wanted to spend the rest of her days alone.

Did she now have the chance to spend her life with a man she really wanted, who she felt needed her?

She needed to know and she had the courage to find out. She realised that she was not going to settle for second best.

"No. I am not." She withdrew her hand from him and slipped the ring from her finger. She placed it in the pocket of her jeans and made a mental note to arrange to see Jason and return the ring to him. He'd get over her.

She looked up at Gabriel and saw a brightness in his dark eyes that she hadn't noticed before. Perhaps she had never really looked beyond the image of him as her captor, the master who had been using her. And she noticed the slight crookedness of his lips as they formed a heartfelt smile that she had missed before.

"Come with me," he said, taking hold of her hand again. He led her out of the main front door to the Hall. There was a gravel path leading off to the left, which continued past the block of garages and down towards an area that gradually became more enclosed by thick bushes.

"I rarely come down here. I hadn't even realised how over-grown it is," he murmured as he squeezed her hand. Then they approached a copse of silver birch and poplar trees. In the middle was a sandstone mausoleum. In stark contrast to the rough grass bordering the path leading here, the building was surrounded by a rich, well-manicured lawn, with beds of winter daffodils and pink and white camellias bordering the domed structure. Someone carried out a lot of maintenance work in this hidden area.

Gabriel let go of her hand and turned a large wrought-iron handle on the distressed oak door. As they stepped inside Grace gazed up at the light flooding in through the glass-domed ceiling. It reflected off four white marble tombs, creating an airy, tranquil ambience. Despite her nervousness, she smiled as she looked around the large chamber. The four tombs were laid out in a horseshoe against the single pale curved wall which formed the mausoleum. Atop each tomb lay a figure, two male and two female, in mottled white marble. Positioned on their sides with their heads propped on their elbows, their animated expressions revealed the fact that some interminable, jovial discussion was in progress. One of the characters gazed for infinity at the entrance, almost inviting any guest with air still in their lungs to join in the frivolities.

Someone had a sense of humour.

Gabriel stood beside the first tomb and caringly caressed the cool marble surface.

"This was my great-grandfather and his wife. This place was constructed following his detailed instructions." He turned to the fourth one. "And this is my father." He ran his hand along its length, his fingers lingering here and there, pausing to trace along some of the lines of the marble effigy.

Grace watched as his hands stroked the face of the lifeless man.

"Hello, Poppa," he said quietly, calmly.

Grace stepped back into a shaded area where the light couldn't quite penetrate at this time of day. She felt like an intruder until he reached out to her. She walked up to him.

"I want you to meet Grace. It's over now, Poppa." His voice quivered, but he continued, "I have done what you ordered and been true to my word. I … I forgive you, Poppa."

He turned to her and smiled weakly, tears glistening in his eyes, but forbidden to fall. Grace squeezed his hand.

"Will you stay with me now?"

"Yes," she said. "We still have another two hundred and sixty-three days to go yet."

He looked surprised, and his lips curled up, adding a charm to his already handsome face. "But you know my secret. I can't keep you as my captive any more."

"I'm here, aren't I? And you said you could never break your word."

"I'm not an easy man to get on with."

"You think I don't know that already? I don't think I'm a walk in the park either."

Gabriel smiled. "My father was a good man, you know. But his priorities were wrong. His plan to save our family was flawed. It nearly destroyed it. I understand now, though, why the family was so important to him. It is to me, too. But I know what is and what isn't acceptable." He paused and Grace waited silently by his side.

Eventually he headed towards the doorway. "Let's get you back to your brother."

Everyone was gathered in the drawing room, with Julian explaining the discipline of fencing to Kit and Rick.

"Are we on for a bout then tonight, and a celebration of families reunited?" he asked his brother, as Gabriel and Grace entered the room.

"Are we going to have a party, Daddy?" John came running over to be scooped up into his father's arms.

"Yes, why not?" he laughed.

Julian and Ellouise glanced at each other, and then looked at Roger. He grinned widely and shrugged.

Something had happened. Their brother was relaxed; liberated in some way.

You know something, Julian stated silently to Roger.

Roger walked over to Gabriel and put his arm around his shoulder, leaning in to whisper, "I think you need to have a talk to a couple of people."

Black glanced over to his siblings and smiled. Then he raised John in the air before placing his feet back on the ground.

"Right. Are we going to be fed before the festivities begin?" he asked jovially.

"I'll check timings with Steve," and Roger went down to the kitchen, still smiling.

At the end of the evening, Julian and Lindsey were the first to leave the party and head off to Julian's suite upstairs. Having spoken with Gabriel and Ellouise, he felt calmer than he ever remembered feeling.

Roger hugged Gabriel and Grace before going to the coach house with Steve. Grace and Kit had enjoyed each other's company as they watched the men fence, their competitive determination creating a tense and enjoyable atmosphere.

Kit then took his leave, exhausted and a little uncomfortable at the nagging desire for some chemical comfort that was building up in him. As he said goodnight to Black, his host sensed his edginess and offered to escort him to his room.

"I hope you're going to stick around, Kit, for a while at least. We can sort out some accommodation for you. And I imagine you'll need some help to adjust," he studied the younger man's reaction before continuing. It was obvious that he was tired, and the darkness lurking in his eyes betrayed Kit's need. "I've got a little something that might take the edge off for now."

"I ..." Kit glanced at him and then ran his hand through his hair. "Thanks, that would be good. I guess I'm going to need to straighten myself out a bit. For her. And thanks for getting me here. I ... I don't want to let you down."

"It's not me that I care about. But do it for her." They had reached the green twin room which had been allocated to Kit. "I'll be back in a minute," Black added.

He retrieved a cannabis cigar from his morning room. He wouldn't need them any more. He went back to find Kit.

As he returned to the drawing room, Grace was chatting with Rick. When Rick saw his employer, he thanked him for a lovely evening and then retired to his room for the night.

"And I'm going to take this very tired young man to bed too. I think we may get a lie-in in the morning." Ellouise smiled as she eased herself off the sofa. Gabriel gently scooped John up and carried him to bed, followed by his sister, who said, "I've got it from here, GeeBee. Go back to Grace. I'm so happy for you, darling. I love you. I always have, you know."

He lowered his head and kissed her cheek. "I know. I love you too. Goodnight, Ellouise. And thanks."

He placed a final kiss on his son's sleepy head and then made his way downstairs.

It was quarter to midnight. Gabriel's body was still adjusting to the time in the UK, and he was struggling to keep his tiredness at bay. As he entered the drawing room, Grace was resting on the sofa. Her eyes were closed but she opened them when she heard him come in. As he came to sit next to her, she shuffled up a little, sitting with her legs curled beneath her.

"Hi," she said softly, smiling and looking a little weary.

"Hi," he responded. "You look like you're ready to go to bed," he added with apprehension and a need which he hoped didn't show.

"Mmm," she sighed. "It's been a long day. But a good one."

"Yes, a very good one. I must thank you for your ..." he hesitated a second and held her gaze, "choice of book. I would never have looked in that book again. She knew that. But enough. Come on." He took her hand and pulled her up, pressing on the remote control in his pocket, extinguishing lights as they made their way upstairs.

As he opened "her" unlocked bedroom door, he stayed on the landing. She looked at him expectantly before a look of concern flickered across her face.

"Are you coming in?" she whispered.

"Are you sure? I won't be able to keep my hands off you." He no longer tried to conceal his need and his voice was low and husky with desire.

"That's the idea," she said and her eyes twinkled with lust.

They stood together in the en-suite and he waited while she brushed her teeth. When she had finished, he asked her reflection, holding her toothbrush up in his hand, "May I?" He was too desperate to see her, to be with her, to go to his room to retrieve his own brush.

"Go ahead. It is yours."

"No, Grace, it's yours. So. May I?"

She turned round to face him and put her hands on his shirt, her fingers stroking his chest.

"Yes. But I may distract you."

"Oh. You already are. Always have. Even the first time I saw you, when I was driving." He winked mischievously.

As he reached around her to put some paste on the brush, Grace began to slowly unfasten the buttons of his shirt, pulling the shirt-tails out from his trousers. He started to brush his teeth and she pushed the shirt down his arms and off his back.

Next she began to unfasten his belt buckle, and as she looked down she could see his erection growing, bulging against the fabric of his trousers.

"It wants to break free," he breathed in her ear as he removed the brush and cast it into the sink, too impatient to clean it thoroughly.

She undid the clasp and lowered the zip, gently easing her hands in between the silk fabric of the lining of his trousers and the soft cotton of his trunks. She pressed her palm lightly against his large penis and lingered a moment before sliding her hand inside the trunks.

He lifted her chin with his fingers as she cupped his testicles, rolling them in her hand. He groaned and placed his lips on hers. He was hungry and impatient as his tongue prised her lips apart, demanding entry. As she yielded, it invaded and explored her mouth, as if for the first time. She felt she would be bruised by the force of his movements, but she yearned for him and her tongue twisted with his, binding him to stay inside a while longer.

The kiss was deep and passionate, with a shared sensual need. It was as if they were getting to know each other at last. Then she pulled away from him and he felt her loss. She had fallen to her knees. With a sense of urgency that could barely be quick enough for him, she pushed his trousers and trunks down to his ankles and raised her face to his groin. She nuzzled in his pubic hair, smelling him, and traced her tongue from the base of his penis along his vein to the tip. It was misted with a wetness and she lapped it up, lightly licking his tip before enclosing her lips around it, taking him in as deeply as she could, smothering him with the warmth of her mouth.

He moaned out her name and she felt him pressing her head to him. "Grace, that is so good. I … I can't hold back much longer …" He needed to give her the chance to pull away from him, afraid she would take stock of all that had happened and be repulsed by him, but his innate need to ejaculate was over-powering him and he throbbed for release.

Grace raised her hand to the base of his penis and held him, sliding him in and then almost out of her mouth, determined to continue and determined to drink him.

As he came, his gasps combined with her moans of pleasure in tasting his sperm, swallowing and keeping it forever. She closed her eyes and fervently hoped he would be able to come again. She had already decided she would give him a child with her eggs. But not how he had planned.

He removed his trousers and trunks from around his ankles and slid his naked body down onto the bathroom floor, pulling her onto his lap. He kissed her tenderly and she reached up for more. She straddled him and ran her fingers through his short black hair, stroking the back of his neck and rubbing his shoulders with her palms, caressing the top of his back. And he continued to kiss her, feeling a pleasure he hadn't known from kissing anyone else, and clasped her to him, fearing he would lose her when reality set in in the morning.

After several minutes, he got to his feet, scooped her up and carried her to bed. He laid her down and slowly began to undress her. As he climbed in beside her naked body, his face showed his concern. "I don't have a condom."

She looked at him, puzzled. It had never bothered him before. And she had just swallowed his seed! What was his problem?

"Why does it matter? You told me you were clean."

"I … I wasn't sure how you would feel, now you know."

She sat up beside him and cupped his chin in her hands. "Don't you realise? It's better now I know. You have no hold on me. We are equal. I'm here now because I want to be. I know you, Gabriel. You're a good father, a good brother, a good friend. And a good son. You once told me the children cannot be blamed for the faults and crimes of their parents. I want to make love with you tonight, now."

A tear escaped and stole down his cheek. She gently caught it with her finger, raised it to her mouth and licked it away. He lay down on his side and pulled her down next to him. As he pressed his body to hers, she could feel his erection before he rolled her onto her back and leaned over her, taking his weight on his knees and placing his outstretched arms on either side of her head.

"I love you, Grace McGuire," and he leaned down and peppered her lips with light feathery kisses.

"Tell me again," she begged, luxuriating in his touch. His kisses were divine.

"I love you. I. Love. You."

She raised her knees slightly and invited him in. He watched her intently as he took one of her legs and carefully eased it up to rest on his shoulder. Seeing that she appeared to be in no discomfort, he raised her other leg to his shoulder and positioned his penis at her vulva. He held it against her soft skin, his palm gently pressing on her clean-shaven pubis.

She reached up to pull him to her. "Come inside me, I want to feel you," and she leaned back as she felt him fill her, stretching her skin in that most delightful way, and pressing her G-spot. Then she felt him reaching between her pubis and his penis. His finger lightly touched her clitoris and she tingled with erotic pleasure. She wallowed in the sensual thrill as his touch grew firmer, locating her exact spot, circling it, tweaking it, to send shivers through her, leaving her breathless as she waited in ever-mounting anticipation. She was climbing higher and higher and his rhythm was accelerating. He began to thrust forwards and pull backwards.

"Breathe, Grace," he murmured and she gasped. Steadily, her pleasure increased and her orgasm approached. The feeling was exquisite and she pushed herself up to him, hoping they could come together.

"Gabriel, I—" As she gasped once more, she cried out with the intense pleasure of her orgasm and beamed with joy as he squeezed his eyes shut and filled her with his seed. After a few moments, he eased her legs down and moved them both onto their sides, staying inside her, not wanting to break their bond.

He brushed the hair from her face.

"Oh, that was wonderful. You make me feel wonderful," she sighed, smiling from ear to ear.

"I'm glad. And ditto." He kissed her again.

Finally, he wrapped his body around her, hugging her and nuzzling the back of her neck. She was enveloped by his warm, soft skin.

They were happy and their sleep was deep and peaceful.

In the morning, Grace rolled over and felt him lying next to her. He had stayed! She propped herself up on one elbow and watched him breathing. He was lying on his back, in the middle of the bed, one nipple exposed above the bedcovers. She felt the urge to nibble it but fought it, not wanting to wake him.

She slipped out of bed and went into the bathroom, smiling as she saw the toothbrush still smeared with remnants of toothpaste as he had been too distracted and impatient to clean it last night.

Had yesterday really happened? Was there a chance for them to have a future together? Either way, their lives had changed. She felt warm at the memory of Kit, and the fact that Gabriel had brought him to her. Yes, things had definitely changed, and for the better.

Standing in the shower, she felt a sudden coolness as the door was opened, and she turned to face him as he stepped in and wrapped his arms around her.

"You're still here," he said as he nuzzled at her neck and then turned her round and pulled her to him for more kisses.

"So are you," she murmured, trembling with delight at his touch and the fact that he was there. She was already soapy from the shower gel, and he began to rub the lather over her body, playfully coating her breasts before lingering with his hand in between her legs and inserting his tongue in her mouth. Gazing up at him, she closed her eyes to the rain from the showerhead in the ceiling and gasped as she felt his finger enter her vagina. He circled her, withdrew and brought his hand to his mouth, breaking free from hers. He watched her as he sucked his finger, and closed his eyes, playfully exaggerating his pleasure at her taste.

After washing himself, slightly distracted by Grace's attention to his balls and penis, he reached for the shampoo and washed first her hair and then his own. After their shower, he passed her the fluffy white towelling robe.

"Gabriel, I was wondering ..." Grace's voice was low and hesitant. "Has anyone asked why Kit and I haven't seen each other in such a long time?"

She wrung her hands, and her head was down. Gabriel stepped towards her, pulled her hands apart and lifted her chin. "Don't worry, Grace, I explained that there had been some family issues and you guys lost touch with each other when Kit moved to Kenya. No one here will ask any questions; they're just very happy for you both." He kissed her gently.

"Thank you," she murmured and she felt his protection, his strength and his love.

Gabriel quickly dried himself and pulled on the black robe.

"I'm going to get dressed and then find John. If you can't find what you need in *your* room, Grace" – he looked intently at her as he said the word "your" – "just ask Ellouise to help you. She's in the room on the right just across the gallery." Then he held her gaze for a moment before turning and walking back to his own room.

As Grace walked into the kitchen wearing yesterday's clothes, but comforted with clean underwear, Steve told her that Gabriel and John had gone to see Satan.

"Have you seen my brother?" she asked Steve as he busied himself preparing vegetables.

"No. Not yet. Do you know which room he is in?"

As she shook her head, he wiped his hands on his apron. "Come on and I'll take you."

"Come in," Kit called when he heard the knock on the door.

"Good morning. Did you sleep well?" Grace smiled as she saw him tucking his shirt into his jeans.

"Yeah, actually, I did. And you?"

She hoped she didn't blush too much as she confirmed it had been a good night.

"I saw Black a short while ago and he suggested that we go to your place. He said we were very welcome to stay here, but maybe we would like a bit of time alone?" He was hesitant, not wanting to drag Grace away from her friends, but hopeful that they could be alone for a while. They had a lot of catching up to do and he wanted to admit some of his own shortcomings to her, so they could start afresh and he hoped his guilt would finally start to leave him. "Would you mind?"

"Of course not. I want to spend more time with you. You can stay at my place for as long as you want and we can talk about what you want to do, in the short term at least." She was surprised how relaxed she felt with him, considering they hadn't seen each other for so long. It was just so lovely to see him and talk to him again.

She wondered for a moment if and how things might move on now between her and Gabriel, fearing slightly that she could have misread things last night and there would be no moving on. He had said he loved her and she believed him. But she knew he was filled with guilt and fear; fear that she would loathe him in the cold light of day. She wasn't too sure that he would give her the chance to show him that she loved him and wanted to be with him. But there was one thing she was sure of: she needed to let Jason know that their relationship was over.

She helped Kit gather his belongings and they went downstairs and placed his bags near the entrance. By the time they entered the kitchen, everyone was up and drinking coffee and juice and nibbling croissants and cheese in the breakfast area. Gabriel immediately got up and walked over to them.

"Come and join us." He reached for Grace's hand. There was a space next to John and she sat beside him as he smiled at her and told her that Daddy had said he could start having fencing lessons. When Gabriel asked what everyone was planning to do that day, Grace saw through his attempt to make it look like a general question when he looked directly at her.

"I'm going to take Kit home with me," she said. "We have a lot of catching up, as you can imagine."

"I'll take you, when you're ready." Gabriel had the only answer he needed and he turned to talk to Julian about a board meeting on Monday.

Grace glanced at Roger, unsure whether his employer was upset about her intention to return home. But hadn't he suggested this to Kit?

"Well, Steve and I are heading over to my sister's and John's coming with us to meet my nephew, aren't you, mate?" and John excitedly confirmed he was looking forward to seeing Andy.

As everyone finished breakfast, Gabriel took Grace aside. "I suggested to Kit that you two may like some time on your own." He paused and rubbed his fingers over the space on her finger where the engagement ring had been. "But that doesn't mean I want you to go. I don't. But I do want you to have time to think about what we could have together, Grace. I mean, if you think there could be anything for us in the future. To share. A lot has happened recently and I know I need to give you some time. And some space. I'm not an easy man to be with, Grace. I have issues. But I want to try to deal with some of those now and you have enabled me to do that. I won't shy away from what I have to do. But I need to know if I have any chance with you." He looked into her hazel eyes and hoped she knew what he was trying to say. "I will try to be worthy of you, Grace, if you want me. But I won't force myself on you. Not any longer. I will accept your decision." He lifted her hand to his lips and slowly covered it in soft kisses.

"I'll take you home now. I won't trouble you for the next few days." He knew this would allow her time to see Jason to tell him it was over, or to decide to put her ring back on. "And then you can let me know if you have made a decision."

"I think …"

He interrupted. "No, don't say anything. I want you to remind yourself how I can be. There are some things in my life I can change now " – they both thought about his mother – "but I'm not so naïve to think I can change everything. Take the time you need to consider what you can and cannot accept about me. And then, if you so choose, we can talk and see if we have something we can build on."

Grace waited, unsure what to say.

544

"Just tell me you will think about what I have said. And I meant what I said last night, Grace. I love you."

Then he let go of her hand and started to walk to the door. Suddenly he stopped and turned back to face her. He put his hand in his pocket.

"I meant to give you this." He took her hand and placed the golden collar in it. "It's worth about eighty thousand pounds, so … if you feel things won't work out for us, sell it and put the money to some good use. For yourself. It really did suit you, Grace."

He left her alone while he went to find Kit and tell him he was ready to take them to Grace's house. Grace stared down at the golden collar, and fingered the simple clasp, missing its padlock.

Chapter 95

On Monday morning, Gabriel walked into the boardroom at Black HQ. He helped himself to coffee and then sat in the black leather chair to the right of the chairperson's at the head of the table. It would be another twenty minutes or so before the other members of the board would arrive.

He rang Roger. "Have the trustees confirmed in writing their agreement to my proposal?"

"Yes, sir, and I spoke with Andrew Cornworthy myself to reassure them of the reasons."

"Good." Gabriel put the phone down.

As the meeting began, it didn't take long for those present to sense that the Chief Executive Officer was in a strange mood.

Favourable financial results were reported and all divisions, with the exception of China, were at least achieving budget. Most questions on the figures were asked by Roger Courtney or Cynthia Black, with Julian helping the managing directors when some issues were raised on a couple of outstanding contracts.

Cynthia was quick to interrogate her younger son, and although his answers were accurate and succinct, it didn't go unnoticed that she remained unsatisfied with the overall progress that was being reported, and appeared to hold Julian responsible, rather than the managing director of the particular subsidiary involved, who had overall responsibility.

Gabriel had remained relatively quiet until a question came up about the early completion of the Canadian Black Armour project. The work had been signed off, payments made and the client had confirmed it would be awarding a further project to the Group in the first quarter of the new year. Everyone was pleased with the outcome and Roger had suggested having a celebratory dinner.

However, Cynthia implied that it had been due more to luck than good management, and Julian should have held a tighter rein on the contract amendments, which could have resulted in lost revenues.

"Nothing was lost, and Julian's involvement with the project was minimal. It was already close to completion when he rejoined the board."

The other members of the board agreed with Gabriel's statement.

There was some shuffling of papers, as the managing directors began to feel a little uncomfortable at the personal battle that was being waged between the chairwoman and her two sons. As Cynthia leaned forward and began to reiterate her accusation, Gabriel stood up.

"Would you excuse us, please? I need to talk to the chairperson in private." He turned to the company secretary. "You too. This is outside of this meeting and not to be minuted."

It was clear that Black expected everyone to leave. Julian looked questioningly at his twin as he gathered his papers together before following Roger and the others out into the lobby.

Cynthia got up from the table, went to the coffee machine and poured herself another cup. Right from the moment Gabriel had told her Julian was coming back onto the board, she had not been happy. She had steadfastly refused to forgive her son for leaving the company all those years ago – when he had also left her. She didn't need to be reminded of that fact by seeing his face at the table at every meeting. The fact that it was also Gabriel's face annoyed her even more. So she questioned his every move, pointed out every risk, and highlighted every weakness in anything the younger twin did or said. Gabriel had known what she was up to from the beginning. Now, having discovered the letter from his father, he was armed with all he needed to put a stop to her psychological torture of all her children.

When the two of them were alone, he slowly got out of his chair, walked over to the door and locked it. He then closed all the blinds along the wall of windows which looked out onto the Hilton Hotel on Deansgate.

"What are you doing?" Cynthia asked, trying to hide her concern by continuing to sip her coffee. *Had she overstepped the mark?*

"I think enough is enough, Mother." He was facing her now and clearing his own papers from the board table, placing them in a neat pile on top of the credenza next to the coffee machine. "It's about time we started being honest with each other, don't you think?"

Cynthia couldn't fail to note the threat in his words. She knew that Gabriel at his worst was a heartless, ruthless man to be feared. After all, she was the one who had made him that way when she had ripped his heart from him that first night when, aged fifteen, she had forced him and his brother to have sex with her.

She also knew that his father had told Gabriel about the way she had been repeatedly unfaithful to him over the course of their marriage. Her son knew about the infidelities which had led George Black to impose such an outrageous duty on his sons. Infidelities which had led to his depraved ill-judgement of how to keep his family together.

Julian and Ellouise had managed to escape her to save themselves. Cynthia realised now it was not too late for Gabriel to escape her too.

He returned to his seat and lounged back, looking calm as his dark eyes burned into her with their hatred. His voice was low, stern and threatening.

"I have discovered the letter from my father," he began, each word filled with warning. "The one you kept from me."

As the colour drained from her face, her trembling hands replaced the coffee cup awkwardly back into its saucer.

Cynthia struggled to respond. "I … I meant to give you the letter. When you found out that Eliza was pregnant. Really, Gabriel, I did." She looked up at him as he approached her, unable to tear her eyes away from him. "But it was too soon, too soon after your father's death. I … I couldn't give you up, Gabriel, I needed you …"

"Too soon?" he spat the words at her. "Too soon? Poppa had been dead *six years*. How fucking long were you going to make me wait?" He stopped. His voice threatened to falter, but he would not permit it to. Anger was seething through him. She had kept him to herself, never allowing him to love anyone.

Then he continued. "You kept me from my son. It was your fault Eliza hated me. I could have had a chance. I might even have fallen in love with her. You made me think I couldn't love anyone. But I love my son. And now I love someone else too."

He towered over her. Roughly, he pulled her to her feet. Before he could stop himself, he pushed her back on to the table.

"Well, I'm going to make you hate me as much as I hate you." He unzipped his trousers. "Remember me like this, Mother. Hell, I'm doing you a favour, so you won't want me any more. You won't want to fucking keep me." He pulled his dick from his trousers and pushed her skirt up to her hips. He leaned over her and pulled her thong to the side.

"Gabriel," she cried, trying in vain to escape him, "please don't do this. I love you."

"Shut the fuck up. Don't say that to me."

He moved to push his dick inside her. He wanted to punish her, hurt her, shame her.

"You made me like this, you bitch. I. Hate. You."

Suddenly he squeezed his eyes shut. He flung himself away from her and banged his fist down hard on the table right next to her head.

You stupid bastard, what are you doing? he silently cried out to himself.

Then his body sagged. He shakily adjusted himself, fastened his trousers and slowly sank onto a chair.

Cynthia lay on the table and sobbed.

"You have to leave. We will accept your resignation. I have contacted the trustees. You cannot influence them any more."

Slowly, she sat up. She wiped her eyes and walked over to her bag to retrieve a tissue. Arrogantly, she stood over her son and looked at him scornfully.

"What are you talking about? You can't force me to resign. I helped to build this company ..."

Gabriel looked at her, his quiet voice emphasising his menacing words.

"I know that you had an affair with the Duke of Woodhall when Father was alive. I wonder how the duchess would feel if she found out one of her closest friends had betrayed her like that?"

Cynthia froze. Amanda Barrington, the Duchess of Woodhall, was a very influential woman in the circles of Westminster, not to mention a popular socialite. Cynthia adored her – as well as the fact that she could move happily in her circle, sit at her table and share dinners, events and influential friends. Cynthia Black would be a social outcast if Amanda ever found out about her affair with the duke.

"You wouldn't dare."

"Don't try me. Resign. Go to Kenya. Armen may be happy to see you. I can't think who else would be." Slowly, he got to his feet.

"I'll get Roger." He looked at her and then changed his mind. "No, I'll get Julian to write to you with a severance package. And just so we both know where we stand" – he withdrew a sheet of paper from his jacket pocket – "here's a copy of the letter I'll send to the duke if you don't sign the agreement. On your way out, let Roger know I'm ready to resume the meeting."

He picked up his papers from the credenza and placed them back on the board table in front of his chair. Then he poured himself a coffee, sat down and turned to the next page of the agenda.

"Gabriel, please, I don't want it to end like this. Don't banish me. I'm your mother."

He looked down at the papers as he spoke. "You lost all rights to be my mother when you fucked with us. I thought we needed you in order for our family to survive. I was wrong. I never want to see you again."

He didn't bother to look up until he heard the door close behind his mother.

Chapter 96

"Well, did she say she would go?"

"Yes. I'll pick her up and take her home."

Gabriel sighed with relief as Roger told him that Grace had agreed to join everyone for the last skiing lesson.

It was Wednesday evening and Roger had been somewhat surprised when his employer asked him to call Grace to check that she would be going to the Chill Factore tomorrow. He knew that something had changed between the school teacher and his employer, and he hadn't failed to notice that she no longer wore her engagement ring. As far as he was concerned that had to be a good thing, so he didn't voice his curiosity to Gabriel.

Roger was also positively ecstatic when Gabriel asked him to help Julian draft a severance package for Mrs Black. Although her personal shareholding in the Black Holdings company was only half Gabriel's, the trustees of the two family trusts, who held the majority of the shares, often looked to the chairwoman for guidance on any voting matters. If Cynthia Black wanted to, she could cause difficulties for Gabriel and his siblings, and Roger's own holding of five per cent would do little to help them. But Gabriel had been in touch with the family solicitor, Andrew Cornworthy, who was also one of the trustees, and had had a very frank discussion with him. He had made it perfectly clear that the position with his mother had become untenable and that he would be seeking her resignation. Andrew was well aware of Gabriel's influential position in the Group, and confirmed in writing the trust's support for the Chief Executive Officer.

Things were definitely looking up. But Roger was perplexed that Grace McGuire and her brother were still absent from Arnford Hall. He had even ventured to ask Ellouise what she thought of the situation, and she confessed that she didn't know what was going on. Gabriel was never the easiest man to understand but, as Ellouise had said, at least he wasn't in a bad mood lately – unlike the days following the revelation of Grace's engagement to Jason Chesters.

So everyone lay low, not troubling Gabriel with their concerns, but patiently hoping there would be further good news to add to the delightful news of Cynthia Black's resignation from the business and from their lives.

Following the board meeting, Gabriel had spoken with his brother and sister and told them their mother would be resigning and might go out to Kenya, for a while at least. He felt he needed to let them know, so they could go and see her at her apartment to say their goodbyes, but he thought, correctly, that he was wasting his breath.

No one would miss her.

He hadn't been so sure about what to tell John about his grandmother, and he regretted allowing her to get close to him. But the time they had spent together had been short and she had never bought the gun she had promised him. (Black had accepted that John wasn't ready, at least yet, to shoot anything, including clay pigeons, which he still really didn't want to hurt, even if they couldn't feel it!)

So after tea on Monday, as they fed Satan, he explained that Grandma would be going away for a while and wouldn't be able to see them again.

Gabriel was both shocked and relieved when John asked, "Can I still have sleepovers sometimes with Roger and Steve, especially when Andy comes to visit them?"

"Of course, John."

He also fervently hoped that John would have someone else in his life who would fill some of the gaps and help to make John's life a happy and loving one.

But he couldn't be certain about this.

Chapter 97

On Friday evening, Grace nervously got off the train at Euston and scanned the crowd of commuters for Jason.

He waved his newspaper as he downed the last of his coffee and walked over to meet her.

"What's the matter, Grace? You didn't sound too happy on the phone last night." He tried to ignore his concern that recent telephone calls had been strained and she had seemed withdrawn, sad even.

"Er … can we find a table and get a drink?" She noticed he didn't lean forward to kiss her and the guilt she had been feeling on the train intensified.

Jason reached for her left hand. "You're not wearing your ring."

"Can we sit down?" She wanted to shrink back from the look of sorrow in his eyes.

"Will it make any difference to what you've got to say to me?"

She wanted him to be cross with her and to see hatred in his eyes, or blankness, as though he didn't care one way or another. But he wasn't, and she couldn't. Instead, he was silent as he looked at her out of sad, tired eyes. He turned to sit at a nearby empty table outside Costa Coffee. He made no attempt to go to the counter.

"Shall I get some coffee?" she asked nervously.

He shook his head. "Not for me, thanks."

"Do you mind if I do?" and she walked over, not waiting for him to answer. She needed a minute to compose herself and try to give the speech she had prepared and repeated a thousand times on the train.

He was fiddling with a handful of paper tubes of sugar when she returned with her regular Americano.

"Have you met someone else?" he asked.

"Well. Yes. But it's not how you think. I never intended to. And I'm not even sure if anything will come of it." She took a long, slow sip, the coffee almost scalding the roof of her mouth, but in a masochistic sort of way she felt she deserved some sort of pain, as she felt guilty that her heart was not broken. Not by the man in front of her, anyway. "I'm not even seeing him."

Jason looked at her, confused, but she continued, not allowing him to interrupt her or try to dissuade her from the decision she had made. "But it has made me realise, I … I don't love you, Jason. I'm sorry. But the proposal, the dinner, the ring. It all happened so quickly. And I thought, why not? We had been seeing each other for over a year, we weren't getting any younger and …"

"You didn't have a better option, is that it, Grace?"

"Yes … I mean no … I mean …" She wrapped her hands around the cup and stared down at the brown liquid. "It just seemed the thing to do. Jason, I never actually said yes that night. You simply put the ring on my finger and assumed my acceptance."

"Aw, come on, Grace. You didn't say no, either."

"No. I didn't say no. And I went home, I handed in my resignation and I felt nothing. I felt nothing, except regret at not seeing my schoolchildren any more." She immediately pictured John Black's tearful face when she had said she would be leaving Arnford Primary School. She closed her eyes a second. "I should have felt happy, excited, hopeful for the future. But I didn't."

"So what are you saying? You would rather carry on as things were? Before we got engaged?"

Oh no, she didn't want him to think they could turn the clock back. She could never turn the clock back. She didn't want to turn the clock back. She wanted to run forward into the unknown, with a powerful, handsome and annoying man and she hoped she could share his family, be a part of it and help to keep it together.

"No, Jason. I'm not saying that. I have changed over the last few days. Well, months, really. Things have happened that have made me think what I have is good, but I want more.

Unfortunately, you can't give me the 'more' that I want. But ..."
She hesitated, knowing she would upset him even more with
her next words, but she knew she needed to end this with him
now, "I have met someone who could give me that 'more'. He
may not, but I need to find out. I can't marry you, Jason. I'm so
sorry."

"So, what are you going to do now?" He tried to sound
matter-of-fact.

Grace looked at her watch. "There's a train in twenty minutes. I'm going to go home, Jason. I'm staying in Cheshire."
Then she added, "You don't have to wait, really."

"Yeah, right. I think I will go. I ... I don't feel too good. I hope
you find what you're looking for, Grace."

There was no kiss, no hug, and no look back as he disappeared into the crowd.

Chapter 98

After dropping John off at school on Wednesday morning, Gabriel instructed Michael to pull up in front of Grace's house, to pick up Kit. They had spoken several times on the phone, when Grace had been at work, and Kit finally admitted he needed some help to control his drinking and the urge to take drugs. He had been getting up after Grace had gone to work, and immediately hitting the bottle. In the evenings, Grace had often worked late, not coming home until after seven. Kit had managed to hold it together when she was there and they had usually shared a meal, something quick and easy to prepare. More often than not, Grace would do some more work in the kitchen and he would lie on the sofa watching some inane programme on TV. As soon as she could, she would come in and join him. When she asked him how his day had been, he had nothing to say. He was bored and it was driving him mad. She would go to bed first and he would tell her he would be up in a minute. He would then drink some more to enable him to fall into a drunken stupor. Then he could look forward to doing the same thing all over again the next day.

So when Black said he would come over to discuss what Kit could do with his time as he sampled life back in the UK, he was actually looking forward to seeing him. They went to the Cottons and Kit had a late breakfast, while Black sipped coffee. He had brought him some information on LAC Flying School in Manchester and also a brochure for a drug and alcohol detox and rehabilitation clinic.

"I'm not saying that you need to see these people. *You* must decide that. If you have a problem, Kit, then you need to face it and deal with it. Have you spoken to Grace?"

"No. I keep wanting to talk to her about it. She knows I'm no angel. But she seems so busy. I don't want to cause her any worry or stress. I think it would help if I had something to do."

"You won't get on the flying course, even to retrain, until you've sorted yourself out."

"Yeah. I know."

"Do you know my sister?"

"Only from meeting her briefly at your place."

"I think you should talk to her." Black hesitated a moment, wondering if Ellouise would be angry if he talked about her to this man. Then he took his phone out and dialled her number.

Half an hour later, he left Kit and Ellouise to chat, seemingly happily, about their shared experiences: needing release, needing to forget and waking up to realise that what they really needed was a new purpose in life …

By Friday, Grace wondered if she would ever hear from Gabriel Black again. The skiing lessons were over, and from the way everyone spoke about the impending Christmas holiday, it still seemed to be taken for granted that she would be part of the group. They were going on Saturday. But he had said nothing.

He told her to take her time to think about accepting him, that they could then talk. But that had been nearly two weeks ago.

When she got home from school at about five o'clock at the end of the school term, Kit asked if she minded if Ellouise called round. She was a little surprised. Kit had told her he had met up with her on Wednesday, but she hadn't thought the two of them would form any sort of friendship. Yet she couldn't help noticing how clean-shaven her brother looked this evening, and she was also pleased that she couldn't smell alcohol on his breath.

He had already confessed to her that he had had a drink problem in Kenya, but he was trying to clean up his act now he was in the UK. Although she had smelled alcohol on his breath most evenings, she thought it was just from having a couple of beers through sheer boredom. She fully intended to have a proper conversation with him about what he wanted to do now with his life, even if that meant going back to Kenya. But because she had been so busy with work, they hadn't had the chance to sit down and talk properly. While she knew she couldn't expect him to stay with her forever, she was sure that they would always stay in touch now and she was determined to make certain of that.

So, an hour later, after she had reassured the unlikely couple that she needed to do a couple of things that evening, she found herself feeling lonely and confused as she waved at them in Ellouise's departing car.

Ellouise had even called, "See you at the airport," as she had closed the driver's door. What airport and when?

She was waiting for the kettle to boil when there was a knock at her door.

"Hi," he said, holding a bottle of champagne and looking incredible in his Versace liquorice-grey silk suit that she had seen him in once before, with a metallic-grey shirt fastened to the neck. He looked incredible and he gave her the sexiest smile she had ever seen. He was calm, confident and totally in control of the situation.

"I hoped now would be a good time to talk. Can I come in?"

Grace couldn't believe he was here. She simply stared at the handsome man still standing in her doorway, beginning to look a little nervous at her silence. Gabriel raised his eyebrow, not quite with impatience. "Grace?"

"Sorry, I … yes … come in," and instead of moving aside to let him in, she turned her back on him and left him to follow her. She heard the door close and then she felt his hand on her shoulder.

"Breathe, Grace," he breathed on her neck.

"I can't," she whispered.

He scooped her up in his arms. "Then I had better hold you and be ready to give you the kiss of life."

He lowered his head to kiss her lips as she placed her hands in his hair.

"Which way do I go?"

She realised he had only ever been in her hallway before. Unable to speak, she pointed to the first doorway off the hall, and he carried her into the lounge and sat down on the sofa, cradling her to him.

"I am going to keep touching you unless you tell me not to." He kissed her again. "Until you tell me you have thought about it," his hands stroked her cheeks, "and you tell me you can't handle me," his right hand began to caress the mound of her left breast over her blouse. "Do you want me to go?"

"No." She swooned as she pushed his hand harder onto her breast and revelled in his kisses. Oh, could he kiss!

"Can I tell my driver to go and come back later?" He was unfastening her buttons and his hand started to roam inside, gently stroking the skin above her breasts while his lips peppered the base of her neck.

"Tell him not to come back. Stay here."

He stopped his attentive actions and looked at her. He smiled. "But we're going skiing tomorrow." He pulled out his Xphone. "Michael, come back in two hours to take us back to the Hall." He placed his phone on the arm of the sofa and continued to undo her buttons. She lay in his arms as he removed her shirt and then her bra.

"I've missed you." He sucked on her nipples and they hardened at his touch. Gasps escaped her, her eyes closing and his touch delighting her. She put her hands in his hair and ran her fingers over his scalp as she pulled him closer to her breasts.

As he began to undo her trousers, she reached between them to remove his belt and unfasten the button, lower the zip and push down the exquisite grey fabric of his trousers. He raised his hips, helping her to push them off. Then he lifted her up and stood her in front of him. He knelt and slid her trousers and knickers down, waiting for her to kick them off.

He raised his face and buried it in the soft mound of her bare pubis. "You smell wonderful." Then he pulled her naked body onto the biscuit-coloured carpet. He laid her before him and quickly removed the rest of his clothes.

She reached up and took hold of his penis, wrapping her hands around it, gently stroking his velvety skin and fondling his balls, before moving her hands behind him to caress his buttocks. She kneaded them, pulling him on top of her. "I want you to take me, Gabriel. Only me." Her eyes held his. "You cannot have anyone else!" She shocked herself with the strength of her words and feelings, knowing she would not share this man, not now, not ever.

"Only you, Grace, I promise," and he closed his eyes, covered her mouth and tasted her with his tongue, wanting to consume her and make her a part of him. "Only you."

He moved his hand down and placed first one and then two fingers in her vagina. He withdrew them and brought them to his mouth, revelling in her taste. "You're beautiful." He raised himself and hovered over her, desperate to be inside her. He felt her hands on his buttocks again as she pulled him onto her, and gasped as he pushed his penis inside her warm, wet vagina. He felt captivated by her passion, her confidence and her acceptance of him and all he had been.

He started to move inside her, filling her deeper and deeper. "I can't make it last long, Grace, I'm going to come!" He desperately moved his hand onto her clitoris, aching to give her release, but too enraptured by the approach of his own blissful pleasure to hold back. His semen flowed into her, as if her body sucked it from him, and his moans echoed around the room. Gradually his breathing slowed and he moved his fingers to stimulate and pleasure her. He wet them and then resumed stroking and caressing her clitoris. His movements created a sensual and pleasurable, long-lasting orgasm.

"Aaaghh," she exclaimed. "I love you. I want you."

"Thank God. You've said it at last." He laid his forehead on hers and their bodies remained connected. Neither of them wanted it to end. Eventually their stillness was broken and they slowly dressed, smiling at each other. Standing in front of her, he ran his hands up and down her arms.

"Can we make this work, Grace?" His gaze held hers as she stretched up to reach his lips, seeking more of his kisses.

"Yes. I'm good at making things work."

His arms enveloped her and she felt safe with him. They would make it work.

"So. You expect me to go on holiday tomorrow when I have nothing ready. And what about Kit?" They were sitting in her kitchen, sipping his champagne from her non-crystal flutes. Her mind was racing with concern and frustration as he just grinned and carried on sipping, enjoying her confusion.

"I love to see you flustered." He was teasing her like a school-girl. "But it's all taken care of. Ellouise has been doing a bit of undercover work."

Grace stared at him. "What do you mean?"

"She has checked out what toiletries you like, already chosen a wardrobe for you, and we have your ski gear all ready. My job is to make sure you get to the airport. And we've arranged for Kit to join us. I'm not sure how he'll take to skiing but I'm sure we can see that he has a good time."

"Does he know?"

"Ellouise is with him, isn't she? She's good at making things happen too," he smiled. "We need to have a talk about Kit. I think he needs some help adjusting to things here." His unspoken question hung in the air.

"Yes. I think he may have a drink problem."

Gabriel reached over and took her hand. "We can get him some help, Grace. And I think he's admitted it to himself. That's a good start. He'll need our support." He decided not to mention his sister's experience in this area. If she wanted to discuss it with Grace, she would.

Grace suddenly turned to Gabriel. "Why did you ask me to come on your family skiing holiday?" Something was bothering her. "You asked me to start the skiing lessons in November, when I thought you were mad at me for referring to you as my fuck buddy."

"I know," he said seriously. "I thought you might appreciate going away somewhere at this difficult time."

She stared at him. "You knew, didn't you?"

"That you wouldn't want to be here? Of course I knew, Grace. I was worried that you wouldn't want to be with me at all, but I wanted to protect you, prevent you from feeling any guilt or anger. You don't have to suffer for your father's crimes, Grace. I know the media will be reporting on the families commemorating their children's deaths, and I know you have to escape from it. We will be in the ski chalet, away from everything, and you and Kit can enjoy your time together."

"Thank you. I think it's time we both moved on and started living our lives. I'm happy to share mine with you and John right now."

He smiled. *Not just for now, Grace. Forever.*

Chapter 99

On Saturday afternoon Gabriel, John, Grace and the Beardlys travelled on one private Learjet 60 XR, with Julian and Lindsey, Kit, Ellouise, Roger and Steve on another.

The groups were reunited at the Blacks' chalet in Meribel. Grace and Carol were still getting over the excitement of travelling in the Learjet: the personal door-to-door service, no queues, no struggling for leg space, and no bored children! They were all way too excited to ask, "Are we there yet?" And the elation didn't cease as they entered the huge chalet on the slopes in the French resort of Meribel in the Three Valleys.

Although it was night-time, the moonlight bouncing off the snow lit up the surrounding area, so the visitors could see the outdoor heated pool and the hot tub resting on a decked veranda, together with garden furniture covered in a light smattering of fresh snow.

Gabriel took Grace's hand as the front door was opened and they were greeted by Amanda, whom Grace recognised from Arnford Hall. "Hello, sir, and welcome to Meribel."

Black's guests gazed around in awe. The hallway led into a vast open space with a dark stone wall housing a huge open fire at one end, the ceiling rising up to an atrium with a galleried landing. There were huge comfortable-looking sofas, tempting one to lounge on them and relax. A large oak island with a sand-speckled granite top divided the room and gave way to a large dining table on the other side.

The room was completed with a wall of glass and wooden frames from floor-to-ceiling that provided a magnificent vista of the twinkling lights shining up from the town of Meribel. A giant Christmas tree decorated in a multitude of coloured garlands, baubles and fairy lights completed a perfect winter picture.

Gabriel wrapped his arms around Grace and whispered, "Breathe, Grace."

Then he turned to the mesmerised Beardlys. "Let's get everyone settled in their rooms and then we can eat."

The children started racing around, whooping as they discovered a games room with table tennis and pool tables, a cinema area with a horseshoe-shaped sofa and giant multimedia screen, a sauna and steam room, and a wooden staircase leading to the mezzanine floor, where they discovered a large bedroom with bunk beds and screens for gaming.

When everyone had gone exploring, and Grace had taken John's hand as he insisted on showing her the games room, Carol turned to her "brother-in-law". "Thank you so much for this, Gabriel."

They were alone and he knew she wanted to say more. "I'm sorry things didn't turn out well for you and Eliza. I can see that you are a wonderful father to John, and I know she would be very happy about that." She hesitated a moment before she continued, "And I think you and Grace make a lovely couple. She seems good for John. I don't fully understand why Eliza drew up the agreement she did with you, but I just want you to know that I can only assume that it served its purpose as John was born and growing up. But I don't think there is any need for it now. I'll be ripping up my copy of it. I wanted you to know that."

Gabriel took her hand. "Thank you, Carol. I'm glad that you and your family are a part of mine now. And, yes, although it's not what you think, we have all changed through Eliza's death, and for me it has been in such a positive way, I can only be grateful to her. I discovered something important recently and realised that things could have been different ..." He paused, and his sombre expression was replaced by a warm smile and he squeezed her hand in his. "Well, it doesn't matter now. Thank you for your understanding and patience. I'm glad that you're all here." Suddenly there were hoots and laughter pouring down from the galleried landing above them and he glanced up. "And I know John's delighted his cousins are here. They're going to have a fantastic time. We all are."

And, bang on cue, everyone started to congregate in the living area and Amanda announced that dinner was served.

Chapter 100

Having finally got four very excited children to bed on Christmas Eve, the adults shared a simple traditional Swiss meal of cheese fondue. As cheese dripped from bread, fine French wine flowed, and they shared stories from their first day on the pistes, the atmosphere was happy and relaxed.

Roger was doing all he could to keep Steve out of the kitchen to leave the French chef that Gilles had organised for the week to get on with it. Ellouise was providing the perfect distraction for Kit not to consume too much alcohol. Carol and James felt like they were on a second honeymoon, despite all the added company. Julian and Lindsey were grateful for this second chance, and were determined to make up for lost time.

And Grace and Gabriel continued to get to know each other. They occupied the master bedroom at the far end of the chalet, almost isolated from the main building by a structure accommodating the sauna and steam room, necessitating a darkened corridor down to their bedroom and bathroom. This end of the building was also single-storey, so any sound that travelled from their room ascended straight to the stars.

Gabriel had warned her that living with him could be a challenge, and Grace soon appreciated that one of the more thrilling challenges was his ravenous appetite for sex. She began to know – and enjoy – his games of masturbation, bondage and oral enjoyments. She admired his strength, stamina and creativity. She loved his attention to her pleasure, and how it was such an integral part of his own. She had known selfish lovers in the past, but this man made her pleasure his prime objective and she could feel how her pleasure increased his.

And she loved to stimulate him in the way he had once asked her and shown her. She would caress his body, lubricate his crease and enhance his orgasm by touching him from inside. That which had frightened her at first now gave her pleasure and allowed her to bask in her power over him.

They joined together so perfectly, like needle and thread, hand in glove, fitting together and making each other whole. He was her man and she was his woman.

After a magical Christmas morning when everyone opened their gifts, Gabriel announced that he and Grace would disappear for a while, leaving everyone to go sledging and, no doubt, snowball fighting.

He hugged John and asked him if it was OK with him if Daddy and Mrs McGuire went away and came back in the morning to take him skiing. He was so excited by his new toys and the prospect of having snowball fights with everyone that he didn't make Gabriel feel guilty for leaving his young son on their first Christmas together. And Gabriel was grateful – there was something he wanted to do, and time was pressing.

As he led Grace back to their bedroom, he instructed her to put her ski clothes on. When he led her to the boot room and began putting on his boots, she stared at him. "But I thought the slopes and lifts were all closed today."

"They are. We're going on a trek." He grinned, not willing to give away any of the surprise he was planning.

Once they were both booted, he led her outside to the back of the chalet. There was a skidoo laden with their skis and a large holdall. He climbed onto the front and asked her to get on behind him.

"Where are we going?" she asked, partly excited but mostly nervous. He was up to something.

"You'll see. Now hold on to me and enjoy," and he twisted the throttle and they were off. The machine glided over the snow and Grace admired the snow-covered trees as they skidded past, the stillness of the empty slopes, the vacant chairs on the chairlifts swaying in the slight breeze. She leaned into Gabriel's back, clasping his waist, and smiled to herself, feeling like a teenager going off for an illicit weekend. In their case it was a matter of sneaking away from a small child, brothers and sisters and the rest of his extended family. After about half an hour, she saw a log cabin in the distance, smoke swirling from its chimney.

He pulled to a stop outside and helped her off the vehicle. He picked up their bag and then took her gloved hand as he led her to the door. He removed his own glove to retrieve a key and then opened the door and stood back for her to enter.

Inside, a fire was blazing in a rustic fireplace. Candles were burning. The space was small and cosy. There was a three-seater sofa covered in faux fur throws, and a shabby armchair in russet cotton twill. There was a small coffee table, a tall cupboard, a washbasin and tap, and an ancient-looking stove with two gas rings.

"Well?" Gabriel started to take off his jacket and salopettes while he watched Grace's expression; her eyes soaked up the interior of this small hut, the pleasant, warming smell of the burning logs permeating her nostrils.

"It's … very cosy." Her voice barely concealed her question: why are we here?

"I have a simple question to ask you and I wanted to ask it in a simple place, with nothing to distract us, no one to disturb us and no luxuries to influence you." He began to help her out of her ski gear, revealing her navy thermals and bright pink ski socks.

"Well, I guess it ticks all of those boxes. Is there a bathroom?"

"No. Just a lean-to at the side."

"Oh," she said and instinctively squeezed her pelvic floor muscles.

"There should be some peppermint tea, and there's a butt of rainwater outside. I'll fill the kettle." As he nipped outside with a dented kettle, Gabriel was beginning to fear his "back to basics" idea might not have been such a good plan. He had brought several women here in the past, for nothing more than a quick shag before taking them back to whichever bar he had picked them up in.

But he loved the hut's remoteness, its solitude, and the fact that he never went anywhere else quite like it. He had thought long and hard about his relationship with Grace and what he hoped for from it. There were so many things to consider when he thought about his future. He was sure John would grow to love Grace, if he didn't already, and while she would never replace Eliza as his mother, he felt certain they could form a relationship that would enable them to live as a family. And now that Carol had solved the problem of the agreement and the reference to a "Mrs Black", he didn't want to wait any longer.

He had not forgotten he had asked her for her eggs, but somehow he had realised that wouldn't be enough. And deep down he knew she wouldn't want to be an absent mother, unknown to her child.

He went back inside and lit the gas burner, placing the kettle on the flame. Grace was curled on the sofa, watching the flames flicker in the fire. There was a comfortable silence between them as they waited for the kettle to sing its declaration that the water was boiling, and he made a cup of tea for Grace and a mug of black coffee for himself. Then he came to sit beside her and held out his arm so she could snuggle into his chest.

"So. My question …" He smelled her hair and sighed.

Without turning to look at him, she spoke softly. "I have something to tell you first."

He sipped from his mug, gently stroking her hair with his free hand.

"Oh?" he asked, clearly not having expected her to interrupt him.

"You asked me for my eggs a few weeks ago." She paused.

He remained silent, his hand still playing with her hair.

"I thought you would want to know what I have decided." She was trying to get a reaction from him but he was deliberately disappointing her. "I can't do what you asked. I couldn't live with myself knowing I had given a child away, knowing I would never have a chance to love it." She leaned forward and placed her cup on the small table. She turned to him and took his cup from his hands. "You know what that was like, don't you?" Her tone was hushed and sympathetic.

"Yes, I know," he said calmly. "She … she found out about me and … me and Mother." He closed his eyes and swallowed. Grace raised his hand to her lips and covered it in kisses. "She said I could never see my child. I entered an agreement with her so he would at least bear my name. And she put certain 'conditions' in place in the event of her death, conditions I had to consent to in order to get custody of my child. It's funny, really. She controlled my life more from the grave than any other woman has ever done." A weak smile passed over his lips. "Knowing about the baby, and my banishment from his life, was the hardest thing for me to live with. I could fuck my mother without caring. I would build a wall around myself and she couldn't penetrate my soul. I tried to believe in myself, and my relationship with Roger – both sexual and professional – enabled me to do that. But Eliza's discovery and subsequent hatred of me destroyed everything I had tried to protect myself with. I not only didn't care about my mother; I didn't care about myself or anything else. I have abused those around me, Grace, including Roger, when I was unfaithful to him with woman after woman. Even Ellouise couldn't bear to be with me any more. I'm sorry I asked you to give up such a part of you. And I'm glad you're denying me." He laid his head back and closed his eyes, feeling a shiver run through him as she stopped kissing his hand.

She was suddenly nervous about saying anything, no longer confident in what he wanted from her. There was still tension and anxiety between them. They were two complicated people, contaminated by the crimes of their parents, and yet they were the rocks the other members of their families depended on, and they both felt the need to hide their own vulnerability, their own desire for someone to be *their* rock.

Couldn't they now be each other's rock? Was their love strong enough to prepare them for whatever life threw at them?

Gabriel interrupted her thoughts as he eased her forward and got off the sofa. Then he got down onto one knee at her feet. "Grace, will you marry me?"

As a surge of happiness engulfed her, she blushed, her eyes sparkled and her smile was so wide it almost hurt. She could barely utter the words, but this time her answer was definitely, "Yes, yes, yes. I thought you would never ask," and she knelt beside him and wrapped her arms around him. They hugged as their lips sought each other's, kissing and tasting each other in blissful happiness.

They hungrily stripped each other's clothes away and rolled naked on the deerskin rugs that covered the stone floor. He sucked at her nipples as she pressed his head to her breasts, pulling at his hair. Their lust intensified as he lifted her, forcing her to wrap her legs around him to pull herself onto his penis. His entry into her vagina was almost painful, as she wasn't quite wet enough and yet she couldn't wait to feel him inside her. He was straining, using all his strength to move within her, to feel his own orgasm build. Eventually he stepped over to the sofa and eased her back on it, not breaking his union with her body. He straddled her and resumed nibbling at her breasts. Then he took her hand and moved it down, guiding it towards her clitoris.

"I want to feel your hand there; know what you are doing to yourself. I want to see you enjoy it, Grace."

And so she pleasured herself in the way which she had found so distasteful when he had first forced her to be with him.

"Come for me, Grace, let me hear you," he gasped in his efforts to reach a climax.

Then they both cried out, and he found himself bowled over by the rapture running through him. He knew it was the same for the woman he loved as they slowed and their heartbeats gradually returned to normal.

As he held her afterwards, she started to shiver. "Come on; let's get dressed," he said as he passed her the discarded clothes from the floor.

Once dressed in thermals, he collected the bag he had left by the door. He took out a rectangular Christmas present and brought it over to her.

"Merry Christmas, Grace," he said, handing her the gift. He sat beside her and held his breath as she tore open the paper to reveal a plain black box. Inside it, she withdrew tissue paper surrounding a tall slim object. Then a yellow tinge appeared through bubble wrap. Grace held her breath as she very carefully revealed the contents. She gasped as she held up a golden orchid, with gold strands running through the petals. The delicate structure ascended from a plinth with the words *My Grace* inscribed on it.

A small piece of black silk ribbon hung down from the principal flower. The ribbon held a platinum ring with two small pear-shaped diamonds protecting a larger central one.

Gabriel encircled Grace with his arm as he carefully removed the ribbon and slipped the ring off it. His eyes held hers as he reached for her hand.

"Just to check if I misheard you … Grace, will you marry me?"

Her eyes remained fixed on his. Her hand didn't move. She simply said, "Yes."

With just the right amount of pressure, he placed it firmly on the third finger of her left hand. Then he raised it to his lips and kissed it. "Thank you," he whispered.

Grace clasped his hands and leaned in to kiss his lips. "I love you, Gabriel Black."

Then she pulled back, beaming like a child, as she stretched out her arm and twirled her finger, admiring the beauty of the ring. "It's beautiful. And it feels so right."

Still smiling, she held up the orchid, examining each facet of the plant. "And this is beautiful too." She turned to face him, letting him see the sheer delight on her face. "Is it one of yours?"

He smiled and touched the gold ornament with his fingers. "Actually, it will be yours, Grace. I'm working on a new strain, but I want it to be yours …" He smiled. "A beauty for a beauty," and he loved the way she blushed.

He reached back into the bag and pulled out a cool bag containing sandwiches, orange juice and a bottle of Dom Perignon. He poured some champagne into the two flutes that were also in the bag.

"To us, Grace." They raised their glasses and clinked them together, their eyes not breaking contact as they savoured the taste, which complemented their wonderful day. They ate a little of the picnic lunch, rewrapping the leftovers to have for breakfast. Gabriel put more wood on the fire to keep the hut warm before telling Grace to get kitted up again so they could venture out to ski in the surrounding area. Grace was so glad he had made her take skiing lessons, as she confidently skied with him on the gentle slopes. She was careful to maintain her balance and relieved she had not yet fallen.

As they cuddled later in front of the fire, still admiring her ring, and sipped some more champagne, she leaned in to kiss him and let him taste the sparkling liquid on her lips.

"Mmm, you taste nice. I need to taste some other parts …" He raised his eyebrows, not hiding the lust on his face. "We will be each other's entertainment for the night. I'll make it my mission to tire you out since, now it's too dark to ski, it's the only way I can ensure you will sleep on that small sofa."

"Well, I haven't given you your Christmas present yet."

"You did when you said yes. I'm taking all of you, Grace, and I won't wait long to officially bind you to me," and he pulled her close to him.

She pressed her hands on his chest and gazed up at him. "I'm pregnant."

He held her at arm's length. A look of incredulity came over his normally assured face. "You are? How, when, why didn't you tell me—?"

She laughed and placed her finger on his lips. "Yes, I am. And you should know how by now. I have missed a period since the first time we really made love in 'my' bedroom at Arnford Hall, the day you brought Kit home to me." Her shining eyes watched him as his began to glisten.

Then he suddenly frowned. "You shouldn't be skiing. Are you warm enough? Have you had enough to eat? Why on earth have you been skiing?" and he stared at the champagne flute.

"Gabriel, it's OK. A little champagne won't hurt. I've only had a few sips since the start of the holiday, in case you hadn't noticed! And I checked with the doctor about skiing on Thursday, when I was sure I was pregnant and Ellouise made it clear she thought I was coming skiing. I wasn't sure about this holiday, remember," she hurriedly continued as she saw a guilty expression appear on his face. "When you said you would give me some space, I didn't know if that meant hours or days. I didn't hear from you for nearly two weeks. And it gave you time to consider what you wanted in the future too. I wasn't sure if that was still going to be me. But I did know I wanted a baby. I wanted your baby just like you wanted mine. Now I know we can both have what we want." She cupped his face in her hands and wiped away a tear that had managed to escape. "And I want to be a part of John's life. I want him to love me too, as I have grown to love him and his father."

"He will, Grace, he will."

He glanced up at the small window. It was pitch black outside. He contemplated trying to make their way back to the chalet on the skidoo, but realised it was too dark and not worth the risk. He now had an even more precious cargo on his hands. But he had been looking forward to this night, alone with the woman who was now going to be his wife. Tomorrow would come soon enough.

He began to nuzzle at her neck. "Is still safe for me to …?"

"Come inside me?" she laughed. "Yes. I won't break, you know, and the baby is well protected where it is. Sex in pregnancy is perfectly safe – mandatory, in fact, to keep the mother happy."

Chapter 101

Gabriel Black had never driven a skidoo so carefully in his life. He finally allowed himself to relax as he helped his precious cargo dismount.

The happy couple had already discussed how they were going to tell John the news of their engagement, over their "make do" breakfast in the cabin. They had agreed that Gabriel would speak to him when father and son went skiing that morning. Grace had said she would understand if Gabriel thought it better for John if they were to delay the announcement. But he had said no, first because he was sure John would be thrilled about it, but also because Gabriel Black couldn't wait!

However, he did concede that news of the baby would initially be for grown-up ears only. Grace's refusal of fine champagne and wine would be too difficult to explain. But they wanted to wait until they were back in Arnford to tell John about his new little brother or sister.

As they walked into the chalet, they found everyone gathered in the living area playing Monopoly, kids' style! Carol came over to greet Grace and bring her to the fire to get warm. She immediately saw the ring. Gabriel put his finger to his lips, silently asking her not to give their surprise away yet.

John ran over to his daddy, who lifted him into a tight hug.

"Hi, Daddy. Will you help me play?"

"I've got a better idea. Let's go skiing, just you and me, like I promised."

John's face lit up.

"We'll take the others," announced Roger, as excitement grew at the prospect of getting ready to go skiing again.

Stopping for a hot chocolate after a brief time on the slopes, Gabriel asked John if he liked his school teacher. He already knew the answer, but he was pleasantly surprised nonetheless when John said, "I think she's the best lady in the world, Daddy. I know you can't have her 'cos you don't love anyone but me and she's going to marry someone else. But if I ever got to have a new mummy, I would want her to be just like Mrs McGuire."

Gabriel wrapped his arms around him and hoped his son wouldn't see his tears.

"Well, John. I have fallen in love with Grace – Mrs McGuire. And I know she loves you. I think she loves me too."

"She does?" John's eyes were like saucers.

Gabriel grinned at his son's lack of faith in him. "Well, maybe when we go back, you can ask her for me, and then come and tell me what she says. You know, I would really appreciate your help, darling."

"OK, Daddy," and John grinned, enjoying the collusion with his father.

As the two Blacks met up with the others, Roger informed them that Grace and Carol were taking it easy on a nearby nursery slope. Gabriel was relieved to hear that Grace was being sensible. He skied over to them with John and then winked at John as he gestured to the boy to go and talk to his teacher.

A moment later he heard, "She loves you, Daddy, she does!" as John came snow-ploughing towards him. "She said she loves me too. Are you going to get married? Then that will mean she's going to come and live with us, won't it, Daddy?"

"Yes, John," Gabriel Black laughed.

Grace came to a stop by his side.

"Will you marry me, Grace McGuire?"

By now Carol had joined them and she beamed with delight and took John's hand, who had a fit of the giggles.

"Yes, Mr Black, I would love to marry you."

"Yuk," said John, as the couple leaned together for a quick kiss.

"I can't wait to tell Craig. And Adam. And Roger."

John fell silent for a moment and Gabriel held his hand.

"We'll tell Mummy when we get back to Arnford Hall, John, OK?"

He nodded. "Daddy, I think she would like Mrs McGuire. Mummy always liked my school teachers and told me I needed to do what they said."

"Your mummy was right."

As she had waited on the slope, Grace realised how nervous she was and how important it was to all three of them that she would be accepted as a new member of John's family. Not as an aunty and not to take Eliza's place, but to be a loving guide: she wanted to protect and nurture John, take care of him and show him she loved him. She wanted to be a mother to him, but knew she couldn't replace the one he had lost.

Gabriel bent down to whisper in his son's ear. "Let's take our skis off and give her a hug, shall we?"

Grace observed them for a moment, nervous that John might stay back from her. But she needn't have worried. He clicked out of his skis, just like Daddy had shown him, and, as Grace held her arms out, John accepted her embrace as she wrapped her arms around him. She felt as if he belonged to her. He felt happy.

Gabriel approached and wrapped his arms around them both. Seeing the other skiers heading their way, he said, "Will you tell everyone our news then, John?"

"Craig! Craig! Guess what!"

As they all congregated back at the chalet for lunch, it was champagne for most and sparkling water laced with elder-flower for one, as everyone gathered round to congratulate the happy couple and John. Kit hugged his sister with an "I knew he loved you" grin on his face, and Ellouise and Carol cried, for different reasons but with the same conclusion: everyone was delighted.

That night Gabriel and Grace volunteered to put all the children to bed. Four excited and seemingly wide-awake children were told in no uncertain terms that it was bedtime. Gabriel sat between John and Craig as Grace read a story, with Abbie by her side, admiring her ring. Then it was lights out and after a short period of chatter, silence and sleep overtook the children.

"Let's go to bed," Gabriel said quietly. "The others won't miss us and I want to be alone with you." He hesitated as he looked at his fiancée. "Is that all right with you?"

Grace reached for his hand and linked her fingers with his as she fought against acknowledging the sad tinge to his voice. She perceived a guilt and a fear in his eyes and voice; remorse

576

for cruel punishments and callous sex. There would be a time when they would have to address this together, but that time was not now. Now she wanted him to feel her love more than anything.

As she climbed into bed beside him, he began to make small circles on her stomach with the softest of touches.

"You know I'm sorry for everything except meeting you and falling in love with you, Grace. I can't expect you to forgive me …"

She cupped his face in her hands and raised her lips to his. She felt his strong arms envelop her and their kiss intensified as their tongues mingled. There was nothing but love between them. He leaned over, careful not to put too much weight on her.

"I won't break," she smiled and pulled him onto her. "Soon I'll be too big for you to do this, and we'll have to experiment with different positions. So let's make the most of the next few weeks." Then she gazed deeply into his eyes, and her hand moved to his penis, to guide it into her as she added, "But don't you ever stop touching me."

"No, I won't, Grace. Just tell me what you want and I'll do it. I'm yours now."

They had had sex so many times, and with so many emotions, but tonight it was gentle, with a gradual rise to orgasm and a shared, unequivocal joy in each other.

They spent the next two days on the slopes, Gabriel and Julian, together with Roger and Steve, skiing off for the odd blast down black runs before returning to join the others on the gentler slopes. Gilles was the perfect guide, and everyone's confidence grew as the week progressed and their skills improved.

All too soon, it was time to go home.

Chapter 102

It was late on Saturday, the thirtieth of December when the cars pulled up at Arnford Hall.

Gabriel was still trying to persuade Grace to stay the night, and every night from now on if he could have his way, with him and John, but she felt that it was too soon for John. It was going to be another big change for him, and the last thing she wanted was for Gabriel's son to feel that she could be taking his daddy from him.

"I think it would be better if I went home with Kit."

She saw the look of disappointment on Gabriel's face as he held a very tired John in his arms at the bottom of the grand staircase.

"Oh, don't worry about that," Ellouise declared as she turned to Kit. "I'll take you home." *And maybe we can call at my place for a late-night glass of juice, or something,* she hoped.

Kit raised his eyebrows as he looked at his sister. "That's fine by me. Stay here, Grace. It's late and I think a certain young fellow will be very happy to see you in the morning." Over the holiday, her brother had come to appreciate the bond Grace had with the children – and one black-haired little boy in particular. And he saw that bond strengthen with the news that she was going to marry his father. Kit was delighted that his sister had found happiness and it inspired him to work to find his own, wherever that might be. But he knew it wouldn't be at the bottom of a glass.

"Come on, let's leave the happy family to get some sleep." This vision of her brother's "new" life made Ellouise's heart swell with love for him. She prayed he would now find the happiness he so deserved.

"Well, I guess I don't have a choice." Grace turned to Gabriel, who had started to ascend the stairs.

"You always have a choice, Grace. No more orders." He stopped and asked quietly, "Do you want to stay?"

"Yes. Just for tonight, though. Then we need to think what will be best for all of us before we're married."

Suddenly he grinned. "Well, we'll start by getting a date organised as soon as possible, because I don't want to be without you. Not ever again."

With John safely tucked up in bed, Gabriel took Grace's hand. She turned towards the door to "her" room. Gabriel stopped for a moment.

"No," he said, "I want you to come into my bedroom."

He opened the door and entered, using his remote to turn the lights on. He placed his arm around Grace as she came to stand beside him. Then he let her go and strode over to the bed, pulling the curtains back and securing them to the posts.

"I have dreamed of being in here with you, Grace – only you. We can make some changes, but the view is beautiful and when the light shines in through the windows it creates a wonderful warmth to the room. Come on through here," and he opened the door to his morning room.

Grace was speechless. She stared at the paintings and the sculpture.

"Oh, Gabriel. Do you lose yourself in here?"

Gabriel commanded the music to play and Grace gazed at him as Perry Como began to sing "And I Love You So".

"Not any more."

Epilogue

Gabriel Black married Grace McGuire on Saturday, the twentieth of January. It was a small affair, and John had a central role at his father's side. They were joined by their siblings, Roger and Steve, and the Beardly family, together with Gabriel's nanny, who was temporarily returning to Arnford Hall again. After some gentle persuasion from his fiancée, Gabriel had agreed to a religious ceremony at Arnford Church and he began to accompany Grace and John to the occasional church service, since his new wife informed him that if she lived in Arnford Hall, so did God. Grace often wore her silver cross and chain, but she loved the way her husband would always look at her, adoration and lust in his eyes, when she wore his necklace of gold.

They delayed their honeymoon until the Easter holidays when both John and Grace were on holiday from school. Of course, Gabriel would happily have told the state what it could do with its holidays-in-term-time policy, but Grace and John insisted on not getting into trouble, particularly now that she was going to be returning to teach at John's school again!

Kit chose to stay in the UK a while longer and, as a result of learning to abstain from alcohol and drugs, and enjoying a different kind of life with Ellouise Black, the chip on his shoulder began to wear away. He regained his pilot's licence and started shuttling high-earning executives around, happily recounting his experiences whenever he went to visit his sister, brother-in-law and nephew. Visits to his niece would also appear soon on his agenda.

After the wedding, John was very emotional: he was filled with love for his father, his Grace, who he had agreed he would call Momma G, and occasional heartbreak at missing his real mummy. As time went on, however, John began to call Grace "Mum", and she would smile at bedtime as she listened to John recount some of the day's activities to a photo of Eliza. No one was ever made to feel awkward.

And Cynthia Black? She never saw Gabriel or Julian again. Ellouise visited her once when she was in hospital to have a hip replacement, after a fall during one of the many holidays she took in Kenya, though she was never able to bring herself to emigrate out there to live with Armen, the one man who seemed to love her. But George Black's widow had enough money to pay people to look after her, and her daughter decided she could definitely live without her mother. No member of the Black family missed her.

Dear Reader,

In my stories I refer to abuse in many forms – brutal, sexual, emotional. My stories are fictional, based on characters and events from my imagination.

But we are all aware that situations can arise in real life that no one should be expected to live through. If you have ever been the victim of abuse, please remember there are people who can help.

Please visit my website at mollieblake.co.uk/help for more information and don't feel that you are alone or unimportant.

Mollie x

To fans of reading,

Please take the time to write a review on Amazon for any story you have read and enjoyed. These words are not only inspirational and encouraging to authors, but reviews are very helpful to those who publish independently.

Thank you to all who have taken the time to write such constructive feedback. Your words are valuable and as an independent writer, I greatly appreciate your comments and suggestions.

Mollie x

Also by Mollie Blake:

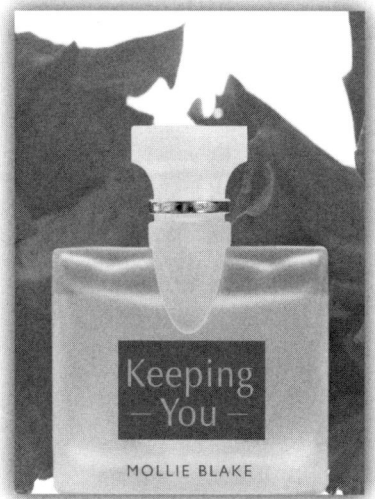

Keeping You

This story of love, loss and lust keeps the reader hoping and guessing to the very last sexy, satisfying page.